Praise fo

'Deborah Crombie just keeps getting
better and better . . . utterly compelling'
Peter Robinson

'Dark and complex contemporary police procedural'
Andrew Taylor

'Comparisons with Elizabeth George are
inevitable . . . Crombie's emotionally intense,
quietly yet exquisitely wrought gems have taken
on a new brilliance with each offering'
The Times

'Crombie has laid claim to the literary territory
of moody psychological suspense owned by
P. D. James and Barbara Vine'
Washington Post

'Crombie's latest Kincaid and James crime story
is as rich in its picture of cultural and racial flux
as it is in its framework of family dynamics . . . and
tells a subtle and moving character-driven story'
Booklist

'Spectacular'
New York Times

'Captivating'
Publishers Weekly

'A solution dazzling in its cunning'
Scotsman

'Deserves to be on the bestseller shelves'
Stuart Pawson

Leave the Grave Green
&
In a Dark House

Deborah Crombie was born and educated in Texas. After living in both England and Scotland, she wrote her first Duncan Kincaid/Gemma James novel. She has since been nominated for the Agatha, Macavity and Edgar Awards and is published across the world. Deborah lives with her family in a small north Texas town and frequently visits the UK.

Deborah Crombie

Leave the
Grave Green
&
In a Dark House

PAN BOOKS

Leave the Grave Green first published in Great Britain 1996 by Macmillan
First published by Pan Books 2009
In a Dark House first published in Great Britain 2005 by Macmillan
First published by Pan Books 2006

This omnibus first published 2011 by Pan Books
an imprint of Pan Macmillan, a division of Macmillan Publishers Limited
Pan Macmillan, 20 New Wharf Road, London N1 9RR
Basingstoke and Oxford
Associated companies throughout the world
www.panmacmillan.com

ISBN 978-0-330-54542-6

1 3 5 7 9 8 6 4 2

A CIP catalogue record for this book is available
from the British Library.

Typeset by IntypeLibra Ltd
Printed in the UK by CPI Mackays, Chatham ME5 8TD

Leave the
Grave Green

For my dad, whose creativity and
enjoyment of life continue to inspire me

Acknowledgements

I'd like to thank Stephanie Woolley, of Taos, New Mexico, whose beautiful watercolours provided the model for Julia's portraits. I am also grateful to Brian Coventry, head cutter at Lilian Baylis House, who took time from his extremely busy schedule to show me LB House and introduce me to the mysteries of Making Wardrobe; and to Caroline Grummond, assistant to the orchestra manager at the English National Opera, who was kind enough to show me both front- and back-of-house at the Coliseum.

My agent, Nancy Yost, and my editor, Susanne Kirk, provided their usual expert advice, and thanks are, as always, due to the EOTNWG for their reading of the manuscript.

Last, but by no means least, thanks to my daughter, Katie, for helping our household run smoothly, and to my husband, Rick Wilson, for his patience and support.

Prologue

'Watch you don't slip.' Julia pushed back the wisps of dark hair that had snaked loose from her ponytail, her brow furrowed with anxious concern. The air felt dense, as thick and substantial as cotton wool. Tiny beads of moisture slicked her skin, and larger drops fell intermittently from the trees to the sodden carpet of leaves beneath her feet. 'We'll be late for tea, Matty. And you know what Father will say if you've not done your homework in time for practice.'

'Oh, don't be so wet, Julia,' said Matthew. A year younger than his sister, as fair and stocky as she was thin and dark, he'd physically outstripped her in the past year and it had made him more insufferably cocksure than ever. 'You're a broody old hen. "Matty, don't slip. Matty, don't fall," he mimicked her nastily. 'The way you carry on you'd think I couldn't wipe my own nose.' His arms held shoulder-high, he balanced on a fallen tree trunk near the edge of the swollen stream. His school rucksack lay where he'd dropped it carelessly in the mud.

Clutching her own books to her thin chest, Julia rocked on the balls of her feet. *Serve him right if he*

1

caught it from Father. But the scolding, even if severe, would be brief, and life in their household would return quickly to normal – normal being that they all behaved, to quote Plummy when she felt particularly exasperated with him, 'as if the sun rose and set out of Matthew's backside'.

Julia's lips twitched at the thought of what Plummy would say when she saw his muddy bookbag and shoes. But no matter, all would be forgiven him, for Matthew possessed the one attribute her parents valued above all else. He could sing.

He sang effortlessly, the clear, soaring treble falling from his lips as easily as a whispered breath. And singing transformed him, the gawky, gap-toothed twelve-year-old vanishing as he concentrated, his face serious and full of grace. They would gather in the sitting room after tea, her father patiently fine-tuning Matthew on the Bach cantata he'd be singing with the choir at Christmas, her mother interrupting loudly and often with criticism and praise. It seemed to Julia that the three of them formed a charmed circle to which she, due to an accident of birth or some inexplicable whim of God, was forever denied admittance.

The children had missed their bus that afternoon. Julia, hoping for a private word with the art mistress, had delayed too long, and the loaded bus had rumbled by them, splattering dark freckles of mud on their calves. They'd had to walk home, and cutting across the fields, had caked their shoes with clay until they had to lift their heavy feet deliberately, like visitors from a lighter planet. When they reached the woods, Matthew had caught Julia's hand and pulled her, slipping and slithering through the trees, down the hillside to the stream nearest their house.

Julia shivered and looked up. The day had darkened perceptibly, and although the November afternoons drew in early, she thought the lessening visibility meant more rain. It had rained heavily every day for weeks. Jokes about the forty days and forty nights had long since grown stale; now glances at the heavy sky were followed by silent and resigned head-shaking. Here in the chalk hills north of the Thames, water leached steadily from the saturated ground and flowed into already overburdened tributaries.

Matty had left his tightrope-walking on the log and squatted at the water's edge, poking about with a long stick. The stream, in ordinary weather a dry gully, now filled its banks, the rushing water as opaque as milky tea.

Julia, feeling increasingly cross, said, 'Do come on, Matty, please.' Her stomach rumbled. 'I'm hungry. And cold.' She hugged herself tighter. 'If you don't come I shall go without you.'

'Look, Julie!' Oblivious to her nagging, he gestured towards the water with the stick. 'There's something caught under the surface, just there. Dead cat, maybe?' He looked round at her and grinned.

'Don't be disgusting, Matty.' She knew her prim and bossy tone would only fuel his teasing, but she was past caring. 'I really will go without you.' As she turned resolutely away she felt an unpleasant cramping sensation in her abdomen. 'Honestly, Matty, I don't feel—'

The splash sprayed her legs even as she whipped around. 'Matty! Don't be such an—'

He'd fallen in, landing on his back with his arms and legs splayed awkwardly. 'It's cold,' he said, his face registering surprise. He scrabbled towards the bank, laughing, shaking the water from his eyes.

Julia watched his gleeful expression fade. His eyes widened, his mouth formed a round *o*.

'Matty—'

The current caught him, pulling him downstream. 'Julie, I can't—' Water washed over his face, filling his mouth.

She stumbled along the bank's edge, calling his name. The rain began to fall in earnest, big drops that splashed against her face, blinding her. A protruding stone caught her toe and she fell. She picked herself up and ran on, only vaguely aware of the pain in her shin.

'Matty. Oh, Matty, please.' Repeated again and again, the words formed an unconscious incantation. Through the muddy water she could see the blue of his school jacket and the pale spread of his hair.

The ground descended sharply as the stream widened and turned away from her. Julia slid down the incline and stopped. On the opposite bank an old oak teetered precariously, a web of roots exposed where the stream had undercut the bank. Here

4

Matthew's body lodged, pinned under the roots as if held by a giant hand.

'Oh, Matty,' she cried, the words louder now, a wail of despair. She started into the water, a warm metallic saltiness filling her mouth as she bit through her lower lip. The cold shocked her, numbing her legs. She forced herself to go on. The water swirled about her knees, tugging at the hem of her skirt. It reached her waist, then her chest. She gasped as the cold bit into her ribs. Her lungs felt paralysed from the cold, unable to expand.

The current tugged at her, pulling at her skirt, shifting her foothold on the moss-covered rocks. With her arms held out for balance, she inched her right foot forward. Nothing. She moved a few feet to one side, then the other, feeling for the bottom. Still nothing.

Cold and exhaustion were fast sucking away her strength. Her breath came in shuddering gasps and the current's grasp seemed more insistent. She looked upstream and down, saw no easier crossing. Not that access to the other side would help her – it would be impossible to reach him from the steep bank.

A little moan escaped her. She stretched her arms towards Matty, but yards separated them, and she was too frightened to brave the current. Help. She must get help.

She felt the water lift and drag her forward as she turned, but she plunged on, digging her heels and toes in for purchase. The current slacked and she clambered out, standing for a moment on the muddy bank as a wave of weakness swept over her. Once more she looked at Matty, saw the outline of his legs twisting sideways in the current. Then she ran.

The house loomed through the dark arches of the trees, its white limestone walls eerily luminous in the dusk. Julia bypassed the front door without thinking. On around the house her feet took her, towards the kitchen, and warmth, and safety. Gasping from the steep climb up the hillside, she rubbed at her face, slick with rain and tears. She was conscious of her own breathing, of the squelching sound her shoes made with each step, and of the heavy wet wool of her skirt scratching her thighs.

Julia yanked open the kitchen door and stopped just inside, water pooling around her on the flags. Plummy turned from the Aga, spoon in hand, her dark hair dishevelled as always when she cooked. 'Julia! Where have you been? What will your mother have to say . . .?' The good-natured scolding faded. 'Julie, child, you're bleeding. Are you all right?' She came towards Julia, spoon abandoned, her round face creased with concern.

Julia smelled apples, cinnamon, saw the streak of flour across Plummy's bosom, registered in some compartment of her mind that Plummy was making apple pudding, Matty's favourite, for tea. She felt Plummy's hands grasp her shoulders, saw her kind and familiar face draw close, swimming through a film of tears.

'Julia, what is it? What's happened? Where's Matty?'

Plummy's voice was breathy now with panic, but still Julia stood, her throat frozen, the words dammed behind her lips.

A gentle finger stroked her face. 'Julia. You've cut your lip. What's happened?'

The sobs began, racking her slight body. She squeezed her arms tight to her chest to ease the pain. A stray thought flickered disjointedly through her mind – she couldn't remember dropping her books. *Matty. Where had Matty left his books?*

'Darling, you must tell me. What's happened?'

She was in Plummy's arms now, her face buried against the soft chest. The words came, choked out between sobs like a tide released. 'It's Matty. Oh, Plummy, it's Matty. He's drowned.'

Chapter One

From the train window Duncan Kincaid could see the piles of debris in the back gardens and on the occasional common. Wooden planks, dead branches and twigs, crushed cardboard boxes and the odd bit of broken furniture – anything portable served as fair game for Guy Fawkes bonfires. He rubbed ineffectually at the grimy window-pane with his jacket cuff, hoping for a better view of one particularly splendid monument to British abandon, then sat back in his seat with a sigh. The fine drizzle in the air, combined with British Rail's standard of cleanliness, reduced visibility to a few hundred yards.

The train slowed as it approached High Wycombe. Kincaid stood and stretched, then collected his overcoat and bag from the rack. He'd gone straight to Marylebone from the Yard, grabbing the emergency kit he kept in his office – clean shirt, toiletries, razor, only the necessities needed for an unexpected summons. And most were more welcome than this, a political request from the AC to aid an old school chum in a delicate situation. Kincaid grimaced. Give him an unidentified body in a field any day.

9

He swayed as the train lurched to a halt. Bending down to peer through the window, he scanned the station carpark for a glimpse of his escort. The unmarked panda car, its shape unmistakable even in the increasing rain, was pulled up next to the platform, its parking lights on, a grey plume of exhaust escaping from its tailpipe.

It looked like the cavalry had been called out to welcome Scotland Yard's fair-haired boy.

'Jack Makepeace. Sergeant, I should say. Thames Valley CID.' Makepeace smiled, yellowed teeth showing under the sandy bristle of moustache. 'Nice to meet you, sir.' He engulfed Kincaid's hand for an instant in a beefy paw, then took Kincaid's case and swung it into the panda's boot. 'Climb in, and we can talk as we go.'

The car's interior smelled of stale cigarettes and wet wool. Kincaid cracked his window, then shifted a bit in his seat so that he could see his companion. A fringe of hair the same colour as the moustache, freckles extending from face into shiny scalp, a heavy nose with the disproportionate look that comes of having been smashed – all in all not a prepossessing face, but the pale blue eyes were shrewd, and the voice unexpectedly soft for a man of his bulk.

Makepeace drove competently on the rain-slick streets, snaking his way south and west until they crossed the M40 and left the last terraced houses behind. He glanced at Kincaid, ready to divert some of his attention from the road.

'Tell me about it, then,' Kincaid said.

'What do you know?'

'Not much, and I'd just as soon you start from scratch, if you don't mind.'

Makepeace looked at him, opened his mouth as if to ask a question, then closed it again. After a moment he said, 'Okay. Daybreak this morning the Hambleden lock-keeper, one Perry Smith, opens the sluicegate to fill the lock for an early traveller, and a body rushes through it into the lock. Gave him a terrible shock, as you can imagine. He called Marlow – they sent a panda car and the medics.' He paused as he downshifted into an intersection, then concentrated on overtaking an ancient Morris Minor that was creeping its way up the gradient. 'They fished him out, then when it became obvious that the poor chappie was not going to spew up the canal and open his eyes, they called us.'

The windscreen wiper squeaked against dry glass and Kincaid realized that the rain had stopped. Freshly ploughed fields rose on either side of the narrow road. The bare, chalky soil was a pale brown, and against it the black dots of foraging rooks looked like pepper on toast. Away to the west a cap of beech trees crowned a hill. 'How'd you identify him?'

'Wallet in the poor sod's back pocket. Connor Swann, aged thirty-five, brown hair, blue eyes, height about six feet, weight around twelve stone. Lived in Henley, just a few miles upstream.'

'Sounds like your lads could have handled it easily enough,' said Kincaid, not bothering to conceal his annoyance. He considered the prospect of spending his Friday evening tramping around the Chiltern Hundreds, damp as a Guy Fawkes bonfire, instead of meeting Gemma for an after-work pint at the pub down Wilfred Street. 'Bloke has a few drinks, goes for a stroll on the sluicegate, falls in. Bingo.'

Makepeace was already shaking his head. 'Ah, but that's not the whole story, Mr Kincaid. Someone left a very nice set of prints on either side of his throat.' He lifted both hands from the wheel for an instant in an eloquently graphic gesture. 'It looks like he was strangled, Mr Kincaid.'

Kincaid shrugged. 'A reasonable assumption, I would think. But I don't quite see why that merits Scotland Yard's intervention.'

'It's not the *how*, Mr Kincaid, but the who. It seems that the late Mr Swann was the son-in-law of Sir Gerald Asherton, the conductor, and Dame Caroline Stowe, who I believe is a singer of some repute.' Seeing Kincaid's blank expression, he continued, 'Are you not an opera buff, Mr Kincaid?'

'Are you?' Kincaid asked before he could clamp down his involuntary surprise, knowing he shouldn't have judged the man's cultural taste by his physical characteristics.

'I have some recordings, and I watch it on the telly, but I've never been to a performance.'

The wide sloping fields had given way to heavily wooded hills, and now, as the road climbed, the trees encroached upon it.

'We're coming into the Chiltern Hills,' said Makepeace. 'Sir Gerald and Dame Caroline live just a bit further on, near Fingest. The house is called Badger's End, though you wouldn't think it to look at it.' He negotiated a hairpin bend, and then they were running downhill again, beside a rocky stream 'We've put you up at the pub in Fingest, by the way, the Chequers. Lovely garden in the back, on a fine day. Not that you're likely to get much use of it,' he added, squinting up at the darkening sky.

The trees enclosed them now. Gold and copper leaves arched tunnel-like overhead, and golden leaves padded the surface of the road. The late afternoon sky was still heavily overcast, yet by some odd trick of light the leaves seemed to take on an eerie, almost phosphorescent glow. Kincaid wondered if just such an enchanting effect had produced the ancient idea of 'roads paved with gold'.

'Will you be needing me?' Makepeace asked, breaking the spell. 'I'd expected you to have back-up.'

'Gemma will be here this evening, and I'm sure I can manage until then.' Seeing Makepeace's look of incomprehension, he added, 'Gemma James, my sergeant.'

'Rather your lot than Thames Valley.' Makepeace gave something halfway between a laugh and a snort. 'One of my green constables made the mistake this morning of calling Dame Caroline "Lady Asherton". The housekeeper took him aside and gave him a tongue-lashing he'll not soon forget. Informed him that Dame Caroline's title is hers by right and takes precedence over her title as Sir Gerald's wife.'

Kincaid smiled. 'I'll try not to put my foot in it. So there's a housekeeper, too?'

'A Mrs Plumley. And the widow, Mrs Julia Swann.' After an amused sideways glance at Kincaid, he continued, 'Make what you will of that one. Seems Mrs Swann lives at Badger's End with her parents, not with her husband.'

Before Kincaid could form a question, Makepeace held up his hand and said, 'Watch now.'

They turned left into a steep, high-banked lane, so narrow that brambles and exposed roots brushed the sides of the car. The sky had darkened perceptibly towards evening and it was dim and shadowed under the trees. 'That's the Wormsley valley off to your right, though you'd hardly know it.' Makepeace pointed, and through a gap in the trees Kincaid caught a glimpse of twilit fields rolling away down the valley. 'It's hard to believe you're only forty miles or so west of London, isn't it, Mr Kincaid?' he added with an air of proprietary pride.

As they reached the lane's high point, Makepeace turned left into the darkness of the beech woods. The track ran gently downhill, its thick padding of leaves silencing the car wheels. A few hundred yards on they rounded a curve and Kincaid saw the house. Its white stone shone beneath the darkness of the trees, and lamplight beamed welcomingly from its uncurtained windows. He knew immediately what Makepeace had meant about the name – Badger's End implied a certain rustic, earthy simplicity, and this house, with its smooth white walls and arched windows and doors, had an elegant, almost ecclesiastic presence.

Makepeace pulled the car up on the soft carpet of leaves, but left the engine running as he fished in his pocket. He handed Kincaid a card. 'I'll be off, then. Here's the number at the local nick. I've some business to attend to, but if you'll ring up when you've finished, someone will come and collect you.'

Kincaid waved as Makepeace pulled away, then stood staring at the house as the still silence of the woods settled over him. Grieving widow, distraught in-laws, an imperative for social discretion ... not a recipe for an easy evening, or an easy case. He squared his shoulders and stepped forward.

The front door swung open and light poured out to meet him.

'I'm Caroline Stowe. It's so good of you to come.'

This time the hand that took his was small and soft, and he found himself looking down into the woman's upturned face. 'Duncan Kincaid. Scotland Yard.' With his free hand he pulled his warrant card from his inside jacket pocket, but she ignored it, still grasping his other hand between her own.

His mind having summed up the words *Dame* and *opera* as *large*, he was momentarily taken aback. Caroline Stowe stood a fraction over five feet tall, and while her small body was softly rounded, she could by no stretch of the imagination be described as heavy.

His surprise must have been apparent, because she laughed and said, 'I don't sing Wagner, Mr Kincaid. My speciality is bel canto. And besides, size is not relevant to strength of voice. It has to do with breath control, among other things.' She released his hand. 'Do come in. How rude of me to keep you standing on the threshold like some plumber's apprentice.'

As she closed the front door, he looked around with interest. A lamp on a side table illuminated the hall, casting shadows on the smooth grey flagstone floor. The walls were a pale grey-green, bare except for a few large gilt-framed watercolours depicting voluptuous, bare-breasted women lounging about Romanesque ruins.

Caroline opened a door on the right and stood aside, gesturing him in with an open palm.

Directly opposite the door a coal fire burned in a grate, and above the mantel he saw himself, framed in an ornate mirror – chestnut hair unruly from the damp, eyes shadowed, their colour indistinguishable from across the room. Only the top of Caroline's dark head showed beneath the level of his shoulder.

He had only an instant to gather an impression of the room. The same grey slate floor, here softened by scattered rugs; comfortable, slightly worn chintz furniture; a jumble of used tea things on a tray – all dwarfed by the baby grand piano. Its dark surface reflected the light from a small lamp, and sheet music stood open behind the keyboard. The bench was pushed back at an angle, as though someone had just stopped playing.

16

'Gerald, this is Superintendent Kincaid, from Scotland Yard.' Caroline moved to stand beside the large rumpled-looking man rising from the sofa. 'Mr Kincaid, my husband, Sir Gerald Asherton.'

'How nice to meet you,' Kincaid said, feeling the response inappropriate even as he made it. But if Caroline insisted on treating his visit as a social occasion, he would play along for a bit.

'Sit down.' Sir Gerald gathered a copy of the day's *Times* from the seat of an armchair and moved it to a nearby end table.

'Would you like some tea?' asked Caroline. 'We've just finished, and it's no trouble to boil the kettle again.'

Kincaid sniffed the lingering scent of toast in the air and his stomach rumbled. From where he sat he could see the paintings he'd missed when entering the room – watercolours again, by the same artist's hand, but this time the women reclined in elegant rooms and their dresses had the sheen of watered silk. A house to tempt the appetites, he thought, and said, 'No, thank you.'

'Have a drink, then,' Sir Gerald said. 'The sun's certainly over the yardarm.'

'No, I'm fine. Really.' What an incongruous couple they made, still standing side by side, hovering over him as if he were a royal guest. Caroline, dressed in a peacock-blue silk blouse and dark tailored trousers, looked neat and almost childlike beside her husband's bulk.

17

Sir Gerald smiled at Kincaid, a great, infectious grin that showed pink gums. 'Geoffrey recommended you very highly, Mr Kincaid.'

By Geoffrey he must mean Geoffrey Menzies-St John, Kincaid's assistant commissioner, and Asherton's old schoolmate. Though the two men must be of an age, there any outward resemblance ended. But the AC, while dapper and precise enough to appear priggish, possessed a keen intelligence, and Kincaid thought that unless Sir Gerald shared that quality, the two men would not have kept up with one another over the years.

Kincaid leaned forward and took a breath. 'Won't you sit down, please, both of you, and tell me what's happened?'

They sat obediently, but Caroline perched straight-backed on the sofa's edge, away from the protective curve of her husband's arm. 'It's Connor. Our son-in-law. They'll have told you.' She looked at him, her brown eyes made darker by dilating pupils. 'We can't believe it's true. Why would someone kill Connor? It doesn't make sense, Mr Kincaid.'

'We'll certainly need more evidence before we can treat this as an official murder inquiry, Dame Caroline.'

'But I thought . . .' she began, then looked rather helplessly at Kincaid.

'Let's start at the beginning, shall we? Was your son-in-law well liked?' Kincaid looked at them both, including Sir Gerald in the question, but it was Caroline who answered.

18

'Of course. Everyone liked Con. You couldn't *not*.'

'Had he been behaving any differently lately? Upset or unhappy for any reason?'

Shaking her head, she said, 'Con was always . . . just Con. You would have to have known . . .' Her eyes filled. She balled one hand into a fist and held it to her mouth. 'I feel such a bloody fool. I'm not usually given to hysterics, Mr Kincaid. Or incoherence. It's the shock, I suppose.'

Kincaid thought her definition of hysteria rather exaggerated, but said soothingly, 'It's perfectly all right, Dame Caroline. When did you see Connor last?'

She sniffed and ran a knuckle under one eye. It came away smudged with black. 'Lunch. He came for lunch yesterday. He often did.'

'Were you here as well, Sir Gerald?' Kincaid asked, deciding that only a direct question was likely to elicit a response.

Sir Gerald sat with his head back, eyes half closed, his untidy tuft of grey beard thrusting forward. Without moving, he said, 'Yes, I was here as well.'

'And your daughter?'

Sir Gerald's head came up at that, but it was his wife who answered. 'Julia was here, but didn't join us. She usually prefers to lunch in her studio.'

Curiouser and curiouser, thought Kincaid. *The son-in-law comes to lunch but his wife refuses to eat with him.* 'So you don't know when your daughter saw him last?'

Again the quick, almost conspiratorial glance between husband and wife, then Sir Gerald said, 'This has all been very difficult for Julia.' He smiled at

Kincaid, but the fingers of his free hand picked at what looked suspiciously like moth holes in his brown woollen sweater. 'I'm sure you'll understand if she's a bit . . . prickly.'

'Is your daughter here? I'd like to see her, if I may. And I will want to talk to you both at more length, when I've had a chance to review the statements you've given Thames Valley.'

'Of course. I'll take you.' Caroline stood, and Sir Gerald followed suit. Their hesitant expressions amused Kincaid. They'd been expecting a battering, and now didn't know whether to feel relieved or disappointed. They needn't worry – they'd be glad to see the back of him soon enough.

'Sir Gerald.' Kincaid stood and shook hands.

The watercolours caught his eye again as he turned towards the door. Although most of the women were fair, with delicate rose-flushed skin and lips parted to show small glistening white teeth, he realized that something about them reminded him of the woman he followed.

'This was the children's nursery,' Caroline said, her breathing steady and even after the three-flight climb. 'We made it into a studio for her before she left home. I suppose you might say it's been useful,' she added, giving him a sideways look he couldn't interpret.

They'd reached the top of the house and the landing was unornamented, the carpeting threadbare in spots. Caroline turned to the left and stopped before a closed door. 'She'll be expecting you.' She smiled at Kincaid and left him.

He tapped on the door, waited, tapped again and listened, holding his breath to catch any faint sound. The echo of Caroline's footsteps had died away. From somewhere below he heard a faint cough. Hesitating, he brushed his knuckles against the door once more, then turned the knob and went in.

The woman sat on a high stool with her back to him, her head bent over something he couldn't see. When Kincaid said, 'Uh, hello,' she whipped around towards him and he saw that she held a paintbrush in her hand.

Julia Swann was not beautiful. Even as he formed the thought, quite deliberately and matter-of-factly, he found he couldn't stop looking at her. Taller, thinner, sharper than her mother, dressed in a white shirt with the tail out and narrow black jeans, she displayed no softly rounded curves in figure or manner. Her chin-length dark hair swung abruptly when she moved her head, punctuating her gestures.

He read his intrusion in her startled posture, felt it in the room's instantly recognizable air of privacy. 'I'm sorry to bother you. I'm Duncan Kincaid, from Scotland Yard. I did knock.'

'I didn't hear you. I mean, I suppose I did, but I wasn't paying attention. I often don't when I'm working.' Even her voice lacked the velvety resonance of Caroline's. She slid off the stool, wiping her hands on a bit of rag. 'I'm Julia Swann. But then you know all that, don't you?'

21

The hand she held out to him was slightly damp from contact with the cloth, but her grasp was quick and hard. He looked around for somewhere to sit, saw nothing but a rather tatty and overstuffed armchair which would place him a couple of feet below the level of her stool. Instead he chose to lean against a cluttered workbench.

Although the room was fairly large – probably, he thought, the result of knocking two of the house's original bedrooms into one – the disorder extended everywhere he looked. The windows, covered with simple white rice-paper blinds, provided islands of calm in the jumble, as did the high table Julia Swann had been facing when he entered the room. Its surface was bare except for a piece of white plastic splashed with bright daubs of paint, and a Masonite board propped up at a slight angle. Before she slid onto the stool again and blocked his view, he glimpsed a small sheet of white paper masking-taped to the board.

Glancing at the paintbrush still in her hand, she set it on the table behind her and pulled a packet of cigarettes from her shirt pocket. She held it towards him, and when he shook his head and said, 'No, thanks,' she lit one and studied him as she exhaled.

'So, Superintendent Kincaid – it is Superintendent, isn't it? Mummy seemed to be quite impressed by the title, but then that's not unusual. What can I do for you?'

'I'm sorry about your husband, Mrs Swann.' He tossed out an expected opening gambit, even though he suspected already that her response would not be conventional.

She shrugged, and he could see the movement of her shoulders under the loose fabric of her shirt. Crisply starched, buttons on the left – Kincaid wondered if it might have been her husband's.

'Call me Julia. I never got used to "Mrs Swann". Always sounded to me like Con's mum.' She leaned towards him and picked up a cheap porcelain ashtray bearing the words *Visit the Cheddar Gorge*. 'She died last year, so that's one bit of drama we don't have to deal with.'

'Did you not like your husband's mother?' Kincaid asked.

'Amateur Irish. All b'gosh and b'gorra.' Then she added more affectionately, 'I used to say that her accent increased proportionately to her distance from County Cork.' Julia smiled for the first time. It was her father's smile, as unmistakable as a brand, and it transformed her face. 'Maggie adored Con. She would have been devastated. Con's dad did a bunk when Con was a baby . . . if he ever had a dad, that is,' she added, only the corners of her lips quirking up this time at some private joke.

'I had the impression from your parents that you and your husband no longer lived together.'

'Not for . . . ' She spread the fingers of her right hand and touched the tips with her left forefinger as her lips moved. Her fingers were long and slender, and she wore no rings. 'Well, more than a year now.'

23

Kincaid watched as she ground out her cigarette in the ashtray. 'It's a rather odd arrangement, if you don't mind my saying so.'

'Do you think so, Mr Kincaid? It suited us.'

'No plans to divorce?'

Julia shrugged again and crossed her knees, one slender leg swinging jerkily. 'No.'

He studied her, wondering just how hard he might push her. If she were grieving for her husband, she was certainly adept at hiding it. She shifted under his scrutiny and patted her shirt pocket, as if reassuring herself that her cigarettes hadn't vanished, and he thought that perhaps her armour wasn't quite impenetrable. 'Do you always smoke so much?' he said, as if he had every right to ask.

She smiled and pulled out the packet, shaking loose another cigarette.

He noticed that her white shirt wasn't as immaculate as he'd thought – it had a smudge of violet paint across the breast. 'Were you on friendly terms with Connor? See him often?'

'We spoke, yes, if that's what you mean, but we weren't exactly what you'd call best mates.'

'Did you see him yesterday, when he came here for lunch?'

'No. I don't usually break for lunch when I'm working. Ruins my concentration.' Julia stubbed out her newly lit cigarette and slid off the stool. 'As you've done now. I might as well quit for the day.' She gathered a handful of paintbrushes and crossed the room to an old-fashioned washstand with basin and ewer. 'That's the one drawback up here,' she said, over her shoulder, 'no running water.'

His view no longer blocked by her body, Kincaid straightened up and examined the paper taped to the drawing board. It was about the size of a page in a book, smooth-textured, and bore a faint pencil sketch of a spiky flower he didn't recognize. She had begun to lay in spots of clear, vivid colour, lavender and green.

'Tufted vetch,' she said, when she turned and saw him looking. 'A climbing plant. Grows in hedgerows. Flowers in—'

'Julia.' He interrupted the rush of words and she stopped, startled by the imperative in his voice. 'Your husband died last night. His body was discovered this morning. Wasn't that enough to interrupt your concentration? Or your work schedule?'

She turned her head away, her dark hair swinging to hide her face, but when she turned back to him her eyes were dry. 'You'd better understand, Mr Kincaid. You'll hear it from others soon enough. The term "bastard" might have been invented to describe Connor Swann.

'And I despised him.'

Chapter Two

'A lager and lime, please.' Gemma James smiled at the barman. If Kincaid were there he would raise an eyebrow at the very least, mocking her preference. So accustomed to his teasing had she become that she actually missed it.

'A raw evening, miss.' The man set the cool glass before her, aligning it neatly in the centre of a beer mat. 'Have you come far?'

'Just from London. Beastly traffic getting out, though.' But the sprawl of western London had finally faded behind her, and she left the M40 at Beaconsfield and followed the Thames Valley. Even in the mist she had seen some of the fine Victorian houses fronting the river, relics of the days when Londoners used the upper Thames as a playground.

At Marlow she turned north and wound up into the beech-covered hills, marvelling that in a few miles she seemed to have entered a hidden world, dark and leafy and far removed from the broad, peaceful expanse of the river below.

'What are the Chiltern Hundreds?' she asked the

barman. 'I've heard that phrase all my life and never known what it meant.'

He set down a bottle he'd been wiping with a cloth and considered his answer. Approaching middle age, with dark, wavy, carefully groomed hair and the beginning of a belly, he seemed happy enough to pass the time chatting. The lounge was almost empty – a bit early for the regular Friday night customers, Gemma supposed – but cosy with a wood fire burning and comfortable tapestry-covered furniture. A buffet of cold pies, salads and cheeses stood at the bar's end, and she eyed it with anticipation.

Thames Valley CID had certainly been up to the mark, booking her into the pub in Fingest and giving her precise directions. When she arrived she'd found a stack of reports waiting for her in her room, and having attended to them, she had only to enjoy her drink and wait for Kincaid.

'The Chiltern Hundreds, now,' said the barman, bringing Gemma sharply back to the present, 'they used to divide counties up into Hundreds, each with its own court, and three of these in Buckinghamshire came to be known as the Chiltern Hundreds because they were in the Chiltern Hills. Stoke, Burnham and Desborough, to be exact.'

'Seems logical,' said Gemma, impressed. 'And you're very knowledgeable.'

'Bit of a local history buff in my spare time. I'm Tony, by the way.' He thrust a hand over the bar and Gemma shook it.

'Gemma.'

'All the Hundreds are obsolete now, but the Stewardship of the Chiltern Hundreds is still a nominal office under the Chancellor of the Exchequer, the holding of which is the only reason one is allowed to resign from the House of Commons. A bit of jiggery-pokery, really, and probably the only reason the office still exists.' He smiled at her, showing strong, even, white teeth. 'There, I've probably told you more than you ever wanted to know. Get you a refill?'

Gemma glanced at her almost-empty glass, deciding she'd drunk as much as she ought if she wanted to keep a clear head. 'Better not, thanks.'

'You here on business? We don't let the rooms much this time of year. November in these hills is not exactly a drawing point for holiday-makers.'

'Quite,' said Gemma, remembering the fine drizzle under the darkness of the trees. Tony straightened glassware and kept an attentive eye on her at the same time, willing to talk if she wanted, but not pushing her. His self-assured friendliness made her wonder if he might be the pub's owner or manager, but in any case he was certainly a likely repository for local gossip.

'I'm here about that drowning this morning, actually. Police business.'

Tony stared at her, taking in, she felt sure, the curling ginger hair drawn back with a clip, the casual barley-coloured pullover and navy slacks. 'You're a copper? Well, I'll be . . .' He shook his head, his wavy hair not disturbed a whit by his incredulity. 'Best-looking one I've seen, I must say.'

Gemma smiled, accepting the compliment in the

same good humour as it was given. 'Did you know him, the man who drowned?'

This time Tony tut-tutted as he shook his head. 'What a shame. Oh, everyone around here knew Connor. Doubt there's a pub between here and London where he hadn't put his head in once or twice. Or a racetrack. A real Jack the Lad, that one.'

'Well liked, was he?' asked Gemma, fighting her prejudice towards a man on such good terms with pints and horses. Only after she'd married Rob had she discovered that he considered flirting and gambling as inalienable rights.

'Connor was a friendly sort of bloke, always had a word and a pat on the back for you. Good for business, too. After he'd had a couple of pints he'd buy rounds for everybody in the place.' Tony leaned forward against the bar, his face animated. 'And what a tragedy for the family, after the other.'

'What other? Whose family?' Gemma asked, wondering if she'd missed a reference to another drowning in the reports she'd read.

'Sorry.' Tony smiled. 'It is a bit confusing, I'm sure. Connor's wife Julia's family, the Ashertons. Been here for donkey's years. Connor was upstart Irish, second generation, I think, but all the same . . .'

'What happened to the Ashertons?' Gemma encouraged him, interested.

'I was just a couple of years out of school, back from trying it out in London.' His white teeth flashed as he smiled. 'Decided the big city wasn't nearly as glamorous as I'd thought. It was just about this time of year, as a matter of fact, and wet. Seemed like it had rained for months on end.' Tony paused and pulled a half-pint mug from the rack, lifting it towards Gemma. 'Mind if I join you?'

She shook her head, smiling. 'Of course not.' He was enjoying himself thoroughly now, and the longer she let him string out the story, the more detail she'd get.

He pulled a half-pint of Guinness from the tap and sipped it, then wiped the creamy foam from his upper lip before continuing. 'What was his name, now? Julia's little brother. It's been twenty years, or close to it.' He ran his fingers lightly over his hair, as if the admission of time passing made him conscious of his age. 'Matthew, that was it. Matthew Asherton. All of twelve years old and some sort of musical prodigy, walking home from school one day with his sister, and drowned. Just like that.'

The image of her own son clutched unbidden at Gemma's heart – Toby half-grown, his blond hair darkened, his face and body maturing from little-boy chubbiness, snatched away. She swallowed and said, 'How terrible. For all of them, but especially Julia. First her brother and now her husband. How did the little boy drown?'

'I'm not sure anyone ever really knew. One of those freak things that happen sometimes.' He shrugged and drank down half his Guinness. 'Quite a hush-hush at the time. Nobody talked about it except in whispers, and it's still not mentioned to the family, I suppose.'

A draught of cold air stirred Gemma's hair and swirled around her ankles as the outer door opened. She turned and watched a foursome come in and settle at a corner table, waving a familiar greeting to Tony. 'Reservations in half an hour, Tony,' one of the men called. 'Same as usual, okay?'

'It'll be picking up a bit now,' Tony remarked to Gemma as he began pouring their drinks. 'Restaurant usually fills up on a Friday night – all the locals out for their weekly bit of fun, minus the kiddies.' Gemma laughed, and when the air blew cool again against her back she didn't turn in anticipation.

Light fingers brushed her shoulder as Kincaid slid onto the barstool beside her. 'Gemma. Propping up the bar without me, I see.'

'Oh, hullo, guv.' She felt the pulse jump in her throat, even though she'd been expecting him.

'And chatting up the locals, I see. Lucky bloke.' He grinned at Tony. 'I'll have a pint of . . . Brakspear, isn't it, that's brewed at Henley?'

'My boss,' Gemma said in explanation to Tony. 'Tony, this is Superintendent Duncan Kincaid.'

'Nice to meet you, I'm sure.' Tony gave Gemma a surprised glance as he put out a hand to Kincaid.

Gemma studied Kincaid critically. Tall and slender, brown hair slightly untidy, tie askew and tweed jacket beaded with rain – she supposed he didn't look like most people's idea of a proper Scotland Yard superintendent. And he was too young, of course. Superintendents should definitely be older and weightier.

'Tell all,' Kincaid said, when he'd got his pint and

31

Tony had busied himself serving drinks to the customers in the corner.

Gemma knew that he relied on her to digest information and spit the pertinent bits back out to him, and she rarely had to use her notes. 'I've been over Thames Valley's reports.' She nodded towards the rooms above their heads. 'Had them waiting for me when I got in, very efficient.' Closing her eyes for a moment, she marshalled her thoughts. 'They had a call at seven-oh-five this morning from a Perry Smith, lock-keeper at Hambleden Lock. He'd found a body caught in his sluicegate. Thames Valley called in a rescue squad to fish the body out, and they identified him from his wallet as Connor Swann, resident of Henley-on-Thames. The lock-keeper, however, once he'd recovered from the shock a bit, recognized Connor Swann as the son-in-law of the Ashertons, who live a couple of miles up the road from Hambleden. He said the family often walked there.'

'On the lock?' Kincaid asked, surprised.

'Apparently it's part of a scenic walk.' Gemma frowned and picked up the thread of her story where she'd left off. 'The local police surgeon was called in to examine the body. He found considerable bruising around the throat. Also, the body was very cold, but rigor had only just begun—'

'But you'd expect the cold water to retard rigor,' Kincaid interrupted.

Gemma shook her head impatiently. 'Usually in drowning cases rigor sets in very quickly. So he thinks it likely that the victim may have been strangled before he went in the water.'

'Our police surgeon makes a bloody lot of assumptions, don't you think?' Kincaid selected a bag of onion-flavoured crisps from a display and counted out the proper coins to Tony. 'We'll see what the post-mortem has to say.'

'Nasty things,' said Gemma, eyeing the crisps distastefully.

Mouth full, Kincaid answered, 'I know, but I'm starving. What about the interviews with the family?'

She finished the last of her drink before answering, taking a moment to shift mental gears. 'Let's see . . . they took statements from the in-laws as well as the wife. Yesterday evening, Sir Gerald Asherton conducted an opera at the Coliseum in London. Dame Caroline Stowe was at home in bed, reading. And Julia Swann, the wife, was attending a gallery opening in Henley. None of them reported having words with Connor or having any reason to think he might be worried or upset.'

'Of course they didn't.' Kincaid pulled a face. 'And none of this means a thing without some estimate of time of death.'

'You met the family, didn't you, this afternoon? What are they like?'

Kincaid made a noise that sounded suspiciously like 'hummmph'. 'Interesting. Might be better if I let you form your own impressions, though. We'll interview them again tomorrow.' He sighed and sipped his pint. 'Not that I'll hold my breath waiting for a revelation. None of them can imagine why anyone would want to kill Connor Swann. So we have no motive, no suspect, and we're not even sure it's murder.' Raising his glass, he made her a mock toast. 'I can't wait.'

A good night's sleep had imbued Kincaid with a little more enthusiasm for the case. 'The lock first,' he said to Gemma over breakfast in the Chequers' dining room. 'I can't get much further along with this until I see it for myself. Then I want to have a look at Connor Swann's body.' He gulped his coffee and squinted at her, adding, 'How do you manage to look fresh and cheerful so early in the morning?' She wore a blazer the bright russet colour of autumn leaves, her face glowed, and even her hair seemed to crackle with a life of its own.

'Sorry.' She smiled at him, but Kincaid thought her sympathy was tinged with pity. 'I can't help it. Something to do with genes, I expect. Or being brought up a baker's daughter. We rose early at my house.'

'Ugh.' He'd slept heavily, aided by one pint too many the night before, and it had taken him a second cup of coffee just to feel marginally alert.

'You'll get over it,' Gemma said, laughing, and they finished their breakfast in companionable silence.

They drove through the quiet village of Fingest in the early morning light and took the lane leading south, towards the Thames. Leaving Gemma's Escort in the carpark half a mile from the river, they crossed the road to the path. A chill wind blew into their faces as they started downhill, and when Kincaid's shoulder accidentally bumped against Gemma's, he felt her warmth even through his jacket.

Their path crossed the road running parallel to the river, then threaded its way between buildings and overgrown shrubbery. Not until they emerged from a fenced passage did they see the spread of the river. Leaden water reflected leaden sky, and just before them a concrete walkway zigzagged its way across the water. 'Sure this is the right place?' Kincaid asked. 'I don't see anything that looks like a lock.'

'I can see boats on the far side, past that bank. There must be a channel.'

'All right. Lead on, then.' He gave a mock-gallant little bow and stepped aside.

They ventured out onto the walkway single file, unable to walk abreast without brushing the tubular metal railing which provided some measure of safety.

Halfway out they reached the weir. Gemma stopped and Kincaid came to a halt behind her. Looking down at the torrent thundering beneath the walkway, she shivered and pulled the lapels of her jacket together. 'Sometimes we forget the power of water. And the peaceful old Thames can be quite a monster, can't it?'

'River's high from the rain,' Kincaid said, raising his voice over the roar. He could feel the vibration from the force of the water through the soles of his feet. Grasping the railing until the cold of the metal made his hands ache, he leaned over, watching the flood until he began to lose his equilibrium. 'Bloody hell. If you intended to push someone in, this would be the place to do it.' Glancing at Gemma, he saw that she looked cold and a little pinched, the dusting of freckles standing out against her pale skin. He placed a hand lightly on her shoulder. 'Let's get across. It'll be warmer under the trees.'

They walked quickly, heads down against the wind, eager for shelter. The walkway ran on another hundred yards or so past the weir, paralleling the bank, then turned abruptly to the left and vanished into the trees.

The respite proved brief, the belt of trees narrow, but it allowed them to catch their breath before they came out into the open again and saw the lock before them. Yellow scene-of-crime tape had been stretched along the concrete aprons on either side of the lock, but not across the sluicegates themselves. To their right stood a sturdy red-brick house. The small-paned windows were symmetrical, one on either side of the door, but the one nearest them sported such a thatch of untrimmed green creeper that it looked like a shaggy-browed eye.

As Kincaid put a hand on the tape and bent to duck under it, a man came out of the door of the house, dodging under stray twigs of creeper, and shouted at them. 'Sir, you're not to go past the tape. Police orders.'

Kincaid straightened up and waited, studying the man as he came towards them. Short and stocky, with grey hair bristle-cut, he wore a polo shirt bearing the Thames River Authority insignia, and carried a steaming mug in one hand. 'What was the lock-keeper's name?' Kincaid said softly in Gemma's ear.

Gemma closed her eyes for a second. 'Perry Smith, I think.'

'One and the same, if I'm not mistaken.' He pulled his warrant card from his pocket and extended it as the man reached them. 'Are you Perry Smith, by any chance?'

The lock-keeper took the card with his free hand and studied it suspiciously, then scrutinized Kincaid and Gemma as if hoping they might be impostors. He nodded once, brusquely. 'I've already told the police everything I know.'

'This is Sergeant James,' Kincaid continued in the same conversational tone, 'and you're just the fellow we wanted to see.'

'All I'm concerned with is keeping this lock operating properly, Superintendent, without police interference. Yesterday they made me keep the sluicegates closed while they picked about with their tweezers and little bags. Backed river traffic up for a mile,' he said, and his annoyance seemed to grow. 'Bloody twits, I tell you.' He included Gemma in his scowl and made no apology for his language. 'Didn't it occur to them what would happen, or how long it would take to clear up the mess?'

'Mr Smith,' Kincaid said soothingly, 'I have no intention of interfering with your lock. I only want to ask you a few questions' – he held up a hand as Smith opened his mouth – 'which I'm aware you've already answered, but I'd prefer to hear your story directly from you, not second hand. Sometimes things get muddled along the way.'

Smith's brow relaxed a fraction and he took a sip from his mug. The heavy muscles in his upper arm stood out as he raised it, straining against the sleeve-band of his knitted shirt. 'Muddled wouldn't be the half of it, if those idiots yesterday set any example.' Although he seemed unaware of the cold, he looked at Gemma as if seeing her properly for the first time, huddled partly in the shelter of Kincaid's body with her jacket collar held closed around her throat. 'I suppose we could go inside, miss, out of the wind,' he said, a bit less belligerently.

Gemma smiled gratefully at him. 'Thank you. I'm afraid I didn't dress for the river.'

Smith turned back to Kincaid as they moved towards the house. 'When are they going to take this bloody tape down, that's what I'd like to know?'

'You'll have to ask Thames Valley. Though if the forensics team has finished, I shouldn't think it would be long.' Kincaid paused as they reached the door, looking at the concrete aprons surrounding the lock and the grassy path leading upriver on the opposite side. 'Doubt they'll have had much luck.'

The floor of the hall was covered in sisal matting and lined with well-used-looking rubber boots, the walls hung with working gear – oilskin jackets and hats, bright yellow slickers, coils of rope. Smith led them through a door on the left into a sitting room as workaday as the hall.

The room was warm, if spartan, and Kincaid saw

Gemma let go of her collar and take out her notebook. Smith stood by the window, still sipping from his mug, keeping an eye on the river. 'Tell us how you found the body, Mr Smith.'

'I came out just after sunrise as always, have my first cuppa and make sure everything's shipshape for the day. Traffic starts early, some days, though not so much now as in the summer. Sure enough, upstream there was a boat waiting for me to operate the lock.'

'Can't they work it themselves?' asked Gemma.

He was already shaking his head. 'Oh, the mechanism's simple enough, but if you're too impatient to let the lock fill and drain properly you can make a balls-up of it.'

'Then what happened?' prompted Kincaid.

'I can see you don't know much about locks,' he said, looking at them with the sort of pity usually reserved for someone who hasn't learned to tie their shoelaces.

Kincaid refrained from saying that he had grown up in western Cheshire and understood locks perfectly well.

'The lock is kept empty when it's not in operation, so first I open the sluices in the head gate to fill the lock. Then when I opened the head gate for the boat to enter, up pops a body.' Smith sipped from his cup, then added disgustedly, 'Silly woman on the boat started squealing like a pig going to slaughter, you've never heard such a racket. I came in here and dialled nine-nine-nine, just to get some relief from the noise.' The corners of Smith's eyes crinkled in what might have been a smile. 'Rescue people fished him out and tried to resuscitate the poor blighter, though if you ask me, anybody with a particle of sense could see he'd been dead for hours.'

'When did you recognize him?' asked Gemma.

'Didn't. Not his body, anyway. But I looked at his wallet when they took it out of his pocket, and I knew the name seemed familiar. Took me a minute to place it.'

Kincaid moved to the window and looked out. 'Where had you heard it?'

Smith shrugged. 'Pub gossip, most likely. Everyone hereabouts knows the Ashertons and their business.'

'Do you think he could have fallen in from the top of the gate?' Kincaid asked.

'Railing's not high enough to keep a tall man from going over if he's drunk. Or stupid. But the concrete apron continues for a bit on the upstream side of the gate before it meets the old towpath, and there's no railing along it at all.'

Kincaid remembered the private homes he'd seen upstream on this side of the river. All had immaculate lawns running down to the water, some also had small docks. 'What if he went in further upstream?'

'The current's not all that strong until you get close to the gate, so if he went in along there,' – he nodded upstream – 'I'd say he'd have to have been unconscious not to have pulled himself out. Or already dead.'

'What if he went in here, by the gate? Would the current have been strong enough to hold him down?'

Smith gazed out at the lock a moment before

answering. 'Hard to say. The current is what holds the gate closed – it's pretty fierce. But whether it could hold a struggling man down . . . unlikely, I'd say, but you can't be sure.'

'One more thing, Mr Smith,' Kincaid said. 'Did you see or hear anything unusual during the night?'

'I go to bed early, as I'm always up by daybreak. Nothing disturbed me.'

'Would a scuffle have awakened you?'

'I've always been a sound sleeper, Superintendent. I can't very well say, now can I?'

'Sleep of the innocent?' whispered Gemma as they took their leave and Smith firmly shut his door.

Kincaid stopped and stared at the lock. 'If Connor Swann were unconscious or already dead when he went in the water, how in hell did someone get him here? It would be an almost impossible carry even for a strong man.'

'Boat?' ventured Gemma. 'From either upstream or down. Although why someone would lift him from a boat downstream of the lock, carry him round and dump him on the upstream side, I can't imagine.'

They walked slowly towards the path that would take them back across the weir, the wind at their backs. Moored boats rocked peacefully in the quiet water downstream. Ducks dived and bobbed, showing no concern with human activity that didn't involve crusts of bread. 'Was he already dead? That's the question, Gemma.' He looked at her, raising an eyebrow. 'Fancy a visit to the mortuary?'

Chapter Three

The smell of disinfectant always reminded Kincaid of his school infirmary, where Matron presided over the bandaging of scraped knees and wielded the power to send one home if the illness or injury proved severe enough. The inhabitants of this room, however, were beyond help from Matron's ministrations, and the disinfectant didn't quite mask the elusive tang of decay. He felt gooseflesh rise on his arms from the cold.

A quick call to Thames Valley CID had directed them to High Wycombe's General Hospital, where Connor Swann's body awaited post-mortem. The hospital was old, the mortuary still a place of ceramic tiles and porcelain sinks, lacking the rows of stainless-steel drawers which tucked bodies neatly away out of sight. Instead, the steel gurneys that lined the walls held humped, white-sheeted forms with toe tags peeping out.

'Who was it you wanted, now?' asked the attendant, a bouncy young woman whose name-tag read 'Sherry' and whose demeanour seemed more suited to a nursery school.

'Connor Swann,' said Kincaid, with an amused glance at Gemma.

The girl walked along the row of gurneys, flicking toe tags with her fingers as she passed. 'Here he is. Number four.' She tucked the sheet down to his waist with practised precision. 'And a nice clean one he is, too. Always makes it a bit easier, don't you think?' She smiled brightly at them, as if they were mentally impaired, then walked back to the swinging doors and shouted, 'Mickey,' through the gap she made with one hand. 'We'll need some help shifting him,' she added, turning back to Kincaid and Gemma.

Mickey emerged a moment later, parting the doors like a bull charging from a pen. The muscles in his arms and shoulders strained the thin fabric of his T-shirt, and he wore the short sleeves rolled up, displaying an extra inch or two of biceps.

'Can you give these people a hand with number four, Mickey?' Sherry enunciated carefully, her nursery-teacher manner now mixed with a touch of exasperation. The young man merely nodded, his acne-inflamed face impassive, and pulled a pair of thin latex gloves from his back pocket. 'Take all the time you want,' she added to Kincaid and Gemma. 'Just give me a shout when you've finished, okay? Cheerio.' She whisked past them, the tail of her white lab coat flapping, and went out through the swinging doors.

They moved the few steps to the gurney and stood. In the ensuing silence Kincaid heard the soft expulsion of Gemma's breath. Connor Swann's exposed neck and shoulders were lean and well formed, his thick straight hair brown with a hint of auburn. Kincaid thought it likely that in life he had been one of those high-coloured men who flushed easily in anger or excitement. His body was indeed remarkably unblemished. Some bruising showed along the left upper arm and shoulder, and when Kincaid looked closely he saw faint dark marks on either side of the throat.

'Some bruising,' Gemma said dubiously, 'but not the occlusion of the face and neck you'd expect with a manual strangulation.'

Kincaid bent over for a closer look at the throat. 'No sign of a ligature. Look, Gemma, across the right cheekbone. Is that a bruise?'

She peered at the smudge of darker colour. 'Could be. Hard to tell, though. His face could easily have banged against the gate.'

Connor Swann had been blessed with good bone structure, thought Kincaid, high wide cheekbones and a strong nose and chin. Above his full lips lay a thick, neatly trimmed, reddish moustache, looking curiously alive against the grey pallor of his skin.

'A good-looking bloke, would you say, Gemma?'

'Probably attractive, yes . . . unless he was a bit too full of himself. I got the impression he was quite the ladies' man.'

Kincaid wondered how Julia Swann felt about that – she hadn't impressed him as a woman willing to sit at home meekly while her husband played the lad. It also occurred to him to wonder how much of his desire to see Connor had to do with assessing the physical evidence, and how much to do with his personal curiosity about the man's wife.

He turned to Mickey and raised a questioning eyebrow. 'Could we have a look at the rest?'

The young man obliged wordlessly, flipping the sheet off altogether.

'He'd been on holiday, but I'd say not recently,' Gemma commented as they saw the faint demarcation of a tan against belly and upper thighs. 'Or maybe just summer boating on the Thames.'

Deciding he might as well imitate Mickey's nonverbal style of communication, Kincaid nodded and made a rolling motion with his hand. Mickey slid both gloved hands beneath Connor Swann's body, turning him with an apparent ease betrayed only by a barely audible grunt.

Wide shoulders, faintly freckled; a thin pale band on the neck bordering the hairline, evidence of a recent haircut; a mole where the buttock began to swell from the hollow of the back – all trivial things, thought Kincaid, but all proof of Connor Swann's uniqueness. It always came, this moment in an investigation when the body became a person, someone who had perhaps liked cheese-and-pickle sandwiches, or old Benny Hill comedies.

'Had enough, guv?' Gemma said, sounding a bit more subdued than usual. 'He's clean as a whistle this side.'

Kincaid nodded. 'Not much else to see. And nothing does us much good until we've traced his movements and got some estimate of time of death. Okay, Mickey,' he added, as the expression on the young man's face indicated they might as well have been speaking in Greek. 'I guess that's it. Let's look up Sherry Sunshine.' Kincaid looked back as they reached the door. Mickey had already turned Connor's body and tidied the sheet as neatly as before.

They found her in a cubbyhole just to the left of the swinging doors, bent industriously over a computer keyboard, cheerful as ever. 'Do you know when they've scheduled the post?' Kincaid asked.

'Um, let's see.' She studied a typed schedule stuck to the wall with Sellotape. 'Winnie can probably get to him late tomorrow afternoon or early the following morning.'

'Winnie?' Kincaid asked, fighting the absurd vision of Pooh Bear performing an autopsy.

'Dr Winstead.' Sherry dimpled prettily. 'We all call him that – he's a bit tubby.'

Kincaid contemplated attending the post-mortem with resignation. He had long ago got over any sort of grisly thrill at the proceedings. Now he found it merely distasteful, and the ultimate violation of human privacy sometimes struck him as unbearably sad. 'You'll let me know as soon as you schedule it?'

'Quick as a wink. I'll do it myself.' Sherry beamed at him.

Out of the corner of his eye Kincaid saw Gemma's expression and knew she'd rag him about buttering up the hired help. 'Thanks, love,' he said to Sherry, giving

her his full-wattage smile. 'You've been a great help.'
He waggled his fingers at her. 'Cheerio, now.'

'You're absolutely shameless,' said Gemma as soon
as they were through the outer doors. 'That poor little
duck was as susceptible as a baby.'

Kincaid grinned at her. 'Gets things done, though,
doesn't it?'

After a few unplanned detours due to her unfamiliarity
with High Wycombe's one-way system, Gemma found
her way out of the town. Following Kincaid's directions, she drove southwest, back into the hidden folds
of the Chiltern Hills. Her stomach grumbled a bit, but
they had decided that they should interview the Ashertons again before lunch.

In her mind she ran through Kincaid's and Tony's
comments about the family, her curiosity piqued. She
glanced at Kincaid, a question forming on her lips, but
his unfocused gaze told her he was somewhere else
entirely. He often got like that before an interview, as
if it were necessary for him to turn inward before
bringing that intense focus to bear.

She concentrated again on her driving, but she
suddenly felt extraordinarily aware of his long legs
taking up more than their share of the room in her
Escort's passenger compartment, and of his silence.

After a few minutes they reached the point where
she had to make an unfamiliar turning. Before she
could speak, he said, 'Just here. Badger's End lies about

halfway along this little road.' His fingertip traced a faint line on the map, between the villages of Northend and Turville Heath. 'It's unmarked, a shortcut for the locals, I suppose.'

Ribbons of water trickled across the pavement where a stream bed ran down through the trees and intersected the narrow road. A triangular yellow road sign warned DANGER: FLOODING, and suddenly the story Gemma had heard of Matthew Asherton's drowning seemed very immediate.

'Hard left,' Kincaid said, pointing ahead, and Gemma turned the wheel. The lane they entered was high-banked, just wide enough for the Escort to pass unscathed, and on either side thick trees arched until they met and intertwined overhead. It climbed steadily, and the high banks rose until the tree roots were at eye level. On the right, Gemma caught an occasional flash through the foliage of golden fields dropping down to a valley. On the left the woods crowded, darkly impenetrable, and the light filtering through the leafy canopy over the lane seemed green and liquid.

'Sledging,' Gemma said suddenly.

'What?'

'It reminds me of sledging. You know, bobsleighing. Or the Olympic luge.'

Kincaid laughed. 'Don't accuse me of poetic fancy. Careful now, watch for a turning on the left.'

They appeared to be nearing the top of the gradient when Gemma saw a gap in the left-hand bank. She slowed and eased the car onto the leaf-padded track, following it on and slightly downhill until she rounded a bend and came into a clearing. 'Oh,' she said softly, surprised. She'd expected a house built with the comfortable flint and timber construction she'd seen in the nearby villages. The sun, which had chased fitfully in and out of the cloud bank, found a gap, making dappled patterns against the white limestone walls of Badger's End.

'Like it?'

'I'm not sure.' Gemma rolled down the window as she turned off the engine, and they sat for a moment, listening. Beneath the silence of the woods they heard a faint, deep hum. 'It's a bit eerie. Not at all what I imagined.'

'Just wait,' said Kincaid as he opened the car door, 'until you meet the family.'

Gemma assumed that the woman who answered the door must be Dame Caroline Stowe – good quality, tailored wool slacks, blouse and navy cardigan, short, dark, well-cut hair liberally streaked with grey – everything about her spoke of conservative, middle-aged good taste. But when the woman stared at them blankly, coffee mug poised halfway to her mouth, then said, 'Can I help you with something?' Gemma's certainty began to waver.

Kincaid identified himself and Gemma, then asked for Sir Gerald and Dame Caroline.

'Oh, I'm sorry, you've just missed them. They've gone down to the undertakers for a bit. Making arrangements.' She transferred the coffee mug to her left hand and held out the right to them. 'I'm Vivian Plumley, by the way.'

'You're the housekeeper?' Kincaid asked, and Gemma knew from the less-than-tactful query that he'd been caught off guard.

Vivian Plumley smiled. 'You might say that. It doesn't offend me, at any rate.'

'Good.' Kincaid, Gemma saw, had recovered both aplomb and smile. 'We'd like a word with you as well, if we may.'

'Come back to the kitchen. I'll make some coffee.' She turned and led the way along the slate-flagged passage, then stepped back and let them precede her through the door at its end.

The kitchen had escaped modernization. While Gemma might sigh over photographs of gleaming space-age kitchens in magazines, she knew instinctively that they provided no emotional substitute for a room like this. Nubby braided rugs softened the slate floor, a scarred oak refectory table and ladder-backed chairs dominated the room's centre, and against one wall a red-enamelled Aga radiated warmth and comfort.

'Sit down, why don't you,' said Vivian Plumley, and gestured towards the table. Gemma pulled out a chair and sat, feeling tension she hadn't been aware of flow out of her muscles. 'Some biscuits?' added Vivian, and Gemma shook her head quickly, fearing they'd lose control of the interview entirely, seduced by the room's comfort.

Kincaid said, 'No, thank you,' and seated himself, taking the chair at the table's end. Gemma took her notebook from her bag and cradled it unobtrusively in her lap.

The drip coffeemaker worked as quickly as its expensive looks implied. It was only a few moments before the smell of fresh coffee began to fill the room. Vivian put together a tray with mugs, cream and sugar in silence, a woman enough at ease with herself not to make small talk. When the coffeemaker had finished its cycle, she filled the mugs and brought the tray to the table. 'Do help yourself. And that's real cream, I'm afraid, not dairy substitute. We have a neighbour who keeps a few Jerseys.'

'A treat not to be missed,' said Kincaid, pouring generously into his cup. Gemma smiled, knowing he usually drank it black. 'Are you not the housekeeper, then?' he continued easily. 'Have I put my foot in it?'

Vivian clinked her spoon around twice in her coffee cup and sighed. 'Oh, I'll tell you about myself, if you like, but it always sounds so dreadfully Victorian. I'm actually related to Caroline, second cousins once removed, to be exact. We're as close to the same age as never-mind, and we were at school together.' She paused and sipped from her cup, then made a slight grimace of discomfort. 'Too hot. We drifted apart, Caro and I, once we'd finished school. We both married, her career blossomed.' Vivian smiled.

'Then my husband died. An aneurysm.' The palms of her hands made a slapping sound as she brushed them together. 'Just like that, he was gone. I was left childless, with no job skills and not quite enough money to get by. This was thirty years ago, mind you, when not every woman grew up with the expectation of working.' She looked directly at Gemma. 'Quite different from your upbringing, I'm sure.'

Gemma thought of her mother, who had risen in the early hours of the morning to bake every day of her married life, then worked the counter in the shop from opening till closing. The possibility of *not* working never occurred to Gemma or her sister – it had been Gemma's driving ambition for the work to be of her own choosing, not something done purely for the necessity of putting food on the table. 'Yes, very different,' she said, in answer to Vivian Plumley's statement. 'What did you do?'

'Caro had two toddlers and a very demanding career.' She shrugged. 'It seemed a sensible solution. They had room, I had enough money of my own not to be totally dependent on the family, and I loved the children as if . . .'

They were your own. Gemma finished the sentence for her, and felt a rush of empathy for this woman who seemed to have made the best of what life had dealt her. She ran her fingers along the tabletop, noticing faint streaks of colour embedded in the wood's grain.

Watching her, Vivian said fondly, 'The children did everything at this table. They had most of their meals in the kitchen, of course. As much as their parents travelled, formal family dinners were a rare treat. School assignments, art projects – Julia did her first paintings here, when she was at grammar school.'

The children this . . . the children that . . . It seemed to Gemma as if time had simply stopped with the boy's death. But Julia had been there afterwards, alone. 'This must all be very difficult for Julia,' she said, feeling her way into the subject delicately, 'after what happened to her brother.'

Vivian looked away, grasping the table's edge with one hand, as if she were physically restraining herself from getting up. After a moment, she said, 'We don't talk about that. But yes, I'm sure Con's death has made life more difficult than usual for Julia. It's made life difficult for all of us.'

Kincaid, who had been sitting quietly, chair pushed back a bit from the table, mug cradled in his hands, leaned forward and said, 'Did you like Connor, Mrs Plumley?'

'Like him?' she said blankly, then frowned. 'It never occurred to me whether or not I should like Connor. He was just . . . Connor. A force of nature.' She smiled a little at her own analogy. 'A very attractive man in many ways, and yet . . . I always felt a little sorry for him.'

Kincaid raised an eyebrow but didn't speak, and Gemma followed his cue.

Shrugging, Vivian said, 'I know it sounds a bit silly to say one felt sorry for someone as larger-than-life as Con, but Julia baffled him.' The gold buttons on her cardigan caught the light as she shifted in her chair. 'He could never make her respond in the way he wanted, and he hadn't any experience with that. So he sometimes behaved . . . inappropriately.' A door slammed in the front of the house and she cocked her head, listening. Half-rising from her chair, she said, 'They're back. Let me tell—'

'One more thing, please, Mrs Plumley,' Kincaid said. 'Did you see Connor on Thursday?'

She sank down again, but perched on the edge of her seat with the tentative posture of one who doesn't intend staying long. 'Of course I saw him. I prepared lunch – just salad and cheese – and we all ate together in the dining room.'

'All except Julia?'

'Yes, but she often works through lunch. I took a plate up to her myself.'

'Did Connor seem his usual self?' Kincaid asked, his tone conversational, but Gemma knew from his still concentration that he was intent on her answer.

Vivian relaxed as she thought, leaning back in her chair again and absently tracing the raised flower pattern on her mug with her fingers. 'Con was always teasing and joking, but perhaps it seemed a bit forced. I don't know.' She looked up at Kincaid, frowning. 'Quite possibly I'm distorting things after the fact. I'm not sure I trust my own judgement.

Kincaid nodded. 'I appreciate your candour. Did he mention any plans for later in the day? It's important that we trace his movements.'

'I remember him glancing at his watch and saying something about a meeting, but he didn't say where or with whom. That was towards the end of the meal, and as soon as everyone had finished I came in here to do the washing up, then went to my room for a lie-down.

You might ask Caro or Gerald if he said something more to them.'

'Thank you. I'll do that,' Kincaid said with such courtesy that Gemma felt sure it would never occur to Vivian Plumley that she'd just told him how to do his job. 'It's strictly a formality, of course, but I must ask you about your movements on Thursday night,' he added almost apologetically.

'An alibi? You're asking me for an alibi for Connor's death?' Vivian asked, sounding more surprised than offended.

'We don't yet know exactly when Connor died. And it's more a matter of building known factors – the more we know about the movements of everyone connected with Connor, the easier it becomes to see gaps. Logic holes.' He made a circular gesture with his hands.

'All right.' She smiled, appeased. 'That's easy enough. Caro and I had an early supper in front of the fire in the sitting room. We often do when Gerald's away.'

'And after that?'

'We sat before the fire, reading, watching the telly, talking a little. I made some cocoa around ten o'clock, and when we'd finished it I went up to bed.' She added with a touch of irony, 'I remember thinking it had been a particularly peaceful and pleasant evening.'

'Nothing else?' Kincaid asked, straightening up in his chair and pushing away his empty mug.

'No,' Vivian said, but then paused and stared into space for a moment. 'I do remember something, but it's quite silly.' When Kincaid nodded encouragement, she continued. 'Just after I'd fallen asleep I thought I heard the doorbell, but when I sat up and listened, the house was perfectly quiet. I must have been dreaming. Gerald and Julia both have their own keys, of course, so there was no need to wait up for them.'

'Did you hear either of them come in?'

'I thought I heard Gerald around midnight, but I wasn't properly awake, and the next thing I knew it was daybreak and the rooks were making a god-awful racket in the beeches outside my window.'

'Couldn't it have been Julia?' Kincaid asked.

She thought for a moment, her brow furrowed. 'I suppose it could, but if it's not terribly late, Julia usually looks in on me before she goes up.'

'And she didn't that evening?'

When Vivian shook her head, Kincaid smiled at her and said, 'Thank you, Mrs Plumley. You've been very helpful.'

This time, before rising, Vivian Plumley looked at him and said, 'Shall I tell them you're here?'

Sir Gerald Asherton stood with his back to the sitting room fire, hands clasped behind him. He made a perfect picture of a nineteenth-century country squire, thought Gemma, with his feet spread apart in a relaxed posture and his bulk encased in rather hairy tweeds. He even sported suede elbow patches on his jacket. The only things needed to complete the tableau were a pipe and a pair of hunting hounds sprawled at his feet.

'So sorry to have kept you waiting.' He came towards them, pumped their hands and gestured them towards the sofa.

Gemma found the courtesy rather disarming, and suspected it was meant to be.

'Thank you, Sir Gerald,' Kincaid said, returning it in kind. 'And Dame Caroline?'

'Gone for a bit of a lie-down. Found the business at the undertakers rather upsetting, I'm afraid.' Sir Gerald sat in the armchair opposite them, crossed one foot over his knee and adjusted his trouser leg. An expanse of Argyle sock in autumnal orange and brown appeared between shoe and trouser cuff.

'If you don't mind my saying so, Sir Gerald,' Kincaid smiled as he spoke, 'it seems a little odd that your daughter didn't take care of the arrangements herself. Connor was, after all, her husband.'

'Just so,' answered Sir Gerald with a touch of asperity. 'Sometimes these things are best left to those not quite so close to the matter. And funeral directors are notorious for preying on the emotions of the newly bereaved.' Gemma felt a stab of pity at the reminder that this burly, confident man spoke from the worst possible personal experience.

Kincaid shrugged and let the matter drop. 'I need to ask you about your movements on Thursday night, sir.' At Sir Gerald's raised eyebrow, he added, 'Just a formality, you understand.'

'No reason why I shouldn't oblige you, Mr Kincaid. It's a matter of public record. I was at the Coliseum, conducting a performance of *Pelleas and Melisande*.' He favoured them with his large smile, showing healthily pink gums. 'Extremely visible. No one could have impersonated me, I assure you.'

Gemma imagined him facing an orchestra, and felt sure he dominated the hall as easily as he dominated this small room. From where she sat she could see a photograph of him atop the piano, along with several others in similar silver frames. She stood up unobtrusively and went to examine them. The nearest showed Sir Gerald in a tuxedo, baton in hand, looking as comfortable as he did in his country tweeds. In another he had his arm around a small dark-haired woman who laughed up at the camera with a voluptuous prettiness.

The photograph of the children had been pushed to the back, as if no one cared to look at it often. The boy stood slightly in the foreground, solid and fair, with an impish gap-toothed grin. The girl was a few inches taller, dark-haired like her mother, her thin face gravely set. This was Julia, of course. Julia and Matthew.

'And after?' she heard Kincaid say, and she turned back to the conversation, rather embarrassed by her lapse of attention.

Sir Gerald shrugged. 'It takes a while to wind down after a performance. I stayed in my dressing room for a bit, but I'm afraid I didn't take notice of the time. Then I drove straight home, which must have put me here sometime after midnight.'

'Must have?' Kincaid asked, his voice tinged with scepticism.

Sir Gerald held out his right arm, baring a hairy wrist for their inspection. 'Don't wear a watch, Mr Kincaid. Never found it comfortable. And a nuisance taking it off for every rehearsal or performance. Always lost the bloody things. And the car clock never worked properly.'

'You didn't stop at all?'

Shaking his head, Sir Gerald answered with the finality of one used to having his word taken as law. 'I did not.'

'Did you speak to anyone when you came in?' Gemma asked, feeling it was time she put an oar in.

'The house was quiet. Caro was asleep and I didn't wake her. I can only assume the same for Vivian. So you see, young lady, if it's an alibi you're after,' he paused and twinkled at Gemma, 'I suppose I haven't one.'

'What about your daughter, sir? Was she asleep as well?'

'I'm afraid I can't say. I don't remember seeing Julia's car in the drive, but I suppose someone could have given her a lift home.'

Kincaid stood. 'Thank you, Sir Gerald. We will need to talk to Dame Caroline again, at her convenience, but just now we'd like to see Julia.'

'I believe you know your way, Mr Kincaid.'

*

'Good God, I feel like I've been dropped right in the bloody middle of a drawing room comedy.' Gemma turned her head to look at Kincaid as she preceded him up the stairs. 'All manners and no substance. What are they playing at in this house?' As they reached the first landing, she stopped and turned to face him. 'And you'd think these women were made of glass, the way Sir Gerald and Mrs Plumley coddle them. "Mustn't upset Caroline . . . mustn't upset Julia,"' she hissed at him, remembering a bit belatedly to lower her voice.

Kincaid merely raised an eyebrow in that imperturbable manner she found so infuriating. 'I'm not sure I'd consider Julia Swann a good candidate for coddling.' He started up the next flight, and Gemma followed the rest of the way without comment.

The door swung open as soon as Kincaid's knuckles brushed it. 'Bless you, Plummy. I'm star—' Julia Swann's smile vanished abruptly as she took in their identity. 'Oh. Superintendent Kincaid. Back so soon?'

'Like a bad penny,' Kincaid answered, giving her his best smile.

Julia Swann merely stuck the paintbrush she'd had in her hand over her ear and stepped back enough to allow them to enter. Studying her, Gemma compared the woman to the thin, serious child in the photo downstairs. That Julia was certainly visible in this one, but the gawkiness had been transmuted into sleek style, and the innocence in the child's gaze had been lost long ago.

The blinds were drawn up, and a pale, watery light illuminated the room. The centre worktable, bare except for palette and white paper neatly masking-taped to a board, relieved the studio's general disorder. 'Plummy usually brings me up a sandwich about this time,' Julia said, as she shut the door and returned to the table. She leaned against it, gracefully balancing her weight, but Gemma had the distinct impression that the support she drew from it was more than physical.

A finished painting of a flower lay on the table. Gemma moved towards it almost instinctively, hand outstretched. 'Oh, it's lovely,' she said softly, stopping just short of touching the paper. Spare and sure in design, the painting had an almost oriental flavour, and the intense greens and purples of the plant glowed against the matte-white paper.

'Bread and butter,' said Julia, but she smiled, making an obvious effort to be civil. 'I've a whole series commissioned for a line of cards. Upscale National Trust, you know the sort of thing. And I'm behind schedule.' Julia rubbed at her face, leaving a smudge of paint on her forehead, and Gemma suddenly saw the weariness that her smart haircut and trendy black turtleneck and leggings couldn't quite camouflage.

Gemma traced the rough edge of the watercolour paper with a finger. 'I suppose I thought the paintings downstairs must be yours, but these are quite different.'

'The Flints? I should hope so.' Some of the abruptness returned to Julia's manner. She shook a cigarette from a pack on a side table and lit it with a hard strike of a match.

'I wondered about them as well,' Kincaid said. 'Something struck me as familiar.'

'You probably saw some of his paintings in books you read as a child. William Flint wasn't as well known as Arthur Rackham, but he did some marvellous illustrations.' Julia leaned against the worktable and narrowed her eyes against the smoke rising from her cigarette. 'Then came the breastscapes.'

'Breastscapes?' Kincaid repeated, amused.

'They are technically quite brilliant, if you don't mind the banal, and they certainly kept him comfortably in his old age.'

'And you disapprove?' Kincaid's voice held a hint of mockery.

Julia touched the surface of her own painting as if testing its worth, then shrugged. 'I suppose it is rather hypocritical of me. These keep me fed, and they supported Connor in the lifestyle to which he'd become accustomed.'

To Gemma's surprise, Kincaid didn't nibble at the proffered bait, but instead asked, 'If you dislike Flint's watercolours, why do they hang in almost every room in the house?'

'They're not mine, if that's what you're thinking. A few years ago Mummy and Daddy got bitten by the collector's bug. Flints were all the rage and they jumped on the bandwagon. Perhaps they thought I'd be pleased.' Julia gave them a brittle little smile. 'After all, as far as they're concerned, one watercolour looks pretty much like another.'

Kincaid returned her smile, and a look of understanding passed between them, as if they'd shared a joke. Julia laughed, her dark hair swinging with the movement of her head, and Gemma felt suddenly excluded. 'Exactly what lifestyle did your husband need to support, Mrs Swann?' she asked, rather too quickly, and she heard an unintended note of accusation in her voice.

Propping herself up on her work stool, Julia swung one black-booted foot as she ground the stub of her half-smoked cigarette into an ashtray. 'You name it. I sometimes thought Con felt honour-bound to live up to an image he created – whiskey, women and an eye for the horses, everything you'd expect from your stereotypical Irish rogue. I wasn't always sure he enjoyed it as much as he liked you to think.'

'Were there any women in particular?' Kincaid asked, his tone so lightly conversational he might have been inquiring about the weather.

She regarded him quizzically. 'There was always a woman, Mr Kincaid. The particulars didn't concern me.'

Kincaid merely smiled, as if refusing to be shocked by her cynicism. 'Connor stayed on in the flat you shared in Henley?'

Julia nodded, sliding off the stool to pull another cigarette from the crumpled packet. She lit it and leaned back against the table, folding her arms against her chest. The paintbrush still positioned over her ear gave her an air of slightly rakish industry, as if she might be a Fleet Street journalist relaxing for a brief moment in the newsroom.

'You were in Henley on Thursday evening, I believe?' Kincaid continued. 'A gallery opening?'

'Very clever of you, Mr Kincaid.' Julia flashed him a smile. 'Trevor Simons. Thameside.'

'But you didn't see your husband?'

'I did not. We move in rather different circles, as you might have guessed,' said Julia, the sarcasm less veiled this time.

Gemma glanced at Kincaid's face, anticipating an escalating response, but he only answered lazily, 'So I might.'

Julia ground out her cigarette, barely smoked this time, and Gemma could see a release of tension in the set of her mouth and shoulders. 'Now if you don't mind, I really must get back to work.' She included Gemma this time in the smile that was so like her father's, only sharper around the edges. 'Perhaps you could—'

'Julia.'

It was an old interrogation technique, the sudden and imperative use of the suspect's name, a breaking down of barriers, an invasion of personal space. Still, the familiarity in Kincaid's voice shocked Gemma. It was as if he knew this woman down to her bones and could sweep every shred of her artifice away with a casual flick of a finger.

Julia remained frozen in mid-sentence, her eyes locked on Kincaid's face. They might have been alone in the room.

'You were only a few hundred yards from Connor's flat. You could have stepped out for a smoke by the river, bumped into him, arranged to meet him later.'

A second passed, then another, and Gemma heard the rustle as Julia shifted her body against the work-table. Then Julia said slowly, 'I could have. But I didn't. It was my show, you see – my fifteen minutes in the limelight – and I never left the gallery at all.'

'And afterwards?'

'Oh, Trev can vouch for me well enough, I think. I slept with him.'

Chapter Four

'Division of labour,' Kincaid told Gemma as they stopped for a quick lunch at the pub in Fingest. 'You see if you can confirm Sir Gerald's alibi – that'll allow you a night or two at home with Toby – and I'll tackle Henley. I want to go over Connor Swann's flat myself, and I want to have a word with – what did Julia say his name was? Simons, that was it – Trevor Simons, at his gallery. I'd like to know a bit more about Julia's movements that night,' he added, and Gemma gave him a look he couldn't interpret.

They finished their sandwiches under Tony's watchful eye, then Gemma ran upstairs to pack her bag. Kincaid waited in the gravelled carpark, jingling the change in his pockets and drawing furrows in the gravel with his toe. The Ashertons were very plausible, but the more he thought about it, the more difficult it became to make sense of what they had told him. They seemed to have been on close terms with a son-in-law their daughter barely tolerated, and yet they also seemed to go to great lengths to avoid confrontation with Julia. He made a *J* in the gravel with his shoe, then carefully raked it over again. How had Julia Swann really felt about her husband? In his mind he saw her again, her thin face composed and her dark eyes fixed on his, and he found he didn't quite buy the tough persona she wore so successfully.

Gemma came out with her case, turning back for a moment to wave goodbye to Tony. The sun sparked from her hair, and it was only then that Kincaid realized it had ventured out from the clouds that had hidden it through the morning.

'Ready, guv?' asked Gemma as she stowed her things in the boot and slid behind the wheel of her Escort. Kincaid put his speculations aside and got in beside her. She seemed to him refreshingly uncomplicated, and he offered up a silent thanks, as he often did, for her competent cheerfulness.

Leaving the hills behind, they took the wide road to Henley. They had a glimpse of the river beneath the Henley Bridge, then it vanished behind them as the one-way system shunted them into the centre of town. 'Can you get back to the pub all right, guv?' Gemma asked as she pulled up to let Kincaid out in Henley's marketplace.

'I'll ask the local lads for a lift. I could pull rank and requisition a car, of course,' he added, grinning at her, 'but just now I think I'd rather not be bothered with parking the bloody thing.'

He stepped out of the car and gave the door a parting thump with his hand, as if he were slapping a horse on its way. Gemma let up on the brake, but before nosing back into the traffic she rolled down the

Escort's driver's-side window and called to him, 'Mind how you go.'

Turning back, he waved jauntily to her, then watched the car disappear down Hart Street. The sudden note of concern in her voice struck him as odd. It was she who was driving back to London, while he merely intended an unannounced interview and a recce of Connor Swann's flat. He shrugged and smiled – he'd quite grown to like her occasional solicitousness.

Henley Police Station lay just across the street, but after a moment's hesitation he turned and instead climbed the steps to the Town Hall. A cardboard sign taped to the wall informed him that Tourist Information could be found downstairs, and as he descended, he wrinkled his nose at the standard public building accoutrements – cracked lino and the sour smell of urine.

Fifty pence bought him a street map of the town, and he unfolded it as he walked thankfully back out into the sun. He saw that his way lay down Hart Street and along the river, so tucking the map in his jacket and his hands in his pockets, he strolled down the hill. The square tower of the church seemed to float against the softly coloured hills beyond the river, and it drew him on like a lodestone. 'St Mary the Virgin,' he said aloud as he reached it, thinking that for an Anglican church the syllables rolled off the tongue with a very Catholic resonance. He wondered where they meant to bury Connor Swann. Irish Catholic, Irish Protestant? Could it possibly matter? He didn't yet know enough about him to hazard a guess.

Crossing the busy street, he stood for a moment on the Henley Bridge. The Thames spread peacefully before him, so different from the thunder of water through Hambleden Weir. The river course wound north for a bit after Henley, curved to the east before it reached Hambleden, then meandered northeast before turning south towards Windsor. Could Connor have gone in the river here, in Henley, and drifted downstream to Hambleden Lock? He thought it highly unlikely, but made himself a mental note to check with Thames Valley.

He took a last look at the red-and-white Pimm's umbrellas beckoning temptingly from the terrace of the Angel pub, but he had other fish to fry.

A few hundred yards beyond the pub he found the address. Next door to the tearoom a discreet sign announced THE GALLERY, THAMESIDE, and a single painting in an ornate gilded frame adorned the shop window. The door chimed electronically as Kincaid pushed it open, then clicked softly behind him, shutting out the hum of sound from the riverside.

The silence settled around him. Even his footsteps were muffled by a thickly padded Berber carpet covering the floor. No one seemed to be about. A door stood open at the back of the shop, revealing a small walled garden, and beyond that another door.

Kincaid looked round the room with interest. The paintings, spaced generously around the walls, seemed to be mostly late nineteenth- and early twentieth-century watercolours, and most were river landscapes.

In the room's centre a pedestal held a sleek bronze

of a crouching cat. Kincaid ran his hand over the cool metal and thought of Sid. He had made arrangements with his neighbour, Major Keith, to look after the cat when he was away from home. Although the major professed to dislike cats, he looked after Sid with the same gruff tenderness he had shown to the cat's former owner. Kincaid thought that for the major, as well as himself, the cat formed a living link to the friend they had lost.

Near the garden door stood a desk, its cluttered surface a contrast to the spare neatness he saw everywhere else. Kincaid glanced quickly at the untidy papers, then moved into the second small room which lay a step down from the first.

He caught his breath. The painting on the opposite wall was a long narrow rectangle, perhaps a yard wide and a foot high, and it was lit by a lamp mounted just above it. The girl's body almost filled the frame. Dressed in shirt and jeans, she lay on her back in a meadow, eyes closed, hat tilted back on her auburn hair, and beside her on the grass a basket of ripe apples spilled over onto an open book.

A simple-enough composition, almost photographic in its clarity and detail, but it possessed a warmth and depth impossible to capture with a camera. You could feel the sun on the girl's upturned face, feel her contentment and pleasure in the day.

Other paintings by the same artist's hand were hung nearby, portraits and landscapes filled with the same vivid colours and intense light. As Kincaid looked at them he felt a sense of longing, as if such beauty and perfection existed forever just out of his reach, unless he, like Alice, could step through the frame and into the artist's world.

He had bent forward to peer at the illegibly scrawled signature when behind him a voice said, 'Lovely, aren't they?'

Startled, Kincaid straightened and turned. The man stood in the back doorway, his body in shadow as the sun lit the garden behind him. As he stepped into the room, Kincaid saw him more clearly – tall, thin and neat-featured, with a shock of greying hair and glasses that gave him an accountant-like air at odds with the casual pullover and trousers he wore.

The door chimed as Kincaid started to speak. A young man came in, his face white against the dead-black of his clothes and dyed hair, a large and battered leather portfolio tucked under his arm. His get-up would have been laughable if not for the look of supplication on his face. Kincaid nodded to Trevor Simons, for so he assumed the man who had come in from the garden to be, and said, 'Go ahead. I'm in no hurry.'

Rather to Kincaid's surprise, Simons looked carefully at the drawings. After a few moments he shook his head and tucked them back into the portfolio, but Kincaid heard him give the boy the name of another gallery he might try. 'The trouble is,' he said to Kincaid as the door chimed shut, 'he can't paint. It's a bloody shame. They stopped teaching drawing and painting in the art colleges back in the sixties. Graphic artists – that's what they all want to be – only no one tells them there aren't any jobs. So they come out of art college like this wee chappie,' he nodded towards the street, 'hawking their wares from gallery to gallery like itinerant peddlers. You saw it – fairly competent airbrushed crap, without a spark of originality. If he's lucky he'll find a job frying up chips or driving a delivery van.'

'You were courteous enough,' said Kincaid.

'Well, you have to have some sympathy, haven't you? It's not their fault they're ignorant, both in technique and in the realities of life.' He waved a hand dismissively. 'I've nattered on long enough. What can I do for you?'

Kincaid gestured towards the watercolours in the second room, 'These—'

'Ah, she's an exception,' Simons said, smiling. 'In many ways. Self-taught, for one, which was probably her salvation, and very successful at it, for another. Not with these,' he added quickly, 'although I think she will be, but with the work she does on commission. Stays booked two years in advance. It's very difficult for an artist who is successful commercially to find the time to do really creative work, so this show meant a lot to her.'

Realizing the answer even as he asked and feeling an utter fool, Kincaid said, 'The artist – who is she?'

Trevor Simons looked puzzled. 'Julia Swann. I thought you knew.'

'But . . .' Kincaid tried to reconcile the flawless but rather emotionally severe perfection of Julia's flowers with these vibrantly alive paintings. He could see similarities now in technique and execution, but the outcome was astonishingly different. Making an attempt to collect himself, he said, 'Look. I think perhaps I ought to go out and come in again, I've made such a muddle of things. My name's Duncan Kincaid' – he extended his warrant card in its folder – 'and I came to talk to you about Julia Swann.'

Trevor Simons looked from the warrant card to Kincaid and back again, then said rather blankly, 'It looks like a library permit. I always wondered, you know, when you see them on the telly.' He shook his head, frowning. 'I don't understand. I know Con's death has been a dreadful shock for everyone, but I thought it was an accident. Why Scotland Yard? And why me?'

'Thames Valley has treated it as a suspicious death from the beginning, and asked for our assistance at Sir Gerald Asherton's request.'

Kincaid had delivered this with no intonation, but Simons raised an eyebrow and said, 'Ah.'

'Indeed,' Kincaid answered, and when their eyes met it occurred to him that he might be friends with this man under other circumstances.

'And me?' Simons asked again. 'Surely you can't think Julia had anything to do with Con's death?'

'Were you with Julia all Thursday evening?' Kincaid said, pushing a bit more aggressively, although the note of incredulity in Simons's voice had struck him as genuine.

Unruffled, Simons leaned against his desk and folded his arms. 'More or less. It was a bit of a free-for-all

in here.' He nodded, indicating the two small rooms.
'People were jammed in here like sardines. I suppose
Julia might have popped out to the loo or for a smoke
and I wouldn't have noticed, but not much longer than
that.'

'What time did you close the gallery?'

'Ten-ish. They'd eaten and drunk everything in
sight, and left a wake of litter behind like pillaging
Huns. We had to push the last happy stragglers out of
the door.'

'We?'

'Julia helped me tidy up.'

'And after that?'

Trevor Simons looked away for the first time. He
studied the river for a moment, then turned back to
Kincaid with a reluctant expression. 'I'm sure you've
seen Julia already. Did she tell you she spent the
night? I can't imagine her being silly enough to protect
my honour.' Simons paused, but before Kincaid could
speak he went on. 'Well, it's true enough. She was here
in the flat with me until just before daybreak. A small
attempt at discretion, creeping out with the dawn,' he
added with a humourless smile.

'She didn't leave you at any time before that?'

'I think I would have noticed if she had,' Simons
answered, this time with a genuine flash of amusement, then he quickly sobered and added, 'Look, Mr
Kincaid, I don't make a habit of doing this sort of thing.
I'm married and I've two teenage daughters. I don't
want my family hurt. I know,' he continued hurriedly,

as if Kincaid might interrupt him, 'I should have considered the consequences beforehand, but one doesn't, does one?'

'I wouldn't know,' Kincaid answered in bland policemanese, all the while thinking, *Does one not, or does one consider the consequences and choose to act anyway?* The image of his ex-wife came to him, her straight flaxen hair falling across her shuttered face. *Had Vic considered the consequences?*

'You don't live here, then?' he asked, breaking the train of thought abruptly. He gestured towards the door across the garden.

'No. In Sonning, a bit further upriver. The flat was included in the property when I bought the gallery, and I use it mainly as a studio. Sometimes I stay over when I'm painting, or when I've an opening on.'

'You paint?' asked Kincaid, a little surprised.

Simons's smile was rueful. 'Am I a practical man, Mr Kincaid? Or merely a compromised one? You tell me.' The question seemed to be hypothetical only, for he continued, 'I knew when I left art school I wasn't quite good enough, didn't have that unique combination of talent and luck. So I used a little family money and bought this gallery. I found it a bit ironic that Julia's opening also marked the anniversary of my twenty-fifth year here.'

Kincaid wasn't inclined to let him off the hook, although he suspected his curiosity was more personal than professional. 'You didn't answer my question.'

'Yes, I paint, and I feel insulted if I'm referred to as

a "local artist" rather than an "artist who paints locally". It's a fine distinction, you understand,' he added mockingly. 'Silly, isn't it?'

'What sort of things do you paint?' Kincaid asked, scanning the paintings on the walls of the small room.

Simons followed his gaze and smiled. 'Sometimes I do hang my own work, but I haven't any up just now. I've had to make room for Julia's paintings, and frankly I've other things that sell better than mine, although I do paint Thames landscapes. I use oils – I'm not good enough yet to paint in watercolour, but one day I will be.'

'Is what Julia does that difficult, then?' Kincaid allowed himself to study Julia's lamplit painting, and discovered that he had been deliberately resisting doing so. It drew him, as she did, in a way that felt both familiar and perilous. 'I always thought that one just made a choice, watercolours or oils, depending on what one liked.'

'Watercolour is much more difficult,' Simons said patiently. 'In oil you can make any number of mistakes and just as easily cover them up, the more the merrier. Watercolour requires a confidence, perhaps even a certain amount of ruthlessness. You must get it right the first time.'

Kincaid looked at Julia's paintings with new respect. 'You said she was self-taught? Why not art college, with her talent?'

Simons shrugged. 'I suppose her family didn't take her seriously. Musicians do tend to be rather one-dimensional, even more so than visual artists. Nothing else exists for them. They eat, sleep and breathe music, and I imagine that to Sir Gerald and Dame Caroline, Julia's paintings were just amusing dabs of colour on paper.' He stepped down into the lower room and walked over to the large painting, staring at it. 'Whatever the reason, it allowed her to develop in her own way, with no taint of graphic mediocrity.'

'You have a special relationship,' Kincaid said, watching the way Trevor Simons's slender body blocked the painting in an almost protective posture. 'You admire her – do you also resent her?'

After a moment Simons answered, his back still to Kincaid. 'Perhaps. Can we help but envy those touched by the gods, however briefly?' He turned and the brown eyes behind the spectacles regarded Kincaid candidly. 'Yet I have a good life.'

'Then why have you risked it?' Kincaid said softly. 'Your wife, family . . . perhaps even your business?'

'I never intended it.' Simons gave a self-mocking bark of laughter. 'Famous last words – I never meant to do it. It was just . . . Julia.'

'What else didn't you intend, Trevor? Just how far did your loss of judgement take you?'

'You think *I* might have killed Connor?' His eyebrows shot up above the line of his spectacles and he laughed again. 'I can't lay claim to sins of that magnitude, Mr Kincaid. And why would I want to get rid of the poor bloke? Julia had already chewed him up and spat out the partially digested remains.'

Kincaid grinned. 'Very descriptively put. And will she do the same to you?'

'Oh, I expect so. I've never been able to delude myself sufficiently to think otherwise.'

Pushing aside an untidy stack of papers, Kincaid sat on the edge of Simons's desk and stretched out his legs. 'Did you know Connor Swann well?'

Simons put his hands in his pockets and shifted his weight in the manner of a man suddenly territorially displaced. 'Only to speak to, really. Before they separated he came in with Julia occasionally.'

'Was he jealous of you, do you think?'

'Con? Jealous? That would be the pot calling the kettle black! I never understood why Julia put up with him as long as she did.'

A passer-by stopped and peered at the painting in the window, as had several others since Kincaid had come into the gallery. Beyond her the light had shifted, and the shadows of the willows lay longer on the pavement. 'They don't come in,' Kincaid said as he watched her move towards the tea shop and pass from his view.

'No. Not often.' Simons gestured at the paintings lining the walls. 'The prices are a bit steep for impulse buying. Most of my customers are regulars, collectors. Though sometimes one of those window-shoppers will wander in and fall in love with a painting, then go home and save up pennies out of the housekeeping or the beer money until they have enough to buy it.' He smiled. 'Those are the best, the ones that know nothing about art and buy out of love. It's a genuine response.'

Kincaid looked at the illuminated painting of the girl in the meadow, her eyes gently closed, her faintly freckled face tilted to the sun, and acknowledged his own experience. 'Yes, I can see that.'

He stood and regarded Trevor Simons, who, whatever his sins, seemed a perceptive and decent man. 'A word of advice, Mr Simons, which I probably shouldn't give. An investigation like this moves out in ripples – the longer it takes the wider the circle becomes. If I were you I'd do some damage control – tell your wife about Julia if you can. Before we do.'

Kincaid sat at the table nearest the window in the tea shop. The tin pot had leaked as he poured, and his cup sat in a wet ring on the speckled plastic tabletop. At the next table he recognized the woman who had stopped at the gallery window a few minutes before – middle-aged, heavyset, her greying hair tightly crimped. Although the air in the shop was warm enough to form faint steamy smudges on the windowpanes, she still wore a waterproof jacket over her bulky cardigan. Perhaps she feared it might rain unexpectedly inside? When she looked up, he smiled at her, but she looked away, her face frozen in an expression of faint disapproval.

Gazing idly at the river again, he fingered the key in his trouser pocket. Gemma had acquired Connor's key, address and a description of the property from Thames Valley along with the initial reports. Until a year ago Julia and Connor had lived together in the flat he thought must be just along the terrace, near the willow-covered islands he could see from the window.

Julia might have stopped in here often for a morning coffee or a cup of afternoon tea. He imagined her suddenly, sitting across the booth from him in a black sweater, smoking jerkily, frowning in concentration. In his mind she rose and went out into the street. She stood before the gallery for a moment, as if hesitating, then he heard the door chime as she opened it and went in.

Shaking his head, Kincaid downed the remains of his tea in one gulp. He slid from the booth and presented his soggy bill to the girl behind the counter, then followed Julia's phantom out into the lengthening shadows.

He walked towards the river meadows, gazing alternately at the placid river on his left and the blocks of flats on his right. It surprised him that these riverside addresses weren't more elegant. One of the larger buildings was neo-Georgian, another Tudoresque, and both were just a trifle seedy, like dowagers out in soiled housecoats. The shrubbery grew rankly in the gardens, brightened only by the dark red dried heads of sedum and the occasional pale blue of Michaelmas daisies. But it was November after all, Kincaid thought charitably, looking at the quiet river. Even the kiosk advertising river trips and boats for hire was shuttered and locked.

The road narrowed and the large blocks of flats gave way to lower buildings and an occasional detached house. Here the river seemed less separate from the land, and when he reached the high black wrought-iron fence he recognized it from the scrawled description in his pocket. He grasped two of the spiked bars in his hands and peered through them. A commemorative ceramic plaque set into the wall of the nearest building informed him that the flats were quite recently developed, so perhaps Julia and Connor had been among the first tenants. They were built to look like boathouses, in a soft-red brick with an abundance of white-trimmed windows, white deck railings and white peaked gables adorned with gingerbread. Kincaid thought them a bit overdone, but pleasantly so, for they harmonized with both the natural landscape and the surrounding buildings. Like the Prince of Wales, he found most contemporary architecture to be a blight upon the landscape.

Dodging an array of parked boats and trailers, Kincaid walked along the fence until he found a gate. The flats were staggered behind a well-tended garden, and none was quite identical to the next. He found the house easily, one of the three-tiered variety, raised above the ground on stiltlike supports. Feeling suddenly as if he were trespassing, he fitted the key in the lock, but no one called out to him from the adjacent decks.

He had expected black and white.

Illogically, he supposed, considering the intensity of colour Julia used in her paintings. This was a softer palette, almost Mediterranean, with pale yellow walls and terra-cotta floors. Casually provincial furniture filled the sitting room and a fringed Moroccan rug softened the tile floor. On a tiled platform against one wall stood an enamelled wood-burning stove. A small painted table in front of the sofa held a chess set. Had Connor played, Kincaid wondered, or had it been merely for show?

A sports jacket lay crumpled over the back of a chair, an untidy pile of newspapers spilled from sofa to floor and a pair of boat shoes peeked from beneath the coffee table. The male clutter seemed incongruous, an intrusion on an essentially feminine room. Kincaid ran his forefinger across a tabletop, then brushed off the resulting grey fuzz against his trouser leg. Connor Swann had not been much of a housekeeper.

Kincaid wandered into the adjoining kitchen. It had no windows, but opened to the sitting room with its view of the river. Unlike the sitting room, however, it looked immaculate. Cans of olive oil and coloured-glass bottles of vinegar stood out like bright flags against the oak cabinets and yellow countertops, and a shelf near the cooktop held an array of well-thumbed cookbooks. *Julia Child*, read Kincaid, *The Art of Cooking. The Italian Kitchen. La Cucina Fresca.* There were more, some with lavish colour photographs that made him hungry just looking. Glass jars filled with pasta lined another open shelf.

Kincaid opened the fridge and found it well stocked with condiments, cheeses, eggs and milk. The freezer held a few neatly wrapped and labelled packages of meat and chicken, a loaf of French bread, and some plastic containers of something Kincaid guessed might be homemade soup stock. A pad beneath the telephone held the beginnings of a grocery list: *aubergines, tomato paste, red-leaf lettuce, pears.*

The descriptions Kincaid had heard of Connor Swann had not led him to expect an accomplished and enthusiastic cook, but this man had obviously not resorted to zapping frozen dinners in the microwave.

The first floor held a master bedroom and bath done in the same soft yellows as the ground floor, and a small room which apparently served as an office or study. Kincaid continued up the stairs to the top floor.

It had been Julia's studio. The wide windows let in a flood of late afternoon light, and over the willow-tops he could see the winding Thames. A bare table stood in the centre of the room, and an old desk pushed against one wall held some partially used sketch pads and a wooden box filled with odds and ends of paint tubes. Curious, Kincaid rummaged through them. He hadn't known that professional watercolours came in tubes. *Winsor Red. Scarlet Lake. Ultramarine Blue.* The names ran through his mind like poetry, but the tubes left the fine dust of neglect on his finger-tips. The room itself felt empty and unused.

He slowly retraced his steps, stopping once more at the door to the bedroom. The bed was hastily made, and a pair of trousers lay thrown over a chair, belt dangling.

The sense of a life interrupted hung palpably in the air. Connor Swann had meant to shop for groceries, prepare dinner, put out the newspapers, brush his teeth, slide under the warmth of the blue-and-yellow quilt on the bed. Kincaid knew that unless he came to an understanding of who Connor Swann had been, he had little hope of discovering who had killed him, and he realized that all his knowledge and perceptions of him were filtered through Julia and her family.

This was Julia's house. Every room bore her imprint, and except for the kitchen, Connor seemed to have only drifted across its surface. Why had Julia left it, like a commander who held all the advantages retreating from the citadel?

Kincaid turned from the bedroom and went into the study. The room contained nothing but a desk and chair facing the window, and a wing-backed chair with a reading lamp. Sitting in the straight-backed chair, he turned on the green-shaded desk lamp and began picking desultorily through the clutter.

A leather-bound appointment book came first to hand. Starting with January, Kincaid flipped slowly through it. The names of the racetracks jumped out first – Epsom, Cheltenham, Newmarket ... They rotated regularly through the months. Some had times written beside them, others sharp exclamation points. A good day?

Kincaid went back to the beginning, starting more carefully. In between races he began to see the pattern of Connor's social life. Dates for lunch, dinner, drinks, often accompanied by a name, a time and the words *Red Lion*. *Bloody hell*, thought Kincaid, *the man had kept up an exhausting social schedule*. And to make it worse, pubs and hotels called the Red Lion were as common as sheep in Yorkshire. He supposed the logical place to start would be the plush old hotel here in Henley, next to the church.

Golf dates appeared often, as well as the notation

Meet with J., followed by a dash and varying names, some cryptic, some, like Tyler Pipe and Carpetland, obviously businesses. It looked as though these weren't all social engagements, but rather business appointments, entertaining clients of some sort. Kincaid had assumed that Connor lived off the Asherton income, and nothing in the Thames Valley reports had led him to think otherwise, but perhaps that hadn't been the case. He closed the book and began shuffling through the papers on the desktop, then had a thought and opened the diary again. *Lunch at B.E.* appeared every Thursday, regular as clockwork.

The stack on the desktop resolved itself into ordinary household bills, betting slips, a set of racing-form books, a corporate report from a firm in Reading, and an auction catalogue. Kincaid shrugged and continued his inventory. Paperclips, paper knife, a mug emblazoned with HENLEY ART FEST, which held a handful of promotional pens.

He found Connor's cheque book in the left-hand drawer. A quick look through the register revealed the expected monthly payments, as well as regular deposits labelled *Blackwell, Gillock and Frye*. A firm of solicitors? wondered Kincaid? An interesting pattern began to form – he returned to the beginning of the register, double-checking. The first cheque written after every deposit was made out to a K. Hicks, and the amounts, although not the same, were always sizeable.

Lost as he was in speculation, it took a moment for the soft click from downstairs to penetrate Kincaid's consciousness. He looked up. Dusk had fallen as he worked. Through the window the outline of the willows showed charcoal against a violet sky.

The sounds were more definitive this time – a louder click, followed by a creak. Kincaid slid from the chair and moved quietly out into the hall. He listened for a moment, then went quickly down the stairs, keeping his feet carefully to the outside of the treads. When he reached the last step, the light came on in the sitting room. He listened again, then stepped around the corner.

She stood by the front door, one hand still on the light switch. The glow from the table lamps revealed tight jeans, a fuzzy pink sweater in a weave so loose it revealed the line of her bra, impossibly high heels, blonde hair permed into Medusa-like ropes. He could see the quick rise and fall of her chest beneath the sweater.

'Hullo,' he said, trying a smile.

She took one gulping breath before she shrieked 'Who the bloody hell are you?'

Chapter Five

Disoriented, Gemma reached out and touched the other side of the double bed, patted it. Empty. Opening her eyes, she saw the faint grey light brightening the wrong side of the room.

She came fully awake. New flat. No husband. Of course. Sitting up against the pillows, she pushed the tangle of hair away from her face. It had been months since she dreamed of Rob, and she had thought that particular ghost well laid to rest.

The hot water had just begun to gurgle through the radiator pipes as the automatic timer switched on the central heating. For a panicked moment she wondered why the alarm hadn't gone off, then relaxed in relief. It was Sunday. She closed her eyes and snuggled down into the pillows, feeling that luxurious laziness that comes with waking early and knowing one doesn't have to get up.

Sleep, however, refused to be coaxed back. The thought of the interview she'd managed to schedule later in the morning at the Coliseum niggled at her consciousness until finally, with a yawn, she swung her feet from under the duvet. The opera had seemed the logical place to start checking out Gerald Asherton's story, and she found herself looking forward to her day with a tingle of pleasure.

When her toes touched the floor they curled involuntarily from the cold, and she fumbled for her slippers as she shrugged into her dressing gown. At least she could take advantage of the time before Toby awakened to have a quiet cup of coffee and organize her thoughts for the day.

A few minutes later the flat was warming nicely and she sat at the black-slatted table in front of the garden windows, cradling a hot mug in her hands and questioning her sanity.

She had sold her house in Leyton – three bedrooms, semi-detached with garden, a symbol in brick and pebbledash of Rob's unrealistic plans for their marriage – and instead of buying the sensible flat in Wanstead she'd had in mind, she'd leased . . . this. She gazed round the room, bemused.

Her estate agent had begged, 'Just have a quick look, Gemma, that's all I ask. I know it's not what you're looking for, but you simply must see it.' And so she had come, and seen, and signed on the dotted line, finding herself the surprised tenant of the converted garage behind a square detached Victorian house in a tree-lined street in Islington. The house itself was unexpected, standing as it did between two of Islington's most elegant Georgian terraces, but it occupied its space with the confidence of good breeding.

The garage was separate from the house, and lower than the garden, so that the hip-high windows which lined one entire wall of the flat were actually ground level on the outside. The owners, a psychiatrist who worked from a shed in the garden, and his wife, had done up the garage in what the agent described as 'Japanese minimalist' décor.

Gemma almost laughed aloud, thinking of it. An exercise in 'minimalist living' would be a fitting description of what it had become for her. The flat was basically one large room, furnished with a futon and a few other sleek, contemporary pieces. Cubbyholes along the wall opposite the bed contained kitchen and water closet, and a storage room with a small window had become Toby's bedroom. The arrangement didn't allow much privacy, but privacy with a small child was a negligible quality anyway, and Gemma couldn't imagine sharing her bed with anyone in the foreseeable future.

Gemma's furniture and most of their belongings had been stored in the back of her parents' bakery in Leyton High Road. Her mum had shaken her faded red curls and tut-tutted. 'What were you thinking of, love?'

A quiet, tree-lined street with a park at its end. A green, walled garden, filled with interesting nooks and crannies for a little boy to hide in. A secret place, filled with possibilities. But Gemma had merely said, 'I like it, Mum. And it's nearer the Yard,' doubting her mother would understand.

She felt stripped clean, pared down to essentials, serene in the room's black-and-grey simplicity.

Or at least she had until this morning. She frowned,

wondering again what had made her feel so unsettled, and the image of twelve-year-old Matthew Asherton came unbidden to her mind.

She rose, put two slices of brown bread in the toaster that stood on the tabletop and went to kiss Toby awake.

Having deposited Toby at her mum's, Gemma took the tube to Charing Cross. As the train pulled away, the rush of wind down the tunnel whipped her skirt around her knees and she hugged the lapels of her jacket together. She left the station and entered the pedestrian mall behind St Martin-in-the-Fields, and rounding the church into St Martin's Lane she found the outside no better. A gust of north wind funnelled down the street, flinging grit and scraps of paper and leaving tiny whirlwinds in its wake.

She rubbed her eyes with her knuckles and blinked several times to clear them, then looked about her. Before her on the corner stood the Chandos Pub, and just beyond it a black-and-white vertical sign said LONDON COLISEUM. Blue and white banners emblazoned with the letters ENO surrounded it and drew her eyes upwards. Against the blue-washed canvas of the sky, the ornate white cupola stood out sharply. Near the top of the dome, white letters spelled out ENGLISH NATIONAL OPERA rather sedately, and Gemma thought they must be lit at night.

Something tugged at her memory and she realized she'd been here before. She and Rob had been to a

play at the Albery Theatre up the street, and afterwards had stopped for a drink at the Chandos. It had
been a warm night and they'd taken their drinks
outside, escaping the smoky crush in the bar. Gemma
remembered sipping her Pimm's and watching the
opera-goers spill out onto the pavement, their faces
animated, hands moving with quick gestures as they
dissected the performance. 'It might be fun,' she'd said
rather wistfully to Rob.

He had smiled in his condescending way and said,
light voice mocking, 'Old cows in silly costumes
screeching their lungs out? Don't be stupid, Gem.'

Gemma smiled now, thinking of the photo she'd
seen of Caroline Stowe. Rob would've fallen over
himself if he'd come face-to-face with her. Old cow,
indeed. He'd never know what he had missed.

She pushed through the lobby doors, feeling a small
surge of excitement at her own entrance into this
glamorous fairy-tale world. 'Alison Douglas,' she said
to the heavy grey-haired woman at the reception desk.
'The orchestra manager's assistant. I've an appointment with her.'

'You'll have to go round the back, then, ducks,' the
woman answered in less than rarefied accents. She
made a looping motion with her finger. 'Round the
block, next to the loading bay.'

Feeling somewhat chastened, Gemma left the
plush-and-gilt warmth of the lobby and circled the
block in the indicated direction. She found herself in
an alleylike street lined with pub and restaurant delivery entrances. With its concrete steps and peeling

paint, the stage entrance to the London Coliseum was distinguished only by the increasingly familiar ENO logo near the door. Gemma climbed up and stepped inside, looking around curiously at the small lino-floored reception area.

To her left a porter sat inside a glass-windowed kiosk; just ahead another door barred the way into what must be the inner sanctum. She announced herself to the porter and he smiled as he handed her a sign-in sheet on a clipboard. He was young, with a freckled face and brown hair that looked suspiciously as if it were growing out from a Mohawk cut. Gemma looked more closely, saw the tiny puncture in his earlobe which should have held an earring. He'd made a valiant effort to clean up for the job, no doubt.

'I'll just give Miss Alison a ring,' he said as he handed her a sticky badge to wear. 'She'll be right down for you.' He picked up the phone and murmured something incomprehensible into it.

Gemma wondered if he'd been on duty after last Thursday evening's performance. His friendly grin augured well for an interview, but she had better wait until she wouldn't be interrupted.

Church bells began to ring close by. 'St Martin's?' she asked.

He nodded, checking the clock on the wall behind him.

'Eleven o'clock on the dot. You can set your watch by it.'

Was there a congregation for eleven o'clock services, Gemma wondered, or did the church cater solely to tourists?

Remembering how surprised she'd been when Alison Douglas had agreed to see her this morning, she asked the porter, 'Business as usual here, even on a Sunday morning?'

He displayed the grin. 'Sunday matinée. One of our biggest draws, especially when it's something as popular as *Traviata*.'

Puzzled, Gemma tugged her notebook from her purse and flipped quickly through it. '*Pelleas and Melisande*. I thought you were doing *Pelleas and Melisande*.'

'Thursdays and Saturdays. Productions—'

The inner door opened and he paused as a young woman came through, then continued to Gemma, 'You'll see.' He winked at her. 'Alison'll make sure you do.'

'I'm Alison Douglas.' Her cool hand clasped Gemma's firmly. 'Don't mind Danny. What can I do for you?'

Gemma took in the short light brown hair, black sweater and skirt, platform shoes, which didn't quite raise her to Gemma's height, but Alison Douglas's most notable characteristic was an air of taking herself quite seriously.

'Is there somewhere we could talk? Your office, perhaps?'

Alison hesitated, then opened the inner door, indicating by a jerk of her head that Gemma should precede her through it. 'You'd better come along in, then. Look,' she added, 'we've a performance in just under three hours and I've things I absolutely must do. If you don't mind following along behind me we can talk as we go.'

'All right,' Gemma agreed, doubting she'd get a better offer. They had entered a subterranean maze of dark green corridors. Already lost, Gemma followed hard on Alison Douglas's heels as they twisted and turned, went up, down and around. Occasionally, she looked down at the dirty green carpet beneath her feet, wondering if she recognized the pattern of that particular stain. Could she follow them like Hansel and Gretel's breadcrumbs? The smells of damp and disinfectant made her want to sneeze.

Alison turned back to speak to her, stopped suddenly and smiled. Gemma felt sure her 'bewilderment had been entirely visible, and thought for once she ought to be grateful her every emotion registered on her face.

'Back-of-house,' Alison said, her brusque manner softening for the first time. 'That's what all the unglamorous bits are called. It's quite a shock if one's never been backstage, isn't it? But this is the heart of the theatre. Without this' – she gestured expansively around her – 'nothing happens out front.'

'The show doesn't go on?'

'Exactly.'

Gemma suspected that the key to loosening Alison Douglas's tongue was her work. 'Miss Douglas, I'm not sure I understand what you do.'

Alison moved forward again as she spoke. 'My boss

– Michael Blake – and I are responsible for all the administrative details of the running of the orchestra. We–' Glancing at Gemma's face, she hesitated, seeming to search for a less complicated explanation. 'We make sure everything and everyone are where they should be when they should be. It can be quite a demanding business. And Michael's away for a few days just now.'

'Do you deal directly with the conductors?' Gemma asked, taking advantage of the opening, slight as it was, but the corridor turned again and Alison pushed aside the faded plush curtain which barred their way. She stepped back to allow Gemma to pass through first.

Gemma stopped and stared, her mouth open in surprise. Beside her, Alison said softly, 'It is rather amazing, isn't it? I begin to take it for granted until I see it through someone else's eyes. This is the largest theatre in the West End, and it has the largest backstage area of any theatre in London. That's what allows us to put on several productions simultaneously.'

The cavernous space bustled with activity. Pieces of scenery belonging to more than one production stood side by side in surreal juxtaposition. 'Oh,' Gemma said, watching a huge section of stone wall roll easily across the floor, guided by two men in overalls. 'So that's what Danny meant. Thursdays and Saturdays Sir Gerald conducts *Pelleas and Melisande* – Fridays and Sundays someone else is doing . . . what did he say?'

'*La Traviata.* Look.' Alison pointed across the stage. 'There's Violetta's ballroom, where she and Alfredo sing their first duet. And there – ' she gestured towards the section of stone wall, now slotted neatly into a recess – 'that's part of King Arkel's castle, from *Pelleas*.' She looked at Gemma, studied her watch, looked once again at Gemma and said, 'There are a few things I simply must see to. Why not have a look round here while I get things in hand? After that I'll try to manage a quarter of an hour in the canteen with you.' She was already moving away from Gemma as she finished, the soles of her platform shoes clicking on the wooden floor.

Gemma walked to the lip of the stage and looked out. Before her the tiers of the auditorium rose in baroque splendour, blue velvet accented with gilt. The chandeliers hung from the dome high above her like frosted moons. She imagined all the empty seats filled, and the expectant eyes upon her, waiting for her to open her mouth and sing. Cold crept up her spine and she shivered. Caroline Stowe might look delicate, but to stand on a stage like this and face the crowd required a kind of strength Gemma didn't possess.

She looked down into the pit and smiled. At least Sir Gerald had some protection, and could turn his back on the audience.

A thread of music came from somewhere, women's voices carrying a haunting, lilting melody. Gemma turned and walked towards the back of the stage, straining to hear, but the banging and thumping going on around her masked even the sound's direction. She didn't notice Alison Douglas's return until the woman spoke. 'Did you see the pit? We jam a hundred and nineteen players into that space, if you can imagine that, elbow to—'

Gemma touched her arm. 'That music – what is it?'

'What – ?' Alison listened for a moment, puzzled, then smiled. 'Oh, that. That's from *Lakme*, Mallika's duet with Lakme in the high priest's garden. One of the girls in *Traviata* is singing Mallika next month at Covent Garden. I suppose she's swotting by listening to a recording.' She glanced at her watch, then added, 'We can get that cup of tea now, if you like.'

The music faded. As Gemma followed Alison back into the maze of corridors she felt an odd sadness, as if she'd been touched by something beautiful and fleeting. 'That opera,' she said to Alison's back, 'does it have a happy ending?'

Alison looked back over her shoulder, her expression amused. 'Of course not. Lakme sacrifices herself to protect her lover, in the end.'

The canteen smelled of frying chips. Gemma sat across the table from Alison Douglas, drinking tea strong enough to put fur on her tongue and trying to find a comfortable position for her backside in the moulded plastic chair. Around them men and women dressed in perfectly ordinary clothes drank tea and ate sandwiches, but when Gemma caught snippets of conversation it contained such obscure musical and technical terms that it might as well have been a foreign language. She pulled her notebook from her handbag and took another sip of tea, grimacing at the tannin's bite. 'Miss Douglas,' she said as she saw Alison touch the face of her wristwatch with her fingertips, 'I appreciate your time. I'll not take up any more than necessary.'

'I'm not sure I understand how I can help you. I mean, I know about Sir Gerald's son-in-law. It's an awful thing to happen, isn't it?' Her forehead creased as she frowned, and she looked suddenly very young and unsure, like a child encountering tragedy for the first time. 'But I can't see what it has to do with me.'

Gemma flipped open her notebook and uncapped her pen, then laid both casually beside her teacup. 'Do you work closely with Sir Gerald?'

'No more so than with any of the conductors – ' Alison paused and smiled – 'but I enjoy it more. He's such a dear. Never gets in a tizzy, like some of them.'

Hesitating to admit she didn't understand how the system worked, Gemma temporized with, 'Does he conduct often?'

'More than anyone except our music director.' Alison leaned over the table towards Gemma and lowered her voice. 'Did you know that he was offered the position, but declined it? This was all years ago, way before my time, of course. He said he wanted to have more freedom to work with other orchestras, but I think it had something to do with his family. He and Dame Caroline started with the company back at Sadler's Wells – he would have been the obvious choice.'

'Does Dame Caroline still sing with the company?

I would have thought ... I mean, she has a grown daughter ...'

Alison laughed. 'What you mean is that she's surely past it, right?' She leaned forward again, her animated face revealing how much she enjoyed teaching the uninitiated. 'Most sopranos are in their thirties before they really hit their stride. It takes years of work and training to develop a voice, and if they sing too much, too soon, they can do irreparable damage. Many are at the peak of their careers well into their fifties, and a few exceptional singers continue beyond that. Although I must admit, sometimes they look a bit ridiculous playing the *ingénue* parts when they get really long in the tooth.' She grinned at Gemma, then continued more seriously. 'Not that I think that would have happened to Caroline Stowe. I can't imagine her looking ridiculous at any age.'

'You said "would have happened". I don't—'

'She retired. Twenty years ago, when their son died. She never sang publicly again.' Alison had lowered her voice, and although her expression was suitably concerned, she told the story with the relish people usually reserve for someone else's misfortune. 'And she was brilliant. Caroline Stowe might have been one of the most renowned sopranos of our time.' Sounding genuinely regretful, Alison shook her head.

Gemma took a last sip of tea and pushed her cup away as she thought about what she'd heard. 'Why the title, then, if she stopped singing?'

'She's one of the best vocal coaches in the country,

if not the world. A lot of the most promising singers in the business have been taught, and are still being taught, by Caroline Stowe. And she's done a tremendous amount for the company.' Alison gave a wry smile, adding, 'She's a very influential lady.'

'So I understand,' said Gemma, reflecting that it was Dame Caroline's influence, and Sir Gerald's, that had dragged the Yard into this investigation in the first place. Seeing Alison straighten up in her chair, Gemma asked, 'Do you know what time Sir Gerald left the theatre on Thursday evening?'

Alison thought for a moment, wrinkling her forehead. 'I really don't know. I spoke to him in his dressing room just after the performance, around eleven o'clock, but I didn't stay more than five minutes. Had to meet someone,' she added with a dimple and a lowering of her lashes. 'You'll have to ask Danny. He was on duty that night.'

'Did Sir Gerald seem upset in any way? Anything different about his routine that night?'

'No, not that I can think—' Alison stopped, hand poised over her teacup. 'Wait. There was something. Tommy was with him. Of course, they've known each other practically forever,' she added quickly, 'but we don't often see Tommy here after a performance, at least not in the conductor's dressing room.'

Feeling the sense of the interview fast escaping her, Gemma said distinctly, 'Who exactly is Tommy?'

Alison smiled. 'I forgot you wouldn't know. Tommy is Tommy Godwin, our Wardrobe Manager. And it's not that he considers one of his visits akin to a divine blessing, like some costume designers I could name – ' she paused and rolled her eyes – 'but if he's here at the theatre he's usually busy with Running Wardrobe.'

'Is he here today?'

'Not that I know of. But I expect you can catch him tomorrow at LB House.' This time Gemma's bewilderment must have been evident, because before she could form a question, Alison continued. 'That's Lilian Baylis House, in West Hampstead, where we have our Making Wardrobe. Here.' She reached for Gemma's notebook. 'I'll write down the address and phone number for you.'

A thought occurred to Gemma as she watched Alison write in a looping, schoolgirl hand. 'Did you ever meet Sir Gerald's son-in-law, Connor Swann?'

Alison Douglas flushed. 'Once or twice. He came to ENO functions sometimes.' She returned the pen and notebook, then ran her fingers around the neck of her black sweater.

Gemma cocked her head while she considered the woman across the table – attractive, about her own age, and single, if her unadorned left hand and the date she'd alluded to were anything to go by. 'Shall I take it he tried to chat you up?'

'He didn't mean anything by it,' Alison said, a little apologetically. 'You know, you can tell.'

'All flash and no substance?'

Alison shrugged. 'I'd say he just liked women . . . he made you feel special.' She looked up, and for the first time Gemma noticed that her eyes were a light, clear brown. 'We've all talked about it, of course. You know what the gossip mill's like. But this is the first time I've really let myself think ...' She swallowed once, then added slowly. 'He was a lovely man. I'm sorry he's dead.'

The canteen tables were emptying rapidly. Alison looked up and grimaced, then bustled Gemma back into the dark green tunnels. Murmuring an apology, she left Gemma once again in Danny the porter's domain.

''Ullo, miss,' said Danny, ever cheerful. 'You get what you came for?'

'Not quite.' Gemma smiled at him. 'But you may be able to help me.' She pulled her warrant card from her handbag and held the open case where he could see it clearly.

'Crikey!' His eyes widened and he looked her up and down. 'You don't look like a copper.'

'Don't get cheeky with me, mate,' she said, grinning. Resting her elbows on the counter-sill, she leaned forward earnestly. 'Can you tell me what time Sir Gerald signed out last Thursday evening, Danny?'

'Ooh, alibis, is it?' The glee on Danny's face made him look like an illustration in an Enid Blyton novel.

'Routine inquiries just now,' Gemma said, managing to keep a straight face. 'We need to know the movements of everyone who might have had contact with Connor Swann the day he died.'

Danny lifted a binder from the top of a stack and

opened it at the back, flipping through the last few pages. 'Here.' He pointed, holding the page up where Gemma could see. 'Midnight on the dot. That's what I remembered, but I thought you'd want – what is it, corroboration?'

Sir Gerald's signature suited him, thought Gemma, a comfortable but strong scrawl. 'Did he usually stay so long after a performance, Danny?'

'Sometimes.' He glanced at the sheet again. 'But he was last out that night. I remember because I wanted to lock up – had a bird waiting in the wings, you might say.' He winked at Gemma. 'There was something, though,' he said more hesitantly. 'That night . . . Sir Gerald . . . well, he was half-cocked, like.'

Gemma couldn't keep the surprise from her voice. 'Sir Gerald was drunk?'

Danny ducked his head in embarrassment. 'I didn't really like to say, miss. Sir Gerald always has a kind word for everybody. Not like some.'

'Has this happened before?'

Danny shook his head. 'Not that I can remember. And I've been here over a year now.'

Gemma quickly entered Danny's statement in her notebook, then closed it and returned it to her bag. 'Thanks, Danny. You've been a great help.'

He passed over the sign-in sheet for her initial, his grin considerably subdued.

'Cheerio, then,' she said as she turned towards the door.

Danny called out to her before she could open it.

'There's one other thing, miss. You know the son-in-law, the one what snuffed it?' He held up his ledger and pointed to an entry near Sir Gerald's. 'He was here that day as well.'

Chapter Six

Eggs, bacon, sausage, tomatoes, mushrooms – and could that possibly be kidneys? Kincaid pushed the questionable items a little to one side with the tip of his fork. Kidneys in steak-and-kidney pie he could manage, but kidneys at breakfast were a bit much. Otherwise the Chequers had done itself proud. Surveying his breakfast laid out on the white tablecloth, complete with china teapot and a vase of pink and yellow snap-dragons, he began to think he should feel grateful for Sir Gerald Asherton's influence. His accommodations when out of town on a case were seldom up to these standards.

As he'd slept late, the more righteous early risers had long since finished their breakfasts and he had the dining room to himself. He gazed out through the leaded windows at the damp and windy morning as he ate, enjoying his unaccustomed leisure. Leaves drifted and swirled, their golds and russets a bright contrast against the still-green grass of the churchyard. The congregation began to arrive for the morning service, and soon the verges of the lanes surrounding the church were lined with cars parked end to end.

Wondering lazily why a parish church would draw such a crowd, he was suddenly struck by the desire to see for himself. He pushed a last bite of toast and marmalade into his mouth. Still chewing, he ran upstairs, grabbed a tie from his room and hastily knotted it on his way back down.

He slipped into the last pew just as the church bells began to ring. As he looked around it occurred to him that this was most likely the Ashertons' church. He wondered who knew them and if some of those gathered had come out of curiosity, hoping to see the family.

None of the Ashertons were in evidence, however, and as the peaceful order of the service settled over him, he found his mind drawn back to the previous evening's revelations.

It had taken him a few minutes to calm her down enough to get her name – Sharon Doyle – and even then she'd taken his warrant card and examined it with the intensity of the marginally literate.

'I've come for me things,' she said, shoving the card back at him as if it might burn her fingers. 'I've a right to 'em. I don't care what anybody says.'

Kincaid backed up until he reached the sofa, then sat down on its edge. 'Who would say you didn't?' he asked easily.

Sharon Doyle folded her arms, pushing her breasts up against the thin weave of her sweater. 'Her.'

'Her?' Kincaid repeated, resigned to an exercise in patience.

'You know. Her. The wife. *Julia*,' she mimicked in an accent considerably more precise than her own. Hostility seemed to be triumphing over fright, but although she moved nearer him, she still stood with her feet planted firmly apart.

'You have a key,' he said, making it a statement rather than a question.

'Con gave it to me.'

Kincaid looked at the softly rounded face, young beneath the makeup and bravado. Gently, he said, 'How did you find out Connor was dead?'

She stared at him, her lips pressed together. After a moment her hands dropped to her sides and her body sagged like a rag doll that had lost its stuffing. 'Down the pub,' she answered so quietly that he read her lips as much as heard her.

'You'd better sit down.'

Folding into the chair across from him as if unaware of her body, she said, 'Last night. I'd gone round to the George. He hadn't rung me up when he said, so I thought, I'm bloody well not going to sit home on my own. Some bloke'd buy me a drink, chat me up – serve Con bloody well right.' Her voice wavered at the last and she swallowed, then wet her lips with the pink tip of her tongue. 'The regulars were all talking about it. I thought they were havin' me on, at first.' She fell silent and looked away from him.

'But they convinced you?'

Sharon nodded. 'Local lad came in, he's a constable. They said, "Ask Jimmy. He'll tell you."'

'Did you?' Kincaid prompted after another moment's silence, wondering what he might do to loosen her tongue. She sat huddled in her chair, arms folded again across her breasts, and as he studied her he thought he saw a faint blue tinge around her lips. Remembering a drinks trolley he'd seen near the wood-stove as he explored the room, he stood and went over to it. He chose two sherry glasses from the glassware on the top shelf, filling them liberally from a bottle of sherry he found beneath.

On closer inspection he discovered that the stove was laid ready for a fire, so he lit it with a match from the box on the tiled hearth and waited until the flames began to flicker brightly. 'This will take the chill off,' he said as he returned and offered the drink to Sharon. She looked up at him dully and lifted her hand, but the glass tipped as she took it, spilling pale gold liquid over the rim. When he wrapped her unresponsive fingers around the stem, he found them icy to the touch. 'You're freezing,' he said, chiding her. 'Here, take my jacket.' He slipped off his tweed sports jacket and draped it over her shoulders, then circled the room until he found the thermostat for the central heating. The room's glass-and-tile Mediterranean look made for a pleasant effect, he decided, but it wasn't too well suited for the English climate.

'Good girl.' He sat down again and lifted his own glass. She'd drunk some of hers, and he thought he saw a faint flush of colour on her cheeks. 'That's better.

Cheers,' he added, sipping his sherry, then said, 'You've had a rough time, I think, since last night. Did you ask the constable, then, about Connor?'

She drank again, then wiped her hand across her lips. 'He said, "Why d'you want to know, then?" and gave me this fishy-eyed look, so I knew it was true.'

'Did you tell him why you wanted to know?'

Sharon shook her head and the blonde curls bounced with the movement. 'Said I just knew him, that's all. Then they started a slanging match about whose round it was, and I slipped out the door by the loo.'

Her survival instincts had functioned well, even in shock, Kincaid thought, a good indication that she'd had plenty of experience looking after herself. 'What did you do then?' he asked. 'Did you come here?'

After a long moment she nodded. 'Stood about outside for hours, bloody well freezing it was, too. I still thought, you know, maybe . . .' She put the fingers of both hands over her mouth quickly, but he'd seen her lip tremble.

'You had a key,' he said gently. 'Why didn't you come in and wait?'

'Didn't know who might come in here, did I? Might tell me I hadn't any right.'

'But today you got up your courage.'

'Needed my things, didn't I?' she said, but she looked away, and Kincaid fancied there was more to it than that.

'Why else did you come, Sharon?'

'You wouldn't understand.'

'Try me.'

She met his eyes and seemed to see in them some possibility of empathy, for after a moment she said, 'I'm nobody now, do you see? I thought I'd never have another chance just to be here, like . . . we had some good times here, Con and me. I wanted to remember.'

'Didn't you think Con might have left you the flat?' Kincaid asked.

Looking down into her glass, she swirled the few remaining drops of sherry. 'Couldn't,' she said, so quietly that he had to lean forward to hear.

'Why couldn't he?'

'Not his.'

The drink didn't seem to have done much in the way of lubricating her tongue, Kincaid thought. Getting anything out of her was worse than pulling teeth. 'Whose is it, then?'

'Hers.'

'Connor was living in Julia's flat?' He found the idea very odd indeed. Why hadn't she booted him out and stayed herself, rather than going back home to her parents? It sounded much too amicable an arrangement for a couple who had supposedly not been speaking to one another.

Of course, he added to himself as he considered the girl sitting across from him, it might not have been true. Perhaps Connor had needed a handy excuse. 'Is that why Connor didn't have you move in with him?'

His jacket slipped from Sharon's shoulders as she shrugged, re-exposing the pale swell of her breasts through the weave of the pink fuzzy sweater. 'He said it wasn't right, it being Julia's house and all.'

Kincaid hadn't imagined Connor Swann being a great one for moral scruples, but then Connor was proving to be full of surprises. Glancing at the open-plan kitchen, he asked, 'Do you cook?'

Sharon looked at him as if he had a slate loose. 'Course I can cook. What do you take me for?'

'No, I mean, who did the cooking here, you or Connor?'

She thrust her lower lip out in a pout. ''E wouldn't let me touch a thing in there, like it was a bloody church or something. Said fry-ups were nasty, and he'd not have anything boiled in his kitchen but eggs and water for the pasta.' Still absently holding her glass, she stood and wandered over to the dining table. She traced a finger across its surface. ''E cooked for me, though. No bloke ever did that. Nobody ever cooked anything for me but me mum and me gran, come to think of it.' Looking up, she stared at Kincaid as if seeing him for the first time. 'You married?'

He shook his head. 'I was once, a long time ago.'

'What happened?'

'She left. Met someone else.' He said the words flatly, with an ease born of years of practice, yet it still amazed him that such simple sentences could contain such betrayal.

Sharon considered that, then nodded. 'Con made me supper – "dinner," I mean – he'd always remind me to say "dinner". Candlelight, best dishes. He'd make me

111

sit while he brought me things – "Try this, Shar, try that, Shar." Funny things, too.' She smiled at Kincaid. 'Sometimes I felt like a kid playing dressing-up. Would you do things like that for a girl?'

'I've been known to. But I'm afraid I'm not up to Con's standards – my cooking runs more to omelettes and cheese on toast.' He didn't add that he'd never been inclined to play Pygmalion.

The brief animation that had lit Sharon's face faded. She came slowly back to her chair, empty glass trailing from her fingertips. In a still little voice she said, 'It won't happen to me again.'

'Don't be silly,' he scolded, hearing the false heartiness in his voice.

'Not like with Con, it won't.' Looking directly at Kincaid, she said, 'I know I'm not what blokes like him go for – always said it was too good to be true. A fairy tale.' She rubbed the sides of her face with her fingers, as if her jaws ached from unshed tears. 'There's not been anything in the papers. Do you know about the . . . arrangements?'

'No one in the family's rung you?'

'Rung me?' she said, some of her earlier aggression returning. 'Who the hell do you think would've rung me?' She sniffed, then added, mincing the names, 'Julia? Dame Caroline?'

Kincaid gave the question serious consideration. Julia seemed determined to ignore the fact that her husband had existed, much less died. And Caroline? He could imagine her performing a distasteful, but necessary, duty. 'Perhaps, yes. If they had known about you. I take it they didn't?'

Dropping her gaze to her lap, she said a little sullenly, 'How should I know what Con told them? I only know what he told me.' She pushed the hair from her face with chubby fingers, and Kincaid noticed that the nail on her index finger was broken to the quick. When she spoke again the defiance had gone from her voice. 'He said he'd take care of us – little Hayley and me.'

'Hayley?' Kincaid said blankly.

'My little girl. She's four. Had her birthday last week.' Sharon smiled for the first time.

This was a twist he hadn't expected. 'Is she Con's daughter, too?'

She shook her head vehemently. 'Her dad buggered off soon as he knew I was going to have her. Rotten swine. Not heard a word from him since.'

'But Con knew about her?'

'Course he did. What do you take me for, a bloody tart?'

'Of course not,' Kincaid said soothingly, and, eyeing her empty glass, unobtrusively fetched the bottle. 'Did Con get on with little Hayley, then?' he asked, dividing the last of the sherry between them.

When she didn't answer, he thought perhaps he'd gone over the mark with the sherry, but after a moment she said, 'Sometimes I wondered . . . if it was really her he wanted, not me. Look.' Digging in her handbag, she pulled out a worn leather wallet. 'That's Hayley. She's lovely, isn't she?'

It was a cheap studio portrait, but even the artificial pose and tatty props couldn't spoil the little girl's beauty. As naturally blonde as her mother might have been as a child, she had dimples and an angelic, heart-shaped face. 'Is she as good as she looks?' Kincaid asked, raising an eyebrow.

Sharon laughed. 'No, but you'd never think it to look at her, would you? Con called her his little angel. He'd tease her, call her names in this silly Irish voice. "Me little darlin'",' she said in a credible Irish accent. 'You know, things like that.' For the first time her eyes filled with tears. She sniffed and wiped the back of her hand across her nose. 'Julia didn't want any kids. That's why he wanted the divorce, but Julia wouldn't give it to him.'

'Julia wouldn't divorce Connor?' Kincaid asked, thinking that although no one had actually said, that wasn't the impression he'd had from Julia or her family.

'When the two years were up he was going to divorce her – that's how long it takes, you know, to obtain a divorce without the other party's consent.' She said the last bit so precisely Kincaid thought she must have memorized it, perhaps repeating something Connor had said in order to comfort herself.

'And you were going to wait for him? Another year, was it?'

'Why shouldn't I have done?' she said, her voice rising. 'Con never gave me reason to think he wouldn't do what he said.'

Why indeed? thought Kincaid. *What better prospect*

had she? He looked at her, sitting back a little in her chair now, with her lower lip pushed out belligerently and both hands clasped around the stem of the sherry glass. Had she loved Connor Swann, or had she merely seen him as an attractive meal ticket? And how had such an unlikely union taken place? He certainly doubted that they had moved in the same social circles. 'Sharon,' he said carefully, 'tell me, how did you and Connor meet?'

'In the park,' she said, nodding towards the river. 'Just there, in the Meadows. You can see it from the road. In the spring, it was. I was pushing Hayley in the swings and she fell out, skinned her knee. Con came over and talked to her, and before you knew it she'd stopped her bawling and was laughing at him.' She smiled, remembering. 'Him and his Irish blarney. He brought us back here to look after her knee.' When Kincaid raised an eyebrow at that, she hurried on. 'I know what you're thinking. At first I was afraid he might be . . . well, you know, a bit funny. But it wasn't like that at all.'

Sharon looked relaxed now, and warm, sitting with her feet in their preposterous shoes stretched out in front of her, sherry glass cradled in her lap. 'What was it like?' Kincaid asked softly.

She took her time answering, studying her glass, the fan of her darkly mascaraed lashes casting shadows on her cheeks. 'Funny. What with his job and all, it seemed like Con knew everybody. Always lunches and dinners and drinks and golfing. Busy, you know, important.' She raised her eyes to Kincaid's. 'I think he was lonely. In between all those engagements, there wasn't anything.'

Kincaid thought about the desk diary he'd seen upstairs, with its endless round of appointments. 'Sharon, what was Con's job?'

''E was in advertising.' Wrinkling her brow, she said, 'Blakely, Gill ... I can never remember. In Reading, it was.'

That certainly made sense of the diary. Remembering the deposit stubs, he recited, 'Blackwell, Gillock and Frye.'

'That's it.' Pleased at his cleverness, she beamed at him.

Kincaid ran back through the cheque book register in his mind. If Connor had helped Sharon out financially, he had done it on a cash basis – there had been no cheques made out in her name. Unless he had passed the money through someone else. Casually, he asked, 'Do you happen to know someone called Hicks?'

'That Kenneth!' she said furiously, sitting up and sloshing what remained of her drink. 'Thought you were him, didn't I, when I first came in and heard you upstairs. Thought he'd come for what he could get, like a bloody vulture.'

Was that why she'd been so frightened? 'Who is he, Sharon? What connection did he have with Con?'

A little apologetically, she said, 'Con liked the horses, see? That Kenneth, he worked for a bookie, ran Con's bets for him. 'E was always hanging about, treated me like I was dirt.'

If that were the case, Connor Swann had not played

the ponies lightly. 'Do you know what bookmaker Kenneth Hicks worked for?'

She shrugged. 'Somebody here in the town. Like I said, he was always hanging about.'

Remembering all the Red Lion notations in the diary, Kincaid wondered if that had been their regular meeting place. 'Did Con go to the Red Lion Hotel often? The one next to the chur—?'

Already shaking her head, she interrupted, 'All tarted up for the tourists, that one. A posh whore, Con called it, where you couldn't get a decent pint.'

The girl was a natural mimic, with a good memory for dialogue. When she quoted Con, Kincaid could hear the cadence of his voice, even the faint hint of Irish accent.

'No,' she continued, 'it was the Red Lion in Wargrave he liked. A real pub, with good food at a decent price.' She smiled, showing a faint dimple like her daughter's. 'The food was the thing, you know – Con wouldn't go anywhere he didn't like the food.' Putting her glass to her lips and turning it end up, she drained the last few drops. ''E even took me there, a few times, but mostly he liked to stay at home.'

Kincaid shook his head at the contradictions. The man had lived a boozing, betting, life-in-the-fast-lane, by all accounts, but had preferred to stay at home with his mistress and her child. Connor had also, according to his diary, had lunch with his in-laws every single Thursday for the past year.

Kincaid thought back to the aftermath of his own marriage. Although Vic had left him, her parents had somehow managed to cast him as the villain of the piece, and he had never heard from them again, not so much as a card at Christmas or on his birthday. 'Do you know what Con did on Thursdays, Sharon?' he asked.

'Why should I? Same as any other day, far as I know,' she added, frowning.

So she hadn't known about the regular lunch with the in-laws. What else had Connor conveniently not told her? 'What about last Thursday, Sharon, the day he died? Were you with him?'

'No. 'E went to London, but I don't think he'd meant to, beforehand. When I'd given Hayley her supper, I came over and he'd just come in. All wound up he was, too, couldn't sit still with it.'

'Did he say where he'd been?'

Slowly, she shook her head. 'Said he had to go out again for a bit. "To see a man about a dog," he said, but that was just his way of being silly.'

'And he didn't tell you where he was going?'

'No. Told me not to get my knickers in a twist, that he'd be back.' Slipping off her high-heeled sandals, she tucked her feet up in the armchair and rubbed at her toes with sudden concentration. She looked up, her eyes magnified by a film of moisture. 'But I couldn't stay, 'cause it were Gran's bridge night and I had to see to Hayley. I couldn't . . .' Wrapping her arms around her calves, she buried her face against her knees. 'I didn't . . .' she whispered, her voice muffled by the fabric of her jeans, '. . . wouldn't even give him a kiss when he left.'

So she had been pouting, her feelings hurt, and had childishly snubbed him, thought Kincaid. A small failing, an exhibition of ordinary lovers' behaviour, to be laughed about later in bed, but this time there could be no making up. Of such tiny things are made lifetimes of guilt, and what she sought from him was absolution. Well, he would give whatever was in his power to bestow. 'Sharon. Look at me.' Slipping forward in his chair, he reached out and patted her clasped hands. 'You couldn't know. We're none of us perfect enough to live every minute as if it might be our last. Con loved you, and he knew you loved him. That's all that matters.'

Her shoulders moved convulsively. He sat back quietly, watching her, until he saw her body relax and begin a barely perceptible rocking, then he said, 'Con didn't say anything else about where he was going or who he meant to see?'

She shook her head without lifting it. 'I've thought and thought. Every word he said, every word I said. There's nothing.'

'And you didn't see him again that night?'

'I said I didn't, didn't I?' she said, raising her face from her knees. Weeping had blotched her fair skin, but she sniffed and ran her knuckles under her eyes unselfconsciously. 'What do you want to know all this stuff for, anyway?'

At first her need to talk, to release some of her grief, had been greater than anything else, but now Kincaid saw her natural wariness begin to reassert itself. 'Had Con been drinking?' he asked.

Sharon sat back in her chair, looking puzzled. 'I don't think so – at least he didn't seem like it, but sometimes you couldn't tell, at first.'

'Had a good head, did he?'

She shrugged. 'Con liked his pint, but he wasn't ever mean with it, like some.'

'Sharon, what do you think happened to Con?'

'Silly bugger went for a walk along the lock, fell in and drowned! What do you mean "What happened to him?" How the bloody hell should I know what happened to him?' She was almost shouting, and bright spots of colour appeared on her cheekbones.

Kincaid knew he'd received the tail end of the anger she couldn't vent on Connor – anger at Connor for dying, for leaving her. 'It's difficult for a grown man to fall in and drown, unless he's had a heart attack or is falling-down drunk. We won't be able to rule those possibilities out until after the post-mortem, but I think we'll find that Connor was in good health and at least relatively sober.' As he spoke her eyes widened and she shrank back in her chair, as if she might escape his voice, but he continued relentlessly. 'His throat was bruised. I think someone choked him until he lost consciousness and then very conveniently shoved him in the river. Who would have done that to him, Sharon? Do you know?'

'The bitch,' she said on a breath, her face blanched paper-white beneath her makeup.

'What—'

She stood up, propelled by her anger. Staggering,

she lost her balance and fell to her knees before Kincaid. 'That bitch!'

A fine spray of spittle reached his face. He smelled the sherry on her breath. 'Who, Sharon?'

'She did everything she could to ruin him and now she's killed him.'

'Who, Sharon? Who are you talking about?'

'Her, of course. Julia.'

The woman sitting beside Kincaid nudged him. The congregation was rising, lifting and opening hymnals. He'd heard only snippets of the sermon, delivered in a soft and scholarly voice by the balding vicar. Standing quickly, he scrabbled for a hymnal and peered at his neighbour's to find the page.

He sang absently, his mind still replaying his interview with Connor Swann's mistress. In spite of Sharon's accusations, he just didn't think that Julia Swann had the physical strength necessary to choke her husband and shove him into the canal. Nor had she had the time, unless Trevor Simons was willing to lie to protect her. None of it made sense. He wondered how Gemma was getting on in London, if she had found out anything useful in her visit to the opera.

The service came to a close. Although the congregation greeted one another and chatted cheerfully as they filed out, nowhere did he hear Connor or the Ashertons mentioned. They glanced curiously and a little shyly at Kincaid, but no one spoke to him. He followed the crowd out into the churchyard, but instead of returning to the hotel, he turned his collar up, stuck his hands in his pockets and wandered among the headstones. Distantly, he heard the sounds of car doors slamming and engines starting, but the wind hummed against his ears. Leaves rustled in the thick grass like small brown mice.

He found what he had been looking for behind the church tower, beneath a spreading oak.

'The family,' said a voice behind him, 'seems to have been more than ordinarily blessed and cursed.'

Startled, Kincaid turned. Contemplating the headstone, the vicar stood with his hands clasped loosely before him and his feet spread slightly apart. The wind whipped his vestments against his legs and blew the strands of thinning, grey hair across his bony skull.

The inscription said simply: MATTHEW ASHERTON, BELOVED SON OF GERALD AND CAROLINE, BROTHER OF JULIA. 'Did you know him?' Kincaid asked.

The vicar nodded. 'In many ways an ordinary boy, transformed into something beyond himself by the mere act of opening his mouth.' He looked up from the headstone and Kincaid saw that his eyes were a fine, clear grey. 'Oh yes, I knew him. He sang in my choir. I taught him his catechism, as well.'

'And Julia? Did you know Julia, too?'

Studying Kincaid, the vicar said, 'I noticed you earlier, a new face in the congregation, a stranger wandering purposefully about among the headstones, but you did not seem to me to be a mere sensation seeker. Are you a friend of the family?'

In answer Kincaid removed his warrant card from his pocket and opened the case. 'Duncan Kincaid. I'm looking into the death of Connor Swann,' he said, but even as he spoke he wondered if that were now the entire truth.

The vicar closed his eyes for a moment, as if conducting a private communication, then opened them and blinked before fixing Kincaid with his penetrating stare, 'Come across the way for a cup of tea. We can talk, out of this damnable wind.'

'Brilliance is a difficult enough burden for an adult to bear, much less a child. I don't know how Matthew Asherton would have turned out, if he had lived to fulfil his promise.'

They sat in the vicar's study, drinking tea from mismatched mugs. He had introduced himself as William Mead, and as he switched on the electric kettle and gathered mugs and sugar onto a tray, he told Kincaid that his wife had died the previous year. 'Cancer, poor dear,' he'd said, lifting the tray and indicating that Kincaid should follow him. 'She was sure I'd never be able to manage on my own, but somehow you muddle through. Although,' he added as he opened the study door, 'I must admit that housekeeping was never my strong suit.'

His study bore him out, but it was a comfortable sort of disorder. The books looked as if they might have leaped off the shelves, spreading out onto every available surface like a friendly, invading army, and the bits of wall space not covered by books contained maps.

Setting his mug on the small space the vicar had cleared for him on a side table, Kincaid went to examine an ancient-looking specimen which was carefully preserved behind glass.

'Saxton's map of the Chilterns, 1574. This is one of the few that show the Chilterns as a whole.' The vicar coughed a little behind his hand, then added, out of what Kincaid thought must be a lifetime's habit of honesty, 'It's only a copy, of course, but I enjoy it nonetheless. It's my hobby – the landscape history of the Chilterns.

'I'm afraid,' he continued with an air of confession, 'that it takes up a good deal more of my time and interest than it should, but when one has written a sermon once a week for close on half a century, the novelty pales. And these days, even in a rural parish like this one, for the most part our work is saving bodies, rather than souls. I can't remember when I've had someone come to me with a question of faith.' He sipped his tea and gave Kincaid a rather rueful smile.

Kincaid, wondering if he looked as though he needed saving, smiled back and returned to his chair. 'You must know the area well, then.'

'Every footpath, every field, or close enough.' Mead stretched out his legs, exhibiting the trainers he had slipped into upon returning to the house. 'My feet must be nearly as well travelled as Paul's on the road to Damascus. This is an ancient countryside, Mr Kincaid – ancient in the sense the term is used in landscape

ment, the southern the dip-slope, with valleys running down it like fingers. Some of these valleys bear rivers – the Lea, the Bulbourne, the Chess, the Wye, and others – all tributaries of the Thames. In others the springs and surface-flow only break out when the water table reaches the surface – during the winter or other times of particularly heavy rain.' Sighing, he gave the map a gentle tap with a forefinger before folding it again. 'Hence their name – winterbournes. It's quite pretty, isn't it? Very descriptive. But they can be treacherous in flood, and that, I'm afraid, was the downfall of poor young Matthew.'

'What exactly happened?' asked Kincaid. 'I've only really heard the story secondhand.'

'The only one who will ever know exactly what happened is Julia, as she was with him,' said the vicar, with an attention to detail worthy of a policeman. 'But I'll do my best to piece it together. The children were walking home from school and took a familiar shortcut through the woods. The rain had given us a brief respite, for the first time in days. Matthew, indulging in some horseplay along the bank of the stream, fell in and was caught by the current. Julia tried to reach him, going dangerously far into the water herself, and, failing, ran home for help. It was too late, of course. I think it quite likely that the boy had stopped breathing before Julia left him.'

'Did Julia tell you the story herself?'

Mead nodded as he sipped his tea, then set his mug down and continued. 'In bits and snatches, rather less than coherently, I'm afraid. You see, she was quite ill afterwards, what with the shock and the chill. No one thought to see to her until hours later, and she'd been soaked to the skin. Even that was Mrs Plumley's doing – the parents were entirely too distraught to remember her at all.

'She developed pneumonia. It was touch and go for a bit.' Shaking his head, he held his hands out towards the electric fire, as if the memory had made him cold. 'I visited her every day, taking it in turn with Mrs Plumley to sit with her during the worst of it.'

'What about her parents?' asked Kincaid, feeling the stirrings of outrage.

Distress creased the vicar's gentle face. 'The grief in that house was as thick as the water that drowned Matthew, Mr Kincaid. They had no room in their minds or hearts for anything else.'

'Not even their daughter?'

Very quietly, almost to himself, Mead said, 'I think they couldn't bear to look at her, knowing that she was alive and he was not.' He met Kincaid's eyes, adding more briskly, 'There, now, I've said more than I should. It's been a long time since I've thought of it, and Connor's death has brought it all back.'

'There's more you're not telling me.' ... forward in his chair, not willing to let the matter drop.

'It's not my place to pass judgement, Mr Kincaid. It was a difficult time for everyone concerned.'

Kincaid translated that as meaning that Mead thought the Ashertons had behaved abominably, but wouldn't allow himself to say so. 'Sir Gerald and Dame Caroline are certainly solicitous of their daughter now.'

'As I said, Mr Kincaid, it was all a very long time ago. I'm only sorry that Julia has had another such loss.'

A movement at the window caught Kincaid's eye. The wind had raised a dervish of leaves on the vicar's lawn. It spun for a moment, then collapsed. A few leaves drifted towards the window, lightly tapping the panes. 'You said you knew Matthew, but you must have come to know Julia quite well, actually.'

The vicar swirled the dregs of his tea in his mug. 'I'm not sure anyone knows Julia well. She was always a quiet child, watching and listening where Matthew would plunge into things. It made the rare response from her all the sweeter, and when she took an interest in something it seemed genuine, not merely the latest enthusiasm.'

'And later?'

'She did talk to me, of course, during her illness, but it was a hotchpotch, childish delirium. And when she recovered she became quite withdrawn. The only time I had a glimpse of the child I knew was at her wedding. She had that glow that almost all brides have, and it softened the edges.' His tone affectionate, the vicar's smile invited Kincaid's understanding.

'I can almost imagine that,' Kincaid said, thinking of the smile he'd seen when Julia had opened the door to them, thinking it was Plummy. 'You said you married them, Vicar? But I thought—'

'Connor was Catholic, yes, but he didn't practise, and Julia preferred to be married here at St Barts.' He nodded at the church, its distinctive double tower just visible across the lane. 'I counselled Connor as well as Julia before the wedding, and I must say I had my doubts, even then.'

'Why was that?' Kincaid had developed a considerable regard for the vicar's perceptions.

'In some odd way he reminded me of Matthew, or of Matthew as he might have been had he grown up. I don't know if I can explain it . . . he was perhaps a bit too glib for my liking – with such outward charm it's sometimes difficult to tell what runs beneath the surface. An ill-fated match, in any event.'

'Apparently,' Kincaid agreed wryly. 'Although I'm a bit confused as to who wouldn't divorce whom. Julia certainly seems to have grown to dislike Connor.' He paused, weighing his words. 'Do you think she could have killed him, Vicar? Is she capable of it?'

'We all carry the seeds of violence, Mr Kincaid. What has always fascinated me is the balance of the equation – what factor is it that allows one person to tip over the edge, and another not?' Mead's eyes held knowledge accumulated over a lifetime of observing the best and worst of human character, and it occurred to Kincaid once again that their callings were not dissimilar. The vicar blinked and continued, 'But to answer your question, no, I do not think Julia capable of killing anyone, no matter what the circumstances.'

'Why do you say "anyone", Vicar?' Kincaid asked, puzzled.

'Only because there were rumours at the time of Matthew's death, and you are bound to hear them if you poke long enough under rocks. Open accusations might have been refutable, but not the faceless whispers in the dark.'

'What did they say, the whisperers?' Kincaid said, knowing the answer even as he spoke.

Mead sighed. 'Only what you might expect, human nature being what it is, as well as being fuelled by her sometimes obvious jealousy of her brother. They insinuated that she didn't try to save him . . . that she might even have pushed him.'

'She was jealous of him, then?'

The vicar sat up a bit in his chair and for the first time sounded a bit irascible. 'Of course she was jealous! As any normal child would have been, given the circumstances.' His grey eyes held Kincaid's. 'But she also loved him, and would never willingly have allowed harm to come to him. Julia did as much to save her brother as anyone could expect of a frightened thirteen-year-old, probably more.' He stood up and began collecting the tea things on the tray. 'I don't possess the temerity to call a tragedy like that an act of God. And accidents, Mr Kincaid, are often unanswerable.'

Placing his mug carefully on the tray, Kincaid said, 'Thank you, Vicar. You've been very kind.'

Mead stood, tray balanced in his hands, gazing out of the window at the churchyard. 'I don't profess to understand the workings of fate. Sometimes it's best not to, in my business,' he added, the twinkle surfacing again, 'but I've always wondered. The children usually took the bus home from school, but they were late that day and had to walk instead. What kept them?'

Chapter Seven

Kincaid reshuffled the files on his desk and ran a hand through his hair until it stood up like a cockscomb. The late Sunday afternoon lull at the Yard usually provided the perfect time to catch up on paperwork, but today concentration eluded him. He stretched and glanced at his watch – past teatime, and the sudden hollow sensation in his stomach reminded him he'd missed lunch altogether. Tossing the reports he'd managed to finish into the out tray, he stood up and grabbed his jacket from the peg.

He'd go home, look after Sid, repack his bag, perhaps grab a Chinese take-away. Ordinarily the prospect would have contented him, but today it didn't ease the restlessness that had dogged him since he left the vicarage and caught the train back to London. The image of Julia rose again in his mind. Her face was younger, softer, but pale against the darkness of her fever-matted hair, and she tossed in her white-sheeted bed, uncomforted.

He wondered just how much political clout the Ashertons wielded, and how carefully he need tread.

It was not until he'd exited the Yard garage into

Caxton Street that he thought of phoning Gemma again. He'd rung periodically during the afternoon without reaching her, although she must have been finished with her interview at the ENO hours ago. He eyed the cellular phone but didn't pick it up, and as he rounded St James's Park he found himself heading towards Islington rather than Hampstead. It had been weeks since Gemma moved into the new flat, and her rather embarrassed delight when she spoke of it intrigued him. He'd just pop by on the off-chance he'd catch her at home.

When he remembered how carefully she had avoided inviting him to her house in Leyton, he pushed it to the back of his mind.

He pulled up in front of the address Gemma had given, studying the house before him. A detached honey-coloured stone, it was one of a hotchpotch of houses lying rather incongruously between two of Islington's Georgian crescents. Its two bow-fronted windows caught the late afternoon sun, and an iron fence surrounded the well-tended garden. From the front steps two large black dogs of indeterminate breed regarded him alertly, ready to protest if he should cross the bounds of the gate. Remembering Gemma's description, he left the car in the nearest space and walked round the corner, following the garden wall.

The garage doors were painted a cheerful daffodil yellow, as was the smaller door to their left. Above it a discreet, black number 2 satisfied him that he had indeed found the right place. He knocked, and when no one answered, he sat down on the step leading up to the garden, eased his back into a comfortable position against the bars of the narrow gate and prepared to wait.

He heard her car before he saw it. 'You'll get a ticket, parking on the double-yellows,' he said as she opened the door.

'Not when it's my own garage I'm blocking. What are you doing here, guv?'

She unbuckled Toby's seat belt and he clambered across her, shouting with excitement.

'Nice to be appreciated,' Kincaid said, slapping Toby's palm, then lifting him up and tousling the straight, fair hair. 'Your engine's developing a bit of a knock,' he continued to Gemma as she locked the Escort.

She grimaced. 'Don't remind me. Not just yet, anyway.' They stood awkwardly for a moment, Gemma clutching a bouquet of pink roses to her chest, and as the silence lengthened he grew ever more uncomfortable.

Why had he thought he could breach her carefully maintained barriers without consequence? His invasion seemed to stand between them, tangible as stone. He said, 'I'm sorry. I'll not come in. It's just that I couldn't reach you, and I thought we should connect.' Feeling more apologetic by the second, he added, 'I could take you and Toby for something to eat.'

'Don't be daft.' She dug in her handbag for her keys. 'Do come in, please.' Smiling at him, she unlocked the door and stood back. Toby darted between them with a whoop. 'This is it,' she said as she entered behind him.

Her clothes hung on an open rack beside the door. Brushing against a dress, he smelled for an instant the floral scent of the perfume she usually wore. He took his time, looking around with pleasure, considering. The simplicity surprised him, yet in some way it did not. 'It suits you,' he said finally. 'I like it.'

Gemma moved as if released, crossing the room to the tiny closet of a kitchen, filling a vase with water for the roses. 'So do I. So does Toby, I think,' she said, nodding at her son, who was busily yanking out drawers from the chest beneath the garden windows. 'But I've had a particularly severe thrashing from my mum this afternoon. She doesn't think it a suitable place for a child.'

'On the contrary,' he said, wandering about the room on a closer tour of inspection. 'There's something rather childlike about it, like a playhouse. Or a ship's cabin, where everything has its place.'

Gemma laughed. 'I told her my granddad would have loved it. He was in the navy.' She placed the roses on the small coffee table, the splash of pink the single accent in the black and grey room.

'Red would have been the obvious choice,' he said, smiling.

'Too boring.' Two pairs of cotton knickers, a bit faded and frayed about the elastic, hung suspended in front of the radiator. Flushing, Gemma snatched them down and tucked them away in a drawer beside the bed. She lit lamps and closed the blinds, shutting out the twilit garden. 'I'll just get changed.'

'Let me take you out.' He still felt he needed to make amends. 'If you don't already have plans,' he added, giving her an easy out. 'Or we'll have a quick drink and catch up, and I'll be on my way.'

She stood for a moment, jacket in one hand and hanger in the other, looking around the room as if assessing the possibilities. 'No. There's a Europa just round the corner. We'll pick up a few things and cook.' She hung the jacket up decisively, then pulled jeans and a sweater from a chest beneath the rack.

'Here?' he asked, eyeing the kitchen dubiously.

'Coward. All it takes is a bit of practice. You'll see.'

'It does have its limitations,' Gemma admitted as they pulled chairs up to the half-moon table. 'But you learn to adapt. And it's not as though I have time to do much fancy cooking.' She looked pointedly at Kincaid as she filled his wineglass.

'Copper's life. You'll get no sympathy from me,' he said with a grin, but in truth he admired her determination. With its long, unpredictable hours and heavy caseload, CID was a tough proposition for a single mother, and he thought Gemma managed remarkably well. It didn't do to let his compassion show, however, as she bristled at anything she could construe as special treatment.

'Cheers.' He lifted his glass. 'I'll drink to your adaptability any time.' They'd cooked pasta on the gas ring and served it with ready-made sauce, a green salad, a loaf of freshly baked French bread and a bottle of fairly respectable red wine – not bad fare from a kitchen the size of a broom closet.

'Oh, wait. I almost forgot.' Gemma slipped out of her chair and rummaged in her handbag, retrieving a cassette tape. She popped the tape into the player on the shelf above the bed and brought the case to Kincaid. 'It's Caroline Stowe, singing Violetta in *Traviata*. It's the last recording she made.'

Kincaid listened to the gentle, almost melancholy strains of the overture. As they shopped, he had told Gemma about his encounter with Sharon Doyle and his visits to Trevor Simons and the vicar, and Gemma had related her interviews at the Coliseum. She'd given her usual attention to detail, but there had been an added element in her recital, an interest which stretched beyond the bounds of the case.

'This is the drinking song,' she said as the music changed. 'Alfredo sings about his carefree life, before he meets Violetta.' Toby banged his cup enthusiastically on the table in time to the rollicking music. 'Listen, now,' Gemma said softly. 'That's Violetta.'

The voice was darker, richer than he'd expected, and even in the first few phrases he could hear its emotional power. He looked at Gemma's rapt face. 'You're fascinated by all this, aren't you?'

Gemma sipped her wine, then said slowly, 'I suppose I am. I never would have thought it. But there's something . . .' She looked away from him and busied herself cutting Toby's pasta into smaller pieces.

'I don't think I've ever seen you at a loss for words, Gemma,' Kincaid said, a little amused. 'You're more likely to be guilty of the opposite sin. What is it?'

She looked up at him, pushing a stray copper hair from her cheek. 'I don't know. I can't explain it,' she said, but her hand went to her chest in a gesture more eloquent than words.

'Did you buy this today?' he asked, tapping the cassette case. A younger Caroline Stowe looked back at him, her delicate beauty accentuated by the nineteenth-century costume she wore.

'At the ENO shop.'

He grinned at her. 'You're converted, aren't you? A proselyte. I'll tell you what – you interview Caroline Stowe tomorrow. We still need a more detailed account of her movements on Thursday evening. And you can satisfy your curiosity.'

'What about the post-mortem?' she asked, wiping Toby's hands with a cloth. 'I'd expected to go with you.' She patted Toby on the bottom as she scooted him out of his chair with a whispered, 'Jammy time, love.'

Watching her, Kincaid said, 'I'll manage it myself this time. You stay in town until you can see Tommy Godwin, then drive to Badger's End and tackle Dame Caroline.'

She opened her mouth to protest, but closed it again after a moment and returned to collecting salad on her fork. Attending post-mortems was a particular point of honour with her, and Kincaid felt surprised she hadn't offered more of an objection.

'I've put Thames Valley on to tracing Kenneth

138

Hicks,' he said, pouring a little more wine into his glass.

'The bookie's runner? Why would he want to get rid of his source of cash? They'll never collect anything from Connor Swann now.'

Kincaid shrugged. 'Maybe they wanted to make an example of him, start a few rumours among the big gamblers – this is what's in store if you don't pay up, mate.'

Gemma finished her pasta and pushed her plate away, then picked up another piece of bread and buttered it in an absent-minded way. 'But he did pay up, regularly. A bookie's dream, I should think.'

'They could have had an argument over a payment. Maybe Connor found Kenneth was skimming off the top, threatened to tell the boss.'

'We don't know that he was.' Gemma stood up and began clearing the table. 'We don't know much of anything, for that matter.' Setting down the stack of plates again, she ticked off on her fingers. 'We need to map out Connor's day. We know he had lunch at Badger's End, and that he was meeting someone, but we don't know who. Why did he go to London? Who did he see at the Coliseum? Who did he go that night, after he came back from London? Who did he see then?'

Kincaid grinned at her. 'Well, that at least gives us somewhere to start,' he said, viewing a return of her usual combativeness with relief.

After Gemma had put Toby to bed, he tried to help with the washing up, but the kitchen would not hold more than one at a time. 'Sardines?' Kincaid suggested as he squeezed in behind her to put away the bread. The top of her head fitted just under his chin, and he was suddenly aware of the curves of her body, aware of how easy it would be to put his hands on her shoulders and hold her against him. Her hair tickled his nose and he stepped back to sneeze.

Gemma turned and gave him a look he couldn't read, then said brightly, 'Try the chair while I finish up.'

Eyeing the curving chrome and black leather article dubiously, Kincaid said, 'Are you sure it's not an instrument of torture? Or a sculpture?' But when he lowered himself gingerly into it, he found it enormously comfortable.

His expression must have given him away, because Gemma laughed and said, 'You didn't trust me.'

She pulled a dining chair near him and they chatted amiably, finishing their wine. He felt at peace, free of the restless tension that had disturbed him earlier, reluctant to manoeuvre himself out of the chair and go home. But when he saw her smother a yawn, he said, 'Early start for both of us. I'd better be off.' She didn't demur.

It was only as he drove home that he realized he hadn't told her of Sharon Doyle's accusations that Julia Swann had killed her husband. Hysteria, he thought, shrugging. Not worth recounting.

A small voice reminded him that neither had he told her of Julia's illness after her brother's death, and his only excuse for this omission was that telling the vicar's story smacked of betrayal in a way he couldn't explain.

Backstage at the Coliseum should have prepared Gemma for Lilian Baylis House, but Alison's description had misled her. 'A big old house, a bit difficult to get to. Used to be a recording studio for Decca Records.' From that Gemma envisaged a genteel place, set back in a large garden, populated by ghosts of rock stars.

'Bit difficult to get to' had proved to be more than an under-statement. Not even her well-thumbed *London A to Z* prevented her from arriving half an hour late for her appointment with Tommy Godwin, flustered, her hair escaping from its clip and her breath coming hard after a three-block sprint from the only available parking space. She felt the beginnings of a blister where her new shoe rubbed her heel.

The dark blue sign with its white ENO legend identified the house easily enough, which was just as well, as it bore no resemblance whatsoever to Gemma's fantasy. A square, heavy house with soot-darkened red brick, it stood sandwiched between a dry cleaners and an auto-parts shop in a busy shopping street just off the Finchley Road.

Squelching the thought that she might not have become so hopelessly muddled if she'd had her mind on her driving instead of Kincaid's visit the previous evening, she tucked a stray hair into place and pulled open the door.

A man leaned against the door jamb of the receptionist's cubicle, chatting with a young woman in jeans. 'Ah,' he said, straightening up and holding a hand out to Gemma, 'I see we won't have to send your colleagues out searching for you, after all, Sergeant. It is Sergeant James, is it not?' He looked down the considerable length of his nose at her, as if assuring himself he hadn't made a mistake. 'Had a bit of trouble getting here, I'd say, from the look of you.' As the young woman handed Gemma a clipboard similar to the one Danny had used at the Coliseum, he looked at her and shook his head. 'You really should have warned her, Sheila. Not even London's finest can be expected to navigate the wilds north of the Finchley Road without a snag.'

'It was rather dreadful,' Gemma said with feeling. 'I knew where you were, but I couldn't get here from there, if you see what I mean. I'm still not quite sure how I did.'

'No doubt you'd like to powder your nose,' he said, 'before you have your wicked way with me. I'm Tommy Godwin, by the way.'

'So I'd gathered,' retorted Gemma, escaping gratefully to the loo. Once safely behind the closed door, she surveyed her reflection in the fly-specked mirror with dismay. Her navy suit, Marks and Sparks best, might as well have been jumble sale beside Tommy Godwin's casual elegance. Everything about the man, from the silk of his jacket to the warm shine of his leather slip-on shoes, spoke of good taste, and of the money spent to indulge it. Even his tall, thin frame lent itself to the act, and his fair, greying hair was sleekly and expensively barbered. A swipe of lipstick and a comb provided little defence, but Gemma did the best she could, then squared her shoulders and went out to regain charge of her interview.

She found him in the same relaxed posture as before. 'Well then, Sergeant, feeling better?'

'Much, thank you. Is there somewhere we could have a word?'

'We might steal five uninterrupted minutes in my office. Up the stairs if you don't mind.' He propelled her forward with a light hand upon her back, and Gemma felt she'd once again been outmanoeuvred. 'This is officially the buying office, the costume co-ordinator's domain,' he continued, ushering her through a door at the top of the stairs, 'but we all use it. As you might guess.'

Every available inch of the small room seemed to be covered – papers and costume sketches spilled from the worktables onto the floor, bolts of fabric leaned together in corners like old drunkards propping one another up, and shelves on the walls held rows of large black books.

'Bibles,' said Godwin, following her gaze. Gemma's face must have registered her surprise, because he smiled and added, 'That's what they're called, really. Look.' He ran his finger along the bindings, then pulled one down and opened it on the worktable. 'Kurt Weill's *Street Scene*. Every production in rep has its own bible, and as long as that production is performed the bible is adhered to in the smallest possible detail.'

Gemma watched, fascinated, as he slowly turned the pages. The detailed descriptions of sets and costumes were accompanied by brightly coloured sketches, and each costume boasted carefully matched fabric swatches as well. She touched the bit of red satin glued next to a full-skirted dress. 'But I thought ... well, that every time you put on an opera it was different, new.'

'Oh no, my dear. Productions sometimes stay in rep as long as ten or fifteen years, and are often leased out to other companies. This production, for instance' – he tapped the page – 'is a few years old, but if it should be done next year in Milan, or Santa Fe, their Wardrobe will be responsible for securing this exact fabric, down to the dye lot, if possible.' He sat on the edge of a stool and crossed his long legs, displaying the perfection of his trouser crease. 'There are some up-and-coming directors who insist that a show they've originated mustn't be done without them, no matter where it's performed. Upstarts, the lot of them.'

Making an effort to resist the fascination of the brightly coloured pages, Gemma gently closed the book. 'Mr Godwin, I understand you attended last Thursday evening's performance at the Coliseum.'

'Back to business, is it, Sergeant?' He drew his brows together in mock disappointment. 'Well, if you must, you must. Yes, I popped in for a bit. It's a new production, and I like to keep an eye on things, make sure one of the principals doesn't need a nip here or a tuck there.'

'Do you usually drop in on Sir Gerald Asherton after the performance as well?'

'Ah, I see you've done your homework, Sergeant.' Godwin smiled at her, looking as delighted as if he were personally responsible for her cleverness. 'Gerald was in particularly fine form that night – I thought it only fitting to tell him so.'

Growing increasingly irritated by Tommy Godwin's manner, Gemma said, 'Sir, I'm here because of the death of Sir Gerald's son-in-law, as you very well know. I understand that you've known the family for years, and under the circumstances I think your attitude is a little cavalier, don't you?'

For an instant he looked at her sharply, his thin face still, then the bright smile fell back into place. 'I'm sure I deserve to be taken to task for not expressing the proper regret, Sergeant,' he said, clicking his tongue against his teeth. 'I've known Gerald and Caroline since we were all in nappies.' Pausing, he raised an eyebrow at Gemma's look of disbelief. 'Well, at least in Julia's case it's quite literally true. I was the lowest of the lowly in those days, junior assistant to the women's costume cutter. Now it takes three years of design school to qualify for that job, but in those days most of us blundered into it. My mother was a dressmaker – I knew a sewing machine inside out by the time I was ten.'

If that were the case he'd certainly done a good job of acquiring his upper-middle-class veneer, thought Gemma. Her surprise must have shown, because he smiled at her and added, 'I had a talent for copying as well, Sergeant, that I've put to good use.

'Junior assistant cutters don't fit the principals' costumes, but sometimes they are allowed to fit the lesser luminaries, the has-beens and the rising stars. Caro was a fledgling in those days, still too young to have mastered control of that marvellous natural talent, but ripe with potential. Gerald spotted her in the chorus and made her his protégée. He's thirteen years older – did you know that, Sergeant?' Godwin tilted his head and examined her critically, as if making sure he had his pupil's attention. 'He had a reputation to consider, and oh, my, tongues did wag when he married her.'

'But I thought—'

'Oh, no one remembers that now, of course. It was all a very long time ago, my dear, and their titles weren't even a twinkle in the Queen's eye.'

The hint of weariness in his voice aroused her curiosity. 'Is that how you met Caroline, fitting her costumes?'

'You're very astute, Sergeant. Caro had married Gerald by that time, and produced Julia. She'd sometimes bring Julia to fittings, to be fussed and cooed over, but even then Julia showed little evidence of being suitably impressed.'

'Impressed by what, Mr Godwin? I'm not sure I follow you.'

'Music in general, my dear, and in particular the whole tatty, overblown world of opera.' Sliding from the stool, he walked to the window and stood, hands in his pockets, looking down into the street. 'It's like a bug, a virus, and I think some people have a predisposition for catching it. Perhaps it's genetic.' He turned and looked at her. 'What do you think, Sergeant?'

Gemma fingered the costume sketches lying loose on the table, thinking of the chill that had gripped her as she heard *Traviata*'s finale for the first time. 'This . . . predisposition has nothing to do with upbringing?'

'Certainly not in my case. Although my mother had a fondness for dance bands during the war.' Hands still in his pockets, he did a graceful little box-step, then gave Gemma a sideways glance. 'I always imagined I was conceived after a night spent swinging to Glenn Miller or Benny Goodman,' he added with a mocking half-smile. 'As for Caroline and Gerald, I don't think it ever occurred to them that Julia wouldn't speak their language.'

'And Matthew?'

'Ah, well, Matty was a different story all together.' He turned away again as he spoke, then fell silent, gazing out of the window.

Why, wondered Gemma, did she meet this stone wall every time she brought up Matthew Asherton? She remembered Vivian Plumley's words: 'We don't talk about that,' and it seemed to her that twenty years should have provided more solace.

'Nothing was ever the same after Caro left the company,' Godwin said softly. He turned to Gemma. 'Isn't that what they always say, Sergeant, the best times of one's life are only recognized in retrospect?'

'I wouldn't know, sir. It seems a bit cynical to me.'

'Ah, but you've contradicted yourself, Sergeant. I can see you do have an opinion.'

'Mr Godwin,' Gemma said sharply, 'my opinion is not in question here. What did you and Sir Gerald talk about last Thursday night?'

'Just the usual pleasantries. To be honest, I don't remember. I can't have been there more than five or ten minutes.' He came back to the stool and leaned against the edge of its seat. 'Do take the weight off, Sergeant. You'll go back to your station and accuse me of dreadful manners.'

Gemma kept firmly to her position, back against the worktable. She was finding this interview difficult enough without conducting the rest of it on a level with Tommy Godwin's elegant belt buckle. 'I'm fine, sir. Did Sir Gerald seem upset or behave in an unusual way?'

Glancing down his long nose, he said with mild sarcasm, 'As in dancing about with a lampshade on his head? Really, Sergeant, he seemed quite the ordinary fellow. Still a bit charged up from the performance, but that's only to be expected.'

'Had he been drinking?'

'We had a drink. But it's Gerald's custom to keep a bottle of good single-malt whisky in his dressing room for visitors, and I can't say I've ever seen him any the worse for it. Thursday night was no exception.'

'And you left the theatre after your drink with Sir Gerald, Mr Godwin?'

'Not straight away, no. I did have a quick word with

one of the girls in Running Wardrobe.' The coins in his pocket jingled softly as he shifted position.

'How long a word, sir? Five minutes? Ten minutes? Do you remember what time you signed out with Danny?'

'Actually, Sergeant, I didn't.' He ducked his head as sheepishly as an errant schoolboy. 'Sign out, that is. Because I hadn't signed in, and that's quite frowned upon.'

'You hadn't signed in? But I thought it was required of everyone.'

'In theory it is. But it's not a high-security prison, my dear. I must admit I wasn't feeling entirely sociable when I arrived on Thursday evening. The performance had already started when I came in through the lobby, so I just gave one of the ushers a wink and stood at the back.' He smiled at Gemma. 'I've spent too much of my working life on my feet, I suppose, to feel comfortable staying in one position for very long.' As if to demonstrate, he left the stool and came to stand near Gemma. Lifting a swatch of tartan satin from the table, he ran his fingers over its surface. 'This ought to do nicely for *Lucia*—'

'Mr Godwin. Tommy.' Gemma's use of his first name caught his attention, and for an instant she saw again the stillness beneath his surface prattle. 'What did you do when the performance finished?'

'I've told you, I went straight to Gerald's—' He stopped as Gemma shook her head. 'Oh, I see what you mean. How did I get to Gerald's dressing room?

It's quite simple if you know your way around the warren, Sergeant. There's a door in the auditorium that leads to the stage, but it's unmarked, of course, and I doubt anyone in the audience would ever notice it.'

'And you left the same way? After you spoke to Sir Gerald and – ' Gemma paused and flipped back through her notes – 'the girl in Running Wardrobe.'

'Got it in one, my dear.'

'I'm surprised you found the doors still unlocked.'

'There are always a few stragglers, and the ushers have to tidy up.'

'And I don't suppose you remember what time this was, or that anyone saw you leave,' Gemma said with an edge of sarcasm.

Rather contritely, Tommy Godwin said, 'I'm afraid not, Sergeant. But then one doesn't think about having to account for oneself, does one?'

Determined to break through his air of polished innocence, she pushed him a little more aggressively. 'What did you do when you left the theatre, Tommy?'

He propped one hip on the edge of the worktable and folded his arms. 'Went home to my flat in Highgate. What else, dear Sergeant?'

'Alone?'

'I live alone, except for my cat, but I'm sure she'll vouch for me. Her name is Salome, by the way, and I must say it suits—'

'What time did you arrive home? Do you by any chance remember that?'

'I do, actually.' He paused and smiled at her, as if

anticipating praise. 'I have a grandfather clock and I remember it chiming not long after I came in, so it must have been before midnight.'

Stalemate. He couldn't prove his statements, but without further evidence she had no way to disprove them. Gemma stared at him, wondering what lay beneath his very plausible exterior. 'I'll need your address, Mr Godwin, as well as the name of the person you spoke to after you saw Sir Gerald.' She tore a page from her notebook and watched as he wrote the information in a neat left-handed script. Running back through the interview in her mind, she realized what had been nagging her, and how deftly Tommy Godwin had sidestepped.

'How well did you know Connor Swann, Mr Godwin? You never said.'

He carefully capped her pen and returned it, then began folding the paper into neat squares. 'I met him occasionally over the years, of course. He wasn't exactly my cup of tea, I must say. It baffled me that Gerald and Caro continued to put up with him when even Julia wouldn't, but then perhaps they knew something about him that I didn't.' He raised an eyebrow and gave Gemma a half-smile. 'But then one's judgement of character is always fallible, don't you find, Sergeant?'

Chapter Eight

The High Wycombe roundabout reminded Kincaid of
a toy he'd had as a child, a set of interlocking plastic
gears that had revolved merrily when one turned a
central crank. But in this case five mini-roundabouts
surrounded a large one, humans encased in steel boxes
did the revolving, and no one in the Monday morning
crush was the least bit merry. He saw an opening in
the oncoming traffic and shot into it, only to be
rewarded by a two-fingered salute from an impatient
lorry driver. 'Same to you, mate,' Kincaid muttered
under his breath as he escaped gratefully from the last
of the mini-roundabouts.

A hold-up on the M40 had delayed him, and he
arrived at High Wycombe's General Hospital half an
hour late for the post-mortem. Kincaid tapped on the
door of the autopsy room and opened it just enough to
put his head in. A small man in green surgical gar-
ments stood facing the stainless-steel table, his back to
Kincaid. 'Dr Winstead, I presume?' Kincaid asked.
'Sorry I'm late.' He entered the room and let the door
swing shut behind him.

Winstead tapped the foot switch on his recorder as

he turned. 'Superintendent Kincaid?' He edged the microphone away from his mouth with the back of his wrist. 'Sorry I can't shake,' he added, holding up his gloved hands in demonstration. 'You've missed most of the fun, I'm afraid. Started a bit early, trying to catch up on the backlog. Should have had your fellow done Saturday, yesterday at the latest, but we had a council housing fire. Spent the weekend identifying remains.'

Tubby, with a mop of curly, greying hair and boot-button black eyes, Winstead lived up to his sobriquet. Kincaid found himself thinking that his vision of Pooh Bear with scalpel in hand hadn't been too far off the mark. And like many forensic pathologists Kincaid had come across, Winstead seemed unfailingly jolly. 'Find anything interesting?' Kincaid enquired, just as glad that Winstead's body blocked part of his view of the steel table. Although he'd grown accustomed to the gaping Y-incision and peeled-forward scalp, he never enjoyed the sight.

'Nothing to jump for joy over, I'm afraid.' He turned his back on Kincaid, his gloved hands again busy. 'One or two things to finish up, then we could nip over to my office, if you like.'

Kincaid stood watching, the cold air from the vents blowing in torrents down the back of his neck. At least there wasn't much smell to contend with, cold water and refrigeration having done a good bit towards retarding the body's natural processes. Although he could look at almost anything, he still had to fight the gag response triggered by the odour of a ripe corpse.

A young woman in scrubs came in, saying, 'Ready for me, Winnie?'

'I'll just leave the tidying up to my assistant,' Winstead said over his shoulder to Kincaid. 'She likes to do the pretty work. Don't you, Heather darling?' he added, smiling at her. 'Gives her a sense of job satisfaction.' He peeled off his gloves, tossed them in a rubbish bin and scrubbed his hands at the sink.

Heather rolled her eyes indulgently. 'He's just jealous,' she said *sotto voce* to Kincaid, 'because I'm neater than he is.' She slipped on a pair of gloves and continued. 'This chap's mum would be proud of him by the time I've finished, isn't that so, Winnie?'

At least Connor Swann's adoring mum had been spared admiring Heather's handiwork, thought Kincaid. He wondered if Julia would defy convention to the extent of avoiding the mortuary and the funeral.

As Winstead ushered Kincaid from the room he said, 'She's right, I'm afraid. I get the job done, but she's a perfectionist, and her hand is much finer than mine.' He led Kincaid down several halls, stopping on the way to retrieve two coffees from a vending machine. 'Black?' he asked, pushing buttons with familiarity.

Kincaid accepted the paper cup and sipped, finding the liquid just as dreadful as its counterpart at the Yard. He followed Winstead into his office and stopped, examining the human skull which adorned the doctor's desk. Attached to the facial surface by pins were small cylinders of rubber, each of varying height with a black number inked on its tip. 'Voodoo or art, Doctor?'

'A facial reconstruction technique, lent to me by an anthropologist chum. A guess as to sex and race is made by measuring certain characteristics of the skull, then the skin depth markers are placed according to information from statistical tables. Clay is added to a thickness that conforms to the markers, and Bob's your uncle, you have a human face again. It's quite effective, actually, even if this stage does look like something from *Nightmare on Elm Street*. Heather is interested in forensic sculpture, and with her hands I don't doubt she'd be good at it.'

Before Winstead wandered too far on the subject of the lovely Heather's attributes, Kincaid thought he had better redirect him. 'Tell me, Doctor,' he said as they settled into worn leather chairs, 'did Connor Swann drown?'

Winstead knitted his brows, an exercise which made him look comical rather than fierce, and seemed to bring himself back to the body in question. 'That's a pretty problem, Superintendent, as I'm sure you very well know. Drowning is impossible to prove by autopsy. It is, in fact, a diagnosis of exclusion.'

'But surely you can tell if he had water in his lungs—'

'Do hold on, Superintendent, let me finish. Water in the lungs is not necessarily significant. And I didn't say I couldn't tell you anything, only that it couldn't be proved.' Winstead paused and drank from his cup, then made a face. 'I'm an eternal optimist, I suppose –

I always expect this stuff to be better than it is. Anyway, where was I?' He smiled benignly and took another sip of his coffee.

Kincaid decided Winstead was teasing him deliberately, and that the less he fussed the faster he'd hear the results. 'You were about to tell me what you *couldn't* prove.'

'Gunshot wounds, stabbing, blunt trauma – all fairly straightforward, cause of death easily determined. A case like this, however, is a puzzle, and I like puzzles.' Winstead uttered this with such relish that Kincaid half-expected him to rub his hands together in anticipatory glee. 'There are two things which contradict drowning,' he continued, holding up the requisite fingers. 'No foreign material present in the lungs. No sand, no nice slimy river-bottom weeds. If one inhales great gulps of water in the act of drowning, one usually takes in a few undesirable objects as well.' He folded down one finger and waggled the remainder at Kincaid. 'Secondly, rigor mortis was quite delayed. The temperature of the water would account for some degree of retardation, of course, but in an ordinary, garden-variety drowning the person struggles violently, depleting the ATP in their muscles, and this depletion speeds up the onset of rigor considerably.'

'But what if there was a struggle before he went in the water? His throat was bruised – he might have been unconscious. Or dead.'

'There are several indications that he died quite a few hours before his body was discovered,' Winstead admitted. 'The stomach contents were only partially digested, so unless your Mr Swann ate a very late supper indeed, I'd guess he was dead by midnight, or as close to it as makes no difference. When the analysis of the stomach contents comes back from the lab you may be able to pinpoint that last meal.'

'And the bruising—'

Winstead held up a hand, palm out like a traffic warden. 'There is another possibility, Superintendent, that would account for Mr Swann having been alive when he went in the water. Dry drowning. The throat closes at first contact with the water, constricting the airway. No water gets into the lungs. But, as the laryngospasm relaxes after death, it is impossible to prove. It would explain, however, the lack of foreign matter in the lungs.'

'What causes a dry drowning, then?' Kincaid asked, willing himself again to be patient and let the doctor have his bit of fun.

'That's one of nature's little mysteries. Shock would probably be your best catch-all explanation, if you must have one.' Winstead paused and drank from his cup, then looked surprised that it hadn't miraculously improved in the interval since his last tasting. 'Now, about this throat business you're so keen on. I'm afraid that's inconclusive as well. There was some external bruising – I understand you visited the morgue?' When Kincaid nodded, he continued, 'You'll have seen it, then – but there was no corresponding internal damage, no crushing of the hyoid processes. Nor did we find any occlusion of the face or neck.'

'No spots in the eyes?'

Winstead beamed at him. 'Exactly. No petechiae. Of course, it's possible that either by accident or design, someone put enough pressure on his carotid arteries to render him unconscious, then shoved him in the river.'

'Could a woman exert that much pressure?'

'Oh, a woman would be quite capable physically, I should think. But I would have expected more than just bruising – fingernail marks, abrasions – and there were none. He was clean as a whistle. And I doubt very much if a woman could have rendered him unconscious without her hands suffering some trauma from the struggle.'

Kincaid digested this for a moment. 'So what you're telling me is' – he touched the tip of one index finger to the other – 'that *a*: you don't know how Connor Swann died, and if you can't give me *cause of death*, I have to assume that *b* follows: you won't hazard a guess as to *manner of death*.'

'Most drownings are accidental, and often alcohol-related. We won't know his blood alcohol until the report comes back from the lab, but I'd be willing to bet it was quite high. However' – up came the traffic warden hand again as Kincaid opened his mouth to speak – 'if you want my off-the-record opinion . . .' Winstead sipped from his coffee again, although Kincaid had long since abandoned his, finding an inconspicuous spot for the cup among the litter on Winstead's desk. 'Most accidental drownings are also fairly straightforward. Bloke goes out fishing with his friends, they all have a few too many, bloke falls in and his friends are too pissed to pull him out. Corroborating stories from several witnesses – end of case. But in this instance' – the intelligent boot-button eyes fixed on Kincaid – 'I'd say there are a good deal too many unanswered questions. No indications of suicide?'

Kincaid shook his head. 'None.'

'Then I'd say there's not much doubt he was helped into that river in one way or another, but I'd also say you're going to have a hell of a time proving it.' Winstead smiled as if he'd just delivered a welcome pronouncement.

'What about time of death?'

'Sometime between when he was last seen and when he was found.' Winstead chortled at his own humour. 'Seriously, Superintendent, if you want my intuitive stab at it, I'd say between nineish and midnight, or perhaps nine and one o'clock.'

'Thank you, I think.' Kincaid stood up and held out a hand. 'You've been . . . um, extremely helpful.'

'Glad to be of service.' Winstead shook Kincaid's hand and smiled, the Pooh Bear resemblance more pronounced than ever. 'We'll get the report to you as soon as the lab work comes back. Can you find your way to the front? Cheerio, then.'

As Kincaid left the office he glanced back. The skull seemed to be superimposed upon Winstead's chubby form, and as Winstead waved Kincaid could have sworn the skull grinned a little more widely.

*

Kincaid left the hospital feeling little further forward than before. Although now more certain of the fact, he still had no concrete proof that Connor had been murdered. Nor had he a plausible motive, or any real suspects.

Hesitating when he reached his car, he glanced at his watch. Once Gemma had managed to track down Tommy Godwin, she would be on her way to interview Dame Caroline, and as long as she was looking into the Asherton end of things, he had better concentrate on Connor. Connor was the key – until he knew more about Connor nothing else would fall into place.

It was time he did a little prying into the part of Connor's life that did not seem to be connected to the Ashertons. Using his phone, he ascertained the address of Blackwell, Gillock and Frye, then took the road south to Maidenhead and Reading.

He never came to Reading without thinking of Vic. She had grown up here, gone to school here, and as he'd entered the city from the north, he made a quick detour down the street where her parents had lived. The suburb boasted comfortable semi-detached houses and well-tended gardens, with an occasional garden gnome peeping tastefully from behind a hedge. He had found the neighbourhood dreadful then, and he discovered that time had done nothing to soften his opinion.

Easing the car to a halt, he let the engine idle while he studied the house. So unaltered did it appear that he wondered if it had been held in some sort of stasis while time eddied around it, and he had changed and aged. He saw it as he'd seen it the first time Vic took him home to meet her parents, down to the determined shine on the brass letterbox. They had looked upon him with well-bred disapproval, dismayed that their beautiful and scholarly daughter should have taken up with a policeman, and with a stab of discomfort he remembered that he had felt faintly ashamed of his less-than-conventional family. His parents had always cared more for books and ideas than the acquisition of middle-class possessions, and his childhood in their rambling house in the Cheshire countryside had been far removed from this tidy, ordered world.

He slipped the Midget into first gear and eased out the clutch, listening to the engine's familiar sputtering response. Perhaps Vic had chosen someone more suitable for the second go-round. He, at least, was well out of it. With that thought came a sense of release and the welcome realization that he did, actually, finally, mean it.

The snarl of Reading traffic hadn't improved since his last visit, and as he sat drumming his fingers on the steering wheel in the queue for city-centre parking, he remembered how much he had always disliked the place. It combined the worst of modern architecture with bad city planning, and the results were enough to make anyone's blood pressure rise.

Once he'd parked the car he found the modern block of offices which housed the advertising agency without too much difficulty. A pretty receptionist greeted him with a smile as he entered the third-floor suite. 'Can I help you, sir?' she asked, and her voice held a hint of curiosity.

He knew she must be trying to catalogue him – not a familiar client or supplier, no briefcase or samples to mark him as a commercial traveller – and he couldn't resist teasing her a bit. Her short bobbed dark hair and heart-shaped face gave her an appealing innocence. 'Nice office,' he said, looking slowly around the reception area. Modular furniture, dramatic lighting, art-deco advertising prints carefully framed and placed – it added up, he thought, to clever use of limited funds.

'Yes, sir. Is there someone you wanted to see?' she asked a little more forcefully, her smile fading.

He removed his warrant card and handed her the open folder. 'Superintendent Duncan Kincaid, Scotland Yard. I'd like to speak to someone about Connor Swann.'

'Oh.' She looked from his face to the card and back again, then her brown eyes filled with tears. 'Isn't it just awful? We only heard this morning.'

'Really? Who notified you?' he asked, casually retrieving his card.

She sniffed. 'His father-in-law, Sir Gerald Asherton. He rang John – that's Mr Frye—'

A door opened in the hallway behind her desk and a man came out, shrugging into a sports jacket. 'Melissa, love, I'm off to the—' His hand up to tighten his tie, he stopped as he saw Kincaid.

'Here's Mr Frye now,' she said to Kincaid, then

added to her boss, 'A man from Scotland Yard, here about Connor, John.'

'Scotland Yard? Connor?' Frye repeated, and his momentary bewilderment gave Kincaid a chance to study him. He judged him to be about his own age, but short, dark, and already acquiring that extra layer of padding that comes with desk-bound affluence.

Kincaid introduced himself, and Frye recovered enough to shake hands. 'What can I do for you, Superintendent? I mean, from what Sir Gerald said, I didn't expect . . .'

Smiling disarmingly, Kincaid said, 'I just have a few routine questions about Mr Swann and his work.'

Frye seemed to relax a bit. 'Well, look, I was just going round to the pub for some lunch, and I've got a client meeting as soon as I get back. Could we talk and grab a bite at the same time?'

'Suits me.' Kincaid realized that he was ravenously hungry, a not unexpected side effect of attending a post-mortem, but the prospect of the culinary delights to be found in a Reading pub didn't fill him with anticipation.

As they walked the block to the pub, Kincaid glanced at his companion. Three-piece suit in charcoal grey, expensively cut, but the waistcoat strained its buttons; midday beard shadow; hair slicked back in the latest yuppie fashion; and as Kincaid matched his stride to the shorter man's, he caught the scent of musky aftershave. He thought Connor had given the same attention to his appearance – and advertising was, after all, a business of image.

They made desultory chitchat until they reached their destination, and as they entered the White Hart, Kincaid's spirits lifted considerably. Plain and clean, the pub had an extensive lunch menu chalked on a board and was filled with escapees from other offices, all busily eating and talking. He chose the plaice, with chips and salad, his stomach rumbling. Turning to Frye, he asked, 'What are you drinking?'

'Lemonade.' Frye grimaced apologetically. 'I'm slimming, I'm afraid. I love beer, but it goes straight to my middle.' He patted his waistcoat.

Kincaid bought him a lemonade and ordered a pint for himself, not feeling the least bit of guilt at giving his companion cause for envy. Carrying their drinks, they threaded their way to a small table near the window. 'Tell me about Connor Swann,' he said as they settled into their seats. 'How long had he worked for you?'

'A little over a year. Gordon and I needed someone to do the selling, you see. We're neither of us really good at it, and we'd acquired enough clients that we thought we could justify—'

'Gordon's your partner?' Kincaid interrupted. 'I thought there were three of you.' He sipped his pint and licked a bit of foam from his lip.

'I'm sorry. I'd better start at the beginning, hadn't I?' Frye sighed and went on. 'I'm *Frye*, of course, Gordon is *Gillock*, and there isn't a *Blackwell*. When we went out on our own three years ago, we thought Gillock and Frye sounded like a fishmongers'.' Frye smiled a little sheepishly. 'The Blackwell was just to add a bit of class. Anyway, I function as creative director and Gordon does the media buying and oversees production, so we were stretched pretty thin. When we heard through a friend that Connor might be interested in an account executive's position, we thought it was just the ticket.'

The barmaid appeared at their table with laden plates. Tall and blonde, she might have been a Valkyrie in jeans and sweater. She bestowed a ravishing smile upon them along with their lunch and made her way back through the crowd. 'That's Marian,' Frye said. 'We call her the Ice Maiden. Everyone's madly in love with her and she enjoys it immensely.'

'Does the adjective refer to her looks or her disposition?' Kincaid looked at Frye's plate of salad and tucked happily into his steaming fish and chips.

'I'm not allowed fried things, either,' Frye said, eyeing Kincaid's food wistfully. 'Marian's disposition is sunny enough, but she's not generous with her favours. Even Connor drew a blank.'

'Did he chat her up?'

'Does the sun rise every morning?' Frye asked sarcastically, pushing a sprig of watercress into the corner of his mouth with his little finger. 'Of course Con chatted her up. It was as natural to him as breathing—' He stopped, looking stricken. 'Oh Christ, that was tasteless. I'm sorry. It's just that I haven't quite taken it in yet.'

Kincaid squeezed a little more lemon on his excellent fish and asked, 'Did you like him? Personally, I mean.'

Frye looked thoughtful. 'Well yes, I suppose I did. But it's not that simple. We were quite chuffed to have him at first, as I said. Of course, we wondered why he would have left one of the best firms in London for us, but he said he'd been having domestic problems, wanted to be a bit closer to home, get out of the London rat race, that sort of thing.' He took another bite of salad and chewed deliberately.

Kincaid wondered if Frye's sorrowful expression reflected his opinion of his lunch or his feelings about Connor. 'And?' he prompted gently.

'I suppose it was naïve of us to have believed it. But Con could be very charming. Not just with women – men liked him, too. That was part of what made him a good salesman.'

'He was good at his job?'

'Oh yes, very. When he put his mind to it. But that was the problem. He was so full of enthusiasm at first – plans and ideas for everything – that I think Gordon and I were rather swept away.' Frye paused. 'Looking back on it, I can see that there was a kind of frantic quality to it, but I didn't realize it at the time.'

'Back up just a bit,' Kincaid said, his forkful of chips halted in mid-air. 'You said you were naïve to have believed Connor's reasons for coming to work for you – did you find they weren't true?'

'Let's say he left a good deal out,' Frye answered ruefully. 'A few months later we began hearing trickles through the grapevine about what had really happened.' He drew his brows together in a frown. 'Didn't his wife tell you? You have spoken to the wife?'

'Tell me what?' Kincaid avoided the question, trying to fit the vivid image of Julia in his mind into that neutral possessive. *The wife.*

Frye scraped ham and shredded carrot into a neat pile in the centre of his plate. 'Con's firm in London handled the ENO account. That's how he met her – at some reception or other. I suppose she must have attended with her family. So when she left him and he had a . . .' Looking rather embarrassed, Frye studied his plate and pushed his food around with his fork. 'I guess you'd call it an emotional breakdown. Apparently he went quite bonkers – broke down crying in front of clients, that sort of thing. The firm kept it all very hush-hush – I suppose they felt they couldn't risk offending the Ashertons by publicly turning him out on his ear.'

They had all been very discreet, Kincaid thought. Had compassion entered into it at all? 'The firm gave him a recommendation when he came to you?'

'We wouldn't have taken him on, otherwise,' Frye answered matter-of-factly.

'When did things begin to go wrong?'

An expression of guilt replaced the embarrassment on Frye's face. 'It's not that Con was a total wash-out – I didn't mean to give you that impression.'

'I'm sure you didn't,' Kincaid said soothingly, hoping to forestall Frye's *let's not speak ill of the dead* qualifications.

'It was a gradual thing. He missed appointments with clients – always with a good excuse, mind you, but after a few times even good excuses begin to wear thin. He promised things we couldn't deliver—' He shook his head in remembered dismay. 'That's a creative director's nightmare. And all those new accounts he was going to bring in, all those connections he had . . .'

'Didn't materialize?'

Frye shook his head regretfully. ''Fraid not.'

Kincaid pushed away his empty plate. 'Why did you keep him on, Mr Frye? It certainly sounds as if he became more of a liability than an asset.'

'Call me John,' Frye said. Leaning forward confidentially, he continued, 'The funny thing is, a few months ago Gordon and I had just about screwed ourselves up to give him the sack, but then things started to improve. Nothing earth-shaking, but he seemed to become a bit more dependable, a bit more interested.'

'Any idea what prompted the change?' Kincaid asked, thinking of Sharon and little Hayley.

Frye shrugged. 'Not a clue.'

'Did you know he had a girlfriend?'

'Girlfriends, you mean. Plural,' Frye said with emphasis. With the resigned air of the much-married, he added, 'Once my wife met him a few times, it was more than my life was worth to have a pint with him after work. She was sure he'd lead me into temptation.' He smiled. 'Fortunately, or unfortunately, depending on your point of view, I never had Connor's knack with women.'

The lunchtime crowd had thinned. Relieved from the crush at the bar, Marian came to collect their empty plates. 'Anything else, lads? A sweet? There's some smashing gâteau left—'

'Don't torment me, please.' Frye put his hands over his face with a moan.

Marian scooped up Kincaid's plate and gave him a most un-icy wink. Smothering a chuckle, he thought that Frye's wife needn't have worried about Connor's influence – her husband's weaknesses obviously lay in other directions. That train of thought reminded him of a particular weakness they hadn't addressed. 'Were you aware of Connor's gambling debts?'

'Debts?' Frye asked, draining the last drop of lemonade from his glass. 'I knew he liked a bit of racing, but I never knew it was that serious.'

'Ever hear of a chap called Kenneth Hicks?'

Frye wrinkled his brow for a moment, then shook his head. 'Can't say that I have.'

Kincaid pushed his chair back, then stopped as another question occurred to him. 'John, did you ever meet Connor's wife, Julia?'

Frye's reaction surprised him. After a moment of rather sheepish throat-clearing, he finally looked Kincaid in the eye. 'Well, um, I wouldn't say I exactly met her.'

Kincaid raised an eyebrow. 'How can you "not exactly" meet someone?'

'I saw her. That is, I went to see her, and I did.' At Kincaid's even more doubtful expression he coloured and said, 'Oh hell, I feel an idiot, a right prat. I was curious about her, after all I'd heard, so when I saw the notice in the paper of her show in Henley . . .'

'You went to the opening?'

'My wife was away at her mum's for the night, and I thought, well, why not, there's no harm in it.'

'Why should there have been?' Kincaid asked, puzzled.

'I want to paint,' Frye said simply. 'That's why I studied art in the first place. My wife thinks it's frivolous of me – two kids to support and all that–'

'–and artists are bad influences?' Kincaid finished for him.

'Something like that.' He smiled ruefully. 'She does get a bit carried away sometimes. Thinks I'd bugger off and leave them to starve, I suppose, if someone waggled a paintbrush under my nose.'

'What happened at the opening, then? Did you meet Julia?'

Frye gazed dreamily past Kincaid's shoulder. 'She's quite striking, isn't she? And her paintings . . . well, if I could paint like that, I wouldn't spend my life doing print layouts for White's Plumbing Supply and Carpet-land.' He gave a self-deprecating grimace. 'But I can't.' Focusing again on Kincaid, he added, 'I didn't meet her, but not from lack of trying. I'd drunk my cheap champagne – not without a good bit of it knocked down my shirt-front by careless elbows – and had almost made my way through the mob to her when she slipped out of the front door.'

'Did you follow her?'

'Eventually I elbowed my way to the door, thinking I'd at least pay my respects on my way out.'

'And?' Kincaid prompted impatiently.

'She was nowhere in sight.'

Chapter Nine

The trees arched overhead, their branches interlocking like twined fingers, squeezing tighter and tighter – Gemma blew a wisp of hair from her face and said, 'Silly goose.' The words seemed to bounce back at her, then it was quiet again inside the car except for an occasional squeaking as the twigs and rootlets protruding from the banks brushed against the windows. The sound reminded her of fingernails on chalkboard. London and Tommy Godwin's urbane civility seemed a world away, and for a moment she wished she'd insisted on attending the post-mortem with Kincaid. He had left a message for her at the Yard, summing up the rather inconclusive results.

She shifted down into second gear as the gradient grew steeper. Kincaid had been with her when she'd driven this way the first time, his presence forestalling any lurking claustrophobia. It was all quite silly, really, she chided herself. It was just a narrow road, after all, and some of her discomfort could surely be put down to her London-bred distrust of the country.

Nevertheless, she spied the turning for Badger's End with some relief, and soon bumped to a stop in the clearing before the house. She got out of the car and stood for a moment. Even in the chill air, the damp scent of leaf mould reached her nose, rich as autumn distilled.

In the stillness she heard the same curious, high-pitched humming sound she and Kincaid had noticed before. She looked up, searching for power lines, but saw only more leaves and a patch of uniformly grey sky. Perhaps it was some sort of generator or trans-former, or – she smiled, her temper improving by the moment – UFOs. She'd try that one on the guv.

Her lips still curved in the hint of a smile as she rang the bell. Vivian Plumley opened the door, as she had before, but this time she smiled as she recognized Gemma. 'Sergeant. Please come in.'

'I'd like a word with Dame Caroline, Mrs Plumley,' Gemma responded as she stepped into the flagged hall. 'Is she in?'

'She is, but she's teaching just now.'

Gemma heard the piano begin, then a soprano voice singing a quick, lilting line. Words she couldn't distinguish interrupted the singing, then a second voice repeated the line. Darker and more complex than the first voice, it possessed an indefinable unique-ness. Even through the closed sitting room door, Gemma recognized it instantly. 'That's Dame Caroline.'

Vivian Plumley regarded her with interest. 'You have a good ear, my dear. Where have you heard her?'

'On a tape,' Gemma said shortly, suddenly reluc-tant to confess her interest.

Vivian glanced at her watch. 'Come and have a cuppa. She should be finished shortly.'

'What are they singing?' Gemma asked as she followed Vivian down the hall.

'Rossini. One of Rosina's arias from *The Barber of Seville*. In Italian, thank goodness.' She smiled over her shoulder at Gemma as she pushed open the door into the kitchen. 'Although in this household that's not the most politically correct thing to say.'

'Because of the ENO's policy?'

'Exactly. Sir Gerald is quite firm in agreeing with their position. I think Caro has always preferred singing an opera in its original language, but she doesn't express her opinion too forcefully.' Vivian smiled again, affectionately. The disagreement was obviously a long-standing family tradition.

'Something smells heavenly,' Gemma said, taking a deep breath. After her previous visit, the kitchen seemed as comforting and familiar as home. The red Aga radiated heat like a cast-iron heart, and on its surface two brown loaves rested on a cooling rack.

'Bread's just out of the oven,' Vivian said as she assembled mugs and a stoneware teapot on a tray. On the Aga a copper kettle stood gently steaming.

'You don't use an electric one?' Gemma asked curiously.

'I'm a dinosaur, I suppose. I've never cared for gadgets.' Turning her attention fully on Gemma, Vivian added, 'You will have some hot bread, won't you? It's getting on for teatime.'

'I had some lunch before I left London,' Gemma said, remembering the cold and greasy sausage roll hastily snatched from the Yard canteen after her interview at LB House. 'But yes, I'd love some, thanks.' She went nearer as Vivian poured boiling water into the pot and began slicing the bread. 'Wholemeal?'

'Yes. Do you like it?' Vivian looked pleased. 'It's my trademark, I'm afraid, and my therapy. It's kneaded twice, and takes three risings, but it puffs up in the oven like a dream.' She gave Gemma a humorous glance. 'And it's hard to stay frustrated with life when you've done that much pounding.'

As they seated themselves at the scarred oak table, Gemma confided, 'I grew up in a bakery. My parents have a small shop in Leyton. Almost everything's done by machine, of course, but Mum could usually be persuaded to let us get our hands in the dough.'

'It sounds a good upbringing,' Vivian said approvingly as she poured tea into Gemma's mug.

A flowery cloud of steam enveloped Gemma's face. 'Earl Grey?'

'You do like it, I hope? I should have asked. It's a habit – that's what I always have in the afternoons.'

'Yes, thank you,' Gemma answered demurely, thinking that if she were to make a practice of taking afternoon tea in houses like this, she had bloody well better learn to like it.

She ate her bread and butter in appreciative silence, wiping the last crumbs from the plate with her fingertip. 'Mrs Plumley—'

'Everyone calls me Plummy,' Vivian said in invitation. 'The children started it when they were tots, and it stuck. I've rather grown to like it.'

'All right, then. Plummy.' Gemma thought the name suited her. Even dressed as she was today, in a brightly coloured running suit and co-ordinating turtleneck, Vivian Plumley had about her an aura of old-fashioned comfort. Noticing that the other woman still wore her wedding ring, Gemma half-consciously rubbed the bare finger on her left hand.

They sat quietly, drinking their tea, and in the relaxed, almost sleepy atmosphere, Gemma found that a question came as easily as if she had been talking to friend. 'Didn't you find it odd that Connor stayed on such close terms with the family after he and Julia separated? Especially with no children involved . . .'

'But he knew them first, you see, Caro and Gerald. He'd met them through his job, and cultivated them quite actively. I remember thinking at the time that he seemed quite smitten with Caro, but then she's always collected admirers the way other people collect butterflies.'

Although Plummy had uttered this without the least hint of censure, Gemma had a sudden vision of a struggling insect pinned ruthlessly to a board. 'Ugh,' she said, wrinkling her nose in distaste. 'I could never stand the thought.'

'What?' asked Plummy. 'Oh, butterflies, you mean. Well, perhaps it was an unkind comparison, but men always seem to flutter so helplessly around her. They think she needs looking after, but the truth of it is that she's quite capable of looking after herself. Personally, I can't imagine it.' She smiled at Gemma. 'I don't think I've ever inspired that desire in anyone.'

Gemma thought of Rob's automatic assumption that she would provide for his every need, both physical and emotional. It had never occurred to him that she might have a few of her own. She said, 'I never thought of it quite like that, but men haven't fallen over themselves trying to look after me, either.' Sipping her tea, she continued, 'About Dame Caroline – you said you were at school together. Did she always want to sing?'

Plummy laughed. 'Caro was front and centre from the day she was born. At school she sang the leading part in every programme. Most of the other girls quite despised her, but she never seemed to notice. She might as well have worn blinkers – she knew what she wanted and she never gave a thought to anything else.'

'She launched her career quite early for a singer, didn't she?' Gemma asked, remembering the snippets she'd heard from Alison Douglas.

'That was partly Gerald's doing. He plucked her out of the chorus and put her centre-stage, and she had the drive and ambition to meet the challenge, if not the experience.' She reached out and broke a corner from a slice of the bread she'd set on the table, then took an experimental nibble. 'Just checking,' she said, smiling at Gemma. 'Quality control.' Taking a sip of her tea, she continued, 'But you realize that this all happened more than thirty years ago, and there are only a few of us who remember Gerald and Caro before they were leading lights.'

Gemma contemplated this for a moment, following Plummy's example and reaching for another slice of bread. 'Do they like being reminded that they were ordinary once?'

'I think there is a certain comfort in it.'

What had it been like for Julia, Gemma wondered, growing up in her parents' shadow? It was difficult enough under any circumstances to shake off one's parents' influence and become a self-governing individual. She washed down a bite of bread with tea before asking, 'And that's how Julia met Connor? Through her parents?'

After a moment's thought, Plummy said, 'I believe it was an ENO fund-raising reception. In those days Julia still occasionally attended musical functions. She was just beginning to make her mark as an artist, and she hadn't completely left her parents' orbit.' She shook her head. 'It took me by surprise from the start – Julia had always preferred the sort of intellectual and arty types, and Con was about as far removed from that as one could imagine. I tried talking to her, but she wouldn't hear a word of it.'

'And were they as ill-matched as you thought?'

'Oh yes,' she answered with a sigh, swirling the tea in the bottom of her mug. 'More so.'

When Plummy didn't elaborate, Gemma asked, 'Did you know that Connor had been seeing someone?'

She looked up in surprise. 'Recently, you mean? A girlfriend?'

'A young woman with a small daughter.'

'No. No, I didn't.' With the compassion Gemma had begun to expect of her, Plummy added, 'Oh, the poor thing. I suppose she will have taken his death quite badly.'

The words *unlike Julia* seemed to hang unspoken between them. 'She's moved back, you know,' said Plummy. 'Julia. Into the flat. I told her I didn't think it looked well at all, but she said it was her flat, after all, and she had the right to do whatever she liked with it.'

Gemma thought of the upstairs studio, empty of Julia Swann's disturbing presence, and felt an unaccountable sense of relief. 'When did she go?'

'This morning, early. She has missed her studio, poor love – I never understood why she let Con stay on in the house. But there's no reasoning with her once she's made up her mind about something.'

The exasperated affection in Plummy's voice reminded Gemma of her own mum, who swore that her red-haired daughter had been born stubborn. Not that Vi Walters was one to talk, Gemma thought with a smile. 'Was Julia always so headstrong?'

Plummy regarded her steadily for a long moment, then said, 'No, not always.' She glanced at her watch. 'Have you finished your tea, dear? Caro should be free by now, and she has another student coming this afternoon, so we'd better sandwich you in between.'

'Caro, this is Sergeant James,' Plummy announced as she ushered Gemma into the sitting room. Then she withdrew, and Gemma felt the draught of cool air as the door clicked shut.

Caroline Stowe stood with her back to the fire, as had her husband when Gemma and Kincaid had interviewed him two days earlier. She stepped towards Gemma with her hand outstretched. 'How nice to meet you, Sergeant. How can I help you?'

Her hand felt small and cool in Gemma's, as soft as a child's. Involuntarily, Gemma glanced at the photograph on the piano. While it had given her a hint of the woman's feminine delicacy, it hadn't begun to express her vitality. 'It's just a routine follow-up on the report you gave Thames Valley CID, Dame Caroline,' said Gemma, and her own voice sounded harsh in her ears.

'Sit down, please.' Dame Caroline moved to the sofa and patted the cushion invitingly. Over white wool trousers she wore a long garnet-coloured sweater. The soft cowl neck framed her face, its colour the perfect foil for her pale skin and dark hair.

Gemma, who had dressed with particular care that morning, suddenly found her favourite olive silk skirt and blouse as drab as camouflage, and as she sat down she felt awkward and clumsy. A flush of embarrassment warmed her cheeks and she said quickly, 'Dame Caroline, I understand from your initial statement that you were at home last Thursday evening. Can you tell me what you did?'

'Of course, Sergeant, if you find it necessary,' Caroline said with an air of gracious resignation. 'I had dinner with Plummy – that's Vivian Plumley – then we watched something on the telly, I'm afraid I can't remember what. Does it matter?'

'Then what did you do?'

'Plummy made us some cocoa, that must have been around ten o'clock. We talked for a bit, then went to bed.' Apologetically, she added, 'It was a very ordinary evening, Sergeant.'

'Do you remember what time your husband came in?'

'I'm afraid not. I sleep quite soundly, and we have separate beds, so he seldom disturbs me when he comes in late after a performance.'

'And your daughter didn't disturb you when she returned in the early hours of the morning?' Gemma asked, wanting to shake Caroline's polished complacency just a bit.

'She did not. My daughter is a grown woman and comes and goes as she pleases. I'm not in the habit of keeping tabs on her whereabouts.'

Bull's-eye, thought Gemma. She'd hit a sensitive spot. 'I understand from Mrs Plumley that your daughter has gone back to the flat she shared with Connor. Did you approve of her being on her own again so soon, considering the circumstances?'

Caroline seemed to bite back a response, then sighed. 'I thought it rather ill-advised, but then my approval has never had much effect on Julia's actions. And she has behaved very badly over Connor's death from the first.' Looking suddenly tired, Caroline rubbed her fingers over her cheekbones, but Gemma noticed that she didn't stretch the skin.

'In what way?' Gemma asked, although she'd had proof enough that Julia wasn't playing the grieving widow to perfection.

Shrugging, Caroline said, 'There are things that must be done, and people have certain expectations . . . Julia has simply not met her obligations.'

Gemma wondered if Julia would have done what was necessary if she hadn't been sure her parents would step in and take care of everything. The fact that Julia seemed to resent them doing so only served to illustrate the perversity of human nature, and Gemma had begun to think that their relationship might be more perverse than most. She turned a page in her small notebook, running through her questions in her mind. 'I believe Connor came here for lunch last Thursday?' At Caroline's nod, she continued, 'Did you notice anything unusual about his behaviour that day?'

Smiling, Caroline said, 'Con was very entertaining, but there was nothing unusual about that.'

'Do you remember what you talked about?' Gemma asked, and as she watched Caroline ponder the question, she realized she'd never before seen a woman capable of furrowing her brow prettily.

'Oh, nothing memorable or weighty, Sergeant. Local gossip, Gerald's performance that night—'

'So Connor knew your husband would be in London?'

Looking perplexed, Caroline answered, 'Well, of course Con knew Gerald would be in London.'

'Do you know why Connor would have visited the Coliseum that same afternoon?'

'I can't imagine. He certainly didn't say anything to us about going to London – are you saying he visited the theatre?'

'According to the porter's sign-in sheet, but no one else admits to seeing him.'

'How very odd,' Caroline said slowly, and for the first time Gemma sensed her departing from a comfortably rehearsed script. 'Of course, he did leave in rather a tiz—'

'What happened?' Gemma felt a prickle of excitement. 'You said he hadn't done anything out of the ordinary.'

'I don't know that I'd describe it as out of the ordinary. Con was never very much good at sitting still. He excused himself for a moment while Gerald and I were having our coffee. He said he meant to give Plummy a hand in the kitchen, and that's the last we saw of him. A few minutes later we heard his car start up.'

'And you thought something had upset him?'

'Well, I suppose we did think it a bit odd that he hadn't said goodbye.'

Gemma turned carefully back through the pages of her notebook, then looked up at Caroline. 'Mrs Plumley said she did the washing up alone. She didn't see Connor again after she left the dining room. Do you think he went upstairs to see Julia? And perhaps they had a row?'

Caroline clasped her hands in her lap, and the shadows shifted on the garnet sweater as she took a breath. 'I can't say, Sergeant. If that were the case I'm sure Julia would have said something.'

Gemma didn't share her sentiments. 'Did you know that Connor had a girlfriend, Dame Caroline? Technically, I suppose she would have been his mistress, since he and Julia were still married.'

'A girlfriend? Con?' Caroline said quietly, then as she looked into the fire she added more softly still, 'He never said.'

Remembering what Kincaid had told her, Gemma said, 'Her name is Sharon Doyle, and she has a four-year-old daughter. Apparently it was a fairly serious relationship, and he ... um, entertained her quite often at the flat.'

'A child?' Caroline returned her gaze to Gemma. Her dark eyes had dilated and Gemma saw the fire reflected in their liquid and luminous surface.

The afternoon had drawn in as they talked, and now the fire and the lamps cast a noticeable glow in the quiet room. Gemma could imagine serene hours spent here with music and conversation, or time whiled away on the comfortably worn chintz sofa with a book, but never voices raised in anger. 'What if Julia found out about Sharon? Would they have argued over it? Would Julia have liked Connor having another woman in her flat?'

After a long moment, Caroline said, 'Julia is often a law unto herself, Sergeant. I can't begin to guess how she would react to a given situation. And why does it matter anyway?' she added wearily. 'Surely you don't think Julia had anything to do with Con's death?'

'We're trying to find an explanation for Connor's behaviour that last afternoon and evening. He made an unexpected visit to the theatre. He also met someone later that evening, after he'd returned to Henley, but we don't yet know who it was.'

'What *do* you know?' Caroline straightened her back and regarded Gemma directly.

'The results of the post-mortem didn't tell us much. We're still waiting on some of the forensic reports – all we can do until then is gather information.'

'Sergeant, I think you're being deliberately vague,' said Caroline, teasing her a little.

Unwilling to be drawn any further, Gemma focused on the first thing that came to mind. She'd been absently examining the paintings Kincaid and Julia had talked about – what had Julia said the painter was called? Flynn? No, Flint. That was it. The rosy bare-breasted women were voluptuous, somehow innocent and slightly decadent at the same time, and the sheen of their satin gowns made Gemma think of the costume fabrics she'd seen that morning at LB House. 'I met an old friend of yours today, Dame Caroline. Tommy Godwin.'

'Tommy? Good God, what on earth could you possibly want with Tommy?'

'He's very clever, isn't he?' Gemma settled back more comfortably on the sofa and tucked her notebook into her bag. 'He told me a lot about the early days, when you were all starting out with the Opera. It must have been terribly exciting.'

Caroline's expression softened. She gazed absently into the fire, and after a moment said, 'It was glorious. But, of course, I didn't realize quite how special it was, because I had nothing to compare it to. I thought that life could only get better, that everything I touched would turn to gold.' She met Gemma's eyes again. 'Well, that's the way of it, isn't it, Sergeant? You learn that the charmed times can't last.'

The words held an echo of such sorrow that Gemma felt their weight upon her chest. The photographs on the piano pulled at her insistently, but she kept her eyes on Caroline's face. She had no need to look at them – Matthew Asherton's smiling image had burned itself upon her memory. Taking a breath, she said, with a daring born out of her own fear, 'How do you manage to go on?'

'You protect what you have,' Caroline said quietly, vehemently. Then she laughed, breaking the spell. 'Tommy wasn't quite so elegant in those days, though you wouldn't think it to look at him now. He shed his background like a snake sloughing off its skin, but he hadn't completed the process. There were still a few rough edges.'

Gemma said, 'I can't imagine,' and they both laughed.

'Tommy was never less than amusing, even at his least polished. We did have some lovely times ... and we had such vision. Gerald and Tommy and I –

we were going to change the face of opera.' Caroline smiled fondly.

How could you bear to give it up? thought Gemma. Aloud, she said, 'I've heard you sing. I bought a tape of *Traviata*. It's marvellous.'

Caroline folded her arms loosely under her breasts and stretched her dainty feet towards the fire. 'It is, isn't it? I've always loved singing Verdi. His heroines have a spiritual quality that you don't find in Puccini, and they allow you more room for interpretation. Puccini you must sing exactly as it's written or it becomes vulgar – with Verdi you must find the heroine's heart.'

'That's what I felt when I listened to Violetta,' Gemma said with delight. Caroline had given definition to her own vaguely formed impressions.

'Do you know the history of *Traviata?*' When Gemma shook her head, Caroline continued, 'In Paris in the 1840s there lived a young courtesan named Marie Duplessis. She died on the second of February, 1846, just nineteen days after her twenty-second birthday. Among her numerous lovers in her last year were Franz Liszt and Alexandre Dumas, *fils*. Dumas wrote a play based on Marie's life called *La Dame aux Camélias*, or *Camille—*'

'And Verdi adapted the play as *Traviata*.'

'You've been swotting,' said Caroline in mock disappointment.

'Not really, just reading the liner notes. And I didn't know that Violetta was based on a real person.'

'Little Marie is buried in the cemetery at Montmartre,

just below the church of Sacre Coeur. You can visit her grave.'

Gemma found herself unable to ask if Caroline herself had made such a pilgrimage – it came too near the forbidden territory of Matthew's death. She shivered a little at the thought of such waste. Marie Duplessis must have held on to her life with all the passion Verdi wrote into Violetta's music.

A bell rang, echoing in the passage outside the sitting room. The front door – Plummy had said Caroline had another student coming. 'I'm sorry, Dame Caroline. I've kept you too long.' Gemma slid the strap of her handbag over her shoulder and stood up. 'Thank you for your time. You've been very patient.'

Caroline rose and once again offered Gemma her hand. 'Goodbye, Sergeant.'

As Gemma neared the sitting room door, Plummy opened it and said, 'Cecily's here, Caro.'

As Gemma passed the girl in the hall, she had a brief impression of dark skin and eyes and a flashing shy smile, then Plummy ushered her gently out into the dusk. The door closed and Gemma stood breathing the cool, damp air. She shook her head to clear it, but that made the dawning realization no less uncomfortable.

She had been seduced.

'A message for you, Mr Kincaid,' Tony called out cheerfully from the bar as Kincaid entered the

Chequers. 'And your room's ready for you.' Tony seemed to do everything around the place, and all with the same unflagging good nature. Now he fished a message slip from beneath the bar and handed it to Kincaid.

'Jack Makepeace called?'

'You've just missed him by a few minutes. Use the phone in the lounge if you like.' Tony gestured towards the small sitting area opposite the bar.

Kincaid rang High Wycombe CID and shortly Makepeace came on the line. 'We've run down a possible lead on your Kenneth Hicks, Superintendent. Rumour from some racing sources has it that he does his drinking in a pub in Henley called the Fox and Hounds. It's on the far side of town, off the Reading road.'

Kincaid had just come through Henley on his way from Reading, and would now have to turn round and go back. He swore under his breath but didn't criticize Makepeace for not contacting him by bleeper or car phone – it wasn't worth the loss of good will. 'Anything known about him?'

'No record to speak of – a few juvenile offences. He's a petty villain from the sound of it, not a serious one. Hand in the till here and there, that sort of thing.'

'Description?'

'Five foot eight or nine, nine stone, fairish hair, blue eyes. No available address. If you want to talk to him I guess you'll have to do a spot of drinking at the Fox and Hounds.'

Kincaid sighed with resignation at the prospect. 'Thanks, Sergeant.'

Unlike the pub where he'd lunched in Reading, the Fox and Hounds turned out to be every bit as dreary as he'd imagined. The sparse late afternoon activity centred around the snooker table in the back room, but Kincaid choose the public bar, seating himself at an inadequately wiped plastic-topped table with his back against the wall. Compared to the other customers, he felt conspicuously well groomed in jeans and a fisherman's jersey. He sipped the foam from his pint of Brakspear's bitter and settled back to wait.

He'd killed half the pint as slowly as he could when a man came in who fitted Kenneth Hicks's general description. Kincaid watched as he leaned on the bar and said a few low words to the barman, then accepted a pint of lager. He wore expensive-looking clothes badly on his slight frame, and his narrow face had a pinched look that spoke of a malnourished childhood. Kincaid watched over the rim of his pint as the man glanced nervously around the bar, then took a seat at a table near the door.

The sneaky bugger's paranoia would have given him away even if his looks hadn't, thought Kincaid, and he smiled in satisfaction. He drank a little more of his beer, then stood and casually carried his glass across to the other man's table. 'Mind if I join you?' he said as he pulled up a stool and sat down.

'What if I do?' the man answered, shrinking back and holding his glass before his body like a shield.

Kincaid could see specks of dandruff mixed with the styling cream that darkened the fair hair. 'If you're Kenneth Hicks, you're out of luck, because I want a word with you.'

'What if I am? Why should I talk to you?' His eyes shifted from one side of Kincaid's body to the other, but Kincaid had sat between him and the door. The grey light from the front windows illuminated the imperfections of Hicks's face – a patch of pale stubble missed, the dark spot of a shaving cut on his chin.

'Because I asked you nicely,' Kincaid said as he pulled his warrant card from his hip pocket and held it open in front of Hicks's face. 'Let me see some identification, if you don't mind.'

A sheen of perspiration appeared on Hicks's upper lip. 'Don't have to. Harassment, that's what that is.'

'Oh, I don't think it's harassment at all,' Kincaid said softly, 'but if you like we'll call in the local lads and have our little chat in the Henley nick.'

For a moment he thought Hicks would bolt, and he balanced himself a little better on the stool, his muscles tensing. Then Hicks set his glass down on the plastic table with a thump and wordlessly handed Kincaid his driving licence.

'A Clapham address?' Kincaid asked, after he had examined it for a moment.

'It's me mum's,' Hicks said sullenly.

'But you stay here in Henley, don't you?' Kincaid

shook his head. 'You really should keep these things current, you know. We like to know where to find you when we want you.' He pulled a notebook and pen from his pocket and slid them across the table. 'Why don't you write down your address for me before we forget? Make sure you get it right, now,' he added as Hicks reluctantly picked up the pen.

'What's it to you?' Hicks asked as he scribbled a few lines on the paper and shoved it back.

Kincaid held out his hand for the pen. 'Well, I have a vested interest in staying in touch with you. I'm looking into Connor Swann's death, and I think you know a good deal about Connor Swann. It would be very odd if you didn't, considering the amount of money he paid you every month.' Kincaid drank another half-inch of his pint and smiled at Hicks, whose sallow skin had faded almost to green at the mention of Connor's name.

'I don't know what you're talking about,' Hicks managed to squeak, and now Kincaid could smell his fear.

'Oh, I think you do. The way I heard it is that you do some unofficial collecting for a bookie here in town, and that Connor was in over his head—'

'Who told you that? If it was that little tart of his, I'll fix her—'

'You'll not touch Sharon Doyle.' Kincaid leaned forward, abandoning his amiable pretence. 'And you'd better hope she's not accident prone, because I'll hold you responsible if she so much as breaks a little finger.

Have you got that, sunshine?' He waited until Hicks nodded, then said, 'Good. I knew you were a bright boy. Now unfortunately, Connor didn't discuss his financial problems with Sharon, so you're going to have to help me out. If Connor owed money to your boss, why did he pay you directly?'

Hicks took a long pull on his lager and fumbled in his jacket pocket until he found a crumpled packet of Benson & Hedges. He lit one with a book of matches bearing the pub's name, and seemed to gather courage as he drew in the smoke. 'Don't know what you're talkin' about, and you can't—'

'Connor may not have taken very good care of some parts of his life, but in others he was quite meticulous. He recorded every cheque he wrote – did you know that, Kenneth? You don't mind if I call you Kenneth, do you?' Kincaid added, all politeness again. When Hicks didn't reply, he continued. 'He paid you large amounts on a very regular basis. I'd be curious to see how those amounts tally with what he owed your boss—'

'You leave him out of this!' Hicks almost shouted, sloshing beer on the table. He looked round to see if anyone else had heard, then leaned forward and lowered his voice to a hiss. 'I'm telling you, you leave him—'

'What were you doing, Kenneth? A little loan-sharking on the side? Carrying Con's debts with interest? Somehow I don't think your boss would take too kindly to your skimming his clients like that.'

'We had a private arrangement, Con and me. I helped him out when he was in trouble, same as he'd have done for me, same as any mates.'

'Oh, mates, was it? Well, that puts a different complexion on it entirely. I'm sure in that case Connor didn't mind you making money off his debts.' Kincaid leaned forward, hands on the edge of the table, resisting the urge to grab Hicks by the lapels of his leather bomber jacket and shake him until his brains rattled. 'You're a bloodsucker, Kenneth, and with mates like you nobody needs enemies. I want to know when you saw Connor last, and I want to know exactly what you talked about, because I'm beginning to think Con got tired of paying your cut. Maybe he threatened to go to your boss – is that what happened, Kenneth? Then maybe the two of you had a little scuffle and you pushed him in the river. What do you think, sunshine? Is that how it happened?'

The bar had begun to fill and Hicks had to raise his voice a little to make himself heard over the increasing babble. 'No, I'm telling you, man, it wasn't like that at all.'

'What *was* it like?' Kincaid said reasonably. 'Tell me about it, then.'

'Con had a couple of really stiff losses, close together, couldn't come up with the ready. I was flush at the time so I covered him. After that it just got to be sort of a habit.'

'A nasty habit, just like gambling, and one I'll bet Con got fed up with pretty quickly. Con hadn't written you a cheque the last few weeks before he died. Was he balking, Kenneth? Had he had enough?'

Perspiration beaded on Hicks's upper lip and he wiped it with the back of his hand. 'No, man, the horses had been good to him the last couple of weeks, for a change. He paid off what he owed – we were square, I swear we were.'

'That's really heart-warming, just like good little Boy Scouts. I'll bet you shook hands on it, too.' Kincaid sipped from his glass again, then said conversationally, 'Nice local beer, don't you think?' Before Hicks could reply he leaned across the little table until he was inches from the man's face. 'Even if I believed you, which I don't, I think you'd look for some other way to soak him. You seem to know a lot about his personal life, considering your *business* arrangement. Looking for another foothold, were you, Ken? Did you find something out about Connor that he didn't want anyone else to know?'

Hicks shrank back. 'Don't know what you're talkin' about, man,' he said, then wiped spittle from his lower lip. 'Why don't you ask that slut of his what she knows? Maybe she found out hell'd freeze over before he'd marry her.' He smiled, showing nicotine-stained teeth, and Kincaid found it no improvement over his sneer. 'Maybe she shoved him in the river – did you ever think about that one, Mr Bloody Know-it-all?'

'What makes you think he wouldn't have married Sharon?'

'Why should he? Get himself stuck with a stupid

little cow like that – take on some other bugger's bleedin' kid? Not on your nelly.' Sniggering, Hicks pulled another cigarette from the packet and lit it from the butt of the first. 'And her with a gob like a fishwife.'

'You're a real prince, Kenneth,' Kincaid said generously. 'How do you know Sharon thought Con intended to marry her? Did she tell you?'

'Too right, she did. Said, "He'll get shut of you then, Kenneth Hicks. I'll make sure of it." Stupid—'

'You know, Kenneth, if you'd been the one found floating face-down in the Thames, I don't think we'd have had to look far for a motive.'

'You threatening me, man? You can't do that – that's—'

'Harassment, I know. No, Kenneth, I'm not threatening you, just making an observation.' Kincaid smiled. 'I'm sure you had Connor's best interests at heart.'

'He used to tell me things, when he'd had a few, like.' Hicks lowered his voice confidentially. 'Wife had him by the balls. She crooked her little finger, he'd come running with his tail between his legs. He'd had a hell of a row with her that day, the bitch—'

'What day, Kenneth?' Kincaid said very distinctly, very quietly.

Cigarette frozen halfway to his lips, Hicks stared at Kincaid like a rat surprised by a ferret. 'Don't know. You can't prove nothing.'

'It was the day he died, wasn't it, Kenneth? You saw Connor the day he died. Where?'

Hicks's close-set eyes shifted nervously away from Kincaid's face and he drew sharply on the cigarette.

'Spit it out, Kenneth. I'll find out, you know. I'll start by asking these nice people here.' Kincaid nodded towards the bar. 'Don't you think that's a good idea?'

'So what if I did have a couple of pints with him? How was I to know it was different from any other day?'

'Where and when?'

'Here, same as always. Don't know what time,' Hicks said evasively, then added as he saw Kincaid's expression, 'Twoish, maybe.'

After lunch, Kincaid thought. Con had come straight here from Badger's End. 'He told you he'd had a row with Julia? What about?'

'Don't know, do I? Nothin' to do with me.' Hicks clamped his mouth shut so decisively that Kincaid changed tack.

'What else did you talk about?'

'Nothin'. We just had a friendly pint, like. Not against the law, is it, havin' a friendly drink with a mate?' Hicks asked, voice rising if he might be working himself up to hysteria.

'Did you see Connor again after that?'

'No, I never. Not after he left here.' He took a last drag on his cigarette and ground it out in the ashtray.

'Where were you that night, Kenneth? From eight o'clock or so on?'

Shaking his head, Hicks said, 'None of your friggin' business, is it? I've had enough of your bleedin' harassment. I ain't done nothin', fuckin' filth got no right to keep after me.' He shoved his empty glass away and pushed back on his stool, watching Kincaid, the whites of his eyes showing beneath the irises.

Kincaid debated the benefit of pushing him any further, and decided against it. 'All right, Kenneth, have it your way. But stay around where I can find you, just in case we need to have another little chat.' Hicks's stool screeched against the floor as he stood up. As he pushed past, Kincaid reached up and sank his fingers into the sleeve of his leather jacket. 'If you even think about disappearing, boyo, I'll have the lads after you so fast you won't be able to find a hole big enough to hide your skinny backside. Do we understand each other, mate?'

After a long moment, Hicks nodded and Kincaid smiled and let him go. 'There's a good boy, Ken. See you around.'

Kincaid turned and watched Hicks scuttle out of the door into the street, then he carefully wiped his fingers against his jeans.

Chapter Ten

Not one to let good beer go to waste, Kincaid drained the last drop of his pint. He considered briefly having another, but the pub's atmosphere didn't encourage lingering.

Out in the street, he sniffed the air curiously. He'd noticed the smell when he arrived in town, but it seemed stronger now. Familiar but elusive . . . tomatoes cooking, perhaps? Finding his car free of sprayed graffiti and still in possession of its hub caps, Kincaid stood still for a moment and closed his eyes. Hops. Of course, it was hops – it was Monday and the brewery was in full operation. The wind must have shifted since he'd arrived at the pub, bringing the rich smell with it. The brewery would be closing soon, as well as most of the shops, he thought as he glanced at his watch – rush hour, such as it was, had begun in Henley.

He'd navigated his way onto the Reading road, intent on exchanging the day's findings with Gemma back at the Chequers, when the signpost for the Station Road carpark caught his eye. Almost without thinking he found himself making the turn and pulling into a vacant slot. From there it was only a few hundred yards' walk down Station Road to the river. On his right lay the boathouse flats, serene behind their iron fence in the dusk.

Something had been niggling at him – he couldn't swear to the date of the last cheque Connor had written Kenneth. Kincaid had never finished his interrupted search of Con's desk, and now he let himself into the flat with the key he'd used earlier, intending to have another look at the cheque book.

He stopped just inside the door. Looking around, he tried to pinpoint why the flat felt different. Warmth, for one thing. The central heating had been switched on. Con's shoes had disappeared from beneath the settee. The untidy stack of newspapers on the end table had gone as well, but something even less definable spoke of recent human occupation. He sniffed, trying to place the faint scent in the air. Something tugged at the fringes of his mind, then vanished as he heard a noise above.

He held his breath, listening, then moved quietly towards the stairs. A scrape came, then a thump. Someone moving furniture? He'd only been a few minutes behind Kenneth leaving the pub – had the little sod beaten him here, bent on destroying evidence? Or had Sharon come back, after all?

Both doors on the first landing had been pulled to, but before he could investigate, the noise came again from above. He climbed the last flight of steps, carefully keeping his feet to the edge of the treads. The studio door stood open a few inches, not enough to give him a clear view into the room. Taking a breath, he used his fist to slam the door open. He charged into the room as the door bounced against the wall.

Julia Swann dropped the stack of canvases she held in her hands.

'Jesus, Julia, you gave me a fright! What the hell are you doing here?' He stood breathing hard, adrenaline still rushing through his body.

'*I* gave *you* a fright!' She stared at him wide-eyed, holding her balled hand to her chest and flattening her black sweater between her breasts. 'You probably just cost me ten years off my life, Superintendent, not to mention damage to my property.' She bent to retrieve her paintings. 'I might ask you the same question – what are you doing in my flat?'

'It's still under our jurisdiction. I'm sorry I frightened you. I had no idea you were here.' Trying to regain a semblance of authority, he added, 'You should have notified the police.'

'Why should I feel obliged to let the police know I'd come back to my own flat?' She sat on the rolled arm of the chair she used for a prop in her paintings and looked at him challengingly.

'Your husband's death is still under investigation, Mrs Swann, and he did live here, in case you'd forgotten.' He came nearer to her and sat on the only other available piece of furniture, her worktable. His feet dangled a few inches above the floor and he crossed his ankles to stop them swinging.

'You called me Julia before.'

'Did I?' Then, it had been instinctive, involuntary.

201

Now he used it deliberately. 'Okay, Julia.' He drew the syllables out. 'So what are you doing here?'

'I should think that would be rather obvious.' She gestured around her and he turned, examining the room. Paintings, both the small flower studies and the larger portraits, had been stacked against the walls, and a few had been hung. Dust had vanished from the visible surfaces, and some of the paints and paper familiar to him from her workroom at Badger's End had appeared on the table. She had brought in a large pot plant and placed it near the blue velvet chair – those, along with the faded Persian rug and the brightly coloured books in the case behind the chair, formed the still-life tableau he'd seen in several of the paintings at the gallery.

The room felt alive once more, and he finally identified the scent that had eluded him downstairs. It was Julia's perfume.

She had slid down into the depths of the chair and sat quietly smoking with her legs stretched out, and as he looked at her he saw that her eyes were shadowed with fatigue. 'Why did you give this up, Julia? It doesn't make any sense.'

Studying him, she said, 'You look different out of your proper policeman's kit. Nice. Human, even. I'd like to draw you.' She stood suddenly and touched her fingers to the angle of his jaw, turning his head. 'I don't usually do men, but you have an interesting face, good bones that catch the light well.' Just as quickly, she sank into the chair again and regarded him.

He still felt the imprint of her fingers against his

skin. Resisting the urge to touch his jaw, he said, 'You haven't answered me.'

Sighing, she ground the half-smoked cigarette into a pottery ashtray. 'I don't know if I can.'

'Try me.'

'You would have to know how things were with us, towards the end.' Idly, she rubbed the nap on the chair arm the wrong way. Kincaid waited, watching her. She looked up and met his eyes. 'He couldn't pin me down. The more he tried the more frustrated he got, until finally he started imagining things.'

Fastening on the first part, Kincaid asked, 'What do you mean, he couldn't pin you down?'

'I was never there for him, not in the way he wanted, not when he wanted . . .' She crossed her arms as if suddenly cold and rubbed her thumbs against the fabric of her sweater. 'Have you ever had anyone suck you dry, Superintendent?' Before he could answer, she added, 'I can't go on calling you Super-bloody-intendent. Your name's Duncan, isn't it?' She gave his name a slight stress on the first syllable, so that he heard in it a Scots echo.

'What kind of things did Connor imagine, Julia?'

Her mouth turned down at the corners and she shrugged. 'Oh, you know. Lovers, secret trysts, that sort of thing.'

'And they weren't true?'

'Not then.' She lifted her eyebrows and gave him a little flirtatious smile, challenging him.

'You're telling me that Connor was jealous of *you*?'

Julia laughed, and the smile that transformed her

thin face moved him in a way he couldn't explain. 'It's so ironic, isn't it? What a joke. Connor Swann, everyone's favourite Lothario, afraid his own wife might be messing him about.' Kincaid's consternation must have shown, because she smiled again and said, 'Did you think I didn't know Con's reputation? I would have to have been deaf, dumb and blind not to.' Her mirth faded and she added softly, 'Of course, the more I slipped away, the more women he notched on his braces. Was he punishing me? Or was he just looking for what I couldn't give him?' She stared past Kincaid at the window he knew must be darkening.

'You still haven't answered my question,' he said again, but this time gently.

'What?' She came back to him from her reverie. 'Oh, the flat. I was exhausted, in the end. I ran away. It was easier.' They looked at each other in silence for a moment, then she said, 'You can see that, can't you, Duncan?'

The words 'ran away' echoed in his mind and he had a sudden vision of himself, packing up only the most necessary of possessions, leaving Vic in the flat they had chosen with such care. It had been easier, easier to start again with nothing to remind him of his failure, or of her. 'What about your studio?' he said, shutting off the flow of memory.

'I've missed it, but I can paint anywhere, if I must.' She leaned back in the chair, watching him.

Kincaid thought back to his earlier interviews with her, trying to put a finger on the change he sensed. She was still sharp and quick, her intelligence always evident, but the brittle nervousness had left her. 'It wasn't easy for you, was it, those months you spent at Badger's End?' She stared back at him, her lips parted, and he felt again that frisson along his spine that came with knowing her in a way more intimate than words.

'You're very perceptive, Duncan.'

'What about Trevor Simons? Were you seeing him then?'

'I told you, no. There wasn't anyone.'

'And now? Do you love him?' A necessary question, he told himself, but the words seemed to leave his lips of their own accord.

'Love, Duncan?' Julia laughed. 'Do you want to split philosophical hairs over the nature of love and friendship?' She continued more seriously, 'Trev and I are friends, yes, but if you mean am I in love with him, the answer is no. Does it matter?'

'I don't know,' Kincaid answered truthfully. 'Would he lie for you? You did leave the opening that night, you know. I have an independent witness who saw you go.'

'Did I?' She looked away from him, fumbling for the cigarette packet that had slipped under the chair. 'I suppose I did, for a bit. It was rather a crush. I don't like to admit it, but sometimes things like that make me feel a little claustrophobic.'

'You're still smoking too much,' he said as she found the packet and lit another cigarette.

'How much is too much? You're splitting hairs again.' Her smile held a hint of mischief.

'Where did you go, when you left the gallery?'

Julia stood up and went to the window, and he twisted around, watching her as she closed the blinds against the charcoal sky. Still with her back to Kincaid, she said, 'I don't like bare windows, once it's dark. Silly, I know, but even up here I always feel someone might be watching me.' She turned to him again. 'I walked along the River Terrace for a bit, had a breath of air, that's all.'

'Did you see Connor?'

'No, I didn't,' she answered, coming back to her chair. This time she curled herself into it with her legs drawn up, and as she moved the bell of her hair swung against her neck. 'And I doubt I was gone more than five or ten minutes.'

'But you saw him earlier that day, didn't you? At Badger's End, after lunch, and you had a row.'

He saw her chest move with the quick intake of breath, as if she might deny it, but she only watched him quietly for a moment before answering, 'It was such a stupid thing, really, such a petty little end note. I was ashamed.

'He came upstairs after lunch, bounding in like a great overgrown puppy, and I lit into him. I'd had a letter that morning from the building society – he'd not made a payment in two months. That was our arrangement, you see,' she explained to Kincaid, 'that he could stay in the flat as long as he kept up the payments. Well, we argued, as you can imagine, and I told him he had to come up with the money.' Pausing, she put out the cigarette she'd left burning in the ashtray, then took another little breath. 'I also told him he needed to think about making other arrangements. It was too worrying, about the payments, I mean . . . and things were difficult for me at home.'

'And he didn't take that well?' Kincaid asked. She shook her head, her lips pressed together. 'Did you give him a time limit?'

'No, but surely he could see that we couldn't go on like that for ever . . .'

Kincaid asked the question that had been bothering him from the beginning. 'Why didn't you just divorce him, Julia? Get it over with, make a clean break. This was no trial separation – you knew when you left him that it couldn't be mended.'

She smiled at him, teasing. 'You of all people should know the law, Duncan. Especially having been through it yourself.'

Surprised, he said, 'Ancient history. Are my scars still visible?'

Julia shrugged. 'A lucky guess. Did your wife file against you?' When he nodded, she continued, 'Did you agree to her petition?'

'Well, of course. There was no point going on.'

'Do you know what would have happened if you had refused?'

He shook his head. 'I never thought about it.'

'She would've had to wait two years. That's how long it takes to prove a contested divorce.'

'Are you saying that Connor refused to let you divorce him?'

'Got it in one, dear Superintendent.' She watched him as he digested this, then said softly, 'Was she very beautiful?'

'Who?'

'Your wife, of course.'

Kincaid contrasted the image of Vic's delicate, pale prettiness with the woman sitting before him. Julia's face seemed to float between the blackness of her turtlenecked jersey and her dark hair, almost disembodied, and in the lamplight the lines of pain and experience stood out sharply. 'I suppose you would say she was beautiful. I don't know. It's been a long time.'

Realizing that his rear had gone numb from sitting on the hard table edge, he pushed off with his hands, stretched and lowered himself to the Persian rug. He wrapped his arms around his knees and looked up at Julia, noticing how the difference in perspective altered the planes and shadows of her face. 'Did you know about Con's gambling when you married him?'

She shook her head. 'No, only that he liked to go racing, and that was rather a lark for me. I'd never been—' She laughed at his expression. 'No, really. You think I had this very sophisticated and cosmopolitan upbringing, don't you? What you don't understand is that my parents don't do anything unless it's connected with music.' She sighed, then said reflectively, 'I loved the colours and the movement, the horses' grace and perfect form. It was only gradually that I began to see that it wasn't just fun for Con, not in the sense it was for me. He'd sweat during the race, and sometimes I'd see his hands tremble. And then I began to realize he was lying to me about how much he'd bet.' Shrugging, she added, 'After a bit I stopped going.'

'But Con kept betting.'

'Of course we had rows. "A harmless pastime" he called it. One he deserved after the pressures at work. But it was only towards the end that it became really frightening.'

'Did you bail him out, pay his debts?'

Julia looked away from him, resting her chin on her hand. 'For a long time, yes. It was my reputation, too, after all.'

'So this row you had last Thursday was old business, in a sense?'

She managed a small smile. 'Put that way, yes, I suppose it was. It's so frustrating when you hear yourself saying things you've said a hundred times before – you know it's useless but you can't seem to stop.'

'Did he say anything different when he left you? Anything that varied from the normal pattern of these arguments?'

'No, not that I can remember.'

And yet he had gone straight to Kenneth. Had he meant to borrow the money for the mortgage? 'Did he say anything to you about going to London that afternoon, to the Coliseum?'

Julia lifted her head from her hand, her dark eyes widening in surprise. 'London? No. No, I'm sure he didn't. Why should he have gone to the Coli? He'd just seen Mummy and Daddy.'

The childish diminutives sounded odd on her lips, and she seemed suddenly young and very vulnerable. 'I'd hoped you might tell me,' he said softly. 'Did you ever hear Connor mention someone called Hicks? Kenneth Hicks?' He watched her carefully, but she only shook her head, looking genuinely puzzled.

'No. Why? Is he a friend?'

'He works for a local bookie, does some collecting for him, among other things. He's also a nasty piece of work, and Connor paid him large amounts of money on a regular basis. That's why I came back, to have another look at Connor's cheque book.'

'I never thought of looking through Con's things,' Julia said slowly. 'I've not even been in the study.' She dropped her head in both hands and said through her splayed fingers, 'I suppose I was putting off the inevitable.' After a moment she raised her head and looked at him, her lips twisting with a mixture of embarrassment and bravado. 'I did find some woman's things in the bedroom and in the bath. I've packed them up in a box – I didn't know what else to do with them.'

So Sharon had not come back. 'Give them to me. I think I can return them to their rightful owner.' Although he read the question in her expression, she didn't speak, and they regarded one another in silence. He sat near enough to touch her, and the desire came to him to raise his hand and lay the backs of his fingers against the hollow of her cheek.

Instead, he said gently, 'He was seeing someone, you know. A quite steady arrangement, from the sound of it. She has a four-year-old daughter, and Con told her that he would marry her and look after them both, just as soon as you'd let him have a divorce.'

For a long moment Julia's face went blank, wiped as clean of expression as a mannequin's, then she gave a strangled laugh. 'Oh, poor Con,' she said. 'The poor, silly bastard.'

For the first time since Kincaid had met her, he saw her eyes fill with tears.

Gemma finished her second packet of peanuts and licked the salt from the tips of her fingers. Looking up, she saw Tony watching her and smiled a little shame-facedly. 'Starving,' she said by way of apology.

'Let me have the kitchen fix you something.' Tony seemed to have adopted her as his own personal responsibility and was even more solicitous than usual. 'We've got lovely pork chops tonight, and a vegetarian lasagne.'

Surreptitiously, Gemma glanced at her watch beneath the level of the bar. 'I'll wait a bit longer. Thanks, Tony.' After leaving Dame Caroline, she had driven to the pub and carried her case upstairs. Suddenly overcome by a wave of exhaustion, she'd stretched out on top of the duvet in her good clothes and slept deeply and dreamlessly for an hour. She'd awakened feeling cold and a little stiff, but refreshed. After a good wash and brush, she'd changed into her favourite jeans and sweater and gone down to wait for Kincaid.

Tony, polishing glasses at the far end of the bar,

still kept an anxious eye on the level of cider in her glass. She had almost decided to let him refill it when he looked towards the door and said, 'There's your boss now, love.'

Kincaid slid onto the stool beside her. 'Has Tony been plying you with drink?' He went on without waiting for an answer, 'Good, because I'm going to ply you with food. Sharon Doyle told me that Connor favoured the Red Lion in Wargrave – only place the food was up to his standards. I think we should suss it out for ourselves.'

'Will you be having a drink before you go, Mr Kincaid?' asked Tony.

Kincaid looked at Gemma. 'Hungry?'

'Famished.'

'Then we had better go straight on, Tony.'

Tony flapped his dishcloth at them. 'Cheerio. Though if you don't mind my saying so,' he added in a slightly affronted tone, 'their food's no better than ours.'

Having lavished reassurances upon Tony, they escaped to the car and drove to Wargrave in silence.

Only when they had settled at a table in the cheerful atmosphere of the Red Lion did Gemma say, 'Tony said you had a message from Sergeant Makepeace. What did he want? Where have you been?'

Kincaid, intent on his menu, said, 'Let's order first. Then I'll tell you. See anything you fancy? Gratin of haddock and smoked salmon? Prawns in garlic sauce? Chicken breast with red and green pepper-corns?' He looked up at her, grinning, and she thought his eyes looked unusually bright. 'Con had it right – no shepherd's pie or bangers and mash to be found here.'

'Are you sure our expenses will run to this?' Gemma asked.

'Don't worry, Sergeant,' he said with exaggerated authority. 'I'll take care of it.'

Unconvinced, Gemma gave him a doubtful glance, but said, 'I'll have the chicken, then. And the tomato and basil soup for starters.'

'Going the whole hog?'

'Pudding, too, if I can find room for it.' She closed her menu and propped her chin on her hands. He had seated her with her back to the crackling fire and the warmth began to penetrate her sweater. 'I feel I deserve it.'

The barman came round to them, his pad ready. He had a dishcloth tucked into his belt, dark, curling hair restrained in a pony-tail, and an engaging smile. 'What will you have?'

Kincaid ordered the gratin for himself and added a bottle of American Fumé Blanc. When they had finished the young man said, 'Right, then. I'll just pass this to the kitchen.' As he slipped back behind the bar, he added, 'My name's David, by the way. Just give me a shout if you need anything else.'

Gemma and Kincaid looked at each other, brows raised, then she said, 'Do you suppose the service is always this good, or is it just because it's slow tonight?'

She looked around the room. Only one other table was occupied – in the far corner a couple sat, heads bent close together.

'I'll bet he has a good memory for customers. After we eat, we'll give it a go.'

When David had returned and filled their glasses with chilled wine, Kincaid said, 'Tell me.'

Gemma related her interview with Tommy Godwin, omitting her rather inglorious arrival. 'I'm not sure I buy the bit about his coming into the theatre from the front and standing up at the back of the stalls. Doesn't feel quite right.'

Their starters came, and as Kincaid tucked into his pâté, he said, 'And what about Dame Caroline? Any joy there?'

'It seems their lunch didn't go quite as smoothly as they claimed at first. Connor excused himself to help with the washing up, but Plummy says he never came into the kitchen, and he left without saying goodbye to Gerald and Caroline.' She scraped the last bit of soup from the cup. 'I think he must have gone upstairs to Julia.'

'He did, and they had a nasty row.'

Gemma felt her mouth drop open. She closed it with a snap, then said, 'How could you possibly know that?'

'Kenneth Hicks told me, then Julia herself.'

'All right, guv,' Gemma said, exasperated. 'You've got that cat-in-the-cream look. Give.'

By the time he'd recounted his day, their main courses had come and they both ate quietly for a few minutes. 'What I can't understand,' he said as he finished a bite of fish and sipped his wine, 'is how a yobbo like Kenneth Hicks managed to hook Connor so thoroughly.'

'Money can be a powerful incentive.' Gemma deliberated between more braised leeks or more roast potatoes, then took both. 'Why did Julia lie about the row with Connor? It seems innocent enough.'

Kincaid hesitated, then shrugged. 'I suppose she didn't think it significant. It certainly wasn't a new argument.'

Fork halfway to her mouth, Gemma said hotly, 'But this wasn't a case of failing to mention something that might or might not have been significant. She deliberately lied. And she lied about leaving the gallery as well.' She returned her fork with its speared chicken to her plate, and leaned towards Kincaid. 'It's not right the way she's behaved, refusing to take care of the funeral arrangements. What would she have done, let the county bury him?'

'I doubt that very much.' Kincaid pushed his plate aside and leaned back a little in his chair.

Although his tone had been mild enough, Gemma felt rebuked. Feeling a flush begin to stain her cheeks, she retrieved her fork, then put it down again as she realized she'd lost her appetite.

Watching her, Kincaid said, 'Finished already? What about that pudding?'

'I don't think I can possibly manage it.'

'Drink your wine, then,' he said, topping up her glass, 'and we'll have a word with David.'

Gemma bristled at this avuncular instruction, but before she could respond he caught the barman's eye.

'Ready for your sweets?' David said as he reached their table. 'The chocolate roulade is heavenly—' As they both shook their heads he continued with hardly a break in stride, 'No takers. Cheese, then? The cheese selection is quite good.'

'A question or two, actually.' Kincaid had opened his wallet. First he showed David his warrant card, then a snapshot of Connor he had begged from Julia. 'We understand this fellow was a regular customer of yours. Do you recognize him?'

'Of course I do,' answered David, puzzled. 'It's Mr Swann. What do you mean, "was"?'

'I'm afraid he's dead,' Kincaid said, using the standard formula. 'We're looking into the circumstances of his death.'

'Mr Swann – dead?' For a moment the young man looked so pale that Kincaid reached out and pulled up a chair from the next table.

'Sit down,' said Kincaid. 'The mob is not exactly queuing up for service at the bar.'

'What?' David folded into the proffered chair as if legless. 'Oh, I see what you mean.' He gave a wan attempt at a smile. 'It's just a bit of a shock, that's all. Seems like just the other night he was here, and he was always so . . . larger-than-life. Vital.' Reaching out, he touched the surface of the photograph with a tentative fingertip.

'Can you remember what night it was you saw him

last?' Kincaid asked quietly, but Gemma could sense his concentrated attention.

David drew his brows together, but said quickly enough, 'My girlfriend, Kelly, was working late on the checkout at Tesco's, didn't finish till half-past nine or thereabouts . . . Thursday. It must have been Thursday.' He glanced at them both, expecting approbation.

Kincaid met Gemma's eyes across the table and she saw the flash of victory, but he only said, 'Good man. Do you remember what time he came in on Thursday?'

'Late-ish. Must have been after eight.' Warming to his tale, David continued, 'Sometimes he came in by himself, but usually he was with people I thought must be clients of some sort. Not that I eavesdropped on purpose, mind you,' he added, looking a bit uncomfortable, 'but when you're a waiter sometimes you can't help but overhear, and they seemed to be talking business.'

'And that night?' Gemma prompted.

'I remember it particularly because it was different. He came in alone, and even then he didn't seem his usual self. He was short with me, for one thing. "Something's really got on his wick," I thought.' Remembering Gemma, he added, 'Sorry, miss.'

She smiled at him. 'Don't mind me.'

'Mr Swann, now, he could put it away with the best of them, but he was always jolly with it. Not like some.' David made a face and Gemma nodded sympathetically. As if that had reminded him of his other customers, he glanced at the table at the back, but its occupants were still too engrossed in each other to notice his lack of attention. 'Then this other bloke came in, and they took a table for dinner.'

'Did they know each other?' Kincaid asked.

'What did—' Gemma interjected, but Kincaid stopped her with a quickly lifted hand.

'Oh, I'm sure they must have done. Mr Swann stood up as soon as the other bloke came in the door. They went straight to their table after that, so I didn't hear what they said – custom was fairly good that night – but things seemed friendly enough at first.'

'And then?' Kincaid said into the moment's pause.

David looked from one to the other, less comfortable now. 'I guess you could say they had a heated discussion. Not a shouting match – they didn't really raise their voices, but you could tell they were arguing. And Mr Swann, well, he always enjoyed the food here, made a point to compliment the chef, that sort of thing.' He paused, as if making sure they fully understood the import of what he was about to say. 'He didn't even finish his dinner.'

'Do you remember what he had?' Kincaid asked, and Gemma knew he was thinking of the still incomplete lab report on the contents of Connor's stomach.

'Steak. Washed down with a good part of a bottle of Burgundy.'

Kincaid considered this, then asked, 'What happened after that?'

David shifted in his chair and scratched his nose. 'They paid their bills – separately – and left.'

'They left together?' Gemma asked, clarifying the point.

Nodding, David said, 'Still arguing, as far as I could tell.' He was fidgeting more obviously now, turning round in his chair to glance at the bar.

Gemma looked at Kincaid, and receiving an almost imperceptible nod, said, 'Just one more thing, David. The other man, what did he look like?'

David's smile lit his face. 'Very elegant, nice dresser, if you know what I mean. Tall, thin, fairish – ' he puckered his brow and thought for a moment – 'in his fifties, I should think, but he'd kept himself well.'

'Did he pay by credit card?' Kincaid asked hopefully.

Shaking his head and looking genuinely regretful, David said, 'Sorry. Cash.'

Making an effort to keep the excitement out of her voice, Gemma congratulated him. 'You're very observant, David. We seldom get a description half as good.'

'It's the job,' he said, smiling. 'You get in the habit. I put names with the faces when I can. People like to be recognized.' Pushing back his chair, he looked questioningly from one to the other. 'All right if I clear up now?'

Kincaid nodded and handed him a business card. 'You can ring us if you think of anything else.'

David had stood and deftly stacked their dirty dishes on his arm when he stopped and seemed to hesitate. 'What happened to him? Mr Swann. You never said.'

'To tell you the truth, we're not quite sure, but we are treating it as a suspicious death,' said Gemma. 'His body was found in the Thames.'

The plates rattled and David steadied them with his other hand. 'Not along here, surely?'

'No, at Hambleden Lock.' Gemma fancied she saw a shadow of relief cross the young man's face, but put it down to the normal human tendency to want trouble kept off one's own patch.

David reached for another dish, balancing it with nonchalant ease. 'When? When did it happen?'

'His body was found early Friday morning,' Kincaid said, watching David with a pleasant expression that Gemma recognized as meaning his interest was fully engaged.

'Friday morning?' David froze, and although Gemma couldn't be sure in the flickering reflection from the fire, she thought his face paled. 'You mean Thursday night . . .'

The front door opened and two middle-aged couples came in, faces rosy with the cold. David looked from them to the couple at the back, who were finally showing signs of restiveness. 'I'll have to go. Sorry.' With a flash of an apologetic smile and a rattle of crockery, he hurried to the bar.

Kincaid watched him for a moment, then shrugged and smiled at Gemma. 'Nice lad. Might make a good copper. Has the memory for it.'

'Listen.' Gemma leaned towards him, her voice urgent.

At that moment the two rosy-faced couples, having ordered drinks at the bar, sat down at the next table. They smiled at Gemma and Kincaid in a neighbourly fashion, then began a clearly audible conversation among themselves. 'Here, David's left us a bill,' said Kincaid. 'Let's settle up and be on our way.'

Not until they had stepped out into the street again was Gemma able to hiss at him, 'That was Tommy Godwin.' Seeing Kincaid's blank expression, she said, 'The man with Connor that night. I'm sure it was Tommy Godwin. That's what I kept trying to tell you,' she added testily.

They had stopped on the pavement just outside the pub and stood holding their coat collars up around their throats, a defence against the fog that had crept up from the river. 'How can you be certain?'

'I'm telling you, it had to be him.' She heard her voice rise in exasperation and made an attempt to level it. 'You said yourself that David was observant. His description was too accurate for it to be anyone but Tommy. It's beyond the bounds of probability.'

'Okay, okay.' Kincaid held up a hand in mock surrender. 'But what about the theatre? You'll have to recheck—'

The pub door flew open and David almost catapulted into them. 'Oh, sorry. I thought I might catch you. Look—' He stopped, as if his impetus had vanished. Still in shirtsleeves, he folded his arms across his torso and stamped his feet a little. 'Look – I had no way of knowing, did I? I thought it was just a bit of argy-bargy. I'd have felt a right prat interfering . . .'

'Tell us what happened, David,' said Kincaid. 'Do you want to go back inside?'

David glanced at the door. 'No, they'll be all right for a bit.' He looked back at them, swallowed and went on. 'A few minutes after Mr Swann and the other bloke left, I came out for a break. Kelly usually drops in for a drink when she gets off work, and I like to keep an eye open for her – a bird on her own at night, you know. It's not as safe as it used to be.' For a moment he paused, perhaps realizing just whom he was lecturing, and Gemma could feel his embarrassment intensify. 'Anyway, I was standing just about where we are now, having a smoke, when I heard a noise by the river.' He pointed down the gently sloping street. 'It was clear, not like tonight, and the river's only a hundred yards or so along.' Again he stopped, as if waiting to be drawn.

'Could you see anything?' Kincaid asked.

'The street lamp reflecting off fair hair, and a slightly smaller, darker figure. I think it must have been Mr Swann and the other bloke, but I couldn't swear to it.'

'They were fighting?' Gemma couldn't keep the disbelief from her voice. She found the idea of Tommy Godwin involved in a physical confrontation almost inconceivable.

'Scuffling. Like kids in a school playground.'

Kincaid glanced at Gemma, his eyebrows raised in surprise. 'What happened then, David?'

'I heard Kelly's car. Loose exhaust,' he added in explanation. 'You can hear the bloody thing for a mile. I went to meet her, and when we came back, they were gone.' He scanned their faces anxiously. 'You don't think . . . I never dreamed . . .'

'David,' said Kincaid, 'can you tell us what time this happened?'

He nodded. 'Quarter to ten, or near enough.'

'The other man,' put in Gemma, 'would you know him if you saw him again?'

She could see the gooseflesh on his arms from the cold, but he stood still, considering. 'Well, yes. I suppose I would. Surely, you don't think he—'

'We might want you to make an identification. Just a matter of routine,' Gemma added soothingly. 'Can we reach you here? You'd better give us your home address and telephone as well.' She passed her notebook to him and he scribbled in it, squinting in the orange glow of the street lamps. 'You'd better see to your customers,' she said when he'd finished, smiling at him. 'We'll be in touch if we need you.'

When David had gone, she turned to Kincaid. 'I know what you're thinking, but it's not possible! We know he was in London a few minutes after eleven—'

Kincaid touched his fingers to her shoulder, gently turning her. 'Let's have a look at the river.' As they walked the fog enveloped them, sneaking into their clothes, beading their skin, so that their faces glistened when caught by the light. The pavement ended and their footsteps scrunched on gravel, then they heard the lapping of water against shoreline. 'It must be close now,' said Kincaid. 'Can you smell it?'

The temperature had dropped noticeably as they neared the water, and Gemma shivered, hugging her coat around her. The darkness before them became denser, blacker, and they stopped, straining their eyes. 'What is this place?'

Kincaid shone his pocket torch on the gravel. 'You

can see the wheel ruts where cars have been parked. Forensic will love this.'

Gemma turned to him, clamping down on her chattering teeth. 'How could Tommy have done it? Even if he'd choked Connor and dumped him in the boot of his car, he would have to have driven like a demon to be in London before eleven o'clock. He couldn't possibly have driven to Hambleden and carried Con's body all that way.'

'But,' Kincaid began reasonably, 'he could have left the body in the boot, driven to London to establish an alibi, and dumped the body later.'

'That doesn't make sense. Why go to the theatre, the one place that would connect him with the Ashertons, and through them, with Connor? And if he wanted to establish an alibi, why not sign in with the porter? It was only chance that Alison Douglas saw him in Gerald's dressing room, and Gerald certainly hasn't mentioned it.' Having forgotten the cold and damp in the heat of her argument, Gemma drew breath for her final salvo. 'And even if the rest of it were true, how could he possibly have carried Con's body from the Hambleden carpark to the lock?'

Kincaid smiled his most infuriating smile, the one that meant he found her vehemence amusing. 'Well, I suppose we had better ask him, hadn't we?'

Chapter Eleven

Alison Douglas protested when Gemma rang her early the next day. 'But, Sergeant, how can I possibly ask the ushers to come in this morning when they worked last night? And some of them have other jobs or school.'

'Do the best you can. The alternative is having them down to the Yard, which I doubt most of them would be too keen on.' Gemma tried to keep the irritation out of her voice. A restless night and a drive back to London in the thick of the commuter traffic had left her feeling shirty, but that was no excuse for taking it out on Alison. And it was not the most reasonable of requests, after all. 'I'll be there before noon,' she told Alison, ringing off.

Replacing the receiver in its cradle, she surveyed with distaste the paperwork swamping Kincaid's desk. She felt none of her usual satisfaction in having appropriated his office, but rather the same discomfort that had kept her awake into the wee hours. Something had been different about Kincaid last night – at first she had only been aware of a rather feverish quality to his behaviour, but as she tossed and turned through

the night she came to the conclusion that his re-
sponses to her had altered as well. Had she only
imagined the easy companionship of the previous
evening in London? He had sought her out. Had his
delight in her flat and evident enjoyment of her
company caused her to drop her barriers a dangerous
notch too far?

She shrugged and rubbed her eyes, trying to mas-
sage away the fatigue, but she couldn't erase the
fleeting thought that the change in Kincaid's manner
had something to do with his visit to Julia Swann.

In the end, Alison managed to bring in four of the
ushers, and they sat cramped together on folding
chairs in her office, looking disgruntled but curious.

Gemma introduced herself, adding, 'I'll try not to
keep you any longer than necessary. Do any of you
know Tommy Godwin, the Wardrobe Manager? Tall,
thin, fairish man, very well dressed?' Looking at them,
she wasn't hopeful that sartorial elegance had a place
in their vocabularies. The three young men were neat
but ordinary, and the girl had managed what Gemma
recognized as low-budget dressing with a bit of flair. 'I
want to know if anyone saw him last Thursday evening.' The young men glanced sideways at one another
from blank faces. Behind them Alison stood with arms
crossed, leaning lightly against the wall, and Gemma
saw her mouth open slightly in surprise.

Shaking her head slightly at Alison, Gemma waited,
letting the silence stretch.

Finally, the girl spoke. 'I did, miss.' Her voice held a trace of West Indian cadence, probably acquired from parents or other family members who were first-generation immigrants, thought Gemma.

Letting out the breath she'd been unconsciously holding, Gemma said, 'Did you? You're sure it was Thursday evening, now? *Pelleas and Melisande*, right?' She hadn't really expected such a positive result, still didn't quite trust it.

'Yes, miss.' The girl smiled as if she found Gemma's doubt amusing. 'I see all the productions – I can tell which is which.'

'Good. I'm glad one of us can.' Gemma smiled, silently kicking herself for sounding patronizing. 'What's your name?'

'Patricia, miss. I'm a design student – I'm interested in costumes, so sometimes I help out a bit with Wardrobe. That's how I know Mr Godwin.'

'Can you tell me about Thursday evening?'

The girl glanced round at Alison as if seeking permission from the nearest authority. 'Go ahead, Patricia, tell the Sergeant. I'm sure it's quite all right,' responded Alison.

'Mr Godwin came into the foyer from the street doors. Usually I stand just inside the auditorium and listen to the performance, but I'd just come back from the Ladies' and was crossing the foyer myself. I called out to him, but he didn't hear me.'

Gemma didn't know whether she felt relief or disappointment – if Tommy had been telling the truth about watching the performance, he couldn't have been in Wargrave with Connor. 'What did he do then, did you see?'

'Went in the next aisle over. Roland's,' she added with a sideways glance at the best-looking of the young men.

'Did you see him?' asked Gemma, turning her attention to him. He smiled at her, comfortable with the sudden attention. 'I can't say for sure, miss, as I don't know him, but I don't remember seeing anyone of that description.'

At least he hadn't called her 'ma'am'. Gemma returned the smile and turned her attention back to Patricia. 'Once you'd gone back to your post in the auditorium, did you see him again?'

The girl shook her head. 'The mob started out just afterwards, and I had my hands full.'

'Interval so soon?' asked Gemma, puzzled.

'No.' Patricia shook her head more forcefully this time. 'Final curtain. I'd only realized I needed to go for a pee' – she sent a quelling glance at the young men – 'just in time.'

'Final curtain?' Gemma repeated faintly. 'I thought you meant he'd come in just after the performance began.'

'No, miss. Five minutes, maybe, before the end. Just before eleven o'clock.'

Gemma drew in a breath, collecting herself. So it might have been Tommy in the Red Lion after all. 'Did you see him later on, Patricia, when you were clearing up?'

'No, miss.' Having entered into the spirit of things,

she sounded as if she genuinely regretted having nothing more to offer.

'Okay, thanks, Patricia. You've been a great help.' Gemma looked at the men. 'Anyone else have anything to add?' Receiving the expected negatives, she said, 'All right, thank you.' Patricia trailed out last, looking back a little shyly. 'Bright girl,' said Gemma as the door closed.

'What is all this about Tommy, Sergeant?' asked Alison, coming to sit on the edge of her desk. She brushed absently at the wrinkles in her brown wool suit. The fabric was the same soft tone as her hair and eyes and made her look, thought Gemma, like a small brown wren.

'Are you quite sure you didn't see him until you went to Gerald's dressing room?'

'I'm positive. Why?'

'He told me he was here in the theatre during the entire performance that night. But Patricia's just contradicted that, and she seems a reliable witness.'

'Surely you don't think Tommy had anything to do with Connor's death? That's just not possible. Tommy is . . . well, everyone likes Tommy. And not just because he's witty and amusing,' Alison said as though Gemma had suggested it. 'That's not what I mean. He's kind when he doesn't have to be. I know you wouldn't think it from his manner, but he notices people. That girl, Patricia – I imagine he gave her some encouragement. When I first started here I tiptoed around everything, terrified of making a mistake, and he always had a kind word for me.'

'I'm sure you're right,' said Gemma, hoping to soothe Alison's hostility, 'but there is a discrepancy here, and I must follow it through.'

Alison sighed, looking suddenly weary. 'I suppose you must. What can I do to help?'

'Think back to those few minutes in Sir Gerald's dressing room. Did you notice anything at all unusual?'

'How can I tell?' asked Alison, her feathers ruffling again. 'How can I be sure my recollection's not distorted by what you've told me? That I'm not making something out of nothing?' When Gemma didn't respond, she went on more quietly. 'I have been thinking about it. They stopped talking when I came into the room. I felt as if I'd put my foot in – you know?' She looked at Gemma for confirmation. 'Then after that awkward bit, they seemed a bit too hearty, too jolly. I think now that's why I only stayed a minute, just long enough to offer the usual congratulations, although I didn't consciously realize it at the time.'

'Anything else?' Gemma asked, without too much anticipation.

'No. Sorry.'

'That's okay.' Smiling at Alison, Gemma made an effort to overcome the lethargy that seemed to be creeping into her limbs. 'I will have to talk to him again, and he's proving rather elusive. This morning I've tried his flat, LB House, and here, with no joy. Any suggestions?'

Alison shook her head. 'No, he ought to be around.'

Seeing the spark of concern in Alison's eyes,

Gemma said thoughtfully, 'I hope our Mr Godwin won't prove too difficult to find.'

High Wycombe CID had obligingly made room for Kincaid at an absent DI's desk, and there he had spent the morning, going through report after inconclusive report. He stretched, wondering if he should have another cup of dreadful coffee, or give it up and have some lunch.

Duty and coffee were grudgingly in the lead when Jack Makepeace put his head round the door. 'Anything?'

Kincaid pulled a face. 'Sod all. You've read them. Any word from the team in Wargrave?'

Makepeace grinned evilly. 'Two crushed lager cans, some foil gum wrappers, the remains of a dead bird and half a dozen used condoms.'

'A popular parking spot, is it?'

'It marks the beginning of a footpath that runs along the river for a bit, then loops around the church-yard. Parking there isn't strictly legal, but people do it anyway, and I dare say a spot of midnight necking goes on as well.' Makepeace fingered his moustache for a moment. 'The forensic lads say the gravel's much too soft and messed about for tyre casts.'

'I expected as much.' Kincaid regarded him thoughtfully. 'Jack, if the body went in the river at Wargrave, could it have drifted downstream to Hambleden by morning?'

Makepeace was shaking his head before Kincaid had finished. 'Not possible. River's too slow, for one thing, and there's Marsh Lock, just past Henley, for another.'

Thinking of Julia's brief escape from the gallery, he said, 'Then I suppose the same would be true of Henley, if he'd gone in along the River Terrace?'

Makepeace levered his bulk away from the door frame and walked over to the area map on the office wall. He pointed a stubby finger at the twisting blue ribbon representing the River Thames. 'Look at all these twists and turns, all making places where a body might catch.' Turning back to Kincaid, he added, 'I think your body went in within a few hundred yards of where it was found.'

Kincaid pushed back the creaky chair, stretched out his legs and laced his fingers behind his neck. 'I'm afraid you're right, Jack. I'm just clutching at straws. What about the houses along the river, above the lock? House-to-house turn up anything?'

'Either they were all sleeping like babies by ten o'clock,' Makepeace said sarcastically, laying his cheek against the back of his hand, 'or they see talking to us as an excuse to trot out their own pet phobias. Remember that flat conversion at the beginning of the weir walkway? Old biddy in one of the riverside flats says she heard voices some time after the late news finished. When she looked out of her window she saw a man and a boy on the walkway. "Poofters," she says. "Queers sinning against the Lord." And motorcycle hoodlums to boot.' Makepeace's eyes crinkled in amusement. 'It seems the boy had longish hair and wore leather, and that was good enough for her. Before my PC could get away, she asked him if he'd been saved by Jesus.'

Kincaid snorted. 'Doesn't make me miss my days on the beat. What about access from south of the river, then? Through the meadows.'

'Need a Land Rover, or something with a four-wheel drive. Ground's like glue after all this rain.' Makepeace studied Kincaid's face, then said sympathetically, 'Bad luck. Oh' – he patted the file tucked under his left arm – 'here's something might cheer you up – final report from pathology.' He handed it across to Kincaid. 'Spot of lunch?'

'Give me ten minutes,' Kincaid said with a wave, then dug into the file.

After a cursory read-through he picked up the phone and eventually managed to reach Dr Winstead in his lair. 'Doctor,' he said when he had identified himself, 'I know now what time Connor ate – nine, or shortly thereafter. Are you sure he couldn't have died as early as ten?'

'Meat and potatoes, was I right?'

'Steak, actually,' Kincaid admitted.

'I'd put it closer to midnight, unless the fellow had stomach acid that would've stripped paint.'

'Thanks, Dr Winnie.' Kincaid rang off and contemplated the scattered reports. After a moment he swept them into a pile, pulled up the knot on his tie and went in search of more pleasant prospects.

*

When Gemma returned to the Yard, she found a message on her desk that read simply, 'Tom Godwin called. Brown's Hotel, three o'clock.'

She went in search of the duty sergeant. 'Was that all, Bert? Are you sure?'

Affronted, he said, 'Have you ever known me to make a mistake with a message, Gemma?'

'No, of course not.' She patted his grizzled head affectionately. 'It's just odd, that's all.'

'That's what the gentleman said, verbatim,' said Bert, slightly mollified. 'The guv'nor wants to see you, by the way.'

'Oh, terrific,' she muttered under her breath, and received a sympathetic glance from Bert.

'He hasn't eaten anyone since lunch, love.'

'Ta, Bert,' said Gemma, grinning. 'That makes me feel ever so much better.'

Still, she went along the corridor in some trepidation. In truth, Chief Superintendent Denis Childs was known to be fair with his staff, but there was something in his pleasant and courteous manner that made her want to confess even imagined misdeeds. His door stood open, as was his policy, and Gemma tapped lightly before entering. 'You wanted to see me, sir?'

Childs looked up from a file. He had recently adopted granny-style reading glasses, and they looked so incongruous perched on his massive moon-shaped face that she had to bite her lip to stifle a giggle. Fortunately, he took them off and dangled them daintily from thumb and forefinger. 'Sit down, Sergeant. What have you and Kincaid been up to the past few days – tiddlywinks? I've had a prod from the assistant commissioner, wanting to know why we haven't produced the expected brilliant results. Apparently Sir Gerald Asherton has put quite a flea in his ear.'

'It's only been four days, sir,' Gemma said, stung. 'And the pathologist only got round to the PM yesterday. Anyway,' she added hurriedly, before Childs could trot out his dreaded maxim – *results, not excuses* – 'we have a suspect. I'm interviewing him this afternoon.'

'Any hard evidence?'

'No, sir, not yet.'

Childs folded his hands across his belly and Gemma marvelled, as she always did, that for all his bulk the man radiated such physical magnetism. As far as she knew, he was happily married and used his appeal for nothing more sinister than keeping the typists working to order.

'All the teams are out just now – we've had a regular rash of homicides. But as badly as I need the two of you, I don't think we want to let the AC down, do you, Sergeant? It's always in our best interest to keep the powers-that-be happy.' He smiled at her, his teeth blindingly white against his olive skin. 'Will you pass that along to Superintendent Kincaid when you talk to him?'

'Yes, sir,' Gemma answered, and, taking that as dismissal, beat a hasty and grateful retreat.

When Gemma returned to Kincaid's office, bars of sunlight slanted into the room. They looked solid enough to touch, the quality of the light almost viscous. Not quite trusting the phenomenon, she went to the window and peered through the blinds. The sky was indeed clear and as blue as it ever managed with the city smog. She looked from the window to the paperwork, lying haphazardly where she'd left it. The angle of the light across the desk revealed streaks of dust and several perfect fingerprints – smiling, Gemma walked over and wiped them away with a tissue. Remove the evidence – that was the first rule. Then she grabbed her bag from the coat stand and made for the lift before anyone could stop her.

She cut through St James's Park, walking quickly, taking in great breaths of the cool, clear air. The English have an instinct for sunshine, however brief its duration, she thought, like a radar early-warning system. The park was busy with others who had heeded the signal, some walking as quickly as she was, obviously on their way somewhere, others strolling or sitting on benches, and all looking oddly out of place in their business clothes. The trees, which in the past few days' drizzle had looked drab as old washing, showed remnants of red and gold in the sunlight, and pansies and late chrysanthemums made a brave showing in the beds.

She came out into the Mall, and by the time she'd made her way along St James's Street to Piccadilly she could feel her heart beating and warmth in her face. But it was only a few more blocks along Albemarle Street, and her head felt clear for the first time that day.

Although she had timed it accurately, arriving a few minutes early, Tommy Godwin was there before her. He waved at her, looking as much at home in the hotel's squashy armchair as he might in his own parlour. She made her way over to him, suddenly aware of her windblown hair and pink cheeks, and of her unfashionably sensible low-heeled shoes.

'Do have a seat, my dear. You look as if you've been exerting yourself unnecessarily. I've ordered for you – I hope you don't mind. Stuffy and old-fashioned as it is' – he nodded at the room, with its wood-panelled walls and crackling fire – 'they do a proper tea here.'

'Mr Godwin, this is not a social occasion,' Gemma said as severely as she could while sinking into the depths of her chair. 'Where have you been? I've been trying to reach you all day.'

'I paid a visit to my sister in Clapham this morning. A gruesome but regular family necessity, one which I fear most of us are subject to – unless one has had the good fortune to come into the world via test tube, and even that has ramifications that don't bear thinking of.'

Gemma tried to straighten her back against the chair's soft cushion. 'Please don't take me round the mulberry bush, Mr Godwin. I need some answers from you.'

'Can't we have tea first?' he asked plaintively. 'And call me Tommy, please.' Leaning toward her confidentially, he said, 'This hotel was the model for Agatha Christie's *At Bertram's Hotel* – did you know that,

Sergeant? I don't believe it's changed much since her day.'

Curious in spite of her best intentions, Gemma looked round the room. Some of the little old ladies seated nearby might have been Miss Marple's clones. The faded prints of their dresses (covered by sensibly woolly cardigans) harmonized with the faded blues and violets of their hair rinses, and their shoes – Gemma's comfortable flats weren't even in the same realm of sensibleness as their stout brogues.

What an odd place to appeal to Tommy Godwin, she thought, studying him covertly. She pegged today's navy jacket as cashmere, his shirt as immaculate pale grey broadcloth, his trousers charcoal and his silk tie a discreetly rich navy and red paisley.

As if reading her mind, he said, 'It's the pre-war aura I can't resist. The Golden Age of British manners – vanished now, much to our loss. I was born during the Blitz, but even during my childhood there were still traces of gentility in English life. Ah, here's our tea,' he said as the waiter brought a tray to their table. 'I've ordered Assam to go with the sandwiches – I hope that's all right – and a pot of Keemun later with the cakes.'

Tea in Gemma's family had run to Tetley's Finest teabags, stewed in a tin pot. Not liking to admit that she had never tasted either, she pounced on his previous remark. 'You only think that time must have been perfect because you didn't live it. I imagine the generation between the wars saw Edwardian England as the Golden Age, and probably the Edwardians felt the same way about the Victorians.'

'A good point, my dear,' he said seriously as he poured tea into her cup, 'but there was one great difference – the First World War. They had looked into the mouth of hell, and they knew how fragile our hold on civilization really is.' The waiter returned, placing a three-tiered tray on their small table. Tiny sandwiches filled the bottom tray, scones the middle, and cakes the top, the crowning touch. 'Have a sandwich, my dear,' said Tommy. 'The smoked salmon is particularly nice.'

He sipped his tea and continued his lecture, a cucumber sandwich poised in his fingers. 'It's fashionable these days to pooh-pooh the Golden Age crime novel as trivial and unrealistic, but that was not the case at all. It was their stand against chaos. The conflicts were intimate, rather than global, and justice, order and retribution always prevailed. They desperately needed that reassurance. Did you know that Britain lost nearly a third of its young men between 1914 and 1918? Yet that war didn't physically threaten us in the same way as the next – it stayed safely on the European Front.'

Pausing to down half the cucumber sandwich in one bite, he chewed for a moment, then said sadly, 'What a waste it must have seemed, the flower of Britain's manhood lost, with nothing to show for it but some newspaper headlines and politicians' speeches.' He smiled. 'But if you read Christie or Allingham or

Sayers, the detective always got his man. And you'll notice that the detective always operated outside the system – the stories expressed a comforting belief in the validity of individual action.'

'But weren't the murders always clean and blood-less?' Gemma asked rather impatiently through a mouthful of sandwich. She'd felt too tired and unsettled to eat lunch, and her walk had left her suddenly ravenous.

'Some of them were in fact quite diabolical. Christie was particularly fond of poisoning, and I can think of no less civilized way to commit murder.'

'Are you suggesting that there are civilized meth-ods of murder?' *Such as drowning your victim in a convenient river*, she thought, wondering at the bizarre turn the conversation seemed to be taking.

'Of course not, my dear, only that I've always found the idea of poison especially abhorrent – such suffering and indignity for one person to inflict upon another.'

Gemma drank a little more of her tea. She rolled it around on her tongue, deciding she liked the rich, malty taste. 'So you prefer your murders quick and clean, do you, Tommy?'

'I don't prefer them any way at all, my dear,' he said, glancing up at her as he poured more tea into her cup. He was playing with her, teasing her, she could see it in the suppressed laughter in his eyes.

Time for a little dose of reality, she thought, licking a crumb from her fingertip. 'I've always thought drown-ing would be quite horrible myself. Giving in at last to that desperate need to draw air into the lungs, then choking, struggling, until unconsciousness comes as a blessed relief.'

Tommy Godwin sat quite still, watching her, his hands relaxed on the tabletop. What beautiful hands he had, thought Gemma, the fingers long and slender, the nails perfectly kept. She found quite inconceivable the idea of him fighting like a common ruffian, using those hands to choke and squeeze, or perhaps to hold a thrashing body under water.

'You're quite right, my dear,' he said softly. 'It was tasteless of me to go on that way, but crime novels are rather a hobby of mine.' He picked up a watercress sandwich and looked at it a moment before returning it to the plate. The eyes that met hers were a surprisingly dark blue, and guileless. 'Do you think poor Connor suffered?'

'We don't know. The pathologist didn't find evidence indicating he'd inhaled river water, but that doesn't rule it out.' She let the silence stretch for a heartbeat, then added, 'I was hoping you might tell me.'

His eyes widened. 'Oh, come now, Sergeant. You can't think—'

'You lied to me about attending the opera that night. One of the ushers saw you come in from the street just minutes before the performance ended. And I have a witness who can place you in a pub in Wargrave, having a not-too-friendly dinner with Connor Swann,' she said, tendering her bluff with all the authority she could manage.

For the first time since she had met him, Tommy Godwin seemed at a loss for words. As she studied his still face, she saw that most of his attractiveness lay not in his individual features, but in the expression of alert, humorous inquisitiveness that usually animated them. Finally, he sighed and pushed away his empty plate. 'I should have known it was no use. Even as a child I was never any good at lying. I had meant to attend the performance that night – that much at least was true. Then I had an urgent message from Connor on my answerphone, saying he needed to see me. I suppose he must have been looking for me when he came to the theatre that afternoon.'

'He asked you to meet him at the Red Lion?'

As Tommy nodded the waiter brought their second pot of tea. Lifting the pot, Tommy said, 'You must try the Keemun, my dear. What would you like with it?'

Gemma had started to shake her head when he said, 'Please, Sergeant, do have something. This was to be a special treat for you – I thought hardworking policewomen probably didn't have too many opportunities to take afternoon tea.'

She heard Allson's words again, and she found that no matter what else Tommy might have done, she couldn't reject this small act of kindness. 'I'll have a scone then, please.'

Having taken a scone for himself, he poured tea into her cup from the fresh pot. 'Taste your tea. You can put milk in it if you like, but I'd advise you not to.'

Gemma did as instructed, then looked up at him in surprise. 'It's sweet.'

He looked pleased. 'Do you like it? It's a north China Congou. The best of the China blacks, I think.'

'Tell me about Connor,' Gemma said, spreading clotted cream and strawberry jam on her scone.

'There's not much to tell, really. I met him at the Red Lion, as you said, and from the beginning he behaved quite oddly. I'd never seen him like that, although I'd heard stories about the weeks after he and Julia first separated. He had been drinking, but I didn't think he'd had enough to account for his manner. It was . . . I don't know . . . almost hysterical, really.'

'Why did he want to see you?'

Tommy washed down a bite of scone with tea. 'I found out soon enough. He said he'd decided he wanted his old job back – that he'd had enough of dealing with two-bit, small-town accounts, and he wanted me to intercede for him.'

'Could you have done it?' asked Gemma in some surprise.

'Well, yes, I suppose so. I've known the firm's senior partner for years. In fact, it was I who encouraged him to go after the ENO account in the first place.' He looked at Gemma over the cup he held cradled in both hands. 'It's unfortunate that we can't foresee the consequences of our actions. If I had not done that, Connor would never have met Gerald and Caro, and through them, Julia.

'But you refused Connor's request.'

'Politely at first. I told him that my reputation would ride on his performance, and that considering his previous conduct, I didn't feel I could risk it. The truth of the matter is,' he added, setting down his cup and looking away from Gemma, 'I never liked him. Not the thing to say when one is suspected of foul play, is it, dear Sergeant?' He smiled, teasing her once more, then said reflectively, 'I can remember their wedding day quite clearly. It was a June wedding, in the garden at Badger's End – I know you won't have seen it, but it can be quite lovely at that time of year. All Plummy's doing, although Julia used to help her quite a bit when she had the time.

'Everyone said how perfect Julia and Connor looked together, and I have to admit they did make a handsome couple, but when I looked at them I saw only disaster. They were completely, utterly unsuited for one another.'

'Do stick to the point, Tommy, please,' said Gemma, wondering how she could impress the gravity of the situation upon him with her mouth full of scone.

He sighed. 'We argued. He became more and more abusive, until finally I told him I'd had enough. I left. That's all.'

Moving her plate out of the way, Gemma leaned towards him. 'That's not all, Tommy. The barman came out just after you and Connor left the pub. He says he saw you fighting down by the river.'

Although she wouldn't have believed that a man with Tommy Godwin's poise and experience could blush, she could have sworn his face turned pink with embarrassment.

There was a moment's pause as he refused to meet her eyes. Finally, he said, 'I've not done anything like that since I was at school, and even then I considered any form of physical violence both undignified and uncivilized. It was the accepted way to get on in the world, beating what one wanted out of someone else, and I made a deliberate choice to live my life differently. It got me labelled a pansy and a poofter, of course,' he added with a hint of the familiar, charming smile, 'but I could live with that. What I couldn't live with was the thought of abandoning my principles.

'When I found myself locked in a ridiculous schoolboy scuffle with Connor, I simply stopped and walked away.'

'And he let you?'

Tommy nodded. 'I think he'd run out of steam himself by that time.'

Had you parked your car on the gravel by the river?'

'No, I'd found a spot on the street, a block or two up from the pub. Someone may have seen it,' he added hopefully. 'It's a classic Jaguar, red, quite distinctive.'

'And then, after you'd returned to your car?'

'I drove to London. Having agreed to see Con, against my better judgement, I'd spoiled my evening, and I felt he'd made rather a fool of me. I thought I'd try to salvage as much of my original plan as I could.'

'Five minutes' worth?' asked Gemma, sceptically.

He smiled. 'Well, I did my best.'

'And you didn't make a point of stopping by Sir Gerald's dressing room in order to establish an alibi?'

Patiently, he said, 'I wanted to congratulate him, as I told you before, Sergeant.'

'Even though you hadn't actually seen the performance?'

'I could tell by the audience's response that it had been particularly good.'

She searched his face, and he returned her gaze steadily. 'You're right, you know, Tommy,' she said at last. 'You are an awful liar. I suppose you went straight home from the theatre.

'I did, as a matter of fact.'

'Is there anyone who can vouch for you?'

'No, my dear. I'm afraid not. And I parked at the back of my building and went up in the service lift, so I didn't see anyone at all. I'm sorry,' he added, as if it distressed him to disappoint her.

'I'm sorry, too, Tommy.' Gemma sighed. Feeling suddenly weary, she said, 'You could have put Connor's body in the boot of your car, then driven back to Hambleden after the performance and dumped him in the lock.'

'Really? What an extraordinarily imaginative idea.' Tommy sounded amused.

Exasperated, she said, 'You do realize that we'll have to impound your car so that the forensics team can go over it. And we'll have to search your flat for evidence. And you will have to come down to the Yard with me now and make a formal statement.'

He lifted the delicate porcelain teapot and smiled at her. 'Well, then you had better finish your tea, my dear Sergeant.'

Chapter Twelve

Lunch with Jack Makepeace improved Kincaid's outlook on life considerably. Replete with cheese, pickle and pints of Greene King ale, they blinked as they came out into the street from the dim interior of a pub near the High Wycombe nick. 'That's a surprise,' said Makepeace, turning his face up to the sun. 'And I doubt it'll last long – the forecast is for cats and dogs.'

The perfect antidote to a morning spent wheel-spinning, thought Kincaid as he felt the faint warmth of the sun against his face, was a good walk. 'I think I'll take advantage of it,' he said to Makepeace as they reached the station. 'You can reach me if anything comes up.'

'Some people have all the luck,' Makepeace answered good-naturedly. 'It's back to the salt mines for the likes of me.' He waved and disappeared through the glass doors.

Kincaid made the short drive from High Wycombe to Fingest, and on reaching the village he hesitated for a moment before turning into the pub's carpark. Although the vicarage looked mellow and inviting in the afternoon sun and the vicar was certainly the authority on local walks, he decided it was much too likely he'd end up spending the rest of the afternoon being comfortably entertained in the vicar's study.

In the end, Tony proved as useful and accommodating on the matter of walks as he had about everything else. 'I've just the thing,' he said, retrieving a book from the mysterious recesses under the bar. 'Local pub walks. Three and a half miles too much for you?' He eyed Kincaid measuringly.

'I think I can just about manage that,' Kincaid said, grinning.

'Fingest, Skirmett, Turville, and back to Fingest. All three villages are in their own valleys, but this particular walk avoids the steepest hill. You might get a bit mucky, though.'

'Thanks, Tony. I promise not to trample mud over your carpets. I'll just go and change.'

'Take my compass,' Tony called out as Kincaid turned away, producing it from the palm of his hand like a conjuror. 'It'll come in handy.'

At the top of the first long climb, some thoughtful citizen had placed a bench on which the winded walker could sit and enjoy the view. Kincaid took brief advantage of it, then toiled on, through woods and fields and over stiles. At first the vicar's brief history rolled through his mind, and as he walked he imagined the progression of Celts, Romans, Saxons and Normans settling these hills, all leaving their own particular imprint upon the land.

After a while the combination of fresh air, exercise and solitude worked its magic, and his mind returned freely to the question of Connor Swann's death, sorting the facts and impressions that he had gathered so far. The pathologist's evidence made it highly unlikely that Tommy Godwin had killed Connor outside the Red Lion in Wargrave. He might, of course, have knocked Connor unconscious and killed him a couple of hours later after returning from London – but, like Gemma, Kincaid could come up with no logical scenario for the later removal of the body from the car to the lock.

Dr Winstead's report also meant that Julia could not have killed Con during her brief absence from the gallery, and David's statement placing Connor in Wargrave until at least ten o'clock made it impossible for her to have met him along the River Terrace and made an assignation for later. Kincaid shied away from the feeling of relief that this conclusion brought him, and forced himself to consider the next possibility – that she had met Connor much later and that Trevor Simons had lied to protect her.

So caught up was he in these ruminations that he failed to see the cowpat until he had put his foot in it. Swearing, he wiped his trainer as best he could on the grass. Motive was like that, he mused as he walked on more carefully – sometimes you just couldn't see it until you fell into it. Hard as he tried, he couldn't come up with a likely reason why Julia would have wanted to kill Con, nor did he believe that having had one row with him that day, she would have agreed to meet him later in order to have another.

Had that lunchtime argument with Julia been the trigger for Connor's increasingly odd behaviour during the rest of that day? Yet it was only after he had left Kenneth that Con had visibly deviated from an expected pattern. And that brought Kincaid to Kenneth – where had Kenneth been on Thursday evening, and why had asking him about his movements sent him from reluctant co-operation into complete and obstinate withdrawal? As he pictured Kenneth, huddled in his bomber jacket as if it were armour, he remembered the female witness Makepeace had mentioned. 'A boy in leather,' she'd said ... Kenneth was slightly built and Makepeace had described him as five foot eight or nine. Next to Connor he might easily have been mistaken for a boy. It was certainly a possibility worth pursuing.

The woods enclosed him again as he left Skirmett. He walked in a dim and soundless world, his footfalls absorbed by the leaf mould. Not even birdsong broke the stillness, and when he stopped, staring after a flash of white that might have been a deer bounding away, he could hear the rush of his own blood in his ears.

Kincaid walked on, following the next tendril that shot out from the amoebic mass of speculation. If Connor had driven away from the Red Lion after his scuffle with Tommy Godwin, where had he gone? Sharon Doyle's face came into his mind – she, like Kenneth, had become belligerent when Kincaid had pushed her about her movements later that evening.

As he came into Turville he looked northwest, towards Northend, up the hill where Badger's End lay hidden under the dark canopy of the beeches. What had brought Julia back to that house, as if drawn by an unseen umbilical cord?

He stopped at the Northend turning and frowned. Some thread ran through this case that he couldn't quite grasp – he felt it move away whenever he approached it too closely, like some dark underwater creature always swimming just out of reach.

Nestled among Turville's cluster of cottages, the Bull and Butcher beckoned, but Kincaid declared himself immune to the temptation of Brakspear's ales and pushed on into the fields again.

He soon came out onto the road that led to Fingest. The sun had dropped beneath the tops of the trees, and the light slanted through the boles, illuminating dust motes and flickering on his clothes like a faulty film projector.

By the time the now-familiar twin-gabled tower of Fingest church came into view, Kincaid found he had made two decisions. He would ask Thames Valley to pick up Kenneth Hicks, and then they'd see how well Hicks's bravado held up in an interview room in the local nick.

And he would pay another visit to Sharon Doyle.

When Kincaid returned to the Chequers, a bit muddy as Tony had predicted and feeling pleasantly tired from his walk, there was still no word from Gemma regarding her progress with Tommy Godwin. He rang the Yard and left a message for her with the duty sergeant. As soon as she finished in London she was to join him again. He wanted her in on the interview with Hicks. And considering Kenneth's obvious dislike of women, Kincaid thought with a smile, maybe she should conduct it.

In Henley, Kincaid left the car near the police station and walked down Hart Street, his eyes on the tower of the church of St Mary the Virgin.

Square and substantial, it anchored the town around it like the hub of a wheel. Church Avenue lay neatly tucked in the tower's shadow, facing the churchyard as if it were its own private garden. A plaque set into the stonework informed him that the row of almshouses had been endowed by John Longland, Bishop of Lincoln, in 1547, and rebuilt in 1830.

The cottages were unexpectedly charming, built of a very pale green-washed stucco, with bright blue doors and lace curtains in every window. Kincaid knocked at the number Sharon Doyle had given him. He heard the sound of the television, and faintly, the high voice of a child.

He had raised his hand to knock again when Sharon opened the door. Except for the unmistakable golden corkscrew curls, he would hardly have recognized her. She wore no makeup, not even lipstick, and her bare face looked young and unprotected. The tarted-up clothes and high heels were gone – replaced by a faded sweatshirt, jeans and dirty trainers, and in the few days since he had seen her she seemed visibly thinner. To his surprise, she also seemed rather pathetically glad to see him.

'Superintendent! What are you doing here?' A sticky and dishevelled version of the child in the wallet photo Kincaid had seen slipped up beside Sharon and wrapped herself around her mother's leg.

'Hullo, Hayley,' said Kincaid, squatting at her eye level. He looked up at Sharon and added, 'I came to see how you were getting on.'

'Oh, come in,' she said, as if making an effort to recall her manners, and she stepped back, hobbled by the child clinging to her like a limpet. 'Hayley was just having her tea, weren't you, love? In the kitchen with Gran.' Now that she had Kincaid in the sitting room, she seemed to have no idea what to do with him, and simply stood there stroking the child's tangle of fair curls.

Kincaid looked around the small room with interest. Doilies and dark furniture, fringed lampshades and the smell of lavender wax, all as neat and clean as if they had been preserved in a museum. The sound of the television was only a bit louder than it had been when he stood outside, and he surmised that the cottage's interior walls must be constructed of thick plaster.

'Gran likes the telly in the kitchen,' Sharon said into the silence. 'It's cosier to sit in there, close by the range.'

The front room might have been the scene of some long-ago courtship, thought Kincaid. He imagined young lovers sitting stiltedly on the horsehair chairs, then remembered that these cottages had been built for pensioners, and any wooing must have been done by those old enough to know better. He wondered if Connor had ever come here.

Diplomatically, he said, 'If Hayley would like to go in with Gran and finish her tea, perhaps you and I could go outside and have a chat.'

Sharon gave Kincaid a grateful glance and bent down to her daughter. 'Did you hear what the superintendent said, love? He needs to have a word with me, so you go along in with Gran and finish your tea. If you eat up all your beans and toast, you can have a biscuit,' she added cajolingly.

Hayley studied her mum as if gauging the sincerity of this pledge.

'I promise,' said Sharon, turning her and giving her a pat on the bottom. 'Go on now. Tell Gran I'll be along in a bit.' She watched the little girl disappear through the door in the back of the room, then said to Kincaid, 'Just let me get a cardy.'

The cardy turned out to be a man's brown wool cardigan, a bit moth-eaten, and ironically reminiscent of the one Sir Gerald Asherton had worn the night Kincaid met him. Seeing Kincaid's glance, Sharon smiled and said, 'It was my granddad's. Gran keeps it for wearing about the house.' As she followed Kincaid out into the churchyard, she continued, 'Actually, she's my great-gran, but I never knew my real gran. She died when my mum was a baby.'

Although the sun had set in the few minutes Kincaid had been inside the house, the churchyard looked even more inviting in the soft twilight. They walked to a bench across the way from the cottages, and as they sat down Kincaid said, 'Is Hayley always so shy?'

'She's always chattered like a magpie, from the day she learned to talk, even with strangers.' Sharon's hands lay loosely in her lap, palms turned up. They might have been disembodied, so unanimated were they, and Kincaid noticed that since he'd seen her last, the small pink nails had been bitten to the quick. 'It's only since I told her about Con that she's been like this.' She looked up at Kincaid in appeal. 'I had to tell her, didn't I, Mr Kincaid? I couldn't let her think he just scarpered, could I? I couldn't let her think he didn't care about us.'

Kincaid gave the question careful consideration before answering. 'I think you did the right thing, Sharon. It would be hard or her now, regardless, and in the long run I'm sure it's better to tell the truth. Children sense when you're lying, and then they have that betrayal to deal with as well as the loss.'

Sharon listened intently, then nodded once when he'd finished. She studied her hands for a moment. 'Now she wants to know why we can't see him. My auntie Pearl died last year and Gran took her to the viewing before the funeral.'

'What did you tell her?'

Shrugging, Sharon said, 'Different people do things different ways, that's all. What else could I say?'

'I imagine she wants some concrete evidence that Con is really gone. Perhaps you could take her to see his grave, afterwards.' He gestured at the graves laid out so neatly in the green grass of the churchyard. 'That should seem familiar enough to her.'

She turned to him again, her hands clenching convulsively.

'There's not been anyone to talk to, see? Gran doesn't want to know about it – she disapproved of him anyway—'

'Why was that?' asked Kincaid, surprised that the woman would not have been pleased at a better prospect for her great-granddaughter.

'Marriage is marriage in the eyes of the Lord,' mimicked Sharon, and Kincaid had a sudden clear vision of the old lady. 'Gran's very firm in her beliefs. It made no difference that Con wasn't living with *her*. And as long as Con was married I had no rights, Gran said. Turned out she knew what she was on about, didn't she?'

'You must have girlfriends you can talk with,' said Kincaid, as there seemed no helpful answer to the last question.

'They don't want to know, either. You'd think I'd got leprosy or something all of a sudden – they act like they're afraid it might rub off on them and spoil their fun.' Sharon sniffed, then added more softly, 'I don't want to talk to them about Con, anyway. What we had was between us, and it doesn't seem right to air it like last week's washing.'

'No, I can see that.'

They sat quietly for a few minutes as the lights

began to come on in the cottages. Indistinct shapes moved behind the net curtains, and every so often a pensioner would pop out from one door and then another, putting out milk bottles or picking up papers. It made Kincaid think of those elaborate German clocks, the kind in which the little people bob cheerfully in-and-out as the hour chimes. He looked at the girl beside him, her head again bent over her hands. 'I'll see you get your things back, Sharon. *She* would want you—' Bloody hell, now he was doing it. 'Mrs Swann would like you to have them,' he corrected himself.

Her response, when it came, surprised him. 'Those things I said, the other night ... well, I've been thinking.' In the fading light he caught a quick flash of her eyes before she looked away from him again. 'It wasn't right, what I said. You know. About her ...

'About Julia having killed Connor, is that what you mean?'

She nodded, picking idly at a spot on the front of her sweatshirt. 'I don't know why I said it. I wanted to hit at someone, I suppose.' After a moment she continued in a tone of discovery, 'I think I wanted to believe she was as awful as Con said. It made me feel better. Safer.'

'And now?' Kincaid asked, and when she didn't answer he continued, 'You had no reason for making those accusations? Con never said anything that made you think Julia might have threatened him?'

Shaking her head, she said so softly that he had to

lean close to catch it, 'No.' She smelled of Pears soap, and the good, clean ordinariness of it suddenly squeezed at his throat.

The twilight deepened, and from some of the cottage windows came the blue flicker of televisions. Kincaid imagined the pensioners, all women that he had seen, having their evening meals early so that they could settle down in front of the box, uninterrupted, isolated from themselves as well as one another. He gave a tiny shudder, shaking off the wave of melancholy that threatened him, like a dog coming out of water. Why should he begrudge them their comfort, after all?

Beside him, Sharon stirred and pulled the cardigan a little closer about her. Rubbing his hands together to warm them, he turned to her, saying briskly, 'One more thing, Sharon, and then you'd better go in before you catch a chill. We have a witness who's certain he saw Connor at the Red Lion in Wargrave after he left you that night. Con met a man who fits the description of Tommy Godwin, an old friend of the Ashertons. Do you know him, or did you ever hear Con mention him?'

He could almost hear her thinking as she sat beside him in the dark, and he thought that if he looked closely enough he would see her brow furrowed in concentration. 'No,' she said eventually, 'I never did.' She turned to him, pulling her knee up on the bench so that she could face him directly. 'Did they . . . were they having a row?'

'According to the witness, it was not a particularly friendly meeting. Why?'

She put her hand to her mouth, nibbling at the nail of her index finger. Nail-biting was a form of self-mutilation that had never tempted Kincaid, and it always made him wince for the damaged flesh. He waited, lacing his own fingers together to stop himself from pulling her hand away from her mouth.

'I thought it was me made him angry,' she said in a rush. 'He came back that night. He wasn't pleased to see me – he wanted to know why hadn't I gone back to Gran's, like I said.' She touched Kincaid's sleeve. 'That's why I didn't say anything before. I felt such a bloody fool.'

Kincaid patted her hand. 'Why hadn't you gone home?'

'Oh, I did. But Gran's bridge finished early – one of the old ladies felt a bit ill – so I came back. I was sorry I'd left in a huff before. I thought he'd be glad to see me and we could—' She gulped, unable to go on, but what she had hoped was painfully clear to Kincaid without any further elaboration.

'Was he drunk?'

'He'd had a few, but he wasn't proper pissed, not really.'

'And he didn't tell you where he'd been or who he'd seen?'

Sharon shook her head. ''E said, "What are you doing here?" and walked past me like I was a piece of bloody furniture or something.'

'Then what? Tell me bit by bit, everything you can remember.'

Closing her eyes, she thought for a moment, then began obediently, 'He went into the kitchen and fixed himself a drink—'

'Not to the drinks trolley?' asked Kincaid, remembering the plethora of bottles.

'Oh, that was just for show. Company. Con drank whisky and he always kept a bottle on the kitchen counter,' she said, then continued more slowly. 'He came back into the sitting room and I noticed he kept rubbing at his throat. "Are you all right?" I asked him. "You're not feeling ill, love?" But he didn't answer. He went upstairs into the study and closed the door.'

'Did you follow him?' Kincaid asked when she lapsed into silence.

'I didn't know what to do. I'd started up the stairs when I heard him talking – he must have rung someone.' She looked at Kincaid and even in the dim reflected light he could see her distress. 'He was laughing. That's what I couldn't understand. Why would he laugh when he'd hardly said boo to me?

'When he came downstairs again, he said, "I'm going out, Shar. Lock up when you leave." Well, I'd had enough by that time, I can tell you. I told him to lock his own bloody door – I wasn't hanging about to be treated like a bloody tart, was I? I told him if he wanted to see me he could pick up the sodding phone and ring me, and I'd think about it if I hadn't anything better to do.'

'What did Connor say to that?'

''E just stood there, his face all blank, like he hadn't heard a word I said.'

Kincaid had heard Sharon in full fury, and he thought Connor must have been very preoccupied indeed. 'And did you? Leave, I mean?'

'Well, I had to, didn't I? What else was I to do?'

'The scene definitely called for a grand exit,' said Kincaid, smiling.

Sharon smiled back a little reluctantly. 'I slammed the bloody door so hard I ripped my nail right off. Hurt like hell, too.'

'So you didn't actually see him leave the flat?'

'No. I stood about for a minute. I guess I still hoped he'd come after me, say he was sorry. Silly cow,' she added bitterly.

'You weren't silly at all. You had no way of explaining Con's behaviour – in your place I think I'd have done exactly the same.'

She took a moment to absorb this, then said haltingly, 'Mr Kincaid, do you know why Con said those things . . . why he treated me like that?'

Wishing he had some comfort to give her, he said, 'No,' then added with more certainty than he felt, 'but I'm going to find out. Come on, let's get you inside. Your gran'll have the police out after you.'

Her smile was as weak as his little joke, and manufactured simply to please him, he felt sure. As they reached the cottage door, he asked, 'What time was it when you left Con, Sharon? Do you remember?'

She nodded at the massive tower behind them. 'Church clock struck eleven just as I came round the Angel.'

After he left Sharon, it seemed the most natural thing in the world to Kincaid that he should continue down the hill and along the river to Julia's flat. He would collect Sharon's things while he was thinking of it, and while he was there he'd question Julia again about her movements after the gallery closed that night.

Or so said the rational, logical part of his mind. Some other part stood back and watched the machinations of the first, an amused and taunting spectator. Why didn't he admit he hoped he might sit with her, watching the warm lamplight reflect from the shining curve of her hair? Or admit that he wanted to see again the way her lips curved up at the corners when she found something he said amusing? Or that his skin still remembered the touch of her fingers against his face?

'Bollocks!' Kincaid said aloud, banishing the spectator to the recesses of his mind. He needed to clear up a few points, that was all, and his interest in Julia Swann was purely professional.

The wind that earlier cleared the sky had died at sunset, leaving the evening still and hushed, waiting expectantly. Lights reflecting on the water's surface made it look ice-solid, and as he passed the Angel pub and walked along the embankment, he felt the chill air hovering over the river like a cloud.

As he came opposite Trevor Simons's gallery, he

saw Simons come out of the door. Hurriedly crossing the street, Kincaid found him still bent over the latch. He touched his arm. 'Mr Simons. Having a bit of trouble with your lock?'

Simons jumped, dropping the heavy key-ring he'd held in his hand. 'Christ, Superintendent, you gave me a fright.' He stooped to retrieve the keys and added, 'It does stick a bit, I'm afraid, but I've done it now.'

'On your way home?' Kincaid said pleasantly, wondering even as he asked if Simons's itinerary included a visit to Julia. Now that she was reinstalled in the flat just down the road, they would have no more need of furtive meetings in the workshop behind the gallery.

Simons stood a little awkwardly, holding his keys in one hand and a portfolio in the other. 'Yes, actually. Did you need to see me?'

'There were one or two things,' Kincaid answered, making a decision as he spoke. 'Why don't we go across the road and have a drink?'

'It won't take more than half an hour, will it?' Simons looked at his watch. 'We're going out for a meal tonight. My wife's sent the children to friends – it's more than my life's worth to be late.'

Kincaid hastened to reassure him. 'We'll just nip across to the Angel. I promise we won't be long.'

They found the pub busy, but it was a sedate crowd – made up, judged Kincaid, mostly of professional people having a quick drink before making their way home after work.

'Nice place,' Kincaid said, as they settled comfortably at a table by one of the windows overlooking the river. 'Cheers. I admit I've developed rather a taste for Brakspear's Special.' Tasting his beer, he watched his companion curiously. Simons had sounded a bit embarrassed about his dinner engagement, yet it had the ring of truth. 'Sounds as though you and your wife have quite a romantic evening planned,' Kincaid said, fishing.

Simons looked away, his earlier discomfort more evident. The silver in his thick brown hair caught the light as he ran a hand through it. 'Well, Superintendent, you know what women are like. She'll be very disappointed if I don't participate with enthusiasm.'

A boat motored slowly under the Henley Bridge, its port and starboard lights gleaming steadily. Kincaid idly pushed his beer mat back and forth with one finger, then looked up at Simons. 'Did you know that Julia's moved back into her flat?'

'Yes. Yes, I did. She rang me yesterday.' Before Kincaid could respond, Simons said more forcefully, 'Look, Superintendent. I took your advice the other day. I told my wife about . . . what happened with Julia.' Simons's fine-boned face looked drawn with exhaustion, and as he sipped his whisky and water, his hand trembled slightly.

'And?' Kincaid said when he didn't continue.

'She was shocked. And hurt, as you can imagine,' Simons said quietly. 'I think that the damage won't be easy to repair. We've had a good marriage, probably better than most. I should never have been so careless with it.'

'You sound as though you don't mean to continue things with Julia,' Kincaid said, knowing it was none of his business, and that his investigation hardly justified crossing the boundary of good manners.

Simons shook his head. 'I can't. Not if I mean to mend things with my wife. I've told Julia.'

'How did she take it?'

'Oh, she'll be all right.' Simons smiled with the same gentle, self-deprecating humour Kincaid had seen before. 'I was never more than a passing fancy to Julia, I'm afraid. I've probably saved her the bother of having to say, "Sorry, old dear, but it was only a bit of a lark."'

It occurred to Kincaid that Simons, like Sharon Doyle, was probably glad of a non-partisan ear, and he pushed his advantage. 'Were you in love with her?'

'I'm not sure "love" and "Julia" exist in the same vocabulary, Mr Kincaid. I've been married almost twenty years – to me love means darned socks and "Whose turn is it to take out the rubbish, darling?"' Grinning, he drank a little more of his whisky. 'It may not be exciting, but you know where you are—' He sobered suddenly. 'Or at least you should, unless one of you behaves like an ass.

'I was infatuated with Julia, fascinated, entranced; but I'm not sure one could ever get close enough to love her.'

As much as Kincaid disliked the necessity, he dug in, his voice suddenly harsh. 'Were you infatuated enough to lie for her? Are you sure she didn't leave the gallery when the party finished that night? Did she tell you that she had to see someone? That she'd be back in an hour or two?'

The pleasant humour vanished from Trevor Simons's face. He finished his whisky and set his glass down deliberately, carefully, in the exact centre of its mat. 'She did not.

'I may be an adulterer, Superintendent, but I'm not a liar. And if you think Julia had anything to do with Connor's death, I can tell you you're barking up the wrong tree. She was with me from the time we closed up the gallery until daybreak. And having burned my bridges, so to speak, by confessing to my wife, I'll testify to that in court if I must.'

Chapter Thirteen

Kincaid rang the bell and waited. He rang again, shifting his weight a bit from foot to foot and whistling under his breath. No sound came from inside the flat, and he turned away, feeling an unexpected stab of disappointment.

The sound of the door opening stopped him. When he turned back he found Julia looking at him silently, registering neither pleasure nor dismay at his presence. She lifted the wineglass she held in a mock salute. 'Superintendent. Is this a social call? You can't join me if you're going to play the heavy.'

'My, my,' he said, taking in the faded red jersey she wore over black leggings, 'an outbreak of colour. Is this significant?'

'Sometimes one has to abandon one's principles when one hasn't done laundry,' she answered rather owlishly. 'Do come in – what will you think of my manners? Of course,' she added as she stepped back into the sitting room, 'it might be my concession to mourning.'

'A reverse statement?' Kincaid asked, following her into the kitchen.

'Something like that. I'll get you a glass. The wine's upstairs.' She opened a cupboard and stood up on her toes, stretching to reach a shelf. Kincaid noticed that she wore thick socks but no shoes, and her feet looked small and unprotected. 'Con arranged everything in the kitchen to suit himself,' she said, snagging a glass. 'And it seems whenever I want anything it's always just out of reach.'

Kincaid felt as if he'd barged in on a party in progress. 'Were you expecting someone? There's no need for me to interrupt – I only wanted a quick word with you, and I thought I'd pick up Sharon Doyle's things as well.'

Julia turned round and stood with her back against the counter, looking up at him, holding both glasses against her chest. 'I wasn't expecting a soul, Superintendent. There's not a soul to expect.' She chuckled a little at her own humour. 'Come on. We had graduated from "Superintendent", hadn't we?' she added over her shoulder as she led him back through the sitting room. 'I suppose I'm the one backsliding.'

She wasn't more than a bit tipsy, Kincaid decided as he climbed the stairs after her. Her balance and co-ordination were still good, although she moved a little more carefully than usual. As they passed the first landing he glimpsed the tumbled, unmade bed through the bedroom's open doorway, but the study door still stood tightly shut.

When they reached the studio he saw that the lamps were lit and the blinds drawn, and it seemed to him that the room had acquired another layer of Julia's personality in the twenty-four hours since he'd seen it last. She had been working and a partially finished painting was pinned to the board on her worktable. Kincaid recognized the plant from the rambles of his Cheshire boyhood – speedwell, the gentian-blue flowers along the pathside that were said to 'speed you well' upon your journey. He also remembered his dismay in discovering that its beauty could not be held captive – the delicate blooms wilted and died within minutes of picking.

The rest of the table's surface held open botanical texts, crumpled papers and several used glasses. The room smelled of cigarette smoke, and very faintly of Julia's perfume.

She padded across the Persian carpet and sank to the floor in front of the armchair, which she used as a backrest. Beside the chair were Julia's ashtray, close to overflowing, and an ice bucket holding a bottle of white wine. She filled Kincaid's glass. 'Sit down, for heaven's sake, Duncan. You can't hold a funeral celebration standing up.'

Kincaid lowered himself to the floor and accepted his drink. 'Is that what we're doing?'

'With a bloody good Cap d'Antibes, too. Con would have liked a wake, don't you think? He was all for Irish tradition.' Tasting what remained of her wine, she made a face. 'Warm.' She refilled her glass, then lit a cigarette. 'I'm going to cut down, I promise,' she said in anticipation of Kincaid's protest, smiling.

'What are you doing, barricading yourself up here like this, Julia? The rest of the house doesn't look like anyone's been in it.' He examined her face, deciding that the shadows under her eyes were more pronounced than they had been the day before. 'Have you eaten anything?'

Shrugging, she said, 'There were still some bits and pieces in the fridge. Con's sort of bits, of course. I would have settled for bread and jam. I suppose I hadn't realized – ' she paused to draw on her cigarette – 'that it would have become Con's house. Not mine. Yesterday I spent most of the day cleaning, but it didn't seem to make any difference – he's everywhere.' She made a circular gesture with her head, indicating the studio. 'Except here. If he ever came up here, he left no traces.'

'What makes you want to eradicate him so thoroughly?'

'I told you before, didn't I?' She knitted her brow and gazed at him over the rim of her glass, as if she couldn't quite remember. 'Con was a first-class shit,' she said, without heat. 'A drinker, a gambler, a womanizer, a lout with a load of Irish blarney that he thought would get him anything he wanted – why would I want to be reminded of him?'

Kincaid raised a sceptical eyebrow and sipped his wine. 'Can we attribute this to Con, too?' he asked, tasting its crisp delicacy against the roof of his mouth.

'He had good taste, and he was surprisingly adept at finding a bargain,' Julia admitted. 'A legacy of his upbringing, I would imagine.'

Kincaid wondered if Connor's attraction to Sharon Doyle stemmed from his upbringing as well – a spoiled only son of a doting mum might have considered devotion his due. He hoped that Con had also seen her value.

Uncannily echoing his thoughts, Julia said, 'The mistress – what did you say she's called?'

'Sharon. Sharon Doyle.'

Julia nodded, as if it fit an image in her mind. 'Blonde and a little plump, young, not very sophisticated?'

'Have you seen her?' Kincaid asked, surprised.

'Didn't need to.' Julia's smile was rueful. 'I only imagined my antithesis,' she said, having a little difficulty with the consonants. 'Look at me.'

Kincaid found it all too easy to oblige. Framed in the dark bell of her hair, her face revealed humour and intelligence in equal measure. He said, teasing her, 'I'll only follow your hypothesis so far. Are you suggesting I should regard you as ancient and world-weary?'

'Well, not quite.' This time she gave him the full benefit of her grin, and Kincaid thought again how odd it seemed to see Sir Gerald's smile translated so directly onto her thin face. 'But you do see what I mean?'

'Why should Connor have wanted someone as unlike you as he could find?'

She hesitated a moment, then shook her head, shying away from it. 'This girl – Sharon – how is she taking it?'

'I'd say she's coping, just.'

'Do you think it would help if I spoke to her?' She

ground out her cigarette and added more lightly, 'I've never quite been sure of the proper protocol in these situations.'

Kincaid sensed how vulnerable Sharon would feel in Julia's presence, and yet she had no one with whom she could share her grief. He had seen stranger alliances formed. 'I don't know, Julia. I think she'd like to attend Connor's funeral. I'll tell her she's welcome, if you like. But I wouldn't expect too much.'

'Con will have told her horror tales about me, I'm sure,' Julia said, nodding. 'It's only natural.'

Regarding her quizzically, Kincaid said, 'You're certainly feeling magnanimous tonight. Is it something in the air? I just had a word with Trevor Simons and he was in the same frame of mind.' He paused, swallowing a little more of his wine, and when Julia didn't respond, he went on, 'He's says he's willing to swear under oath that you were together the entire night, regardless of the damage to his marriage.'

She sighed. 'Trev's a decent sort. Surely it won't come to that?' Wrapping her arms around her calves, she rested her chin on her knees and looked at Kincaid steadily. 'You can't really think I killed poor Con, can you?' When Kincaid didn't answer she lifted her head and said, '*You* don't think that, do you, Duncan?'

Kincaid ran the evidence through his mind. Connor had died between the closing of the gallery show and the very early hours of the morning, the time for which Trevor Simons had given Julia a cast-iron alibi. Simons was a decent sort, as Julia had so aptly put it, and Kincaid had disliked goading him, but he felt more certain now than ever that he would not have compromised himself by lying for Julia.

But even as he set out these facts, he knew that they had little to do with what he felt. He studied her face. Could one see guilt, if one had the right skills, the right information? He had sensed it often enough, and his rational mind told him the assessment must be based on a combination of subliminal cues – body language, smell, shadings in the voice. But he also knew that there was an element to it that transcended the rational – call it a hunch, or a feeling, it didn't matter. It was based on an innate and inexplicable knowledge of another human being, and his knowledge of Julia went bone-deep. He was as certain of her innocence as of his own.

Slowly, he shook his head. 'No. I don't think you killed Connor. But someone did, and I'm not sure we're getting any closer to it.' His back had begun to ache and he stretched, recrossing his legs. 'Do you know why Connor would have had dinner with Tommy Godwin the night he died?'

Julia sat up straight, her eyes widening in astonishment. 'Tommy? Our Tommy? I've known Tommy since I was this high.' She held out a hand, toddler height. 'I can't imagine anything less likely than the two of them having a social get-together. Tommy never quite approved of Con, and I'm sure he made it clear. Very politely, of course,' she added fondly. 'If Con had meant to see Tommy, surely he would have said?'

'According to Godwin, Con wanted his old job back, and thought he might help.'

Julia shook her head. 'That's piffle. Con had a screaming nervous breakdown. The firm wouldn't have considered it.' Her eyes were peat-dark, and guileless.

Kincaid closed his eyes for a moment, in the hope that removing her face from his sight would allow him to gather his thoughts. When he opened them again he found her watching him. 'What did Connor say that day, Julia? It seems to me that his behaviour only became out of the ordinary after he left you at lunchtime. I think you've not quite told me the whole truth.'

She looked away from him, fumbling for her cigarettes, then pushed the packet away and stood up, as graceful as a dancer. Moving to the table, she unscrewed the top of a paint tube and squeezed a drop of deep blue colour onto her palette. Choosing a fine brush, she dabbed a little of the colour onto the painting. 'Can't seem to get the bloody thing quite right, and I'm tired of looking at it. Maybe if I—'

'Julia.'

She stopped, paintbrush frozen in mid-air. After a long moment, she rinsed the brush and placed it carefully beside the drawing, then turned to him. 'It began ordinarily enough, just the way I told you. A little row about money, about the flat.' She came back to the arm of the chair.

'Then what happened?' He moved closer to her and touched her hand, urging her on.

Julia captured his hand between her palms and held it tightly. She looked down, rubbing the back of his hand with her fingertips. 'He begged me,' she said so softly Kincaid had to strain to hear. 'He literally got

274

down on his knees and begged me. Begged me to take him back, begged me to love him. I don't know what set him off that day. I'd thought he had pretty well accepted things.'

'What did you tell him?'

'That it was no use. That I meant to divorce him as soon as the two-year limit had passed, if he still refused to co-operate.' She met Kincaid's eyes. 'I was perfectly beastly to him, and it wasn't his fault. None of it was.'

'What are you talking about?' Kincaid said, startled enough to forget for a moment the sensation of her fingers against his skin.

'It was all my fault, from the very beginning. I should never have married Con. I knew it wasn't fair, but I was in love with the idea of getting married, and I suppose I thought we'd muddle through somehow.' She laughed, letting go his hand. 'But the more he loved me, the more he needed, the less I had to give. In the end there was nothing at all.' Softly, she added, 'Except pity.'

'Julia,' Kincaid said sharply, 'you were not responsible for Connor's needs. There are people who will suck you dry, no matter how much you give. You couldn't—'

'You don't understand.' She slipped from the arm of the chair, moving restlessly away from him, then turned back as she reached the worktable. 'I knew when I married Con I couldn't love him. Not him, not anyone, not even Trev, who hasn't asked for much except honesty and affection. I can't, do you see? I'm not capable.'

'Don't be absurd, Julia,' Kincaid said, pushing to his feet. 'Of course you—'

'No.' She stopped him with the one flat word. 'I can't. Because of Matty.'

The despair in her voice banished his anger as quickly as it had come. He went to her and drew her gently to him, stroking her hair as she laid her head against his shoulder. Her slender body fitted into the curve of his arms as easily as if it had always been there, and her hair felt as silky as feathers against the palm of his hand. She smelled faintly, unexpectedly, of lilac. Kincaid took a breath, steadying himself against the wave of dizziness that swept over him, forcing himself to concentrate on the matter at hand. 'What has Matty to do with it, Julia?'

'Everything. I loved him, too, you see, but that never seemed to occur to anyone . . . except Plummy, I suppose. She knew. I was ill, you know . . . afterwards. But it gave me time to think, and it was then I decided that nothing would ever hurt me like that again.' She pulled away from him just enough to look up into his face. 'It's not worth it. Nothing is.'

'But surely the alternative – lifetime of emotional isolation – is worse?'

She came back into his arms, resting her cheek in the hollow of his shoulder. 'It's bearable, at least,' she said, her voice muffled, and he felt her breath, warm through the fabric of his shirt. 'I tried to explain it to Con that day – why I could never give him what he wanted . . . a family, children. I had nothing to go by, you see, no blueprint for an ordinary life. And a child

– I could never take that risk. You do you see that, don't you?'

He saw himself with uncomfortable clarity, curling up like a wounded hedgehog after Vic had shattered his safe and comfortable existence. He had protected himself from risk as surely as Julia. But she, at least, had been honest with herself, while he had used work, with the convenient demands of a cop's life, as an excuse for not making emotional commitments. 'I do see it,' he said softly, 'but I don't agree with it.'

He rubbed her back, gently kneading the knotted muscles, and her shoulder blades felt sharp under his hands. 'Did Connor understand?'

'It only made him more angry. It was then I was beastly to him. I said—' She stopped, shaking her head, and her hair tickled Kincaid's nose. 'Horrid things, really horrid. I'm so ashamed.' Harshly, she added, 'It's my fault he's dead. I don't know what he did after he left Badger's End that day, but if I hadn't sent him away so cruelly—' She was crying now, her words coming in hiccuping gulps.

Kincaid took her face in his hands and wiped the tears from her cheeks with his thumbs. 'Julia, Julia. You don't know that. You can't know that. You were not responsible for Connor's behaviour, or for his death.' He looked down at her, and in her tousled hair and tear-streaked face he saw again the child of his vision, alone with her grief in the narrow white bed. After a moment he said, 'Nor were you responsible for Matthew's death. Look at me, Julia. Do you hear me?'

'How can you know that?' she asked fiercely.

'Everyone thought . . . Mummy and Daddy never for-gave—'

'Those who knew and loved you never held you responsible, Julia. I've spoken to Plummy. And the vicar. You're the one who has never forgiven yourself. That's too heavy a burden for anyone to carry for twenty years. Let it go.'

For a long moment she held his gaze, then he felt the tension drain from her body. She returned her head to his shoulder, slipped her arms round his waist and leaned against him, letting him support her weight.

Thus they stood, quietly, until Kincaid became aware of every point where their bodies made contact. For all her slenderness, her body seemed suddenly, undeniably solid against his, and her breasts pressed firmly against his chest. He could hear his blood pounding in his ears.

Julia gave a hiccuping sigh and raised her head a little. 'I've gone and made your shirt all soggy,' she said, rubbing at the damp patch on his shoulder. Then she tilted her head so that she could look into his face and added, her voice husky with suppressed laughter, 'Does Scotland Yard always render its services so . . . enthusiastically?'

He stepped back, flushing with embarrassment, wishing he had worn less-revealing jeans rather than slacks. 'I'm sorry. I didn't mean—'

'It's all right,' she said, drawing him to her again. 'I don't mind. I don't mind at all.'

Chapter Fourteen

He woke to the sound of Tony's voice. 'Morning tea, Mr Kincaid,' he said as he tapped on the door and entered. 'And a message for you from Sergeant Makepeace at High Wycombe. Something about catching the bird you wanted?'

Kincaid sat up and ran a hand through his hair, then accepted the cup. 'Thanks, Tony,' he said to Tony's departing back. So they had found Kenneth Hicks and brought him in. They wouldn't be able to hold him long without cause. He should have checked in last night – hot tea sloshed onto his hand as awareness came flooding into his still groggy brain.

Last night. Julia. Oh, bloody hell. What have I done? How could he have been so unprofessional? With the thought came the memory of Trevor Simons's words, 'I never meant to do it. It was just . . . Julia,' and of his own rather supercilious comments about the man's loss of judgement.

He closed his eyes. Never, in all his years in the force, had he crossed that line, hadn't even thought, really, that he needed to protect himself from the temptation. Yet even in his self-reproach he found that there was a part of him that felt no remorse, for their union had been clean and healing, a solace for old wounds and a destruction of barriers too long held.

It was not until he entered the Chequers' dining room and saw Gemma seated alone at a table that he remembered the message he'd left for her yesterday. When had she arrived, and how long had she waited for him?

Sitting down across from her, he said, 'You're an early bird,' with as much aplomb as he could manage. 'We'll need to get on to High Wycombe as soon as we can. They're holding Kenneth Hicks for questioning.'

Gemma answered him without a trace of her usual morning cheeriness. 'I know. I've spoken to Jack Makepeace already.'

'Are you all right, Gemma?'

'Headache.' She nibbled without much enthusiasm on a piece of dry toast.

'Tony pour you one drink too many?' he said, attempting to humour her, but she merely shrugged. 'Look,' he said, wondering if the flush of guilt he felt were visible, 'I'm sorry about last night. I was . . . delayed.' She must have rushed here from London and waited for him, might even have been worried about him, and he had sent no word. 'I should have rung you. It was thoughtless of me.' Tilting his head, he studied her, measuring her mood. 'Shall I grovel some more? Would a bed of hot coals do?'

This time she smiled and he gave an inward sigh of relief. Searching for a change of subject, he said, 'Tell me about Tommy Godwin.' Just then his breakfast arrived, and he tucked into eggs and bacon while Gemma briefly recounted her interview.

'I took a statement, and I've had the forensics lads go over his flat and car.'

'I saw Sharon Doyle again, and Trevor Simons,' he said through a mouthful of toast. 'And Julia. Connor went home again after his scuffle with Tommy, Gemma. It looks as though Tommy Godwin's out of the frame unless we can prove he met Con again later. He did ring someone from the flat, though – problem is, we've no earthly idea who it was.'

Julia. There had been a familiarity, an unconscious intimacy, in the way Kincaid said her name. Gemma tried to concentrate on her driving, tried to ignore the certainty that was growing in the pit of her stomach. Surely she was imagining things? And what if it were true? Why should it matter so much to her if Duncan Kincaid had formed a less-than-professional relationship with a suspect in a murder investigation? It was common enough – she'd seen it happen with other officers – and she'd never thought he was infallible. Had she?

'Grow up, Gemma,' she said under her breath. He was human, and male, and she should never have forgotten that even gods sometimes have feet of clay.

But those reminders made her feel no less miserable, and she was thankful when the High Wycombe round-abouts claimed all her attention.

'I've had Hicks warming up nicely for you the last half-hour,' Jack Makepeace said in greeting when they found him in his office. He shook their hands, and Gemma thought he gave hers an extra little squeeze. 'Thought it would do him a world of good. Too bad he didn't quite manage to finish his breakfast.' Makepeace winked at Gemma. 'He's made his phone call – his mum, or so he says – but the cavalry's not come to the rescue.'

Having been briefed earlier on the telephone by Makepeace, Kincaid had brought Gemma up to date in the car and suggested that she begin the interview. 'He doesn't care for women,' Kincaid said as Makepeace left them at the nondescript door of Room A. 'I want you to upset his balance a bit, prime him for me.'

One interview room seldom differed much from another – they could be expected to meet some vari-ation of small and square, and to smell of stale ciga-rette smoke and human sweat, but when Gemma entered the room she swallowed convulsively, fighting the instinctive urge to cover her nose. Unshaven and all too obviously unbathed, Kenneth Hicks reeked of fear.

'Christ,' Kincaid muttered in Gemma's ear as he came in behind her. 'We should've brought masks.' He coughed, then added at full volume as he pulled out a chair for Gemma, 'Hullo, Kenneth. Like the accommodation? Not quite up to the Hilton, I'm afraid, but then what can you do?'

'Go fuck yourself,' Hicks said succinctly. His voice was nasal, and Gemma pegged his accent as South London.

Kincaid shook his head as he sat down beside Gemma, facing Hicks across the narrow laminated table. 'I'm disappointed in you, Kenneth. I thought you had better manners. We'll just record our little conversation,' he said, pushing the switch on the tape recorder. 'If you don't mind, of course. You don't mind, do you, Kenneth?'

Gemma studied Kenneth Hicks while Kincaid nattered pleasantly on and fiddled with the recorder. Hicks's narrow, acne-spotted face seemed permanently stamped with a surly expression. In spite of the warmth of the room, he had kept on a black leather bomber jacket, and he rubbed nervously at his nose and chin as Kincaid's patter continued. There seemed something vaguely familiar about him, and Gemma frowned with frustration as it hovered on the fringe of her mind.

'Sergeant James will be asking you a few questions,' Kincaid said, pushing his chair back from the table a bit. He folded his arms and stretched out his legs, as if he might catnap through the interview.

'Kenneth,' she said pleasantly, when they had completed the recorded preliminaries, 'why don't you make it easy for everyone and tell us exactly what you were doing the night Connor Swann was killed?'

Hicks darted a glance at Kincaid. 'I already told the

other bloke, the one as brought me in here. Big ginger-haired berk.'

'You told Sergeant Makepeace that you were drinking with friends at the Fox and Hounds in Henley until closing, after which you continued the party in the friends' flat,' said Gemma, and the sound of her voice brought Hicks's eyes back to her. 'Is that right?' she added a little more forcefully.

'Yeah, that's right. That's just like I told him.' Hicks seemed to gain a little confidence from her recital. He relaxed in his chair and stared at Gemma, letting his eyes rest for a long moment on her breasts.

She smiled sweetly at him and made a show of consulting her notebook. 'Thames Valley CID took statements last night from the friends you named, Kenneth, and unfortunately none of them seems to remember you being there at all.'

Hicks's skin turned the colour of the room's nicotine-stained walls as the blood drained from his face. 'I'll kill 'em, the friggin' little shits. They're lying their bloody heads off.' He looked from Gemma to Kincaid, and, apparently finding no reassurance in their expressions, said a little more frantically, 'You can't do me for this. I never saw Con after we had that drink at the Fox. I swear I didn't.'

Gemma flipped another page in her notebook. 'You may have to, unless you can come up with a little better accounting of your movements after half-past ten. Connor made a telephone call from his flat around then, and afterwards said he meant to go out.'

'Who says he did?' asked Hicks, with more shrewdness than Gemma had credited him.

'Never mind that. Do you want to know what I think, Kenneth?' Gemma asked, leaning towards him and lowering her voice confidentially. 'I think Connor rang you and asked you to meet him at the lock. You argued and Connor fell in. It could happen to anybody, couldn't it, Ken? Did you try to help him, or were you afraid of the water?' Her tone said she understood and would forgive him anything.

'I never!' Hicks pushed his chair back from the table. 'That's a bleedin' lie. And how the bleedin' hell am I supposed to have got there without a car?'

'Connor picked you up in his car,' Gemma said reasonably, 'and afterwards you hitched a ride back to Henley.'

'I didn't, I tell you, and you can't prove I did.'

Unfortunately, Gemma knew from Thames Valley's reports that he was correct – Connor's car had been freshly washed and vacuumed and forensics had found no significant traces. 'Then where were you? Tell the truth this time.'

'I've told you already. I was at the Fox, then at this bloke's. Jackie – he's called Jackie Fawcett.'

Kincaid recrossed his ankles lazily and spoke for the first time since Gemma had begun. 'Then why wouldn't your mates give you a nice, tidy alibi, Kenneth? I can see two possibilities – the first is that you're lying, and the second is that they don't like you, and I must say I don't know which I think is the more likely.

Did you help out other friends the same way you helped Connor?'

'Don't know what you're on about.' Hicks pulled a battered cigarette pack from the pocket of his jacket. He shook it, then probed inside it with thumb and forefinger before crumpling it in disgust.

Gemma took up the thread again. 'That's what you argued about, isn't it, Kenneth? When you met Con after lunch, did you tell him he had to pay up? Did he agree to meet you later that evening? Then when he turned up without the money, you fought with him.' She embroidered as she went along.

An element of pleading crept into Hicks's voice. 'He didn't owe me nothin', I told you.' He kept his eyes fixed anxiously on Kincaid, and Gemma wondered what Kincaid had done to put the wind up him like that.

Straightening up in his chair, Kincaid said, 'So you're telling me that Con paid you off, and yet I happen to know that Con was so hard up he couldn't make the mortgage on the flat. I think you're lying. I think you said something to Connor over that little social pint at the Fox that sent him over the edge. What was it, Kenneth? Did you threaten to have your boss call out his muscle?' He stood up and leaned forward with his hands on the table.

'I never threatened him. It wasn't like that,' Hicks squeaked, shrinking away from Kincaid.

'But he did still owe you money?'

Hicks looked at them, sweat beading on his upper lip, and Gemma could see him calculating which way to turn next. *Rat in a trap*, she thought, and pressed her lips together to conceal her satisfaction. They waited in silence, until finally Hicks said, 'Maybe he did. So what? I never threatened him like you said.'

Moving restlessly back and forth in the small space before the table, Kincaid said, 'I don't believe you. Your boss was going to take it out of your skin if you didn't come up with the ready – I don't believe you didn't use a little persuasion.' He smiled at Hicks as he came near him again. 'And the trouble with persuasion is that sometimes it gets out of hand. Isn't that so, Kenneth?'

'No. I don't know. I mean—'

'Are you saying that it wasn't an accident? That you intended to kill him?'

'That's not what I meant.' Hicks swallowed and wiped his hands on his thighs. 'I only made him a suggestion, a proposition, like.'

Kincaid stopped pacing and stood very still with his hands in his pockets, watching Hicks. 'That sounds very interesting, Kenneth. What sort of proposition?'

Gemma held her breath as Hicks teetered on the edge of confession, afraid any move might nudge him in the wrong direction. Listening to the ragged cadence of his breathing, she offered up a silent little incantation to the god of interviews.

Hicks spoke finally, with the rush of release, and his words were venomous. 'I knew about him from the first, him and his hoity-toity Ashertons. You would've thought they were the bleedin' Royals, the way he talked, but I knew better. That Dame Caroline's just a

287

jumped-up tart, no better than she should be. And all
the fuss they made over that kid what drowned, well,
he wasn't even Sir Gerald's kid, was he, just a bleedin'
little bastard.' Matty. He was talking about Matty,
Gemma thought, trying to make sense of it.

Kincaid sat down again, pulling his chair up until
he could rest his elbows on the table. 'Let's start again
from the beginning, shall we, Kenneth?' he said very
quietly, very evenly, and Gemma shivered. 'You told
Connor that Matthew Asherton was illegitimate, have
I got that right?'

Hicks's Adam's apple bobbed in his skinny throat
as he swallowed and nodded, then looked in appeal at
Gemma. He'd got more than he bargained for, she
thought, wondering suddenly what Kincaid might have
done if she hadn't been in the room and the tape
recorder running.

'How could you possibly know that?' Kincaid asked,
still soft as velvet.

''Cause my uncle Tommy was his bleedin' dad,
that's how.'

In the silence that followed, Kenneth Hicks's ragged,
adenoidal breathing sounded loud in Gemma's ears.
She opened her mouth, but found she couldn't quite
formulate any words.

'Your uncle Tommy? Do you mean Tommy
Godwin?' Kincaid said finally, not quite managing to
control his surprise.

Gemma felt as if a giant hand were squeezing her

diaphragm. She saw again the silver-framed photograph of Matthew Asherton – the blond hair and the impish grin on his friendly face. She remembered Tommy's voice as he spoke of Caroline, and she wondered why she had not seen it before.

'I heard him telling me mum about it when the kid drowned,' said Hicks. He must have interpreted the shock in their faces as disbelief, because he added on a rising note of panic, 'I swear. I never said nothin', but after I met Con and he went on about them, I remembered the names.'

Gemma felt a wave of nausea sweep over her as the corollary sank in. 'I don't believe you. You can't be Tommy Godwin's nephew, it's just not possible,' she said hotly, thinking of Tommy's elegance, and of his courteous patience as she'd taken him through his statement at the Yard, but even as she resisted the idea, she felt again that odd sense of familiarity. Could it be something in the line of the nose, or the set of the jaw?

'You go to Clapham and ask me mum, then. She'll tell you soon enough—'

'You said you made Connor a proposition,' Kincaid dropped the words into Hicks's protest like stones in a pool. 'Just what was it, exactly?'

Hicks rubbed his nose and sniffed, shifting away from eye contact with them.

'Come on, sunshine, you can tell us all about it,' Kincaid urged him. 'Spit it out.'

'Well, the Ashertons have got to be pretty stinking with it, haven't they, what with their titles and all.

Always in the newspapers, in the gossip sections. So I figured they'd not like it put about that their kid was wrong side of the blanket, like.'

The intensity of Kincaid's anger seemed to have abated. 'Do I take it that you suggested to Connor that he should blackmail his own in-laws?' he asked, regarding Hicks with cool amusement. 'What about your own family? Did it occur to you that this might damage your uncle and your mother?'

'He wasn't to say I was the one told him,' Hicks said, as if that absolved him of any culpability.

'In other words, you didn't care how it might affect your uncle as long as it couldn't be traced back to you.' Kincaid smiled. 'Very noble of you, Kenneth. And how did Connor react to your little proposition?'

'He didn't believe me,' said Hicks, sounding aggrieved. 'Not right away. Then he thought about it a bit and he started to get all strung up. He said how much money was I thinking about, and when I told him "start with fifty-thousand quid and we'd split it, we could always ask for more later," he bloody laughed at me. Told me to shut my friggin' face and if I ever said another word about it, he'd kill me.' Hicks blinked his pale lashes and added, as if he still couldn't quite believe it, 'After everything I did for him!'

'He really didn't understand why Connor was angry with him,' Kincaid said to Gemma as they stood at the zebra crossing separating High Wycombe Station from the carpark where they had left Gemma's Escort. 'He's more than a few bricks short of a load in the morals department, is our Kenneth. I imagine it's only the fact that he's such a "timorous wee beastie" that's kept him to petty villainy – although I think the comparison does an injustice to the poor mouse,' he added, brushing at the sleeve of his jacket.

It was one of his favourites, Gemma noticed with the detachment that had overtaken her, a fine blue-and-grey wool that brought out the colour of his eyes. Why was he waffling on as if he'd never come across a small-time crook before?

The oncoming traffic came to a halt and they crossed on the stripes. Kincaid glanced at his watch as they reached the opposite pavement. 'I think we can manage a word with Tommy Godwin before lunch if we drive like the hounds of hell are after us. In fact,' he said as they reached the car and Gemma dug the Escort's keys out of her bag, 'since it looks as though we may not need to come back here, we'd better pick up our things and get my car back to London as well.'

Without a word, Gemma started the engine as he slid in beside her. She felt as though a kaleidoscope inside her head had shifted, jumbling the pieces so that they no longer made a recognizable pattern.

Kincaid touched her arm. 'Gemma, what is it? You've been like this since breakfast. If you really don't feel well—'

She turned towards him, tasting salt where she had bitten the inside of her lip. 'Did you believe him?'

'Who, Kenneth?' asked Kincaid, sounding a bit puzzled. 'Well, you have to admit, it does make sense of things that—'

'You haven't met Tommy. Oh, I can believe that Tommy was Matthew's dad,' she conceded, 'but not the rest of it. It's a cock-and-bull story if I ever—'

'Just improbable enough to be true, I'm afraid,' said Kincaid. 'And how else could he have found out about Tommy and Matthew? It gives us the missing piece, Gemma – motive. Connor confronted Tommy over dinner that night with what he'd found out, and Tommy killed him to keep him quiet.'

'I don't believe it,' Gemma said stubbornly, but even as she spoke little slivers of doubt crept into her mind. Tommy loved Caro, and Julia. You could see that. And Gerald he spoke of with respect and affection. Had protecting them been enough reason for murder? But even if she could swallow that premise, the rest still didn't make sense to her. 'Why would Connor have agreed to meet him at the lock?'

'Tommy promised to bring him money.'

Gemma stared blindly at the drizzle that had begun to coat the windscreen. 'Somehow I don't think that Connor wanted money,' she said with quiet certainty. 'And that doesn't explain why Tommy went to London to see Gerald. It can't have been to establish an alibi, not if Connor was still alive.'

'I think you're letting your liking for Tommy Godwin affect your judgement, Gemma. No one else has a shred of motive. Surely you can see—'

The anger that had been building in her all morning broke like a flash flood. 'You're the one that's blind,' she shouted at him. 'You're so besotted with Julia Swann that you won't consider that she might be implicated in Connor's death, when you know as well as I do that the husband or wife is most likely to be involved in a spouse's murder. How can you be sure Trevor Simons isn't lying to protect her? How do you know she didn't meet Connor before his dinner with Tommy, before the gallery opening, and arrange to meet him later that night? Maybe she thought a scandal involving her family would damage her career. Maybe she wanted to protect her parents. Maybe . . .' She ran down, her fury quickly spent, and sat waiting desolately for the inevitable backlash. This time she had really crossed over the line.

But instead of giving her the dressing-down she expected, Kincaid looked away. In the silence that followed she could hear the swishing of tyres on the damp road, and a faint ticking that seemed to be inside her own head. 'Perhaps you're right,' he said finally. 'Perhaps my judgement can't be trusted. But unless we come up with concrete physical evidence, it's all I have to go on with.'

They made the journey back to London in separate cars, meeting again at Kincaid's flat as they had arranged. The drizzle had followed them, and Kincaid drew the cover over the Midget before locking it. As he climbed into Gemma's car he said, 'You really must do something about your tyres, Gemma. The right rear is as bald as my grandad's head.' It was an often-repeated nag, and when she didn't rise to the bait, he sighed and continued, 'I rang LB House on the mobile phone. Tommy Godwin didn't come in today, said he was unwell. Didn't you say his flat was in Highgate?'

Gemma nodded. 'I have the address in my note-book. It's quite near here, I think.' A formless anxiety settled over her as she drove, and it was with relief that she spotted the block of flats. She left the car in the circular drive and hopped out, jiggling her foot in impatience as she waited for Kincaid to lock his side of the car and catch her up at the building's entrance.

'Christ, Gemma, is there a fire no one bothered to tell me about?' he said, but she ignored the barb and pushed through the frosted-glass doors. When they presented their identification to the doorman, he scowled and grudgingly directed them to take the lift to the fourth floor.

'Nice building,' Kincaid said as they rose creakingly in the lift. 'It's been well maintained, but not overly modernized.' The fourth-floor landing, tiled in a highly polished black-and-white geometric design, bore him out. 'Deco, if I'm not mistaken.'

Gemma, searching for the flat number, had only been listening with half an ear. 'What?' she asked, knocking at 4C.

'Art Deco. The building must date from between—'

The door swung open and Tommy Godwin regarded them quizzically. 'Mike rang me and said the Bill were paying another call. Very disapproving he was, too. I think he must have had unfortunate dealings with the law in a previous existence.' Godwin wore a paisley silk dressing gown and slippers, and his usually immaculate blond hair stood on end. 'You must be Superintendent Kincaid,' he said as he ushered them into the flat.

Having assured herself that Tommy hadn't gone and put his head in the oven or something equally silly, Gemma felt irrationally angry with him for having worried her. She followed slowly behind the men, looking about her. A small, sleek kitchen lay to her left, done in the same black and white as the landing. To her right, the sitting room carried on the theme, and through its bank of windows she could see a grey London spread before her. All the lines of the furniture were curved, but without fussiness, and the monochromatic color scheme was accented by a collection of pink frosted glass. Gemma found the room restful, and saw that its gentle order fitted Tommy like a second suit of clothes.

A Siamese cat posed on a chair beneath the window. Paws tucked under her chest, she regarded them with unblinking sapphire eyes.

'You're quite right, Superintendent,' Tommy said as she joined them, 'these flats were built in the early thirties, and they were the ultimate in advanced design for their day. They've held up remarkably well, unlike most of the post-war monstrosities. Sit down, please,' he added as he seated himself in a fan-shaped chair that complemented the swirling design on his dressing gown. 'Although I must say, I think it must have been a bit nerve-racking during the war, as high above the city as we are. You'd have felt like a sitting duck when the German bombers came over. A chink in the blackout and—'

'Tommy,' Gemma interrupted severely, 'they said at LB House that you weren't well. What is it?'

He ran a hand through his hair, and in the clear grey light Gemma saw the skin beginning to pouch a little under his eyes. 'Just a bit under the weather, Sergeant. I must admit that yesterday rather took its toll.' He stood and went to the drinks cabinet against the wall. 'Will you have a little sherry? It's appropriately near lunchtime, and I'm sure Rory Alleyn always accepted a sherry when he was interrogating suspects.'

'Tommy, this isn't a detective novel, for heaven's sake,' said Gemma, unable to contain her exasperation.

He turned to look at her, sherry decanter poised in one hand. 'I know, my dear. But it's my way of whistling in the dark.' The gentleness of his tone told her that he acknowledged her concern and was touched by it.

'I won't refuse a small one,' said Kincaid, and Tommy placed three glasses and the decanter on a small cocktail tray. The glasses were sensuously scalloped in the same delicate frosted pink as the fluted lampshades and vases Gemma had already noticed, and when she tasted the sherry it seemed to dissolve on her tongue like butter.

'After all,' said Tommy as he filled his own glass and returned to his chair, 'if I'm to take the blame for a crime I didn't commit, I might as well do it with good grace.'

'Yesterday you told me you'd been to Clapham to visit your sister.' Gemma paused to lick a trace of sherry from her lip, then went on more slowly. 'You didn't tell me about Kenneth.'

'Ah.' Tommy leaned against the chair back and closed his eyes. The light etched lines of exhaustion around his mouth and nose, delineated the pulse ticking in his throat. Gemma wondered why she hadn't seen the grey mixed in with the gold at his temples. 'Would you admit to Kenneth, given a choice?' Tommy said, without moving. 'No, don't answer that.' He opened his eyes and gave Gemma a valiant attempt at a smile. 'I take it you've met him?'

Gemma nodded.

'Then I can also assume that the whole sordid cat is out of the bag.'

'I think so, yes. You lied to me about your dinner with Connor. There wasn't any question of him going back to his old job. He confronted you with what Kenneth had told him.' This seemed to be her day for making accusations, she thought, finding that she took Tommy's deception personally, as if she'd been betrayed by a friend.

'A mere taradiddle, my dear—' Catching Gemma's expression he stopped and sighed. 'I'm sorry, Sergeant. You're quite right. What do you want to know?'

'Start from the beginning. Tell us about Caroline.'

'Ah, you mean from the very beginning.' Tommy swirled the sherry in his glass, watching it reflectively. 'I loved Caro, you see, with all the blind, single-minded recklessness of youth. Or perhaps age has nothing to do with it ... I don't know. Our affair ended with Matthew's conception. I wanted her to leave Gerald and marry me. I would have loved Julia as my own child.' Pausing, he finished his sherry and returned the glass to the tray with deliberate care. 'It was a fantasy, of course. Caro was beginning a promising career, she was comfortably ensconced at Badger's End with the backing of the Asherton name and money. What had I to offer her? And there was Gerald, who has never behaved less than honourably in all the years I've known him.

'One makes what adjustments one must,' he said, smiling at Gemma. 'I've come to the conclusion that great tragedies are created by those who don't make it through the adjustment stage. We went on. As "Uncle Tommy" I was allowed to watch Matty grow up, and no one knew the truth except Caro and me.

'Then Matty died.'

Kincaid set his empty glass on the cocktail tray, and the click of glass against wood sounded loud as a shot in the silent room. Gemma gave him a startled glance – so focused had she been on Tommy that for a moment she had forgotten his presence. Neither of them spoke, and after a moment, Tommy continued.

'They shut me out. Closed ranks. In their grief Caro and Gerald had no room for anyone else's. As much as I loved Matty, I also saw that he was an ordinary little boy, with an ordinary little boy's faults and graces. The fact that he was also extraordinarily gifted meant no more to him than if he'd had an extra finger or been able to do lightning calculus in his head. Not so, Gerald and Caro. Do you understand that? Matty was the embodiment of their dreams, a gift God had sent them to mould in their own image.'

'So how did Kenneth come into this?' asked Gemma.

'My sister is not a bad sort. We all have our crosses – Kenneth is hers. She was still at school when our mother died. I was barely making ends meet at the time and wasn't able to do much for her, so I think she married Kenneth's dad out of desperation. As it turned out, he stayed around just long enough to produce his son and heir, then scarpered, leaving her with a baby to look after as well as herself.'

Gemma saw an echo of her own marriage in Tommy's account of his sister, and she shuddered at the thought that in spite of all her efforts, her own little son might turn out to be like Kenneth. It didn't bear thinking of. She finished her sherry in one long swallow, and as the warmth spread to her stomach and suffused her face, she remembered she'd gone without breakfast that morning.

Tommy shifted in his chair and smoothed the fold of his dressing gown across his lap. The cat seemed to take that as an invitation, leaping easily up and settling herself under his hands. His long, slender fingers stroked her chocolate-and-cream fur, and Gemma found she could not force herself to see those hands wrapped around Connor's throat. She looked up and met Tommy's eyes.

'After Matty died,' he said, 'I went to my sister and poured out the whole story. There was no one else.'

Clearing his throat, he reached for the decanter and poured himself a little more sherry. 'I don't remember that time very clearly, you understand, and I've just been piecing things together myself. Kenneth can't have been more than eight or nine, but I think he was born a sneak – possessive of his mother, always hiding and eavesdropping on adult conversations. I had no idea he was even in the house that day. Can you imagine how shocked I was when Connor told me what he had heard, and who had told him?'

'Why did Connor come to you?' asked Kincaid. 'Did he ask for money?'

'I don't think Connor knew what he wanted. He seemed to have got it into his head that Julia would have loved him if it hadn't been for Matty's death, and that if Julia had known the truth about Matty, things would have been different between them. I'm afraid he wasn't very coherent. "Bloody liars," he kept saying, "They're all bloody hypocrites."' Tommy laced his fingers together and sighed. 'I think Con had bought the Asherton family image lock, stock and barrel, and he couldn't bear the disillusionment. Or perhaps he just needed someone to blame for his own failure. They had hurt him and he had been powerless, unable to nick even their armour. Kenneth put the perfect weapon into his waiting hands.'

'Couldn't you have stopped him?' Kincaid asked.

Tommy smiled at him, undeceived by the casual tone. 'Not in the way you mean. I begged him, pleaded with him to keep quiet, for Gerald's and Caro's sake, and for Julia's, but that only seemed to make him angrier. In the end I even tussled with him, much to my shame.

'When I walked away from Connor I had made up my mind what to do. The lies had gone on long enough. Connor was right, in a sense – the deception had warped all our lives, whether we realized it or not.'

'I don't understand,' said Kincaid. 'Why did you think killing Connor would put an end to the deception?'

'But I didn't kill Connor, Superintendent,' Tommy said flatly, weariness evident in the set of his mouth. 'I told Gerald the truth.'

Chapter Fifteen

Gemma started the Escort's engine and let it idle while Kincaid buckled himself into the passenger seat. She had been silent all the way from Tommy's flat down to the car. Kincaid glanced at her, feeling utterly baffled. He thought of the usual free give-and-take of their working relationship, and of dinner at her flat just a few nights ago, when they had shared such easy intimacy. At some level he had been aware of her special talent for forming bonds with people, but he had never quite formulated it. She had welcomed him into her warm circle, made him feel comfortable with himself as well as her, and he had taken it for granted. Now, having seen the rapport she'd developed with Tommy Godwin, he felt suddenly envious, like a child shut out in the cold.

She swatted at a spiralling wisp that had escaped her plait and turned to him. 'What now, guv?' she said, without inflection.

He wanted urgently to repair the damage between them, but he didn't quite know how to proceed, and other matters needed his immediate attention. 'Hold on a tick,' he said, and dialled the Yard on the mobile phone. He asked a brief question and rang off. 'According to forensics, Tommy Godwin's flat and car were as clean as a whistle.' Feeling his way tentatively, he said, 'Perhaps I was a bit hasty in my conclusions about Tommy. That's more your style,' he added with a smile, but Gemma merely went on regarding him with a frustratingly neutral expression. He sighed and rubbed his face. 'I think we'll have to see Sir Gerald again, but first let's have something to eat and see where we are.'

As Gemma drove he closed his eyes, wondering how he might mend their relationship, and why the solution to this case continued to elude him.

They stopped at a café in Golders Green for a late lunch, having rung Badger's End and made sure that Sir Gerald would see them whenever they arrived.

Much to Kincaid's satisfaction, Gemma ate her way steadily through a tuna sandwich without any of the reluctance she'd shown at breakfast. He finished his ham-and-cheese, then sipped his coffee and watched Gemma as she polished off a bag of crisps. 'I can't make sense of it,' he said when she had reached the finger-licking stage. 'It can't have been Gerald whom Con phoned from the flat. According to Sharon, Con made that call at a little after half-past ten, when Gerald was busy conducting a full orchestra.'

'He might have left a message,' said Gemma, wiping her fingertips with a paper napkin.

'With whom? Your porter would have remembered. Alison what's-her-name would have remembered.'

'True.' Gemma tasted her coffee and made a face. 'Cold. Ugh.' She pushed her cup away and folded her arms on the tabletop. 'It would make much more sense if Sir Gerald rang Con after Tommy had left.'

According to Tommy, Gerald had expressed neither shock nor outrage at his revelation. He gave Tommy a drink, as if nothing out of the ordinary had occurred, then said as if to himself, 'The worm ate Arthur's empire from the inside, too, as he always knew it would.' Tommy had left him sitting slumped in his makeup chair, glass in hand.

'What if the call Sharon overheard had nothing to do with Connor's murder? We have no proof that it did.' Kincaid drew speculative circles on the tabletop with the damp end of his spoon. 'What if Con didn't follow Sharon out of the flat? He didn't tell her he meant to leave right away.'

'You mean that if Gerald had rung him after Tommy left, he might still have been there? And he might have agreed to meet him at the lock?' continued Gemma with a spark of interest.

'But we've no proof,' said Kincaid. 'We've no proof of anything. This entire mess is like a pudding – as soon as you sink your teeth into it, it slides away.'

Gemma laughed, and Kincaid gave thanks for even a small sign of a thaw.

By the time they reached Badger's End, the drizzle had evolved into a slow and steady rain. They sat for a moment in the car, listening to the rhythmic patter on roof and bonnet. Lamps were already lit in the house, and they saw a flick of the curtain at the sitting room window.

'The light will be gone soon,' said Gemma. 'The evenings draw in so early in this weather.' As Kincaid reached for the door handle, she touched his arm. 'Guv, if Sir Gerald killed Connor, why did he want us in on it?'

Kincaid turned back to her. 'Maybe Caroline insisted. Maybe his friend, the assistant commissioner, volunteered us, and he didn't think he should protest.' Sensing her discomfort, he touched her fingers and added, 'I don't like this, either, Gemma, but we have to follow it through.'

They dashed for the house under the cover of one umbrella, and stood huddled together on the doorstep. They heard the short double ring as Kincaid pushed the bell, but before he could lift his finger, Sir Gerald opened the door himself. 'Come in by the fire,' he said. 'Here, take your wet things off. It's beastly out, I'm afraid, and not likely to get any better.' He shepherded them into the sitting room, where a fire blazed in the grate, and Kincaid had a moment's fancy that it was never allowed to go out.

'You'll need something to warm you inside as well as out,' said Sir Gerald when they were established with their backs to the fire. 'Plummy's making us some tea.'

'Sir Gerald, we must talk to you,' said Kincaid, making a stand against the tide of social convention.

'I'm sorry Caroline's out,' said Gerald, continuing

in his hearty, friendly way as if there were nothing the least bit odd about their conversation. 'She and Julia are making the final arrangements for Connor's funeral.'

'Julia's helping with the funeral?' asked Kincaid, surprised enough to be distracted from his agenda.

Sir Gerald ran a hand through his sparse hair, and sat down on the sofa. It was his spot, obviously, as the cushions had depressions that exactly matched his bulk, like a dog's favourite old bed. Today he wore another variation of the moth-eaten sweater, this time in olive green, and what seemed to be the same baggy corduroys Kincaid had seen before. 'Yes. She seems to have had a change of heart. I don't know why, and I'm too thankful to question it,' he said, and gave them his engaging smile. 'She came in like a whirlwind after lunch and said she'd made up her mind what should be done for Con, and she's been putting us through our paces ever since.'

It would seem that Julia had made peace with Con's ghost. Kincaid pushed the thought of her aside and concentrated on Gerald. 'It's you we wanted to see, sir.'

'Have you found something?' He sat forward a bit and scanned their faces anxiously. 'Tell me, please. I don't want Caroline and Julia upset.'

'We've just come from Tommy Godwin, Sir Gerald. We know why Tommy came to see you at the theatre the night Connor died.' As Kincaid watched, Gerald sank back into the sofa, his face suddenly shuttered. Remembering the comment Sir Gerald had made to

Tommy, Kincaid added, 'You knew that Tommy was Matthew's father all along, didn't you, sir?'

Gerald Asherton closed his eyes. Under the jut of his eyebrows, his face looked impassive, remote and ancient as a biblical prophet's. 'Of course I knew. I may be a fool, Mr Kincaid, but I'm not a blind fool. Have you any idea how beautiful they were together, Tommy and Caroline?' Opening his eyes, he continued, 'Grace, elegance, talent – you would have thought they'd been made for one another. I spent my days in terror that she would leave me, wondering how I would anchor my existence without her. When things seemed to fizzle out between them with Matty's conception, I thanked the gods for restoring her to me. The rest didn't matter. And Matty ... Matty was everything we could have wanted.'

'You never told Caroline you knew?' put in Gemma, disbelief evident in her tone.

'How could we have gone on, if I had?'

It had started, thought Kincaid, not with outright lies but with a denial of the truth, and that denial had become woven into the very fabric of their lives. 'But Connor meant to wreck it all, didn't he, Sir Gerald? You must have felt some relief when you heard the next morning that he was dead.' Kincaid caught Gemma's quick, surprised glance, then she moved quietly to stand by the piano, examining the photographs. He left the fire and sat in the armchair opposite Gerald.

'I must admit I felt some sense of reprieve. It shamed me, and made me all the more determined to get to the bottom of things. He was my son-in-law, and in spite of his sometimes rather hysterical behaviour, I cared for him.' Gerald clasped his hands and leaned forward. 'Please, Superintendent, surely it can't benefit Connor for all this past history to be raked over. Can't we spare Caroline that?'

'Sir Gerald—'

The sitting room door opened and Caroline came in, followed by Julia. 'What a perfectly horrid day,' said Caroline, shaking fine drops of water from her dark hair. 'Superintendent. Sergeant. Plummy's just coming with some tea. I'm sure we could all do with some.' She slipped out of her leather jacket and tossed it wrong-side-out over the sofa back, before sitting beside her husband. The deep red silk of the jacket's lining rippled like blood in the glow from the fire.

Kincaid met Julia's eyes and saw pleasure mixed with wariness. It was the first time he had seen her with her mother, and he marvelled at the combination of contrast and similarity. It seemed to him as if Julia were Caroline stretched and reforged, edges sharpened and refined, with the unmistakable stamp of her father's smile. And in spite of her tough mannerisms, her face was as transparent to him as his own, while he found Caroline's unreadable.

'We've been to Fingest church,' said Julia, speaking to him as if there were no one else in the room. 'Con's mum would have insisted on a Catholic funeral and burial, with all the trappings, but it didn't matter the least bit to Con, so I mean to do what seems right to me.' She crossed the room to warm her hands by the fire. Dressed for the outdoors, she wore a heavy oiled-wool sweater still beaded with moisture, and her cheeks were faintly pink from the cold. 'I've been round the churchyard with the vicar, and I've picked a gravesite within a stone's throw of Matty's. Perhaps they'll like being neighbours.'

'Julia, don't be irreverent,' said Caroline sharply Turning to Kincaid, she added, 'To what do we owe the pleasure of your company, Superintendent?'

'I've just been telling Sir Gerald—'

The door swung open again as Plummy came through with a laden tea tray. Julia went immediately to her aid, and together they arranged the tea things on the low table before the fire. 'Mr Kincaid, Sergeant James.' Plummy smiled at Gemma, looking genuinely pleased to see her. 'I've made extra, in case you've not had a proper lunch again.' She busied herself pouring, this time into china cups and saucers rather than the comfortable stoneware mugs they'd used in the kitchen.

Refusing the offer of freshly toasted bread, Kincaid accepted tea reluctantly. He looked directly at Gerald. 'I'm sorry, sir, but I'm afraid we must go on with this.'

'Go on with what, Mr Kincaid?' said Caroline. She had taken her cup from Plummy and returned to perch on the arm of the sofa, so that in spite of her small stature she seemed to hover protectively over her husband.

Kincaid wet his lips with a sip of tea. 'The night Connor died, Dame Caroline, Tommy Godwin visited your husband in his dressing room at the Coliseum. He told Sir Gerald that he had just had a very unpleasant encounter with Connor. Although Connor was a little drunk and not terribly coherent, it eventually became clear that he had discovered the truth about Matthew's parentage, and was threatening to make his knowledge public with as much attendant scandal as possible.' Kincaid paused, watching their faces. 'Connor had discovered, in fact, that Matthew was Tommy's son, not Gerald's.'

Sir Gerald had sunk into the sofa cushions again, eyes closed, his hand only loosely balancing the cup on his knee.

'Tommy and Mummy?' said Julia. 'But that means Matty . . .' She subsided, her eyes wide and dark with shock. Kincaid wished he could have softened it for her somehow, wished he could comfort her as he had yesterday.

Vivian Plumley also watched the others, and Kincaid saw in her the perpetual observer, always on the edge of the family but not privy to its deepest secrets. She nodded once and compressed her lips, but Kincaid couldn't tell if her expression indicated distress or satisfaction.

'What utter nonsense, Superintendent,' said Caroline. She laid her hand lightly on Gerald's shoulder. 'I won't have it. You've overstepped the bounds of good manners as well as—'

'I am sorry if it distresses you, Dame Caroline, but I'm afraid it is necessary. Sir Gerald, will you tell me exactly what you did after Connor left you that night?'

Gerald touched his wife's hand. 'It's all right, Caro. There can't be any harm in it.' He roused himself, sitting forward a little and draining his teacup before he began. 'There's not much to tell, really. I'd had quite a stiff drink with Tommy, and I'm afraid I kept on after he left. By the time I left the theatre I was well over the limit. Shouldn't have been driving, of course, very irresponsible of me, but I managed without mishap.' He smiled, showing healthy pink gums above his upper teeth. 'Well, almost without mishap. I had a bit of a run-in with Caro's car as I was parking mine. It seems my memory misled me by a foot or so as to its position, and I gave the paintwork a little scrape on the near side. It must have been close on one o'clock when I wobbled my way up to bed. Caro was asleep. I knew Julia was still out, of course, as I hadn't seen her car in the drive, but she's long past having a curfew.' He gave his daughter an affectionate look.

'But I thought I heard you come in around midnight,' said Plummy. She shook her head. 'I just opened my eyes and squinted at the clock – perhaps I misread it.'

Caroline slipped from the arm of the sofa and went to stand with her back to the fire. 'I really don't see the point of this, Superintendent. Just because Connor was obviously disturbed does not mean we should be subjected to some sort of fascist grilling. We've already been over this once – that should be enough. I hope you realize that your assistant commissioner will hear about your irrational behaviour.'

She stood with her hands clasped behind her back and her feet slightly apart. In her black turtleneck, with fitted trousers tucked inside soft leather riding boots, she looked as though she might have been playing a trouser role in an opera. With her chin-length dark hair and in those clothes, she could easily pass for a boy on the verge of manhood. Her colour was a little high, as befitted the hero/heroine under trying circumstances, but her voice, as always, was perfectly controlled.

'Dame Caroline,' said Kincaid, 'Connor may have been emotionally distraught, but he was also telling the truth. Tommy admitted it, and Sir Gerald has confirmed it as well. I think it's time—' He caught a movement out of the corner of his eye. Caroline's jacket slid from the back of the sofa to the cushion with a rustling sound, the soft black leather as fluid as running water.

An odd sensation came over him, as if he had suddenly receded down a tunnel, distorting both his hearing and his vision. Blinking, he turned again to Caroline. Rearrange a few insignificant pieces in the pattern, and the whole thing shifted, turning on itself and popping into focus, clear and sharp and irrefutable. It amazed him now that he hadn't seen it all from the beginning.

They were all watching him with various degrees of concern. Smiling at Gemma, who had frozen with her cup poised midway in the air, he set his own empty cup firmly upon the table. 'It wasn't the doorbell you heard that night, Mrs Plumley, it was the telephone. And it wasn't Gerald you heard coming in a few minutes after midnight, but Caroline.

'Connor rang this number from the flat a little before eleven o'clock. I think it likely that he was looking for Julia, but it was Caroline who answered the phone.' Kincaid rose and went to stand against the piano, so that he could face Caroline directly. 'He couldn't resist baiting you, could he, Caroline? You were the architect of the deception he felt had cost him his happiness, after all.

'You thought you could calm him down, make him see reason, so you said you'd meet him. But you didn't want him making a scene in a public place, so you suggested somewhere you wouldn't be overheard – what could have been more natural than your favourite walk along Hambleden Lock?

'You dressed quickly, I imagine in something quite similar to the things you're wearing just now, and put on your leather jacket. The night was cold and damp, and it's a good brisk walk from the carpark to the river. You slipped quietly out of the house, making sure not to wake Plummy, and when you reached the river you waited for Con at the beginning of the weir.'

He shifted his position a bit, putting his hands in his trouser pockets. They all watched him, as mesmerized as if he were a conjuror about to pull a rabbit from a hat. Julia's eyes looked glazed, as if she were unable to assimilate a second shock so soon after the first.

'What happened then, Caroline?' he asked. Closing his eyes, he pictured the scene as he spoke. 'You walked along the weir, and you argued. The more you tried to reason with Con, the more difficult he became. You reached the lock, crossing over it to the far side,

313

and there the paved path ends.' He opened his eyes again and watched Caroline's still, composed face. 'So you stood with Connor on the little concrete apron just upstream of the sluicegate. Did you suggest turning back? But Con was out of control by that time, and the argument disintegrated into—'

'Please, Superintendent,' said Sir Gerald, 'you really have gone too far. This is all absurd. Caro couldn't kill anyone. She's not physically capable – just look at her. And Con was over six feet tall and well built . . .'

'She's also an actress, Sir Gerald, trained to use her body on the stage. It may have been something as simple as stepping aside when he rushed at her. We'll probably never be certain of that, or know what actually killed Connor. From the results of the post-mortem I think it likely he had a laryngospasm – his throat closed from the shock of hitting the water, and he died from suffocation without ever drawing water into his lungs.

'What we do know,' he said, turning back to Caroline, 'is that help was less than fifty yards away. The lock-keeper was at home, he had the necessary equipment and expertise. And even had he not been available, there were other houses just a bit further along the opposite bank of the river.

'Whether Connor's fall into the river was an accident, or self-defence, or a deliberate act of violence, the fact remains that you are culpable, Dame Caroline. You might have saved him. Did you wait what seemed a reasonable time for him to come up again? When he didn't surface, you walked away, drove home and climbed back into bed, where Gerald found you sleeping peacefully. Only you were a bit more flustered than you thought, and didn't quite manage to leave your car exactly as it had been.'

Caroline smiled at him. 'That's quite an amusing fiction, Mr Kincaid. I'm sure the chief constable and your assistant commissioner will find it most entertaining as well. You have nothing but circumstantial evidence and an overactive imagination.'

'That may be true, Dame Caroline. We will have forensics go over your car and your clothes, however, and there's the matter of the witness who saw a man and, she assumed, a boy wearing a leather jacket on the weir walkway – she may recognize you in an identity parade.

'Whether or not we can build a case against you that will hold up in court, those of us here today will know the truth.'

'Truth?' said Caroline, at last allowing her voice to rise in anger. 'You wouldn't know truth if it came up and bit you, Mr Kincaid. The truth is that this family will stand together, as we always have, and you can't touch us. You're a fool to think—'

'Stop it! Just stop it, all of you.' Julia rose from the sofa and stood shaking, her hands clenched and her face drained of colour. 'This has gone on long enough. How can you be such a hypocrite, Mummy? No wonder Con was furious. He'd bought your load of rubbish and taken on my share of it, too.' She paused for a breath, then said more evenly, 'I grew up hating myself because I never quite fitted into your ideal circle, thinking that if I'd only been different, better somehow, you would have loved me more. And it was all a lie, the perfect family was a lie. You warped my life with it, and you would have warped Matty's, too, if you'd been given a chance.'

'Julia, you mustn't say these things.' Sir Gerald's voice held more anguish than when he'd defended his wife. 'You've no right to desecrate Matthew's memory.'

'Don't talk to me about Matty's memory. I'm the only one who really grieved for Matty, the little boy who could be rude and silly, and sometimes had to sleep with his light on because he was frightened of his dreams. You only lost what you wanted him to be.' Julia looked at Plummy, who still sat quietly on the edge of her seat, her back straight as a staff. 'I'm sorry, Plummy, that's unfair to you. You loved him – you loved both of us, and honestly.

'And Tommy – as ill as I was I remember Tommy coming to the house, and now I can understand what I only sensed then. He sat with me, offering what solace he could, but you were the only one who might have comforted him, Mummy, and you wouldn't see him. You were too busy making high drama of your grief. He deserved better.'

In two lightning steps, Caroline crossed the space that separated her from Julia. She raised her open hand and slapped her daughter across the face. 'Don't you dare speak to me like that. You don't know anything. You're making a fool of yourself with this ridiculous scene. You're making fools of us all, and I won't have it in my house.'

Julia stood her ground. Even though her eyes filled with tears, she neither spoke nor lifted a hand to touch the white imprint on her cheek.

Vivian Plumley went to her and put an arm gently around her shoulders. She said, 'Maybe it's time someone made a scene, Caro. Who knows what might have been avoided if some of these things had been said long ago?'

Caroline stepped back. 'I only meant to protect you, Julia, always. And you, Gerald,' she added, turning to him.

Wearily, Julia said, 'You've protected yourself, from the very beginning.'

'We were all right as we were,' said Caroline. 'Why should anything change?'

'It's too late, Mummy,' said Julia, and Kincaid heard an unexpected note of compassion. 'Can't you see that?'

Caroline turned to her husband, hand out in a gesture of supplication. 'Gerald—'

He looked away.

In the silence that followed, a gust of wind blew a spatter of rain against the window, and the fire flared up in response. Kincaid met Gemma's eyes. He nodded slightly and she came to stand beside him. He said, 'I'm sorry, Dame Caroline, but I'm afraid you'll need to come with us to High Wycombe and make a formal statement. You can come in your own car, if you like, Sir Gerald, and wait for her.'

Julia looked at her parents. What judgement would she pass on them, wondered Kincaid, now that they had revealed themselves as all too fallibly human, and flawed?

For the first time Julia's hand strayed to her cheek. She went to Gerald and briefly touched his arm. 'I'll wait for you here, Daddy,' she said. Then she turned away and left the room without another glance at her mother.

When they had rung High Wycombe and organized the preliminaries, Kincaid excused himself and slipped out of the sitting room. By the time he reached the top landing he had to catch his breath, and he felt a welcome ache in his calves. He tapped lightly on the door of Julia's studio and opened it.

She stood in the centre of the room, holding an open box in her arms and looking about her. 'Plummy's cleaned up after me, can you tell?' she said as he came in.

It did look uncharacteristically clean and lifeless, as if the removal of Julia's attendant clutter had stripped it of its heart.

'There's nothing left I need, really. I suppose what I wanted was to say goodbye.' She gestured around the room with her chin. The mark of her mother's hand stood out clearly now, fiery against the pale skin of her cheek. 'I won't be back here again. Not in the same way. This was a child's refuge.'

'Yes,' said Kincaid. She would move on now, into her own life. 'You'll be all right.'

'I know.' They looked at one another and he

understood that he would not see her again, that their coming together had served its purpose. He would move on now as well, perhaps take a leaf from Gemma's book – she had been hurt, as he had, but she had put it behind her with the forthright practicality he so admired.

After a moment, Julia said, 'What will happen to my mother?'

'I don't know. It depends on the forensic evidence, but even if we turned up something fairly concrete, I doubt we'll make anything stiffer than involuntary manslaughter stick.'

She nodded.

Near to the eaves as they were, the sound of the rain beating against the roof came clearly, and the wind rattled the windows like a beast seeking entrance. 'Julia, I'm sorry.'

'You mustn't be. You only did your job, and what you knew was right. You couldn't violate your integrity to protect me, or my family. There's been enough of that in this house,' she said firmly. 'Are you sorry about what happened with us, as well?' she added, with a trace of a smile.

Was he sorry? For ten years he had kept his emotions safely, tightly reined, until he had almost forgotten how it felt to give another person access. Julia had forced his hand, made him see himself in the mirror of her isolation, and what he found frightened him. But probing beyond the fear, he felt a new and unexpected sense of freedom, even of anticipation.

He smiled back at Julia. 'No.'

Chapter Sixteen

'We should have taken the Midget,' Kincaid said testily as Gemma pulled up the Escort in front of the Carlingford Road flat.

'You know as well as I do that the bloody thing leaks in the rain,' she retorted, glaring at him. She felt as miserable and bedraggled as a cat forced into the bath, and he wasn't much of an improvement. As she watched, a rivulet of water trickled down his forehead from his matted hair.

He wiped it away with the back of his hand, then burst out laughing. 'Gemma, look at us. How can you be so stubborn?'

After what seemed an interminable session at High Wycombe, they had started back to London on the M40, only to have a puncture before they reached the North Circular Road. Gemma had pulled over to the verge and plunged out into the driving rain, refusing his help in changing the tyre. He had stood in the rain, arguing with her while she worked, so that in the end they were both soaked to the skin.

'It's too late to collect Toby tonight,' he said. 'Come in and get some dry things on before you catch your death, and have something proper to eat. Please.'

After a moment, she said, 'All right,' but the words she'd meant to be acquiescent came out grudging and sullen. Her bad temper seemed to be out of control, feeding on itself, and she didn't know how to break the cycle.

They didn't bother with umbrellas as they crossed the road to Kincaid's building – how could they get any more wet, after all? – and the pellets of water stung against her skin.

When they reached the flat, Kincaid went straight to the kitchen, leaving a dripping trail on the carpet. He pulled an already uncorked bottle of white wine from the fridge and poured two glasses. Handing her one, he said, 'Start on this. It will warm you up from the inside. Sorry I haven't anything stronger. And in the meantime I'll get you something dry to put on.'

He left her standing in the sitting room holding her glass, too wet to sit down, too exhausted to sort out her own feelings. Was she angry with him because of Julia? She had felt a communion between them, an understanding that excluded her, and the strength of her reaction dismayed her.

She tasted the wine, then drank half the glass. Chill in her mouth, it did seem to generate some warmth in her middle.

Or was she angry with Caroline Stowe for having taken her in, and Kincaid merely happened to be the nearest available target?

Perhaps it was just the waste of it all that made her feel like chucking something.

Sid uncurled himself from his nest on the sofa, stretching, and came to her. He elongated his sleek body as he rubbed around her ankles and butted his head against her legs. She bent to scratch him in the soft spot under his chin, and his throat began to vibrate under her fingertips. 'Hullo, Sid. You've got the right idea tonight – warm and dry. We should all be so lucky.'

She looked around the familiar and comfortable room. Light from the lamps Kincaid had switched on spilled out in warm pools, illuminating his collection of brightly coloured London transport posters. The coffee table held a haphazard pile of books and an empty mug, and the sofa a crumpled afghan rug. Gemma felt a sudden pang of longing. She wanted to feel at home here, wanted to feel safe.

'I didn't know about underthings,' said Kincaid, returning from the bedroom carrying a stack of folded clothes with a big fluffy towel on the top. 'I suppose you'll have to make do.' He deposited the jeans and sweatshirt on the sofa and draped the towel around her shoulders. 'Oh, and socks. I forgot socks.'

Wiping her face with one end of the towel, Gemma began fumbling with her sodden plait. Her fingers were too numb with cold to work properly, and she felt tears of frustration smart behind her eyelids.

'Let me help,' he said gently. He turned her around and deftly worked her hair loose, combing it out with his fingers. 'Now.' Rotating her until she faced him again, he began rubbing her head with the towel. His hair stood on end where he had scrubbed at it, and his skin smelled warm and damp.

The weight of his hands against her head seemed to crumble her defences, and she felt her legs go limp and boneless, as if they could no longer support her weight. She closed her eyes against the faintness, thinking *too much wine, too quickly*, but the sensation didn't pass. Reaching up, she put a hand over his, and a buzz ran through her like electric current as their skin made contact.

He stopped his towelling of her hair, looking at her with concern. 'Sorry,' he said. 'Did I get carried away?'

When she managed to shake her head, he let the towel slide to her shoulders and began gently rubbing her neck and the back of her head. She thought disjointedly of Rob – he had never looked after her like this. No one had. And nowhere in her calculations had she reckoned with the power of tenderness, irresistible as gravity.

The pressure of his hand on the back of her head brought her a stumbling step forward, against him, and she gasped with shock as his weight pressed her icy clothes to her skin. She turned her face up, and of its own volition her hand reached for him, cupping the back of his damp head, pulling his mouth down to meet hers.

Drowsily, Gemma raised herself on one elbow and looked at him, realizing she'd never seen him asleep.

His relaxed face seemed younger, softer, and the fan of his eyelashes made dark shadows on his cheeks. His eyelids fluttered for an instant, as if he were dreaming, and the corners of his mouth turned up in the hint of a smile.

She reached out to smooth the unruly chestnut hair from his brow and froze. Suddenly, in that small act of intimacy, she saw the enormity, the absurdity, of what she had done.

She drew her hand back as if stung. Oh dear God, what had she been thinking of? What on earth had possessed her? How could she face him at work in the morning, say, 'Yes, guv, no, guv, right-oh, guv,' as if nothing had happened between them?

Her heart racing, she slid carefully from the bed. They'd left a trail of wet clothes across the bedroom, and as she disentangled hers from the jumble she felt tears fill her eyes. She swore under her breath. *Silly, bloody fool.* She never cried. Even when Rob had left her, she hadn't cried. Shivering, she pulled on damp pants, slipped her soggy jumper over her head.

She had done what she'd sworn she'd never do. As hard as she'd worked to earn her position, to be considered an equal, a colleague, she'd shown herself no better than any tart who slept her way up the ladder. A wave of dizziness swept over her as she stepped into her skirt and she swayed.

What could she do now? Ask for a transfer? Everyone would know why – she might as well wear a sign and save them speculating. Resign? Give up her dreams, let all her hard work turn to dust in her fingers? How could she bear it? Oh, she would have sympathy and a plausible excuse – too hard a life for a single mum, a need to spend more time with her son – but she would know how badly she had failed.

Kincaid stirred and turned, freeing an arm from the covers. Staring at him, she tried to memorize the curve of his shoulder, the angle of his cheek, and her heart contracted with longing and desire. She turned away, afraid of her own weakness.

In the sitting room she squelched her bare feet into her shoes and gathered up her coat and bag. The dry jeans and sweater he'd brought her still lay neatly folded on the sofa, and the towel he'd used to dry her hair lay crumpled on the floor. She picked it up and held its soft nap against her cheek, imagining that it smelled faintly of shaving soap. With exaggerated care she folded it and placed it beside the clothes, then let herself quietly out of the flat.

When Gemma reached the street door, she found the rain still coming down in relentless sheets, a solid wall of water. She stood for a moment, watching it. In her traitorous mind she imagined running back up the stairs and into the flat, shedding her clothes and climbing back into bed beside his sleeping form.

She pushed open the door, stepped slowly out into the rain and crossed the road, making no effort to shield herself. The dim outline of the Escort was familiar, comforting even. Scrabbling for the handle as if she were blind, she wrenched the door open and half fell into the driver's seat. She wiped her streaming face with her hands and started the engine.

The radio blared into life and instead of hitting the off switch, she reflexively jammed a tape into the player. Caroline Stowe's voice filled the car as Violetta sang her last aria, begging for life, for love, for the physical strength to match her courageous will.

Gemma put her head down against the steering wheel and wept.

After a moment she mopped her face with some tissues and put the car into gear, and when the music finished the only sound was the drumming of the rain against the roof.

The soft click of a door penetrated Kincaid's consciousness. He struggled towards the surface of sleep, but it clung to him tenaciously, dragging him down again into its cotton-wool depths. His body felt boneless, warmly lethargic, and his eyelids seemed to have acquired surplus weight. Rousing himself enough to tuck his exposed arm under the covers, he felt the sheet cool and empty beside him. He blinked. Gemma. She must have gone to the loo – women always had to go to the loo – or perhaps to the kitchen for a glass of water.

He smiled a little at his own stupidity. What he wanted, needed, had been right under his nose all along and he'd been too blind to see it. Now he felt as if his life had come round full circle, complete, and he imagined the pattern of their days together. Work, then home, and at day's end he would find sanctuary beside her, entangling himself in the curtain of her coppery hair.

Kincaid stretched his arm across her pillow, ready to enfold her when she returned. The rain beat steadily against the windowpane, counterpoint to the warmth of the room. With a sigh of contentment, he drifted once again into sleep.

In a Dark House

To the memory of Fleur Lombard
Who died in the line of duty
4 February, 1996
Avon Fire Brigade, England

Why have you suffer'd me to be imprison'd,
Kept in a dark house . . .

William Shakespeare,
Twelfth Night

Acknowledgements

Thanks to Nancy Yost, with Lowenstein-Yost Associates, New York, best of agents and friend, for her good advice and infinite patience, to Arabella Stein with Abner Stein, UK, to Sarah Turner at Pan Macmillan, and to Canon Bill Ritson for his hospitality and knowledge of Southwark.

To those who have read the manuscript, Steve Copling, Dale Denton, Jim Evans, Diane Sullivan Hale, Gigi Sherrell Norwood, and Viqui Litman, thanks for your dedication, suggestions (and our many dinners at La Madeleine) and to Kate Charles, Marcia Talley, and particularly Diane Hale for your creative input.

Jan Hull has provided moral support, as always. My husband, Rick, has kept all my IT systems up and running, and my daughter, Kayti, has kept my *life* running smoothly while I wrote. I'm sure I couldn't have done it without you all.

Chapter One

London . . . Smoke lowering down from chimney-pots, making a soft black drizzle, with flakes of soot in it as big as full-grown snowflakes – gone into mourning, one might imagine, for the death of the sun.

Charles Dickens
Bleak House

It took no more than a match, nestled beneath the crumpled paper and foil crisp packets. The flame smouldered, then flared and crackled, and within seconds tongues reached out for the bottom layer of furniture stacked so conveniently on the ground floor of the old warehouse. Nothing burned like polyurethane foam, and the cheap chairs, sofas and mattresses removed from the flats on the upper floors of the building were old enough not to have been treated with fire retardants.

A gift. It was a gift. He could hardly have asked for more if he had assembled the ingredients for a perfect fire himself. The furniture would generate enough heat for flashover, then the old wooden floorboards and ceiling joists would blaze with a beautiful fury. The fire would take on a life of its own, separate from its creator.

1

And the fire had power, that he had learned early on; power to exhilarate, power to transform, power to induce wonder and terror. He had first read about the great Tooley Street fire of 1861 in school, which seemed to him now an odd place to have discovered a life's calling.

The conflagration had burned for two days and consumed over three hundred yards of wharf and warehouse, damage unequalled since the Great Fire of 1666, damage not to be seen again until the Blitz.

There had been other fires, of course: the Mustard Mills in 1814, Topping's Wharf in 1843, Bankside in 1855; it seemed to him that fire was as necessary to Southwark as birth and death, that it provided an essential means of growth and regeneration.

Heat began to sear his face; the skin across his cheekbones and forehead felt stretched, his nostrils began to sting from the smoke and escaping gas. The blaze was well under way now, burrowing deep into the pile of furniture, then licking out in unexpected places. It was time for him to go, but still he lingered, unable to tear himself from the energy that gave him more than a sexual charge – it was a glimpse into the heart of life itself. If he gave himself up to it, let it consume him, would he at last know the truth?

But still he resisted complete surrender. Shaking himself, he blinked against the stinging in his eyes and took a last look round, making sure he had left no trace. Satisfied, he slipped out the way he had come. He would watch from a distance as the fire mounted to its inevitable climax *and then . . . then there would be other fires. There were always other fires.*

Rose Kearney liked night duty best, when the station was quiet except for the muted murmur of voices in the staff room as everyone went about their assigned tasks. There was something comforting about the camaraderie inside held against the dark outside, and in the easing of the adrenalin rush after a call out. And she considered herself lucky to have ended up at Southwark, the station where she had trained and the most historic in the London Fire Brigade.

She and her partner, Bryan Simms, were checking their breathing apparatus after the first bell of the night – a little old lady in a council flat, having decided to make herself a bedtime snack, had dozed off with the chip pan on the stove. Fortunately, a neighbour had seen the first sign of smoke, the blaze had been easily contained, and the woman had escaped serious injury.

But every fire call, no matter how minor, required a careful examination of any equipment they had used. Tonight she and Bryan had been assigned to BA crew and their lives depended on the efficiency of their breathing apparatus – and on each other. Simms, at twenty-three a year older than Rose, was as steady and reliable as his square, blunt face implied, and not inclined to panic.

He looked up at her, as if sensing her regard, and

frowned in concentration. '"What's in a name?"' he asked, as if continuing a conversation. '"That which we call a rose by any other name would smell as sweet."'

For a moment, Rose was too startled to respond. Not that she wasn't used to being teased about her name, or her fair looks, but this was the first time one of her fellow firefighters had resorted to Shakespeare.

Taking her silence as encouragement, Bryan went on, grinning, '"But earthlier happy is the rose distilled, than that which withering on the virgin thorn grows, lives, and dies in single blessedness—"'

'Piss off, Simms,' Rose interrupted, smothering a laugh. She had to admit she was impressed he'd gone to the trouble of memorizing the lines. 'I'd never have taken you for a Shakespeare buff.'

'I like the second one. It's from *A Midsummer Night's Dream*,' said Simms, and she wondered if she had imagined a blush in his dark skin as he bent again over his task.

'You don't say,' Rose retorted with a smile. 'And *Romeo and Juliet* as well. Aren't you the clever one.' Her father, a secondary-school English teacher, had begun quoting Shakespeare to her before she could talk. 'Look sharp there,' she added, glancing at his neglected equipment. 'You don't want to miss a crack in that hose.'

She'd started at the Southwark station six months before Bryan, and she never missed an opportunity to remind him of her seniority. It was hard enough, being female in what was still basically a man's profession,

4

and she certainly couldn't afford a partner with some half-baked romantic idea about their relationship.

Rose meant to go far, perhaps even divisional officer one day, and she wasn't about to let an entanglement stand in her way. Not that she was averse to a night out and a bit of a recreational cuddle, but not with someone on her own ground. And the job left no time for a real relationship. If you wanted to be good, you had to eat it, sleep it, breathe it. She wanted more than the ability to put a fire out; she wanted to understand the why and how, and fire investigation was a way to move up the ranks.

It was now after midnight, and she intended to use her time to study if things remained quiet. She'd just stowed the BA set and pulled out her books when the bells went for the second time that night.

Rose felt the familiar jolt of adrenalin, and then she and Bryan and the rest of the watch were running for the pole. Descending to the appliance bay, they began pulling on fire gear as the duty officer called out 'Pair' over the tannoy, meaning that both the pump and the pump ladder were needed. As if of their own volition, Rose's hands performed the familiar rituals: fastening her tunic, tightening the throat buckle, pushing back her hair before slipping on her helmet and adjusting the chin strap, clasping her belt so that the weight of the small axe rested against her hip.

The station officer, Charlie Wilcox, ripped the call slip off the teleprinter. 'It's just round the corner – warehouse in Southwark Street,' he told them. 'Sounds like it's well away – we'll need sets on this one.'

Within seconds they were aboard the appliance and rolling into Southwark Bridge Road, sirens wailing and blue lights flashing. A fine drizzle blurred the September night, slicking the tarmac and haloing the street lamps. As they swung round into Southwark Street, Wilcox called out from the front, 'It's showing.'

As the pump came to a stop, Rose saw a bank of smoke hanging heavily over the street, and in the lower windows of a brick Victorian warehouse the telltale red-orange flicker of light. Acrid smoke stung her nostrils as she leapt from the appliance and pulled on her mask. She caught a glimpse of huddled bystanders as Wilcox said, 'Rose, Bryan. It looks as though the worst of it is still confined to the ground floor. Take in a guideline and check for occupants.' He turned to his sub officer, Seamus MacCauley. 'Check round the back, will you, Seamus? See what we've got.'

The other BA team from the pump ladder was already laying hose line as Rose and Bryan tallied in their breathing apparatus, checked their radios. 'Door's open,' she heard Wilcox shout as she pulled her visor down, and she registered faint surprise before focusing again on her task.

They went in low, Rose leading, peering through the smoke, feeling their way into the dense blackness. The heat seared, even through their coats, and she could hear the groaning and cracking of a well-estab-lished fire. She fell against something soft and bulky, went down on her knees. Through a momentary thin-ning of the smoke she saw shapes piled above her like

6

a giant child's tower of blocks. The disjointed images suddenly coalesced.

'It's furniture,' she said. 'Someone's piled up bloody furniture.' The polyurethane foam used in furniture cushions and mattresses was highly flammable – the thought of the devastating fire that had started in the furniture department of the Manchester Woolworth's crossed her mind, but she banished it, concentrating on the job at hand.

Still on her knees, she moved forward, feeling her way round the obstacles, trying to find a suitable place to tie off the line. Suddenly, there was a loud crack, then a series of pops, and the heat bloomed as debris rained down on them.

'Flashover,' shouted Bryan. She felt him grab her waist belt. 'We've got to get out of here. Forget the line, Rose.'

Even with Bryan's weight dragging at her, her momentum carried her another foot, her hand still outstretched with the line.

'I said forget the fucking line, Rose. Evacuate! Evacuate!'

Even though her stubbornness, her refusal to let the fire get the better of her, was one of the things that made her good at her job, she knew he was right. Going on would be suicidal, and nothing could have survived this blaze without protection.

Hemmed in on one side by a sofa, on the other by what seemed to be stacks of lumber, Rose tried to turn back. As she manoeuvred her body round, her gloved hand came down on something that yielded beneath her fingers. It felt malleable, like flesh, with the brittleness of bone beneath.

Rose looked down, blinking eyes burning and swollen from the heat, and felt the bile rise in her throat. 'Jesus Christ,' she said. 'We've got a body.'

On this morning there had been no drifting slowly into consciousness, no lingering in imagined wholeness, no savouring the memory of life as it used to be.

Franny Liu opened her eyes and took stock, reluctantly. It was later than usual, that she could tell by the angle of light in the sitting room window, but still overcast, as it had been the previous day. She slept, as she had since she'd become unable to manage the stairs, on an old velvet-covered chaise longue that had belonged to her mother. For once in her life her small stature was a blessing – a few inches taller and her feet would have hung over the end of her makeshift bed. At night the arms of the chaise cradled her, offering a solid comfort; in the daytime her bedding could be tucked away, allowing her to maintain an illusion of normality.

Elaine had argued with her, of course, wanting to put a bed in the sitting room, but for once Franny's soft refusal had held sway over her housemate's brisk efficiency. The wheelchair was bad enough. For Franny, a bed in the sitting room would have meant admitting the possibility that she might not improve.

Her cat, Quinn, still lay curled on her feet. The

only sound in the flat was his faint purring. It was the silence that had awakened her, Franny suddenly realized. There were no footsteps upstairs, no sound of movement in the kitchen. Elaine was always up first, making coffee and pottering around the house. Before leaving for her job as an administrative assistant at Guy's Hospital, she allowed time to make Franny tea and toast and helped her with her morning routine.

Perhaps Elaine had overslept, thought Franny – but no, Elaine was as punctual as Big Ben. Could she be ill? 'Elaine?' Franny called out tentatively, pulling herself up by using the arms of the chaise. Her voice seemed to echo emptily, and a spark of fear shot through her. 'Elaine?'

There was no answer.

Suddenly, Franny remembered her dream, a jumbled nightmare of doors closing softly, and felt again the dream's inexplicable sense of loss. It made her think of the deathbed watches she'd kept as a private nurse before her illness, of the way she'd felt when she'd awakened from an inadvertent doze and known instantly that her patient had died while she slept.

Just as she knew, now, as the silence closed around her, that the house was empty. The sound of the door closing in the night had been no dream.

Elaine was gone.

There was nothing Harriet Novak hated more than having to tell strangers that she attended Little Dorrit

School. Grown-ups would smile and coo as if it were disgustingly sweet – which made Harriet wonder how many of them had ever actually read *Little Dorrit* – and kids looked at her as if she'd just teleported from another planet.

Not that the school itself was all that bad, she allowed, digging the toe of her trainer in the playground dirt as she waited for the first bell. It was just that it sounded so God-awfully sickening – like telling people you were called Tiny Tim.

It helped to be prepared, Harriet had learned, knowledge a necessary defence against living in a Dickens-infested neighbourhood. She'd read the biography in the school library and could tell people more about Dickens than most wanted to know. Charles Dickens's father had been briefly imprisoned in Marshalsea Prison, just up the road, and twelve-year-old Charles had lived in lodgings nearby. This experience had stayed with him all his life, working its way into many of his books, and his creations had come back to haunt the Borough. Not only did the area boast a Little Dorrit Court and a Little Dorrit Street, there was a Marshalsea Road, a Pickwick Street and a Copperfield Street.

At least there was nothing named after Oliver Twist. Harriet thought Oliver a right little tosser, too sweet to be borne. Davey Copperfield she liked better. He was a bit soft on his dead mum, but at least he *had* bitten his horrid stepfather. Davey knew how to stand up for himself.

Harriet scowled, only half aware of the smoky tang

IN A DARK HOUSE

in the air and the pupils straggling in the school gate. Her thoughts settled into a well-worn groove. Would it be better to have a wicked stepfather, like Davey, rather than a father who had walked out? He said he loved her, her dad, but if that was true, how could he have left them?

He told her lots of parents got divorced, that it was just something they would all have to learn to live with, but that didn't stop her missing him. Nor had his moving out stopped her parents' rows. She heard them when he came to pick her up, and other times she heard her mum on the phone with him.

The last argument had been the worst, when her dad had taken her home hours late after her last weekend at his flat. Her mum had been sitting on the doorstep of their house, watching for them, and she'd run to the car as Harriet was getting out.

'You bastard, Tony, you selfish little shit,' her mother had shouted – her mother the surgeon, who was always in control, who had never raised her voice before this began. Her curly dark hair bloomed round her head as if energized by her anger; her jeans and jumper hung loosely on her too-thin frame, making her bones look as sharp as her voice. 'You're late; you don't answer your bloody phone – does it ever occur to you that I might worry? Anything could have happened.'

Harriet stood frozen on the pavement. She'd glimpsed a movement in the open window of the flat next door and knew their neighbour was listening. In the street, a couple walking by with their dog pointedly looked away and increased their pace. She felt her face flush scarlet with embarrassment. 'Mum, we only—'

'For God's sake, Laura,' her father broke in. 'We went to the bloody zoo. It was a nice day, and we stayed longer than we meant. Is that a crime?' His voice was level, tight, his face pinched.

'You were supposed to have Harriet back hours ago. You know the rules—'

'Mum, please,' said Harriet, hearing the mortifying quaver in her voice. Her throat ached, and a sharp pain seared her chest. 'I'm fine, really. Can we please go in?'

Her father shot her an anguished glance. 'Laura, let it go, okay? You're upsetting Harriet—'

'*I'm* upsetting Harriet?' Her mother stepped back from the car, looking suddenly, dangerously, calm.

'Listen, it won't happen again,' Tony said quickly, as if realizing his mistake. 'Next time I'll—'

'There's not going to be a next time,' her mum had said quietly, taking Harriet's arm in a vice-like grip and turning them both towards the door. As they reached the building, Harriet looked round and saw her dad pulling away, and if he had tried to ring her since, her mum hadn't told her.

Harriet hadn't dared ask her mother what she'd meant, but the words had stayed with her over the past few days, disturbing her sleep and haunting her waking hours.

She shifted her backpack and frowned again, aware

of a headache coming on. She hadn't eaten her breakfast and her empty stomach was starting to cramp.

That was one of the worst things about her parents'
separation: now, with her dad gone, when her mother
had to work night duty at the hospital, she left Harriet
with old Mrs Bletchley, who lived in one of the cottages across from the school. Mum said Mrs B was
lonely and enjoyed having children stay with her, but
the woman reminded Harriet of the witch in *Hansel
and Gretel*, and her house smelled of cats. That morning she had given Harriet some sort of unspeakable
hot cereal for breakfast, which Harriet had mushed
around in the bowl and then tipped in the bin when
Mrs B wasn't looking.

A shiny black Range Rover pulled up to the school
gate and a boy climbed from the back, shrugging into
his backpack with impossible-to-imitate eleven-year-
old cool. Shawn Culver was a year ahead of Harriet,
and the most popular boy in the school.

'Hey, Harry,' he called out, seeing her watching.
She nodded without smiling, determined not to appear
impressed, but she didn't object to his use of the hated
nickname. She tugged her hair more tightly into its
bunch, suddenly aware that she looked as if she hadn't
bothered to wash that morning – which she hadn't.
And if her hair weren't bad enough at home, when she
could smooth it down with some of her mum's gel, on
a Bletchley morning it was impossible.

The bell rang. She'd turned to follow Shawn with a
studied nonchalance when the sound of a car braking

fast made her look back. It was a dark green Volvo, like her dad's – no, it was her dad's. As she made out his face through the tinted glass, she saw that he was motioning to her. What was he doing here, before school?

She started towards the car slowly, aware of the second ring of the bell, of the playground emptying behind her. As she neared the car she realized there was a person in the passenger seat, a woman, and for a moment her heart flared in wild hope.

Then her dad reached back and swung open the rear door, and she saw that the woman was not her mother, but someone she had never seen before.

'Want some coffee, guv?' asked Doug Cullen, popping his head into Detective Superintendent Duncan Kincaid's office. 'I mean real coffee, not that slop,' Cullen added, nodding at the mug on Kincaid's desk.

Kincaid grimaced at his sergeant and laid down his pen, stretching the stiffness out of his shoulders. 'You just want an excuse to get out, and we've not been here an hour.' They'd come in early the past few days, catching up on accumulated paperwork, and the warren of cubicles that made up Scotland Yard's CID had begun to seem more like a prison than an office.

'Guilty.' With his thatch of straight blond hair and wire-framed spectacles, Cullen looked more like a schoolboy than a detective sergeant. But in the year since Kincaid's former partner, Gemma James, had been promoted to detective inspector and posted to Notting Hill Station, he had learned to work well with Cullen, respecting the younger officer's intelligence and dogged persistence when faced with a problem.

Not that Cullen or anyone else could truly replace Gemma as a colleague. Although he and Gemma had been living together since the previous Christmas, he found he still missed working with her.

Glancing out his window, he was tempted to play truant along with Cullen, but the pile of paper on his desk argued against it. Besides, the day had got perceptibly greyer since he'd come in, and he wasn't in the mood to get drenched. 'Okay,' he said, stifling a sigh. 'A coffee. But just coffee, mind you; no poncey lattes.'

Cullen grinned and gave him a mock salute. 'Right, boss. Back in a tick.'

It was a bad sign, Kincaid thought, when going out on such a dreary morning seemed preferable to work, but administrative reports had never been his strong suit. Not that he didn't have the aptitude for it; he just lacked the patience. He hadn't joined the force to become a bloody bureaucrat, yet that seemed more and more the case. And he had reached the point in his career where he felt increasingly pressured to seek promotion, but such a move would mean still less work in the field.

Could he stay where he was, watching the university fast-trackers like Cullen pass him by, without becoming bitter? It was not a prospect he wanted to consider, so with a scowl he turned his attention back to the performance survey on his desk. But when his phone rang a moment later, he leapt on it like a drowning man.

It was his guvnor's secretary, summoning him to a meeting with the chief superintendent. Kincaid straightened his tie, grabbed his jacket from the coatrack, and was out the door with only a twinge of regret for his missed coffee.

Chief Superintendent Denis Childs had moved office recently, now commanding a view of the parks and the river, but in spite of his elevated status the man remained as Buddha-like as ever. His round, heavy face betrayed little emotion, but Kincaid had learned to read the slightest flicker in the deep brown eyes half hidden by folds of skin. Today he detected apology, annoyance and what might have been a trace of worry.

'I'm sorry to dump this on you, Duncan,' said Childs, his voice surprisingly soft for a man his size.

Not a promising start, Kincaid thought, settling himself in a chair. Perhaps he should have stayed with the paperwork after all. 'But?'

'But as you have nothing pressing on at the moment, and as you have a knack for soothing ruffled feelings' – Childs's lips turned up in the smallest of smiles – 'you seemed the best man for the job.'

'I'm not going to like this, am I?'

'You can look on it as a diplomatic challenge. It will mean liaising with the Fire Investigation Team and Southwark CID. A fire broke out in the early hours of this morning in a warehouse on Southwark Street. Do you know it?'

'Southwark Street? That's near London Bridge Station, isn't it? But why send me?'

'Patience, boyo, patience. I'm getting there.' Childs leaned back in his chair and steepled his fingers together, a familiar gesture. 'This particular building is Victorian, and was in the process of being converted into luxury flats. The fire apparently started on the ground floor, but by the time the brigade got there it had done considerable damage to the upper floors and had begun to threaten the building next door.'

'The warehouse was empty, then, if it was undergoing renovation?'

'Not quite. When the brigade got inside, they found a body among the debris. Quite badly burned, I'm afraid. And no identification.'

'A tramp, smoking—'

'Possibly, although tramps aren't usually found naked with no effects. And it gets a bit more complicated. This particular building happens to be owned by one of our more illustrious MPs, Marcus Yarwood.'

'Yarwood?' Kincaid sat up a bit straighter in surprise. 'I didn't know Yarwood was developing property.' The vocal and abrasive Yarwood leaned far to the left of the government Labour party and was often heard publicly castigating anyone capitalist enough to make a profit. 'This could be awkward for him, I take it? And the press will be on it like flies.'

'An understatement. A public relations nightmare in the making, to be more accurate, especially with an important by-election coming up. Not to mention that the loss adjusters are already sniffing round and muttering about possible insurance fraud. And I've heard rumours from other quarters – one of my golfing mates who's in the property market – that Yarwood hasn't had the early interest in his leases that he expected.'

'Ouch.' Kincaid winced. 'So he might have a very costly liability on his hands – or he did until last night.'

'Not that he'd admit it. But the powers-that-be are worried enough that someone from Number Ten rang the assistant commissioner and called in a favour.'

'And that's where I come into it?' Kincaid said, enlightenment dawning.

'The word is they only want to be sure the investigation is given high priority—'

'Meaning they want to be sure Yarwood's interests are well represented.' Kincaid weighed the prospect of taking on such a politically sensitive case against going back to his performance reviews. It could prove messy, both literally and figuratively. He hated self-important politicians, and fire scenes had always given him the creeps.

'You can refuse, of course,' said Childs, with a deceptive gentleness Kincaid recognized. Not only did Childs want him on the investigation, he knew that Kincaid needed the good mark in the AC's book.

'Is the body still in situ?' Kincaid asked.

Childs permitted himself another small smile. 'I told them to wait for you.'

Chapter Two

'But let him look at me, in prison, and in bonds here.
I endure without murmuring, because it is appointed
that I shall so make reparation for my sins.'

Charles Dickens
Little Dorrit

The Reverend Winifred Catesby Montfort was finding
it more difficult than she'd expected to adjust to life in
London. After the past few years at her country church
outside Glastonbury, the concrete and grime of urban
South London seemed a barren landscape to a soul
parched for the gentle spread of green across the
Somerset Levels.

But her exile was only temporary, she told herself
for the hundredth time as she searched the unfamiliar
cupboards of St Peter's Rectory, hoping that something
would materialize for her lunch. She also reminded
herself that her exile was of her own making, and that
she had no real cause for complaint. When her old
friend and theological college mentor, Roberta Smith,
had developed asthma so severe that her doctor

ordered her to leave the city for a few months, Winnie had suggested that they swap parishes.

At the time it had seemed the right thing to do, as if God had offered her an opportunity to serve too obvious to refuse, but now she wondered if it had been merely her ego jumping at a chance to be seen as a rescuer – *St Winnie saves the day.* And so she had abandoned her husband of less than a year, as well as others at home and in her parish who depended on her, to minister to what she had imagined as the poor and huddled masses.

Instead, she found a fairly comfortable and disinterested parish, the same round of bureaucratic meetings she'd left behind, and an ache of homesickness and longing for Jack that plagued her like a missing organ.

Well, there was nothing for it now but to get on with things, she chided herself as she rooted out a tin of tuna from the cupboard shelf and checked its use-by date. Too much self-examination smacked of self-absorption and was unproductive to boot – and her situation did have its compensations.

The rectory, a flat in Mitre Road across from St Peter's Church, was cosy, filled with the bright wall hangings and artefacts Roberta had collected on her trips to Africa and Asia. Southwark Cathedral was only a few streets away, and Winnie found the frequent exposure to cathedral life both fascinating and moving.

Then there was Borough Market, nestled up against the side of the cathedral, its bustle and colour an unending source of culinary and sensual delight.

When Jack could get up to London for the weekend, they began it with a trip to the market.

She now had a family connection in London as well, Jack's cousin Duncan, and Duncan's partner Gemma and their two boys. With the zeal of the newly wed, Winnie hoped that she might encourage the couple to take the same step. She knew the dangers of meddling, of course, but she also knew that sometimes a sympathetic ear and a bit of a gentle nudge were all it took to set things in motion.

And then there were her parishioners, some of whom she was beginning to know and like. One in particular was her neighbour, Frances Liu, a woman near her own age who had been stricken a few years ago by the mysterious and debilitating Guillain-Barré syndrome. As Franny remained partially paralyzed and housebound, Winnie had quickly got into the habit of stopping in after work as often as she could, and she took the sacraments to her on Sundays.

On the latter occasions Winnie felt the disapproval of Franny's housemate Elaine, but she hadn't discovered whether the woman's hostility was personal or ideological. Nor had she quite worked out the exact nature of the relationship between the two women, but she sensed that Elaine perceived her as a threat and knew she must tread carefully. Winnie had no wish to make Franny's life any more difficult. Perhaps if she could learn more about Elaine, she could draw her out – and then there was the fact that Elaine was a striking woman, and Winnie's curiosity was naturally piqued.

Resolving to make more of an effort next time she saw them Winnie finished her sandwich and began tidying up. She'd just dried her plate and cup when the rectory phone rang.

'I was just thinking of you,' she said when she heard Franny Liu's voice. 'I thought I'd pop by after work—'

'Winnie, can you come now?' Franny's words were hurried, breathy.

Winnie frowned in concern. 'Are you all right?'

'I . . . It's Elaine. She wasn't here this morning, and when I called the hospital, they said she hadn't turned up for work.'

'You mean she wasn't in the house at all?' Winnie asked, puzzled. 'Perhaps she went for a walk—'

'At dawn, in this foul weather, when she never goes walking? Why would she do that?' Franny's voice rose. 'And even if she had, why not come home or go to work?'

She could have felt ill, Winnie thought, but doubted the suggestion would dampen her friend's growing panic. 'Did she leave a note?' she asked instead.

'Not that I can find,' Franny said tightly, and Winnie imagined her frustration, her search limited by the range of her wheelchair. Nor would Franny have been able to check upstairs, she realized, thinking of a young woman in her home parish who had died suddenly of an aneurysm. What if Elaine, upstairs, alone, had fallen ill and been unable to call for help?

'Look, I'll be right over.' She gathered up her bag and jacket, forcing a lightness she didn't feel into her tone. 'But I imagine she's just decided to play truant for a day. Everyone deserves to play truant once in a while, even Elaine.'

'No,' said Franny, refusing to be placated, her voice level now. 'Something dreadful's happened to her. I know it.'

The rain began as they crossed Waterloo Bridge. Kincaid had been glad to let Cullen drive, and now could look out at the Thames with the pleasure he always felt when crossing the river. He glanced upstream, at grey water melding into grey sky, then downstream, towards Blackfriars Bridge obscured by the curtain of rain. Beyond the bridge lay Tate Modern, the Millennium Bridge, the Globe, all part of trendy new Bankside, which so recently had been crumbling dockside. The transformation had been due, in part, to the vision of men like Marcus Yarwood.

Cullen, who had been quickly briefed, seemed to pick up Kincaid's thoughts. 'Have you ever met Yarwood?'

'No, just seen him on the telly.' Yarwood was not easily forgotten – stocky and balding, with a face mashed flat like a bulldog's, his speech and manner as blunt as his looks. In spite of his ingrained scepticism of all politicians, Kincaid had found himself both impressed and intrigued by the man.

'Why all the fuss about him making a bob or two on a property venture?' asked Cullen, deftly negotiating the turn from Waterloo Road into Stamford Street.

Kincaid thought about it for a moment. 'It's not that he's ever taken an anti-development position, but he's supported projects that benefit the community as a whole—'

'And bringing in yuppie flat owners with money to spend doesn't?' Cullen asked with evident sarcasm.

'Yes, the new residents patronize restaurants and shops,' Kincaid said, finding himself in the role of advocate. 'But what happens to the lower-income locals displaced by the renovation? They can't afford alternative housing in the area, and it's these people who are the backbone of Yarwood's constituency.' Yarwood had come from just such a working-class Southwark family, with roots in the neighbourhood that went back generations.

'Well, I'd be happy enough to contribute to the economy by buying one of his flats, if I could afford it.' There was an edge of bitterness in Cullen's voice. Kincaid knew how much his sergeant disliked his dreary Euston flat, and he suspected that Cullen's girlfriend, the well-off and well-connected Stella Fairchild-Priestly, had friends with flats in the Borough or Bankside.

'How *is* Stella, by the way?' Kincaid asked.

Cullen glanced at him as if surprised by his apparent non sequitur, but answered readily enough. 'Bloody insufferable. She's been promoted.'

Kincaid knew that Stella, a buyer for an up-market

home-furnishings shop, would only be content with Cullen's choice of job if he were suddenly and miraculously promoted to chief constable, and he suspected that her impatience would only increase as her career advanced. 'Bully for her,' he told Cullen, keeping his reservations to himself. 'We'll have to have you over sometime soon, to celebrate,' he added cheerfully, knowing Gemma would view the prospect with as much enthusiasm as root canal work. Although Gemma got on well with Cullen, her few encounters with Stella had not been successful.

The traffic began to back up as they reached Blackfriars Road, slowing to a crawl as they eased into Southwark Street. 'Looks like they've still got things partially blocked off,' said Cullen.

Ahead, Kincaid could just make out the red bulk of the fire appliances and the blue flash of lights on the Met patrol cars. A brigade utility lorry was pulled up behind the fire engine. 'There's no bloody place to put the car,' Cullen grumbled.

'Then you'll have to make one, won't you, Dougie?'

Cullen flashed Kincaid a grin and pulled the Astra up, half on the double yellows and half on the pavement. As a uniformed constable trotted over to wave them away, Cullen held his ID up to the window.

Kincaid saw with relief that the rain had eased to a drizzle and he abandoned his umbrella, merely turning up the collar of his mac as he climbed from the car.

With his first breath, the smell hit him in a tangible wave, the bitterness of charred wood mingling with the darkness of wet ash in the back of his mouth. Looking up to the right, he saw what remained of Marcus Yarwood's Victorian warehouse. He recognized the building immediately, having noticed it when passing by because of its particularly attractive architecture.

Its four storeys were a solid grey-brown brick relieved by the graceful arches of large windows. The square edges of its corners were softened by gentle curves, its dark facade lightened by touches of cream brick round windows and roof.

Now the roof sagged and the front door hung crookedly from its hinges. The shattered windows glared like blind eyes, those on the front of the building ringed by the black stain of smoke. A firefighter in helmet and tunic raked through the broken glass and smouldering debris littering the pavement. Hoses still snaked inside from the brigade engine, along with cables from the utility lorry.

The building and the surrounding area had been cordoned off with crime scene tape. Pedestrians milled outside the barrier, a few sporting the telltale notebooks and cameras of the press. A sole television van remained, waiting, Kincaid assumed, for the removal of the body and a statement from the police.

Well, they could wait a bit longer, but he'd have to deal with them eventually. Speaking to the media was a necessary part of a senior police officer's job, but he didn't particularly enjoy it. Giving a brief thought to the tie he'd put on that morning, a loud Liberty print Gemma's mum had given him the previous Christmas, he shrugged and smiled to himself. Maybe he'd set a police fashion trend.

As they neared the warehouse entrance, Kincaid saw a uniformed fireman with an Alsatian dog. Beside him stood a tall man wearing a firefighter's tunic over civilian clothes and a woman in a suit and tan wool coat. The tall man Kincaid pegged as a member of the Fire Investigation Team, and there was something in the woman's bearing that marked her unmistakably as CID. There was a tension in their postures, as if they'd been arguing.

'You'll be Scotland Yard, I expect,' said the tall man, turning towards Kincaid and Cullen with an air of relief.

Kincaid introduced himself. 'And you're . . .'

'Fire Investigation Officer Farrell, South-East FIT,' the man acknowledged. He was balding and bearded, with a lined, intelligent face and eyes that seemed narrowed in a permanent squint, as if he'd spent too many hours poring over minute fragments of evidence. 'I was just telling Inspector Bell here that we'd wait until you arrived to view the scene – the less disturbance inside, the better. My team and the Home Office pathologist should be here any moment.'

The woman nodded at them but kept her hands firmly in her coat pockets. 'Maura Bell, Southwark CID.' Her voice held a trace of Glasgow Scots. She was dark-haired, thirtyish, with a thin, sharp-boned face and a less than welcoming expression. 'I've been asked to help you coordinate the local area investigation. We'll set up an incident base for you at the station.'

Bell might have been asked to assist, Kincaid thought, but that didn't necessarily make her happy about having Scotland Yard on her patch. He'd have to tread carefully if he wanted more than minimal cooperation from her. She must have guessed why they'd been called in, even if she hadn't been told outright – Southwark CID would have been responsible for informing Yarwood of the damage to his building.

Farrell turned to the uniformed firefighter. 'This is Sub Officer Jake Martinelli, and Scully.'

'That's a name to live up to,' Kincaid acknowledged, admiring the dog. She was black and tan, with dark comma-shaped patches above her eyes that gave her a quizzical expression. 'Search and rescue or explosives?' The Alsatian sniffed his proffered fingers, then went back to gazing expectantly at her handler.

Martinelli gave Kincaid a friendly grin. 'Neither. Scully's an accelerant detection dog. Her nose is a hundred times more sensitive than the mechanized hydrocarbon sniffers—'

'Don't let him start,' broke in Farrell. 'He'll bend your ear till it's blue. Not that Scully isn't a good advertisement, but as I was just saying to Inspector Bell, we can't take her in until the scene has cooled down sufficiently.' The dog whined and moved restively, as if aware her name had been mentioned, and Martinelli stroked her head.

'Easy, girl,' he said to her, then added, 'She knows what she's here to do, and she's eager to get started.'

'Do you have reason to suspect arson at this point?' Kincaid asked.

'There's always a possibility of arson with a fire, but no one's reported a man running from the scene with a can of petrol.' Farrell grinned. 'We should be so lucky.'

In Kincaid's experience, fire investigation officers tended to be a cautious species, refusing to commit themselves to anything less obvious than whether or not the sun was shining until they had irrefutable evidence, and sometimes not even then. At least this one appeared to have a sense of humour. 'What *do* you have so far?' Kincaid asked without great expectation.

'The alarm came in at twelve thirty-six,' Farrell began deliberately, ignoring the impatience radiating from the angular Inspector Bell as well as the drizzle, which was steadily growing heavier again. It occurred to Kincaid that perhaps Inspector Bell's temper was not improved by being wet.

Nor was his, and he was beginning to sympathize with Cullen's craving for hot coffee.

'Called in by someone next door, a resident in one of the flats who looked out the window and saw flames,' Farrell went on, nodding towards the adjacent building, of similar but less elaborate architecture. Together, the two structures had formed a bastion of grace among an array of concrete shopfronts.

'Could it have been the arsonist?' Kincaid asked, knowing that sometimes fire-raisers called in their own fires.

'Not likely. According to Control it was a woman, and there were small children audible in the background.'

'No sign of anyone hanging about when the brigade arrived?'

'No, and the response time was under three minutes. The appliances came from Southwark Fire Station, just up the road. The station officer believed the fire had been in progress ten to fifteen minutes when they arrived. It was well established on the ground floor and beginning to take hold on the upper floors.'

'The door wasn't locked.' The soft voice came from behind Kincaid and he turned, startled. A young woman stood there, dressed in jeans and anorak. Her corn-fair hair was tied back in a ponytail and she looked tired, her eyes red-rimmed. 'I'm Leading Firefighter Kearney,' she explained, seeing their expressions. 'My partner and I were first on the scene, BA crew.'

Farrell seemed to assess her dishevelled appearance. 'You're just off your watch, then?'

'Yes, sir. Thought I'd make sure the relief had it all under control.' Kearney smiled but shifted on her feet as if she felt a bit awkward under their scrutiny. 'And I thought, if you had any questions, I'd save you waiting until the watch came back on duty tonight.'

'You're interested in fire investigation?' Farrell asked with a trace of amusement.

'Yes, sir.' The girl met his gaze squarely, her chin up. Although her face was scrubbed pink, her bare neck still bore traces of soot, and the contrast struck Kincaid as rather endearing. Both Cullen and Martinelli were eyeing her with obvious interest, but she didn't seem to notice.

'Were there persons reported when you went in?' Farrell asked.

'No, sir. We were just doing a routine search, trying to lay a guideline for the hose. But it got really hot, and when Simms and I started to evacuate, I crawled into . . . it.' She made a faint grimace. 'We could see there was no point in rescue.'

'Any smell of petrol before you went in?' Martinelli asked.

Kearney frowned, then shook her head. 'Not that I remember. And then afterwards I had my mask on . . .'

'You said you found the door wasn't locked,' Kincaid said. 'Is there more than one entrance?'

'There's a side door,' Farrell told him, gesturing towards the narrow street on their right. 'It was open when we got here as well. There's no sign of damage to it, and none of the crew reported forcing entry.'

'So someone with legitimate access opened the doors?'

'Too soon to say,' Farrell cautioned.

'The builders might have left them unlocked accidentally,' offered Cullen.

'One, maybe, but both?' Farrell shook his head. 'I suppose it's possible, but not all that likely, in my opinion. Which takes us back to an illegitimate entry, but if that's the case, we've not turned up anything noteworthy on the preliminary outside search.'

The station officer came up and spoke to Farrell. 'The SOCOs have finished their preliminary examination, guv, and the structure seems stable. I think it's cool enough for the dog, if she wears her booties.' He gave the dog a friendly pat, but she ignored him, all her attention focused on the building. When Martinelli pulled a set of paw protectors from his tunic pocket, she began to dance and strain at her lead.

'All right, girl, all right,' he soothed, kneeling to slip the rubber boots over her paws.

'Let me get my kit from the van, will you?' Farrell said, adding, 'It's Rose, is it? Since you're here, Rose, you can go through the scene with us, tell us if anything strikes you.'

Farrell strode to the brigade van, returning with a bulky evidence collection bag and a notebook. 'Right, then, let's have a look.'

They queued up behind Farrell single file – Indian file, Kincaid would have said as a child, and he felt a flicker of regret for a politically correct age in which his children would never be encouraged to play cowboys and Indians, or soldiers. He had done both, and had still grown up relatively civilized.

But any pleasant thoughts of childhood were quickly banished as he stepped through the warehouse doorway behind Farrell and Rose Kearney. If the smell had been bad outside, in here it was choking, a physical substance that permeated skin, hair, clothing, sinuses. As he blinked his watering eyes, he detected another odour beneath the pervasive char, the faint, oily sweetness of roasted flesh.

Water from the firefighters' attack had pooled on the warehouse floor, standing several inches deep in places, and Kincaid made a mental note to be careful where he placed his feet. Swallowing hard against the burning in his throat, he focused his attention on Farrell, who had stopped a few feet into the interior. 'Stay behind me if you can,' Farrell said. 'We don't want to muck things up more than necessary.'

'I'm not sure *muck* is the appropriate word,' Cullen muttered, and Kincaid heard what might have been a snort of agreement from Inspector Bell.

They stood in a large, open area, lit by floodlights powered from generators on the brigade lorry and by what weak daylight filtered in through the intact windows, but the illumination made only a feeble sally against the encroaching blackness. Walls, ceilings, floors, the unidentifiable objects that filled the room – all might have been black holes, absorbing light into a dense and solid darkness.

As his eyes adjusted, Kincaid began to differentiate shapes. To his left, near the windows, a long object resolved itself into a stack of lumber, but Kincaid couldn't tell if it had been new or salvaged from the renovation. Four posts, equidistant from the room's centre, rose floor to ceiling, and he assumed they were the structural supports left behind when interior walls had been removed.

The charring on the posts seemed fairly shallow, but he still gave an anxious glance at the ceiling.

Then, to the left of the posts, he saw a large, lumpy pile of objects, an obscene parody of furniture. Blackened coils and springs protruded from the mass at odd angles, like a bizarre modernist sculpture.

Martinelli moved away from the group, murmuring words of encouragement to the dog as he began a careful circuit of the area's perimeter.

'Tell us what you saw,' Farrell said to Rose Kearney.

'We *couldn't* see. Not more than a foot or two. The smoke was low, and black.' She turned slowly in a circle, examining the space. 'We must have come straight in, but after a few yards there was nothing but the line to anchor us. We didn't know there weren't any walls, so when I bumped into that' – she gestured towards the furniture – 'I thought I'd hit a wall or some sort of room divider. Then I realized it felt soft, but it still didn't make sense for a few seconds – you don't expect furniture to tower over your head.'

At the invitation of a mate in the fire service, Kincaid had once suited up and gone into a burn house on a training exercise. The memory of the searing heat and complete disorientation still made him shudder, but the experience had given him tremendous respect for anyone who could face such a situation on a daily basis.

'Where was it burning hottest?' Farrell asked. 'Could you tell?'

'The fire was everywhere – it must have been close to flashover. But' – Kearney frowned, nodding towards the furniture – 'I'd say it was most intense there.'

Turning to his little group of followers, Farrell said, 'The first thing we do in a fire investigation is identify the point of origin. Look.' He pointed at the floor surrounding the furniture. 'See, the char is deepest here, as if it burned the longest. And there' – he nodded at the rear wall, a few feet behind the piled furniture – 'see the V pattern?'

Kincaid found that he could make it out, now that his attention had been directed to it – a faint lightening of the soot in a pattern wider at the top than at the bottom.

'Fire tends to travel upward and outward, and to burn longer and more intensely near the point of origin. The expanding gases typically leave such a pattern, but there are other indicators, of course.'

'You're telling us that the fire started in the furniture?' said Inspector Bell, sounding interested in spite of herself. She edged forward so that she stood in front of Kincaid.

'That would be my guess, but that doesn't tell us whether the cause of ignition was deliberate or accidental.'

'But surely if it started in the furniture, it must have been arson,' Bell insisted.

'Not necessarily. First off, until we interview the job foreman, we don't know whether the furniture was stacked up by the builders or by an unknown party.' Farrell ticked one forefinger against the other, striking off an imaginary list. 'Then, even if the builders left the furniture this way, that still doesn't tell us if the fire was started by accident or design. The foam in these cushions and mattresses is highly flammable. One of the workmen could have dropped a cigarette, left it to smoulder. Or there might have been a spark from the wiring they've torn loose.' He pointed to a flex hanging from the ceiling, shrugged, then called out to Martinelli, 'Any hits yet?'

'No. She's not picking up anything definite,' Martinelli answered. 'She's feeling a bit frustrated,' he added as the dog whined and nosed at his tunic pocket.

'If the dog doesn't find an accelerant, can you rule out arson?' asked Cullen.

'Oh, no.' Farrell sounded almost gleeful. 'The accelerant could have burned off completely, or the fire could have been started without an accelerant. Amateur fire-raisers love to splash the petrol around, but often more practised arsonists prefer to start a fire using only what's available at a scene. More of a challenge that way, I should think.'

Kincaid was beginning to sympathize with the dog's frustration and Inspector Bell's impatience. 'Well, we do have one without-a-doubt fact here. Someone died, whether it was before, during or after the fire. What do you say we have a look at the body?'

'There.' Rose Kearney stepped forward gingerly. 'We must have gone past the furniture, then turned slightly to the right.'

Kincaid followed her, and as they edged into the gap between the furniture and the rear wall, he saw it.

The remains were identifiably human, at least. The body lay on its back, arms and legs drawn up in the pugilistic pose caused by muscular contraction, the skin blackened, the teeth showing in a grotesque parody of a smile. The few remaining tufts of hair were charred, and there were no traces of clothing.

Although the tissue damage was extensive, the breasts were still recognizable, and that somehow made it worse. Kincaid swallowed against the sudden rise of bile in his throat.

Rose Kearney's hand had flown to her mouth, but as Kincaid glanced at her she forced it back to her side.

'Bloody hell,' Cullen mumbled, looking a bit green, and even Inspector Bell seemed momentarily to have lost her composure.

When a light female voice spoke from the warehouse doorway they all spun round as if they'd been caught at something unspeakable.

'I take it I've the right address?' said the white-suited figure, and with a flash of pleasure Kincaid recognized Kate Ling, his favourite Home Office pathologist. Now they might get some answers.

Tony Novak pulled things from the bureau drawers and threw them into the open suitcase on his bed, the largest he'd been able to find. Laura would have criticized his untidiness, but then Laura would not only have packed neatly, she would have made a list of essentials for the journey and ticked it off as she stowed each item.

And, of course, Laura would have criticized his impulsiveness, but there were times when impulsiveness could be a virtue. And, he reminded himself, it no longer mattered what Laura thought.

They had been polar opposites from the beginning

of their relationship, first attracted by their differences, then, as time went on, just as fiercely repelled. If she'd teased him at first, saying he'd bluffed his way through medical school, he'd thought there was some part of her that had admired his recklessness. Later, she had seen that quality only as a character defect to be mended.

What she had never understood was that his failings were also his strengths, interwoven with an intuitive understanding and an ability to make quick decisions, and it was these qualities that had made him a success at emergency medicine.

When they'd closed down Accident and Emergency at Guy's his loyalty to the hospital had kept him on in Out Patients, but days spent dealing with flu and broken fingers, with objects inappropriately placed in body orifices, had quickly soured. He missed the adrenalin rush, the sense of flow that came only in a crisis, when time seemed to telescope in on itself. Glancing up, he caught a glimpse of himself in the bureau mirror, his face lean and tired, with new lines about the mouth.

Work was only a small part of the discontent he'd felt lately – it was nothing compared with the gaping hole left in his life by the absence of his daughter since he and Laura had separated. He looked down at the suitcase, at the few things Harriet had accumulated during her weekends in his dreary rented flat on Borough High Street, and felt the familiar despair.

For a moment his courage failed him. But no, he had gone too far, and he knew Laura too well. He knew about her increasing involvement with the women's shelter, and he knew that the agency made it possible for women to disappear with their children. And he'd known, when she'd threatened him on Sunday, what it was she meant to do.

Well, she'd lost her chance, he thought, his resolve returning. Hadn't it occurred to her that two could play at that game, and that he had the advantage? There was no place easier to vanish into with a child than Eastern Europe, and he had family in the Czech Republic who would help him. A change of name, a new set of papers, a job in a backwater town where doctors were desperately needed, all easily accomplished. He and Harriet would start a new life together, and nothing would separate them again.

The hospital would be in a bind for a bit, no doubt, losing him without notice, but there were other doctors who could bandage cuts and prescribe antibiotics.

It was Harriet that mattered, and he had Harriet safely tucked away – he hadn't dared wait until later in the day to pick her up. Once he'd set things in motion, he'd been driven by a mounting sense of urgency. Now, all that remained was a trip to the bank, and Harriet's passport. The passport meant he had to get into Laura's flat, and he had to do it when he could guarantee no one would be at home.

Nor could he take Harriet with him, as he hadn't yet told her what he meant to do, so he'd been forced to call on the one person he felt he could trust to take Harriet for a few hours. He'd arranged to meet them at London Bridge Station at noon, and then he'd tell

Harriet he had a surprise planned for her, an adventure. The truth could wait until they were across the Channel, away from England and all the misery of the past months. He would tell her when he felt the time was right, and he smiled at the thought that from now on, as far as his daughter was concerned, only his decisions mattered.

Chapter Three

... trifles make the sum of life.
Charles Dickens
David Copperfield

'Well, we're not likely to get an accurate temperature on this one, are we?' Kate Ling said drily. She squatted beside the body, balancing on the balls of her feet with an ease that made Kincaid envy her thigh muscles. With anyone else the position would have looked awkward, but the Home Office pathologist even managed to carry off her white crime-scene overalls with grace.

Kincaid had worked with Kate Ling on a number of cases, and found her not only good at her job but genuinely interested in helping the police with their investigations, a trait not every pathologist exhibited. Some of them seemed to become almost territorial about the bodies in their possession, behaving as if it were a point of pride to reveal as little information as possible.

Kate pulled on her thin latex gloves. 'Anything to go on here? Witnesses? Missing person connected with the scene?' She probed the corpse gently with a gloved finger.

'Nothing so far,' Kincaid told her, with a glance at Farrell for confirmation.

'And no identifiers?'

'Nothing obvious.' Farrell squatted beside her, his notebook open. 'Unless there's something under the body. We'll do a grid sift, of course, once you're finished here.'

'Odd.' A tiny crease puckered Kate's forehead. 'I've seen clothing literally fused to the skin, but the condition of the body doesn't indicate that sort of heat. Nor is there any jewellery that I can see. This woman may have been stripped before the fire.' She lifted what remained of the victim's left hand, and Kincaid heard a stifled protest from someone in the group. 'Some trace of a wedding ring usually survives a fire, even if the digits are completely destroyed.'

'Any guess as to the victim's age?' Kincaid asked.

'Hard to say without X-rays and measurements. She seems on the slight side, but the heat can cause shrinkage as well.'

'Race?'

'The lab analysis will tell us, and I'd rather not speculate in the meantime.'

'A homeless person would explain the lack of jewellery,' Cullen suggested. 'Someone sheltering from the rain, maybe starting a little fire to keep warm, not realizing the furniture was highly flammable.'

'When have you seen a rough sleeper without a bin liner or a shopping trolley full of possessions?'

Inspector Bell said dismissively. 'And surely someone would have noticed a naked person wandering the streets?'

'You've a better suggestion?' retorted Cullen.

'Any lividity visible?' Kincaid asked, heading off an altercation. He wondered if she was as sharp with her own officers – it was not the best technique for fostering confidence in the ranks.

Kate lifted one side of the torso gently. There was a distinct lack of charring on the floorboards beneath the body, but the underside of the corpse still looked dark to Kincaid. 'There might be some bruising, yes, but I'll have to get into the tissue to be sure. And there is something else,' Kate added, lowering the torso and edging her fingertips beneath the head. 'It feels like there may be quite a severe fracture to the back of the skull, but there's no way to tell whether it's post-mortem or ante-mortem until I can have a look in the lab. The heat alone can cause shattering of the skull.'

Kincaid knew that even if the pathologist could verify that the trauma had occurred prior to death, that wouldn't rule out an accidental injury. His gut instinct, however, told him that this death had not occurred by chance.

With that knowledge came the realization that his likelihood of spending the weekend with Gemma and the boys was rapidly evaporating. They had planned a Saturday morning excursion to Portobello Market, weather permitting, with a particular mission in mind.

Having shared a bedroom with five-year-old Toby since they'd moved to the Notting Hill house, Kit had asked if he could move into the third bedroom, the room they had meant for the nursery. When Kincaid had started to object, Gemma had stopped him, saying, 'That's fine, Kit. We'll do it up for you.'

'Gemma, are you sure—' Kincaid had begun, but Gemma had stopped him with a shake of her head. 'No, it's all right. Kit needs his own space.'

That was true, Kincaid had to admit. Since Kit had turned thirteen at the end of June, he'd been finding it increasingly difficult to share with Toby, and now, with the beginning of the new school term, it was becoming clear that he would need a more private space for his school work.

Gemma had immediately thrown herself into planning and decorating the room, but to Kincaid her enthusiasm seemed brittle. It had been almost a year since her miscarriage, and on the one occasion he'd gingerly brought up the idea of trying again, she'd looked away and changed the subject. It was still too soon, he'd told himself, but now he wondered if her willingness to give up the nursery to Kit meant she'd rejected the idea altogether. The thought struck him with a fierce and unexpected sense of loss.

'I think that's all I can do here,' said Kate Ling, drawing Kincaid back to his surroundings. 'Let's bag and tag, and I'll get to the post-mortem as soon as I can.'

Kincaid chided himself for letting his attention wander, and as he gazed at the charred remains of the body he felt a twinge of guilt for his aggravation over the change in his plans, surely a trivial thing when a human life had been so brutally snuffed out.

'Can you rule out self-immolation?' Doug Cullen asked as Ling stood and stripped off her gloves.

Farrell answered, 'Again, it seems unlikely unless we turn up some trace of clothing or a positive on accelerant. Let's give the electronic sniffer a try,' he added, removing the bulky hydrocarbon detector from his evidence collection bag and taking Ling's place beside the body. After running the collection nozzle over the remains and the surrounding charred area, he shook his head. 'I'm not getting a reading.'

He motioned to Martinelli, who had almost completed his outer circuit of the room. 'Jake, try over here, will you?'

The others edged out of the way as Martinelli brought the dog over, giving the team room to work.

Kincaid found himself standing beside Rose Kearney. The young woman stood with her hands shoved firmly in the pockets of her anorak, her shoulders hunched. 'Is this your first body?' he asked quietly.

When she glanced at him in surprise, he saw that her eyes were a clear cornflower blue. 'How did you know?'

He shrugged. 'I'm not sure. I've seen a lot of coppers at their first crime scene.'

She seemed to consider this for a moment, then she looked back at the group surrounding the victim and said thoughtfully, 'I've pulled people from buildings who I knew weren't going to make it, tried to revive them. And I've worked my share of fatal road accidents. But this is different, somehow. Maybe it's not having a job to do. In a fire or a rescue, you only have time to think about what you're going to do next.'

'It must have been bad in here.' As Kincaid looked round the ruined space, he realized that water was seeping into his shoes.

'The worst I've seen,' Rose agreed. 'I didn't realize how fast you could lose it, you know? One minute you're on top of it, you're in charge, then the next it all goes to hell.'

'Do you want to go back?' he asked, studying her, his curiosity roused by her candour.

An unexpected smile lit her face. 'Oh, yeah. Absolutely. There's nothing like it.'

'No joy,' Martinelli called out, patting the dog who looked as if she took her failure personally. 'If anything was used here, it's burned up. We'll keep looking, but if there's nothing at the seat of the fire, I'm not hopeful.'

The station officer appeared in the doorway and signalled to Farrell. 'The mortuary van's here, Chief.'

'About time.' Farrell turned to the others. 'Let's get out, let them get on with it. Try to keep to the same track you used coming in.'

Kincaid felt an unanticipated shudder of relief as they stepped out onto the pavement again. He realized he'd been tensing his shoulders as if personally preventing the ceiling from collapsing.

As the mortuary attendants and the white-suited

crime scene specialists conferred with Farrell, he decided he'd grab the opportunity to ring Gemma. It was still raining, a steady and relentless drizzle. Ducking across the street, he sheltered in the doorway of an office building and dialled Gemma's mobile number.

He'd been half expecting her voicemail, but she answered herself, a lift of pleasure in her voice. 'I wasn't expecting to hear from you until later today. Don't tell me; you're off early.' Her tone was half teasing, half hopeful, and he hated having to puncture her mood.

'No. Sorry, love. Something's come up. A special request from the guvnor. It's a fire in Southwark, with a possible homicide. I'll fill you in on the details later.'

There was a moment's hesitation before she said, 'You'll be tied up for the weekend, at least. Kit will be disappointed about tomorrow.'

'Go to the market without me. It's better than postponing.'

'And tonight?'

It was only then that he remembered they'd had plans to take Gemma's friend Erika out for a meal. 'Oh, bugger. You'd better cancel, at least on my part.' Erika Rosenthal was an older woman of whom Gemma had become quite fond, and Kincaid had been promising to meet her for months. 'Maybe we can reschedule for next weekend.'

'Right. Look, I've got to dash,' Gemma said a bit abruptly. 'Ring me when you can.'

*

Winnie pushed the bell at the Ufford Street house, then let herself in when she heard Franny's voice, knowing it was hard for the invalid to get to the front door in her wheelchair.

She stepped directly into the sitting room, marvelling, as she always did when she came here, that a woman of Chinese descent would choose to create a room that was more English than the English. Shelves on the pale green walls held pottery jugs filled with dried flowers, 1930s green glassware, clocks and hand-painted china; the open spaces between the shelves were filled with cottage watercolours, crewelwork still lifes and, in the place of honour above the mantel, a large print of a contemplative black and white cat among pots of flowers.

The furniture was pine, the squashy settee chintz, and in the back of the room, strategically placed for the view into the tiny garden, was a green velvet chaise longue.

Beside the chaise, the small Asian woman sat in her wheelchair, and if her cotton print dress and beaded cardigan seemed coordinated with the room, the metal frame of the chair provided a harsh contrast. Her delicate hands were twisted in the cashmere shawl on her lap, the smooth oval of her face etched with worry.

'Thanks for coming,' Franny said, her voice quavering as Winnie came across and clasped her cold hands. 'I didn't know who else to call.'

'Let's start with some tea, shall we?' said Winnie. 'You can tell me everything, then we'll see what's to be done.' She went into the kitchen at the rear of the house. Toaster and kettle, along with the necessities for both, were arranged on a low table in front of the window. Although Franny had had a small bathroom with roll-in shower built off the scullery, she'd told Winnie she refused to have the cabinets and worktops refitted to wheelchair height. Nor had she put in a wheelchair lift for the stairs. To her, both those things had seemed like admissions of defeat.

Franny was determined to walk again, and while Winnie had learned that people often did make at least a partial recovery from Guillain-Barré syndrome, she knew it could be a slow and laborious process.

'Is there anything you need doing?' she called out as she put the kettle on to boil.

'No. I can manage the basics pretty well on my own,' Franny answered from the sitting room, her voice steadier. 'It's just the getting out that's difficult.'

As she gathered the tea things, Winnie looked round for anything odd or out of place in the small kitchen, but everything seemed the same as on her previous visits. Carrying the steaming mugs back into the sitting room, she pulled a worn wooden chair up to Franny's and sat down.

'Let's go back a bit,' she said. 'Was Elaine at home last night?'

'Yes. Although she was a bit late getting in from work, but she's been late several times a week the past few months, and I didn't think anything of it.'

'Was there anything else unusual? Did she seem upset or worried?'

Franny wrapped her hands round the mug and frowned into its depths. 'No, no, not really. She made us scrambled eggs on toast for supper, then we watched a bit of telly. She didn't stay down to watch the ten o'clock news with me, but she made my milky drink before she went up.'

'Could she have been feeling unwell?' Winnie asked, remembering her earlier fears.

'Not that she said.' Franny looked up, fear in her dark eyes. 'You don't think . . . Surely I'd know . . .'

'Why don't I start by having a look upstairs.' Forcing a reassuring smile, Winnie found a spot on the mantel for her mug and crossed the room to the stairs, which rose from near the front door. She climbed quickly, trying to ignore the dread tingling at the base of her neck.

There were three doors on the landing. She opened the first door on the right with trepidation, then gave a small sigh of relief. The room, obviously Franny's, with its inlaid mahogany bed covered by a lilac quilt, was tidy and had the slightly musty odour of disuse.

Winnie closed the door softly and tried the next. It was the bathroom, tidy as well. Both the towels on the rack and the soap in the dish on the basin were dry, and cold air poured in through the partially opened window. An escape route? Winnie wondered, but as she pulled the window closed she saw that it was a straight drop down to the small paved patio outside the scullery. Not unless Elaine had grown wings.

That left the third door, the room that faced the front of the house. Winnie knocked softly, then, realizing she was holding her breath, exhaled deliberately and pulled open the door.

The room might have been a monk's cell. The starkness came as an almost physical shock after the cocooning clutter of the rest of the house. A single bed stood against the wall, its worn white quilt reminding Winnie of the one on her parents' bed when she was a child. A pine bedside table held a clock and a small lamp – nothing else. The surface of a matching chest of drawers bore nothing other than a faint layer of dust. Beside the chest a straight-backed chair stood awkwardly, like an uninvited guest. No prints or pictures graced the magnolia walls, and there was no mirror.

The bed looked as if it had been made hastily, a lack of care that seemed oddly in contrast to the rest of the room. Winnie opened the doors to the built-in wardrobe. A few hangers hung empty among the trousers and jackets, but she had no way of knowing whether the bare spaces indicated clothing removed for flight or the ordinary breeding of hangers in cupboards. There were no other signs of packing or of hasty departure.

Winnie left the room and descended the stairs more slowly than she'd gone up, wondering what could possibly have happened to Elaine.

'She's not here,' she said when she reached the sitting room and saw Franny's anxious face. 'And I can't tell whether or not she's taken anything away. Are you sure you didn't hear anything in the night?'

'No.' Frowning, Franny picked at the fringe of the

shawl in her lap. 'I only remembered sensing something wrong as soon as I woke this morning. It's odd – I don't usually sleep quite so soundly. Oh.' She looked up, her eyes widening. 'I dreamed I heard a door close.'

'It must have been Elaine, as it doesn't look as though she went out a window, and she can't have vanished into thin air. Have you any idea what time this was?'

'No. I'm sorry. I'm not usually so groggy.'

'And you said you rang Elaine's work and she hadn't come in? Did they tell you if she'd called?'

'No. Only that she wasn't there. They're not allowed to give out more information than that over the phone.'

'Well, that's the first thing, then,' Winnie said with relief, glad to have a goal. 'I'll go and have a word with them. She works at Guy's?'

'Yes, in Medical Records.'

'What about family? Does Elaine have anyone you could ring?'

Franny shook her head and a strand of her fine dark hair came loose from its clip. 'No. There's no one. Her parents are dead and she hasn't any siblings. That was one of the things that—' She stopped, her eyes filling with tears. 'We were both alone.'

Winnie knelt by Franny's chair and gave her hand a squeeze. 'You're not alone. I'll help any way I can.'

Returning the pressure, Franny forced a smile. 'Thanks. Sorry for being so wet.'

'You're just fine,' Winnie reassured her, then added

hesitantly, 'Franny, if we find that Elaine hasn't been in touch with the hospital, I think we should call the police.'

'No!' Franny jerked her hand free.

'Why ever not?' Winnie asked, startled.

'But . . . surely that's not necessary. If she's just out for a lark or something, she'd be furious.'

'You're afraid that if she's all right, she'll be angry with you? Wouldn't she understand that you were concerned?' Winnie was beginning to feel there was something very odd here.

'Yes, but . . . you have to understand. Elaine's a very private person. She doesn't like . . . I don't think . . . I think we should wait. After all, she did leave of her own accord,' Franny added, but she looked even more worried.

'It does seem that way, but—' Winnie stopped, deciding this was not the time to express her own uneasiness. And hadn't she heard that the police wouldn't allow a person to be reported missing until twenty-four hours had passed? She needed advice, and suddenly she knew exactly whom to call.

'Look,' she said to Franny. 'Don't worry. I've a much better idea.'

There was no point taking her disappointment out on Duncan, Gemma told herself, regretting her hastiness as soon as she'd hung up. She'd sounded a right cow, and it wasn't as if she hadn't had to duck out of family plans herself, especially in the past few months, but somehow that didn't make being on the receiving end any easier.

She knew the investigation that had lately consumed so much of her time and energy had disturbed her equilibrium, but that was no excuse for acting the harpy.

A child had gone missing on her patch, a six-year-old girl, and the current easing of her workload was due not to a resolution, but to the fact that the case had gone cold. Not only was it the first time Gemma had dealt personally with such a case, but as SIO, she felt responsible for her team's failure.

The parents' grief and anger had been particularly hard to bear, and she'd not been able to shake off the case outside working hours, something she knew to be essential if one were to survive the job. Her fears for the missing child seemed to have transferred themselves to Toby and Kit, and she found herself worrying whenever they were out of her sight.

Which was all the more reason to take the boys to Portobello on her own, where she'd have both of them under her nose for the day. She'd promised Kit they'd look for an antique specimen cabinet for his room, and having begun the redecorating project, she didn't dare falter. They'd already framed sets of nineteenth-century botanical and zoological drawings they'd unearthed at one of the market's print stalls; she'd painted the walls a strong aqua, and set up bookcases and a desk complete with microscope and dissecting instruments.

Although Kit had seemed thrilled with the idea of

organizing his new room around his scientific interests, Gemma hadn't neglected a concession to adolescent fashion – she'd covered a portion of one wall with cork squares, ready for his growing collection of music posters.

But in spite of Kit's enthusiastic response to her efforts, she knew that nothing she did could compensate for Duncan's lack of participation. It shouldn't matter, she told herself, slamming her desk drawer and pinching her finger in the process. She swore loudly and shook her injured hand, realizing she'd failed to find the pen she'd been rooting for in the drawer when her phone had rung.

There was a knock on her office door and Melody Talbot, the PC who often assisted her, looked in. 'You all right, boss?'

'Just a little accident with the drawer,' Gemma said, embarrassed by her outburst. 'What's up?' she added, as Melody seemed inclined to linger.

'It's the sergeant's birthday. Some of us were planning to go along to the pub after work, buy him a round or two. Want to come?'

Gemma had worked hard to improve her relationship with Sergeant Talley, who had initially resented her posting. It would certainly be politic to join in the festivities, even if only for a few minutes. Could she juggle things with the children, now that she knew Duncan would be late – if he got home at all? 'I'll try—' she began, when her mobile phone rang again.

Melody gave her a little wave of acknowledgment and slipped out the door.

Assuming it was Duncan ringing her back, Gemma flipped open the phone without checking the ID. 'Look, I'm sorry. I was—'

'Gemma?' The voice was female and puzzled. 'It's Winnie. I've a favour to ask.'

He mingled with the crowd, moving around the fringes, careful to keep his expression neutral, careful not to watch too greedily. He'd left the scene last night before the brigade arrived – staying to watch a burn was a luxury he'd long since learned to deny himself – and had only come back after full daylight, when they'd begun to clear up.

A purposeful air was an essential part of his camouflage. A morning coffee, a bit of shopping, a paper from the newsagent – he'd even brushed deliberately against one of the detectives as the man sheltered in the doorway of an office building, making a phone call.

He'd seen the CID arrive, of course, and smiled to himself as they poked through the debris, looking for clues he hadn't left.

He'd seen the pathologist, too, and had watched the removal of the body bag with mild surprise. The body was a first, a bonus, like the prize in a Christmas cracker after the pop. He felt no remorse, only curiosity and an unexpected spike of excitement. The future might prove more interesting than even he had thought.

Chapter Four

The Borough of Southwark ... consisteth of divers
streets, ways, and winding lanes, all full of buildings.
As a subsidy to the king, this borough yieldeth about
... eight hundred pounds, which is more than any one
city in England payeth, except London.

John Stow
Survey of London, 1598

As she hunched her shoulders against the persistent
drizzle Maura Bell grimaced at the stench coming from
the damp wool of her coat. Even in the relatively fresh
air outside the building the cloth held the rankness of
smoke and a faint scent of corruption. The coat was
new as well, carefully budgeted for and put on for the
first time early that morning. To think she'd been
pleased at the drop in temperature, unusual for September, that had allowed her to wear her purchase
early. Now she'd have to send the coat to the dry-
cleaner as soon as she could change, and God knew if
even that would salvage it.

It amazed her to think that there were those, like
Farrell and Jake Martinelli, who chose to work fire

scenes on a daily basis – but then there were plenty who'd say the same about her choice of profession. Not that there weren't days when she'd agree with them, and this was certainly looking like one of them.

She'd organized the uniformed constables into search teams for the house-to-house – or rather building-to-building – and was now awaiting the arrival of the warehouse's construction foreman, one Joe Spender. In a futile effort to keep out the damp she hitched her collar up and wished it were possible to organize a crime scene while holding a brolly. That was all she needed, to prance about like Mary bloody Poppins when she had Scotland Yard on her patch.

In retrospect, the day had begun well enough. She'd got into the station early, beating the traffic from her flat on the Isle of Dogs. She liked to drive rather than take the train and the tube; the time cocooned in her car allowed her to sort her thoughts, gear up or unwind, and having the car in the Borough gave her the freedom to follow up case leads without depending on the station motor pool.

First on the rota, she'd been pleased to draw a major case, a suspicious fire with a possible homicide, and when a trace on the building's ownership had returned a holding company linked with Marcus Yarwood, she'd felt a shiver of excitement. Sensitive, yes – Yarwood was an important presence in the Borough – but this was the sort of case that could add rocket fuel to a career.

Then her chief superintendent had called her into

his office and told her Marcus Yarwood had requested that the Yard be brought in, and she'd been fuming with resentment ever since. Power and influence, that was what it was all about, and if she'd thought the job was proof against that sort of corruption, she'd been a fool.

And what had high-and-mighty Scotland Yard accomplished so far? They'd slouched through the crime scene; the superintendent had nipped off to make a phone call, and the sergeant was chatting up one of the female SOCOs. Even had she been disposed to feel charitable towards the Scotland Yard superintendent sent to pour oil on the waters, his casual demeanour would have raised her hackles. You'd have thought he was out for a walk in the park for all the urgency in his manner, and he was too good-looking by half. Maura distrusted handsome men in general, and found the combination of looks and rank particularly threatening.

The sergeant, now, he wasn't so bad, although a bit rabbity with his fair English colouring and his Harry Potter glasses. Not her type, of course; she liked her men big and brawny, but he seemed friendly enough and not too full of himself.

She fished in the pockets of her coat for the cigarettes she'd been trying to give up. Might as well be hung for a sheep as a lamb, she thought with a grimace. Surely no one could complain that her hair and clothes smelled of cigarette smoke, not after her exposure to the fire reek. Not, she reminded herself, that there was anyone likely to complain.

'Inspector Bell.' It was the sergeant, Cullen, followed by an enormous man in a flat cap and yellow safety jacket. 'This is Joe Spender, the job foreman.'

'Mr Spender.' Maura hastily stuffed the unlit cigarette back in her pocket and forced herself not to step back as Spender loomed over her. He must have been all of six foot five, with a belly that hung over his belt, and the florid complexion indicative of high blood pressure. 'What can you tell us?'

He was shaking his head even as she spoke, his eyes flicking towards the ruin of the warehouse. 'I can't believe it. Couldn't believe it when Mr Yarwood rang me this morning.' His accent was East End, comfortable. 'Yesterday, when we finished up, everything was shipshape.'

Kincaid, the Scotland Yard man, had finished his phone call and come across to the group, but he stood a few feet back, listening.

'You didn't leave anyone behind in the building?' asked Maura.

'No. But that's the first thing I thought when I heard. What if one of my blokes forgot his lunch box or something and went back? But I checked right off, and all my crew are accounted for. Crazy idea, anyway, as I'm the only one with a key.'

'And you locked the premises before you left?'

'Course I did,' Spender said vehemently, but Maura thought she saw a bit of the colour leach from his flushed face. 'I always lock up, side door and then the front. Yesterday was no different.'

'Anyone else have access to your key?' asked the

superintendent. When Spender gave him a startled glance, he introduced himself. 'Scotland Yard. I'm Superintendent Kincaid.'

Spender glanced at his warrant card, shaking Kincaid's hand a little more enthusiastically than he had Maura's. 'Not unless you count my wife and my two girls at home in Poplar. They're eight and six, by the way, my girls.'

'What about the furniture?' Maura put in quickly, determined not to lose control of the interview. The man would be pulling out wallet photos of his kiddies if she wasn't careful. 'Where did it come from?'

Spender turned back to the building. 'Cheap furnished flats, that's how the place was being used when Mr Yarwood bought it. Not much better than squats. He had a time getting the last of the tenants out, had to cut the power and water, but then we were able to get in.

'We started on the ground floor, pulling out walls to make the restaurant space. Then we moved all the furniture from the flats downstairs, ready for the skips. Should have come yesterday, the skips, but there was a delay.'

'Restaurant space?' Kincaid asked, frowning.

'Luxury flats upstairs, restaurant downstairs. A celebrity chef, you know, like what's his name, the cheeky chappy. But now . . .' Spender sighed, shrugged. 'Who knows how long it will take to get this sorted, if at all.'

'Problem with the insurance?' Kincaid commented easily, as if it was to be expected, but Spender's reply was wary.

'Not that I know of. It's just these things take time. You know how it is.'

Kincaid gazed at the building, hands in the pockets of his Burberry. 'Word has it the leases haven't sold as fast as Mr Yarwood had hoped.'

'It's too soon to say that.' Spender's voice held the first trace of irritation. 'There's no doubt they'd have sold, a place this close to the South Bank and London Bridge Station.'

'Let's get back to the furniture, shall we?' said Maura, grinding her teeth. 'How did you leave it yesterday?'

'Piled in the middle of the bloody room, wasn't it? To give us as much working space as possible.'

'It didn't occur to you it was a fire danger?'

'What else were we going to do with the stuff? Put it out in the street for a traffic hazard?'

'What about your boys? Any of them smoke?'

'Look, Inspector.' Spender took a breath and seemed to gain another inch or two in height. The friendly aura had vanished. 'None of my lads left a fag end to smoulder and set that furniture alight, if that's what you're thinking. They've more sense than that, and I've told you I checked the building over before I locked up. We left nothing out of place.'

'And you're absolutely positive you locked both doors?' she asked.

'Of course I'm bloody sure. Do you take me for an idiot?'

Maura saw Sergeant Cullen glance at her and thought she read a trace of amusement. 'Mr Spender,' she began tightly, 'we do need your cooperation here—'

'Mr Spender, excuse me,' Kincaid broke in with his easy smile. 'You may be able to account for your key, but surely there's more than one?'

Following Winnie's instructions, Gemma took the tube to Waterloo and walked south along Waterloo Road, passing the hulk of the railway terminal and the grimy brickwork of the lock-ups that abutted it. The rain had let up, but puddles stood on the pavement and the sky was still as solidly grey as gunmetal.

How odd, she mused as she picked up her stride, that she should find herself on the edge of Southwark, when Duncan had only that morning been summoned out to a case in the same borough. And odder still, the call from Winnie Montfort, who was not one to make spur-of-the-moment demands.

Fortunately, Gemma hadn't anything too pressing scheduled for her Friday afternoon, and as her lunch usually consisted of a sandwich brought up from the canteen she didn't feel terribly guilty about taking a longer than usual lunch break. She had, in fact, been feeling rather restless and unsettled, and was glad of an excuse to stretch her legs and breathe in the cool, damp air flowing from the river.

She and Duncan had managed to see Winnie only once since Winnie had come up to London from her Somerset parish, and that had been on one of the weekends when Jack had joined her. Winnie and Jack had come to Notting Hill, duly admiring the house and giving Gemma the opportunity to try out her very unpolished cooking and entertaining skills. Gemma had never had much time to cook and, until now, had certainly never lived anywhere with the space or atmosphere conducive to giving dinner parties.

There had been times that evening, watching the group around her candlelit dining room table, when she'd felt like a child playing at dressing-up. But if she'd felt like an impostor in her own home, she had also, rather to her surprise, enjoyed herself. Not that she was in any danger of turning into Stella Fairchild-Priestly, Cullen's girlfriend, who was the queen of hostesses, but perhaps her social life had begun to evolve past spag bol and a bottle of plonk.

Of course she and Winnie had ended the evening with promises to get together soon, but then work had intervened on her part and she supposed the same had been true for Winnie. It was a shame, she thought now, as she was beginning to realize how desperately she missed having a close female friend since Hazel Cavendish had gone.

Reaching The Cut, she turned left, passing the Old Vic on one side and a council estate on the other. Winnie had suggested they meet for a quick lunch at a pub called the Hope and Anchor, near her church and her temporary accommodation. Then, Winnie had promised, she'd explain why she'd rung.

The Cut, for all its unusual name, was an unremarkable street, lined with small grocer's shops, cafes and tapas bars that had become trendy. Damp squares of betting slips littered the pavement outside a bookie's premises, and Gemma smelled a faint tang of cigarette smoke beneath the traffic fumes.

Just as she spotted the pub's name above an unassuming shop front, she saw Winnie standing outside, watching for her. If Winnie Montfort was not classically beautiful, most people forgot this as soon as she smiled. Her pleasant face radiated honesty and humour, and she had the knack of making those she spoke to feel they had her undivided attention. Today, her soft brown hair curled about her face in the damp, and her clerical collar provided a slash of contrast beneath her cherry-coloured raincoat.

Her face lit with pleasure at Gemma's approach, and she gave her a quick hug. 'Gemma, thanks for coming. They're holding a table for us – I've just checked.'

'Busy place?' Gemma asked as she followed her inside.

'It's gaining quite a reputation as a gastropub,' Winnie told her, grinning. 'Awful term, isn't it? Always makes me think of some unmentionable complaint. But the food *is* good, and it's more or less my local.'

The bar, with simple wooden tables and an upright piano in the corner, took up the right-hand side of the space, while partially drawn velvet curtains marked off the restaurant area to the left. A waiter seated them at a small table near the back of the restaurant and handed them laminated menu cards.

When they'd ordered – cod and greens for Gemma, a chicken and mushroom pie for Winnie – they settled back with their drinks. 'All right, first things first,' said Gemma, spreading a piece of brown, crusty bread with pale butter. 'How's Jack? Is he coming up to town this weekend?'

''Fraid not. The commission in Bristol is keeping him busy. He may not get away again until the job's complete.'

'Can you not go to him?'

'I only have one day off a week – not long enough to go to Glastonbury and back. And even that day is subject to emergencies.'

'Sounds a bit like the police,' Gemma said ruefully. 'Good thing you picked an understanding bloke.'

'It is, isn't it?' agreed Winnie, sipping at the glass of Pinot Grigio she'd ordered with her meal. 'Although sometimes I wonder if I'd feel less guilty about juggling the job and the relationship if he *weren't* so understanding. What about Duncan and the boys? Any news on the Eugenia front?'

'We've a preliminary hearing scheduled next week.' As if their family situation weren't already complicated enough, Kit's maternal grandmother, Eugenia Potts, had applied for custody of him. Kit's mother, Victoria, had been Kincaid's ex-wife. It was only after Vic's murder the previous year that Kincaid had realized her son might be his child, born without his knowledge not long after their separation. Vic's second husband, Ian McClellan, was still Kit's legal guardian, but since he had moved to Canada, he had allowed Kit to live with Duncan and Gemma.

Eugenia, however, appeared to blame Duncan for

her daughter's death, and could not bear the idea of her grandson living happily with his father. And although Kit despised his grandmother, who had treated him badly after his mother's death, he'd not been willing to take the DNA test that would prove Duncan's paternity without a doubt, thus giving Duncan clear legal rights. The boy seemed to be afraid that if the test proved negative he would lose his new family, and Duncan and Gemma's reassurance of their commitment to him, regardless of the test outcome, had not managed to convince him otherwise.

Kit's stubbornness over the testing meant that Duncan and Gemma would be forced to rely on the understanding of the family court judge, and on the hope that the judge would see Kit as old enough to decide where and with whom he wanted to live. It was all very worrying, and since Eugenia had filed her petition the previous May tensions had been running high in their household.

'We had an outing planned to Portobello Market tomorrow to look for some things for Kit,' Gemma told Winnie, and found herself expressing feelings she hadn't been able to articulate to herself. 'I really thought we should all be together, as a family, to reassure Kit that we'll continue to be a family . . . But Duncan can't make it . . .'

'Work?'

Gemma nodded. 'A case came up. Here in Southwark, as a matter of fact.'

'I wouldn't worry about your outing,' said Winnie. 'Kit knows how committed you are, and the last thing he needs now is to feel any sort of divisiveness between you and Duncan.'

'I'm sure you're right,' Gemma admitted. 'It's just nerves. I suppose I hate the idea of being put on show as a model family. What if we don't measure up?'

'You measure up as far as Kit's concerned, and I'm sure that's what counts.' Winnie buttered a slice of bread for herself. 'What about your friend Hazel? I'm sure she'd testify on your behalf.'

'She would, but she's in Scotland.'

'Trying to make a go of her distillery?'

Gemma nodded, fighting back the sudden, mortifying prickle of tears. After the tragic events of the previous spring she'd encouraged Hazel to do what she thought right, even if it meant staying in Scotland, but she hadn't realized what it would mean to lose the supportive presence of her closest friend.

She took a sip from her half pint of cider, concentrating on the feel of the bubbles against her tongue, hoping that her voice wouldn't betray her. 'She and Tim are talking, at least, and they've agreed for the time being not to sell the Islington house.'

'Any hope of a reconciliation?'

Gemma sighed. 'I don't know. It would be hard, after what's happened, for either of them.' Their meals arrived, and Gemma was glad of an excuse to change the subject.

'Now, why don't you tell me why you rang?' she said, picking up her cutlery as a cloud of steam rose from the perfectly arranged food on her plate. 'I'm dying of curiosity.'

'Well, I hope I haven't been hasty,' confessed Winnie. 'But this is outside my experience, and I wasn't sure if it was a matter for the police, so you seemed the obvious person to consult. And my parishioner wasn't too keen on the idea of going to the police . . .'

'I was the unofficial solution?' Gemma asked, a little amused, imagining a teenager caught stealing or an accumulation of unpaid parking tickets. She hoped she hadn't been called out for a kitten stranded up a tree, but in any case it looked as if she was going to get a good lunch for her time.

As Winnie began to tell her about Frances Liu's missing housemate, her amusement quickly faded.

'I've been round to Guy's Hospital, where Elaine works,' Winnie continued, 'and got them to tell me that not only did she not turn up for work this morning, she didn't call in. Her colleagues say she's very punctual and dependable; she's seldom missed work at all, and never without notice.'

'Does she have family you could ring? Boyfriend? Ex-husband?'

'Not that Franny knows of, and that strikes me as a bit funny as well. I mean, how many people do you know without connections of some sort?'

'Had she been behaving oddly?'

'Not that Franny noticed . . . or not that Franny admits noticing, anyway.'

Deciding her food had cooled enough to taste, Gemma took a bite of meltingly tender white fish and sautéed greens. 'Blimey,' she said, closing her eyes in bliss. 'This is wonderful.' Swallowing, she forced her attention back to the matter at hand. 'What about the local hospitals? Did you check to see if she'd been admitted?'

'I checked Guy's and St Thomas',' answered Winnie. 'No one by that name and no one unidentified. And that left me at a dead end. I thought that perhaps if you were to talk to Franny, you could convince her to report Elaine missing.'

'Do you know why she's so reluctant?'

The pub had filled to capacity since they'd come in, and Winnie leaned a little closer in order to be heard above the rising babble of voices. 'She said Elaine's very protective of her privacy, and would be angry if Franny called attention to her unnecessarily.' Winnie frowned and toyed with a forkful of her chicken pie. 'But I also think that Franny has a horror of making a fuss, of being seen as the hysterical invalid.'

'That's understandable, I suppose,' Gemma said thoughtfully. 'But although the most likely explanation is that her friend has done a runner, I think the situation is odd enough for her to sound an alarm. Does she live nearby, then?' she added, thinking reluctantly of the work that would be piling up on her desk at Notting Hill. She wouldn't be getting away early that evening to toast Sergeant Talley's birthday.

'Not five minutes from here, just across from my church.' Winnie smiled. 'It'll give me a chance to show you where I slave away my days.'

*

Kath Warren shut herself in the toilet adjoining her office and leaned against the basin, holding on to the cold porcelain edge as if it were the only anchor in an unstable universe. She took deep breaths, counting in, counting out, and after a moment she turned on the cold tap and held her wrists beneath the stream. When the faintness began to pass, she shut the water off and reached for the towel, only to find it had disappeared from the hook – nicked by one of the shelter residents, she supposed, as per bloody usual. Tearing off a bit of toilet tissue from the roll, she dried her hands and gazed at herself in the fly-specked mirror over the basin.

She saw carefully streaked hair, expensively feathered over her ears and at the nape of her neck; regular features, nose a bit turned up, skin taut and evenly tanned from weekly sessions in the tanning salon. A good face, she told herself, an attractive face, but in the cold light filtering through the toilet window there was no denying it was the face of a forty-five-year-old woman.

How could she possibly have convinced herself it didn't matter? She'd risked her job, her marriage, her children, her comfortable semi-detached house in Peckham, all for a few quick encounters on the stained and threadbare sofa in her office.

Encounters. That was a euphemism even shabbier than *passed on* or *developmentally challenged.* She could at least be honest with herself. It had been *sex* – sweaty, pulse-racing, heart-pounding, skin-tingling sex

71

– and she had wanted it with a ferocity she hadn't known she possessed.

And she had believed that it mattered as much to him as it did to her. She had been an utter fool, a stupid, pathetically middle-aged fool, and now she would have to deal with the consequences.

The phone call had come that morning as Marcus Yarwood was downing a last cup of coffee in his Birmingham hotel room before beginning the first day of a three-day Labour conference. While the official agenda listed topics such as 'Communicating with Your Constituents' and 'The Question of Tax', the real purpose of the meeting was to meet and greet, to make or cement alliances that would further one's political ambitions. If he had been naive enough in his early days as an MP to think that his own convictions mattered, he had long since realized the error of his ways. But if he'd learned to play the game, he'd also learned to enjoy it for its own sake, and he'd been looking forward to the weekend as a way to take his mind off more personal troubles.

Then the police had rung his London office, and the dominoes began to topple. His secretary had rung him, her voice squeaky with distress; he had taken the first available train, then a taxi from the station, stopping only to drop off his overnight bag at his flat. Now he stood staring in disbelief at the remains of his building, struggling for breath as if he'd just been kicked in the chest by a carthorse. He hadn't imagined it would be so bad, hadn't really visualized the gaping windows, the piles of rubble on the pavement.

Reduced to rubble. Maybe it was fitting for a brick-layer's son with aspirations above his station. He'd been eighteen when he'd bought his first small delivery van with the earnings from his second job; twenty-five when he'd stood for his first council seat. He'd balanced his roles as business owner and Labour activist by his rejection of the greed-driven methods of big business and his unswerving dedication to improving his borough. Until, driven by his worries over Chloe, he'd given in to the temptations of the property market, and now he was facing financial disaster.

His secretary had informed him that the prime minister's office had unofficially requested that Scotland Yard oversee the case, and that was the last thing he needed.

Or maybe there was worse. A movement caught his eye. Turning, he saw a reporter coming towards him, accompanied by an assistant wielding a hand-held videocam like an unnatural appendage. For a moment he wondered wildly if he had conjured them up from the depths of his imagination. But no, they were real enough. The red eye of the camera held him mercilessly, and he struggled to resurrect his public face as the reporter held out a mike.

But before the reporter could speak, there was a touch on his shoulder and a quiet voice said, 'Mr Yarwood? I'm with the police. If we could have a word.'

*

Kincaid had recognized Yarwood immediately, but had been content to observe him for a few moments. The man was smaller in stature than he appeared on television; he did not seem to have the assurance that had always leapt from the screen. Was it shock, Kincaid wondered, or did the camera amplify certain character traits?

Yarwood wore no overcoat – he had not, perhaps, planned to spend his day standing in the rain – and the fit of his dark suit suggested Savile Row. No amount of tailoring, however, could make the man look as though he belonged in a suit. He was too burly, too barrel-chested, his arms and shoulders out of proportion to the rest of his body, his legs short as a wrestler's.

It had seemed strange to see Yarwood's bulldog face wiped clean of its usual cheerful belligerence; stranger still to see his expression of dismay at the journalists' approach.

Seeing no advantage to letting the press have their way with Yarwood just yet, Kincaid hurried to the rescue. When he'd introduced himself, deftly turning Yarwood away from the camera, he looked round for a place where they could talk.

The rain seemed to have stopped for the moment at least, making shelter less of a necessity, but it was still difficult to find somewhere that afforded privacy and less likelihood of being trampled by firefighters with rakes and axes. The side street between Yarwood's warehouse and the similar building next door had been blocked off completely with crime scene tape. Making a quick decision, Kincaid ducked under the tape and led Yarwood towards a spot by the opposite building's side door.

Cullen was busy taking details from Spender, the job foreman, but DI Bell caught his eye and came to join them. Kincaid introduced them, but Yarwood seemed not to take it in. He stared at the burned building as if mesmerized.

'The body – they say you found a body – is it still . . .' His eyes shifted towards the building like an involuntary tic.

'No,' Kincaid told him. 'It's been taken away for examination. Have you any idea how a woman ended up dead in your building, Mr Yarwood?'

'A woman?' Was it Kincaid's imagination, or had he seen a jolt of panic in the man's eyes? If so, Yarwood managed to disguise it, shoving his hands in his pockets and rocking on the balls of his feet. 'My guess would be that the builders left the building open and some poor soul wandered in off the street.'

'That occurred to us as well,' Kincaid said agreeably. 'But Mr Spender, your foreman, says he checked the locks himself when they finished for the day, and both doors were well fastened.'

'Well, perhaps he's mistaken,' Yarwood ventured after a moment's pause. It was obvious he didn't want to call his foreman a liar.

'Or maybe someone came along later and unlocked it again,' suggested Bell, her Scots accent sounding clearly. 'Where were you last night, Mr Yarwood?'

Yarwood stared at her in surprise. 'You're not suggesting—'

If Kincaid had needed a partner in good cop/bad cop, he had certainly got one. 'It's routine, you understand, Mr Yarwood. We have to ask these things, and it's to your benefit to get the facts clear from the beginning.'

'My benefit?' Yarwood sounded puzzled.

'We have a possible murder and possible arson here. As you are the owner of the property, the Fire Investigation Team will naturally need to rule you out – as will your insurance company. Insurance fraud is more common than you'd think.'

Yarwood ran a hand through his short, thinning hair, and seemed to gather himself. 'Of course. I understand that. I was in Birmingham, at a party conference. I had dinner in the hotel restaurant with some other attendees, then went to bed.'

'Mr Spender says you have the only other set of keys to the warehouse. Did you have them with you?' asked Bell.

'No, they're at home in my flat. Why would I carry them with me?'

'Why indeed?' agreed Bell lightly, but there was no humour in her voice. 'We'll need the details, of course, Mr Yarwood, but even if you were safely up in the Midlands last night, that doesn't rule out a bit of professional help.'

'Now look, Inspector, you can't accuse me of setting my own warehouse alight.' Yarwood glared at her with a return of his characteristic attitude, as if he were suddenly on firmer ground.

'No, not at this stage, anyway.' Bell allowed herself

a small smile. 'But there are rumours going round that you were in financial trouble, that the flats weren't selling fast enough to cover your construction costs.'

'That's simply not true,' Yarwood said with assurance. 'The project's barely off the ground, and we never expected to sell off all the leases until the flats were finished.' He frowned at Bell, his heavy forehead creasing. 'You said *possible arson*. That means you've no proof that the fire wasn't an accident.'

'Not yet.' Bell's tone implied that it was only a matter of time, and she gave him a challenging stare.

Kincaid thought he should intervene before they resorted to blows. 'Mr Yarwood, let's just say that we find that the fire was started deliberately. Have you any idea why someone would want to burn your warehouse?'

'*No.* Absolutely none.' Yarwood's denial was firm, accompanied by a sharp shake of his head, but this time Kincaid had no doubt. He'd seen the flash of fear in the man's eyes.

Chapter Five

The chief features in the still life of the street are green shutters, lodging-bills, brass door-plates, and bell-handles; the principal specimens of animated nature, the pot-boy, the muffin youth, and the baked-potato man.

Charles Dickens
The Pickwick Papers

Gemma and Winnie left the pub, crossing the busy road, then turned into the aptly named Short Street. Winnie pointed out her church, a nondescript brown brick structure built parallel to the street on their left.

'And that's Mitre Road.' Winnie gestured to the street of neat Victorian terraces that ran off to the right. 'My flat's about halfway along, first floor. It's quite nice – cosy compared to my draughty vicarage at home. I promise I'll have you both over for a meal.

'And Franny's house is just there,' she added as Short Street came to an abrupt end at Ufford Street. 'Practically on my doorstep.'

They were neat as dolls' houses, thought Gemma as she studied the two-storeyed terraces lining Ufford

Street. The houses looked cheerful even on such a grey day, the red tile roofs steeply peaked, the gables white, the narrow front doors a glossy black. Most of the houses, she noticed, sported flowered number plaques and hanging baskets. A black iron fence ran the length of the terrace, separating tiny front gardens from the street. A glance towards the end of the street revealed a massive grey brick warehouse and, looming above it, the unexpected silhouette of the Millennium Wheel.

'It's easy to forget how close we are to the Thames,' said Winnie, following Gemma's gaze as they crossed the road. 'And that everything here in Southwark used to revolve around the river. The churches still hold remembrance masses for those lost at sea.' She opened one of the iron gates and led Gemma up to a porch. A wheelchair ramp bridged a slight incline to the front door. She rang the bell, then opened the door and called out, 'Franny? It's Winnie. I've brought a friend.'

'Oh, what a lovely smell,' exclaimed Gemma as she followed Winnie into a sitting room as green and flowery as a cottage garden brought indoors.

'Do you like it?' The woman in the wheelchair rolled towards them, her small oval face lit with pleasure. 'It's one of my candles. I make them from soy wax and essential oils. This one's a blend of bergamot, lavender and ylang-ylang – it's meant to be calming.' On a small table near her chair a candle burned in a green glass jar. Beside it lay a cordless phone.

'Franny single-handedly supports the church bazaar,'

added Winnie, when she'd introduced Gemma. 'Her candles are the biggest seller. It's not only the scents that are wonderful – she uses all sorts of things for containers. Teacups, antique glass jars, flowerpots—'

'Basically, anything I can get my hands on,' Franny explained. 'I used to haunt car boot sales; now I have to make do with what friends bring me. Elaine—' She stopped, her voice suddenly unsteady.

Winnie pulled up a chair for Gemma before sitting on the end of the chaise longue. 'Have you heard from her?' she asked Franny.

On closer inspection, Gemma saw that Franny Liu looked tired, and that her dark eyes were red-rimmed as if she'd been weeping.

'No.' Franny shook her head. 'Nothing. I tried her office again, just in case.'

'And you've rung her mobile phone?' Gemma asked.

'She doesn't have one. An unnecessary expense, she said. Elaine likes to mind her pennies.' Franny studied Gemma for a moment, her head tilted to one side. 'Winnie said you had something to do with the police, that you could advise us. But you're not quite what I expected.'

'No uniform?' Gemma smiled. 'I'm in CID. We wear plain clothes. Why don't you tell me about your friend?' she added, leaning forward in her chair, her hands clasped on her knee. 'Start from the beginning.'

'Her name is Elaine Holland. She . . .' Franny's voice wavered and cracked. 'She . . . she works in the

Medical Records department at Guy's Hospital. She's an administrative assistant.'

'Winnie said she rents a room from you,' prompted Gemma, when Franny paused. 'How did the two of you get together?'

'I posted a notice on the hospital board. I was a nurse before my illness, so I knew it was a good way to find someone compatible. I offered a reduced rent in return for help with chores around the house and shopping. Elaine was the first applicant I had.'

'How long ago was that?'

'Almost two years.'

Gemma smiled. 'So you must have got on quite well.'

'I . . . Yes, we did. We do.'

'You said this morning that her parents were dead, and she hadn't any brothers or sisters,' put in Winnie. 'But what about a boyfriend or an ex-husband? Or a school friend? Is there anyone else she might have gone to?'

'Elaine didn't— Elaine doesn't like to talk about personal things,' Franny said quietly, not meeting their eyes, and Gemma thought that Elaine's reticence must have hurt her. 'But I don't think she's ever been married. Somehow I can't imagine her married,' she added, trying for a smile.

'And she never brought anyone here, to the house?'

Franny shook her head. 'Never. I told her she was welcome to have her friends in, when she first arrived, but then after a while the subject just never came up. I suppose we got into a routine.'

A slight thump came from the kitchen, and a black and white cat appeared in the sitting room doorway. It regarded them seriously for a moment, as if assessing their suitability as guests, before jumping into its mistress's lap and curling into a ball. 'This is Quinn,' Franny explained to Gemma, stroking the cat. 'He has his own cat flap so I don't have to let him in and out. Elaine's allergic to cats, so it's better if he doesn't spend all day in the house. She's all right as long as he stays out of her bedroom, but you know how cats are – it's a battle of wits between them. If she leaves her door open for a minute he's in like a shot.'

Gemma smiled, thinking of their cat, Sid, and his unerring talent for picking out those with a feline phobia. 'Did Elaine have any other health problems that you know of?' she asked. 'Fits? A bad heart?'

'No, not that she ever mentioned. But she was good at looking after others – I mean, she knew how to do . . . things.' A flush of embarrassment rose in Franny's cheeks. 'I asked her once, in the beginning, if she'd done any nursing, but she said no. She was a bit sharp about it, to be honest.' She looked up, meeting Gemma's gaze. 'You think she's fallen ill somewhere, don't you. But Winnie's already rung the hospitals . . .'

'I think it's a possibility we have to consider.' Gemma looked round the room, suddenly aware of the one thing missing in the clutter. 'Franny, do you have a photo of Elaine?'

'No.' She frowned as if the realization surprised

her. 'I can't remember there ever being an occasion to take one.'

'She didn't bring any photos of her own?'

'Not unless they're upstairs in her room.'

Winnie gave Gemma a quick negative shake of her head.

Glancing at her friend, Gemma thought it was no wonder Winnie had rung her. All her instincts told her there was something not quite right here. 'Why don't you give me a description, then?' she suggested to Franny.

'Well, she's about my age, mid-thirties, I'd say.' Franny looked at Winnie as if for verification and Winnie nodded.

'You don't know exactly?' Gemma asked, curious.

'Elaine didn't hold with birthdays,' Franny murmured, her hands twisting in the cat's fur, but he only stirred a little and narrowed his eyes.

'Okay.' Gemma smiled, trying to put her at ease. 'What else?'

'Um, she's tallish. Fair complexion. Brown hair, about like this' – Franny held a hand level with her chin – 'with a bit of wave to it. Light brown eyes.'

'I think that's good enough for a report. We can just ring—'

Franny was shaking her head, her eyes wide with distress. 'I told Winnie I didn't want anything official. I don't want—'

'Look, I understand you don't want to upset your friend.' Gemma tried to soothe the woman's agitation. 'But I think you have a serious concern here, and for

Elaine's sake you must report her disappearance to the police. What if she's lying ill somewhere and needs help? We'll ring the local station, then Winnie and I can wait with you until they send someone round.'

'You'd do that?' Franny sounded surprised, and Gemma wondered how much support Elaine had actually provided.

'Of course we would,' Winnie assured her.

Franny closed her eyes for a moment, her hands still on the cat's back. Then she sighed, as if coming to a decision, and looked up at Gemma. 'Okay. But will you call?' She nodded towards the phone. 'I . . . I don't want to have to explain why I can't come in to the station.'

'It's all right. They won't expect it,' Gemma told her, but she was happy enough to comply. She rang the local station directly, and identified herself. The duty officer said he'd send someone round as soon as he could, but they were a bit short-handed because they'd had a fire.

'Got half my constables tied up with house-to-house and perimeter control,' the officer responded. 'Southwark Street, not far from your address.'

It was close, Gemma thought as she hung up, visualizing the page of the *A–Z* she'd glanced at before meeting Winnie. Maybe she could take the tube from London Bridge Station, rather than Waterloo, when she returned to the office. Her route would take her right past Southwark Street; she could see what was going on, have a word with Duncan.

In the meantime, however, she had another idea.

As Winnie volunteered to make them all a cup of coffee, Gemma said, 'Franny, do you mind if I have a look at Elaine's things? I might see something that Winnie missed this morning.'

Franny gave her a bleak smile. 'If something's happened to her, it won't matter that she wouldn't like it.'

Gemma climbed the narrow stairs and looked in the first room at the top. The flowers and antiques identified it as Franny's, but it had the desolate feel acquired by rooms whose inhabitants had died. An ornate mahogany dressing table held the personal photos she had expected to see downstairs – Franny as a girl, posed between a well-dressed Asian couple who looked both proud and rather formal, as if the portrait had been an occasion. Franny playing in a garden with a Border collie, laughing into the camera. Franny alone, in a nursing sister's uniform, her expression grave. Gemma touched the photo with a fingertip, then went out, closing the door firmly behind her.

She examined the bathroom more closely, this time looking for traces of Elaine Holland. The medicine cabinet held only paracetemol, plasters, cotton buds, a bottle of over-the-counter cough remedy. If Franny took prescription medicines, she must keep them downstairs. Frowning, Gemma tried the cupboard above the toilet. It held only toilet tissue, tampons, a few bars of inexpensive soap and a bottle of Boots bubble bath.

Perhaps Elaine kept her personal things in her

bedroom, Gemma thought, moving on to the third room in the corridor and opening the door. Winnie had told her over lunch that the room was bare, but the description hadn't prepared Gemma for the bleakness that met her eyes as she stood on the threshold.

In Gemma's experience the need to stamp one's personality on one's living space seemed a basic human need, one that surfaced as soon as the essentials of food and shelter were provided. She'd seen prostitutes' rooms decorated with ribbons, pictures – only bits of tat from the street markets, but much loved tat nonetheless. She'd seen nursing-home rooms filled with personal mementos. She'd even known rough sleepers on the streets guard their few possessions as fiercely as they did their blankets, as if those possessions allowed them to keep a remnant of the identity life had stripped away.

But this room bore no more imprint than a cheap hotel room slept in for a night – it was as if Elaine Holland had vigilantly erased herself every day of the two years she had lived in this house. There were no photos, no books, no magazines or CDs, no clothes haphazardly strewn across the bed or the chair. Gemma crossed to the chest of drawers and ran a finger across its surface – there was only a light coating of dust.

Methodically, she opened the drawers. At least the woman wore underwear, she thought with a grin, although it was nondescript Marks and Spencer cotton knickers and bras. One drawer held a pad of cheap writing paper with matching envelopes, a few stamps, elastic bands, and pens marked with the hospital logo, but there were no bills or personal documents.

She went on to the built-in wardrobe with as little success. A few pairs of sensible shoes, trousers and jackets in neutral colours suitable for work and, Gemma noted, in the same size she wore. A shelf held neatly folded blankets and bed linen. The wardrobe was quite deep and, on an impulse, Gemma lifted down the linen, then pulled over the chair and climbed up on it so that she could reach all the way to the back of the shelf.

Her fingers closed on a small cardboard box and she drew it into the light, exclaiming as she saw the bright colours. It was the packaging for an Orange phone, and it was empty.

So, in spite of her protestations to Franny, Elaine owned a mobile phone. But why had she lied?

Flushed by her success, Gemma climbed down from the chair and stood back, surveying the storage space. There had to be more – she was sure of it. Pushing all the hanging clothes aside, she was rewarded for her diligence. A low door was set into the back wall of the cupboard, a not unusual feature in many old houses. The extra storage space was remarkably easy to access, once you knew of its existence, and the latch was a simple hook and eye.

Kneeling, Gemma swung open the door. A faint odour of old mothballs wafted out, and she saw immediately that she had struck gold. Some of the open boxes on the floor held strappy, high-heeled shoes, others an assortment of lacy lingerie. Folded over hangers on a low bar were sequined tops and sleek skirts, a few low-cut cocktail dresses, a beaded vintage cardigan.

Gemma sat back, wondering what to make of her find. One thing was certain – there was more to Elaine Holland than her housemate had dreamed.

When asked by her fellow firefighters why she still lived at home Rose would say the decision was purely practical – there was room in her parents' house, after all, and why should she waste money paying rent when she could be saving towards a deposit on a place of her own? Living in London was prohibitively expensive, and firefighters' earnings were towards the low end of the scale.

She didn't talk about her father's unexpected death from heart failure the previous year, nor about her reluctance to leave her mother alone in the house her parents had shared for the thirty years of their marriage. She was even less likely to admit that she couldn't yet bear the thought of leaving the house that still bore such tangible reminders of the father she'd adored.

The drive from Southwark south-east to suburban Forest Hill usually came as a relief at the end of her watch. With some of the money she saved on rent she'd splashed out on her car, a fire-engine-red Mini with a Union Jack painted on the top. She loved the way the little car handled, and the sense of physical engagement she felt as she drove helped her shed the stresses of her shift. The blokes teased her about the car, of course, but it was the good-natured ribbing of approval. They could understand her attachment to a collection of nuts and bolts.

But today not even the drive had helped her unwind, and as she pulled up in front of the semi-detached house not far from the main parade in Forest Hill she realized she had the steering wheel clenched in a white-knuckled grip. She flexed her fingers and stretched the kinks from her neck, making a conscious effort to ease the tension from her body. It was a ritual with her, trying not to take the job inside, even though she knew her mum would be at work. The house was her sanctuary, the one place she could be entirely herself.

She gazed at the familiar curve of the bay window, the gingerbread of the porch gable with the distinctive crosses at the bottom ends, the stained glass of the front door. At work, only Bryan Simms knew she lived in a 'Christmas' house. The passion for the house had been shared with her dad, and it was an area still too tender for public exposure.

Edward Christmas's company thrived between 1888 and 1930, and while his houses weren't as well known as those by Arts and Crafts architects such as Voysey and Lutyens, they had a wealth of detail and a unique charm. Her parents had bought the place cheaply in the late seventies, before the resurgence of interest in the builder's work, and throughout her childhood her father had spent his spare time lovingly restoring each distinctive feature. And she'd helped him, becoming comfortable early on with woodworking and power tools, brick pointing and glass repair – all things that had stood her in good stead in the male culture of the fire station. *Hey, get a load of that! The flower can use a chainsaw!* The memory of her sub officer's surprise still made her smile.

A magpie landed on the gate a few feet from the car and examined her, its bright, beady eye mocking as if it knew the truth about her. She'd worked so hard at showing she could do the job, at fitting in – had she blown it all that morning? What would her station officer say when he heard she'd gone back to the scene, off duty, without clearing it with him first? Charlie Wilcox was a good boss, a fair man who preferred encouragement to criticism, but she had a sinking feeling that she'd violated some unwritten protocol, made a fool of herself, and by association of her watch. There was nothing worse than that. The magpie took off with a sharp clap of wings, and her shoulders jerked involuntarily.

What had possessed her? Had she been afraid she'd missed something, made some mistake that would come to light? In the three years she'd been in the fire service, she'd only worked half a dozen large-structure fires, and last night was one of the few times she'd had the nozzle. To have the nozzle, be first on the hose, that was what every firefighter lived for – it was the ultimate experience, it was what made you real. She could still feel the exhilaration in her veins, and in an instant of clarity she knew she hadn't done anything wrong, she'd simply done what she'd been trained to do, and she'd never felt more whole in her life.

Then why did her brain keep replaying the spongy feel of flesh beneath her gloved hand, the glimpse of the contorted face with the bared and blackened teeth? She'd seen worse, for God's sake – why did *this* one somehow seem to be her responsibility?

She had to let it go. She had to sleep or she'd be useless on her watch tonight. That she couldn't afford, especially with the FIT coming in to question the rest of the watch. Her visit to the fire scene was bound to come out; there was no avoiding it. She'd just have to take the flak from Wilcox and the others, if necessary, and put the whole episode behind her.

Not wanting to say anything about her discoveries in front of Franny, Gemma waited until the constable had come and gone, then spoke briefly to Winnie as they stood outside the church office.

Winnie shook her head in bewilderment. 'Why go to so much trouble to hide things away when she knew Franny couldn't climb the stairs? And why hide the things at all? Don't most single women have a few pairs of sexy knickers?'

'If they don't, they should,' Gemma replied, grinning. In spite of her newly married status, Winnie could still display an endearingly innocent honesty. 'What about the phone?' she asked. 'Do you suppose Elaine thought Franny would be a nuisance if she knew she could reach her on a mobile?'

'It's always seemed to me that Franny goes out of her way not to make demands on Elaine.' Winnie shrugged. 'But maybe Elaine perceived it differently. I can't guess at this point. Should we have told the constable about these things?'

'I don't think having a stash of slightly tarty clothes and a mobile phone constitutes significant detail. But it has made me curious,' she added. 'Will you let me know if she turns up? Do you think Franny will be all right?'

'I'll look in on her this evening,' Winnie told her. 'Thanks for all your help.'

After a quick hug Gemma went on her way, cutting up Blackfriars Road into Union Street. The rain had begun again, a drizzle too light for umbrellas but heavy enough to be annoying. She turned up the collar of her coat and clutched it closed at her throat, trying to keep the occasional drops from slipping down the back of her neck.

There was one thing she'd noticed that she hadn't felt comfortable sharing with Winnie. Franny had frequently used the past tense when talking about her friend, although she'd corrected herself a few times. Did she know more about Elaine's disappearance than she'd let on?

'That's a nasty suspicious mind you've got,' Gemma chastised herself aloud, earning a surprised glance from a passing man in a pinstriped suit. The woman was confined to a wheelchair, for heaven's sake, she went on to herself – she couldn't possibly have had anything to do with her friend's mysterious disappearance.

And Gemma certainly had enough on her plate, with her own caseload and Kit's hearing coming up on

Monday, without taking on another problem. She'd lost half her afternoon as it was, and she imagined Melody Talbot beleaguered, ready to send out a search party for her. Fishing her phone from her bag, she gave Melody a quick call, explaining that something had come up but that she was now on her way back to the station.

Her ruminations and her phone call having taken her as far as Southwark Bridge Road, she took a moment to orient herself before turning north, towards the river, then right into Southwark Street. She caught sight of the distant cluster of emergency vehicles almost immediately, but it wasn't until she was almost upon them that she was able to see the scene of the fire itself.

Her first thought was one of regret, for the building had been beautiful, its form and symmetry a striking example of the best of Victorian architecture. How could someone wilfully damage something so lovely? she wondered, then remembered that Kincaid had called it a *suspicious* fire. It might not have been arson.

The appliances had gone but the generator lorry remained, and against the grey sky the lower windows of the warehouse glowed with the eerie brightness of the floodlights. Piles of blackened rubble had been raked out onto the pavement, and even from a distance the stench made her throat constrict.

There were several marked police cars and a couple of unmarked but vaguely official-looking vans. She recognized Doug Cullen's slightly battered Vauxhall Astra parked over the kerb. She was about to ask one of the constables guarding the perimeter where she might find Kincaid when she saw him, standing a few yards down the side street with Cullen and a dark-haired woman in a tan coat.

Gemma's lips curved in an involuntary smile; familiarity hadn't dulled the jolt of pleasure she felt on seeing him after a few hours' separation. Then he looked up and saw her, his eyes widening in surprise.

'Gemma!' he said, hurrying towards her. 'What are you doing here? Is everything all right? The boys—'

'No, no, they're fine,' she hastened to reassure him. 'It's just that I was in the area – Winnie rang and asked me to lunch – and I thought I'd stop by and see how you were getting on.'

'Very slowly,' he said, slipping an arm round her shoulders for a quick hug and giving her a grin that told her he was glad to see her as well.

Gemma realized that the dark-haired woman was watching her with a less than welcoming regard. 'I don't want to trespass on your patch. If it's inconvenient—'

'You're fine. Don't worry about the grim-visaged Inspector Bell,' he added in her ear. 'She improves as she thaws. We're just about to have a word with the woman who reported the fire. Come along with us – I'll be glad to have your take on this. Then you can tell me about Winnie.'

They'd reached the others. Doug Cullen took her hand warmly, then introduced her to DI Maura Bell. Bell put out her hand in response to Gemma's, but jerked it free after the slightest press of fingers. *Slam-*

bam-thank-you-ma'am, Gemma thought, amused. This was a woman who obviously did not relish physical contact or having an uninvited investigator on her case.

'While we're waiting for the fire investigation officer, Bill Farrell, I can give you a quick rundown of what we have so far,' Kincaid said, ignoring Bell's scowl. 'The building belongs to Marcus Yarwood, the MP, who was in the process of turning it into luxury flats with a restaurant on the ground floor. The emergency call came in just after half past twelve last night, and the fire was well advanced by the time the brigade arrived. They entered through the front door, which they found unlocked, and they later discovered the side door unlocked as well.' He gestured towards the door facing them across the narrow side street. The rear of the building jutted out in a sort of attached tower with a window at each level, leading Gemma to assume that the door opened onto a rear staircase.

'The firefighters found their progress into the ground-floor space impeded by a pile of soft furniture gathered in the centre of the room,' Kincaid continued. 'Behind the furniture they discovered the charred body of the victim. Bill Farrell, the FIO, thinks it likely that the fire started in the furniture, but they've found no obvious signs of arson.'

'Does that mean the death may have been accidental?' asked Gemma.

'Possible, but I'd say not likely, as Kate Ling found a massive fracture to the back of the skull.'

'Kate was here?' Gemma felt a twinge of jealousy. She knew that Kate fancied Kincaid, but how he felt

about Kate she'd never quite been able to work out.
Obviously, he respected the doctor professionally, and
just as obviously he found her attractive, but it never
seemed to occur to him that the feeling might be
reciprocated. Men could be so clueless, thought
Gemma, but in this case Kincaid's blind spot was a
blessing. She just hoped he never saw the light where
Kate Ling was concerned.

'Been and gone. She'll get to the post-mortem as
soon as she can.' He turned to greet a tall, balding
man. 'Here's Farrell now.'

'Are these flats, then?' asked Gemma when she'd
been introduced, looking up at the building they were
about to enter. It was larger than its burned neighbour,
and a bit more ornate, but it showed obvious signs of
decay and neglect. 'You said someone called from here
after midnight.'

'Not flats,' Farrell told her. 'It's a family violence
shelter.' He pointed out a small plaque near the door
which bore the legend HELPING HANDS. 'It was one of
the residents who called in the fire. We're going to
have a word with the director before we interview the
young woman. I've got the entry code from the constable who took the original statement.'

The street door stood open, showing a small entry
hall floored with stained coconut matting, but as
Gemma tailed after the others, she saw that an interior
door had been fitted with an expensive new security
keypad. Farrell entered a code and, when the door
swung open, led them into a dingy stairwell. Looking
back over his shoulder, he said, 'First off, we need to

make sure they haven't misplaced a resident who fits our victim's description.'

'I doubt they were expecting a delegation,' Maura Bell muttered as they climbed.

'A delegation of detectives?' Kincaid quipped. 'Or would a murder of detectives be more appropriate? I rather like that.'

Gemma touched Kincaid's arm. 'Wait. Are you saying your victim was female? I just assumed, when you said you had a possible murder, that the victim was male, someone to do with the site.'

'No. We've got a female, no ID, and burned beyond recognition. Why?'

Gemma's mind raced. Surely it was too much of a coincidence – but was it? The fire scene was only a few streets from Franny Liu's house . . . But what would Elaine Holland have been doing in an empty warehouse at night?

Unless she'd been moonlighting as a prostitute, and that might explain the hidden clothes and shoes, the secret mobile phone. Gemma remembered hearing that call girls worked Union Street at night – a doorway in nearby Southwark Street might have provided a quieter rendezvous, a bit more privacy. But then—

'Gemma?' Kincaid's voice snapped her out of her speculations. They had reached the top of the stairs.

She shook her head. 'Nothing. Just a wild idea. I'll tell you later.'

A woman awaited them in the first-floor corridor. 'Hi, I'm Kath Warren, Helping Hands' director. You're the police?' She'd started to offer her hand but let it fall to her side, seemingly daunted by their number. Gemma guessed the woman to be in her well-preserved forties, with an air of no-nonsense competence. She wore a honey-coloured trouser suit that complemented her fair skin, and her green eyes held a hint of wariness.

Farrell stepped easily into the breach. 'I'm Bill Farrell, from the fire brigade.' He nodded at the others, clustered behind him like ducklings, as he made the introductions. 'Superintendent Kincaid, Scotland Yard. Sergeant Cullen. Inspector Bell. Inspector James,' he added last, with a questioning glance in her direction to assure himself he'd got it right.

Kath Warren looked round the corridor as if realizing its unsuitability for conversation. 'Um, perhaps we'd better go into my office. It's not much larger, but at least there's somewhere to sit.'

'I should say *our* office,' she added as they followed her into the first room off the corridor. 'This is Jason Nesbitt, the agency's assistant director.'

The room held two utilitarian desks, a sagging sofa, several mismatched straight-backed chairs, and ranks of metal filing cabinets. A young man sat at the second desk, one hand on the telephone, the other balancing a manila file folder. At their entrance he returned the handset to its cradle and stood up.

'It's the police, Jason,' said Kath, motioning them to the assorted furniture as she slipped behind the other desk.

'So I gathered. We must be important.' His grin was sardonic but engaging. He was tall, rail-thin, with blond-tipped hair and a wide, expressive mouth. His dark shirt and tie hinted at a certain vanity, and a closer look made Gemma revise her estimate of his age to nearer thirty than twenty.

'Please sit down. You'll have to excuse our lack of elegance,' said Kath, with a shrug that indicated the office. 'The place is a bit of a tip, but we're funded primarily by the council, and that leaves no room for frills.'

Cullen and Bell sat rather awkwardly together on the sofa, while Farrell and Gemma perched on two of the hard-backed chairs. Kincaid remained standing, resting his hip against a filing cabinet.

'You take in women who've been abused by their husbands?' said Gemma, forgetting for a moment that it wasn't her place to ask. Bell gave her a dark look.

'Women and their children, more often than not.' Kath Warren seemed more comfortable behind her desk. 'Not that men aren't sometimes victims of spousal abuse, but the council makes other arrangements in that case. We give women a safe haven, a chance to sort things out, and if that's not possible we help them move on to new lives.'

'How many rooms do you have?' Kincaid asked.

'Ten, all full at the moment. Not the most salubrious of accommodation, but that may not matter for much longer. It looks as if our time here is limited. This building, like the one next door, is ripe for redevelopment. The front half is already vacant, and the asking price for the property will be much more than the council can afford.'

It seemed to Gemma that what had begun as a practised spiel had become personal, that the impending loss of the agency's premises affected Kath Warren in some intimate way. 'What will happen then?' she asked.

'Oh, they'll find a new spot for us eventually, but it may mean our shutting down for some time. The council will do their best to find places for our residents with other agencies, of course.' She forced a smile. 'But I'm waffling on about things that don't concern you when I'm sure you have questions.'

Jason Nesbitt had been listening, his eyes darting occasionally from Kath to the others, but his mobile face was unreadable. It occurred to Gemma that the impending closure might mean that both Nesbitt and Kath Warren would be out of a job.

'Your residents, Ms Warren,' interjected DI Bell, almost springing from her seat in her impatience, 'are they all accounted for?'

'Yes, of course. The residents must sign a log when they exit or enter the building, and we have a ten p.m. curfew. Sometimes at night the women start to miss their husbands and the curfew helps prevent lapses. And it's Mrs Warren, by the way,' she added, but she looked down at her hands as she spoke, twisting her wedding ring, rather than at DI Bell. 'We saw the mortuary van, you know, and the attendants loading the . . . body . . . into it. Does this mean you don't know who it was?'

'An unidentified female,' said Bill Farrell. 'That's been released to the media and is really all we can say at the moment. Now, we understand that one of your residents notified the fire brigade of the fire?'

'Yes, Beverly Brown-Mouse, we call her. Both her kids have got bad colds at the moment, and she was up with one of them when she looked out the window and saw the flames. She had to use the phone in the hall – we can't allow residents to have mobile phones. Again, it makes access too easy for both parties.'

Nesbitt stood up. 'I'll just get Mouse, shall I?' Without waiting for an answer, he eased his way round his desk, and as he passed her Gemma caught the musky scent of expensive cologne.

'That seems rather an infringement of their rights,' ventured Cullen, speaking for the first time.

'They come here voluntarily, but to enter the programme they must agree to the rules. It's a waste of our time and theirs if they're not willing to make changes – that's the only way to break the pattern of habitual abuse.' Kath Warren stood, as if the waiting made her nervous. 'Can I get you all some coffee? We keep a pot going in the kitchen.'

By the time they had all refused and Kath had answered a few more questions about the shelter's programme, Jason Nesbitt had come back with his charges. He ushered the woman and the two children into the room, then stood behind them protectively.

If ever someone looked in need of protection, it was this woman, thought Gemma. She was small and slight, appearing hardly more than a child herself in her T-shirt and combat trousers. Her skin had a junkie's pallor, and a streak of pure white hair sprang from her widow's peak, making her look more like a little badger than a mouse. Her face was pinched with fright, and Gemma guessed that talking to a roomful of coppers was not her idea of a good time.

The children were girls, perhaps two and five, pale as their mother and snotty nosed. They clung to their mother's legs, ducking their faces behind the meagre barricade she provided. A good thing too, thought Gemma, as she had to fight the temptation to pull tissues from her bag and give their faces a good scrubbing.

'Do you want to sit down, Beverly?' asked Kath Warren, but the woman shook her head. 'These people are trying to find out what caused the fire last night, and they need to ask you a few questions. I'm sure it won't take long.'

'It's all right, Mouse,' said Jason Nesbitt. 'They won't bite you.'

Beverly nodded, eyes wide, but didn't speak.

Bill Farrell shifted his chair to face her. 'Beverly, can you tell me exactly what you saw last night? You can start by describing what you were doing before-hand.'

'It was Brittany,' she said in a soft, high voice that made the reason for her nickname evident, pulling the older child out from behind her leg as if wanting to prove her existence. 'Her cough was that bad, she couldn't sleep.' The child coughed on cue, a racking sound that made Gemma cringe. 'I went down to the kitchen to boil a pan of water for her to breathe. When I came back to the room I made her sit over it, you know, with a towel to keep the steam in. Ten minutes, I told her, and I promised to watch the clock. That's when I looked out the window.' Her voice had grown stronger, as if she was encouraged by their interest. 'At first I thought it was weird, you know, there was a red light in the building across the street. I thought why would someone have a red light, must be a wild party. And then I saw it flicker, and suddenly I go wow, it's not a light, it's a fire.'

'And that's when you called 999?'

'Yeah. They were fast, you know. Couldn't have been much more than a minute before we heard the sirens.'

'And you kept watching?'

'Well, yeah. It was exciting.' She ducked her head, as if not sure that was an acceptable response. 'Brandy woke up too, so we all watched.'

Farrell smiled at her. 'There's nothing like a good fire. I'd be the first to agree with you on that. Now, did you see anything else before the brigade arrived? Anyone on the street or coming out the side door?'

'No. There wasn't nobody.'

'The building would have burned down if it hadn't been for Mummy,' piped up Brittany. She wiped a fist across her nose and glared at Farrell, as if daring him to contradict her.

'That's right, sweetheart,' Farrell said kindly. 'Your mummy saved the day. Now, you know what to do if you see a fire, don't you?'

'Call 999,' Brittany informed him, puffing out her little chest in its stained Scooby Doo T-shirt. 'I know where nine is on the phone. Three nines. I can count them.'

'That's great, sweetheart.' Farrell turned back to her mother. 'Beverly, did you see anything before you noticed the fire? Or hear anything unusual?'

Beverly shook her head perhaps a bit too quickly, Gemma thought. 'No. I was asleep. It was only Brittany's coughing that woke me up.'

'What about earlier in the evening, before you went to bed?' Kincaid asked. 'Did you see anything then?'

'No. I didn't look, did I? I was putting the girls to bed.' She turned to Kath Warren. 'Can I go now, Kath? I have to take Brittany to the clinic.'

Kath glanced at Bill Farrell, who nodded.

Farrell handed Beverly a card. 'There's my number, if you think of anything else,' he told her.

'Yeah, okay,' she said, with an obvious lack of enthusiasm. She slipped out the door, her children still clinging like limpets, and Gemma noticed that she adroitly managed to avoid touching Jason Nesbitt.

'Is there somewhere we can talk?' Gemma shielded her eyes against the rain, which was coming down harder now, the drops stinging her skin like biting midges.

Kincaid looked round at the warehouse frontages and at the office buildings across Southwark Street, none of which offered any protection from the downpour; then he shouted at Doug Cullen, who was conferring with Farrell and a firefighter with an Alsatian. 'Hey, Dougie! Lend us your keys for a minute, will you?'

Cullen tossed them over with a grin. 'Careful you don't fog up my windows.'

They sprinted for the car, and when Kincaid had managed to get the doors unlocked, fell inside, laughing.

'I left my brolly at the office,' he admitted, wiping his face.

'Me, too,' said Gemma. 'I thought it had stopped.' She could almost feel her hair curling from the moisture, springing free from its clip.

'Here.' Kincaid retrieved a box of tissues from among the gum wrappers and crisp packets littering the car floor. 'Will these help?'

Gemma pulled out a few tissues and dried her face. Then, looking round for somewhere to put the soggy remains, she grimaced at the mess. 'This car's a tip. I wouldn't have thought it of Doug.'

'I think he's rebelling against having to keep his flat spotless for Stella. Now.' He turned towards her. 'Tell me what's up with Winnie. Are she and Jack all right?'

'Of course.' Touching his cheek, she remembered his reaction when he'd seen her. She was so close she could see the tiny patch of stubble he'd missed when he'd shaved that morning and smell the damp warmth of his skin. 'You're a bit mother hen-ish today.'

'Maybe I don't like fires,' he confessed with a shrug. 'There's something about a burned body, as illogical as it is.'

Gemma felt the lump of Franny Liu's candle inside the bag on her lap, a sudden burden weighted with possibility. 'Okay. I know this is going to sound far-fetched.' She took a breath and proceeded to tell him about Winnie's phone call, about Franny Liu and her missing housemate Elaine Holland, and about her theory that Elaine might have been moonlighting on the street and somehow ended up in Yarwood's ware-house.

Kincaid tapped his fingers on the steering wheel for a moment when she'd finished, gazing out at the warehouse through the slanting curtain of rain. 'It is far-fetched, I'll give you that,' he said slowly. 'But it's the first report of a missing woman we've had that fits the time frame. I think that alone makes it worth consideration. But say, just for the moment, that you're right and she was with a punter, sheltering in the doorway. How did she end up inside the building?'

'Maybe the client had a key?'

His eyes widened. 'Right now, that would narrow it down to Marcus Yarwood and his foreman Spender. We're already checking their alibis for last night. But there are other possibilities. Estate agents, former owners, cleaning services . . .'

'I don't envy you that,' Gemma said, thinking of the massive amount of paperwork involved in following up these leads. 'What about Elaine Holland? Will you want to speak to Franny again today? What about a proper search of the house?'

He thought for a moment, then shook his head. 'No, let's wait until we get the results of the post-mortem. There's no point in jumping the gun here. For all we know, at this point the PM may tell us something that would rule her out entirely – say, the victim was a teenager or non-white. Kate said she'd try to schedule the PM tonight or first thing tomorrow, and she'll keep me informed. We'll go from there. But in the meantime I'd better fill in the others.' He turned back to her and reached out to cup her cheek in his hand. 'I don't know when I'll get home.'

'I know.'

'Then we'd better make the most of the moment,' he said, sliding his fingers down to her chin and turning her face so that he could brush his lips against hers. He tasted very slightly of coffee.

Gemma struggled, laughing, as he nuzzled her neck. 'Don't do that. Someone will see us.'

'That's the idea. You wouldn't want to disappoint Doug, would you?'

Why the hell didn't the woman answer her bloody phone?

Tony Novak stood in London Bridge Railway Station, mobile phone in hand, panic rising in his throat. He'd told Beth to bring Harriet to meet him at the flower stall at twelve o'clock, and there he'd been standing for the last hour.

After half an hour had passed, he'd started ringing Beth's mobile, but the stupid fucking thing went directly to voicemail. It was only then that the truth began to dawn – he had a name and a mobile number, nothing else, and he'd left his daughter with her.

Dear God, what had he been thinking? Sweat stung his armpits, stuck his shirt to his back, and his knees felt suddenly as if they might give way. He sank down onto the large suitcase, rubbing his face with his free hand. People milled past him, wheeling luggage, clutching briefcases, as if the world hadn't come to a dead stop. A pretty girl slowed, gave him a tentative smile, then looked away and hurried on as if something she'd seen in his face had frightened her. Good bloody riddance.

They had always been his downfall – girls, women. He attracted them like flies to honey, and in spite of the best of intentions, he had never learned to say no. This little weakness had ruined his marriage to Laura, as well as every other relationship he'd had since adolescence.

And that was how he'd met Beth, in the bar at the George Inn in Borough High Street, near his flat. An attractive woman, obviously looking for company; he in the throes of post-separation shock, an easy mark. When she'd chatted him up, he'd seen no reason to refuse. He'd taken her back to his flat that night, surprised but intrigued by her ferocity.

Afterwards, lying naked in his bed, she'd told him she was married, her husband a commercial traveller, a jealous man. She said she would come to him again if he wanted, and he *had* wanted it. It helped fill the hours, numbed his mind, and he had liked the fact that she was married, unavailable for more than their regular trysts.

Lately, though, things had begun to change. He should have seen it coming – he'd never known a woman to remain satisfied with simple sex. He recognized the signs easily enough – hints of dissatisfaction with her marriage, hints that things might be different between them – and he'd begun to think of finding a way to terminate the relationship.

Then things had blown up with Laura and his life had spun out of control. His plans hastily conceived, he'd realized he needed someone to watch Harriet while he retrieved her documents from Laura's flat and withdrew his funds from the bank, and Beth had seemed the logical choice.

It was only now that he remembered the odd look on her face last night when he'd told her what he meant to do, but then she'd smiled and said yes, of course she'd help him, and in his hurry and his relief he'd quickly buried any uneasiness.

A garbled announcement came over the tannoy, a train departing for some unidentifiable location. The sound made his head hurt. He rubbed at his face again, trying to clear his mind, trying to bring back any little titbits of information that Beth had revealed in post-coital conversations.

She worked in an estate agent's in the Borough; she had told him that much. She'd grown up in South Africa, a daughter of missionaries, and had only come to London in her late teens. She'd been married once before, but it hadn't worked out.

Fat lot of good any of that did him. What was he going to do, go round to every estate agent's in the Borough, hoping to find her? He might as well ring directory inquiries and ask for a listing for *Beth*. It was madness.

Mary, mother of Jesus, how could he have been so stupid? He stood again, looking round wildly, as if his daughter's face might suddenly appear in the crowd.

Had Beth taken Harriet to the authorities? But in that case wouldn't she have also told them where he was? He'd been waiting in the same spot for close on an hour and a half now, and no one had approached him.

But the alternative was more terrifying still. If she had not reported him, what in hell had she done with his child?

Chapter Six

Five jails, or prisons, are in Southwark placed,
The Counter once St Margaret's Church defaced,
The Marshalsea, the King's Bench, and White Lyon,
Then there's the Clink where handsome lodgings be.

John Taylor, 1630

Rose had drawn kitchen duty for that night's watch, her least favourite chore. Growing up, she'd not had any interest in cooking, while her mother had enjoyed it and had been content to let her help her dad with his projects rather than insisting she do her share in the kitchen.

But cooking, she quickly discovered, was an essential skill in the fire service, and she'd set out with her usual diligence to become competent. Now, at least the other members of the watch didn't roll their eyes and suggest a Chinese takeaway when it was her turn to prepare meals.

She'd come in a half-hour early, hoping to have a word with Station Officer Wilcox before her shift began. It would be better if he heard about her visit to the fire scene from her rather than the FIT.

But Wilcox hadn't yet come in, so she decided to get the dinner ready to go in the oven before roll call. That way she had more chance of getting the meal finished if they had a busy night, and it would give her something to do while she kept an eye out for Wilcox. Using a mallet, she pounded chicken breast halves into an even thickness before coating them in seasoned bread crumbs and drizzling them with olive oil. Then she scrubbed and quartered potatoes for roasted potato wedges; both dishes could be popped in the oven later. She could throw a salad together at the last minute, and there was ice cream in the freezer for a sweet.

Yawning as she finished her tasks, she rubbed at eyes burning from lack of sleep. Although a nap and a shower had helped, she still felt frayed round the edges. It would be a long night, but she knew better than to wish for a quiet one – that only seemed to guarantee that the bells would go non-stop.

Bryan Simms wandered into the kitchen as she was finishing, carrying a takeaway coffee. 'You look knackered,' he offered after examining her critically.

'Thanks.' She shot him a sour glance. 'You really know how to boost a girl's confidence.'

'Anytime.' He grinned at her. 'Dinner looks good, though.' He reached for a slice of potato but she snatched it away.

'Don't eat raw potato, it's disgusting. You'll get a disease or something.'

'Hasn't hurt me yet.' Lounging against the oven, he sipped his coffee and watched her wipe the worktops. 'Besides, I need something to keep my strength up. I've got phone duty, and I hear the press calls about last night's fire have been coming in non-stop. I'm to refer all queries to Lambeth PR.'

Rose dried her hands on a tea towel, debating whether to tell him about her visit to the scene that morning. 'Bryan—'

The blare of the tannoy drowned out her words as roll call was announced. 'Never mind,' she said, patting her hair to make sure it was tucked up in regulation fashion. 'Tell you later.'

But later never seemed to materialize. During roll call MacCauley informed them that the FIT was expected at seven o'clock and would be debriefing the entire watch in the lecture room, so from roll call they scattered to complete their routine maintenance of the equipment and appliances.

Wilcox was closeted in his office with MacCauley, and as she'd caught up on her kitchen chores Rose offered to fill in for one of the pump ladder crew on a call to a nearby office building, a person stuck in a lift. By the time they returned and she'd dashed into the kitchen to put the food in the oven, the rest of the watch had gathered in the lecture room. Having missed her chance to talk to Wilcox, Rose slid into a chair in the back. The tension that had been temporarily dissipated by the call returned with a vengeance.

As she looked round the room, she thought how seldom she saw them all gathered together, except on the rare occasions when both crews managed to sit down to a meal at the same time. It was a good watch, the best she'd ever had, due in part to the personalities of the men themselves and in part to Charlie Wilcox's scrupulous refusal to tolerate any sort of harassment or bullying in his team. Rumours of Wilcox's potential promotion to divisional officer circulated with distressing regularity. What might be a gain for the fire service administration would be a loss for Southwark Station.

Their sub officer, Seamus MacCauley, at fifty-four the oldest member of the watch, was nearing retirement, and Rose suspected he had never actively sought promotion. A whipcord-thin Geordie with an unlikely Scots–Irish name, he was a good and patient teacher, a mediator whose easy-going manner helped keep conflict to a minimum.

As if aware of her regard, he looked over at her from his position by the door and smiled. 'You ready for the inquisition, flower? Mean bastards, this lot,' he added, and winked.

'Just as long as they don't keep me from my dinner,' said Simon Forney from the row in front of her. Simon and the man beside him, Steven Winston, although not in fact brothers were usually referred to as Castor and Pollux, the mythological Gemini twins, because of their uncanny resemblance to each other. Round-headed, barrel-chested, and proud of their strength, they'd only begun to accept her when she'd proved she could swing an axe and haul a hose as well as any bloke.

The buzz of conversation in the room died away as Wilcox came in with the investigators. He introduced Station Officer Farrell and Sub Officer Martinelli, then the three detectives Rose had met that morning. Kincaid, the superintendent, caught Rose's eye and nodded in recognition.

Rose hadn't really noticed Martinelli earlier that day – any attention she'd turned in that direction had been focused on his dog – but now she realized he was younger than she'd thought, perhaps only in his early thirties. His Italian heritage was evident in his dark colouring, but the slant of his cheekbones and the shape of his eyes hinted at another racial component, Asian or maybe Polynesian. He gave her a friendly grin and she looked away, embarrassed that she'd been caught staring.

'We'll keep this informal,' Farrell told them as he hitched himself up on the table at the front of the room. The others stood about a bit awkwardly until Kincaid took charge, pulling chairs from the empty front row and turning them round so that they could sit facing the group. 'You'll need to make individual statements for the coroner's report,' Farrell continued, 'as is always the case with a fatality fire, but first I'd like to hear if anyone noted anything unusual at the scene last night. We've already heard from Firefighter Kearney earlier today about her discovery of the victim.'

Rose felt a sudden intensifying of attention in the room. Simms gave her a surprised glance, frowning as he turned back to Farrell.

'No one saw anyone loitering near the scene?' Farrell prompted. 'Or smelled anything unusual?'

After a few silent moments, Simms spoke up. 'Sir. You think it was arson, then?'

'We haven't found any obvious use of accelerants, but of course that's not conclusive,' replied Farrell evasively.

'What about the videos from the appliances?' Simms continued, undiscouraged. The pump and pump ladder carried cameras mounted in their cabs which provided investigators with a view of any suspicious activity en route to a scene.

'No joy there, I'm afraid.'

'What about CCTV, sir?' put in MacCauley.

'Those tapes are still being collected,' answered Superintendent Kincaid. 'We'll be having a look at them in the morning, but our findings shouldn't prejudice your observations. We would appreciate your cooperation on this,' he added.

A ripple of bodies shifting in chairs and a few mutters signalled the watch's interest.

From the doorway MacCauley directed a comment to Farrell. 'It seems we've had an unusual number of structure fires in the Borough the last few months, guv. Might be worth checking to see if there's some sort of pattern.'

'We'll keep that in mind.' Farrell stood. 'Okay, if there's nothing else, we'll get your statements. It shouldn't take long.'

Superintendent Kincaid and the other detectives stood as well. Kincaid murmured something in Farrell's ear, then flashed a smile at Rose as the three detectives left the room. The FIT officers moved round to the far side of the table to take statements. As she slipped into the rough queue formed by the firefighters, Rose wondered at the generous police presence. She'd been too frazzled that morning to pay much attention to the rumours flying round the scene that the building belonged to Marcus Yarwood, the Labour MP, but she supposed that would account for the amount of attention being given the case.

Beside her, Steven Winston said quietly, 'You ought to remember to wipe your nose, Kearney.'

She reached up instinctively, then flushed and dropped her hand as she realized what he meant. Although his tone had been teasing, his eyes were cold. Before she could respond, he nudged her and added, 'Boss wants you.'

Turning, she saw Wilcox watching her from the door. When he had her attention, he jerked his head in the direction of his office. 'Rose. A word.'

She followed him, her throat tight, very much aware of the stares directed at her retreating back. Expecting the worst, she stepped into the room and, at Wilcox's nod, closed the door behind her.

He stood behind his desk, studying her for a moment, then said quietly, 'Initiative is a good thing, Rose, up to a point. But we don't need freelancers on the watch. No loose cannons, on the fire ground or off. If you know, or remember, anything that might be relevant to last night's fire, you talk to me first and from there we'll take it through the proper channels. Understood?'

Rose swallowed and resisted the urge to explain herself. 'Yes, sir.'

The days when aggression in a firefighter was

prized above all else were gone. Freelancing – charging into a fire, or any situation, without thought for partner or team – was as frowned upon now as going into a fire without a mask.

'I don't want any unnecessary entanglements with the FIT on my watch. It complicates things. And you don't want the rest of the team feeling you've gone behind their backs. You're a good firefighter, and you handled yourself well last night. Don't do anything to screw up your record.' Wilcox sat down at his desk and picked up a stack of reports, effectively dismissing her.

'Sir.' Knowing she'd got off lightly, Rose breathed a sigh of relief and headed for the door. Then, her hand on the knob, she turned back, her curiosity overcoming her better judgement. 'Guv, about those other warehouse fires. Wouldn't the brigade database—'

'Let the FIT do their job, Rose,' growled Wilcox, looking up at her with irritation. 'You've done yours. Leave it alone.'

The phone rang twice before the voicemail clicked in, just as it had the last dozen times Yarwood had called. 'You've reached Tia and Chloe,' the soft, drawling voice informed him. 'We're busy at the moment, but leave a message and we'll get back to you.'

It was not Chloe's voice, but Tia's. The girl's Sloane Ranger upbringing was apparent in her stretched vowels, and Yarwood had recently noticed that Chloe had begun to imitate her flatmate, something that made him furious. He slammed down the phone in frustration.

He'd been trying to reach his daughter, either at her flat or on her mobile, since he'd left the fire scene that morning, with no success. The only possibility he hadn't tried was Chloe's mother, Shirley. He might be worried, but he wasn't yet desperate enough to call his ex-wife.

Yarwood went back to pacing the sitting room of his flat, stopping to stare out the window at the fading light in Hopton Street. He felt edgy and confined. It was ironic, really, as until Shirley's last decorating binge had swathed the room in pale blue and green fabrics and filled it with ornate gilded furniture, he'd always found the small space comforting.

That was just before she'd run off with the interior designer, damn the bitch. The pair was now living in happily wedded bliss, according to Chloe, catering to the tastes of the blue-rinse set in Brighton. Good riddance to them both as far as he was concerned.

It was a shame about the flat, though. The building was one of the oldest in Southwark and deserved something more in keeping with its character. He'd bought the flat years ago, when the Globe Theatre had been merely Sam Wanamaker's dream, and living in the hulking shadow of Bankside Power Station had not been seen as an advantage. Now the Globe had become a reality, the power station had metamorphosed into Tate Modern, and Bankside had become a major destination for the tourists and the trendy.

Of course, the value of the flat had increased

exponentially, and Shirley had nagged him incessantly to sell it. They could buy a place in the country, she'd said, or one of those new flats on the river.

But he hadn't wanted to let the old place go. It was part of Bankside, part of who he was, part of what he believed in. And trying to make him into a country gentleman was about as ridiculous as putting a pig in a tutu.

After what had happened last night, however, selling up might be his only option. How else could he get his hands on the cash he needed, and get it quickly enough?

A current of fear snaked between his shoulder blades and he clenched his fists as if he could physically subdue it. He'd always considered himself tough, a self-made man who could tackle anything that came his way, but the thought of the charred remains of his warehouse, and of the body he'd seen loaded into the mortuary van, made him feel sick.

Had the fire been a warning, the body a reminder of what could happen to his daughter if he didn't pay the men who were threatening him over his daughter's debts?

He strode to the sideboard and poured himself a tumbler of whisky from the bottle he kept mostly for guests. He'd never been much of a drinker, on the theory that it took a clear head to get on in the world, but tonight he needed something to numb the worry clutching at his gut like a claw.

Did Chloe have any idea what she'd got herself

into? Or did she think she could wheedle her way out of this, as she had everything else in her life?

The girl had always preferred her mother's company – not that he'd given her much choice, with his schedule – but when her mother had taken off with that ponce of a designer, Chloe had chosen to stay in London with her father. She'd been eighteen then, and she'd thought exile to a seaside town like Brighton a fate worse than death.

But nothing Yarwood had done in his life had prepared him for dealing single-handedly with a spoiled and angry teenager, and he'd failed miserably. He'd insisted she get a job or stay enrolled in some sort of college or university course, but she didn't seem able to stick at anything long enough to make a success of it. After two years of failures, his patience at an end, he'd told Chloe he'd no intention of continuing to support a layabout, and he'd kicked her out.

He hadn't counted on Tia Foster taking her in as a charity case. Tia, whose wealthy parents had endowed her with more money than sense, had moved Chloe into the spare bedroom in her flat, and Chloe managed to survive by scrounging off Tia and begging the occasional handout from her mother.

Christ, how could he not have seen how vulnerable his daughter was? Or how vulnerable she had made him?

Now he didn't dare talk to the police for fear of reprisals. He could do nothing but pay for the consequences of his own stupidity, and try to keep Chloe safe. He picked up the phone and jabbed a blunt finger at the keypad once more.

He knew the value of a uniform. Clothes made the man. Or so his mum had always told him – the old cow – and then she'd reinforced the maxim with a few well-placed smacks. It had been years since he'd had to put up with that, but he still ironed his shirts as if his mother were watching over his shoulder.

Collar first, then shoulder, then sleeves. He slipped a fresh section of pale blue cloth over the end of the board and sprayed on some starch. His routine never varied. Every evening before reporting for work he unfolded the old ironing board in the middle of his sitting room and laboured over his uniform shirt until it could stand on its own; then he touched up his navy-blue trousers and jacket.

Radio Two droned in the background, not quite loudly enough to cover the murmur of traffic that drifted up from Blackfriars Road through his partially open window. His mum had been big on fresh air in all weathers, convinced that sealing a dwelling would result in a build-up of deadly gases. Bollocks, of course, he knew that, but still the habit stayed with him, and he liked the way the smell of curry from the takeaway beneath his flat mingled with the exhaust fumes and the clean soapiness of the starch.

It was odd the way the mind could divide itself, one part occupied with the identifying of familiar scents – the motion of his arm holding the iron, the babble of sound from the radio – while the other part seethed and bubbled with excitement from last night's burn.

It had been – what was the word he'd read some-where? – serendipitous, that was it. The walk home after his half shift, the sliver of darkness beckoning him from the open door, the interior prepared for him as if by some grand design.

Could it be that his own carefully prepared plan fitted into something larger, dovetailed within it like a nut inside its shell? The thought was so heady it made him shiver. 'Careful, careful,' he whispered, his voice a thread of sound in the room.

The possibilities were laid out in his mind like a series of jewels on a map of the Borough, all carefully researched and explored, waiting to be plucked when the time seemed right. Did last night's gift mean he should act sooner than he'd planned?

Anticipation pumped his heart, made the breath puff from his nostrils. He whipped his shirt from the board and switched off the iron, his mind alight with the thrill of choice.

'That was a frigging waste of time,' Maura Bell muttered as she walked out of the fire station into Sawyer Street, Kincaid and Cullen on either side of her. The rain had stopped at last, and above them a few patches of dusky purple sky showed against the banks of pewter cloud. The temperature had dropped with the sunset. Glancing back, she saw warm light spilling from the windows in the fire station's red bay doors, a glimpse of a closed and comforting world. She shrugged the collar of her coat closer around her throat.

Kincaid glanced at her, raising an eyebrow, as Cullen said easily, 'Maybe, maybe not,' as if he'd nothing better to do than sit around watching a bunch of surly firefighters shuffle their feet and look clueless. 'Somebody may remember something. Never hurts to plant a seed. Listen,' Cullen added as they reached his car, left in the fire station car park, 'we'll give you a lift back to the nick. There's not much more we can do tonight.'

'I've a better idea,' Kincaid said. 'Why don't we all have a drink. My treat. We can map out our agenda for tomorrow.'

Her response was automatic, instinctive. The last thing she wanted to do was have a chummy pint with Scotland Yard. 'I've things to do at the station.'

'Surely they can wait a bit,' Kincaid said lightly. 'Call it conference time, if it will ease your guilty conscience, but I think we could all use a break.'

'The CCTV films—'

'That's what constables are for,' chimed in Cullen, opening the car's back door for her. 'You have to learn to delegate.'

Maura shifted some of the papers that had slid back into the space she'd cleared on Cullen's backseat on the short ride from Southwark Street to the fire station. The task gave her a moment to think.

She'd checked in with the incident room staff just before their meeting at the fire station, so she knew there were no breaking developments that urgently needed her attention.

She was also aware that a refusal to socialize with

the other detectives could mark her as a bad sport, and possibly a prig – not the reputation she wanted to establish on her first outing with Scotland Yard. 'Okay, just a quick one, then,' she said, trying to give in gracefully. 'I know a good pub in Borough High Street. Or there's this one.' She pointed at the pub that occupied the bottom corner of the fire station premises. 'The Goldsmith—'

'If I'm buying, I get to choose,' interrupted Kincaid, sounding amused. He glanced at Cullen. 'The society?'

Cullen nodded. 'Right.'

'But—'

'Don't worry,' Kincaid assured her. 'We'll have you back before you turn into a pumpkin.'

With this, Maura had to be content. She sank back into her seat, curiosity beginning to override her indignation.

In moments they were crossing Blackfriars Bridge. The river caught the remnants of the sunset in a gleaming swathe of gold, and beyond it the floodlit dome of St Paul's was haloed by the fading pink sky. Cullen drove with an assurance she had somehow not expected, and Kincaid sat beside him without criticizing, unlike some of her superior officers.

Once in the City, Cullen sped up New Bridge Street and around Holborn Circle, into Hatton Garden, the heart of the diamond district. Maura knew this part of town only by reputation. 'Doing a little after-hours shopping, are we?' she asked as Cullen slipped the car into a vacant parking space on the street.

'We should be so lucky,' said Cullen, his fingers

barely brushing her elbow as they followed Kincaid across the street. 'But this is almost as good. You'll see.'

Maura relaxed a bit as they came to a cheerful-looking pub, but Kincaid passed it by, ducking into the narrow alleyway that ran alongside it. He stopped at a sleek door made of pale wood and keyed an entry pad.

Maura hung back. 'What—'

'Never fear, it's not a brothel.' Grinning, Cullen guided her inside. The pair reminded her of her older brothers playing a prank – not an auspicious omen.

The foyer opened directly onto a staircase made of more blonde wood and brushed steel. 'Private club,' Kincaid said over his shoulder as he started to climb. 'The Scotch Malt Whisky Society. Good whisky's the best antidote to the taste of a fire scene.'

She knew what he meant. The acrid smoke seemed to have settled permanently in her sinus cavities and at the back of her throat, and the sandwich she'd managed to snatch for lunch had tasted of ashes.

They had reached the first floor. Maura followed the men through a cloakroom area and into a large room that contradicted all her preconceived notions of a private club. There was a handsome bar down one side, but the furniture was contemporary, more Habitat than gentleman's club, and the white walls were splashed with bright, abstract paintings. The room was quite full, but Kincaid spied an empty table in the far corner and led them to it. 'Shall I choose?' he asked as they settled into their chairs.

Picking up a booklet from the low table, Maura found the pages filled with lists of whiskies identified only by numbers and rather fulsome descriptions.

'The society does its own bottling, straight from casks it buys directly from the distilleries,' Kincaid explained. 'It assigns a number to each bottling, but there is a key that links the numbers with the names of the distilleries, if you're interested.'

She shook her head and closed the booklet. 'I'll trust you on this. So, are you some sort of whisky connoisseur?'

'Not really. It's just that we've a friend who's trying to get a small Highland distillery back on its feet, so I'm doing my bit to support the industry.'

'Very noble of you, I'm sure.'

'Yeah.' He grinned at her, and for the first time she was aware of the power of his smile. She suspected he used it like a weapon and dislike surged through her. 'Why don't I see what they have on special tonight?' Kincaid added, then stood and threaded his way to the bar.

'Your superintendent's quite the charmer,' she said to Cullen.

'He has his moments,' Cullen agreed, as if unaware of her sarcasm. 'He's a good guvnor, the best I've had.'

How like a man, she thought furiously, to defend another male no matter how inexcusable his behaviour. 'And does he snog all his female officers when he gets them in a car?' she blurted.

'Snog?' Cullen looked at her as if she'd lost her

mind. 'In a car . . . oh, you mean Gemma?' Enlightenment dawned in his face. 'In my car. Did he really?
Good for him.' He gave a whoop of laughter.

'How can you—'

'Look, Inspector – Maura – I'm afraid you've got
the wrong end of the stick. Duncan's not Gemma's
boss. She works out of Notting Hill Division, not the
Yard. They live together. She was in Southwark today
for personal reasons. And I've never seen Duncan
behave inappropriately with any female officer under
his command, if that's what you're thinking.'

Maura felt the blood rising in her face. 'But . . . I
thought—' Kincaid returned at that moment, balancing
three tumblers. She gave Cullen a pleading glance,
hoping he wouldn't mortify her further by repeating
her comment.

'This is a lighter Speyside,' Kincaid said as he
handed round glasses filled with pale gold liquid. 'I
thought it might be more to your taste than some of
the heavily sherried or peated whiskies.' She had no
idea what he was talking about but forced a smile. She
opened her bag to reach for a cigarette, then, realizing
that neither of them smoked, thought better of it and
closed the bag.

Kincaid took a small pitcher of water from the
table and added a splash of water to his glass and
Cullen's, but Maura shook her head when he offered
it to her. She was a Scot, in case he hadn't noticed,
and the one thing she did know was that Scots drank
their whisky neat. 'Cheers,' she said, and tipped back
her glass for a hearty swallow.

Fire ripped at her throat and knifed down into her chest. A spasm of coughing racked her, and by the time she caught her breath, her eyes were streaming. 'For Christ's sake,' she gasped. 'What is this stuff, turps?'

Both Cullen and Kincaid were barely containing their smirks. 'It's cask strength,' Kincaid told her. 'I should have explained. The alcohol by volume is well over fifty per cent on most of these. Here, have some water.'

This time she accepted the pitcher and added a good dollop before attempting another very small sip. 'Have I passed some sort of initiation, then?' she asked, scowling at them.

'With flying colours,' said Cullen. 'At least it's not the Hellfire Club.'

She wasn't sure whether it was the effects of the whisky or the fact that she didn't see how she could possibly make a bigger fool of herself than she already had, but Maura felt a pleasant sense of ease spread through her muscles.

'Now.' Kincaid set down his glass and leaned forward. 'I had a call from Kate Ling while I was at the bar. She's scheduled the PM for nine in the morning, at St Thomas's. We're to meet her at the morgue. After that, we'll at least have something to go on. Maura, you've not heard anything new from Missing Persons?'

'Not as of an hour ago.'

He frowned. 'Gemma's report must not have been processed yet – either that or it didn't get flagged.'

Cullen looked surprised. 'Gemma's report?'

'I haven't had a chance to tell you,' Kincaid explained, including Maura with a glance. 'And I'm not at all sure it's relevant. My cousin's wife is an Anglican priest on a temporary placement here in Southwark. She rang Gemma today, wanting some advice because one of her parishioners said her house-mate had disappeared overnight. That's why Gemma was in Southwark. She talked to the woman, con-vinced her to report it.'

Cullen gestured excitedly, sloshing a little whisky over the edge of his glass. 'But that's—'

'Gemma also said it looked as if the woman might have decamped voluntarily. It sounds as if she stole out of the house sometime in the night – by which time our victim may already have been dead – and that she might have taken personal items with her, perhaps an overnight bag. Nothing like that has turned up at the scene.' He paused, sipping his drink. 'I thought we should wait until we knew a little more about the victim before we pursue it further.'

'What's the woman's name?' Maura pulled a note-book from her bag and was surprised to find it took a bit more effort than usual to grip the pen.

'Elaine Holland. Mid-thirties. White. Lives in Ufford Street and works at Guy's Hospital. Right now, how-ever, I'm more concerned about Marcus Yarwood and his foreman. I want to make sure their alibis are solid.'

'I've asked Birmingham to send someone to make inquiries at Yarwood's hotel,' said Maura, glad to have her notes handy. 'And I've got a DC from our station checking on Spender.'

'What do you know about Yarwood?' Kincaid asked.

She shrugged. 'Just what you read in the papers or see on the telly. I'd never met him before today, but I've never heard anything dodgy about him either. Seems to be a pretty straight guy. I think he's divorced, with a twenty-something daughter. He started up his own fleet of delivery vans when he was just a kid, before he went into politics. I think this warehouse is his first venture into property.'

'He didn't strike me as the sort to go in for insurance fraud,' Kincaid mused, swirling the dregs in his glass. 'And I think he was genuinely distressed over the loss of the building, but he was also nervous. I want to know why.'

'You think it was more than knowing the press would be on him like sharks?' asked Cullen.

'Yarwood's spent his whole career dealing with sharks. That's what politicians do. My guvnor – that's Chief Superintendent Childs—' he explained to Maura, 'mentioned rumours that Yarwood's flats weren't selling as fast as expected, but both Yarwood and Spender denied it. We need to find out where that's coming from and whether or not it's true.'

Cullen looked pleased. 'That's right up my alley. I'll see what I can dig up on the Internet tonight. Then I can follow up leads tomorrow.'

'And I'll have a word with Childs. We also need to talk to Yarwood's insurance agent, if we can track him down on a Saturday.' Turning to Maura, Kincaid added, 'And you've got the CCTV in hand?'

As was her habit when collecting her thoughts, she

started to reach again for a cigarette, then checked herself and sipped at her drink instead. 'We should have the tapes collected and scanned by morning. There's only a view of the front door, though, and even that was a lucky break. The office building across the street recently put in a camera as they've been having some security problems. We've also collected tapes from the other cameras in the area, just in case they've picked up something suspicious.'

'What about the fires the sub officer mentioned tonight?' Kincaid asked. 'Do you know anything about that?'

She frowned, trying to recall snippets of talk she hadn't given much attention. 'I do remember hearing about a couple of fires in the past few months, but I don't think they were tagged as arson.'

'Nor is this one, yet. But my gut tells me that Farrell is certain of it; he's just not willing to commit himself without evidence. Farrell's sharp, and if there's anything to this, I think he'll ferret it out.' Kincaid glanced at his watch. 'Blast. I'd better dash. Toby'll be in bed, but I'd like to at least say good night to Kit, since our plans for tomorrow are shot to hell.'

'I can run you back to the Yard, guv.' Cullen started to rise, but Kincaid waved him back.

'I'll get the tube from Chancery Lane; worry about the car in the morning. Can I get you two another round before I go?'

Maura shook her head. She'd be legless if she had another.

'I'd better not,' said Cullen, and she noticed his whisky was barely touched. He seemed to hesitate before adding, 'How *is* Kit, guv?'

'As well as can be expected, I suppose, under the circumstances.' Kincaid stood, and although his response had been polite, Maura sensed it was a subject he didn't want to pursue. 'I'll leave things in your capable hands, then.' He nodded at them both. 'See you in the morning.'

Maura watched him walk away, her curiosity aroused. 'Who's Kit?'

'His son,' Cullen said, his expression guarded as if he regretted bringing it up, and he quickly changed the subject. 'Are you sure I can't get you another drink? I can have them put it against Duncan's membership.'

'No, thanks. I'd better get the tube as well. I left my car at the station, and I've things to check on before I go home.'

'Then let me run you back to Borough High Street. It's right on my way.'

She gave him a quizzical glance. 'Where do you live?'

'Um . . .' He grinned. 'Euston.'

'You've an odd way of getting there. Over the river and back again.'

'I find driving relaxing,' he told her, poker-faced. 'What do you say we get a bite to eat first? I'm starved, and the pub downstairs is brilliant.'

'No little missus waiting with dinner for you at home, Sergeant?'

'That'd be a fine thing.' He grimaced. 'My flat runs to a bit of mouldy cheese in the fridge, along with a beer or two if I'm lucky. What about you?'

She took a mental inventory. 'Olives, shrivelled. Some *good* cheese from Borough Market. A half bottle of wine going bad.'

'Does that make us even? I think the least we could do for the sad state of our affairs is to join forces for a decent meal.'

Maura thought about the dark flat awaiting her, considered the prospect of cheese and biscuits eaten in front of the flickering light of the telly, and suddenly rushing home didn't seem all that appealing.

She knocked back the last of her Scotch, her eyes watering, and set her glass down on the table with a thump. Some small part of her mind wondered if it was only the whisky talking, but she found she didn't really care.

'Okay,' she said. 'Why not?'

Winnie stirred a heaped spoonful of Horlicks into the mug of milk she'd heated for Franny in the microwave, then popped the drink back in for a few more seconds while she rooted in the cabinets for a packet of biscuits. She'd made them both omelettes for dinner, then helped Franny get ready for bed and settled her on the chaise longue.

She'd been surprised to learn that Franny could stand on her own, if only briefly. 'It's not like a spinal cord injury,' Franny had explained as Winnie helped her into her nightdress. 'Although I was completely paralyzed the first few months; I even had to have help breathing the first weeks in intensive care.'

'How long were you in hospital?' Winnie asked.

'Six months, although I don't remember much of the first part. GBS comes on very suddenly, and they still don't know the cause. I am getting better, though,' she'd added brightly. 'It's just that . . . sometimes it's hard to be patient.'

Winnie had been about to say 'I can imagine' when she realized she couldn't, and that there was no aphorism adequate for Franny's everyday struggles.

Silently, she'd tucked Franny up under her faded quilt. Then she'd come into the kitchen and rattled things about in an effort to vent the anger she was feeling towards Elaine Holland. If Elaine had been dishonest with Franny about a small thing like the mobile phone, what else had she lied about? Although Winnie cautioned herself against jumping to conclusions, she couldn't shake the feeling that Elaine had been using Franny in some way.

She'd located the biscuits, on the low table that held a toaster, an electric kettle, bread, tea and most of the other necessities that allowed Franny to function fairly independently during the day. When the microwave dinged, she carried the mug and biscuits into the sitting room, breathing in the malty aroma of the Horlicks with a smile. 'Isn't it odd how smells seem to connect with our memories so directly?' she asked as she positioned the things on Franny's table. 'One sniff of Horlicks and I'm five years old, staying the night with my gran, just as if it were yesterday.'

'We drank cocoa when I was a child, but after I got sick I couldn't tolerate the caffeine,' Franny said, pushing herself up on the chaise so that she could reach the cup. 'The Horlicks was Elaine's idea. She made it for me every night, even when she was late getting in.'

Winnie tried to reconcile this small nurturing act with what she'd seen of Elaine, without much success. 'Franny,' she asked slowly, pulling up a chair, 'what do you and Elaine find to talk about? It doesn't seem as if you have much in common.'

'Oh, well . . . we talk about her work, and the hospital – it makes me feel I'm still a bit involved – and about the daily household things, you know, what we need from the shops, what to have for supper. Sometimes we watch telly together.' Franny's face took on a faraway look. 'Sometimes we'd plan holidays we were going to take when I was well enough, somewhere in the sun. Italy or Majorca. I always liked to imagine Elaine on the beach, going brown as a nut, and I thought that if she could get away for a bit, she wouldn't *mind* things so much.'

'Mind things?'

'Oh, you know. She'd get her feelings hurt easily . . . if someone said something at work or if she felt she'd been passed over. And sometimes she'd take against people for no real reason, like—' Franny stopped, a little colour rising in her pale cheeks.

'Like me, you mean?' asked Winnie gently. 'It's all right, I don't mind.'

'I don't think it was you personally. More the Church in general.'

Winnie had suspected Elaine of being jealous of her. Now she wondered if Elaine had been afraid of having her own relationship with Franny too closely inspected.

'I thought she was beginning to soften up a bit recently, though,' Franny went on. 'At least she stayed when you brought the Eucharist on Sundays. She'd always made a point of being out of the house when Roberta came.'

'I'm flattered,' Winnie said with a smile. 'Although I can't imagine anyone not liking Roberta.' She took Franny's empty cup. 'Will you be all right on your own tonight? I can stay if you like.'

'You've done too much as it is.' Franny reached out and gave Winnie's hand a squeeze. 'I do have some tablets, though, that I take sometimes when I have a bad night. Maybe I should take one of those.'

'Good idea. I'll fetch them for you.'

Having been directed to the drawer in the kitchen, Winnie found the bottle and shook a small oval white tablet into her hand. She recognized the name of a mild hypnotic, but frowned as she glanced at the prescription date. The prescription was only a week old but the bottle seemed at least half empty. She poured the remaining tablets out into her palm and counted them – there were ten left out of thirty.

She suspected this type of medication was addictive. Was Franny taking more than the prescribed dose? And how could she go about asking her?

The room had grown dark. Harriet lay on a narrow bed, still half dreaming, disjointed images flitting through her mind.

Beneath her a musty, sour smell rose from the mattress when she moved. It made her think of the time her friend Samantha had come to stay and had wet the bed, and of old Mrs Bletchley.

A spark flared in her mind. Mrs Bletchley's, that's where she was. She'd overslept for school. But no – the images came crowding back, fuzzy and jittering like an old newsreel she'd seen in history class.

Her dad – she remembered seeing her dad, and ducking down to slide into the back seat of his car. Her backpack had caught on the door frame, and the lady in the front seat had looked back at her and smiled.

She drifted again, riding a current of flickering movement – her dad saying something – she could see his lips moving, but she couldn't hear the words.

More darkness. A lamp globe made of swirly orange glass swam into view. Coffee, she'd smelled coffee. It made her think of their flat in the morning, of her mother getting ready for work . . . But no, that wasn't right . . .

She struggled to pull herself out of the dream. Not home. Starbucks. The lady had taken her to Starbucks. But where was her dad?

Movement again, the world tilting. Another car ride – no, a taxi. She remembered the shiny black door. A man's face asking a question, his blue eyes kind. She felt the warmth of a body against hers, heard a woman's voice saying, 'She's not feeling well . . . bit of a bug . . .'

Walls rose, taller than she could see, blocking out the light. Grey brick, topped with broken glass and strands of wire that curled.

Then, a gate – or had it been before? Her mind fixed on it, trying to hold the image. A silvery arch, like a keyhole, filled with black flowers. And through the keyhole, a flash of green.

The bright colour receded and winked out, as if a door had closed at the end of a tunnel, and the darkness descended like a weight.

Chapter Seven

Now, what I want is, Facts . . .Facts alone are wanted in life.

Charles Dickens
Hard Times

'Are you sure you don't want me to run you to the tube station?' Gemma asked as Kincaid gulped at a cup of scalding tea and folded toast and bacon into a makeshift sandwich. 'Then you'd have time to eat your breakfast sitting down.'

'Thanks, love, but I think I'd rather walk. Make hay while the sun shines – isn't that what they say?' The morning had dawned bright and windy, but with a promise of more rain later in the day.

'Have you been listening to *The Archers* again?' she teased, turning from the fridge with a carton of juice in one hand.

'I confess. It's my secret vice.' He set down his mug and gave her a one-armed hug. 'No, seriously, I don't mind the walk, and you've got to get the boys up if you're going to make it to Portobello before the market's jammed.' What he didn't say was that he needed that brief time on his own to fold away the morning's images, the bright kitchen filled with comforting smells, Gemma dishevelled before the warmth of the Aga, the boys still safe in their beds upstairs. These were not things he wanted to carry too close to the surface when he walked into the morgue at St Thomas'.

'I'm sorry about this morning, about not going with you,' he added as she disengaged herself to turn a second batch of bacon cooking in the frying pan.

'You know it can't be helped,' she answered, not glancing up from her task.

He hesitated, knowing this was not the time to discuss it, but he couldn't be sure when he'd have another chance. The dogs, Kit's little terrier Tess and Gemma's cocker spaniel Geordie, were underfoot, tails wagging as they watched him expectantly, so he divided the last bite of his sandwich between them. 'It worries me that Kit won't talk about Monday.'

This time she did look at him. 'He'll be fine.' She gave him a reassuring smile. 'We'll be fine. We'll have our treasure hunt at the market, maybe lunch at Otto's, then after my piano lesson I'm taking them to tea at Erika's.' Putting down her tongs, she came to him and grasped the lapels of his jacket. 'Ring me when you know something. I'll keep my phone with me.'

Her hair was sleep-tousled, her skin still free of the light make-up she wore during the day. With his thumb he traced the faint pattern of freckles on her cheekbone. She turned her face into his hand. The tenderness of the gesture moved him to say what he'd been keeping back for weeks. 'Gemma, are you sure about giving up the nursery? I think we should talk—'

'We can't disappoint Kit now. You know that.' She stepped back, the momentary softness of her expression replaced by a bright smile. He had ventured onto forbidden ground and she'd withdrawn again. 'Now go,' she added briskly, 'or you'll be late.'

She was right, of course, he admitted to himself a few minutes later as he walked up Lansdowne Road, towards Holland Park tube station. Kit had to come first now, but acknowledging that didn't make it any easier to deal with Gemma shutting him out – or the realization that she was, whether consciously or not, using the situation with Kit as an excuse to avoid talking about her miscarriage and the possibility of having another child.

And to add insult to injury he'd had no luck trying to get Kit to discuss his feelings about Monday's impending hearing. Arriving home a bit before ten the previous evening, he'd found Gemma at the piano in the dining room, practising for her Saturday afternoon lesson. She'd been working on a simple Bach piece, and although she didn't have much time to play, he could tell she was improving. Her tempo was still a little slow, but her fingertips moved lightly and surely over the keys.

Pausing, she'd looked up and smiled, but he'd waved her on. 'Don't stop. I'm going to check on the boys.'

He'd started up the stairs, and the dogs, having dutifully met him at the front door, settled back into position on the first landing. This had become their usual strategy for dealing with divided loyalties when the family was split between up and downstairs. Their cat Sid, on the other hand, operating on the principle of *all things come to those who wait*, would be curled on the foot of their bed.

He had looked in on Toby, now sleeping alone in the room he'd shared with Kit until a few weeks ago. The five-year-old lay sprawled on his stomach, covers thrown back to reveal his train-printed pyjamas, his teddy bear tossed to the floor. Kincaid carefully tucked in the bear and pulled up the duvet, but there was no change in the rhythm of Toby's slightly whuffly breathing.

Kincaid had moved on to the room along the landing once intended as the nursery. When his light knock brought no answer, he opened the door. Kit sat at his desk hunched over a sheet of paper, drawing. A set of headphones explained his lack of response, and Kincaid could hear the tinny, muted sound of the personal CD player from across the room.

Rapping more loudly on the open door, Kincaid called out, 'Hey, sport.'

Kit turned, startled, and yanked off the headphones. 'Sorry. Didn't hear you.'

'I'm not surprised.' Kincaid thought of all the times his mother had told him he was going to ruin his hearing, and refrained from further comment on the volume. 'What are you listening to?' he asked instead, sitting down on the bed. Tess had followed him upstairs and now jumped up beside him.

'The Mighty Diamonds.' Kincaid must have looked blank because Kit added, in the *don't you know anything?* tone that had been creeping into his voice more frequently of late, 'It's reggae. Classic eighties.'

'Oh, right. I must have been listening to the Police in the eighties, myself.'

'But the Police were influenced by reggae, and by Bob Marley,' Kit told him with great seriousness, and Kincaid had congratulated himself on inadvertently getting something right. He suspected that would become more and more difficult, but he meant to keep trying.

'Did you borrow the CD from Wesley?' Wesley Howard, a young man they'd met on a previous case, often helped out with the children, as well as working at Otto's Cafe and studying photography at college.

'He said I could.' Kit's reply was unexpectedly defensive. 'I haven't scratched it or anything.'

'No. I'm sure you haven't. You're very good at looking after things,' Kincaid assured him, thinking he'd have to ask Wes for a crash course on reggae on the sly. In the meantime he'd try an easier topic. He glanced at the paper on Kit's desk. 'Are you sketching?'

Kit held up a drawing of a tortoise, copied from the open zoology book beside it. 'Galapagos tortoise.' The boy's latest hero was Dr Stephen Maturin, the surgeon/naturalist from Patrick O'Brien's *Master and*

Commander novels, and he'd become determined to learn to draw.

'Wow, that's terrific,' Kincaid said, and the sincere admiration in his voice elicited a smile from Kit.

'I could do with some better watercolour pencils. There's an art supply shop off Portobello, near Otto's. I thought maybe I could get them tomorrow.'

'Listen, sport. About tomorrow. I'm going to have to miss out on our shopping expedition. Something's come up—'

'I know. Gemma told me.' Kit's expression was neutral, reserved.

'I'm sorry. I wanted—'

'Don't worry about it.' Kit had shrugged and turned back to his desk. 'It doesn't matter.'

The absolution cut Kincaid to the quick.

When Kincaid arrived at the morgue, Farrell, Cullen and Bell were there before him, and Kincaid suspected that Cullen, at least, derived some satisfaction from getting one up on his boss.

He joined them in the post-mortem theatre gallery, where they looked down on Kate Ling and her assistant, and on the grotesque and blackened form on the steel dissection table. The smell made Kincaid wish he'd forgone even his hurried breakfast.

Dr Ling and the assistant pathologist wore long green plastic aprons tied over their scrubs which, viewed from the back, made him think of gunslingers in chaps. Perhaps it was something in the assurance of their stance, feet apart, ready to take on the grim reaper himself.

Ling turned and saw him, her eyes crinkling in a smile above her mask. She switched off her mike. 'Duncan, I was just saying to your colleagues that we've finished the preliminary exam. As I'm sure you all know, we can learn a good bit simply from measurements and radiology, even when the corpse is quite severely damaged.' She gestured towards the far wall, where a series of X-rays were mounted on light boards. 'These things tell us that our victim was an adult female, of medium height – probably five five or six. Although fire can cause some shrinkage of bone, in this case I don't believe the heat was that severe.'

'Could you narrow "adult" down a bit, Doc?' Kincaid asked.

'Post-adolescent, definitely. In females, by the age of twenty, the lower epiphysis – that's one of the bony plates at either end of the forearm – and radius have fused. Shortly thereafter the upper epiphysis and radius fuse as well, as is the case here.

'The collarbone gives us our next marker – it has usually finished growing by the age of twenty-eight or so – but as the victim's upper torso has suffered the most severe fire damage, I can't give a definitive opinion on that.

'As to the upper end of the spectrum, older subjects show signs of degeneration around the edges of the vertebrae, and joints may show signs of arthritis.

Neither of those are evident here, but we may want to have a forensic anthropologist take another look.'

'So you're saying twenty to . . .'

'Mid-thirties, possibly forty.'

Kincaid winced at the idea that, according to a pathologist's estimate, he was already going downhill. He caught a glimpse of the pained expression on Bill Farrell's face and guessed the thought had occurred to him as well.

'Twenty to forty. That's a big bloody help,' Cullen muttered in Kincaid's ear. While his sergeant might approach the most tedious and time-consuming data search with equanimity, post-mortems made him grumpy.

'Any chance the victim could be older than forty, Doc?' Kincaid asked.

'With good genes, maybe. As I said, I'm no expert. Let's move on to the exterior physical examination. Although it's not unusual to find a burn victim's clothing fused to the skin, we were unable to discover any fabric traces. Officer Farrell, has your team turned up any evidence of clothing at the scene?'

'Not so far. Even if the fire destroyed all fabric, we'd expect to turn up a bit of button or zip, or a fragment of shoe leather. Her clothing may have been taken away from the scene, or she arrived there starkers.'

Ling nodded, as if he were a promising pupil. 'That leads us to another interesting point. The stripping of a female victim usually implies some sort of sexual assault, but this woman shows no obvious signs of sexual trauma. Of course, that doesn't completely rule out a sexual motive, but it does narrow things down a bit. We'll know more when we get the results of the swabs.'

'What about race, Doctor?' asked Maura Bell. 'The skin looks black, but the hair that's left seems reddish.'

'Neither skin nor hair are good indicators here. The dark colour of the skin is due to charring, but the hair colour is also misleading. Dark hair can often lighten due to oxidation. My guess is that this woman was a Caucasian brunette.'

Bell looked puzzled. 'Caucasian? But you've just said you couldn't tell the colour of the skin.'

'We can't.' Ling smiled. 'But we can tell the shape of the skull, both from visual assessment and from X-rays.' She touched a gloved finger to the head of the corpse. 'This skull is high and wide. The nasal opening is narrow. The cheekbones do not project, nor does the jaw. These are all defining Caucasian characteristics.'

'Okay, Doc,' said Kincaid. 'We've got white, female, brunette, medium height, between twenty and forty. But did she die in the fire?'

'Patience, Duncan, patience. I'm just getting to the interesting bit. Let's take a closer look at the skull. We noted at the scene that there was fracturing, but we also know that intense heat can cause fracturing. In that case, however, the plates of the skull tend to separate at the sutures. What we can see here, on closer examination, is more consistent with a depressed fracture due to blunt force trauma.'

'Clear as mud,' Cullen said, and Kincaid gave him a silencing frown.

'Microscopic examination of the edges of the fractured bone will tell us more,' Ling went on. 'But there's also evidence of frontal trauma, moderate LeFort fractures. The nose has been broken' – she traced the bridge of the nose with her finger – 'as has one cheekbone.'

'Excuse me, Doctor.' Bell stepped forward, resting her hands on the gallery railing. 'Are you telling us this woman was killed by a blow – or blows – to the head, rather than by the fire?'

'No, I'm merely saying that it's more than likely the skull fractures were not *caused* by the heat from the fire. That doesn't rule out the possibility that the victim was alive at the time of the fire, or that these injuries were sustained *during* the fire. Although the last scenario is unlikely, I'll admit, as there was no evidence of structural collapse at the scene, and it's not very plausible that the victim could have fallen and injured both the front and back of her head at the same time.

'There is some soot visible in the nose and mouth, which could indicate that she was still breathing, but it might also be a result of settling, as she was lying face up. We won't know for sure until we've examined the airway and lungs. So let's have a look.' Switching her mike back on, Ling turned to her assistant, who had been patiently standing by, and accepted a scalpel. 'Thanks, Sandy. Let's begin with the larynx and trachea.'

Kincaid had never quite got over the instinctive flinch brought on by the pathologist's first incision, but he forced himself to watch as Ling made a precise cut, murmuring a detailed description into the microphone. The mortuary cold had begun to make his bones ache, but at least, he realized, his nose had gone numb, acclimatized to the smell. Stealing a glance at his companions, he saw that Cullen looked increasingly cross, Farrell impassive, and Bell wore a glazed expression that made him think of a deer caught in the headlamps of a car.

'Ah, now this is interesting,' said Kate Ling, glancing up at them. 'There's no sign of soot in the windpipe, but there is something else – bruising of the underlying tissues of the throat that was not visible on the skin.'

'She was choked?' Kincaid asked, surprised.

'The hyoid bone is intact, but yes, I'd say so. She could have lost consciousness long enough to have been bashed in the head and face.'

'And the absence of soot means she was dead when the fire started?'

'Well, there is always the possibility of vagal inhibition – that's a reflexive constriction of the pharynx – from inhaling hot gases, but considering her other injuries I'd say yes, it's likely she was dead when the fire started.'

'Hallelujah!' breathed Cullen, and a smile flickered across Bell's face.

'Can you tell us what was used to inflict the blunt trauma injuries?' asked Farrell.

'We'll know more when we get into the skull, of course, but I'd say something with a fairly large surface area.'

While Kate Ling continued with her examination, Kincaid let his mind wander over the implications of what she'd told them. Although Farrell still hadn't found any definitive evidence of arson, this made it look as if they were dealing with a fire started to cover up a murder – which in turn made it less likely that insurance fraud was the motive. But did that mean Marcus Yarwood was out of the frame?

It didn't explain how the murderer had gained access to the building, and Kincaid still harboured a strong feeling that Yarwood was somehow involved.

It hadn't escaped him that he'd been asked to look after Yarwood's interests, but if Yarwood's bosses had thought that appealing to their connections at Scotland Yard would guarantee favouritism, they'd been much mistaken. As far as Kincaid was concerned, his brief was simply to make sure Marcus Yarwood was not accused without grounds.

Kincaid also realized that Ling's description of the victim could fit the profile of Winnie's friend's missing housemate. He'd have to ring Gemma as soon as they were finished at the hospital and arrange to get a sample of the woman's DNA for the lab. He could put in a sample request through official channels, of course, as a report had been filed, but out of consideration for Winnie he preferred to take care of it in person.

And he had to admit his curiosity had been aroused by Gemma's description of the house and the missing woman's odd lifestyle. If there was any chance the woman in the warehouse might turn out to be Elaine Holland, he wanted to see both house and housemate for himself.

As Dr Ling began the Y incision that would allow her to remove and examine the victim's internal organs, Maura Bell's phone rang. She stepped back, shielding the phone and speaking quietly so as not to disturb the procedure, but when she rang off her face shone with barely suppressed excitement.

'That was the station,' she said. 'About the CCTV footage. They've found something.'

Congratulating herself on her luck, Gemma slipped the car into a parking space in Pembridge Gardens, just off the top of Portobello Road. A spot so near Portobello Market on a Saturday morning was not to be passed up, although the location meant she'd have a struggle with Toby when they walked past the library. He'd begun to read simple books on his own, and their usual Saturday visits to the library were the highlight of his week, but today they had another agenda.

Having let the boys skip breakfast at home in the

interests of speed, she distracted Toby with a reminder of her promise to buy them hot cocoa and croissants from the street stall at Mr Christian's Deli. That way they could eat and shop at the same time.

Soon they joined the lemming-like flood of pedestrians pouring into the top of Portobello Road. With one hand firmly gripping Toby and the other her handbag, Gemma relaxed into the flow, letting herself enjoy the colour and bustle of the crowd. Beside her, Kit looked happier than she'd seen him in weeks.

She loved the view from the top end of Portobello Road, and it was never more beautiful than on a sunny autumn morning. Below them the street curved gently, lined on both sides with houses and shopfronts painted every hue of the rainbow.

It made her feel she'd been picked up out of ordinary London and plonked down in the middle of somewhere more exotic – a village in Italy or maybe the south of France – except that this, too, was typical of London, where it was not unusual for colourful and eccentric pockets to adjoin areas of sedate Victorian villas. Snatches of music came from the buskers farther down the road, fading in and out as if someone were twirling the dial on a cosmic radio, and the odour of garlic cooking wafted up from a basement kitchen as they passed.

It took Gemma a moment to put a name to the feeling that welled up inside her. With a start of surprise she realized it was contentment. It wasn't only the view she loved, but all of Portobello and Notting Hill, and the house she shared with Duncan and the boys. She loved the connections they had made – friends, neighbours, shopkeepers – and it came to her that she had never before felt so at home. Not in Islington, not even in Leyton where she had grown up.

Her parents had known that sense of community, of belonging, she was sure, but she'd always been focused on moving on, getting out, making her own life. Then, during her marriage to Rob, her pregnancy, Toby's babyhood, she'd always been looking round the corner, anticipating what came next. Her life had been a litany of afters – *after the wedding, after the baby, after she returned to work, after the divorce, after promotion.* Even living in Hazel's garage flat her perceptions had been coloured by the knowledge that it could only be a stopgap, a temporary measure.

But now . . . now she didn't want to move on. Perhaps it was partly her worry over Kit; perhaps it was the sense of life's fragility that still lingered from her miscarriage; or perhaps it was watching the collapse of her friend Hazel's seemingly perfect marriage.

Whatever the reason, she knew only that she wanted fiercely to hold on to things just the way they were and not take any risks that might bring about change.

The crowd thickened as Gemma and the boys crossed Chepstow Villas and entered the heart of Portobello's antique market, and she gripped Toby's hand a little tighter. When Kit veered off to the right, towards the antique sporting goods shop that was one of his favourites, she pulled him back firmly. 'Food first. Then we shop.'

A few minutes later, armed with hot drinks in paper cups and flaky chocolate croissants, they started a thorough perusal of the street stalls and arcades.

Gemma hadn't expected finding an antique specimen cabinet would be easy, but three hours and four arcades later she was beginning to despair. As the clock crept towards noon, the heat in the arcades had become suffocating, the crowds aggravating rather than exhilarating. Kit's face had grown longer and longer, and Toby was whining because he was hungry and because she'd refused to buy him an outrageously expensive Matchbox car. If she hadn't been so hot and tired, she'd have laughed at the look on his face when she'd tried to explain that the toys were not meant to be played with, only looked at. The concept of collecting made no sense to a five-year-old.

'What do you say we take a break for lunch?' she said, sighing with relief as they emerged once more onto the pavement. 'We could go to Otto's. Is Wes working today?'

'Yeah, I think so,' answered Kit, displaying none of his usual enthusiasm for food or for a visit to their friend Otto's café. 'Couldn't we look just a bit longer?'

'Maybe after lunch—' Gemma broke off, realizing that the tinny sound she'd been hearing above the noise of the mob was her mobile phone. It was

Duncan, she saw as she fished it from her bag, and she had a sudden sinking feeling that it was not good news.

When she answered, he gave her the gist of the pathologist's report. 'We'll need a sample of Elaine Holland's DNA. I thought you might want to let Winnie know that I'll be calling on her friend.'

'I'll have to get in touch with Winnie. I'll ring you when I've contacted her, and you can meet us there.'

'Gemma, you don't have to come,' Kincaid protested. 'You said the house is right opposite Winnie's church. Why don't I just ask her to pop over and meet me?'

She thought of the boys and of another missed piano lesson, and for a moment she was tempted to agree. But then she recalled Franny Liu's frightened face and the comfort Franny had seemed to derive from her presence, and she felt ashamed of her selfishness. 'Yes,' she said reluctantly. 'I think I do.'

When she rang off, both boys were watching her.

'You have to go, right?' Kit said flatly.

'Yes,' she admitted ruefully. 'But maybe we can grab a bite of lunch first.'

'And the cabinet?'

'What about next Saturday?'

'Next Saturday? But . . .' Kit shrugged and turned away, studying the display of antique jewellery on a street stall with great concentration, but she'd seen the flash of panic in his eyes. Was he so worried about Monday's hearing at the family court that he feared there wouldn't be another Saturday?

Gently she said, 'Kit, there's no reason we can't do this next Saturday. Maybe Duncan can—'

'Gemma . . .' Kit was pointing at the jewellery display.

'—come with us. You know he wanted—'

'Gemma, look.'

'At the jewellery? Whatever for?' But frowning she followed his gaze, and then she saw what he had seen.

The glass-fronted display case lay on its back, covering most of the table's surface. But the cabinet, although large, was shallow, and its interior was divided into dozens of small, square compartments. In the case's current position, the compartments formed pockets, each of which held a small display of jewellery, but if it were stood upright it would make a perfect specimen cabinet.

Their exchange had drawn the dealer's attention. Gemma gave Kit's shoulder a warning squeeze and said as casually as she could manage, 'This for sale?'

The man lit a cigarette and squinted at her through narrowed eyes. 'Well, now, that depends, luv. I'd have to find something else to put my stock in. Just how much are you willing to offer?'

The three detectives and Bill Farrell sat huddled round the video monitor in the room they'd been temporarily assigned at Borough High Street Station. After Bell's phone call, they'd left Kate Ling to finish the postmortem. Ling had promised to let them know immediately if she found anything else significant; otherwise, she'd get the report to them as soon as the lab results came back. Kincaid, for his part, had been glad for an excuse to miss out on the sawing and slicing.

The CCTV tape had been loaded into the VCR, and even with the videotape in pause mode, the black and white image on the television screen looked blotchy and faded. Kincaid silently cursed cheap security measures that encouraged reusing videotapes until they were useless.

'This is from the building across the street and a few yards to the east of the warehouse's front entrance,' said the DS in charge of running the tape. 'We were lucky to find a private camera scanning more than the building's foyer, but as this is a credit reporting business they tend to be a bit paranoid about external security. Unfortunately, the view isn't great, as you can see.'

It took Kincaid a moment to match what he was seeing on the screen with his memory of the warehouse entrance. Then he realized that the camera's field of vision ended at the western edge of the warehouse door. This meant that not only could they not see the side door, but they had no view of the street on which it faced.

'Any luck finding a view of the side door?' he asked.

'No, sorry.' The DS, a young Asian woman, sounded as if she took the failure personally. 'There's nothing there except the shelter, and they said that although they'd considered a security camera, they hadn't managed to work it into their budget.' She picked up the remote control and continued more briskly, 'Now, we're just coming up to the critical time, if you'll bear with me.' The time display in the screen's bottom corner read 9:55. As she advanced the tape, a figure popped into view on the left-hand side of the screen and moved quickly across – a man, head down, coat collar pulled up high – then vanished on the right. 'A harmless pedestrian,' said the sergeant, 'but then things get more interesting.' She fast-forwarded the tape until 10:00 showed on the screen, then slowed to normal speed.

This time the figures came from the right, walking more slowly, and stopped before the warehouse door. Although their backs were to the camera, they were recognizable as male and female. The woman wore a short skirt with some sort of blouson jacket; the man was several inches taller and wore what looked like a set of motorcycle leathers. There was something oddly lumpy about the back of the man's head, but Kincaid couldn't quite make out what it was.

The couple shuffled and bumped against each other as if they were a bit tipsy, while the woman dug in her handbag and the man threw an arm briefly across the woman's shoulders. Something glinted in her hand as she let the bag drop to her side, and then, for just an instant, she turned round and surveyed the street.

The DS froze the frame and they all gazed at the face looking eerily back at them, as if the woman were aware of their regard. The image was blurred and grainy, but still an identifiable likeness.

At first Kincaid thought that she was too young to fit their profile, but as he studied her face more closely he decided she could be in her early twenties, maybe even older. Although it was hard to be certain because of the poor quality of the image, she appeared to be white and a brunette. Her lips were pursed in a pout of concentration.

'Anyone recognize her?' the DS asked. When no one responded, she said, 'We've printed photos from this frame – it's the best shot – and so far none of our regular beat officers has recognized her either. That makes it less likely she's a prostitute but doesn't rule it out altogether. I had my doubts about the skirt anyway – doesn't look short enough for a girl on the game.'

'Were those keys in her hand?' Kincaid asked.

'She did pull something from her handbag. It might have been keys or lock picks, but it could just as well have been a small torch or even a light sabre.'

'A warrior princess.' Kincaid grinned, then just as quickly sobered as he thought of what might have happened to this woman. 'Okay, what next?' he asked.

'Go forward again, slowly, Sarah,' instructed Maura Bell.

As the tape jerked into motion, the woman turned back to her companion. Having evidently decided the coast was clear, they both stepped forward into the doorway. After a moment the shadows round them seemed to darken. Then the couple disappeared.

The man's face had never been visible to the camera.

'We've got two more hours of tape before the fire,' explained Sarah, 'and neither of them comes out again – at least not by this door.' She pointed the remote at the screen. 'I'm going to fast-forward again. You'll see a few pedestrians, then, at a few minutes past ten, this man.' A few jerky figures crossed the screen without giving the doorway so much as a glance; then, as the tape slowed, a man in a dark coat came into view, again from the right. His head swivelled towards the doorway as he passed. He seemed to hesitate for an instant, then went on. 'And that's it,' said Sarah, 'until the fire brigade arrives twenty-odd minutes later.' The camera had never caught the man's face, and nothing else distinguished him.

'Did he see the open door and disregard it?' Cullen mused aloud. 'Or hear someone moving about?'

'We can't very well ask him, can we?' Kincaid said, venting his frustration in sarcasm. 'And troops could have been moving in and out on the side street, for all we know, with a marching band and Hannibal's elephants.'

'We've a photo of the girl that's good enough for an ID,' Maura Bell said sharply, as if wanting to make sure her team got the credit they deserved. 'I say we start by showing it to Marcus Yarwood and his foreman.'

'I can take a batch and canvas the street,' offered the DS, showing commendable initiative.

Kincaid thought of the arrangements he'd made to meet Gemma. Could this woman possibly be old enough to fit the description of Elaine Holland? The camera could be deceiving, and it was dangerous to make assumptions at this stage of an investigation. And even if Winnie's friend did not identify the woman in the photo as her missing housemate, they had no proof that the woman was in fact the victim found in the fire more than two hours later.

As much as he wanted to question Yarwood and the foreman about the photo himself, it made more sense to delegate. 'Doug, why don't you and DI Bell try to track down Yarwood and Joe Spender? I'm going to follow through on the missing housemate, and I'll need an evidence collection kit.'

Kincaid was tempted to regret his decision a few minutes later when Gemma rang to say she'd been delayed.

'Something came up,' she said enigmatically. 'And I had to get the boys some lunch. Besides, Winnie's tied up on a pastoral visit and won't be free for another hour.'

'We could go without her,' suggested Kincaid, chafing at the delay.

'I'd rather not,' Gemma told him. 'Franny Liu is going to need all the support she can get. Besides, by the time I get the boys sorted and get there myself, it wouldn't save us that much time. I'll ring you back when I've spoken to Winnie.'

With that he had to be content, and a moment's thought reconciled him to the setback. As efficient as Bell's young DS seemed to be, he wanted to show the photo to the shelter's staff himself, and the delay would give him time. Although Kath Warren had assured him that all the current residents were accounted for, the woman could have lived there formerly or have some connection with one of the current residents.

Bill Farrell was also heading back to the fire scene to supervise the ongoing collection of evidence. 'I've got a murder weapon to find,' he told Kincaid, 'and at least now I have some idea what to look for.'

Kincaid found a parking space near Farrell's van and walked down the side street to the shelter's entrance. The front door stood open, as it had the previous day, but the inner door was closed, and there was no answer when he rang the bell. There was no sound or sign of activity, and he doubted the residents answered the bell when the staff were out.

Glancing at his watch, he decided to grab a sandwich then give it another go. He walked back to South-wark Street and stood for a moment trying to decide which direction offered the best prospect of food. As he scanned the street he noticed a girl standing in the shadow of an office doorway. Something furtive in her posture drew his attention; then he realized her face was familiar. Her straight blonde hair was loose today, half hiding the curve of her cheek, but he'd no doubt it was the young firefighter he'd met yesterday.

'Rose?' he said, going up to her. 'It is Rose, isn't it? What are you doing here?'

Chapter Eight

They mounted up and up, through the musty smell of
an old close house, little used, to a large garret bedroom.

Charles Dickens
Little Dorrit

The patch of light moved across the wall above Harriet's bed. She watched its slow progress for a long
time, thinking about the roses on the wallpaper. They
were old roses, faded roses, on a background the
colour of tea stains. Sleepily, she wondered how her
mum could have forgotten that she hated flowery,
girly things, but the thought drifted lightly away.

She felt very odd, as if she were hovering outside
her own body, watching herself, but when she gave
her toe an experimental wiggle, it moved reassuringly.
It was only then that Harriet realized she was still
wearing her shoes. Why had she gone to bed in her
shoes?

Frowning, she pushed aside the rough blanket
covering her chest. Where was her duvet? And why
was she still wearing her sweatshirt, the same one

she'd put on for school that morning at Mrs Bletchley's? Wait . . . was that this morning? Or had that been yesterday morning? It had been dark, and she knew, somehow, that she had slept for a long time.

She felt a sickening lurch of panic as fragments of memory coalesced. Her dad . . . the lady in the front seat of the car . . . the grey walls . . . being half carried, half dragged, up narrow and twisting stairs . . . the darkness closing in . . .

Harriet sat up, her heart pounding. Her eyes focused on the light pouring in from the rectangle of window on the far wall, but her relief was short-lived. There was daylight coming in through the window, but it wasn't her window. Her mind finally wrapped itself around the truth it had been refusing to accept. It wasn't her room.

She forced herself to look around. Assess things, her mother was always telling her – have all the facts before you act. The room was larger than her bedroom at home. There was the window in the wall opposite the bed, and in the right-hand wall, a door. The left-hand wall sloped down, as if it was set into the eaves of the house. The walls were lined with odds and ends of discarded furniture, and a bookcase under the eaves held a few tattered, hardback volumes. There were a stool and a tin bucket in one corner, and beside the window a chest of drawers. On the chest stood a china basin and jug, patterned in faded pink roses, like the wallpaper.

Carefully, Harriet slid from the bed, and as she moved the sour, musty smell rose again from the mattress. The odour brought back the memory of the darkness, but she pushed it away.

The bare floorboards had once been painted grey, but the colour had aged to that of dust, and the surface was marred with scuff and drag marks. She placed her feet carefully, afraid to make a noise. Making her way to the window, she looked out of the grimy, spider-webbed panes.

A grim prospect greeted her. Below, she saw a small back garden infested with weeds and rubbish. Across the garden, another wall of grey brick, feature-less. Beyond the wall, she could make out the peaks of higher roofs, but nothing looked familiar. She tried the window, but it had been nailed or painted shut. Not that she'd have been able to get out that way, anyway – she could see that it was a straight drop of several floors. Nor did it look as if anyone would hear her if she called for help.

The choking panic rose in her throat again.

Where was she? What was this place? Why was she here?

Harriet gripped the window sill as dizziness swept over her. She realized suddenly that she was starving. How long had it been since she'd had anything to eat? A day, two days? The fact that she wasn't certain frightened her even more.

And she had to pee. The thought made her decide to try the door. The unpainted wood looked ancient and scarred, and there was a web of scratches around the old-fashioned keyhole. The knob turned in her fingers, but the door didn't budge.

Gripping the knob more tightly, she turned it hard to the right and leaned back with all her weight, but the door didn't even quiver. She let go and rubbed her smarting palms against her jeans, then crouched down to peer through the keyhole. There was nothing to see but darkness.

For a moment the urge to call out was almost overpowering, but she pressed her hand hard to her mouth. A shout might bring something worse than being alone and hungry.

Then she heard a noise. A creak, and then another, the soft footfalls of someone climbing the stairs. Harriet's first instinct was to hide. She looked round wildly, but there was no cover, not even beneath the frame of the old iron bed.

Her logical mind told her it wouldn't matter, that whoever was coming knew she was there, but her body obeyed a different instruction. She ran to the bed and wrapped the blanket around herself, as if the tattered fabric could give her a layer of protection, and huddled back against the wall. Then came the sound of bolts being drawn back, and the clicking of the tumblers as the key turned in the lock. The door swung open.

'Superintendent.' Rose Kearney looked as though he were the last person she wanted to see. Kincaid might have been tempted to take it personally, except that she'd been friendly enough yesterday, and her behaviour seemed decidedly odd. She didn't strike him as the type to be skulking in doorways.

'Are you all right?' he asked when she didn't step forward. She was dressed much as she had been at the fire scene yesterday, but with her hair loose rather than pulled back in a ponytail she looked younger, less professional.

'I . . .' She glanced past him, as if seeking a means of escape, then appeared to resign herself to the conversation. 'I was hoping to have a word with Station Officer Farrell.'

Kincaid nodded towards the warehouse. 'He's there now, working on the crime scene.'

Rose looked more uncomfortable still. 'I . . . it's just that . . . if my guvnor finds out I've been here without clearing it with him, he'll be livid. But our next duty's not until tomorrow morning, and there's something I thought Officer Farrell should know.'

'Something you've remembered?' Kincaid asked, his interest quickening.

She shook her head. 'No. But I've been looking into some things . . .' She drew farther into the doorway. 'It's nothing, really. Probably a stupid idea. And if any of the lads from my watch see me here—'

'Look.' He recalled now that there was a tea shop a short way up the road. If he was lucky, the place might have sandwiches, too. 'Let me buy you a cup of tea, and you can tell me about it. Then I can pass your idea along to Farrell if you don't want to speak to him yourself.'

After considering for a moment, she said, 'Okay. I don't suppose it's likely I'll run into anyone I know in a tea shop.' She smiled for the first time.

'Any rule against you being seen with a detective?' he asked as they headed east on Southwark Street.

'Not as long as it was you wanting to talk to me, but I'd rather not have to explain.'

They reached the place Kincaid remembered. He saw that it was a museum as well as a tea shop, housing displays on the history of tea and collections of teapots, but they could use the restaurant without buying a ticket for the tour. Rose ducked inside with obvious relief.

When they'd found a table near the back and placed their orders – tea and sandwiches for him, tea and a scone for her – he said, 'Anyone would think you were hiding from a jealous boyfriend.'

'Rather that than get on the wrong side of my guvnor. Or the lads – that's even worse. But no. No boyfriend, jealous or otherwise.'

He wondered what had motivated her to risk being disciplined or ostracized, but thought it better not to push until she'd relaxed a little. 'Are you the only woman on your watch?' he asked.

'Yeah, at the moment. We had another, a probationer, when I first transferred in, but she got posted to another station.'

'It must be hard.'

Rose shrugged as the waitress brought their tea. 'Sometimes, but not like it used to be. The fire service is changing. Some of the old lags may not like women coming in, but they know there's nothing they can do about it. And the good officers, like my guvnor, realize that women have things to offer that are as important as brute strength. Not that I'm not strong, mind you,' she added, with another small smile. 'But I think the strength thing is overrated. I can haul hoses and lift ladders with the best of them, but there are techniques that women, or smaller men, can use to make things easier. It seems to me that should be the point – getting the job done as efficiently as possible. Safer for personnel, safer for victims, safer for property.' Her face was alight with enthusiasm, and Kincaid found himself hoping that the wear and tear of the job wouldn't erode too much of her crusading spirit.

'What about harassment? Is that still a problem?' Kincaid asked as their food arrived.

Rose considered for a moment. 'There's teasing, of course. It's part of the culture, and I think that if you're going to make it as a woman in the fire service, you have to let a certain amount roll off your back.' She frowned and added slowly, 'The tough part is knowing when to draw the line, because eventually you must, with someone. I'm sure it must be the same for women in the police.'

Kincaid thought of the difficulties Gemma had had with one of the sergeants under her command at Notting Hill. It had taken a delicate combination of tact and authority for her to establish a good working relationship with the man, but then she'd had the advantage of rank.

He was watching Rose slather butter on her scone and congratulating himself a bit because he'd never felt particularly threatened by female police officers when it occurred to him that he'd never worked with a woman who outranked him. If he did, would he find he was a hypocrite, and a self-righteous one at that? It was an uncomfortable thought. He made an effort to concentrate on his sandwich, but he couldn't help wondering if he'd condescended to Maura Bell in a way he wouldn't have if she'd been male.

'What about you?' asked Rose. 'We've established that I don't have a jealous boyfriend. Are you married?'

Kincaid looked up, startled, and tried not to choke on his tuna sandwich. 'Um, no. But I live with my partner and our two sons.'

'That sounds very progressive of you.' Her smile was a little too quick, and he saw a telltale flush of colour stain her cheeks as if she'd embarrassed herself by asking. 'Bohemian.'

'It's not, really.' He hesitated, imagining himself trying to explain their family situation, or telling her how hard it had been just to persuade Gemma to live with him. God forbid he should mention marriage. That was a can of worms he didn't want to contemplate himself, much less reveal to a stranger. 'Long story,' he said at last, then, not wanting to seem abrupt, added, 'We're both in the job, so it complicates things. We used to work together.'

'Really?' Rose sounded interested. 'What happened?'

'She put in for promotion and a transfer.' More than ready to change the subject, he said quickly, 'Why don't you tell me what it was you wanted with Bill Farrell?'

Now, Rose seemed to feel awkward. With her fingertip, she pushed scone crumbs into a pile on her plate. 'I don't want to sound like I'm trying to tell Station Officer Farrell how to do his job, but after the meeting last night I was curious, so I started looking back through the fire reports for the Borough in the last year.' She pulled some folded papers from her jacket pocket and spread them out on the table. 'I found five structure fires in the past seven months that seem to fit a pattern.'

He could see that the top pages were fire brigade incident reports. 'I'm sure Farrell will have checked for arson reports as a matter of routine—'

'But that's just the thing,' interrupted Rose. 'None of these fires were ever definitely flagged as arsons. They were all listed as 'undetermined cause'. Here, I've marked them on a map.' She pushed the bottom sheet across the table to him. It was a photocopy of an area map, showing six scattered red rings. He recognized one location, the Southwark Street warehouse.

'They started small,' Rose said, tapping the ring on the map's western boundary. He noticed that her nails were short and unpolished, her hands slender. 'The first one was in a lock-up behind Waterloo Station. Accumulated rubbish, no sign of accelerants, no more than one point of origin. Multiple points of origin are usually a dead giveaway for arson.'

He frowned. 'So you're saying it *didn't* look like arson?'

'No, wait, hear me out.' She tapped another circle, this one to the east, near the top of Borough High

Street. 'Number two was a vacant basement flat in a council estate. Same scenario, more bang. Keep in mind that basements are ideal for starting a good fire, because fire spreads upwards.

'Then a small grocer off the Borough Road. The fire started in accumulated polystyrene meat-packing trays, a great accelerant. That's how the fire was started in Leo's Grocery in Bristol. Anyone with an interest in fires would know that.' The terrible blaze had been started deliberately by an employee, and it had killed a young firefighter named Fleur Lombard, the first female firefighter to die in the line of duty in the UK.

'Number four, a paint store.' She touched a spot near Blackfriars Road. 'That burned for two days, and took two adjoining buildings with it.'

'And the fifth?'

'A warehouse near Hay's Galleria. Stored fabric for a clothing manufacturer. Went up a treat.'

'And you think last night's fire was the sixth,' Kincaid said, intrigued now. 'What about access in the first five?'

'No sign of forced entry in any instance. The only place with an alarm was the warehouse, but it was an old building and the system wasn't sophisticated.'

'So what makes you think there's any connection? Why not a series of accidents? Or if they were arson, unrelated attempts at insurance fraud?'

'You can rule out insurance fraud on the first two. The lockup was abandoned, the flat vacant. It's a possibility with the others, but the investigators would have looked for financial problems or insurance irregularities. As for connections . . .' Rose ate the last bite of her scone and leaned towards him. 'What do all these fires have in common?'

Kincaid felt like a slow pupil. 'Besides the fact that they weren't proved arson? I don't know. But I think you're dying to tell me.'

'Okay.' She gave him a cheeky grin. 'Most people think that arsonists go about splashing petrol all over the place and setting off timing devices, but that's not always true. A pro will use fuels available at the scene, and the simpler the ignition, the better. If you have a good fuel load, you can use a very small amount of accelerant to get things going and there won't be a trace left after the burn. You put a bit of petrol or paraffin on a pile of loose paper or some plastic cartons, light it with a cigarette lighter, and presto!' She sat back, looking pleased with herself.

Kincaid popped his last bite of sandwich into his mouth while he thought it over. 'And all these places had the right sort of material for fuel, and were pretty well guaranteed to burn on their own from a small ignition?' She nodded. 'Say you're right,' he continued. 'What makes you think last night's fire fits the pattern?'

'It would be hard to find a better fuel load than a pile of old furniture filled with polyurethane foam. The stuff was highly flammable, and arranged for maximum burn. It was perfect. And the time between fires has been getting progressively shorter. There were only two weeks between the last warehouse fire and this one.'

He didn't like where this was leading at all. 'So what you're telling me is that you think we have a pro, and that he's escalating? A serial arsonist?'

The satisfaction faded from Rose's face. 'I could be wrong. But . . .'

'But if, by some chance, you were right, it would be impossible to prove.'

'Well, yeah. Unless there were witnesses that haven't come forward. Or some forensic evidence left at the scenes that no one knew to look for.' Looking less happy by the minute, Rose traced a pattern on the tablecloth with her teaspoon, then set the spoon down and began gathering up her papers. 'I'm sorry. This isn't much use to you, is it?'

There were arguments against her theory, but he certainly didn't think they could afford to dismiss it. 'Maybe not,' he said, 'but that doesn't mean you shouldn't discuss this with Bill Farrell. He's been concentrating on the crime scene, so he may not have had a chance to research these fires as thoroughly as you have.'

She stopped, papers half folded, and looked up at him.

'If I give him your number and he rings you, then you won't be in trouble with your boss, right?' Kincaid continued. 'After all, you can't refuse to talk to the FIT.' Farrell, he thought, might want to encourage her, regardless of whether her theory was pertinent to last night's fire. Rose Kearney had the makings of an investigator. Although her station officer might consider her insubordinate, Kincaid had found a streak of independence essential in a good detective.

'No, I suppose not.' The corners of her mouth curved up, and he found he liked making her smile.

'Are those photocopies?' He gestured towards the papers, and when she nodded, said, 'Why don't you give them to me, and I'll pass them along to Farrell along with your number. But, Rose . . .' He debated how much he could tell her. 'There are reasons why this fire may not fit your pattern. I can't give you any details from the post-mortem, but it looks as though this fire may have been set to cover up a murder.'

Her face tightened. 'I hadn't forgotten the body. But it's not unheard of for serial arsonists to escalate to murder.'

'No, but think about it. You saw the victim. She'd been stripped. The most logical explanation is that the killer wanted to conceal her identity. Why would a serial arsonist want to hide his victim's identity?'

'For the same reason anyone would. To prevent a connection being made between killer and victim. Do you have any idea who she was?'

Kincaid pulled the CCTV photo from the folder he had with him and handed it across the table. 'This woman entered the building a couple of hours before the fire. We've no way of knowing when – or if – she left. Do you recognize her, by any chance?'

Rose studied the photo for a long moment before reluctantly shaking her head. 'No. She looks young, doesn't she? I hate to think . . .' She started to hand the photo back, then stopped and looked at it again. 'There is something about her, though, that looks familiar. I just can't quite put my finger on it. Maybe she looks like someone on the telly?'

As the waitress came with their bill, Rose gave an apologetic shrug and let him slip the photo back into his folder. Glancing at his watch, Kincaid realized he was running short of time if he meant to go back to the shelter before meeting Gemma.

Rose scribbled a number on the photocopied sheets, then stood and handed him the papers. 'I won't take up any more of your time. I've put down my mobile number if Station Officer Farrell wants to talk to me. Thanks for the tea.' She met his eyes. 'And thanks for not telling me I'm crazy.'

'I don't think you're crazy. But I hope you're wrong.'

'Yeah. Me, too,' Rose said slowly.

This time, when Kincaid buzzed at the shelter's entrance, Kath Warren answered immediately. When he identified himself and asked if he could come up, however, she hesitated, then said she'd come down. A moment later the door clicked open and she slipped into the vestibule.

'I'm sorry,' she said a bit breathlessly. 'It's just that having the police in yesterday upset a number of the residents. You have to understand that these women live on the edge of paranoia at the best of times, and anyone coming into their space is perceived as a threat. It's my fault – I should have realized.'

The crisp efficiency she'd displayed the previous day seemed a little frayed round the edges, and her careful make-up didn't quite conceal the shadows beneath her eyes.

'I'm the one that should apologize,' he told her. 'We shouldn't have tramped in like an invading army.'

Kath smiled and seemed to thaw a bit. 'We've conspiracy theories going round like a virus, I can tell you. First, it was that someone's husband had started the fire so that the women would have to evacuate the building. Now, it's some sort of police infiltration plot, but I haven't quite worked that one out.'

'Do the women's husbands know where they are?' Kincaid asked, curious.

'No – at least we hope not. We don't advertise what we do here, but the women do go out during the day; they're not prisoners. There's always the chance of a slip-up, either from someone being seen and followed, or – and I'm sorry to say it's more likely – from one of the residents giving out the location in a weak moment. It's not a perfect system, but we do the best we can.'

'You don't place any credence in the evacuation idea?'

Kath shrugged. 'I suppose it's possible. But in that case why not start the fire in this building? The front half is vacant, and I imagine it would be easy enough for someone to break in.'

'Would one of these men be desperate enough to endanger his own children?'

Kincaid's scepticism must have shown in his voice, because Kath said sharply, 'These men are abusers. Many of them beat their children as well as their wives or partners. And they're very good at justifying what they do, both to themselves and to other people.'

She was right, Kincaid knew, and right about the security risk from the derelict front half of the building. Uneasily, he thought of Rose Kearney's hypothetical arsonist. This building would make a perfect target, and he wondered how easily the shelter could be evacuated in the event of a fire. He'd have a word with Bill Farrell about it when he passed along Rose's papers.

'It's not just the fire, of course,' continued Kath, 'but the woman's death. It's upset everyone. I don't suppose you've any idea yet who she was?'

'Nothing definite, as yet.' Kincaid pulled out a copy of the photo. 'But a CCTV camera caught this woman entering the building a couple of hours before the fire. That's why I came. Do you recognize her?'

Kath took the paper from him and studied it carefully before shaking her head. 'No. No, sorry. I don't think I've ever seen her.'

'Not one of your former residents?'

'No. Not since I've been here, and that's been five years.'

'Would you mind showing the photo to the residents, and to your assistant? Maybe it will ring a bell with someone.'

'Jason's out today, but I'll be glad to hand it round the wom—'

Kath was facing the outside door. Kincaid saw her eyes widen in surprise. He spun round just as a tall man pushed roughly past him and grabbed Kath by the shoulders.

'Hey!' Kincaid called out. 'What do you think you're doing? Let her—' He fell silent as Kath held up a cautionary hand.

'Where's my wife?' the man shouted at Kath, giving her a shake.

Before Kincaid could intervene, Kath said, 'Tony? What's wrong? What's happened?' She looked concerned, but not frightened, and Kincaid checked himself, waiting to see what this was about.

'You know bloody well what's happened,' said the man she'd called Tony, his voice rising to a sob. 'She's gone, and so is Harriet. I want to know what you've done with them.'

'Laura's gone?' Kath gave Kincaid a startled glance. 'Tony, I haven't seen her. I don't know anything about it.'

Stepping forward, Kincaid said quietly, 'Hey, why don't you let Kath go. Then we can talk about this.'

'I don't want to talk about it; I want to find my daughter,' Tony snapped back, but he seemed to take in Kincaid's presence for the first time. After a moment he dropped his hands and stepped back a pace.

Kincaid got his first good look at the man. He was tall and thin, with a long face and the sort of dark, brooding looks Kincaid suspected women would find appealing under better circumstances. Now, however, he looked exhausted, and his well-shaped mouth was twisted in an effort to hold back tears.

'This is Tony Novak,' explained Kath, making a game attempt at normality. 'His wife is on our board of directors. Harriet's his daughter. Tony's a doctor at Guy's. He's helped us with some of our residents—'

'I'd never have lifted a finger if I'd known what I know now. Laura told me, you know. And she threatened me. She knew you'd help her.'

'Help her do what, Tony?' Kincaid asked, forestalling Kath.

'Disappear. Disappear with my daughter. That's what they do here. They help women disappear. But I'm not standing for it.' He turned back to Kath Warren, menace visible now beneath the hysteria. 'You're going to get me my daughter back.'

'Tony, I've told you. I haven't seen her. I haven't seen either of them. This is Superintendent Kincaid from Scotland Yard. You should tell him—'

Kincaid's phone rang, startling them all. Pulling it from his belt, he glanced at the name on the caller ID and jabbed a key. 'Gemma,' he said quickly, 'I'll ring you right back – Hey!'

In the instant Kincaid had been distracted, Tony Novak had turned and vanished into the street.

Chapter Nine

> . . . a smattering of everything, and a knowledge of
> nothing . . .
>
> Charles Dickens
> *Sketches by Boz*

Kincaid sprinted to one end of the short street, then to
the other, but there was no sign of Tony Novak in
either direction. When he returned to the shelter, he
found Kath Warren standing on the pavement, looking
out for him anxiously. 'Did you see him?' she asked.

Shaking his head while he caught his breath, he
resolved to take up jogging. His weekly games of
football with the boys were obviously not keeping him
as fit as he'd thought. Nor did the weather help – a
dark bank of cloud was building to the west, and the
char-tinged air felt heavy as treacle in his lungs. 'No,
not a sign,' he told her when he could speak. 'Who the
hell was that guy, anyway? Is he completely barking
mad?'

'No. At least I don't think so,' Kath qualified, frowning. 'I've certainly never seen him act like that. He
really does work in Out Patients at Guy's, and his wife

– his ex-wife – is one of our board members. Laura helps out in our office when she can, but I haven't seen her for several days.'

'Do you think there's any truth to his abduction story?'

'I can't imagine Laura would do something like that. But then . . .' Kath hesitated. 'You never really know about people, do you? I got the impression it was a bitter divorce, but I believe they had a shared custody arrangement that worked well enough. Laura's not the type to wash her dirty laundry in public, though.'

'She wouldn't have confided in you?'

'We're not close friends. I'm not sure Laura *has* any close friends, to tell the truth. She's very focused on her job, her child, and her volunteer work. She's a doctor, too, a surgeon at Guy's.'

Kincaid studied Kath. Her words were polite enough, but her body language said she didn't much care for Laura Novak. 'What did Novak mean when he said you helped women disappear?' he asked.

Her throaty laugh sounded forced. 'We don't bury bodies in the fields, Superintendent, in spite of how Tony made it sound. It's all perfectly legal. Sometimes it becomes obvious that counselling and trial separation are not going to do the trick. At that point, if it seems that a resident, or a resident and her family, are in serious physical danger, we make arrangements for them to start again somewhere safe. In these cases it's essential that the husband or partner not be told their whereabouts. Unfortunately,' Kath added with a sigh, 'as I said earlier about the shelter, the system's not foolproof. We've had several cases recently where the man has discovered the family's new location. In one instance a woman was killed.

'Even if the woman is convinced she mustn't contact her abusive partner, there's a chance she won't be able to resist staying in touch with someone else, say, a mother or sister, and' – she shrugged – 'the information invariably leaks out.'

'Okay. I understand that. But that still doesn't explain where Tony Novak would get the idea you were going to help his wife "disappear".'

'I don't know.' Kath looked genuinely puzzled. 'I can't believe Laura would tell him something like that.'

'Did she ever give you reason to think he was abusive?'

'No. But as I said, she keeps herself to herself, and I've enough experience with these things to know that abuse can happen where you'd least expect it. Look.' Kath touched Kincaid's arm. 'Shouldn't we make sure she's all right? If she and Tony had a fight that got out of hand, maybe she's hiding from him. She could be hurt.'

'I'll need an address,' Kincaid told her with an inward sigh. This was just what he didn't need – a domestic, on top of an unidentified murder victim, a possible arsonist, and a disabled woman's missing housemate. But he couldn't ignore it, especially if Laura Novak really did turn out to be missing. 'And a description,' he added, fishing his notebook from his jacket pocket.

'I can give you her address without looking it up,' said Kath. 'She lives in Park Street. We talked about it often enough, because Laura's always involved in all the local issues. Her latest project was Crossbones Graveyard – you know, the old cemetery just a street that way.' She nodded in the direction of London Bridge Station.

'I'll need a specific address,' Kincaid said, trying to steer her back to the subject. Time was passing, and Gemma and Winnie would be waiting for him.

Kath gave him a house number, adding, 'The house is unmistakable. It's early nineteenth century. She's very proud of it.'

'Can you describe Laura for me?'

'Um, I'd say mid-thirties . . . I know her daughter is ten, and I think Laura had finished medical school when Harriet was born.'

'Looks?' prompted Kincaid.

'Medium height. Thin and wiry. Dark curly hair. Naturally curly, not permed.'

'But fair-skinned?'

'Oh, yes. Freckles. Brown eyes, I think – I never paid that much attention.'

Kincaid realized with an unwelcome chill that Laura Novak matched the pathologist's description of their victim. He'd have to move this up on his priority list. But the woman in the warehouse had been alone, which didn't account for the missing child. 'And the daughter?' he asked. 'You said her name is Harriet? Can you describe her, too?'

'Not really. I've never met her. But from what Laura says, she sounds a precocious kid. I think she goes to Little Dorrit School, though, in Redcross Way. That's one reason Laura was up in arms about the graveyard. Harriet had to walk right past it going to and from school, and it's just the sort of place where perverts or drug dealers might hang about.'

'And what about Tony? Do you have an address for him?'

'I remember Laura saying he'd rented a flat in Borough High Street, near the George Inn, but I'm afraid that's all I know,' Kath offered apologetically.

'Don't worry. I'm sure we can find him,' Kincaid assured her. 'What concerns me more at the moment is *you*. This guy is obviously volatile, and he's targeting you as having something to do with his wife's disappearance – or supposed disappearance. He knows how to find you. What if you walk out of this building by yourself and he's waiting for you? Next time he might do more than give you a shake.'

Kath paled. 'I hadn't thought of that. He was a little scary. If you hadn't been here . . .'

'Is there anyone who can escort you in and out of the building for the time being, make sure you get home safely? What about your colleague – Jason, isn't it?'

'Jason's gone to Kent for the day, to his aunt's. A family emergency.' Her lips tightened, as if she weren't happy about Jason's absence, excuse or not.

'Is there anyone else?'

Kath brightened. 'I could get my son to come in on the train and drive back with me. He's sixteen—'

'I'm not sure a sixteen-year-old—'

'And he has a black belt in kick-boxing,' Kath finished with a grin. 'I'll be fine.'

Kincaid's phone rang again. When he looked at the caller ID, he said, 'Maybe I should keep your son with me. I could use a little protection from my partner about now.'

When he reached Gemma on the phone, she and Winnie were waiting for him at Franny Liu's house. Her voice sounded strained, and he guessed the visit was proving awkward.

'Something came up,' he explained, 'but I'm on my way now.' He'd not had time to speak to Bill Farrell about Rose, so he would have to track him down later.

'Are you all right?' Gemma asked. 'I was worried about you.'

'Yeah, I'm fine, but we may have another candidate for our mystery woman. I'll tell you about it after we've seen your friend.'

The drive to Ufford Street was short, but he used the time to check in with Doug Cullen. His sergeant informed him that he and Bell had seen Marcus Yarwood's insurance agent, but had had no luck finding either Yarwood or his foreman Joe Spender. 'We've left messages,' Cullen told him, 'asking them to call back as soon as possible.' Kincaid promised to meet

Cullen and Bell in Borough High Street as soon as he'd finished at Franny Liu's.

He found the house in Ufford Street easily, parking his ancient MG behind Gemma's mauve Ford. As he removed his small evidence collection kit, he gave the car an affectionate pat. One day soon he was going to have to part with the old thing. It was a testament to the Midget's condition that Cullen preferred driving them about in his battered Astra to riding in it. The car was completely unsuitable for family life as well, and needed more work than Kincaid was willing to invest in it, but he hadn't quite brought himself to contemplate joining the four-wheel-drive-owning hordes.

Gemma had apparently been watching for him, as she answered the door before he could push the bell. 'We haven't told her yet – about the fire,' she whispered as she led him inside. 'We thought it would be better coming from you.'

'Thanks,' he muttered, taking stock of his surroundings as she led him into a cluttered, flowery sitting room. The room's fussiness brought on instant claustrophobia, made worse by the sweet smell pervading the air. Near the back of the room, Winnie sat beside a small Chinese woman in a wheelchair.

'Winnie,' Kincaid said as she stood to greet him. He gave her a peck on the cheek, thinking how trim and tidy she looked in her clericals.

'Franny,' Gemma was saying as he turned back to her, 'this is Duncan Kincaid. He's a superintendent with Scotland Yard.'

Kincaid found himself towering awkwardly over Franny Liu, who looked up at him with frightened eyes. 'Do you mind if I sit down?' he asked.

'Oh, I'm sorry. Excuse my lack of manners.' Her voice was soft, her words carefully enunciated. As Kincaid pulled up a chair and sank down to her level, she went on: 'It's just that I can't imagine Gemma and Winnie would have asked you here to give me good news.'

'We've nothing definite to tell you about your friend,' he said quickly, 'but there is a possibility we think needs looking into.' There was no gentle way to present the situation, and he knew from long experience that it was best to get the shock over as quickly as possible. 'The night before last there was a fire in a warehouse in Southwark Street, not far from here. A woman's body was found. I'm afraid she was badly burned, and she had no identification.'

'Oh, no.' Franny shook her head in denial. 'You can't possibly think it's Elaine.' Her words held an anguished appeal.

'It's an option we need to rule out, at least. The victim fits your housemate's general description, but there are several other possibilities we're exploring as well.' Seeing Gemma's quick glance, he realized he'd had no time to tell her about the woman captured by the CCTV.

Franny's skin, pale when he had come in, had blanched to the colour of parchment, but she asked steadily, 'What do you need to do?'

'First, I need to show you a photo, an image

captured by the closed-circuit security camera in the building across the street from the warehouse.' Gemma came to stand behind his chair as he opened his folder and took out a photocopy.

Franny took it with a trembling hand, pulse beating visibly in her slender throat. She stared at the photo for a long moment, then leaned back in her chair and closed her eyes. 'It's not her,' she whispered. 'That's not Elaine. This woman's much too young.'

'We had to be sure. But even if the woman in the photo isn't Elaine, it doesn't necessarily rule out Elaine as the victim. This woman entered the warehouse at least two hours before the fire. She may have left again by the door not covered by the security camera, and by the same logic someone else may have entered.'

'But why would Elaine have been in this warehouse?'

'Do you have any idea if Elaine knew Marcus Yarwood?' he countered.

'The MP?' Franny looked startled. 'No. Why would you think she did?'

'The warehouse where the body was found belongs to Yarwood. It was being converted to luxury flats. If Elaine knew Yarwood, it's possible she might have met him there.'

Franny looked from Kincaid to Gemma. 'I don't understand.'

'We don't either,' Gemma said gently, and from her tone Kincaid suspected she thought he was handling Franny a little roughly. 'Listen, Franny,' Gemma went on. 'The only way we can positively eliminate Elaine is to compare a sample of her DNA against the victim's.'

'If you let me have a look, I'll see what I can find,' Kincaid said.

'It can't be Elaine,' Franny protested. 'That's just not possible.' They all waited silently, giving her time to come to terms with the idea. After a few moments, she glanced at Winnie as if for confirmation, before letting her breath out in a sigh. 'Okay. Do whatever it is you have to do.'

'Good.' Kincaid gave her a reassuring smile. 'Believe me, the sooner we get this done, the better for everyone. Now, I understand you don't use the upstairs bathroom. Is that right?' When Franny nodded assent, he turned to Gemma and Winnie. 'Did either of you use the basin or throw anything away in the bathroom?'

Winnie shook her head as Gemma said, 'I didn't. But I think we both looked in the medicine cabinet, and I looked in the cupboard over the toilet.'

'Your hair should be fairly easy to rule out if you shed one or two in the basin.' He shot her an affectionate glance. Gemma's shoulder-length hair was the rich copper of new pennies, and wavy. 'But I'll try the bath first, as that way we can eliminate Winnie more easily. What about the bed? Did either of you turn back the sheets?'

Gemma gave Winnie a questioning look before answering for them both. 'No.'

Kincaid turned back to Franny. 'Anyone else have access to the upstairs?'

'No. I can't remember when anyone else has been up there, until Winnie and Gemma came yesterday. Elaine did the cleaning herself. I told her I'd pay someone to come in, but she always wanted to save me money.'

'Right, then. I'll get started.'

As Kincaid climbed the stairs, he felt a profound sense of relief. It wasn't just the suffocating atmosphere in the room, he realized – Franny Liu herself had made him uncomfortable. He was accustomed to dealing with people suffering from the grief and shock that accompanied a tragedy. Was it her illness that put him off? Of course he felt sorry for her but, if forced, he'd have to admit his pity was tinged with revulsion.

Feeling a flush of shame at his reaction to someone handicapped, he stopped at the head of the stairs. For a moment he imagined Gemma struck down with some unexpected and devastating disease, confined to a wheelchair. Would he respond in the same way? The thought horrified him.

But Gemma would rail against fate – she would be grumpy and difficult, and she would find a way to get on with her life. It was not Franny's physical condition that bothered him, he realized, but the fact that she radiated neediness. The woman wore her vulnerability like a flag. If Elaine Holland had taken advantage of her, it would come as no surprise. But if Franny Liu was the victim in that relationship, what had happened to Elaine Holland?

*

Gemma had to force herself not to follow Kincaid as he left the room. Her natural instinct was always for action. She wanted to be doing something, not sitting in the too-quiet room, watching as Franny seemed to shrink before her eyes. It seemed to her that the woman's flesh had melted away from her bones just since yesterday, and with Kincaid's departure Franny had sunk even further into herself, as if she'd used up all her energy reserves.

The creaking from Kincaid's footsteps as he moved about above them was clearly audible. Gemma found herself straining for the next sound, willing him to hurry. Beside her, Winnie sat quietly, and Gemma envied her supportive patience. But then she'd never been much good at hand-holding, even as a constable, and fortunately these days her job allowed her to delegate such things to those more suited for it.

Then Winnie's phone rang, breaking the silence. After a murmured conversation, Winnie rang off and stood. 'I'm sorry. I've got to run over to the church office for a bit. Franny, I'll be back as soon as I can.' She leaned down to give Franny a brief hug, then said quietly to Gemma as she went out, 'Stop in at the office before you go?'

Winnie's departure seemed to have roused Franny. She sat a little straighter in her chair and focused her dark gaze on Gemma. 'I still don't understand why Elaine would have been in a warehouse. It doesn't make any sense.'

'Maybe she didn't know Marcus Yarwood, but could

she have been meeting someone else?' suggested Gemma, quick to take advantage of the opening.

'Who? Elaine went to work and came home. She didn't socialize.'

'Someone from work, then?'

'She didn't really like anyone in her department. She never went along when the other women met at the pub, or got together for birthday lunches. They invited her, but she said they were catty, all of them, and she'd rather spend her time with . . .' Franny faltered for the first time. 'With me. And even if she had met someone, what happened to the other person? Why weren't they burned in the fire?'

Gemma wasn't about to tell her that, according to the pathologist, the woman in the warehouse had been brutally murdered and left to burn by her companion. Maybe by the time that information was made public and Franny's knowledge of it had become unavoidable, they'd have a positive ID on both murderer and victim. 'We don't know,' she said simply. She did, however, think it was time Franny knew a little more about her housemate. 'Franny, you said Elaine never went out. But when I was checking her room yesterday, I found a number of evening things.' When Franny looked at her blankly, she elaborated. 'You know, fancy outfits, high-heeled shoes . . . Did you ever see her wearing them?'

'Elaine?' Franny smiled. 'No. I can't imagine. Maybe she used to go out more, before we . . . before she moved in with me.'

Gemma was unconvinced. She could have sworn

that some of the things she'd seen were a good deal less than two years old. 'The really odd thing,' she continued, 'was that these clothes were hidden away. Did you know there was a cupboard at the back of the wardrobe in that room?'

Franny shook her head. 'No. I only bought this house after my parents died, and I got ill not long after. I never really used that room for anything. But why would Elaine want to *hide* her things?'

'Why would Elaine tell you she didn't have a mobile phone?' countered Gemma. 'I found the box on the shelf in her wardrobe.'

'Elaine has a phone?' Franny whispered.

'It certainly looks that way.' Gemma thought for a moment. 'Franny, didn't you say that the evening before Elaine disappeared she was late home from work?'

'Yes. But that wasn't unusual. Elaine often worked late. She said she could get more done when everyone else had gone home.'

It was the classic excuse, thought Gemma, used by many an errant husband or wife, but it had obviously never occurred to Elaine's housemate to doubt her. 'Did you never ring her at work after hours?' she asked, wondering how Franny could have been so gullible.

'No. I wouldn't have wanted to interrupt her. She—' Franny stopped as they heard Kincaid's tread on the stairs.

'I'll be off, then,' he said from the doorway. 'The sooner I get these samples off to the lab, the better.

Miss Liu – Franny – we'll let you know as soon as we have a result. Gemma, a word?' He jerked his head towards the door.

Gemma said a quick goodbye to Franny and followed him out into the street, fuming at being summoned like a lackey. 'Did I fail to notice the house was on fire?'

'What? Oh, sorry,' he said distractedly as he unlocked his car and put the collection kit on the passenger seat. 'I just got a call from Cullen. Marcus Yarwood's coming into the station to look at the CCTV tape. They're waiting for me.'

'Did you get anything?' She gestured at the kit.

'Yeah. Quite a bit of hair from the bath plughole and a few from the bed. And I found some tissues in the bathroom waste bin. Looks like someone had a good cry, and if it wasn't you or Winnie, we'll have to assume it was Elaine Holland.' He shoved a hand through his hair impatiently. 'Listen, I've got to—'

'I'm going to Guy's Hospital,' said Gemma, making the decision even as she spoke. 'I want to see if I can talk to someone in Elaine's department.'

Kincaid stared at her, his momentum temporarily checked. 'Gemma, it's not your case.'

'Someone needs to do it. Someone should already have done it.'

He frowned at the implied criticism. 'We've had other priorities. You know this is a long shot. If you were working the case you'd have a bit more perspective.'

Gemma knew he was probably right, but she didn't

like being dismissed. And besides she was too curious now to let it go. 'Maybe you need someone without perspective, then. And what harm can it do? It'll save your team a job.'

'All right, go,' he said after a moment's hesitation. 'We'll talk about it when I get home. Then you can tell me how I'm going to clear this with DI Bell.'

'Anyone would think the woman was going to bite your head off,' Gemma retorted.

'Oh, I think she might do much worse than that.' He flashed his familiar grin at her as he folded himself into the little car. 'You'd better hope I'm still intact by the time this case is over.'

It was only as he drove away that Gemma realized she was going to miss yet another piano lesson. 'Bloody hell,' she swore as she glanced at her watch, wondering if she could go to the hospital and still get back in time to take the boys to Erika's for tea. She could, she decided, if she didn't dally.

She rang Wendy, her piano teacher, and made her excuses, then went in search of Winnie.

Gemma found her in the tiny church office, staring in dismay at the stacks of leaflets covering her desk. 'The printer's made a mistake on the Order of Service,' she explained. 'Again. Oh well, perhaps no one will notice we're singing a hymn about crossing the barren *dessert*.'

Gemma laughed. 'Maybe they'll think you've run out of buns to serve at coffee mornings.' She went on to update Winnie on her plans, then added, 'I feel guilty, leaving Franny like that. If this were an ordinary case – if we had a definite identification of a victim, or even some evidence of foul play – I'd have a constable or a family liaison officer stay with her until we could get a friend or family member in.'

With a sigh, Winnie said, 'Except in this case there doesn't seem to be anyone. It's usually only the elderly who are so isolated. I've offered to have volunteers from the congregation take it in turn to stay with her, but she won't have it. I'm learning that Franny can be unexpectedly stubborn when she has a mind to.'

Gemma perched on the edge of Winnie's visitor's chair. 'I know she lost her parents, but do you suppose she had any friends before her illness?'

'She lost touch with her co-workers, obviously. She was hospitalized for months. And I suppose other friends may have drifted away because they didn't know what to say or do – I suspect that happens more often than we care to think. But I've never heard her mention anyone other than Elaine. It's as if Franny's life started when Elaine Holland moved into her house.'

'Winnie, doesn't the relationship between these two women strike you as odd?'

'If you're implying that two single women living together must be lesbians,' Winnie said a little tartly, 'I thought that sort of prejudice went out with our parents' generation.'

'And our parents may have been right more often than we credit,' Gemma replied with a quick smile, 'because it was socially unacceptable to tell the truth. But that's less true now, especially as neither Elaine nor Franny has family to disapprove. And anyway it's not their sexual orientation that worries me, it's the whole emotional set-up. It just feels wrong. There's Elaine's secretiveness, and Franny's dependence . . . At first it seemed that Elaine was taking advantage of Franny, but now I'm not so sure. I'm beginning to wonder who really pulled the strings in the relationship.'

'Franny had no trouble going against Elaine when it was something that mattered to her, like having me bring in Communion on Sundays. Elaine didn't care for that at all.' Winnie fingered the small silver cross she wore over her clerical collar, a habit Gemma had observed she had when she was thinking. After a moment she said, 'There's something else. Some of Franny's prescription sleeping tablets seem to be missing, but I don't know if Franny's been overdosing or if Elaine might have taken them.'

Gemma frowned. 'Enough for a suicide attempt?'

'I doubt it. But still, it's odd . . .'

'I think there was more going on here than Franny's told either of us,' Gemma agreed. The question is, does it have anything to do with Elaine's disappearance? Maybe if you could talk to Franny—'

'Gemma, you know I couldn't pass on anything Franny told me in confidence.'

'No,' Gemma agreed ruefully, 'I suppose not. But you could encourage her to talk to *me*. That wouldn't be against regulations.'

Winnie smothered a laugh. 'It's not the God police, you know. It's my conscience that's the issue. But I promise I'll try.' Then, sobering, she gazed at Gemma for a moment before she said, 'Gemma, about this body in the warehouse. I know you said it was only a possibility . . . but do you really think Elaine Holland is dead?'

As he drove to Borough Station, Kincaid rang his long-time contact in the Home Office lab, Konrad Mueller. Mueller, in spite of his Germanic name, was half Egyptian and, although in his late thirties, still lived the life of a lad in a flat overlooking the Grand Union Canal.

Kincaid had met him in his early days at Scotland Yard, when Mueller had been working as a crime-scene tech, and had watched his rise through the forensic science service with interest. He'd kept up the connection, although he tried not to ask favours too often.

He'd made a point, however, of getting Mueller's home phone number when he discovered they were near neighbours, thinking he'd invite him round for drinks some weekend, and now his forethought came in handy.

Rather to his surprise, Mueller answered right away. When Kincaid explained what he wanted, Mueller gave a gusty sigh audible over the phone.

'You do realize there's a football match tomorrow, mate?' he asked, sounding aggrieved. 'Not to mention the fact that I just met this really hot chick at the supermarket and made a date for tonight.'

The odd contrast between Mueller's olive skin and the gelled spikes of his bleached-blond hair didn't seem to deter women. Kincaid had never known him not to have at least two on the go.

'I wouldn't ask, Konnie,' he said, 'but I've got the AC's office breathing down my neck on this one, and I can't get anywhere with it until I have a positive ID on the victim. You won't have to run the sample against the database,' he added, knowing that was the most time-consuming stage in the DNA testing process. 'I just need a simple match.'

After a pause in which Kincaid could hear the insistent thump of techno music in the background, Mueller gave in with another resigned sigh. 'All right, mate. I'll see if I can get to the lab some time tomorrow. But you owe me big time for this one.'

'Anything short of providing you with your own personal harem,' Kincaid agreed, ringing off with a grin.

When he reached Borough Station, he turned his samples over to Bell's sergeant, Sarah, with a request to send them directly to Mueller at the lab.

After taking down his instructions, she directed him to an interview room that had been set up with a television and a VCR in readiness for Yarwood's visit. As Kincaid opened the door, Cullen was saying something in Bell's ear and she was laughing in response. It was the first time Kincaid had seen her face lit by a genuine smile, and he realized she was actually quite pretty when she wasn't brooding like a disgruntled hawk.

Then the pair registered his presence. Both their faces froze into the instant solemnity of guilty children.

'Spoiled the party, have I?' Kincaid asked. Seeing their blank expressions, he couldn't resist taking the piss a bit more. 'Are you two going to let me in on the secret?'

Bell glowered at him and Cullen blushed an unbecoming blotchy red. 'It's nothing, guv, just a joke,' Cullen told him.

'I like jokes,' Kincaid said, at his most innocent. 'Do tell me.'

'It wasn't that sort of a joke, sir.' Cullen's face was now puce, and Kincaid thought he might explode at any moment.

Knitting his brows, Kincaid said sternly, 'You're not telling rude jokes to the female officers again, Dougie? We've had words about this before—'

'I'll just let you two get on with it while I check on Yarwood,' broke in Bell, giving them both a scathing glance as she marched from the room.

'What in hell are you on about?' Cullen hissed furiously as soon as the door shut behind her.

Kincaid had braced himself against the conference table and was laughing so hard he had to wipe his eyes. 'Sorry,' he managed to gasp. 'It was just your faces. You looked like you'd been caught with your knickers down in the playground, and then you blushed—'

'You made me feel a complete idiot.'

'I am sorry, Doug, really.' Kincaid made a valiant effort to control his mirth, but the corner of his mouth twitched involuntarily. 'You must like her. I didn't realize.' He had wondered, when he'd left them at the club last night, if they might find more in common on their own, but they seemed to have exceeded expectations. If Cullen had actually managed to slip Stella's lead long enough to enjoy himself, he didn't deserve Kincaid giving him a hard time.

'I don't mind so much being made a fool of,' Cullen said with a return of his usual good humour, 'but I don't think Maura takes well to being teased.'

'Good God, Doug, how's she going to survive in the job if she can't deal with a little friendly ragging? How's she stuck it out this long, for that matter?'

Bell came back in before Cullen could reply. 'Got it all out of your systems, now, have you?' she asked. In spite of her poker face, Kincaid thought he saw a gleam in her eye, and he wondered if Cullen was underestimating her. 'Yarwood's PA says he's on his way,' she added. 'He's coming from his office, apparently. Station Officer Farrell should be here soon, as well.'

'Why did Yarwood offer to come in rather than have us bring a photo round?' Kincaid asked.

'He didn't say, and ours is not to reason why,' Bell replied. 'We're just the police.'

'What did you find out from his insurance agent?'

Cullen took a chair at the table and rocked it back in what Kincaid recognized as his 'preparing to lecture' position. 'He's not over-insured, according to Mr Cohen. He hasn't changed the policy and, as far as Cohen knows, he's not having financial difficulties with the project. He suggested those rumours might have come from a competitor. Of course, their loss adjuster will be working with Bill Farrell, but at least for now they don't consider Yarwood a likely candidate for arson. But' – Cullen paused long enough to make sure he had their attention – 'I did some phoning round this morning. I have a contact at one of the tabloids who told me that *her* contact in the Vice Squad said there are rumours lately of Yarwood dealing with some pretty heavy hitters.'

'What sort of heavy hitters?' Kincaid asked, trying to imagine Marcus Yarwood the public figure involved with drugs or prostitution. That would be a scandal worth murdering to cover up.

'West End gambling. Just because these posh club owners wear bespoke suits doesn't mean they don't collect their debts.'

'Yarwood, gambling?' Kincaid supposed it was not unlikely that Yarwood's political connections frequented West End clubs, but it still seemed out of character for Yarwood himself. He turned to Bell. 'Any luck verifying his alibi for Thursday night?'

'I had a message from Birmingham CID. Yarwood was seen at dinner at his hotel, then in the bar until at least ten o'clock. He'd have been hard-pushed to get back to London to start a fire a little after midnight.'

'He could have hired someone,' Kincaid mused.

'But that wouldn't explain the body. Why would a paid arsonist have killed a woman before starting the fire?'

'If it was the couple in the video, maybe she protested when she realized what he meant to do,' suggested Bell. 'They struggle; he kills her, then strips her so she can't be identified.'

'I've another possibility for our victim.' Kincaid told them about his encounter with Tony Novak at the shelter and Novak's claim that his wife and daughter had gone missing. 'We'll have to follow up. I've got an address for the wife, and we should be able to find the husband easily enough.'

'You going to charge him with assault, guv?' asked Cullen with a grin.

'No. But I think he might be dangerous. I've told Kath Warren to watch herself until we can talk to the man again.'

Before they could speculate further, the sergeant popped her head in the room. 'Excuse me, ma'am. Mr Yarwood's here.'

'Bring him in, will you, Sergeant?' said Bell. 'I don't think we'll wait on Farrell,' she told Kincaid and Cullen. 'We can fill him in afterwards.'

A moment later the sergeant ushered in Marcus Yarwood. If Yarwood had come straight from his parliamentary office, he had dressed casually for a Saturday's work. His polo shirt emphasized his massive shoulders and chest, and his heavy features seemed more prominent without the distraction of a tie. His eyes, however, still seemed as penetrating as they did on the telly, as he raked an impatient glance round the three of them.

'Your message said you found something on CCTV,' he said abruptly, clearly in no mood for pleasantries.

Kincaid saw Bell bristle and guessed she wasn't about to relinquish control of the interview without a fight. The woman would give herself a heart attack if she didn't learn to ease up a bit. Before she could lock horns with Yarwood again, he said, 'Why don't you have a seat, Mr Yarwood, and we'll cue it up for you.'

'I'll stand, thanks. Let's just get on with this, can we?' Yarwood was the picture of the busy politician, not bothering to expend charm on those who didn't matter, but there was a tension in his posture that made Kincaid wonder if his rudeness was due to worry rather than irritation.

Kincaid nodded at Cullen. 'Let's have a look, then, Doug. As you'll see,' he continued to Yarwood, 'it's just coming up to ten o'clock on the night of the fire. Let us know if you want to freeze the image.'

Yarwood stood with his hands plunged in his pockets as the screen came to life, his head lowered in the familiar bulldog pose. After a moment the two figures moved into view, then stopped before the warehouse door. Yarwood suddenly reached out, his finger pointed as if he might touch the screen. Then, as the woman turned towards the camera, the colour drained from his face. He reached blindly for the back of the nearest chair, grasping it for support.

'Are you all right, Mr Yarwood?' Kincaid hovered with a hand near Yarwood's elbow, in case the man went all the way down, while motioning to Cullen to stop the tape.

Yarwood looked at him, as if trying to recall who he was. 'Dear God,' he whispered. 'That's my daughter.'

Chapter Ten

I only ask for information.
Charles Dickens
David Copperfield

Having neither lived nor worked south of the river, Gemma had never before had occasion to visit Guy's Hospital. She knew that the two great hospitals, St Thomas' and Guy's, had once faced each other across St Thomas Street, until St Thomas' had been moved to its present location in Lambeth to make room for the building of London Bridge Station.

Winnie had told her to be sure to have a look at the chapel, so when she'd parked the car on St Thomas Street, she entered the hospital's main quadrangle. It was an imposing vista, although the symmetry of the eighteenth-century buildings was marred, in her opinion, by the addition of a sixties tower block. After taking a moment to examine the statue of Sir Thomas Guy in the quadrangle's centre, she saw a small sign designating the chapel on the right-hand side.

Gemma passed through the chapel's unassuming

entrance with little expectation, then caught her breath in delight. She felt she might have stepped inside a Fabergé Easter egg. The cream walls were touched with gilt and aquamarine; the arched stained-glass windows glowed like living gems; the rich wood of the simple pews shone with years of polish. The air smelled faintly of lilies.

The chapel was empty, the quiet so intense it felt like a physical force. Gemma stood, letting the silence seep into her. How many had come to this place over the years, seeking solace from their worry or grief? Had they found comfort here . . . or did the air hold a weight of accumulated sorrow?

Her thoughts strayed to the parents of the child she'd failed to find. There would be no consolation for their loss, here or anywhere else. Gemma turned and went out into the grey austerity of the quadrangle.

'Mr Yarwood, did you have some reason to think your daughter might have been in the building?' Kincaid asked, remembering the tension he'd seen in Yarwood's body before the tape began.

They had encouraged Yarwood to sit, and Cullen had fetched him a cup of water. Now, while Cullen and Bell stood back, Kincaid took the chair across the table from him. He could see Yarwood beginning to pull himself together, and he wanted answers while the man was still vulnerable from shock.

'No, no, of course not.' Yarwood set down the plastic cup and scrubbed a hand across his face. 'It's just that I hadn't spoken to her for a few days, and I was a bit worried.'

The room, small and poorly ventilated, had become stuffier as the afternoon warmed. Kincaid thought he detected, beneath the musty odour of the building itself, the acrid smell of fear. 'Your daughter doesn't live with you, then?'

'No. Chloe shares a flat with a friend, near Westbourne Grove. She's twenty-one, and you know how kids are. She's very independent.'

'But you speak to her every day on the phone?'

'No,' Yarwood said again. 'It's just that I'd been trying to ring her since the fire. I didn't want her to read about it in the papers or see it on the telly. I thought she might worry.'

'Have you spoken to her flatmate?'

'No. No one answered the phone or the door. Look, that tape . . . The time said ten o'clock, and the fire didn't start until after midnight, so there's no reason to think . . .' Yarwood gave Kincaid a look of appeal.

'Mr Yarwood,' Kincaid said gently, 'unless we find some proof that your daughter left the building again, or we can get in touch with her, I'm afraid we do have to consider her as a possible victim. She fits the parameters given by the pathologist.'

Marcus Yarwood pressed both hands flat against his face, but not before Kincaid had seen his lips twist in a spasm of distress. 'Let me see the body,' he said, his voice muffled.

'There's nothing you could recognize. I'm sorry.'

Yarwood was silent for a moment. Then he dropped his hands and stared hard at Kincaid. 'DNA, then. Can't you do a DNA test?'

'I'm sure we can get a DNA sample from your daughter's flat. We could also take a sample of your blood, if necessary, and we can check your daughter's dental records if they're easily available. But it seems to me we're jumping the gun a bit here. First, have you any idea *why* your daughter was at the warehouse?'

'No. I can't imagine.'

'Do you have any idea how your daughter got into the warehouse?' put in Bell. 'Did she have a key?'

'No, of course not. Why would I have given her a key?'

'Did she have access to your key, then?' Kincaid asked.

'N—' Yarwood hesitated. 'Well, I – I suppose it's possible. I left the key at the flat. I had no reason to carry it around with me.'

'And Chloe has access to your flat?'

'Of course she does. It's her home.'

'So she could have copied the key,' stated Bell, making a note.

'Again, I suppose it's possible, but I can't imagine why she'd do such a thing. Why are you assuming she did?'

Kincaid leaned forward, so that only the width of the tabletop separated his face from Yarwood's. 'The way I see it, there are three possibilities. One, your foreman lied about locking the door and he left the building open. But in that case how would Chloe have known she could get into the building?

'Two, whoever entered the building picked the lock. It's obvious from the CCTV footage that your daughter and her companion entered almost immediately, which makes that option highly unlikely.

'Three, your daughter had a key, more than likely a copy she had made from yours. And that implies premeditation on her part. Do you get on well with your daughter, Mr Yarwood?'

'What sort of question is that?' Yarwood rose out of his seat until he was halfway across the table. 'What the hell are you getting at?'

Kincaid didn't back away. 'I'm wondering if your daughter had any reason to set fire to your warehouse.'

After a moment, Yarwood sank back into his chair. 'No. Chloe wouldn't do something like that,' he said slowly, but Kincaid thought he heard the slightest hesitation.

'What about the man with her?'

'I don't know. I've never seen him before. Look, I've told you all I know. You've got to find out if that's my daughter. I can't bear—'

'We'll do everything we can,' Kincaid assured him. 'But first we're going to need some information from you.'

'And you'll keep this from the press?'

'Until we have a definite identification—'

'Sir,' interrupted Bell, 'could I have a word?' She gestured towards the door, and after a moment's hesitation Kincaid excused himself and followed her into the corridor.

'What—'

'Sir, shouldn't we be asking him about the gambling connection?'

Kincaid made an effort to control his own impatience. It showed restraint on Bell's part that she'd bothered to consult him at all, rather than charging ahead with the questioning on her own. 'Look, Maura, we're dealing with a man who thinks he may have lost his only daughter. We can't in good conscience accuse him of something based on completely unsubstantiated rumour. We'll talk to him about it if and when we have something to back it up.'

'I doubt you'd be so delicate if you didn't have instructions to treat the man with kid gloves,' she retorted, her dark eyes flashing with disapproval.

Kincaid's forbearance vanished. 'I'm not treating Marcus Yarwood differently than I'd treat anyone else in such circumstances. And you, Inspector, are out of order.'

The interview room door swung open and Cullen came out.

'Do you want to broadcast everything to the entire station, guv?' He glared at them both, then added, with his usual peacemaker's instinct, 'Look, I've got Chloe Yarwood's address. I say we find out if the girl's really missing before we go any further with this. Maybe she just doesn't want to talk to Daddy.'

Kincaid turned to Cullen. 'Right. Okay, Doug, you and I will pay a visit to Chloe Yarwood. Inspector Bell,

I'd like you to stay here and look into a couple of things. Run a check on Tony Novak's wife. Then see if you can get an address for him, and send somebody round to have a word.'

'Sounds like a nutter, guv,' put in Cullen. 'His wife's probably done a runner with the kid to get away from him, just like he said.'

'Probably. But we can't afford to leave any stone unturned at this point, and I don't like the connection with the shelter. It's just too close for comfortable coincidence.'

Bell scribbled down the names and Laura Novak's address in grim silence, then said, 'You'll tell Mr Yarwood he can go, then? I'm sure he'll appreciate your diplomatic skills.'

She directed a tight smile at them both and walked away.

'Bit hard on Inspector Bell, weren't you, guv?' Cullen said as they crossed the river yet again and snaked through the City, heading towards Notting Hill in Kincaid's car. 'You always encourage *me* to say what I think.'

'I don't encourage you to be insubordinate,' Kincaid snapped. 'Inspector Bell has yet to learn the difference between offering an opinion and questioning a senior officer's judgement.'

'So you sent her to the salt mines because she disagreed with you? Anyone could have checked up on Tony Novak.'

Kincaid took his eyes from the road long enough to give Cullen a quelling glance. 'I'm beginning to think the inspector's a bad influence on you, Dougie. You'd better watch yourself.'

Greeting this admonition with the silence it deserved, Cullen stared pointedly out of the window.

Great, Kincaid thought. Now he had two sullen detectives on his hands, and he still had to account for authorizing Gemma to conduct interviews on someone else's patch. His day seemed to be rapidly deteriorating.

And yet, aggravated as he was, he began to wonder if Cullen was biased simply because he fancied Maura Bell, or if Bell's criticism had been justified. Would he have been harder on Yarwood if he hadn't been worried about the fallout from higher up? It was an unpleasant thought, and to top it off he suddenly realized he'd completely forgotten about passing Rose Kearney's notes on to Bill Farrell.

Having navigated her way through the warren of buildings that made up Guy's Hospital, Gemma eventually found her way to the administrative section. A young woman sat at the front desk in Medical Records, her long nails clicking on her computer keyboard as she typed. She looked up as Gemma entered, a slight frown creasing her brow.

'Can I help you?' she asked. 'Do you have permission to be up here?'

Gemma produced her warrant card, which she'd

needed to get through the main security checkpoint, although on Winnie's earlier visit her dog collar seemed to have worked just as well. 'Hi, I'm Inspector James, Metropolitan Police. I just wanted to ask a few questions about a member of your staff, Elaine Holland.'

The young woman dropped her hands from the keyboard and appraised Gemma with frank interest. 'Someone came yesterday, too, a priest. Nice lady. I'm Tasha, by the way.' Her smile revealed deep dimples in her cheeks. She was dark-skinned, with a round, friendly face emphasized by her elaborately plaited hair. Her long nails, Gemma noticed when Tasha reached across the desk to shake her hand, were lime green, each one decorated with its own unique design. 'Everyone else is out at the moment – we've a skeleton staff at the weekends – but I work with Elaine. Isn't it unusual to call in the police just because someone misses a day of work?'

Pulling up a chair, Gemma explained, 'She's been missing from home since yesterday morning. After twenty-four hours we begin to get concerned. I understand she didn't call in sick yesterday?'

'No. And that's unheard of for Miss Conscientious. You'd expect Elaine to give two weeks' notice if she was going to take a long lunch.' There was enough satisfaction in Tasha's voice to make Gemma suspect that Elaine hadn't minded criticizing those who didn't meet her standards – and that Tasha had not cared much for her workmate. Nor could she imagine, from the little she knew of Elaine, that Elaine would have found this bright, outspoken girl her cup of tea.

'Did she give you any indication before yesterday that she might be planning to go somewhere, or that there was anything unusual going on in her life?'

'No. But then Elaine's not one to sit down for a good girly gossip.'

'Has she any particular friends in the department?'

Tasha thought for a moment, idly rubbing the tip of one of her long thumbnails. 'No, not really. I suppose if she was going to talk to anyone, it would be me, just because I'm the most available body. But when she does get in the mood to talk, it's not because she's interested in what anyone else has to say. It's more like every so often she has an urge that needs satisfying – a sort of vocal masturbation,' Tasha added, giving Gemma a cheeky grin.

Gemma smiled back, refusing to be shocked. 'What sort of things does she talk about when one of these . . . um . . . *urges* strikes her?'

'Oh, it's usually some sort of rant about the disgraceful state of the government, or her glorious childhood in the Gloucestershire countryside with Mummy and Daddy. Sometimes you'd swear she's a relic from the Great War, instead of a woman in her thirties.'

'I take it she's not a fan of the Labour government, then?' asked Gemma, making a mental note that Elaine wasn't likely to have volunteered for Marcus Yarwood's election campaign.

'No. And I can tell you something else,' Tasha added, 'she didn't come from Gloucestershire.'

'How do you know?' Gemma asked, interested.

'Because I was born and bred right here in Southwark, and I know a Southwark accent when I hear
one. I belong to a local drama group,' Tasha confided,
'and accents are my forte. I'd guess Elaine Holland's
never spent more than a month outside the Borough.'

'Where am I from, then?' Gemma asked, fairly
confident that her years in the job disguised any give-
aways from her old neighbourhood.

'Is this a test?' Tasha asked, grinning. 'Okay, let me
think.' She closed her eyes, making a great show of
concentrating. 'London, obviously. Um, north of the
river, but not within the sound of Bow Bells. Not posh,
though . . . and I think north-east rather than north-
west. I'd say Wanstead, or thereabouts.'

Gemma laughed aloud. 'Got it within a mile. It's
Leyton. I grew up in Leyton High Road.'

'So you'll take my word about Elaine?'

'I will. And I'll come and see you at the Old Vic
one of these days. Your talents are definitely wasted
here.'

'It pays the bills. And it's all right, really.' Tasha
looked a little ashamed. 'I suppose I shouldn't have
been catty about Elaine. I mean, I hope nothing's
happened to her. I just assumed she'd finally lost it.
Or gone off with that guy she's been hinting about.'

Gemma nearly jumped out of her chair. 'What
guy?'

'I don't know,' said Tasha, sounding less sure of
herself. 'She's never really said anything. It's just the
last few months there's been something different . . . a
sort of smugness whenever anyone else is blathering

on about their boyfriends. She listens with this little *cat-who's-got-the-canary* smile. And then . . . One of the other girls is getting married, and she made some comment about spinsters. I don't think she really meant it as a dig at Elaine, not directly, but Elaine just went off. I'd never seen her like that. "I'll bloody well show you," she shouted, and slammed out of the office.'

'When was this?'

'A couple of weeks ago. A half-hour later Elaine came back in, as calm as you please, and never said another word about it.'

Gemma struggled to fit this in with the secret wardrobe and her suspicions about Elaine's relationship with Franny. 'Tasha, did it ever occur to you that Elaine might be gay?'

'Gay?' Tasha frowned. 'Well, you never know these days, do you? But even with the severe suits, no, I never really considered it.'

'And did Elaine ever talk about her home life?'

'She said she had a nice flat, near the river. But as she never invited anybody round she could have been taking the piss, I suppose.'

'She never mentioned her housemate?'

'No.' Tasha looked surprised. 'She has a housemate?'

'She's shared a house with another woman for a couple of years. It was her housemate who reported her missing.'

'Oh. The lady priest said it was a friend.'

Trust Winnie to be discreet, Gemma thought.

Seeing the light of speculation in Tasha's eyes, and conscious of time passing and the boys waiting, she decided to wind up the interview. Gesturing at the laminated ID tag clipped to Tasha's blouse, she said, 'We've not been able to find a picture of Elaine, but she must have an ID photo.'

'Personnel will have it on file, I'm sure. I could show you—'

'I'm sure I can find it.' Smiling, Gemma stood. 'Thanks, Tasha. You've been a great help.' She turned back as she reached the door. 'One more question. Did Elaine often work late?'

'Elaine? She's as regimented about that as she is about everything else. She clocks in and out on the dot.'

'Okay.' Kincaid broke the silence a few minutes later as they passed Paddington Station and swung into Bishop's Bridge Road. 'Maybe I was a bit hasty with Bell. And ratty with you. Sorry.'

'Tact doesn't seem to be Bell's strong point,' Cullen answered equably.

'While it is yours.'

'Well, I try.' Cullen smiled.

'Don't get too cocky. I'm not saying she was right. I don't like shooting in the dark, and we simply don't know enough yet. Nor am I going to badger a man who's afraid he's lost his child, regardless of his position.'

'Do you think he was telling the truth about why he was trying to ring Chloe?'

'No. But I haven't figured out why he would lie.' Bishop's Bridge had morphed into Westbourne Grove, and Kincaid pulled up at a red traffic light. 'What was that address?'

Cullen consulted his notes. 'It's Denbigh Road. Do you need me to check the map?'

'No, I know the street.' Denbigh Road ran parallel to Portobello, but the mere block's separation made the difference between a quiet backwater and a teeming hive of activity.

Having passed the organic food market on Westbourne Grove where Gemma liked to shop, Kincaid turned left into Denbigh Road. Although Notting Hill was becoming increasingly expensive and gentrified, there were still unreconstructed pockets, and Kincaid wondered which sort of flat Chloe Yarwood inhabited.

The address, which he found easily, turned out to be a pre-war mansion block, in solid and unpretentious red brick. The first-floor flat was listed under Tia Foster's name. They rang the bell, and after Cullen explained briefly who they were Chloe's flatmate buzzed them in.

Tia Foster answered the door wearing tight jeans and a loose white cotton sweater, rubbing at her dripping hair with a towel. 'Sorry,' she told them. 'I've just got back from a few days' holiday in Spain. Had to wash off the travel grunge.' She was an elegant-looking woman in her mid-twenties, her lightly tanned face free of make-up, her shower-damp hair a dark blonde. More attractive than pretty, she had the good bone structure that promised her looks would last into middle age. 'You said you were wanting Chloe?' she asked when they'd introduced themselves.

'Have you seen your flatmate recently, Miss Foster?' Kincaid asked.

'Not since I left for Spain on Wednesday. Look, can I get you some coffee or something? I was just making a pot.'

'Yeah, that'd be great,' Cullen answered before Kincaid could decline. 'Can I give you a hand?' Cullen added, following her into the kitchen with the alacrity of an eager puppy. Kincaid wondered if his sergeant's enthusiasm had something to do with the fact that the girl didn't appear to be wearing a bra beneath her thin sweater.

Taking the opportunity to examine the flat rather than its occupant, Kincaid looked round the room. The place had definitely been recently upgraded. Pale wood floors gleamed throughout; the creamy paint was new, the ceiling fitted with high-tech light fixtures. And because the mansion block had been purpose built, the rooms, unlike those in many flats in converted Victorian houses, were spacious and well laid out. How could two young women afford a place like this? Was Marcus Yarwood contributing to his daughter's upkeep?

There were signs, however, that money was not unlimited. An expensive leather sofa anchored the room, but the rest of the furnishings were sparse and looked like they might have come from Ikea. The abstract prints on the walls were obviously inexpensive reproductions.

As Cullen came out of the kitchen carrying a tray with cups and a cafetière, Tia reappeared minus the towel, running a brush through her hair. She was still barefoot, however, and glancing at her slender, tanned feet, Kincaid was reminded of the Victorians' fascination with a briefly bared ankle. Sometimes a slice was more alluring than the whole cake.

'So what's my little flatmate been up to that the police want a word with her?' asked Tia as she settled herself on the sofa, one foot tucked up beneath her. Abandoning the brush, she lifted the cafetière and filled the cups with an easy grace, but the glance she gave Kincaid was sharper than he'd expected.

'Her father's worried about her,' Kincaid answered, accepting the cup she handed him. 'He's been trying to get in touch with her for a couple of days with no luck.'

'So he called the police? That seems a little excessive, even for Mr Yarwood. And a senior officer.' She gave Kincaid an assessing look.

'Did he call here asking for her?'

'There were a couple of messages on the answerphone, yeah.'

'But you weren't concerned about Chloe?'

'I'm not Chloe's keeper. It wouldn't be the first time she's gone off for a day or two. She does her own thing.'

'Would you mind looking to see if any of her things are missing?'

'But I'm sure— Well, okay, I suppose I can do that.' Tia Foster stood up with a look that said she thought he was wasting her time, and disappeared into the rear of the flat.

Leaning closer to Kincaid, Cullen said quietly, 'Don't you think we should—'

Kincaid raised his hand, mouthed, 'Just give it a minute.'

Tia came back, shaking her head. 'I can't tell that she's taken anything, but that doesn't mean—' She must have seen something in their faces because she paused, looking alarmed for the first time. 'What?' she asked. 'What aren't you telling me?'

'We have CCTV footage of Chloe Yarwood entering her dad's warehouse about ten o'clock on the night before last,' Kincaid said, placing his coffee cup carefully on the table. 'Two hours later a fire was reported in the building. The firefighters found the body of a woman who has yet to be identified.'

'Oh my God.' Tia sank onto the sofa, graceless as a marionette whose strings had been cut. Beneath her even tan Kincaid could see the colour leach from her face. 'And you – you think it's Chloe? But . . . that's just not . . . I know she's a bit of an idiot sometimes – you know, reckless – but she couldn't be *dead*.'

Kincaid had never known recklessness to be proof against death; in fact, it was much more likely to be the opposite. 'How do you mean, reckless?'

'She's just a kid. She likes to party, stay out late, that kind of thing. Look, I know Marcus Yarwood doesn't like me, that he thinks I'm some sort of bad influence on his daughter, but I never meant . . . I didn't realize she'd be so eaten up with it.'

'Eaten up with what?' asked Cullen, apparently picking the last part of her statement to unravel first.

'I *know* people. I grew up in Chelsea. My family has money. I can't help that any more than Marcus Yarwood can help having been born into a family of bricklayers, or whatever they were. But Chloe, Chloe was so impressed with it all . . . the right people, the right parties, the right clubs . . . It really went to her head.

'At first I thought it was sort of sweet, you know – made me feel a bit like a fairy godmother. I thought she'd get over it, that she'd see it for the crap it is, but she didn't, and she was . . . out of control.

'I – I'd asked her to move out. If she was in that warehouse – if something happened to her because . . .'

'Why would Chloe have been there because you asked her to move out?' Kincaid asked, not sure he was seeing the connection. 'You didn't put her out on the street, I take it?'

'No, no. I told her I needed someone in the flat who could pay half the mortgage, that I was worried about my job and about money. My parents made me a gift of the deposit on this place so that I could get onto the property ladder, but that was it. Chloe was supposed to be paying me rent, but she was always behind, and lately she hadn't been paying me at all. At first, I didn't mind so much, but . . .'

'I'd say you were bloody generous to put up with it as long as you did,' Cullen remarked stoutly. 'But I still don't see what that had to do with the warehouse.'

'It was the flats,' Tia explained. 'Chloe got the idea she could talk her dad into letting her have one of the flats when they were finished. I don't know why she thought that – he'd kicked her out of his own place because she wouldn't stay in college or keep a job – he certainly wasn't going to pay to set her up on her own. But she kept asking me to let her stay until the flats were ready. I thought she was just playing for time. That's why, when I got back and heard those messages from her dad, and she wasn't here, I was a little . . . relieved.' Tia dropped her head into her hands and rocked back and forth. Her hair, drying now, fell across her face like wisps of barley. 'I'll never forgive myself if something's happened to her,' she whispered.

'So Chloe wouldn't have gone there needing a place to sleep,' Kincaid mused. 'And why take the guy with her when she still had a room here, and plenty of privacy with you away?'

'What guy?' Tia's eyes grew wide with trepidation.

Kincaid drew out the CCTV photo and handed it to her. 'Do you recognize him?'

'Oh, God.' She shook her head, not as a negative but in apparent dismay. 'It's Nigel. Nigel Trevelyan.'

'You're sure?'

'Absolutely. I'd recognize that wanker anywhere.'

'Would he have hurt Chloe?'

'No way. He's a poser. Goes round in motorcycle leathers and chains, with his earring and his bandanna, when the closest he's ever been to a Harley is a pushbike. And all the working-class thing is pure bollocks – his family lives in Ealing, overlooking the golf course. Nigel wouldn't say boo to a fly.'

'Do you know how we can get in touch with him?'

'Not a clue. I mean, Chloe hangs out with him, but I wouldn't be caught de— Oh, God, sorry. I didn't mean that.' Tia's eyes filled with tears and she gave a little hiccuping sob.

Cullen moved over to the sofa as if his physical presence might comfort her. 'Don't worry about it,' he told her gently. 'Everyone says things like that. It's just a figure of speech.'

'We don't know for certain that it *is* Chloe in the warehouse,' Kincaid reminded them. 'We'll need some samples for the lab. Hair would be best. If you could tell me—'

'Chloe's things are on the right-hand side of the basin in the bathroom. I hadn't even unpacked my stuff yet, just used what I needed for my shower straight out of my travel kit. That's how I knew she hadn't taken her things – her hairbrush is still there.'

Leaving Tia to Cullen's ministrations, Kincaid excused himself and found the bathroom. The basin had been set into an oak dresser, leaving a generous amount of space on either side. The left-hand side was clear, the right covered with opened bottles, spilled cosmetics and a purple plastic hairbrush, its bristles matted with brown hair. There was also a toothglass, its rim smudged with traces of lipstick and saliva.

Kincaid bagged both items, then stood, gazing at

the snapshot that had been stuck into the edge of the gilt-framed mirror. It was a casual shot of the two girls, arms round each other's shoulders, laughing into the camera. Chloe was easily recognizable from the CCTV image, but the colour and sharpness of the photo seemed to give her substance. And here her youth was obvious, as it had not been in the brief glimpse captured by the hidden camera.

Although Kincaid had empathized with Marcus Yarwood's shock and worry, his sympathy had been abstract. Now, for the first time, he made an emotional connection between the laughing, pretty girl in the snapshot and the burned thing in the warehouse. Chloe Yarwood had become real.

He stood for a moment with his eyes closed, resting his hands on the basin's edge. Dear God, he hoped the body they'd found did not belong to this girl.

Chapter Eleven

The debilitated old house in the city, wrapped in its
mantle of soot, and leaning heavily on the crutches
that had partaken of its decay and worn out with it,
never knew a healthy or a cheerful interval, let what
would betide.

Charles Dickens
Little Dorrit

As she was running late for tea, Gemma phoned the
boys and asked them to meet her at Erika Rosenthal's
house in Arundel Gardens, only a few minutes' walk
from their own.

Before leaving the hospital she'd visited Personnel
and asked them make her a copy of Elaine Holland's
ID photo. Now she tucked the small colour likeness
into her windscreen visor and glanced at it every so
often as she drove towards Notting Hill. Whatever her
imagination had conjured up from the various things
she knew – or thought she knew – about Elaine, it had
not been the haunting face that looked back at her.

There was an austerity in the magnolia-pale skin,
the jaw-length auburn bob, the eyes that looked dark

in the photo but that Gemma suspected held the same red-gold highlights as the hair, the prominent cheekbones, the rather thin mouth set in an uncompromising line – *that* she had expected. But when Gemma visualized the addition of a bit of make-up, the relaxing of the firmly held mouth, she knew the results would be stunning. She began to have a slightly clearer picture of the woman who had held everyone at arm's length but kept a secret wardrobe tucked away in her cupboard.

She was still mulling over the contradictions when she reached Arundel Gardens. Rather to her surprise, Erika, who had never been demonstrative, greeted her with a hug.

'Gemma, how lovely to see you. The boys are here already and have made a start on the tea and sandwiches.'

'I'm sorry about having to cancel at such short notice last night,' said Gemma as Erika ushered her into the house.

'Not to worry. I'm afraid these days I find I'm just as happy to stay in by the fire with a book. And I will get to meet your young man eventually, I'm sure.'

Gemma thought it would amuse Kincaid, who had recently inched past forty, to be referred to as her 'young man' – it made him sound like a callow suitor paying court – but she was a little concerned about Erika. Her friend seemed more frail than when Gemma had seen her last, and when she had hugged Gemma, her bones felt as delicate as a sparrow's. But Erika's back was as straight as ever, her snowy hair swept as neatly into its twist, her bright black eyes sparkling with their usual humour.

Gemma had first met Erika Rosenthal, a noted historian, the previous year, when the older woman had reported a burglary. Shortly afterwards, when Gemma was researching a case, she'd run across Erika's name on a scholarly monograph on the history of goddess worship and had consulted her professionally. They had become friends, and Gemma tried to visit her as often as her chaotic schedule allowed.

Now in her nineties, Erika was alert and independent, her mind sharp and engaged. Gemma often used her as a sounding board when she was stumped over a case and, more and more frequently with Hazel so far away, confided feelings she was unlikely to reveal to anyone else. Erika's wisdom and sense of perspective gave Gemma a comfort she'd never experienced, and it devastated her to think that her friend might be beginning to fail.

Entering the sitting room, she found the boys huddled over Erika's little piecrust table, attacking a huge plate of sandwiches.

'Don't scold them for not waiting,' Erika entreated. 'I told them to go ahead. Boys need feeding regularly.'

'Like tigers,' added Toby, looking pleased with himself. 'Look, Mum, Erika's made scones, too.' Another table held a plate of scones and the teapot.

'Oh, Erika, you shouldn't have gone to so much trouble,' said Gemma, 'especially when I meant to treat you.'

'Nonsense. It's nice to have someone to bake for. I wouldn't do it for myself.'

Sitting down on the red-brocaded settee as Erika insisted on pouring her tea, Gemma looked round the room with her usual pleasure. Having grown up in a household ruled by the telly and by what her mother referred to as 'practical' furnishings, she loved the rich and cluttered collection of books and paintings and the antique German furniture Erika had accumulated to replace the things lost by her family during the war. The room always held a large arrangement of flowers, and then, of course, there was the piano. Until Duncan's unexpected gift of a piano of her own the previous Christmas, Erika's baby grand had been the object of Gemma's envy.

Now she looked at it with a pang of regret for her missed lesson as she accepted a still-steaming cup of tea from Erika. 'Did you get your cabinet organized?' she asked Kit when she'd placed a few sandwiches on her plate.

'Um, not entirely,' said Kit, with a glance at his brother. 'Toby was helping,' he added, putting it tactfully.

'I can imagine. Sorry to leave you in the lurch.' She stopped herself from adding, *Something came up*. It was a phrase used much too often in their household.

Kit's shrug spoke volumes. As she looked at the two boys sitting side by side, she thought how it never failed to amaze her that they were not, in fact, related by blood. Both had straight blond hair and blue eyes, but while Kit looked like both his late mother and Duncan, Toby was surely a changeling. He resembled neither her nor her deadbeat ex-husband Rob.

Watching them, she realized that Toby, usually an unadventurous eater, was wolfing down smoked salmon and cucumber sandwiches as if he ate them every day, while Kit was merely picking. She'd hoped that the morning's expedition would have taken his mind off his worries over Monday's hearing, but it had obviously not done the trick.

Seeming to sense that Kit was troubled, Erika made an effort to draw him out as they finished their tea, asking him about his interests and collections. 'And what field do you want to study eventually?' she added. 'Botany? Zoology?'

'Um . . .' Kit looked a bit taken aback by being put on the spot but said gamely, 'My friend Nathan's a botanist, and that's really cool . . . but I like animals, too. I'd like to study animal behaviour like Konrad Lorenz or Gerald Durrell. And then there's anthropology, and palaeontology, and geology . . . I don't know how I'll choose.'

'You will have to narrow it down a bit for practical purposes,' Erika agreed, 'but a diversity of interests is a good thing. It contributes to analytical thinking. And I believe that the problems the world faces today can only be solved by those who can synthesize ideas and think outside the traditions of their disciplines.'

Setting down her cup, Erika stood and went to one of the bookcases lining the wall. She ran a finger down the spines, then pulled out a book and handed it to

Kit. 'You might enjoy this. Stephen Jay Gould was a Harvard professor of geology with a lifelong interest in palaeontology. He was a brilliant and original thinker whose interests were as varied as yours.'

'Thanks.' Kit examined the book, his face alight with interest. 'I'll take good care of it.'

Toby, meanwhile, bored with books and biology, had slipped from his chair and begun to sidle round the room, his hands clasped carefully behind his back in the 'don't touch' position he'd been taught.

Suddenly, he paused, his body tensing like a retriever on point, and forgot himself so far as to reach out with a finger. 'Mummy, look! There're little men, and horses!'

'It's a chess set, silly,' Kit told him. He joined his brother, the book clasped under his arm.

Gemma had noticed the set before, but as she didn't play, she hadn't paid it much attention. The intricately carved pieces sat on a small table against the far wall, with a chair drawn up on either side.

'It was my husband's,' said Erika. 'One of the few things he managed to smuggle out of Germany.'

'Don't touch it, either of you,' warned Gemma, alarmed, visions of irreparable damage dancing in her head.

'No, it's quite all right,' Erika assured her. 'Do you play, Kit?'

'A little. My da— Ian showed me a few moves.'

'Why don't you teach your brother, then? Go on,' she added as Gemma started to protest again. 'I promise it's indestructible.' As the boys began arguing over who would take the black and the white pieces, Erika sank back in her chair as if suddenly exhausted.

Gemma stood and began gathering the tea things. 'We've tired you out. Let me do the washing up; then we'll let you rest.'

'I have more than enough time for that,' Erika said with an unexpected touch of wistfulness. 'And I like having the boys here. Back in my teaching days the house was always full of students.' She roused herself. 'But I will let you help with the washing up, if you promise to let me keep you company.' Together, they collected the china and carried it into the kitchen.

When Gemma had filled the basin with soapy water and persuaded Erika to sit at the kitchen table, Erika said, 'I see you've been in the papers again. I've been following your case. Is there any more news about the missing child?'

Gemma shook her head. 'No. And every day that passes makes it less likely she'll be found.'

'Oh, I *am* sorry, my dear. It must be terribly hard for everyone concerned.'

Gemma could only nod. To all appearances, the six-year-old had simply walked out of her front door while her mother had been busy in the kitchen, then vanished in broad daylight. The ordinariness of it terrified Gemma more than anything else.

'You cannot protect your children from everything,' Erika said softly, as if she'd read Gemma's mind. 'You can only do what seems sensible, and trust in fate.'

Gemma spun round, her soapy hands dripping on

the kitchen floor. 'How can you, of all people, trust in fate?' Erika, a German Jew, had lost every single member of her family during the war.

'Because the only other option is to live in constant fear, which to me seems hardly worth doing. And I prefer to put my energies into nurturing minds like your son's. Has he heard from his father – or should I say stepfather? I'm never sure what to call him.'

'I can think of several things to call Ian,' said Gemma, with a grimace of irritation. 'But Kit hasn't heard from him lately, no. Pressures of the new term at his university, and pressures of the new wife, apparently.' She turned back to her task. 'But he has sent an affidavit for the family court judge, saying that as Kit's legal guardian, he believes it best for Kit to live with us rather than be uprooted to Canada, and he feels that for Kit to have any contact with his grandmother would be damaging to his emotional well-being.'

'And yet the grandmother still insists on pursuing custody?'

'Yes. Our first court hearing is on Monday.'

Erika considered this in silence for a few moments, then said, 'Even my tolerance has limits. Someone needs to shake some sense into that woman.'

Dusk was painting shadows in the corners of the garden as Rose got up from the computer, shoving her chair under the desk in a gesture of frustration. The conservatory off the kitchen, with its built-in computer nook, had been one of her father's last projects. Ordinarily, it was her favourite room in the house and she loved working or reading there, daydreaming as she gazed out into the garden.

That afternoon, however, she'd looked from the clock to the phone to the computer and back again, growing increasingly edgy and unsettled. She'd had a run and a shower, and tried to nap, but her sleep had been disturbed by half-remembered nightmares. Giving up on rest, she'd made coffee and called up the fire brigade database once again, thinking she might see something she'd overlooked earlier, while she hoped Station Officer Farrell might call.

But the phone had not rung, and as the hours passed she felt more and more foolish for having attempted to contact him. Why had she thought she'd discovered something the investigating team wouldn't turn up on its own? And what good would it do even if she had? There was nothing anyone could prove, or that would help the investigators predict the location of another fire. Her guvnor had been right; she should have kept her nose out of it.

The fading daylight told her she should be hungry. Padding barefoot into the kitchen, she peered into the fridge but found nothing appealing. Her mum had gone out for a meal with friends, and Rose couldn't be bothered cooking just for herself.

There was, however, half a bottle of her mum's Australian Chardonnay, and after a moment's deliberation Rose poured herself a glass. She wasn't much of a drinker. Although she sometimes went to the pub with the lads after a day shift, she usually nursed a half pint through the evening. Tonight, though, she thought the alcohol might help her relax.

Taking her glass to the open conservatory door, Rose gazed out into the garden. The day had stayed warm, and the faint breeze that had made the humidity bearable seemed to have faded with the sunset. She took a deep breath, trying to dispel the lingering sense of claustrophobia that had plagued her all day. It was absurd – she was used to wearing a mask, and she had never panicked in a fire, even as a raw recruit. Why should she feel now as if she had a weight on her chest?

She thought back to her meeting with the superintendent from Scotland Yard, the only time that day that the heaviness had lifted. Duncan, he'd said to call him. A nice name, and he was bloody good-looking, too. He hadn't made fun of her theory, but perhaps he'd just meant to be kind. She was wondering about his partner, and about his reluctance to discuss his domestic situation, when her mobile rang.

She rushed over to the computer desk where she'd left her phone, flipping it open with one hand while she juggled her wine in the other.

'Hey.' The voice was not Station Officer Farrell's, but one much more familiar.

'Bryan,' she said, making an effort to disguise her disappointment.

'What's up, Petal?'

'Not a lot.' Away from the station, she didn't bother complaining about the nickname. 'You?'

'I thought you might fancy a drink.'

It was the first time he'd ever rung her off duty and asked her to do something socially, and she heard his slight hesitation.

'Um, I don't think I'm up for it,' she said awkwardly. 'What with the early start tomorrow and all.'

'I just thought you might want some company.' Bryan paused, then added, 'Are you all right, Rose?'

They hadn't really had a chance to talk since she'd been hauled over the coals by Wilcox, and for a moment she was tempted to tell Simms what she'd been doing. She knew she could trust him to keep it to himself, but it was clear from the concern in his voice that he thought she needed looking after, and she didn't want to encourage that. Nor was she in the mood to have her ideas shot down, however kindly.

'I'm okay,' she said. 'I'm fine, really. We'll talk tomorrow, yeah? I'll see you at roll call in the morning.'

'Right. Cheers, then.'

When they'd rung off, she walked slowly back to the garden door. There she stood for a long time, cradling her still-untouched glass of wine against her chest, searching the darkening sky for a telltale smudge of smoke.

Having quickly familiarized herself with Franny's kitchen, Winnie had prepared supper, pasta with a simple marinara sauce, some cheese she'd bought at Borough Market, and a salad. She'd hoped that something both light and comforting would encourage

Franny to eat, but she'd watched with growing frustration as Franny pushed the food around on her plate, and she'd felt guilty for her own appetite.

'I'm sorry,' Franny said at last. 'You've done so much already – I would hate you to think I don't appreciate it. It's not your cooking, I promise you. It's just . . . I can't . . .'

'Don't worry about it.' Winnie stood and gave her a pat on the shoulder. 'I'll do the washing up, then we can have a cup of tea and a biscuit. And' – she delved into the bag she'd brought with her – 'I thought we might watch a video.'

She kept a collection that she thought of as her 'ailing parishioner kit'. Through experience, she'd discovered that prayer had its place, but that there was nothing more healing to those who were ill or worried than a good belly laugh. Tonight she'd got out two of her personal favourites, *A Fish Called Wanda* and *Waking Ned Devine*, plus some old episodes of *Fawlty Towers*. They were all irreverent, but in her opinion reverence was highly overrated, and she even had a secret fondness for the ecclesiastical absurdities of *Father Ted*.

'Oh, Winnie.' Franny seemed to sag in her chair. 'I don't think I could manage it. Could we just have the tea . . . and chat?'

'Of course. I'll just help you settle in for the night, shall I?'

Winnie made short work of the dishes, and when she'd put the kettle on she turned to see Franny fingering the videos she'd left out on the table.

'Elaine would never have watched these,' said Franny, looking up at her. 'Nor my parents. I remember how much my mother hated *Fawlty Towers* when I was growing up. There's nothing the Chinese find more offensive than rudeness, and to her Basil Fawlty was the devil incarnate. "That awful man," she called him.'

Winnie filled their mugs and sat down at the table. 'I bet you watched it on the sly, then.'

'I did, whenever I could manage.' Franny grinned, remembering, and Winnie realized it was the first time she'd ever seen a real, unfettered smile on her friend's face. The difference it made was astonishing. 'And worried about getting caught,' Franny went on. 'It was probably the worst thing I ever did. They had such expectations, my parents, and I never wanted to disappoint them.'

'What about Elaine?' asked Winnie, beginning to see disturbing parallels between Franny's home life and her relationship with Elaine Holland. 'What did she like to watch?'

'Oh, serious things. Old movies, sometimes. I didn't like to complain. She . . .'

'She what?' Winnie prompted when Franny didn't continue.

'She – she could be . . . unkind.' Franny gazed down at her mug, as if unwilling to meet Winnie's eyes.

Holding herself very still, Winnie measured her words. 'Unkind, how?'

'Oh . . .' The cat, Quinn, came in through his door

and jumped onto Franny's lap, kneading her with his front paws. 'She – she would say I was lucky to have her . . . that no one else would want to be saddled with me, the way I am.' Franny stroked the cat's back and he butted his head against her shoulder, purring loudly. 'She would say I was never going to get better, that I was fooling myself. But that was only when she'd had a particularly bad day, and I thought it was all right, really, because she'd had such a hard time in her own life.'

Looking down, Winnie saw that her knuckles on the hand round her cup were white. 'What sort of hard time?'

'I at least had parents who cared for me. I mean, they were strict, but I *mattered* to them, more than anything else. Elaine . . . Elaine's mother committed suicide when she was twelve, in their shower so that Elaine would find her when she came home from school. What kind of mother would do that to her own child? And after that her father cared nothing for her, but when he got sick she took care of him until he died.'

'She told you this?'

'In bits and pieces, most of it when she was particularly . . . cross. She was – she could be – she *did* care for me, in spite of how it sounds.'

'You're very forgiving,' Winnie managed to say. 'But you know that neither of the things she said about you were true.'

Franny looked down at her body in the chair. 'It's getting harder and harder to imagine anything else.'

'That will change, I promise,' said Winnie, vowing that she would make sure of it.

At least Franny had begun to speak of Elaine in the past tense, which Winnie could only see as a positive step. Whatever had happened to Elaine Holland, Winnie hoped that Franny, having made such a confession, would not be willing to take her erring housemate back with open arms. And as much as it shamed her, Winnie found herself wishing, just for a moment, that Elaine Holland would never walk through Franny's door again.

Kincaid leaned against the door jamb, watching Gemma in the bath. The tub, an old-fashioned roll-top, was one of the things Gemma loved most about their house, and tonight she'd made the most of her retreat. Candles flickered, the water foamed with something flowery, and a piano nocturne drifted from the CD player. All were signs that she'd had a particularly stressful day.

'Is this the ritual bath?' he asked lightly.

'It's much easier on the goat this way,' she said without turning, but he heard the smile in her voice. She'd pulled her hair up on top of her head, and sat with her arms wrapped round her knees, exposing the slender line of her neck and the curve of her back. In the candlelight, her skin looked pale as alabaster. 'Are the kids in bed?' she asked.

'I've read to Toby, and Kit's curled up with a book he says Erika gave him.' He'd helped Kit arrange the last of his birds' eggs and bits of stone and bone in his display case, and had promised to try to work out some way to light it. 'The cabinet's great, by the way. He seems pleased.'

'He's had a good day, I think, between that and Erika. He's quite impressed now with her being a famous historian, with oodles of published papers.'

'*Oodles?* Is that in the dictionary?' Grinning, he crossed to the dressing table stool and sat down so that he could see her face.

'Do I care?' She flashed a smile at him, then said, 'Duncan, do you suppose we'll be an embarrassment to him one day?'

'What? You think he'll be apologizing for "my parents the plods" as he's accepting his Cambridge degree? Let's hope he has the opportunity,' he added, sobering as he thought of Eugenia's custody suit.

'Duncan, this case . . . You won't let anything keep you from making the hearing on Monday . . .'

'Of course not. I've discussed it with Doug. He'll cover for me if necessary.' He took off his watch and began rolling up his shirtsleeves. 'Shall I do your back?'

'Please.'

He took her nylon bath ball and lathered it with soap. 'If I get the DNA results from Konnie tomorrow, we'll at least be able to narrow things down from there. Maybe then we'll be able to make some real progress.'

Cullen had taken the samples they'd collected from Chloe Yarwood's flat back to the station, and had sent them off to the lab immediately, flagged for Konrad Mueller's immediate attention.

Kincaid had updated Gemma on Marcus Yarwood's identification of the girl in the CCTV image as his daughter, and she'd shared the results of her interview at Guy's Hospital with him. While interested in what she'd learned, he'd decided there was no point trying to trace Elaine's phantom boyfriend until they had the results of the DNA tests, and that copying her photo for the team could wait until the next morning. He had, however, set Cullen the immediate task of trying to find Nigel Trevelyan, the man who had been with Chloe Yarwood on the night of the fire.

Kneeling by the tub, he began soaping Gemma's neck, working his way down to her shoulders with a circular motion. When he had lather the consistency of shaving cream, he dropped the nylon ball in the tub and began massaging her shoulders and back with his hands.

'Um . . . can I hire you on a permanent basis?' Gemma asked, leaning into the pressure.

'Depends on the benefits. I'm open to offers.' Her skin slipped like satin under his fingers. He began to think about the possibilities of the bath mat, and whether or not the boys were well and truly down for the night.

'Gemma . . .'

She turned suddenly, splashing him. 'I've just remembered. You never told me what happened before you came to Franny's house, when you were at the shelter.'

Sighing, he sat back on his heels. He knew her well enough to realize she wouldn't be sidetracked until her curiosity had been satisfied. He told her about Tony Novak accusing the shelter of helping his wife and daughter disappear. Earlier in the evening he'd heard from Maura Bell, who'd said they'd had no luck finding either Novak or his wife. There was no one at the Park Street address Kath Warren had given him for Laura Novak, and although they'd found an address on Borough High Street for a Dr Anthony Novak, there was no answer there, either.

'There's a missing child?' said Gemma, a note of alarm in her voice.

'We don't know that for sure,' he answered reasonably. 'It's more than likely that the wife has gone off with the daughter, if they're really even missing at all.'

'If that were the case, wouldn't she have asked for Kath Warren's help?' Gemma sloshed water on her shoulders, rinsing off the suds.

'Maybe Kath wasn't telling me the truth.'

'Why would she lie, if there's nothing illegal about helping someone relocate?'

'All right, then,' Kincaid said, a little aggravated over the mood obviously lost for the moment. 'Maybe Laura Novak didn't trust Kath Warren not to tell Tony? Or Tony not to find out on his own? After all, Tony has had access to the shelter, and possibly to the shelter's records.'

'How old is the little girl?'

Kincaid searched his memory for details. 'I think Kath said she was ten.'

'How long have they been missing?'

'I don't know. He buggered off before I had a chance to ask him.'

Gemma leaned back into the curve of the tub, her expression thoughtful. 'What were you talking about when Novak ran off?'

He frowned. 'Kath was saying she hadn't seen the wife and daughter, and then she introduced me—'

'By rank?'

'Yes. And then you called, and when I turned round from answering the phone, he was gone. Maybe he thought I was going to nick him for assaulting Kath.'

'Or maybe he'd done something he didn't want to tell the police about.'

'If he'd hurt his wife or his daughter, why would he have been accusing Kath of abducting them?' Kincaid argued.

'At this point, you don't know what sort of a nutter this guy is,' Gemma countered. 'You've got to talk to him again. And make every effort to find his wife and daughter. What if—'

'Gemma—' He stopped himself telling her he knew perfectly well how to run an investigation because he was beginning to have a niggling doubt as to whether he'd given Tony Novak's missing wife enough weight. 'Look, I'll look into it myself in the morning, starting with Laura Novak's house. If she's not there, I'll check with the neighbours.'

'I'm going with you.' Gemma sat up and reached for a towel.

'Gemma, that's not necessary.'

'You need Cullen and Bell for other things. And I want to come.'

He moved out of her way as she pulled the plug and got out of the bath. Her face was flushed pink from the heat, and her face set in the stubborn expression he knew well.

'Gemma,' he said slowly, 'it's not your fault you haven't found the little girl that's missing.'

She put her foot up on the edge of the tub and gave great attention to drying her toes. 'I know that,' she said, but she didn't meet his eyes.

He watched her in silence, knowing there was nothing he could say that would convince her, any more than he would be able to convince himself if it had happened on his watch.

She had been all right until the light started to fade.

The woman who had brought her to the house had come twice during the day, locking the door when she left each time. The first time, that morning, she'd brought Harriet breakfast on a tray – a bowl of instant cereal and some dried fruit. She hadn't spoken at first, and it was only when Harriet saw she meant to put the tray down and leave that she'd got up the courage to speak.

'Why have you brought me here?' she asked, still huddled under her blanket. 'Where's my dad?'

'Your father wants you to stay here for a few days,' the woman said, turning back from the door.

'My dad wouldn't leave me in this place.'

'No? Maybe your father has a little surprise planned for you.'

'Let me talk to him,' Harriet begged.

'He's not here at the moment. But you'd better do what he wants.' The woman reached for the doorknob again.

'My mum.' Harriet stood up, the blanket still wrapped round her shoulders. 'My mum will be worried about me. She'll find me.'

'I don't think so.' The woman smiled, and Harriet felt cold in the pit of her stomach.

'Wait, please,' said Harriet in desperation. 'I have to go to the toilet.'

'Use the bucket.' The woman gestured towards the old tin bucket Harriet had noticed against one wall.

'But I—' It was too late. The door swung shut behind the woman, and Harriet heard the bolts click into place.

She'd cried then, big gulping snotty sobs that made her chest hurt and her throat ache. When the sobs began to subside, she realized there was nothing to wipe her streaming eyes and nose on except the tattered cover around her shoulders. Still hiccuping, she sniffed as hard as she could, then fastidiously dabbed at her nose with the edge of the blanket.

After a while, she gave in to hunger. The cereal had congealed into a cold and slimy mass, but she ate it anyway, then nibbled at what she thought were dried apricots.

Eventually, she used the bucket, as well, because she had no choice, then pushed it into the very farthest corner of the room.

With her stomach filled, a terrible sleepiness came over her again. She fell upon the bed, curling herself once more beneath the blanket.

She woke sometime later, as suddenly as she had fallen asleep, and this time with perfect clarity. She knew instantly where she was and how she had got there, although she still had no idea why.

The light had changed. The sun had moved away from the window, and as she had no other way of telling the time, Harriet thought it must now be afternoon. She was hungry again, and beginning to feel thirsty.

Time passed. She gazed out of the window at the grey rooftops, and when she tired of that, she thumbed through the books in the bookcase. There were a few of Enid Blyton's Famous Five adventures, an Arthur Ransome, a very tattered edition of *Black Beauty*, and a copy of *Peter Pan*. Had this been a child's room, wondered Harriet, some long time ago?

The room had grown warm and stuffy as the afternoon lengthened. She thought about breaking one of the window panes, but realized she'd get cold if it turned chilly in the night. Nor was she sure what sort of retribution such an action would bring.

She realized that she was beginning to smell, as was the bucket in the corner of the room. It occurred to her that she had never in her life been dirty or failed to have clean clothes. Trying to ignore her

growing thirst, she settled against the wall with one of
the Enid Blytons. Her mother was always nagging her
about reading when she should be doing other things,
but here there was nothing else *to* do. The thought of
her mother made her throat ache again. Blinking, she
stared resolutely at the page until the feeling eased.

It was only when she found herself squinting to
make out the print that she realized the light was
fading. She had put down the book when she heard
the creak that signalled footsteps on the stairs. She
waited, heart thumping, hoping it was her dad come
to take her away.

But the woman came in alone, with a tray, as she
had that morning. This time it held some biscuits,
more of the dried fruit, and what looked like some
sort of tinned meat. There was also, Harriet saw to her
relief, a glass of water.

'Where's my dad?' she said, straightening her stiff
legs as she pushed herself up against the wall.

'He's been . . . delayed. Maybe he's forgotten about
you.'

This was a mistake on the woman's part, because
if Harriet knew one thing, it was that her dad would
not forget about her. Fear struck through her, worse
than anything she'd felt before. Had something happened to her dad? Something that had kept him from
coming for her?

She thought about trying to bolt through the door,
but the woman seemed to read her mind. 'I wouldn't
try it,' she said with the smile Harriet had seen earlier.
'The front door locks from the inside and I have the

key. There is no phone. *And* I'd have to drag you back up.' Her tone made it clear that Harriet would not want her to do that. She smiled again and went out, locking the door behind her.

As the footsteps faded, Harriet fell on the food, devouring the stale biscuits and the disgusting tinned meat. Even the water tasted stale and flat, as if it had been stored for some time. She drank a little of it, then realized she'd better save as much as she could – and that the more she drank, the sooner she'd have to use the bucket again.

While she'd finished her brief meal, the room had grown dimmer. Harriet had already noticed that there were no lamps. Now she realized there was no ceiling light either. Trying to quell her rising panic, she searched along the walls, moving furniture when she could. When she'd completed the circle, she did it once more, then went back to the bed and sat. There were no electrical sockets in the room, no paraffin lamps or candles, not even a match. There would be no light.

She lay down and closed her eyes, but the darkness seemed to press on her eyelids. When the panic threatened to choke her, she got up and fumbled her way to the door, kicking at it and shouting until she'd worn herself out, but the house was silent as a tomb.

Crawling back to the safety of the bed, she stared into the encroaching gloom. After a while she began to realize that it had not got any darker. She could see her hand when she held it in front of her face, and the window stood out as a silvery rectangle. It was the reflected light of the city, and it gave her a strange comfort to think that there were people outside this house, moving and laughing and talking, eating and drinking. She was not entirely alone.

Chapter Twelve

Look here. Upon my soul you mustn't come into the
place saying you want to know, you know.

Charles Dickens
Little Dorrit

The rain that had threatened all day on Saturday
passed through in the night, but it did not clear the
air. Kincaid woke to an overcast sky, and when he
walked out onto the small balcony off their bedroom,
the pavements shone greasily with damp. The air felt
pregnant with moisture.

Leaving Gemma sleeping, he'd slipped out of bed
and quietly bathed and dressed, but when he came in
from his perusal of the weather, she sat up and blinked
at him sleepily.

'Is it nice?' she asked, yawning.

'No, not very. Rather damp and looming.' He sat
on the edge of the bed.

'Will it be all right for the boys?' They had arranged
for Wesley to take the boys to the park that morning,
and then to his mother's house for a meal. It would
be a family gathering, filled with chatter and music

and West Indian food, and Kincaid had convinced himself the outing would provide the most distraction for Kit.

'Should be, unless it pours buckets. You know boys are oblivious to the finer nuances. Should we try to slip out without waking them?' He knew that Toby had crept into Kit's room last night, and he'd heard them still up, talking and giggling, when he went to bed.

'Too late.' Gemma sat up and pushed the hair from her face. 'Can't you smell the bacon? When Kit was cataloguing his choice of professions for Erika yesterday, I can't believe he forgot executive chef.'

Like any teenager, Kit had to be dragged from bed on school mornings, but at weekends he was often up early, pottering about in the kitchen. He'd confided once to Kincaid that he used to make breakfast for his mother but had made him promise to keep the information to himself.

Gemma would be touched if she knew, Kincaid thought. She walked a fine line between trying to be a mum to Kit and not making him feel as if she meant to replace his mother. He didn't envy her the job; in a way, his own was made easier by the fact that Ian had let Kit down so badly.

'Go on,' said Gemma, giving him a gentle shove. 'I'll be down as soon as I'm dressed. I want to get away as soon as possible.'

A night's sleep had obviously not changed Gemma's mind about accompanying him to Laura Novak's, and in spite of the procedural difficulties,

Kincaid realized that he was pleased at the prospect of having her with him.

The terraced row of houses looked Georgian in its four-square simplicity, its only ornamentation the scrollwork arches above the glossy black front doors and the white shutters framing the ground-floor windows. Although not ostentatious, Laura Novak's Park Street address spoke of financial comfort. In London location was everything, and this house had it all – no more than two or three minutes' walk from the river in one direction and Borough Market in the other, and another minute or two past Borough Market would bring you to London Bridge Station. It was also, Kincaid mused, a mere hop and a skip from Marcus Yarwood's Southwark Street warehouse.

'It's very close, isn't it?' Gemma said uneasily, echoing his thoughts as they got out of the car.

Locating the number Kath had given him, he looked up at the house. Although the day was already warm and many of the other houses had windows open, Laura Novak's were sealed and her curtains drawn. The flowers in the window boxes looked parched and wilted despite the brief shower in the night.

Kincaid rang the bell and they waited, listening, but there was no answer.

'Could she be hiding from Tony?' whispered Gemma.

'Bloody suffocated if she is. Let's give the neighbours a try.' He nodded to the right.

This time their ring was followed by the quick
tapping of heels, and the door was flung open by a
small Asian woman. 'Jamie, how many times have I
told you—' She stopped, staring at them in surprise.
'Sorry, I thought you were my son. He's always forgetting his keys. Can I help you?'

Producing his warrant card, Kincaid introduced
himself and Gemma. 'We wondered if we might talk
to you about your next-door neighbour, Laura Novak.'

'Why?' she answered with a frown of concern. 'Is
Laura in some kind of trouble?'

'We're just checking on her at this point. She hasn't
been seen for a couple of days.'

'Would you like to come in? Oh, I'm Monica –
Monica Karimgee, by the way.' She led them down a
hall and into a bright kitchen at the back of the house.
The room smelled of coffee and cinnamon, and the
pages of the *Observer* were spread across a small oak
table.

'Sorry to disturb your peaceful Sunday morning,'
said Gemma, with the genuine warmth that made her
so effective in interviews.

Monica Karimgee smiled and gestured at the table.
'It's my vice, reading the Sunday paper from cover to
cover, and I always make an effort to get my husband
and son out of the house. I tell them I'm encouraging
father–son bonding, but my motives are really more
selfish.' She was a pretty woman in her forties, a little

plump, her glossy dark hair lightly threaded with grey. 'Would you like some coffee? I've just made a pot.'

'Yes, please. It smells wonderful,' answered Gemma, and Kincaid concurred. Sitting where she indicated at the table, he examined their surroundings as Mrs Karimgee fetched mugs from a cabinet. The coffee machine was German and looked as though it required programming by a computer; the rest of the kitchen was German and high-tech as well. Kincaid glanced at Gemma for signs of envy, but she looked merely comfortable and interested.

'Mrs Karimgee,' he began when she joined them, 'when—'

'It's Ms, if you insist, not Mrs. My husband's name is Hodge. Why don't you just call me Monica?'

'Right, then.' Kincaid smiled and sipped carefully at his coffee. It was as good as it smelled, and he regretted that she hadn't offered them whatever smelled so enticingly of cinnamon, as well. 'Monica, when did you last see Laura Novak?'

She thought for a moment before answering. 'Sometime during the week. I'm not quite sure, but I think it must have been Tuesday or Wednesday.'

'Did you speak to her?'

'No. I just saw her coming in with Harriet as I was getting the post. It *has* been awfully quiet next door over the weekend, come to think of it, but I just assumed it was one of Harriet's weekends with her dad and that Laura was working. No, wait' – she frowned as she thought – 'that can't be right. I know Harriet was with Tony last weekend because he and

Laura had a row when he brought Harriet back. Laura's very strict about visits and she'd never agree to Tony having Harriet two weekends in a row.'

'This argument,' said Gemma, 'did you hear what it was about?'

Monica fidgeted with her cup and looked away. 'I don't want to sound like a snoop. It was unavoidable, really. My office is at the front of the house – I'm a commercial illustrator and I work from home – so if someone's shouting in the street it's a bit hard to ignore. All I can tell you is that Laura seemed to be angry with Tony, but then that's not unusual. I worry about Harriet – it can't possibly be good for her, all the dissension.'

'No,' Kincaid agreed, thinking of the damage their own difficulties with Eugenia had caused Kit. 'Do you know why Laura's always angry with Tony?'

Again Monica looked uncomfortable. 'Look, I really don't want to gossip. Surely that's their affair.'

'Under ordinary circumstances, yes,' Gemma told her earnestly, 'but Tony Novak has reported both his ex-wife and his daughter missing. The more we know about what was going on between Tony and Laura, the more likely we are to get to the bottom of this quickly.'

Monica blanched. 'But you said Laura. Harriet's missing, too?'

'Her father thinks so, and there's no answer next door. You're sure you didn't see any signs that Laura and Harriet were going away for the weekend?'

'No. It is odd, though, now that I think about it,'

Monica said slowly. 'On Friday – Friday morning, it would have been – I think I saw Tony's car. I just happened to look out the window, then I had a phone call, and when I looked out next it was gone. It's a dark green Volvo, not all that common. When Tony and Laura split up, Laura kept the house and Tony got the car – not a great sacrifice for Laura, as she thinks it wrong to own a non-essential car.'

'A non-essential car?' Kincaid echoed, puzzled.

'You know. She's very green-minded – one should use public transport at all times. I dare say the world would be a better place if we all went along with that, but most of us aren't willing to make Laura's sacrifices.'

'So if Laura had suddenly decided to take Harriet away somewhere for an extended period, she couldn't just have popped a few things in the boot and left,' Kincaid said, thinking aloud. 'She would have had to hire a car or a taxi.'

'But why would Laura want to take Harriet away?' Monica asked.

'Perhaps she was afraid of Tony. It appears he has a bit of a temper.'

'Tony?' Monica looked surprised. 'It's Laura who's always flying off the handle, not Tony.'

Kincaid thought of the man he'd met yesterday at the shelter. Had Tony Novak kept his aggressive tendencies well hidden outside the family, or had yesterday's behaviour been an aberration? 'You're sure you didn't actually see Tony, just his car?'

'I'm positive.'

'Did you hear anything from next door during that time?'

Monica shook her head. 'No. And the car can't have been there more than five or ten minutes, tops. I wasn't on the phone for that long.'

Gemma leaned forward, creating a little zone of intimacy between the two women. 'You said before that it was Laura who was always angry. Was it Laura who wanted to end the marriage?' she asked with an air of frank curiosity that invited confidence.

'Oh, yes, she made that clear to anyone who would listen. I don't know if it was one woman or many, but Tony obviously got caught out. Well,' Monica added, 'with Tony's looks I suppose it wasn't surprising he should be tempted to play away from home – I suppose even Heathcliff needed some light relief occasionally.' As soon as the words were out of her mouth, she looked ashamed. 'Oh, I'm sorry. That was really uncalled for. Look, I really do hope nothing's happened to Laura. It's just that she's not an *easy* person. And Harriet – Harriet's a lovely girl. Surely she's all right?' There was an appeal in her voice.

'Does Harriet get on with her dad?' Kincaid asked, sidestepping the question.

'Adores him. And vice versa. He must be frantic with worry.'

That, Kincaid thought, certainly described Tony Novak's state the previous day. But in that case why had he not informed the police of his concerns? And what had he been doing at the house on Friday morning?

'We will need descriptions of Laura and Harriet, if you wouldn't mind,' he told her.

'But didn't Tony—'

'We just need verification.'

Gemma pulled out her notebook for the first time.

'Well, Laura's in her mid-thirties, about my height, but thin, with curly dark hair and dark eyes. And Harriet – Harriet's about average height for a ten-year-old. She's thin like her mother, and she inherited her mother's hair, but she looks more like her dad.'

'Eye colour?' asked Gemma, her pen poised.

'Umm, grey. A dark grey.' Monica looked increasingly distressed.

Kincaid finished his coffee with regret and pulled a card from his pocket. 'If you think of anything else, or you see Laura or Harriet, please call.'

Monica studied the card, then looked up at him. 'I didn't really take it in when you introduced yourself, the fact that you were a superintendent. Aren't you a little overqualified for this sort of call?'

'There's a possibility that Laura Novak's disappearance may be related to some other matters we're investigating, but I'm afraid that's all we can say at the moment.' Before she could pursue it further, he stood, and Gemma followed his cue.

Monica saw them to the door, her pleasant face etched with worry. When they reached the threshold, she stopped suddenly. 'What about Mrs Blakely – Bleckley – something like that. Have you spoken to her?' Seeing their blank expressions, she went on. 'The woman who looks after Harriet when Laura has to work nights. When Tony and Laura were together, they made sure to arrange their night duties so that one of them could be at home, but now Laura has to use a child minder. Not that I haven't offered to have Harriet here, but Laura didn't like to be beholden to anyone.'

'Can you give me an address?'

'No, not exactly. I know she lives in those cottages in Redcross Way, opposite the school. That made it convenient for Harriet to get to school on the mornings she had to stay.' Her lips curved in a half smile. 'Harriet's always telling my Jamie that the woman's a witch. I've had to reassure him that that's there's no such thing.'

'I hope you're right,' Kincaid said with a passing thought for his former mother-in-law.

'Did you by any chance notice a little bias in favour of Tony Novak?' said Gemma as they climbed back into her car. 'How often do other women side with the straying husband rather than the wronged wife?'

'Monica Karimgee wasn't just forgiving his apparent lapses, she was almost justifying them,' mused Kincaid. 'Which makes me think that either she's smitten with him herself or that Laura Novak does not endear herself to people.'

Gemma gave him a sidelong glance. 'You didn't tell me he was good-looking.'

'Didn't occur to me. But I suppose he is, in a dark and brooding sort of way. Hence the Heathcliff reference. What I don't understand is why, if it wasn't his weekend to have Harriet, Novak was so sure she and Laura were missing.' Rubbing his thumb over his chin, Kincaid stared at the house. 'And what was he doing here? I doubt very much that he's welcome to come and go as he pleases. Did Laura let him in? Or did he go in on his own?'

'Maybe he saw something in the house that made him think Laura had taken Harriet, but he didn't want to admit he'd been inside. But that wouldn't explain why he was there in the first place. And you'd think, given the hostile state of their relationship, that Laura would have changed the locks.' Gemma fished her *A–Z* from the driver's door pocket. 'What about this child minder? She might be able to tell us something.' Redcross Way, she saw from the map, was very close, just the other side of Union Street.

Glancing at his watch, Kincaid said, 'Possibly, but I think the most urgent things on our agenda are finding Tony Novak and, barring that, getting a warrant to search Laura Novak's house. And right now I've got to meet Cullen and Bell at Borough Station. I'm late as it is.'

Gemma touched his arm. 'I want to be there when you interview Tony Novak. I promise I won't inter-fere,' she added, forestalling his protest. 'I'll be quiet as a mouse.'

'Right.' He raised both eyebrows, an indication of extreme scepticism.

'And while you're at the station, I'll see if I can find Mrs Whatever. Then I'll ring you.'

'I don't suppose I could stop you, anyway,' he said with resignation.

Gemma smiled and put the car into gear. 'You should know better.'

When Gemma had dropped Kincaid at the top of Borough High Street, outside the police station, she looped back round to Union Street and turned right into Redcross Way. She saw the primary school immediately and, across the street, a parched little park facing a row of almshouses, undoubtedly the cottages Monica had mentioned. There was nothing for it but to knock on doors.

She had success on her second try. A sweet-faced little white-haired woman answered the door and blinked up at her.

'Excuse me,' said Gemma, 'but do you know where I could find Mrs Blakely?'

The woman stared at her so blankly that Gemma wondered if she might be deaf, or senile, but at last the woman said, 'Oh, is it Agnes Bletchley you're wanting? That'll be next door, and good luck to you.' She slammed the door before Gemma could reply.

After that reception, Gemma tried the cottage next door with some trepidation. She could hear the television blaring even through the closed door. She knocked, waited, then knocked again more loudly.

She'd raised her fist to try once more when a voice shouted from inside, 'Just hold your damned horses, will you?' The door swung open and a woman leaning on a stick scowled out at her. 'What do you want?'

'Mrs Bletchley?'

'What's it to you?' She was tall and angular, with short hair dyed a lifeless brown, and a long face scored with hatchet lines of perpetual discontent.

Gemma showed her warrant card. 'I'd like to talk to you about Harriet Novak.'

'What's the little brat done? Robbed a bank?' Mrs Bletchley sniggered at her own humour, then added ungraciously, 'I suppose you'd better come in, then.' She turned away, leaving Gemma to follow her into a dark little sitting room dominated by the still-blaring television. The remainder of the room was stuffed with a three-piece suite covered in a flowered moquette fabric. The furniture clashed horribly with the thread-bare carpet, and the acrid smell of cat urine made Gemma flinch. What on earth had Laura Novak been thinking to leave her child here? she wondered in horror.

'Mrs Bletchley,' she said, trying to pitch her voice above the noise of the telly, 'can you tell me when you last saw Harriet?'

The woman lowered herself onto the settee but didn't invite Gemma to join her – not that Gemma was at all eager to sit on the furniture, but standing made it difficult for her to look Mrs Bletchley in the eye.

A yellow cat as bony and angular as its mistress slunk in from the kitchen, stared balefully at Gemma, then began washing its paw.

'When did you last see Harriet?' Gemma repeated,

shifting her position until she was blocking the woman's view of the television.

With a grimace of irritation, Mrs Bletchley lifted the remote control and muted the volume. 'No need to shout. Bloody nuisance, that child. Always complaining about this and that. *Missy doesn't want fish fingers for her supper, she wants beefburgers. Missy doesn't want cornflakes for her breakfast, she wants frozen waffles.* Does she think I can afford those on my pension?'

Her patience rapidly deteriorating, Gemma said, 'Mrs Bletchley—'

'If you want to know when I saw her last, she was getting into that car.'

Gemma's heart seemed to dive into her stomach. 'What car? When was this?' She sat down in spite of herself and leaned closer to the old woman.

'Well, it was on the Friday morning, when else would it have been? I'd come out with the cats, after she left for school. I could see her in the playground, hanging about by the school gate. Then a car pulled up and she got in.'

'Are you saying that Harriet stayed with you on Thursday night?' asked Gemma, trying to find a solid point of reference.

'What else would I mean? Her mother had to work, rang me at the last minute. Bloody inconvenient, wasn't it, as I had nothing to suit little Missy's taste. In my day—'

'Mrs Bletchley, did you see Laura Novak on Thursday night?'

'She didn't stop except to pay me. Cash, I always ask for, so as not to have to bother with the bank.'

'What time was this?'

'Nearly ten, it must have been. The news was coming on as she left. At least I didn't have to find the child any supper.'

'Did Laura say anything to you about going away?'

Mrs Bletchley looked at her as if she were daft. 'I told you she didn't stop. In and out, always in a hurry, that woman.'

Gemma was beginning to feel desperate. 'Did Harriet say anything about going away?'

'What's all this about going away? Why should she talk to me about going away?'

'Mrs Bletchley, Harriet and her mother appear to be missing. Can you tell me about the car you saw Harriet getting into?'

The woman shrugged. 'It was dark. Newish. Blue, maybe, or green.' She frowned and the hatchet lines deepened. 'I think it was green.'

'Dark green?' Gemma's heart plunged a little further as she took in the implications.

'Are you deaf?'

'I'm sorry. I just need to make sure. Could it have been a Volvo?'

Rolling her eyes, Mrs Bletchley didn't deign to answer.

'Did you see the number plate?' tried Gemma.

'Do I look like I could see the number plate at that distance?'

'Okay.' Gemma took a breath. 'Could it have been Harriet's father who picked her up?'

Mrs Bletchley glared at her with undisguised dislike. 'How would I know? Never seen the man, have I? And the windows were dark. She got in from the school side, so I never saw inside the car at all.'

Gemma realized then that she'd insisted on pursuing this case partly out of concern for Harriet Novak, but partly because a positive resolution would ease her conscience over the child she'd failed to find. Now she felt as if she were caught in a repeating nightmare. 'Mrs Bletchley,' she said, and it seemed to her that the words were weighted with lead, 'I'm going to need a description of the clothes Harriet was wearing on Friday morning.'

Kincaid found Doug Cullen leaning against the water cooler outside their temporary incident room in Borough Station, grasping a plastic cup as if his life depended on it. Cullen looked pale, and behind his spectacles his eyes were puffy and red-rimmed.

'Whoa, mate,' Kincaid said, grinning. 'Night on the tiles?'

'I wish.' Cullen straightened up, draining his cup and tossing it accurately into the waste bin. 'Clubbing, yes. Fun, no. I got the names of some spots where Chloe Yarwood hangs out from Tia Foster. Thought I might find the boyfriend. This Trevelyan bloke's got no phone number listed, and no driving licence.'

Kincaid would have been more impressed with his sergeant's sacrifice of his evening if he hadn't suspected Cullen of wanting an excuse to ring Tia Foster again. 'No luck, I take it?'

'No. And I wish they'd make bloody smoking illegal,' Cullen added, rubbing at one eye just as Maura Bell came up to them.

'So who made you boss?' she asked, giving him a defensive glare. She'd livened up her black suit that morning with a deep pink sweater, and her hair looked freshly washed. Kincaid wondered if the effort had been made for Cullen's benefit, and if Cullen had failed to notice.

'I did find out something, though,' Cullen continued, ignoring the barb. 'A bloke at one of the West End clubs recognized Nigel Trevelyan. Said the guy's a real sponger, always coming up with schemes to separate people from their money.'

'Including Chloe Yarwood? Or Chloe Yarwood's father?' Kincaid suggested. 'That could prove interesting, if it's true. Maybe he convinced her that her dad needed to collect the insurance on his warehouse.'

'Then they torched the place together?' said Cullen, looking brighter.

'Aren't you overlooking a few things?' asked Bell acidly. 'How does that account for the body, unless Trevelyan killed Chloe and left her there, and in that case how would he gain from Yarwood's insurance settlement?'

Cullen absently rubbed at his eyes again, knocking his glasses askew. 'What if Chloe came up with the idea herself? Maybe she needed money, and she thought that if Dad had a sudden cash infusion, he'd help her out. And it backfired on her.'

The comment brought Kincaid a sudden clear vision of the charred body, and of Chloe Yarwood's young face in the photo he'd found in her bathroom.

'We'll talk to Yarwood again today, see if we can get some answers,' he said. 'But first we need to find Tony Novak. I've just spoken to Laura Novak's neighbour. She says she hasn't seen mother or daughter since some time last week, but that she glimpsed Tony's car outside the house on Friday morning.'

'I checked with the hospital,' said Bell. 'Tony Novak didn't show up for his scheduled shift on Friday morning, and neither did his ex-wife. But I don't understand why you're wasting time on what sounds a simple domestic when we've proof Chloe Yarwood was at the scene.'

Kincaid locked eyes with her. 'I'm not discounting anything – or anyone – until we get the results of those DNA samples. That includes Laura Novak, Elaine Holland and my aunt Martha if she happens to turn up missing between now and then. Is that clear?'

'Sorry, guv,' Bell said after a moment, dropping her gaze. The capitulation was so unexpected that Kincaid wondered if Cullen had had a word with her. 'Will we be needing a warrant for Laura Novak's house?'

'Yeah. Could you see to it? In the meantime, I'm going to try Novak's flat again.'

'I've sent a constable round twice with no luck,' Bell protested. 'What makes you think you'll do any better? Didn't you say he ran away from you at the shelter?' Bell's efforts at concurrence obviously hadn't lasted long.

'Then we'll get a bloody warrant for his place as—'

'Guv,' broke in Cullen quietly, 'Station Officer Farrell's here, and I'd swear he's smiling.'

Looking up, Kincaid saw Farrell coming down the corridor. While he wasn't sure he'd go so far as to call it a smile, the fire investigator's long face bore an expression of cautious enthusiasm.

'Got something for us, Bill?' he asked.

'Possible murder weapon,' said Farrell as he joined them. 'Charred fragment of a two-by-four, buried under debris. Your classic blunt instrument. Luminol brought up a bloodstain on the underside, which was somewhat protected from the fire. The lab will check the blood against the victim's.'

'The way this case is going, we may find one of the workmen cut his thumb,' Kincaid murmured, but he was pleased to have something concrete to go on.

This time Farrell did actually smile. 'If that's not good enough for you, we found several partial prints on the wood as well, one in the blood. If you come up with a suspect, we may be able to place him at the scene. Or if you're really lucky, the guy has a record and the database will give you a name.'

Kincaid thought suddenly of Rose Kearney's suspected serial arsonist. Arsonists often began with petty crimes. If the man existed, he might well have a record. Patting his jacket pocket, he found to his relief that he still had the papers. 'Do you remember the firefighter who came to the scene?' he asked, handing Farrell Rose's list and map.

'The young woman?'

'I ran into her yesterday. She's convinced some of the fires that have occurred in Southwark the past few months form a pattern. I said I'd ask you to ring her – her mobile number's on the sheet.'

Cullen grinned. 'Sounds like you've got yourself a nutter, boss, but at least she's good-looking.' This earned him a disgusted glance from Bell and a scowl from Kincaid.

Farrell, on the other hand, after an initial look of scepticism, was scanning the papers with interest. 'Why didn't she take this to her guvnor?' he asked.

'She was off duty yesterday. Said she didn't want to wait until her shift began this morning. And I think her guvnor warned her off pursuing it.'

'So would I, in his place, and I'd recommend her for a stress debriefing,' said Farrell, folding the papers. 'But as I'm not her boss, and it looks as though she might have come up with something interesting, I'll give her a ring.'

Realizing there was still something in his pocket, Kincaid fished out the photo Gemma had given him the previous evening and handed it to Bell. 'Elaine Holland. From her hospital file. Can you get it into the system?'

'How did you—' she began, but Kincaid was saved by the ringing of his phone.

*

Gemma had parked opposite the primary school and, having escaped from Mrs Bletchley, sat for a moment in the car trying to make sense of what she'd learned. She stared at the school's bright blue iron fence and low brick buildings, picturing a ten-year-old girl, her curly dark hair pulled back with an elastic, wearing jeans and trainers and carrying the inevitable backpack, getting into a dark green car.

Had Harriet been loitering deliberately by the gate, waiting by some prearranged plan? Or had she been surprised to see her dad when the car had pulled up beside her?

But if Tony Novak had picked up Harriet, why had he accused Laura of taking her? Could he have left Harriet at Park Street when Monica Karimgee had seen his car there, and maybe Harriet had later been taken somewhere by her mother?

Or could the green car have been mere coincidence? What if Harriet had not been picked up by her father at all? For all Gemma knew, Laura Novak had hired a green car and fetched Harriet herself, or it might have been a stranger who had enticed Harriet away. The thought made her blood run cold.

Realizing she wasn't going to get any further without more information, Gemma pulled out her mobile phone and rang Kincaid.

When he answered, she gave him a condensed report of her conversation with Mrs Bletchley, adding, 'Laura Novak must be daft to leave her child with that woman. It wouldn't surprise me if she'd buried Harriet in the garden, except she hasn't got one.'

'Gemma, did you say Laura Novak told the child minder that she had to work on Thursday night?'

'Yes. Why?'

'Because we've been in touch with the hospital. Laura was scheduled to work on Friday during the day, but she didn't turn up or call. Nor did Tony Novak.'

'Laura lied to Mrs Bletchley?'

'So it would seem.'

Gemma felt more confused than ever. Lying seemed out of character for a woman so devoted to her principles that she refused to drive a car. Why would Laura Novak have done such a thing? And where was she now?

'Tony Novak didn't turn up, either?' she repeated. 'We have to talk to him.'

'Hang on a sec,' said Kincaid. Gemma heard the murmur of background conversation, then he came back on the line. 'Here's the address. I'll meet you there. But, Gemma, don't go in without me. He could be dangerous.'

Gemma parked the car in front of Guy's Hospital, as she had the previous day, and walked round the corner into Borough High Street. As she looked for the address Kincaid had given her, she passed the George, the last of the ancient galleried inns of Southwark. The Tabard and the Queen's Head had long since disappeared, but the George, with only one of its galleries intact, had not only survived but did a booming business.

Tony Novak had certainly gone for convenience, she thought as she found the address a bit farther along. It was a block of flats over a shopfront, not particularly inviting but a stone's throw from Guy's Hospital.

She was about to push the entrance buzzer when a parting of the pedestrian traffic revealed a man sitting on the kerb, a few yards along. He was hunched over, his head cradled in his hands, his feet in the gutter. People were giving him a wide berth, as they usually did the drunk or the homeless, although you seldom saw either sitting half in the road, and the man looked ill as well as unkempt.

Although the distraction was unwelcome, Gemma couldn't pass by without attempting to help.

She smelled the sour stench of alcohol before she reached him and felt a bit more sympathy for those who hadn't bothered to stop. From a few feet away, she said, 'Excuse me, sir. Are you all right?'

When he didn't respond, she crouched down and looked at him more closely. He was dark-haired and tall – that much was apparent even in his present position – and slender. His clothes, although crumpled, seemed clean and of good quality, and on his wrist, bared where his shirt cuff had fallen back, was an expensive-looking watch. The man was no vagrant, and Gemma had a sudden flash of intuition. If she was wrong, she had nothing to lose.

She touched his shoulder. 'Tony.'

This time he raised his head, slowly, and stared at her with bloodshot eyes. His face was long and thin and covered with several days' stubble, and his eyes were hollow, but Gemma could see that under better circumstances he would be handsome. He didn't speak.

'Tony,' she said again. 'My name's Gemma.' Here she hesitated but decided that if she wanted to gain his trust she'd better be honest from the beginning. He didn't look in any state to run off. 'I'm a police officer, and I think you need some help.'

He stared at her a moment longer, then grasped her arm with surprising strength. 'You've found her. Harriet. Tell me . . . Is she—'

'We haven't found your daughter. We're hoping you can help us do that. But first let's get you up to your flat, okay? Can you stand?'

'Don't know,' he mumbled, but let her pull him to his feet. He swayed a little but seemed steady enough to walk without help. Gemma began to think he was not so much drunk as hung-over and exhausted.

He had not lost his keys, at least, and Gemma let him lead the way up the stairs to his flat. She had to help him unlock the flat door, and once in the sitting room, he sank down on the nearest available chair as if his legs had given out.

The flat was no more inviting from the inside than it had looked from the street. Obviously hastily converted to take advantage of the property boom, it had cheap fittings, and the walls and ceiling were already beginning to show patches of damp. The sitting room held a few pieces of nondescript furniture, and an open suitcase spilled its contents onto the floor.

'How long has it been since you've had anything

to eat or any sleep?' Gemma asked, as Tony looked in danger of nodding off again.

'Don't know. Don't remember.' He frowned and rubbed at his stubble. 'Couple of days, I think.'

'Right.' Gemma went into the tiny kitchen and took stock. There was part of a loaf of bread on the counter and some cheese and butter in an otherwise pathetically empty fridge. 'You're going to have something to eat, and then we'll talk.' She buttered bread and sliced cheese for a sandwich as the kettle boiled, then made a big mug of strong, sweet tea.

When she returned to the sitting room he had closed his eyes, but he sat up and took the food from her without protest. After the first bite, he wolfed down the sandwich as if suddenly starving, then gulped at the tea, even though it must still have been scalding.

When he looked up at her again, his eyes were more clear and focused. Picking at his shirt, he said, 'God, I stink. Must have spilled the bottle.'

'Yeah.' Gemma smiled. 'You do. But that can wait. First we need to talk about Harriet.'

His dark eyes filling with tears, Tony said with a sob, 'Oh, God. It's my fault.'

Gemma controlled her alarm. 'What's your fault, Tony?'

'I should never have left her.'

'Left Harriet?'

Just then the buzzer sounded from the street door. Tony jerked as if he'd been shot, then stood up, looking round wildly. 'Laura. She'll kill me . . .'

'It's not Laura,' Gemma said, gambling that she was right. She pressed the release for the street door latch. 'It's my friend Duncan. You met him the other day.' She gave Kincaid a minute to climb the stairs, then opened the flat door before he could knock. At his startled expression, she gave a quick shake of her head and held up a hand in warning before turning back to Tony.

'Tony and I are just having a chat,' she said. 'About Harriet. He's very worried about her.'

Tony sat down again slowly, his expression wary.

She saw Kincaid take in the open suitcase, but he followed her lead and pulled up a chair without speaking.

'Tony,' she said quietly, as if they hadn't been interrupted, 'where did you leave Harriet?'

He looked from Gemma to Kincaid, then back at Gemma. 'With a friend,' he whispered. 'It was just for a few minutes. I – I had something to do.'

'Was this after you picked Harriet up from school?'

His eyes widened, but after a moment he nodded. 'It was a treat. I was taking her out for the day, for a treat.'

'Did Laura agree that you should take Harriet out of school for the day?'

'God, no.' His face twisted in a grimace. 'It was going to be our secret, Harriet's and mine. But then I had to— She wanted some things from the flat, and I said I'd get them, but I couldn't take her with me.'

Gemma felt Kincaid's stir of impatience, but she nodded as if it all made perfect sense. 'So you left her with your friend while you went to the flat. Was Laura there?'

He looked at her blankly. 'Laura? Of course not. She was at work, or I'd never have gone.'

'Okay,' she said. 'So you picked up Harriet's things. Then what happened?'

He rubbed a trembling hand across his stubble again. 'I was supposed to meet them – Harriet and my friend. But they didn't come. And I realized I'd no idea how to get in touch with her.'

'Your friend?'

'Beth. Her name's Beth. I . . .' He shook his head. 'We'd been going out for a while, but she always came here. She said there was someone else, and I never—'

'But you must have had some way to reach her?'

'Only her mobile, and now it just goes straight to voicemail. She said she worked at an estate agent's here in the Borough, so yesterday I went round to every office, but no one knew anyone called Beth.'

Kincaid could contain himself no longer. 'Are you saying you don't know this woman's last name?'

'It was only casual sex, for God's sake. I never thought – I never meant—'

'You left your daughter, on the spur of the moment, with a woman whose name you didn't even know?'

'It wasn't like that,' protested Tony. 'I needed help, and I couldn't think of anyone else to ask, anyone who didn't—'

'Know your wife,' Gemma finished for him, the light dawning. 'Is that why you didn't want to leave

Harriet on her own, because you were afraid she'd call her mum?' She looked at the suitcase crammed with clothing, a little girl's T-shirt spilling over the side. 'You weren't packing for a day away, Tony; that much is obvious. You'd never have thought you could just take Harriet off for a day without Laura suing to revoke your access. And you'd have been in trouble with the hospital for failing to let them know you were going to be absent.' She tilted her head to one side, thinking, then said slowly, 'Unless it didn't matter, because you weren't coming back. Where were you taking her, Tony?'

He stared at her defiantly, and for a moment she thought he would deny it. Then he closed his eyes, and the tension seemed to seep from his body.

'Prague,' he whispered. 'I was taking her to Prague.'

Chapter Thirteen

> There is a passion for hunting something deeply
> implanted in the human breast.
>
> Charles Dickens
> *Oliver Twist*

'It's a beautiful place, Prague, the city of the spires,'
Tony went on dreamily, as if repeating a story he'd
told himself many times. 'My family's Czech. I thought
they could help us. There's always a need for qualified
doctors in Eastern Europe – I was sure I could find a
job, start again.'

'Wait a minute,' Kincaid said, his voice rising in
disbelief. 'I don't care what you meant to do. Why the
hell did you come bursting into the shelter accusing
Kath Warren of helping your wife abduct your child,
when all the time you knew you'd left Harriet with
someone else?'

Tony Novak raised his head and blinked at him.
His hung-over state was still evident in his glazed and
red-rimmed eyes, but he spoke clearly enough. 'At
first I thought Harriet might have asked Beth to take
her home or to the hospital, and that Harriet might

have told her mother I'd taken her out of school. Laura would've gone spare, I can tell you.

'But then, the longer I tried to find Beth, the odder it seemed that she'd just vanished without a trace. If Beth had taken Harriet to Laura, why wouldn't she have rung me or met me where we'd arranged, to tell me what happened?'

'Did Beth know what you meant to do?' asked Gemma.

Tony nodded, draining the last of the tea Gemma had made him. 'I'd rung her the night before. I told her I thought Laura was planning to abduct Harriet – that Laura had been threatening me with it for months and that on Sunday, when I brought Harriet back late, she was furious. She said it would be the last time I'd have that chance, and I could tell she meant to do something drastic. I was afraid if I didn't take Harriet, I'd never see my daughter again.'

'But why did you need to go to the house after you'd picked Harriet up? Surely you could have bought Harriet anything she needed?'

'I had to get her passport. Laura kept all the legal documents, and I couldn't get Harriet into Prague without her passport.'

'Then why not pick Harriet up after you'd got the passport,' Kincaid said, 'rather than involving Beth at all?'

'I needed Harriet's key. When I dropped off Harriet and Beth, I kept Harriet's backpack. And I had to pick Harriet up before school started because, once she'd gone inside, the school wouldn't release her to me.

Laura's instructions, thanks to the shelter's advice,' Tony added, his face tightening with anger and resentment.

Kincaid stood and took a few steps. The smell of sweat and stale alcohol in the small, stuffy room was making him edgy. 'Where did you drop them?' he asked, trying to keep Tony on track.

'We talked for a bit. I told Harriet I had a surprise for her, a treat, but that first Beth was going to take her shopping. Then I dropped them at London Bridge Station and said I'd pick Harriet up there in three hours. I wanted to be across the Channel before Laura realized Harriet hadn't come home from school.'

'You didn't think Harriet would object to leaving her home and her mother?' Gemma asked sharply, her disapproval obvious for the first time.

Tony rubbed at his face again, avoiding her gaze. 'Harriet loves me,' he said. 'She never wants to leave me after our weekends together, and I know she was worried that Laura meant to separate us. I thought . . . I thought I'd explain things to her once we'd left England, ask her to give it a try. If she didn't like it after a few weeks, she could go home. And I meant to let Laura know Harriet was safe, as soon as we were well away.'

'It's still inexcusable, taking a child away from her mother—'

'What gives mothers special dispensation?' Tony retorted, anger flaring again. 'What would you do if someone was going to take your child away from you? How would you feel?'

Kincaid saw Gemma glance at him, eyes wide, and he knew they were both thinking of Kit.

'Tony,' she said, 'why would Laura be so determined to separate you and Harriet? Is there something you're not telling us?'

'What?' He glared at her. 'You think I mistreat my child? Is that what you're suggesting?'

'No. I—'

'Then you can just bloody well fuck yourself.' He half rose from the sofa, his fists clenching. 'I told you, I love my daughter. I've never done anything worse than have her back a few minutes late from one of our weekends.' He sank down again, his face contorting, and pressed his knuckles hard against his mouth to stop it trembling. 'Oh, Jesus. I couldn't bear it if something's happened to Harriet.'

'Then why—'

'Laura's jealous. That's the truth of it. She's always been jealous of the fact that Harriet preferred me to her. When she found out about the women I'd been seeing that was just an excuse to end the marriage, because she could never admit the truth, even to herself.'

Kincaid's first response was to put Tony's statement down to self-justification, the bitter fall-out of a failed relationship. Then he thought of Kath Warren's tactfully expressed dislike of Laura Novak and of the equally unflattering portrait painted by Laura's next-door neighbour. But if Tony's assessment was accurate, did that tell them anything about what had happened to Harriet?

He said, 'Tony, if Laura had been planning to disappear with Harriet, don't you think Harriet would have told you?'

'Laura can be . . . harsh, if she feels Harriet's disobeyed her. Harriet might have been afraid to speak.'

'She didn't say anything when you picked her up on Friday morning?'

'No. But I didn't give her a chance. Beth was there and I – I put Harriet off when she tried to talk to me. I thought she was just worried that her mum would be angry I was taking her out of school. I didn't think it would matter, once we were gone.'

Leaning forward, Gemma said intently, 'I don't see how Laura could have gone away with Harriet without alerting the neighbours. She'd have to have taken a few things—'

'You don't know Laura. She could have had an emergency getaway kit stashed at the hospital.'

Gemma was shaking her head. 'Tony, none of this makes sense. Laura wasn't at the hospital. She didn't turn up for work on Friday. And she left Harriet with the child minder on Thursday night, saying she had to work night duty, but she didn't. We've checked.'

He stared at her. 'What?'

'You're *sure* she wasn't at home when you went in to get Harriet's passport?'

'Of course I'm bloody sure! Do you think she'd have let me walk merrily out of the house with Harriet's passport in my pocket?'

'If she wasn't at work and she wasn't at home, how could Beth have left Harriet with her?'

'But if Laura didn't take Harriet, it must have been Beth, and that makes even less sense,' protested Tony. 'Why would she do such a thing?'

'You tell us,' Kincaid said, still prowling the room. He could tell his movements made Novak nervous, and he wanted the man unsettled. 'You're the one who knew this woman well enough to take her into your confidence.'

'But I—' Tony picked up his empty mug, tilted it, set it down again. 'I told you, she never said much. Odd, really, as most women tell you their life stories in the first five minutes.'

Gemma raised an eyebrow at this, but didn't comment. Taking Tony's mug, she stepped into the adjoining kitchen and snapped the kettle on. She threw a tea bag and a few spoonfuls of sugar into the cup in the few seconds it took the water to boil, then carried the tea back to Tony. 'How did you meet her?' she asked, perching again on the edge of her chair.

'In the George. One night a couple of months ago. I'd never seen her in there before. She was . . . different. Most women who come into a bar alone, they're either obviously looking for company or just there for a drink. But Beth . . . She had this aloofness, yet at the same time she never stopped watching everyone. It was as if she was working out what made them tick, and she didn't much like what she saw. But when I saw her studying me, I offered to buy her a drink, and she accepted.' He looked as if it still puzzled him. 'Then later . . . she went home with me. After that she'd come over a couple of times a week, but we never talked much.' Tony stopped to sip at his steaming tea.

'Can you describe her?' Kincaid asked.

'Um, mid-thirties, medium height, brown hair . . . not beautiful, really, but attractive in an unusual sort of way.'

Another missing brunette? Kincaid's eyes met Gemma's and she gave her head a barely perceptible shake, as if warning him not to pursue it further. He let her continue.

'Tony,' she said quietly, leaning forward until she could almost touch him, 'we're going to need you to come down to the station to make a formal statement."

Panic flared in his eyes again. 'I – I can't . . . I've got to find Harriet.'

'We're going to help you find Harriet. I promise you.' She touched his knee lightly. 'But you have to cooperate with us. There's nothing you can do on your own that you haven't already tried.'

'I–'

'You get yourself cleaned up. We'll wait for you.'

'But I . . .' Tony picked at his shirt again, holding it away from his body as if suddenly aware of his revolting state. 'All right.' He stood, still a little unsteadily, but when he looked at the open suitcase his eyes filled with tears.

'Here. Let me help you.' Gemma quickly knelt beside the case, fishing out shirt and trousers, clean socks and pants with the practised efficiency of a mother of boys. She bundled the articles into Tony's arms and nudged him in the direction of the bathroom.

When he'd disappeared behind the closed door, Gemma turned back to Kincaid. Her face was strained.

'You realize we now have four missing women that potentially fit the description of one body?' he said.

Gemma knelt and dug through the suitcase again. 'And a missing child who very well may not be with her mother.' With a grunt of satisfaction, she pulled out a framed photograph and sat back on her heels, studying it for a moment before handing it to Kincaid.

The girl stared into the camera with the defiant seriousness of a child refusing to smile for the photographer. She had wiry dark hair pulled back tightly from her thin face, and her grey eyes held an adult intelligence. She might, Kincaid thought, be heartbreakingly beautiful in ten years' time.

Dusting off her knees, Gemma came to stand beside him. 'I'm not so sure there are *four* missing women,' she said, touching Harriet Novak's face with a fingertip. 'Do you still have Elaine Holland's photograph?'

Kincaid frowned at her. 'No. I gave it to Bell. What are you—'

'Think about it. Elaine Holland left work every day on the dot, but several evenings a week she told Franny she had to work late. She'd been hinting recently to a co-worker that she had a boyfriend. She had clothes tucked away that Franny never saw. She lied to Franny about having a mobile phone, yet Tony had no number for Beth other than a mobile phone. And the physical description . . . Elaine has a striking face. Not beautiful, but you can see how a man could be fascinated—'

Kincaid's phone rang. He snapped it open with a grimace of irritation, but his impatience vanished when he heard Konnie Mueller's voice. He listened, nodding, then said, 'And nothing yet on the other one? Okay. As soon as you have a result. Right.'

As he rang off, Gemma said, 'Konnie?'

He nodded. 'He's narrowed our options by one. Whoever – and wherever – Elaine Holland may be, she didn't die in Thursday night's fire.'

It was another ordinary Sunday lunch in the Warren semi-detached house in Peckham – Kath's sixteen-year-old son shovelling in his food, eager to finish and get out of the house; her thirteen-year-old daughter picking at hers, eager to resume an interrupted phone call in her room; Kath's husband, a commercial traveller home for the weekend, eager to make the most of his well-deserved Sunday afternoon nap.

Kath, who had long tried to practise a daily litany of counting her blessings, felt a tide of irritation threaten to swamp her. She slammed plates coated with congealing gravy into the sink and, for once, walked off and left them.

'I've got to go into work for a bit,' she called out as she grabbed her handbag and keys.

'I'll come with you,' her son volunteered. 'What about that crazy guy?'

'I'll be fine.' Tony Novak had not made another appearance, and Kath had more pressing things to worry about.

As she climbed into the car she realized she'd added another lie to the tally that had grown past counting. It wasn't that she had to go into work, but that she couldn't bring herself to stay away.

When she reached Southwark Street, she found that the crime-scene tape still fluttered round Yarwood's warehouse like the ribbon on a giant Christmas present, and that the smell of burning still lingered in the air like a fog. She looked away as she walked by, wondering if she would ever be able to pass the building without seeing the ambulance men manoeuvring their burden carefully out of the door.

The shelter's residents were unsettled as well. She'd spent yesterday – without Jason's help – comforting and consoling, and trying to quell the rumours flying round the shelter like contagious ghosts.

She found Jason where she'd expected, in the office, head bent over a filing cabinet. She stood in the doorway for a moment, watching him, knowing he was aware of her presence but that he wouldn't look up until she spoke.

He wore jeans, as he usually did when he took Sunday duty, rather than the designer shirts and ties he favoured during the week, and the contrast between the rough clothes and the elegant planes of his face made the breath catch in her throat. God, one would think that knowing oneself for a fool would be enough to effect a cure, but the self-knowledge only made her despise her desire.

'How was your visit to your aunt?' she asked, when the silence had gone on as long as she could bear.

Jason looked up. 'Great-aunt. She fell. She needed Mum to stay with her, and you know my mother doesn't drive. It couldn't be helped, Kath.' His voice was cool, dispassionate, the message clear. She was nagging, and he wasn't going to apologize for leaving her in the lurch on a chaotic Saturday – or for anything else.

She came into the room and perched on the edge of her desk, making a pretext of straightening papers. 'You missed all the excitement. Tony Novak turned up, accusing us of helping his wife run off with their child.'

Frowning, Jason paused with a sheet half into a folder. 'Dr Novak? Why would he do that?'

'He says Laura threatened him, and now she and the little girl have both disappeared.'

The sheet of paper slid neatly into its ordained spot and Jason closed the file drawer. 'Not very clever to give advance warning, if she meant to do a runner. It's odd that she didn't come to us for help, though.'

Kath rubbed her thumb across the rough edge of a fingernail. 'I thought maybe there was something you weren't telling me.'

'Me?' His wide, mobile mouth twitched in irritation. 'Don't be daft, Kath. You know Laura's not that fond of me. If she'd come to anyone, it would have been you.' He studied her. 'Look, if this is about the other night, something came up.'

'I waited,' she said, the words spilling out like acid. 'And you let me down.'

'It's not always about you, Kath. Did that ever occur to you? You've no idea what it's like for me, living with— My mum's difficult. It was a bad night.'

'Your mum?' she spat back. 'I lied to my kids.'

'And it's not my sodding fault if you feel guilty. Give it a rest, Kath.'

They stared at each other, poised on the edge of a fully fledged row. Then, to her surprise, Jason looked away. 'I did come, you know,' he said. 'But you were gone. And it's just as well we weren't both here when all hell broke loose.' He flashed her one of his smiles, and she felt her anger start to melt.

Standing, he came over to her and ran his fingertip very lightly from her cheek to the corner of her mouth. She turned her face into his hand with as little volition as a moth flying into a flame.

'Am I forgiven?' he said softly.

'I—' She glimpsed a shadow at the office door, a whisper of movement that was somehow familiar. 'Mouse?' she called out. 'Beverly?'

But there was no answer, and when she went out into the corridor, no one was there.

'It's not correct procedure,' hissed Maura Bell. She'd drawn Kincaid down to the far end of the corridor outside the interview room at the station. A shocked

Tony Novak, having identified the photo of Elaine Holland as the woman he knew as Beth, waited inside the room, while at the other end of the corridor Gemma spoke animatedly to Doug Cullen.

'I don't care if it's correct bloody procedure.' He glanced over at Gemma, then jabbed a finger at Bell. 'She's the one who got Tony Novak to cooperate. She's the one who made the connection between Elaine Holland and Beth. She's the one who insisted we had a child at risk. She's going to sit in on the interview if she bloody well wants.'

'We don't know that the child isn't somewhere with her mother,' protested Inspector Bell.

'We don't know that Tony Novak didn't bash his wife over the head in the ten minutes he was inside her house. We won't know until we get the search warrant. If you want to be useful instead of obstructive, why don't you see if you can hurry the damned thing up?'

'Excuse me, ma'am.' Bell's sergeant had appeared at her elbow. 'A Mrs Teasdale is here to see you. She says she's Chloe Yarwood's mother.'

When Bell hesitated, Kincaid said, 'You've got another interview room?' At her nod, he went on. 'I'll take her up personally. We'll have to put Novak on hold until we see what the former Mrs Yarwood has to say – in fact, let Novak go when he's signed his statement, but have a constable keep an eye on him. I'd just as soon wait to talk to him again until after we've searched his wife's house, but I don't want him disappearing on us.'

'Is there . . . is there any news on Chloe Yarwood, sir?' asked the sergeant, with a quick glance at her boss.

'Not yet. The lab hasn't finished running the match, and I hate to think what Konnie Mueller is going to say when I ask him to run a sample from Laura Novak's house.'

Gemma and Cullen had joined them and were listening intently.

'Sir . . . ma'am . . .' said the sergeant, obviously having difficulties with the issue of temporary authority, 'that warrant's just come through. I was coming to tell you when the duty sergeant rang up about Mrs Teasdale.'

Kincaid considered, trying to work out the most expedient division of labour with the least amount of territorial moaning on Bell's part. 'Doug, why don't you and Gemma go along to Laura Novak's house with the uniforms? Maura, you and I will talk to Mrs Teasdale. Then when we've finished we'll meet the others at Park Street.' Bell might think she'd drawn the plum job, but the truth was that he trusted Gemma's assessment of whatever they might find at the Novak house as well as his own.

Maura Bell drew breath as if to protest, then seemed to think better of it. Turning to the sergeant, she said, 'Right. You'll need a locksmith.'

'No, we won't.' Gemma's lips curved in a very small smile. 'We've got the keys.'

*

Sundays were supposed to be civilized, Rose thought grumpily as she hung her turnout coat on the drying rack for the second time that day. A day of rest, a day of roast beef and Yorkshire pud, of dozing in front of the telly or taking the kiddies to the park.

God knows she'd hoped for a quiet day after a night of dream-haunted, interrupted sleep, but instead they'd had half a dozen road traffic accidents, as many medical calls, and two fires. Both had been nuisance fires, one in a rubbish skip, the other scrub set alight on waste ground at the edge of a park, but both times when she'd seen the smoke her mouth had gone dry and her hands had been unsteady as she pulled on her gear.

Surely she was just tired and not losing her nerve, she thought as she pushed a stray hair from her face with a grubby hand. What she felt seemed more a bone-deep foreboding than fear.

There was certainly no one she could talk to about it. Even if she had been tempted to confess to Simms, he'd been distant and abrupt with her all day. Last night's phone call hung unmentioned between them.

Nor had she heard from Station Officer Farrell, and she'd begun to think she'd made a complete ass of herself. She'd meant to talk to her own guvnor about her theory, but as the day went by the prospect seemed less and less appealing. If she had any sense, she'd take Wilcox's advice and forget the whole thing.

When she'd had a wash, she wandered into the kitchen. Their lunch had been interrupted by the bells an hour ago, and bowls of congealing chilli con carne still stood on the table. Simon Forney came in, whistling tunelessly, and popped his into the microwave, but after a moment's hesitation Rose scraped hers into the bin. The smell made her feel sick, and the last thing she needed was to bring up her lunch on the next call.

She made up her mind to speak to Bryan Simms, see if she could clear the air between them. At least she could tell him she appreciated his concern. She left the control room and went down to the turnout bay, where she found Bryan washing the mud off the appliance from the last call.

'Hey,' she said, grabbing a cloth and following along behind him.

'Hey, yourself.' His voice was casual, but he didn't meet her eyes.

'Busy day, yeah?' she offered, but this brilliant sally met with no more than a nod.

She stopped in mid-wipe. 'Look, Bryan. About last night. It's not that I . . . It just wasn't a good—'

'You two are gluttons for punishment,' said a voice behind her, and she spun round, startled. It was Steven Winston, the other half of Castor and Pollux, and the look he gave her was speculative. He was assigned to the pump ladder, and had not been needed on the last call. 'Someone rang you while you were out. Station Officer Farrell, the arson bloke. Said you didn't answer your mobile. He left a number where you could reach him.' Simon handed her a Post-it with a number scribbled on it.

Rose felt a flush of excitement, quickly dampened

by the wary looks on both men's faces. She'd left her bloody mobile in her locker. She'd have to retrieve it, then hope she could snatch some privacy to ring Farrell back. 'Bloody nuisance,' she said, thinking quickly. She made a face. 'I've already told him everything I—'

The bells went with a deafening clamour, and the men turned away, running for their gear. After an instant's hesitation, Rose followed, feeling more alone than she had since her first day at Southwark.

Chapter Fourteen

So near the fire as we could for smoke; and all over
the Thames, with one's face in the wind, you were
almost burned with a shower of the drops.

Samuel Pepys's
description of the Great Fire of London in 1666

Harriet woke as the room began almost imperceptibly
to lighten. She lay in the narrow bed, watching as the
shadows gradually took on familiar shapes and as the
square of window grew from a slightly lighter black,
to pearly rose, to a dull grey. It was funny; she'd never
realized how long it took for night to become day, and
vice versa, because she was always doing other things.

When she could see well enough, she climbed out
of bed and used the bucket. Then she stood at the
window, her face pressed to the murky glass. She
heard church bells, faintly, and then the whoop of a
fire engine's siren. Were they coming for her? But the
sound grew fainter until at last she heard only the
echo in her mind.

After a bit, as the light grew stronger, she began to
prowl the room, re-examining every nook and cranny

as if something different might have materialized in the night.

She was now more certain than ever that the room had once belonged to a child. There was the small bed, with its odour of old and secret accidents. There was the wooden stool, which she found, on closer inspection, bore the faint remnants of a painted design. In one of the drawers of the chest beneath the window she discovered a chipped wooden horse and a yellowed deck of playing cards.

And of course there were the books, all worn and fragile as if the pages had been turned again and again, as she had turned them the past two days. It was in *Peter Pan*, on the blank page before the back cover, that she found the writing. Tiny and cramped, done with a dull pencil, each line the exact repetition of the one above.

I promise I will be good.

The words made Harriet feel sad and frightened, but nothing frightened her as much as the scratches around the keyhole of the door. What had happened to the child who had tried to get out of this place?

She curled up under the worn blanket, even though the room was warm and stuffy, clutching the copy of *Peter Pan* to her chest. Her stomach was beginning to ache with hunger as if something were gnawing it from the inside. It was getting late, she could tell that by the light, and the lady hadn't brought her any breakfast.

Where was her dad? Why would he have left her here in this house with this strange woman? Why had he picked her up from school, especially when it wasn't his weekend? She screwed her face up in concentration, trying to sort out the fuzziness in her mind.

She remembered that her dad had said it was a treat, and that he'd looked a little odd, nervous and excited, his long fingers tapping on the steering wheel. She remembered that the woman had turned and smiled at her, and that her dad had told her the woman's name, but she couldn't remember what he'd said. It was as if there were a blank space in her brain where the memory should be, all mixed up with the Starbucks and hot cocoa.

Had the woman put something in her drink that made it hard for her to remember? Things only came back to her in a nauseating jumble of images that reminded her of the kaleidoscope her father had given her one Christmas.

Suddenly, Mrs Bletchley's face came into focus, creased in a suspicious scowl. Mrs Bletchley had been watching from her front garden and Harriet had wondered if the old cow would tell her mother that her dad had picked her up from school. Her mum would be furious.

The thought made her stomach churn. Would her mother keep her from seeing her dad ever again? A little whimper of distress escaped her and she pressed her hand to her mouth. She loved her dad, but she hated it when her mother was upset. Her mum was always feeling sorry for people, except for her dad, and everything he did made her angry. He tried, he really did, but somehow everything always seemed to go wrong.

She felt a longing for her dad then, so fierce that her throat tightened in a sob. She wanted them all to be at home, in their own house, together. When she was very small it had been different. Her parents had laughed, and her mother had sung to her when she'd tucked her into bed at night.

Was it something she'd done that had made things change?

Harriet pulled the blanket tighter, and after a while she dozed again, but it was a fitful and feverish sleep. She woke suddenly, sweating, and then she realized she'd heard the creak of footsteps on the stairs.

She sat up, her heart thumping in panic. She had to get out. There must be a way, if she could just think how, if she were just clever enough. Maybe if she could distract the woman, she could make a dash for the door. Maybe the lady had been lying when she'd said only she could open the front door. Maybe there really was a phone, or maybe there was someone else in the house who would help her.

Harriet knew she had to make an attempt – she couldn't bear to be shut alone in this room another minute.

When the door opened, she stood and tried to smile.

As she waited in the second interview room, Maura Bell wasn't sure if she was flattered or insulted that

Kincaid had chosen her to join him in talking to Yarwood's ex-wife. Not that she liked to admit that his decision mattered to her – yet as infuriating as she found his easy authority, there was a small part of her that wanted his approval.

Nor did she want to admit that she'd been hoping for a few minutes alone with Doug Cullen. She was beginning to think she'd imagined the chemistry between them on Friday night, and she felt a fool. Seeing the obvious camaraderie between Doug and Gemma James hadn't improved her mood one bit, and she frowned as she thought of them searching Laura Novak's house together. It was bad enough that Kincaid had brought James into the investigation without so much as a by your leave—

The opening of the interview room door interrupted her uncharitable thoughts. Kincaid ushered in a small woman in a lilac trouser suit, saying, 'Mrs Teasdale, this is Detective Inspector Bell.'

Mrs Teasdale offered her small, cool hand, leaving no doubt that she'd been a well-trained politician's wife, and Maura saw that her perfectly manicured nails matched her suit. Maura guessed her to be in her very-well-preserved mid-forties, but not even the flawless make-up and carefully styled strawberry-blonde hair could hide the lines of stress round her eyes and mouth.

'I've come about me daughter,' she said as she took the chair Kincaid held out for her, and the high voice and working-class accent caught Maura by surprise. 'My Chloe. I want to know if you've found her –

if you've found . . . anything? Marcus says—' She stopped, clutching at the handbag she held in her lap. 'He says you're certain it was her, going into the warehouse.' Her eyes, pale beneath her mascaraed lashes, darted from Kincaid to Maura.

'Both your husband – ex-husband – and Chloe's flatmate have identified her from the CCTV photo as going into the warehouse, yes,' Kincaid answered. 'But we're not sure of anything more at this point. There are tests—'

She shook her head, cutting him off as if refusing to contemplate it. 'He's keeping something from me. He's in some kind of trouble, and if he's hurt Chloe . . .' As she clenched her hands, her nails scored the soft leather of her handbag.

Kincaid hesitated, as if trying to decide which point to address first, but before Maura could speak he said, 'Why do you think he's in trouble, Mrs Teasdale?'

'He told me he wants to sell the flat. He says he's found a buyer.'

Maura frowned. 'I'm not sure I under—'

'It's a listed building. Just round the corner from the Tate. I've been trying to get him to sell it for years, even before the divorce, but he wouldn't have it. Oh, no, he said, it was only fitting that the Member of Parliament for the Borough should show respect for the old places.' Venom had crept into her voice. 'Never mind that it was built for pygmies and the plumbing only works when it's in the mood. Never mind that it's worth a small fortune these days, and Trev – that's my husband, Trevor – Trev and me could use the cash for our business.' She leaned forward and tapped a nail on the table with a brittle sound that made Maura's teeth hurt. 'I'm telling you,' Marcus Yarwood's former wife went on, 'he's into something, and he's got our Chloe mixed up in it somehow. He's gone out, and he wouldn't tell me where he was going.'

Was the woman more interested in stitching up her husband than in finding her daughter? wondered Maura. Had she not understood that Chloe might be dead? She'd taken a breath to speak when Kincaid fixed Mrs Teasdale with a sympathetic smile.

'Mrs Teasdale – it's Shirley, isn't it?' he asked. When Mrs Teasdale nodded, he went on. 'Did you ever know your husband to have a problem with gambling?'

She stared at him as if he were daft. 'Marcus? Gambling? He was brought up Chapel – he can hardly bring himself to have a drink.'

'Then what sort of trouble do you think he might be in?' asked Maura, trying to emulate Kincaid's tone.

Shirley Teasdale seemed to sag in her chair, her momentary umbrage forgotten. 'I don't know. He won't talk to me, but I know him – I know he's keeping something back. He's never forgiven me for Trev, but this is our daughter. He keeps saying she must be all right, but . . . she'd have rung me, wouldn't she?' The look she gave them was pleading. 'I can't imagine why she wouldn't have rung me.'

'I'm sure Chloe must confide in you, about her life, boyfriends, things like that,' Kincaid said. 'Do you know anything about the man she was with in the video, Nigel Trevelyan?'

Shirley hesitated, and it seemed to Maura that even the crisp lilac suit lost a little starch. 'You have to understand. Chloe likes to tease her dad with things. I think . . . I think she likes knowing she can make him angry. It's like waving a red flag under the nose of a bull. She said . . .' Her voice dropped to a whisper. 'She said if her dad knew about Nigel, he'd kill him. But it's not Nigel that's dead, is it?'

As she drove the now familiar route between Borough Station and Park Street, Gemma glanced at the dashboard clock and gave a little groan of dismay. It was already mid-afternoon. She should be at home; the boys would be back from their outing with Wesley, and she'd let the weekend slip by without doing any of the things necessary to prepare for the coming week. Tomorrow would be especially difficult, as she planned to take the afternoon off for the court hearing.

'Are you okay?' asked Doug Cullen, beside her.

'The boys will be at home on their own by now. I never meant to abandon them for the entire day.'

'If you need to go, go,' he said with his usual earnestness. 'I'll do the search, then wait for Duncan. No one could expect you to do more on this case—'

'And I should mind my own business, at least according to Detective Inspector Bell.' She softened the words with a smile. 'Can't say I blame her.' She wasn't used to encountering such obvious hostility from other female officers, and she was surprised by how uncomfortable it made her feel.

'She's all right, really,' Doug said quietly. 'When you get to know her a bit.'

When she glanced at him, he was studying the spots on her windscreen with great deliberation. Gemma seemed to remember hearing him say the same thing once about Stella Fairchild-Priestly, but with less conviction.

'I suppose you've not had much time for Stella this weekend,' she ventured, her curiosity roused.

'She's away. Another country house party.' Doug didn't meet her eyes. 'And I suppose I'm in the doghouse for not joining her.'

Gemma had always wondered what the very polished Stella saw in a lowly detective sergeant who didn't share her social aspirations, but if he was developing an interest in prickly Maura Bell, he might be jumping out of the frying pan into the fire. 'Doug,' she began, meaning to deliver the standard warning about the pitfalls of relationships on the job, then realized how absurd that would sound coming from her. And besides, Doug and Maura didn't normally work on the same patch, and who better to understand the demands of the job than another copper?

Having reached Park Street, she parked the car in front of Laura Novak's house and said instead, 'I want to come in with you, Doug, just for a bit. But thanks for the offer.' She'd come too far not to see for herself if the house held any clues that would tell them what had happened to Laura and Harriet.

Nor could she go home until she'd done one other thing. Franny Liu would have to be told that her housemate was alive, and that she might have abducted a child.

Gemma knocked and rang the bell, then stood listening for a response. The air was hazy and still, the neighbourhood quiet as if its inhabitants had all decamped for fresher climes. She heard the rustle of Doug's jacket as he shifted beside her and the quick rhythm of her own breath, but there was no sound from within the house. Next door, the Karimgees' curtains were drawn.

Slipping on a pair of latex gloves, Gemma put the key in the lock and called out, 'Police! We're coming in.' Her voice echoed back at her, an intrusion into the close silence, and she felt a bit silly.

The door swung open easily and they stepped into the hall. The house smelled stale and a little musty, as if no one had been in for several days, but there was no dreaded hint of decay.

Gemma let out a breath she hadn't realized she'd held.

'No body, then,' said Doug, and she knew he'd been thinking the same thing. 'There'd be no question, in this warm weather.'

'I thought, when Laura left Harriet with the sitter on Thursday night and lied about having to work, that she might have meant . . .'

'To kill herself?' Doug's eyes widened behind his round glasses. 'That hadn't occurred to me. I was thinking more along the lines of Novak having conveniently forgotten to tell us he'd offed his wife when he stopped by on Friday morning.'

Gemma stooped to gather the mail scattered on the tiled floor. There was nothing more personal than a few advertising circulars and credit card offers – one still addressed to Dr Anthony Novak – and a couple of bills. The postmarks bore Thursday's and Friday's dates, so Gemma assumed the mail represented both Friday's and Saturday's deliveries.

On a narrow table against the wall, more post was neatly stacked, but when Gemma examined it she found only junk mail and a few pizza delivery menus.

An umbrella stand in the corner contained a large black umbrella and a cricket bat, while a few pegs mounted on the wall held a woman's fleecy jacket and a smaller Gap anorak in dark green. Harriet's, Gemma thought, her heart contracting. Kit had one identical.

Doug moved forward, opening doors, peering into empty rooms, and Gemma followed. The house was long and narrow, with the same beautiful proportions and detailing as the neighbours' next door, but here no effort had been made to highlight the period features. A sitting room faced the front of the house, then came a dining room, then the kitchen – all neat enough, but none showing any evidence of visual or sensual flair. The furniture was of good quality, and a few pleasant prints were hung haphazardly on the magnolia walls, but Gemma saw little that reflected a personal life. The house obviously belonged to a woman whose interest lay in other things. For the first time Gemma wondered about Laura Novak's background. There were no family photos, not even of Harriet.

'No sign of a struggle or of a hurried exit,' she said as they reached the kitchen. Nor was there any obvious sign that a child inhabited the house. The refrigerator door, unlike her own, held no school reports or drawings, and there was no sign of a calendar marked with family schedules. 'Look, Doug,' Gemma added, frowning as she drew closer to the sink. 'This is odd, don't you think? For a woman this tidy, she's not done the washing up.'

Two plates, two glasses and a saucepan had been stacked and hastily rinsed. The pot still bore traces of what looked like marinara sauce, and there was a very faint smell of spoiled food.

'Maybe she meant to come back and do it?' suggested Doug. 'That's what you do when you're in a hurry. Or at least that's what I do.'

Was this Thursday evening's supper? wondered Gemma. Mrs Bletchley said Harriet had already eaten when she arrived. Had Laura meant to come straight back after she'd dropped Harriet off? And if so, what had prevented her?

'Let's have a look upstairs,' she suggested, and let Doug lead the way back to the stairs in the entrance hall. The first floor contained two bedrooms and a bathroom, the front-facing room obviously Laura's. It was more feminine than Gemma had expected, papered in pale blue and cream, with cream curtains at the window and a cream quilt on the double bed.

The bed was made, but a blouse and trousers had been left tossed across a chair. Beneath the chair lay a pair of shoes, one turned over on its side. There was no sign of packing or any indication that anything had been removed from the room or the wardrobe.

A white-painted dressing table held a few cosmetics and a hairbrush, and in a silver frame a black and white photo of a toddler with curly dark hair. Harriet, wondered Gemma, or Laura herself?

Lifting the brush with a gloved hand, Gemma saw hair nestled in the bristles. 'Doug . . .'

'I've got it,' he said, opening the evidence collection bag he'd brought with him and taking the brush from her.

Gemma thought of all the times she and her sister had sat at their mother's dressing table, using her hairbrush and trying out her lipsticks. 'We can't be sure that some of the hair doesn't belong to Harriet,' she said.

Using a pair of tweezers, Doug carefully transferred the curling dark strands into the bag. 'It should be a close enough match, regardless.'

Leaving him to it, Gemma glanced briefly into the bathroom. Towels hung on the warmer, bottles of shampoo and bubble bath crowded the tub's edge, and on the basin a ceramic cup held two toothbrushes.

She carried on into the back bedroom, undoubtedly Harriet's. The hastily made bed sported a navy coverlet with gold stars. Under the window brightly coloured plastic crates held a jumble of books and school projects, and above the desk a corkboard was jammed with drawings and photos of pop singers and film stars, cut from glossy magazines.

Next to the desk stood a wardrobe, one of its doors half open, spilling out a jumper and a pair of frayed jeans. Opening the doors all the way, Gemma checked the built-in drawers and found them stuffed to bursting with T-shirts and panties and mismatched socks – all expected and all heartbreakingly ordinary.

Hearing a step behind her, Gemma turned as Doug came into the room. 'I've had a look upstairs,' he told her. 'There's a box room and an office. The boffins will have to have a go at the computer, but I found this under the mouse mat.' He handed her a piece of rough paper. In blue ink, in a neat, firm hand, was a list of women's names.

Mary Talbot. Amy Lloyd. Tanika Makaba. Clover Howes. Ciara Donnelly. Debbie Rufey.

The first three and the last had been ticked off; the fourth and fifth bore tiny pencilled question marks.

'It could be anything,' said Gemma. 'An invitation list for a birthday party or a school outing. A professional group . . .' She took out her notebook and copied down the names, then glanced up at Doug. 'But it was under the mouse mat?'

'Just a corner showing. There was nothing else obviously interesting on the desk itself, just the usual bills and household paperwork, and stacks of literature from different causes, mostly neighbourhood things – meals for the homeless at St John's Waterloo, the food bank, family violence outreach. Oh, and the file drawer containing personal documents was standing half open. Seems to support Novak's story about the passport.'

Gemma's phone rang. Even from her pocket the sound was unexpectedly loud in the quiet house. Her first guilty thought was of the boys, needing her at home, but a look at the ID told her it was Kincaid.

When she answered, he said without preamble, 'I've just had a call from Konnie Mueller.'

Gemma felt her doubts dissolve, leaving a hard and implacable certainty, and a spasm of grief for a woman she would never meet. 'It's not Chloe Yarwood, is it?'

'How did you know?'

She thought of the dirty dishes in the sink, the kicked-off shoes, the unopened mail, all the small telling details of a life interrupted. 'Because Laura Novak didn't run off with her daughter,' she said. 'Because when Laura Novak walked out of this house on Thursday night, she had every intention of coming back.'

'We need to talk,' said the message from Kincaid as Gemma checked her voicemail an hour later. 'Ring me and we'll meet somewhere . . . How about the Anchor, Bankside.'

Gemma stood by her car in Ufford Street, having just come away from an exhausting visit with Winnie to Franny Liu. When she'd told Franny that Elaine Holland's DNA did not match that of the victim of the warehouse fire, Franny had pressed a hand to her mouth, stifling a sob of relief.

But Franny's relief soon turned to dismay when Gemma explained, as gently as she could, that they thought Elaine might have abducted ten-year-old Harriet Novak. She told of Elaine masquerading as the mysterious 'Beth', of her affair with Tony, of her agreeing to help him kidnap his daughter, then of her disappearance with Harriet on Friday morning.

As Gemma spoke, Franny seemed to retreat further and further into herself, mutely shaking her head and clutching at the shawl in her lap. 'No,' she whispered when Gemma stopped. 'No. I don't believe it. I don't believe any of it. She was . . . We were . . . I thought we were . . . happy.'

'I don't think there's any doubt. Tony Novak identified Elaine's photo. It explains so many things, including why she left without telling you on Thursday night.' Gemma reached out and took Franny's cold hand in her own. Beneath her fingers, the bones felt as delicate as a bird's. 'Do you have any idea why she would have taken a child? Or where she might have gone?'

'No. I . . . No. No, I can't imagine.'

'Did she ever say—' began Gemma, then stopped as she saw Winnie give a barely perceptible shake of her head. 'I'm sorry,' she said instead, and pressed Franny's hand before letting it go. 'I know this is a shock. We can talk more tomorrow.' Even as she spoke, impatience gnawed at her. She knew Winnie was right, that she couldn't push Franny past the limits of her physical and emotional endurance. But she also knew that Harriet's safety might be at stake, and that no one knew Elaine better than Franny. 'Ring me tonight, please, if you think of anything at all,' she added, standing to go.

Franny's tears had stopped. The face she turned to Gemma was bleak and empty as a husk, and she drew herself up with obvious effort. 'She's not coming back, ever,' she'd said then, coldly, clearly. 'She might as well be dead.'

Gemma felt the skin tighten between her shoulder blades as she remembered Franny's expression. There was nothing more cruel than betrayal, and here they had a web of betrayals. There was Laura, who had perhaps meant to betray Tony; Tony, who meant to betray Laura; and Elaine, who had betrayed both Tony and Franny. But while Tony's and Laura's motivations seemed at least understandable, Elaine's did not.

And if it was Laura Novak who had died in the warehouse, who had killed her? Where were Elaine and Harriet, and how did Chloe Yarwood fit into it all? For if they had proof of anything, it was that Chloe Yarwood had been in the warehouse that night.

Kincaid was right; they had to talk.

Setting a fire in daylight took nerve and cunning, but he had both, and he was more than ready for the challenge. Since the burning of the warehouse on Thursday night he had slept only feverishly, his brain teeming with images of flames and shouting firefighters.

The pleasure had been more intense than any he'd experienced, and yet it had left him with a niggling shard of discontent. He'd held the open flame of the lighter to the furniture – oh yes – but he'd missed the careful planning and plotting that had preceded his other fires; it had been like orgasm without foreplay. Now he knew he had to own the fire from beginning to end, and the desire to get it right drove him like an itch under his skin.

But this one, this one he'd worked out well in advance. He knew the building from a job he'd had some years ago, and he'd marked it then on the map he carried always in the back of his mind. The place was perfect, a neglected Victorian warehouse set back from any main thoroughfare. This meant not only that he'd be less likely to be seen, but that the blaze would have more time to take hold before it was reported. And best yet, he knew the building had an illegal propane tank. Once he'd set alight the cardboard boxes accumulated on the ground floor, the warehouse would burn like fury.

They would come, the firemen – firefighters, he corrected himself, his lip curling at the politically correct term – like little gods in their coats and helmets and boots, and he would show them.

He thought of the photograph he kept by his bed, a faded sepia image of a Victorian fire company, all Southwark men, in full regalia. They might look like Gilbert and Sullivan caricatures to the modern eye, with their luxuriant whiskers and pointed helmets, their mongrel dogs in their laps, but these men had been real firefighters *who had fought real fires. Heroes. They had been heroes the like of which the fire service would not see again.*

They had breathed smoke like dragons, and they had conquered fire with the poor means at their disposal. And if sometimes the fire had conquered them, there had been no shame in it.

Stepping out of the shadows, he crossed the empty road and eased open the ground-floor door of the warehouse. He'd cut the padlocks the previous night, on his way home from work, gambling that the damage wouldn't be noticed on a Sunday. He looked round the cavernous space, adjusted a cardboard box filled with the crisp packets he'd collected for the purpose, and pulled his lighter from his pocket.

Oh, they would come, these great new firefighters, little gods in their arrogance – and then they would run like rats.

Kincaid was waiting for her on the terrace of the Anchor, leaning on the railing overlooking the Thames. The day had stayed damp and dull, and now water, sky and the City across the river seemed to meld one into the other, like a Turner painting with all the colour leached out.

'Samuel Pepys watched the City burn from here, did you know that?' He gestured at the prospect as Gemma joined him.

'From the Anchor?'

'I don't think the Anchor was built until a century or so after the Great Fire. But somewhere near here, on the Southwark bank. It must have been terrifying, but thrilling in a way, as well,' he added, his gaze fixed on the distance.

Gemma had no patience at the moment with day-dreaming about fires. They had more concrete matters to deal with. 'I've rung the boys,' she said, accepting the half pint of cider he'd bought for her. 'They've been home to let the dogs out and have gone back to Wesley's. They're having a jam session, apparently, with Wes's cousins, and eating until they're sick.'

'That's good for Kit.' Kincaid looked relieved. 'He's hardly touched anything for days.'

'I've got to get home soon,' said Gemma, her guilt over her absence only slightly tempered by the knowledge that the boys were in good hands. 'I want to be there when they get back.'

'I know. But I'll be a while yet.' Running a hand through his hair, as was his habit when he was tired or exasperated, he sighed, then drank some of his pint. 'God, what a day. I've rushed Laura Novak's hair sample to Konnie. He's not happy, I can tell you, but he said he'd start on it straight away.' He turned from the river to study Gemma's face. 'You've not much doubt, have you, that it was Laura's body in the warehouse?'

'No. I don't think Laura took Harriet. And if she's not with her daughter, there's only one thing that would keep her from moving heaven and earth to try to find her. But if Laura's dead, who killed her, and why?'

'Novak's the obvious suspect,' Kincaid said. 'Maybe

he decided he couldn't keep Laura from taking Harriet back, even in Prague, so he arranged to meet her on Thursday night. He killed her, intending to take Harriet out of the country the next day, before Laura's death was discovered. And he'd have wanted to delay identification of the body, hence the stripping and the fire.'

Gemma was shaking her head even before he'd finished. 'Why would Laura have arranged to leave Harriet with Mrs Bletchley if she were just meeting Tony for a talk? Why would she have lied about having to work that night? Why would she have agreed to meet Tony in an empty warehouse? That wouldn't make sense even if they'd been on good terms. And' – she waved a hand to stop him from interrupting – 'you didn't see Tony's face when you rang the bell at his flat and he thought it was Laura. He was genuinely terrified.'

'He'd also been on a bender and was barely coherent. Maybe he was having guilt-induced hallucinations. Like Lady Macbeth.'

'Now you're really stretching it.' She wrinkled her nose at him.

Kincaid grinned. 'Admitted. But tell me if you've a better idea.'

Resting her elbows on the railing, Gemma gazed out at the river, as he had done. A train rumbled by over the railway bridge, but the pedestrian walkway along Bankside was fairly quiet. The weekend was winding down, the time she could give to this case was running out, and it seemed they'd made little progress. 'Why would Laura have gone to Marcus Yarwood's warehouse? Is there some connection between them we haven't seen?'

'I've got Doug out looking for Yarwood as well as Chloe. Yarwood's ex-wife says he's not been home since earlier today, and that he's desperately trying to raise money, even trying to find a quick buyer for his flat, which he's always refused to sell.'

Gemma frowned. 'That might make it more likely that he torched the warehouse for the insurance money, if it weren't for the small matter of the body—'

'Not if he needed immediate cash. Insurance payouts are never quick.'

'Forget the fire for a bit,' Gemma said slowly. 'What would you think if you had a missing child and a prominent father trying to raise immediate cash on the quiet?'

Kincaid stared at her. 'Ransom. Bloody hell.'

'It could be an attempt to collect Yarwood's gambling debts. They – whoever he's in hock to – lured Chloe to the warehouse, snatched her, then set the place alight to prove they meant business.'

After a moment's thought Kincaid said, 'It might be plausible but for two things. Yarwood's ex-wife, who has nothing kind to say about him, swears he'd never gamble. And—'

'The body.' Gemma grimaced and rubbed at her face. Her head was starting to ache. 'It doesn't explain the body, whether it's Laura's or not. It doesn't explain the list of names Doug and I found in Laura's flat.' She showed him the copy she'd made. 'And none of this is getting us any closer to finding Elaine and Harriet Novak.'

'Did you have any luck talking to Franny?'

'No. She was too shocked. I'm not sure she took it in about Harriet. Winnie's promised to stay on with her.'

'I'll talk to Franny again tomorrow,' he said. 'And to Tony Novak, and to Yarwood, if we can find him.'

'You won't have much time.' The thought of the court hearing hovered in the back of her mind like a shadow, and she felt her stomach knot.

'I know.' He touched her shoulder, turning her to face him. The reflection of the river had turned his eyes grey as slate. 'It'll be all right,' he said, and she wasn't sure if he meant to reassure her or himself. In the distance a siren began to wail, then another. After a few moments the sound faded away.

Franny sat, chill and silent, as the light in the green room faded to grey. She seemed not to hear Winnie's soft queries, or to feel Winnie's rubbing of her hands, or to notice the butting, purring overtures of Quinn the cat.

Winnie lit the lamps and the candles, hoping to restore some sense of normality. Then she made a cup of tea, to warm her hands if she could not warm Franny's. She sat close beside Franny's chair and saw her own face reflected in the darkening window, lit by the flickering candle flames.

The petition came to her without thought. She had

said it every night since her ordination so that it was now as automatic as breathing. As the words ran through her mind, she realized she was speaking them aloud, her voice a rising and falling murmur of sound.

'Keep watch, dear Lord, with those who work, or watch, or weep this night, and give your angels charge over those who sleep. Tend the sick, Lord Christ; give rest to the weary, bless the dying, soothe the suffering, pity the afflicted, shield the joyous; and all for your love's sake. *Amen*.'

When she'd finished, the silence seemed deeper. Franny sat with eyes closed, her face so pale and pinched that Winnie began to think she had better call a doctor. But before she could rise, the cat jumped up on her lap. She stroked him for a moment then put him down, and when she glanced at Franny once more, she saw that her face was wet, her eyes open.

At first the tears slipped silently down Franny's cheeks, as if she were unaware of them. And then her mouth began to twist, her shoulders to shake, and she was crying with the grief of the bereaved.

Winnie pulled her chair as close as she could and wrapped her arms around Franny's thin shoulders. 'It's all right,' she whispered. 'You'll be all right.'

'How could she do it?' choked out Franny. 'How could she let me think she loved me?'

To this Winnie had no immediate answer. She could only keep patting Franny's back, and when the sobs subsided to an occasional gulp, she provided a clean handkerchief from the pocket of her cardigan and sat back to let Franny blow her nose.

'I think,' Winnie said slowly, when Franny looked up at her with red and swollen eyes, 'I think perhaps she was in terrible pain. I know there are people who are simply wicked, who hurt others for the pleasure of it . . . but because Elaine was good to you in so many ways I can't find it in my heart to believe that of her. She said, didn't she, that her mother committed suicide and her father died from an illness when she was young? That might have—'

'She said a lot of things that turned out not to be true,' countered Franny. 'Why should we believe that?'

'Why would she have lied? Unless . . . unless there was something worse . . . something she couldn't bear to talk about or perhaps even to remember.' Winnie shook her head. 'We're grasping at straws, love, and we may never know the truth.'

'I can understand, a little, about the doctor. I mean, people have affairs all the time . . . And it's not as though there was anything physical, really, between us.' Franny looked away as if ashamed to have mentioned it. 'There were only things that I might have . . . misinterpreted . . . But why . . . why would she take a *child*?'

'Did Elaine want children?' Winnie had seen it in her pastoral work: women – single or married – who reached a certain age and found themselves suddenly obsessed with a desire for a child so strong that it drove them beyond reason. It was a thought she'd kept in the back of her mind, a slender thread of hope on which to hang the safety of Harriet Novak.

'No,' whispered Franny, the brief animation fading from her face. 'No. She didn't care for children at all.'

Rose sat in the rear cab of the pump with Bryan and Steven Winston. Seamus MacCauley was driving and Station Officer Wilcox rode beside him. Beneath her heavy tunic, she could feel her T-shirt plastered wetly to her back. The day had gone from bad to worse – two more nuisance fires, one in a rubbish tip and the other in an abandoned car, two medical calls, then a road traffic accident with an injured child. She'd never had a chance to dry out properly from the morning's fires, much less the afternoon's, nor had she had any opportunity to return Station Officer Farrell's call. And now they were on their way to another fire.

'Better gear up,' said Bryan. 'We're almost there.' In this warm and humid weather they resisted pulling up their Nomex hoods as long as they could. The fire-resistant fabric stopped any air circulation inside their tunics, turning their already sweltering coats into sweatboxes.

They were heading west, along Webber Street, the pump ladder speeding along right behind them. A fire had been reported in a warehouse tucked back between Webber Street and Waterloo Road. As they slipped on their hoods and resettled their helmets, the pump swung round a curve and Rose saw the smoke.

'Christ,' said Steven, his voice filled with awe. The building was old – Victorian, Rose thought, although with none of the architectural grace of the Southwark

Street warehouse – and in poor repair. Its concrete surround was cracked and patched with weeds, a wire fence sagged listlessly to the ground in places, and broken windows gaped like sightless eyes. From the third- and fourth-floor windows smoke dark as coal pumped furiously out. It looked as though a bomb had gone off inside.

Pedestrians milled about in the street, shouting and pointing. MacCauley had to sound the siren to scatter them so he could manoeuvre the pump into position near the hydrant. As soon as they rolled to a stop, Rose could hear the fire, crackling and hissing and groaning like a live thing. They spilled out of the appliance and she felt her chest tighten.

'Seamus,' Wilcox shouted, 'get on to Control. Tell them to make pumps four. Then get us police back-up, and get these people out of the way until the police get here to take over crowd control.' He turned to the others. 'You three, rig in BA. We'll need to get a hose in through the main doors and make an assessment.'

Wilcox turned to the ladder crew. 'Get us entry, then get a ladder up to the roof. And someone have a look round the back side, see what the status is there.'

Both crews sprang into action. It was chaos, but it was the controlled chaos of those who knew their jobs and were prepared to give whatever was required of them. As Rose settled the BA pack on her back and handed in her tally, marked with her set number and the amount of air in her cylinder, she felt the tightness in her chest ease. A rush of adrenalin surged through her, making her feel light-headed and razor-sharp. She was going to be okay.

She had comms, the breathing apparatus radio, and would be responsible for letting Wilcox know what they found inside. As they unreeled the hose, the ladder crew broke down the remainder of the fence and charged at the main doors, axes swinging. The doors splintered under the blows and Rose had a brief glimpse of the padlock flying, then she and Bryan and Steven were pushing through, Bryan leading.

A blast of heat jetted out, knocking them back. They crouched, moving forward again, Bryan sending controlled pulses from the hose into the dense black smoke. The jets turned instantly to roiling steam, and Rose felt her face sear through the faceplate of her mask.

Bryan pulsed the hose another half a dozen times, but there was no change in the temperature. They could see nothing but black clouds of smoke mixed with steam, and then, out of the corner of her eye, Rose caught a flicker of flame within the fumes: flashover.

'Guv!' she shouted over the radio. 'It's all going to shit in here. We can't control it!'

'Back out!' Wilcox yelled in her ear. 'Get out now.'

She grabbed Bryan and Steven and pulled at them, feeling the heat of their tunics even through her gloves. 'Out,' she repeated. 'We're moving out.'

They backed out the way they'd come, Bryan continuing the short bursts from the hose, Rose keeping a grip on them both. She only knew they'd reached the door when Bryan's helmet materialized in front of her.

As they staggered away from the building they heard a rumble and a pop, and a jet of flame shot out, licking at them. 'Jesus,' she heard Steven say as they scrambled away.

When they reached Wilcox and MacCauley, they pulled their masks off and Rose took a deep, gulping breath. In the distance she heard the faint double tone of sirens.

'We're going to have to tackle this bastard from the outside,' said Wilcox. 'And we're going to need help. I've made it pumps six. Get the hose back on the door—'

'Hey!' The shout had come from the crowd. A man's finger pointed upwards, and among the milling pedestrians, Rose caught a glimpse of a pale face and the blue arm of a uniform sleeve. 'There's somebody in there! I saw somebody in there!'

'Where?' said Wilcox, scanning the building.

'Third floor,' the man called out. 'In the window. Third from the left. A face.'

Rose looked, saw nothing but billowing smoke.

'Persons reported,' Wilcox called over the radio. 'I'm sending crew up.' He turned to Rose and Bryan. 'The ladder crew's venting the roof. You two will have to take a look.'

Bryan gave her a quick bright grin, then they moved in unison, raising the ladder and hauling up the hose, Rose leading the way. She felt a moment's relief that the constraint between them had vanished; then she thought of nothing but the job at hand.

When she reached the window, she grabbed the frame and straddled the sill, feeling her way with her foot. She could feel the wood's heat through her gloves, but there was no flame showing inside, only the dense, oily smoke.

'Okay,' she said as her foot found solid floor. Swinging her other leg over, she inched forward, testing the surface with the toe of her boot. She kept hold of the window frame with one hand and groped outwards with the other, exploring the darkness like a blind person in an unfamiliar room.

She'd expected, if there had been someone at the window, to find them crumpled beneath it, but she felt only the solid floor. Bryan climbed in behind her, bumping against her as he crouched and steadied the hose on his knee. He gave two bursts of the jet, and this time she felt the temperature drop.

'Anybody here?' Bryan shouted, his voiced muffled by his mask.

Rose listened, her senses straining, hearing nothing but the hiss and crackle of the fire.

Rising, Bryan pulsed the hose again, then stepped forward. Rose felt a sudden vacuum beside her, heard an exclamation cut short. She swung her arm out wildly, towards the spot where Bryan had stood a moment before, and almost lost her balance as she encountered only air.

'Bryan!' She fell to her knees and inched forward, her hands sweeping in an arc through the smoke.

When her knee touched something solid she gasped in relief, but her exploring fingers felt not a leg, but the round shape of the charged hose.

'Bryan!' she shouted again, panic rising in her throat. She felt along the hose until she touched the nozzle, then swept her hands across the floor in front of it. He must have caught his foot on something, fallen, but she would find him, she would get him out.

She tried to think calmly, to regulate her breathing. She couldn't afford to use up all her air. Keeping one hand on the stationary hose as a guide, she crept forward, her free hand patting the floor. Vaguely, she heard a voice shouting into her headset, but she shut it out. Her world had narrowed to the tips of her gloved fingers.

Then, the floor disappeared beneath her hand. She jerked back instinctively, then felt again. Nothing. She ran her hand sideways, touched the hard edge of the floor, then she reached forward again. Nothing. The other side was the same. The floor dropped away in front of her, as far as she could reach.

'Bryan!' she screamed, but only her own voice echoed back inside her mask.

She kept calling, gripping the edge of the pit, until strong arms came round her from behind and pulled her away.

Chapter Fifteen

Oh, Captain Shaw!
Type of true love kept under!
Could thy Brigade
With cold cascade
Quench my great love, I wonder!
Gilbert and Sullivan
Iolanthe, 1882

Whenever Harriet closed her eyes, the darkness seemed to press against her eyelids with a smothering weight, so she stared at the paler patch of dark she knew was the window. She had no idea how long it had been since nightfall; she'd lost all perception of the passage of time.

She shifted slightly on the narrow bed but kept her left arm tight against her chest. She thought her arm was broken, but not badly. Her mum had told her about fractures: with a compound fracture the bones might stick right through the skin, but a simple fracture was just what it sounded like, a clean break.

Her forearm was swelling, and it hurt to move it, but the skin wasn't broken and nothing felt jagged when she probed gently with her fingers. Still, she felt feverish and nauseated, and miserably thirsty.

At last, in spite of her discomfort, her eyelids fluttered and she drifted towards the edge of sleep.

Oh, God, she was falling, falling, she couldn't stop herself . . . the dark wooden banisters flashed by in a sickening whirl and she felt the impact as the hard steps came up to meet her . . . then hands gripped onto her ankles, the weight of a body crushed the breath from her lungs, and a searing pain tore through her arm.

Harriet jerked awake, gasping, her arm throbbing from the involuntary movement. Slowly, she eased herself up until she was half sitting against the wall. After a bit the falling sensation faded away, but she couldn't stop the images replaying in her mind.

She had stood up, and smiled.

The lady had paused, a slight look of surprise on her face, then she'd carried on into the room and set the tray she carried on the low chest.

'It's warm in here,' Harriet managed to say, even though her heart was thumping. 'Could I – could we – could we have the window open a bit, for some air?'

The woman had turned and gazed at her with a very strange look, as if she'd forgotten Harriet could speak. Then she had stepped to the window and touched one of the fogged panes, her fingers lingering on the glass in what seemed almost a caress.

'It doesn't open,' she said, her voice rusty. 'It hasn't opened for years. You'll have to live with the heat.'

Harriet stared at her, then at the books and at the narrow bed, and a dreadful knowledge filled her. 'This was your room,' she whispered. 'These were your books. You wrote in them. You wrote—'

'Only when I was bad,' said the woman. She smiled. 'But then I was bad quite often.'

'But why did you . . . How could you bring me here, when you knew what it was like?'

'I didn't intend to, not at first.' The woman frowned as she spoke, as if it puzzled her. 'But your father . . .' Her eyes fixed on Harriet, sharper now. 'Your father was going to leave, and he never thought of taking me with him . . . I don't think he'd have even bothered to tell me he was going if he hadn't needed my help.'

'But—'

'I couldn't have that, you see.'

Her dad didn't know, then. He didn't know where she was. Harriet felt a rush of relief that he hadn't put her in this place, then a cold fear as she realized what that meant. Desperate to keep the woman talking, she said, 'No. No, you couldn't. It was selfish of him. My mum's always saying he's selfish.' She flushed with shame at her disloyalty, but she had to go on. 'I'm sure he's sorry. He should have known better.'

'Yes, he should.' The woman looked pleased at Harriet's understanding.

'If he's learned his lesson,' Harriet said carefully, trying to keep her voice level, 'maybe you could let me go.'

'Oh, I don't think so,' the woman said, as if she'd given it long consideration. 'Because then I'd be in trouble, and I don't want to be in trouble.'

'I wouldn't tell.'

'Yes, you would.' Her face hardened, and Harriet knew her deception wasn't going to work. From the corner of her eye she glimpsed the door, not quite pulled shut. She had to take her chance, but she needed a distraction.

'Are those your cards?' she asked, nodding towards the chest. 'I saw them, the playing cards, in the drawer. I could play with you, if you like.'

There was a softening, a flicker of pleasure, perhaps of memory, in the woman's eyes, and then she glanced towards the chest. In that instant, Harriet dived at the door, yanked it fully open, and plunged down the stairs.

The steps were steep and hard, the carpeted runner worn thin as tissue. Harriet skidded on the first step and tumbled, crashing down, and the woman came behind her like a fury. She'd fallen on Harriet, pinning Harriet's slighter body beneath her, ignoring her cries of pain. Then she pulled her to her feet and marched her back up the stairs.

'You tricked me,' she hissed, her breath panting hot in Harriet's ear. 'You tricked me, and you're going to be sorry.' She shoved Harriet into the room, slamming the door so hard the walls shook and the china basin on the chest made a chinking sound.

For a long time Harriet lay where she fell, too afraid to move. The room brightened, then grew dimmer as the sun passed its zenith. At last, driven by the pain in her arm, she shuffled across the floor and climbed up on the bed. Shivering in spite of the heat, she pulled the blanket round her.

The hours passed, the room grew dim as the afternoon faded to evening, and nothing stirred in the house. Harriet's head swam with hunger as well as pain. She'd had nothing to eat or drink since last night's meagre supper. The tray still sat on the chest where *she* had left it, hours before. Trying not to make a sound, Harriet got up and crossed the room.

Congealed cereal, dried fruit, a cup of warm, flat water. Harriet drank all the water, no longer caring if she had to use the bucket, then made herself eat a few bites of the cereal and nibble a piece of fruit. But she had felt ill, too dizzy to stand for long, and she soon crawled back into bed.

Now, as she lay staring into the dark, her stomach cramped with emptiness.

She recalled again what she'd seen in the brief moments of her flight. A landing. An open door. A room as dusty and disused as the one that held her. The bottom of the stairs had yawned dark as a cavern – there had been no light, no sound, anywhere in the house.

Harriet thought of the meals she'd been given: the dried food, the stale water. Then she thought of the utter silence that surrounded her, and of the way she heard the sound of the boiler and the grumble of the plumbing when she lay in her own bed at night.

This house was dead, she realized, abandoned. There was no power, no water, and no one had lived here for a long time, until the woman had brought her here.

It made it worse, somehow, to think of the house so desolate, so empty, and she felt very cold and very afraid. Suddenly, she wanted her mother more than she had ever wanted anything in the world. She cried out in the darkness, but her mother didn't come.

Kincaid groped for the alarm, trying to shut off the insistent ringing. His fingers found the snooze button, but the sound didn't stop. 'Bloody hell,' he muttered. It was the phone, not the alarm.

Squinting at the digital readout of the clock as he fumbled for his handset, he saw that it was only a few minutes after six, and that a dusky light had just begun to show at the gap in the bedroom curtains. Gemma groaned and pulled the pillow over her head as he put the phone to his ear.

'Kincaid,' he croaked.

'Duncan, it's Bill Farrell here. Sorry to ring so early, but I thought you'd want to know.'

He pulled himself up against the headboard, coming fully awake. 'Know what?'

'There was another warehouse fire in Southwark yesterday evening, just before the day watch ended. I was off duty yesterday, so another team took the initial investigation. I didn't hear about it until I got up this morning.'

'What hap—'

'I only know it was a bad fire, fully involved, and that a firefighter was killed.'

'Jesus.' Kincaid remembered Rose telling him she was working a day shift yesterday. 'Do you know who it was?'

'Not yet. I'm meeting Martinelli at the scene. I thought you might want to come. It's just off Waterloo Road – at Webber Street.'

'Give me half an hour.'

When Kincaid hung up, he found Gemma awake and watching him, her eyes wide with alarm.

'Another fire in Southwark,' he said, before she could ask. 'I've got to go.'

He drove east, into a glorious rising sun, and tried to think of anything other than Rose Kearney. The city was just coming to life, its pulse quickening in anticipation of the coming day, and when he crossed the Thames at Waterloo, the water reflected the sky in a molten sheet of pink. Such beauty seemed incongruous with death, and it made the dread weigh more heavily on his heart.

As he turned off the Waterloo Road, following Farrell's directions, he realized how close the fire had been to Ufford Street and Franny Liu's house. Then he saw the blackened hulk of the building, stark against a sky turning quickly to gold. The roof of the warehouse had fallen in, and the remaining walls stuck up like jagged, rotting teeth. The surrounding yard was filled with piles of burned debris and broken fencing, and the rank smell of the fire penetrated the car. The perimeter of blue and white crime-scene tape fluttered lightly in a rising breeze.

He recognized Bill Farrell's van parked in the road, and saw Farrell himself gazing up at the remains of the warehouse. With him was Jake Martinelli, and Scully.

The men turned to greet him as he climbed from the car, and the dog wagged her tail in recognition. Kincaid bent to stroke her, burying his hands in the thick ruff of fur on her neck. Still clasping the dog, he looked up at Farrell. 'Did you—'

'I stopped at the station. It was a young firefighter named Bryan Simms. He was Rose Kearney's partner.'

Kincaid felt a flood of relief, then shame. Why should this death be any less tragic because he had not known the victim? Why did it matter so much to him that Rose was safe?

Seeking a moment's distraction to get his emotions under control, he rubbed the dog's head and said to her, 'Have you got a job today, girl?' Scully licked his ear obligingly. Then he stood, turning to Farrell. 'How did it happen?'

'They'd had to abandon an interior attack when a person was reported on the third floor. Simms and Kearney went up on the aerial ladder. There was no flame showing, so they went in through the window.' Farrell looked away, gazing at the building. 'The smoke was heavy; they were blind. It was an unsecured lift shaft. He fell to the bottom. It was three hours before the crews could get the fire damped down enough to get to him.' He rubbed at his jaw. 'Wouldn't have mattered, though, if that's a blessing. Some falling debris partially protected the body. There was enough left that they could tell he'd broken his neck.'

'Oh, Christ.' Kincaid swallowed. 'And Rose?'

Farrell shrugged. 'They've given her leave, of course. It wasn't her fault, though I doubt she believes it. The floor within four or five feet of the window was solid, so they had no warning of the drop. Simms stepped in front of her.'

'What about the person on the third floor? Did they get him out?'

'They didn't find anyone – at least not yet. We'll see what my lads turn up when it's full light.'

'Was she right?' Kincaid asked, thinking of the papers Rose had given him that he had carried around so carelessly for a day. Had he been in some way responsible for this? 'Was there a pattern?'

'There was a propane tank in the building,' said Martinelli. 'We won't know if an additional accelerant was used until we get the lab results. But like the other fires there seems to be only one obvious point of origin. And the overhaul crew turned up a few bits of cardboard that could have been used as the initial fuel.'

'And we found this, this morning.' Farrell pointed at the ground a few yards from the twisted doors. Kincaid moved closer and peered down. It was a heavy-duty padlock, rusty from exposure, but a bright gleam of metal showed where the hook had been sheared clean through.

'The entry crew . . .'

'They didn't cut it. This was done before the fire.'

Kincaid looked up and met Farrell's eyes.

'We may not find any more hard evidence,' said Farrell, 'but I'd stake my career that this was arson. He's clever, but he's not clever enough. And I'm going to nail the bastard to the wall.'

Rose had held on to a flicker of hope until they carried Bryan's body out of the ruins of the fire.

She'd made a sound then, and Seamus MacCauley had tried to hold her, to turn her away, but she'd pushed herself free of his encircling arm. The others had stepped back in silence, had let her walk beside Bryan to the waiting ambulance. She owed him that, and so much more.

Their relief had arrived, an hour into the fire, but the entire watch had stayed on, watching and waiting. You didn't leave a mate, not like that. The paramedics had stood by as well, even though any hope that they would be needed faded as the fire blazed unabated, and the minutes lengthened into hours.

The pumpers poured out hundreds of thousands of gallons, and it seemed, for a long while, that the water only fed the flames. Then the roof had begun to cave, the inrush of oxygen sending up sparks and new tongues of fire, but it had been the beginning of the end. The glow had dimmed, the fierce heat fading, until she had felt the night air cool against her face. At last, the ladder crew had gone in, to search out the last stubborn, smouldering pockets, but victory had come at too great a price.

Rose reached out as the stretcher slid into the ambulance, but Station Officer Wilcox stilled her hand with his own, and the doors clanged shut.

As the ambulance pulled away, he said, 'He didn't suffer, Rose. And there was nothing you could have done.'

She looked at those gathered round her, their eyes red-rimmed, their faces stained with snot and soot, and she knew she couldn't belittle their grief by giving way to hers. Nodding, she stepped back.

Steven Winston and Simon Forney came up to her. 'We're taking you home, Rose,' said Steven. 'I'll drive you, and Simon will bring your car.'

'But I can—'

'Just do as you're told and don't argue for once, Kearney,' interrupted Simon, and the familiar hectoring tone had eased the tightness in her chest.

She rode with Steven in silence, after they'd dropped their gear at the station and Simon had picked up her Mini. There was nothing to say, and when they reached the house in Forest Hill and Simon had handed over her car keys, they'd stood in awkward silence for a moment.

'Get some rest, Rose,' Steven had said. 'A day or two, then we'll see you back on duty.'

'Right. A day or two,' she'd agreed, and gone in.

She found her mother sitting up in the reading chair in the conservatory, a book face-down in her lap.

'Rose?' she called, putting the book aside and standing up. In her dressing gown, with her face scrubbed free of make-up and the grey showing visibly in her blonde hair, she suddenly looked all of her fifty-two years. 'Rose, Officer MacCauley called me. I'm so sorry.' She reached out, but Rose stepped away from her.

'No, Mum, please. I can't. I just can't.' She couldn't bear sympathy now – it would dissolve the fragile glue that was holding her together. Steven and Simon had known that.

After a moment, her mother nodded and sank back into the chair. 'Can I get you something to eat? Or something hot to drink?'

'No, Mum. I just want to sleep.' Rose leaned down and quickly brushed her lips across her mother's forehead. 'But thanks. I – we'll talk in the morning.'

Once upstairs, she showered, scrubbing her skin until it stung, then fell into her clean white bed. But the forgetfulness of sleep, so longed for, evaded her. She eventually dozed, in fits and starts, always waking with the same urgent feeling of having forgotten something crucial, of needing to be somewhere, needing to do something, if only she could remember what.

She woke fully when the first light of dawn began to pale the windows, her mind suddenly preternaturally clear and alert. Throwing on a sweatshirt and jeans, she left a scribbled note in the kitchen and crept out of the house. The early-morning air smelled clean and fresh, making her think suddenly of the years her father had helped her with a paper delivery. There had been a secret pleasure in getting up together while the world still slept.

She chased away the thought before it could progress to longing – she had no time for that now – and climbed into the Mini. Laying a copy of the map she had shown Kincaid carefully on the passenger seat, she drove north to Southwark.

Traffic was still light, and nothing impeded her as she drove slowly past the scene of every fire she'd marked on the map. The Southwark Street warehouse was last on her list, and last on her route. There, she parked the car and got out. After a moment's hesitation, she turned towards the river. She needed to walk, needed the physical movement in order to sort out all the ideas tumbling wildly through her mind.

She cut through Borough Market, which bustled with the early-morning wholesale trade as it had for centuries. Then she crossed the cathedral yard and climbed the steps to London Bridge.

When she reached the bridge's centre, she stopped, gazing first at St Paul's to the north-west, its dome glowing golden in the light of the rising sun. Then she turned back to the south until she could see the square tower of Southwark Cathedral. She remembered reading somewhere that this was the only spot in England from which one could see two cathedrals, and she thought that on another day she might find that a wondrous thing.

Then her gaze swept on, to all that lay beyond. She recalled what she had thought she'd known about the fires, and what she had seen that morning, and the pattern began subtly to shift. The shadowy form flitting from fire to fire took on clarity and substance, and moved easily into the nightmare of last night's blaze.

She saw him in her mind; she understood what made him act, and then – then she saw something so terrible that she sagged against the railing, her hand pressed to her mouth to stop the rising bile.

The squeal of car tyres tore Kincaid's attention away from the remains of the padlock. A jaunty red Mini swerved, too fast, round the corner into Webber Street, then jerked to a halt behind his car. As the dog began to bark at the unexpected commotion, Rose Kearney got out and ran towards them.

She halted before Farrell, her breath coming hard, her eyes wide and dilated.

'Rose!' said Kincaid. 'What is it? What are you doing here?'

She glanced at him, then turned her attention back to Bill Farrell. 'I rang the station. They told me you were here. I've just realized . . . I was wrong – or at least only partly right – about why he sets the fires. He has picked sites that haven't required added accelerant because he wants to prove he's smarter than we are, but that's only an added ingredient, icing on the cake.'

Martinelli, who had calmed the dog, looked baffled. 'What are you—'

'I've looked at the map, and I've looked at the sites themselves, one after the other. I think he's recreating historic fires.'

'I don't understand,' said Farrell.

'Well, maybe not the first one, the Waterloo lock-up. That might have been a practice run, testing his skills. But the others have been either Victorian warehouses or he's re-created an aspect of a Victorian warehouse fire.' Impatiently, Rose shoved a stray hair behind her ear, and Kincaid saw that her hand was trembling. 'Look at the contents. Groceries. Paint. Fabric.'

Understanding began to bloom in Farrell's craggy face, but Kincaid was completely at a loss.

'Tooley Street?' said Farrell, and she nodded.

'Scovell's warehouses and Cotton's Wharf. Tea, rice, sugar. Paint. Rum. Hemp, cotton and jute.' Rose turned to Kincaid. 'The Tooley Street fire burned for two days in 1861. It did over two million pounds' worth of damage. It was the worst fire to strike London since the Great Fire, and it wouldn't be equalled until the Blitz.'

Martinelli was nodding now too. 'It's wild, but yeah, I can see it. But why?'

'I don't know why,' said Rose. 'But I think he's escalating – building up to something much bigger than anything we've seen. And . . .' She stopped, her hands clenching and unclenching at her sides.

'What?' said Farrell gently. 'Tell us, Rose.'

She took a ragged breath. 'I think . . . I think I saw him. Last night. The man who shouted that there was someone at the window on the third floor. It was a bogus call. There was never anyone in this building. But he wanted us to go in. He wanted to kill a firefighter. And I saw him. I saw his face.'

'Can you describe him?' asked Farrell, his voice tight now.

'Tall. Youngish. Dark hair, pale skin.' Rose closed her eyes, frowning with the effort of recollection. 'And his sleeve . . . it was dark blue, a uniform sleeve.'

'Bloody fucking hell,' said Martinelli, and at the anger in his tone Scully growled and raised her hackles. 'Are you saying it was a fireman? A fucking fireman?'

Rose shook her head. 'No— I don't know. It wasn't a brigade uniform. I'd have seen that instantly. This was something else, almost like a mock-up of a real uniform. But wait . . . Say he has a grudge, this guy, against firefighters. Or maybe not just firefighters, but the whole brigade. Look at the dates of the fires from the first one. When was the last recruitment?'

'Jesus.' Farrell rubbed at his beard furiously, as if it had caught a cinder. 'You think this guy might have been a rejected applicant? And you think you'd recognize him, if you saw him again?'

Rose nodded once.

'Right,' muttered Farrell, half to himself. Then he grasped Rose by the shoulder. 'We'll go to the station, go through the entire brigade files if we have to. Jake, can you oversee the forensics team when they get here?' He turned to Kincaid. 'And, Duncan, I still don't see where the Southwark Street body fits into this, but say Rose is right and Bryan Simms's death is murder. Can you—'

But Kincaid's phone was ringing, and he excused himself, turning away as he unclipped it from his belt.

When he answered, Konnie Mueller said, 'Bingo.'

'Sorry, Konnie – what was that?'

'I said "Bingo", mate.' Konnie sounded tired but jubilant. 'One out of three is not bad. You've got a match on all points. Your body is – or was – Laura Novak.'

Chapter Sixteen

> . . . a being, erect upon two legs, and bearing all the
> outward semblance of a man, and not of a monster . . .
>
> Charles Dickens
> *The Pickwick Papers*

Kincaid felt a growing unease as he returned to Borough Station. They'd made progress with the discovery that Bryan Simms's death was a possible murder and the positive identification of Laura Novak as the victim in the Southwark Street fire, but he couldn't shake the sense that he was missing something crucial, and that his time was running out.

He'd taken what action he could, leaving the search for the arsonist in the capable hands of Bill Farrell and Rose and mobilizing every resource in the search for Harriet Novak and Elaine Holland, but now he had to face giving Tony Novak the news about his ex-wife.

He'd had Novak brought into the interview room where they had spoken the previous day. The man looked a bit more tidy this morning, clean-shaven and dressed in a pressed shirt and chinos, but more hollow-eyed and gaunt than ever.

Cullen had rung while Kincaid was at the fire scene, saying he was still trying to trace Chloe Yarwood and Nigel Trevelyan, so Maura Bell would be assisting with the interview.

'Is there some news about Harriet?' demanded Tony as soon as Kincaid and Maura had taken their seats.

'No, we've heard nothing about your daughter,' Kincaid said, unwilling to keep him in suspense any longer than necessary. 'But I'm afraid I have some bad news. It's your wife. She's dead. I'm sorry.'

'Laura?' Tony sounded shocked, but it seemed to Kincaid that there was the slightest easing of tension in the man's body, as if the news had been expected. 'But why . . . How did you . . .'

'We informed you yesterday that we were going to search your ex-wife's house, Mr Novak,' said Bell. 'Her DNA sample matched that of the victim of the warehouse fire.'

'Dear God,' Tony whispered, blanching. 'That fire . . . Laura . . . I can't—'

'We think she was already dead when the fire started, if that's any comfort,' Kincaid told him. 'She didn't suffer from the burns.'

'But who would . . . You don't think Beth—'

'What time did Beth – Elaine Holland – leave you on Thursday evening?'

'It wasn't late. Before ten, I think.'

Was it possible, Kincaid wondered, for Elaine to have left Tony's flat, somehow lured Laura to the warehouse, killed her, then returned to Franny's in time to watch the ten o'clock news without a speck of blood on her? And what would she have done with Laura's clothes? She had no car, and she couldn't possibly have walked out of the search area in that time. Nor did that explain the fire.

'Why would she do such a thing?' Tony asked.

'I don't think she did.' Maura leaned towards Tony as if inviting a confidence. 'I think Laura found out what you meant to do. I think she left Harriet with the child minder and came to confront you. You argued. Things got out of control. Maybe you didn't mean to kill her, but she was dead, and you had to dispose of the body. You took her to the warehouse, stripped her of any identification, then set the place alight. Then you drove out of London and dumped her clothes.'

Tony stared at her as if she'd gone utterly daft. 'I live in Borough High Street, for God's sake. How am I supposed to have carried Laura's body out to my car without anyone noticing?'

'Wrapped in something, of course,' retorted Maura. 'People carry rubbish out all the time, and no one thinks anything of it.'

'That's bollocks, and you know it.' Tony had begun to let his temper show, and Kincaid had to give Maura credit for knowing how to wind up a suspect. Wearing a black leather coat and a bright blue sweater this morning, she looked tough and surprisingly sexy. He sat back, content to let her play bad cop for the moment.

'Okay,' she said, and smiled, but before Tony could relax, she dived at him again like a pecking gull. 'Maybe Laura didn't find you out, but you were afraid she would. Maybe you tried earlier on Thursday to get the passport, and a neighbour saw you. You knew it was only a matter of time before Laura heard you'd been in the house, and then she'd never let you get your hands on Harriet. So you lured her to the warehouse—'

'You think Laura would have agreed to meet me in a deserted building?' Tony shook his head in disgust. 'You really are crazy.'

'I didn't say she agreed to meet you. I think you needed Elaine Holland's help for more than one thing. You got Elaine to call Laura that night, pretending to be an abused woman who needed her help. You knew that was the one appeal she couldn't resist.'

'No,' said Tony, but he was beginning to look frightened.

'That would explain why Laura left Harriet with Mrs Bletchley. Perhaps she thought she'd have to bring this distressed woman back to her own house.

'Of course you didn't tell Elaine you meant to kill Laura,' continued Maura, her eyes alight with conviction. 'She came to help you with Harriet on Friday morning, just as you'd agreed. Then, when she learned about the fire and the body, she realized what had happened. That's why she took Harriet, to keep her safe from you.'

It was good, Kincaid admitted, inspired even. But there was one problem with Bell's scenario. He didn't believe it.

There were too many gaps. It didn't explain what Chloe Yarwood had been doing at the warehouse that night, or what had happened to her. It didn't explain

Elaine Holland's strange and secretive behaviour with Franny, or how she could have managed to disappear with a ten-year-old child without leaving a trace. Why, if she had believed Tony guilty of murder, had she not come to the police?

Nor did it leave a place for Rose Kearney's arsonist, unless that fire had not been part of the pattern – and yet it fitted too well. After last night's blaze, he was convinced that Rose was right and they were dealing with a serial arsonist.

And then there was Gemma. Kincaid had learned to trust Gemma's instincts, and Gemma didn't believe Tony Novak was a murderer.

Tony turned to Kincaid with a look of desperate appeal. 'Tell her. Tell her it's not true. I'd never have hurt Laura.'

'I'm sorry, Tony,' Kincaid said with genuine sympathy. 'We have to follow up every possibility. Our forensics teams are searching your flat and your car.'

Tony stared at him as if he'd just become Judas Iscariot; then he leaned forward, gripping the table edge until his knuckles turned white. 'Search all you want. Think what you want. I don't care what you do. Just find my daughter.'

When they had first interviewed Tia Foster, Doug Cullen had made a note of her saying that Nigel Trevelyan's family lived near the golf course in Ealing. He'd found two telephone listings that seemed likely prospects, and had tried both numbers on a regular basis over the weekend, without result. This morning one of them had answered. The woman had sounded Punjabi, and had disavowed any knowledge of a Nigel Trevelyan.

Having exhausted all his other leads for Chloe, and having found Marcus Yarwood in his office at last, but ensconced in a committee meeting, Cullen had decided to check out the second address in person.

He'd also had another agenda, a personal one, and was glad of an excuse to drive west from his flat in Euston rather than south to the Borough. It took him half an hour in morning traffic to reach Kensington High Street, and the closer he got, the more reluctant he became to carry out his intentions.

But he knew if he backed out now he might never get his courage up again, so he steeled himself and went on. He found a parking spot on a back street behind St Mary's Church, and walked quickly to the High Street.

It was too early for the shops to open for business, but when he peered in the window of the home furnishings boutique, the sales assistant recognized him and unlocked the door with a smile.

'Doug! What are you doing here?'

'I've come to see Stella,' he said, feeling his mouth go dry. 'Is she in yet?'

'In the stockroom. Go on through.'

He made his way through aisles lined with ribbon-tied linens and bundles of dried flowers, silk-tasselled lampshades, vases, mirrors, gardening implements – the inclusion of which he found very odd – and things he couldn't even put a name to. He felt, as he always did in this place, like the proverbial bull in the china shop.

The scent of pot-pourri wafted out from the stockroom, and he stopped for a moment in the doorway, stifling a sneeze. Stella stood with her back to him, carefully refolding a flower-sprigged quilt. She wore a twinset in a pale yellow that set off her icy blonde looks, with the cardigan draped casually over her shoulders, and pearls. She was flawless, and faultless, and he'd come to the terrible realization that he didn't love her.

'Maddie,' she said, sensing a presence behind her, 'if you could hand me another bolt of the raffia—'

'Stella.'

She whirled around, dropping the cord she'd lifted to tie round the quilt. 'Dougie! What are you doing here? Are you . . . Is everything all right? I've been ringing you since Friday. You said you'd come down if you could get away.'

'I know.'

She'd left half a dozen messages on his voicemail, the first few cross, the last, uncharacteristically for Stella, sounding uncertain and even a little frightened. 'I'm sorry,' he said. 'It's this case. We've had a woman murdered, and now her little girl is missing.' He saw her mouth begin to thin in an expression of disapproval and irritation, as it did whenever he talked about a case, and he held up his hand to stop her.

'Stella, don't. This is not going to change. I'm not going to change. You're not going to change. I think it's time we gave it a rest.'

She stared at him. 'I . . . You don't mean—'

'I'm good at my job, Stella. I can't go on apologizing for it.'

'But things will be different when you're promoted.'

'No, they won't. I'll only have more responsibility, and you wouldn't like it any better.' He smiled at her, trying to ease the sting. 'Besides, there must be dozens of blokes with trust funds dying to take you away for a country weekend.'

Her pale blue eyes grew hard. 'Meaning you don't care?'

'No, of course I care. I only meant—'

'You've found some bloody policewoman to shag, haven't you, Dougie?' she spat at him, crossing her arms tightly beneath her small breasts.

'No, I . . . I only want what's best for both of us,' he protested, cursing the flush he felt staining his cheeks. 'Stella, listen—'

'You always were a lousy liar, Doug, and too innocent to walk God's earth. What do you think I've been doing all those weekends you couldn't be bothered to join me?' She saw his shock and smiled. 'What did you expect, Sleeping Beauty?' Turning away from him, she began retying the folded quilt. 'Now, just bugger off, will you, and don't keep your prison wardress waiting.' The raffia snapped in her fingers.

The address in Ealing wasn't on the golf course, but near enough that Cullen thought Nigel Trevelyan might have felt justified in fudging his geography a bit. The house was detached, built of rose-coloured brick with white paintwork, set back on a tree-lined road.

As he pulled up across the street, Cullen saw that leaves had accumulated in the shadow of the porch, and a collection of advertising circulars decorated the doorstep. He swore aloud. No wonder the people hadn't answered their bloody telephone.

Now he really *was* buggered. His last lead was gone, and so was a good part of a morning that could have been spent pursuing something more productive. The day, which had begun with such promise, had darkened, and a splatter of raindrops rattled across the windscreen on a gust of wind.

Well, he could at least talk to the neighbours, find out if he had the right Trevelyans. He sighed and reached for the door handle, then sat back, resting his hands on the steering wheel as he replayed Stella's parting words once again. Stung pride, guilt and relief jumbled together in his mind, and he couldn't begin to sort them out. There would be time for that, he knew, and time for regret as well, but now he had a job to get on with.

Checking for oncoming traffic before reaching again for the door handle, he glanced in the side mirror and froze. A girl was walking up the street towards the house and his car. Young, a brunette, she trudged head down, hands laden with two plastic carrier bags. He caught only a glimpse of her face as she shrugged her hair back with an irritated twitch of her shoulder, but he would have known it anywhere. He had seen it, over and over, on a loop of security videotape.

Chloe Yarwood looked younger than she had in the film, and thinner. Her skirt was too short, and made her white legs look oddly vulnerable rather than sexy. As she passed the car, he reached for the cold coffee in his console and glanced away from her as he sipped. That was the one good thing about his old Astra – the car that had so humiliated Stella – it attracted no notice at all.

Once Chloe had passed him, he watched her again, openly. She turned into the drive of Nigel's house and walked, not towards the front door, but towards the back of the property, and he saw what he hadn't noticed before – there was an outbuilding at the end of the drive, set back behind the house. When she reached it, she transferred both bags to one hand, unlocked the door, and slipped inside.

Cullen jumped out of the car and followed. He didn't want to give her time to get comfortable. There were no cars in the drive and he hoped he'd caught her alone. It was only as he knocked on the door that he remembered Nigel Trevelyan didn't have a driving licence, but then it was too late for caution.

There was no answer, and not a peep of sound from within. The quiet seemed suddenly to hold a palpable sense of fear, and he knew she was listening just the other side of the door.

'Chloe Yarwood? I'm Detective Sergeant Cullen, from Scotland Yard. I'd like a word with you.' He waited, then knocked again. 'Come on, Chloe. I know you're in there. If you don't open up I'll have to call for a patrol car. I'm not going away.'

Another long minute passed. 'Chloe!' He'd raised his hand again when the door swung open. Chloe Yarwood stared out at him. She looked ill, and terrified, and relieved.

'I'm sorry,' she whispered. 'I thought you were *them.*'

The story came out in fits and starts, between small hiccuping sobs. Cullen sat beside her on an old sofa covered with a woollen rug. The place had obviously been converted from a garage at some point in its history. The floor was still concrete, covered only with a couple of dirty rugs, and the interior walls were unfinished. There was a small cooker and fridge to one side, and a curtain that he assumed hid the bathroom facilities. The room's only ambience came from the half-dozen Harley-Davidson posters tacked to the bare walls. It was cold, even now, on a fairly mild day, and Cullen thought the place must be unbearable in winter.

'Where's your friend Nigel?' he asked, wanting to settle that little matter straight away.

Chloe seemed to take it for granted that he knew who Nigel was. 'Gone to France. His family's there for the month. They have a farm in Normandy.'

'And he didn't take you with him?'

'He didn't want any trouble. I can't blame him. It

wasn't Nigel's fault – none of it was. He said I could stay here, as long as I wanted.'

'That was good of him,' said Cullen, and Chloe nodded, seemingly unaware of the sarcasm.

Now that he knew he didn't have to worry about Nigel Trevelyan popping in unannounced with a shotgun or a blunt instrument, he relaxed a little and studied her more closely. It was hard to see a trace of the smiling girl in the photo Kincaid had found at Tia's flat. 'Why don't you start from the beginning, Chloe, and tell me why you went to your father's warehouse on Thursday night.'

'You know about that, too? How did you—'

'Security camera in the building opposite. It caught you and Nigel going in.'

'Oh.' She didn't ask who had identified her from the photo, and he didn't volunteer the information.

'Come on,' he encouraged. 'What were you doing in the place?'

'There were these blokes, see.' She pulled at the hem of her skirt, which had ridden up even farther when she sat down. 'I'd been to this club, in the West End. My mum gave me a little money, when I moved out from Dad's, but then Tia didn't charge me rent . . .'

'And?'

She hesitated, picking at a spot on her cheek, then locked her fingers in her lap and said with a sigh, 'There were cards. I won a bit at first. But then I lost. They let me keep playing, these blokes, saying I'd be sure to make it back. And it was fun. It was like, every time, anything was possible. But I kept losing.'

So it was not Marcus Yarwood who had been gambling, but Chloe. It all began to make sense. Doug didn't bother to tell her that the mark always lost, and that the only reason they'd let it ride so long was that they'd seen the potential for making a bigger profit.

'And then' – she gave another little hiccup – 'then one night they turned me away from the table. They . . . they told me how much I'd lost.' She paled even at the memory of it. 'They said I had to give them the money. When I said I didn't have it, they said I'd have to get it or . . . or they'd hurt me.'

'They wanted you to ask your dad?'

Nodding, she tugged harder at the skirt. 'But I couldn't. He'd kill me. I mean, it was one thing to make him angry over things like moving out or not finishing my college course, but this – something like this could ruin his career.' She shook her head. 'I couldn't. They gave me a few days, and I thought if I just didn't go back to the club . . .'

Cullen groaned inwardly. And to think Stella had called *him* innocent. 'But they came to you.'

'First at Tia's. Then they came to Nigel's friend's flat, where he'd been staying. I don't know how they knew . . .'

If the police had an information network half as good as the London gangsters', thought Cullen, they'd solve every case on the books. Chloe Yarwood had been a perfect pigeon, had possibly even been marked before she ever set foot in the club. Had the gallant Nigel been in on it? he wondered.

'So I thought . . . maybe I could stay at the warehouse at night, and just hang out somewhere in the daytime, you know, where no one knew me, until . . .' Her expression was bleak. She'd have realized by that time that they weren't going to forget about her, but she'd been cornered.

'You had a key to the warehouse?' Cullen prompted her, gently.

'I'd made it for a lark. I'd told Nigel that Daddy was going to give me the top-floor flat, when it was finished, and I wanted to show it to him. I got him to go with me that night. He was going to leave for France, after the blokes came round to his friend's flat, and I didn't want . . .'

'You didn't want to be alone.'

'No.' She glanced up at Cullen, then back at her hands. 'We went in, and I showed him round a bit. I had a torch. We went upstairs . . . and after a while we heard voices. I thought – I thought it was those guys, looking for me, but then we heard a woman. It was a woman and a man, and they were arguing. There was something . . . I don't know.' Her shoulders jerked. 'I got really scared. We got our— Nige and I got ourselves together again, you know? And then we ran down the stairs as quietly as we could, and out the back door.

'Nige left. He went – I don't know, to another friend's, I think. He – he didn't want to take me with him. But I was afraid to go back to Tia's, and I kept thinking about the woman I'd heard. She'd sounded frightened. I walked for an hour or two, and then I went back.

'But the warehouse was on fire. It was . . . terrible. The heat and the smoke, and the shouting. I thought maybe *they'd* done it, to show me they meant business. And then, the next morning, when I heard about the body, I thought maybe they'd thought it was me . . . or, I don't know what I thought. I just wanted to disappear, and I couldn't bear my dad finding out it was all my fault . . . His building . . . He loved that building . . .'

'Chloe . . .' Doug tried to sort out the relevant bits of her story. 'Could you or Nigel have started the fire? Did either of you smoke, or light a match, while you were there?'

'No.' She looked horrified. 'We don't smoke, and I told you, I had a torch. Why would I light a match?'

He thought about the CCTV film and what it had not shown. 'Chloe, did you unlock the side door before you and Nigel went upstairs?'

'Well, yeah. I was showing him my private entrance, like, and we looked up at the balconies. Then we went up. I never thought of anyone coming in.'

'When you and Nigel ran out, did you see anything? Did you see the man and the woman?'

She shook her head.

'Did you recognize the voices?'

'No.' She frowned and chewed on a fingernail. 'No, but I heard her say something like "How could you, of all people, when you knew what would happen?" It didn't make any sense.'

'And him? Did you hear what he said?'

'No. It was just that one bit, as we went out the door.'

'Do you know what time it was, when you left the warehouse that first time?'

'We can't have been there more than half an hour,' she said slowly. 'Half past ten, maybe.'

'Good girl.' He patted her shoulder. 'One more thing, and then we'll get you out of here. Did you ever know a woman named Laura Novak?'

'No. Who is she?'

'Right.' Doug stood up, avoiding the question. It would be some time before they released Laura Novak's name. 'Get your things together, luv. You'll need to come to the station with me, to make a statement, but first we're going to your dad's office.'

'My dad?' Her voice rose in a squeak. 'But I don't want him to—'

'Chloe, your dad's been desperate with worry,' he said, adding with certainty, 'The blokes from the club went to him, probably when they didn't get anything out of you on the first try. Your dad thought the fire was a warning to him that they'd kill you if he didn't find the money. And then, for a while, after he saw the videotape, he thought the body was yours.'

At daybreak Harriet got up and crossed the room to the chest by the window. Trying to ignore the growing pain in her arm, she ate the last of the apricots and picked at the dried crust of cereal in the bowl. Then she tilted the cup above her mouth, licking at the last drops of water. That made her dizzy, and she crawled unsteadily back to bed.

She waited, then, for the sound of footsteps and the creaking of the door, at first with dread and then, as her hunger and thirst grew worse, with dread and longing, but no one came.

After a while, even that ceased to matter so much. Her arm was swollen and hot to the touch, and she shivered and sweated in turn.

She thought she heard the patter of rain against the window, but the sound faded away as she drifted in and out of a restless sleep. In her dreams, she wandered in a long corridor filled with endless rows of doors, hearing voices she could never quite reach.

As noon approached, Kincaid called Maura Bell and Cullen, who had returned to the station with Chloe and Marcus Yarwood, into their temporary office. 'Maura, will you take charge of coordinating the searches of Tony Novak's flat and car? Doug, you can take the statements from the Yarwoods. I've got to go, but I'll be back as soon as I can.' He meant to get a bite of lunch, then to meet Gemma, Kit and their solicitor at the family court. 'You'll let me know if there's any news about Harriet?'

'Right, guv,' said Cullen, then he hesitated a moment before adding, 'Good luck with the hearing.'

Kincaid nodded his thanks and left the station, his mind occupied with sifting and sorting what they'd learned to date.

When Gemma had called a few minutes earlier to say she'd pick Kit up from school, he'd told her about

Rose Kearney's theory, and the news about Laura and Chloe.

She'd listened in silence as he confirmed what she'd already guessed. After a moment, she said quietly, 'You know Harriet's running out of time, don't you? Every hour she's missing lessens our chances of finding her alive.'

'I know,' he told her, 'but I've run out of ideas.' They'd put out a general alert now that they were sure the child was not with her mother. He and Bell had sent uniformed officers to interview the children and personnel at Harriet's school, to re-interview hospital staff who had worked with Laura and with Elaine Holland, and to search for any useful background information on Elaine.

At least they had reunited one child with a parent. Marcus Yarwood, Cullen said, had crushed his daughter to him in a spasm of relief, then shaken her and called her an idiot, then hugged her again. Yarwood admitted that the men from the club had threatened him, and that he'd feared Chloe dead when he couldn't reach her after the fire. He'd gone on hoping desperately that the fire had only been a threat, trying to raise the money, trying to find Chloe, and cursing the involvement of Scotland Yard.

'I couldn't very well protest when the assistant commissioner asked you to look into things,' he'd said to Kincaid when he arrived at the station. 'Not without buggering my own pitch.'

'You should have been honest with us from the beginning,' Kincaid had told him, but without grea̶ conviction. In Yarwood's place, he might have with-held the truth, too.

'Do you think those bastards were responsible for this?' Yarwood asked, beginning to sound like a crusading politician again. 'Do you think they killed that poor woman as an example? Or because they thought she was Chloe?'

Kincaid thought back over what Cullen had told him. 'No. First of all, I don't think they wanted Chloe dead. That would have meant killing the goose before it laid the golden egg. And from what Chloe's told us, it seems pretty obvious that the victim knew her killer.'

'Then why kill her in my warehouse? And why burn it?' Yarwood shook his head. 'I'm sorry. That sounds callous. I only meant—'

'We don't know. We don't know if the fire was set as a last attempt to hide the victim's identity, or if there was an unrelated motive. We may never, in fact, prove that the fire was set at all.' Kincaid couldn't broadcast the fact that they suspected they might be dealing with a serial arsonist turned murderer, not to someone with Yarwood's media connections, and not when Yarwood stood to gain by making such news public.

But the conversation had started him thinking about Rose's theory again, and as he paid for his sandwich at a takeaway near the station he had an idea. Glancing at his watch to make sure he could squeeze in a few more minutes, he went back to the station and found Sarah, the sergeant who had helped with the CCTV video.

'Can you print me another still from the tape?' he asked. When he'd shown her what he wanted, he ate his sandwich while waiting for the photo, then drove to Southwark Fire Station.

He found Rose and Bill Farrell sequestered in an unused office, surrounded by a mountain of files. They both looked tired and discouraged. The London Fire Brigade only hired new staff irregularly, and then they were inundated with thousands of applications for a few hundred positions.

'No possibles?' he asked, and they both shook their heads.

Rose sat on the floor against the back wall, her knees drawn up, a box of files beside her.

Kincaid handed her the print he'd made. 'Maybe this will help.'

She took it and stared at it. 'What – where did you get this?'

Hearing the excitement in her voice, Farrell joined her and bent to look.

'It's the man who walked by the Southwark Street warehouse a few minutes after Chloe Yarwood and her friend went inside. He only hesitated a moment as he passed, so we didn't think anything of it. Do you recognize him?'

'Yes. I . . . I think so.' She looked at the time stamp on the print. 'But this was only a little after ten. The fire wasn't reported until after midnight.'

'Maybe he came beck,' Kincaid suggested.

'At midnight?' asked Farrell.

'Or earlier, if he killed Laura Novak.' Kincaid told

them what they'd learned from Chloe Yarwood. 'We've no way of knowing exactly when she died, and even if it was nearer ten than twelve, we don't know how long he spent . . . preparing the body.'

Rose flinched. 'But why this particular woman? I mean, I can understand, in a bizarre sort of way, his wanting to kill a firefighter if he has some sort of grudge against the brigade. But why Laura Novak?'

Kincaid thought again of the words Chloe had overheard. Could Laura have learned about the fires and confronted the arsonist? But how could she have discovered something like that? What connection could she have had with this man?

His phone rang and he snapped it open, irritated at the interruption when he knew he was in danger of running late for Kit's hearing. It was Maura Bell.

'Guv, we've found another body.'

'What? Where?' He felt a sick dread. 'It's not Harriet—'

'No. But you'd better come. It's Crossbones Grave-yard, just behind the Southwark Street warehouse. And we've met her. It's Beverly Brown, the young woman who reported the fire.'

'The woman from the shelter? Mouse?' He saw instantly the pinched little face, the hair with its badger-like white streak.

'Yes. And it looks like she's been strangled.'

Chapter Seventeen

Let us be moral. Let us contemplate existence.

Charles Dickens
Martin Chuzzlewit

They met in the judge's chambers. It was a comfortable room centred around a long, polished, mahogany table. The Honorable Sophie O'Donnell, an attractive woman in her fifties with smartly styled, blonde-streaked hair, sat at the head.

On one side were Kit's maternal grandparents, Eugenia and Bob Potts, and their solicitor, a rabbity-faced man named Cavanaugh; on the other, Gemma, Kit, and Miles Kelly, their solicitor. It was shaping up to be the battle of the Irish, thought Gemma, but she couldn't summon a smile. The large clock on the wall behind the judge read exactly two o'clock, and Kincaid hadn't arrived.

Neither party had spoken to the other. Eugenia was in full war paint, her fair hair freshly sprayed, but it seemed to Gemma that her clothes hung too loosely and there was a feverish look to her eyes. Bob merely looked diffident and distressed, the classic hen-pecked husband, and Gemma wondered if he might someday snap and bite the hand that had led him such a merry dance.

Miles Kelly glanced at Gemma, raising very black eyebrows over very blue eyes, and she gave a tiny, worried shrug. Beside her, Kit sat silent and strained. She'd bought him new grey flannels and a navy blazer for the occasion, and he looked painfully grown up.

The judge glanced at her watch and cleared her throat. 'I think, Mr Kelly, that we should begin, but we seem to be missing your client.'

'I know Superintendent Kincaid is on his way, Your Honour,' replied Kelly with his most charming smile. 'Perhaps he's been detained in traffic. If you could give us just a few more moments—'

Gemma jumped as the mobile phone clipped to her waist began to vibrate. A quick glance at the caller ID told her it was Kincaid. After looking at the judge, who nodded permission, she excused herself and moved a few steps away from the table, turning her back to the room before she answered.

She listened briefly, spoke in monosyllables, and rang off. Then she stood for a moment, trying to get her dismay under control before she faced the others.

When she turned round, Kit said, his voice tight, 'He's not coming, is he?'

'Something's happened, Kit,' she answered quietly, then spoke to the judge. 'Your Honour, Superintendent Kincaid has been unavoidably detained on urgent police business. He apologizes to the court and asks if we can reschedule this meeting at a later time.'

'Do sit down, Ms James,' said the judge, sounding very displeased.

As she slipped into her chair, her face blazing with embarrassment, Gemma caught the flash of triumph in Eugenia Potts's eyes.

'This is very irregular,' Judge O'Donnell went on, frowning. 'Under ordinary circumstances I would not be inclined to grant such a request, but considering the nature of Mr Kincaid's job, I will think about it.' Before Gemma could breathe a sigh of relief, she continued: 'However, I must say this gives me serious doubts about Mr Kincaid's suitability as a guardian for Christopher.'

Seeing the protest forming on Kit's face, she raised a hand to silence him. 'I've had a brief discussion with Christopher before we began this meeting, and I'm aware of his feelings on the matter. I've also looked over Christopher's father's rather unusual petition requesting that you, Ms James, and Mr Kincaid be allowed to provide care for Christopher until he comes of age.

'I'm always most reluctant to disrupt what seems to be a stable home situation, particularly when a child has suffered a loss.' She fixed Gemma with a sharp eye. 'But the demands of a police officer's job are both heavy and unpredictable, as Mr Kincaid has demonstrated today, and as both of you are officers of senior rank, I'm not sure you can provide the sort of environment Christopher needs. And as neither of you can prove any blood tie to the boy, and we don't know what Christopher's mother would have wished for him, I'm inclined to give consideration to his grand-parents' petition for custody.'

Gemma felt Kit's physical recoil. She touched his arm in reassurance and leaned forward. 'Ma'am, may I speak?' When Judge O'Donnell nodded, she said, 'You're right. The job is demanding and unpredictable. But there are two of us, and one of us has always managed to be there—'

'That's all very well for the time being. But you'll forgive me, Ms James, if I say I've seen no evidence of a long-term commitment on the part of you and Mr Kincaid.'

A black pit seemed to open before Gemma. How could she answer that? 'I . . .'

'There's also the matter of Christopher's education. His grandparents have assured the court that they have the means to send him to public school—'

'I don't want to go to public school,' broke in Kit, tears of fury starting up in his eyes. 'I like it where I am.'

'Your Honour.' Eugenia spoke for the first time. 'It's just this sort of disrespectful behaviour that concerns us. Christopher is obviously living in a household where this is considered acceptable. Nor is he being encouraged to show the interest in his future fitting for a boy his age—'

'You don't know anything,' Kit shouted at his grandmother. 'I'm going to Cambridge. Lots of kids from comprehensives get into Cambridge.'

Judge O'Donnell rapped her knuckles sharply on

the table once. 'That's enough, son. I'll not tolerate displays of temper in my chambers, nor reward them.' When Kit subsided, his hands clenched in his lap, she turned to Eugenia. 'Mrs Potts, it does worry me that Christopher seems to feel a great deal of hostility towards you.'

Eugenia seemed to pale beneath her make-up, but she smiled. 'He has some childish grievance over a dog. I'm sure, in time, that it can be overcome.'

Clapping a hand on Kit's shoulder, as if fearing the boy might not be able to restrain himself, Miles Kelly said hurriedly, 'Ma'am, may I remind you that Kit's father, Ian McClellan, feels that Mr and Mrs Potts have never given Kit the proper emotional support in his grief over his mother's death.'

'You may remind me all you like, Mr Kelly, but I don't have to give it credence. It doesn't seem to me that Mr McClellan has demonstrated much in the way of emotional support himself, by taking a job in Canada and leaving his son behind in England.'

Eugenia whispered urgently in Cavanaugh's ear, and when she'd pulled away, he addressed the judge. 'Is Your Honour aware that at the time of the late Mrs McClellan's death, she and Mr McClellan were separated? That Mr McClellan was, in fact, living in the south of France with a young woman? We feel this demonstrates a long-standing lack of responsible behaviour concerning his son.'

'That's enough, Mr Cavanaugh,' said the judge with a glance at Kit. 'We will adjourn this hearing until further notice.' She sighed and stood. 'I may very well find that neither party is a fit guardian, without evidence to the contrary.'

She had seemed pathetic in life; death had not given her dignity.

Kincaid looked down at Beverly Brown's twisted body. It lay at the far end of a vacant expanse of cracked and weed-infested concrete. Her head was pillowed on a drift of wind-blown rubbish, her small, trainer-clad feet pushed against the bottom of a rusted metal drum.

When Maura Bell had said Crossbones Graveyard, he'd thought of a churchyard, with a bit of grass and headstones; not this wasteland, its fence adorned with fluttering ribbons and a few faded wreaths.

The police surgeon had certified death, and they were now waiting for the arrival of the pathologist, the photographer and the forensics team. The minutes ticked by as slowly as hours, and as the time set for Kit's hearing drew nearer Kincaid's frustration turned into despair. But this was his case, and as senior investigating officer, he could not delegate this latest in a series of crimes to a junior officer. His personal concerns, no matter how urgent, would have to wait until he had put the case behind him.

Turning away from the others, he rang Gemma.

'What is this place?' he asked Maura a few moments later, trying to banish thoughts of the dismay he'd heard in Gemma's voice as he'd explained the situation.

'It was a medieval cemetery, an unconsecrated burial ground for prostitutes and others who couldn't afford proper burial,' Maura answered. 'When London Transport began work here on the Jubilee Line extension a few years ago, they started digging up bodies. Work was stopped, and the place has been in limbo since. The local residents want a park, with some sort of fitting commemoration for those buried here. Meanwhile, the heroin addicts have a field day.'

'I suspected she might be a junkie, when we met her,' he said, remembering the girl's edgy pallor.

'She could have met someone here, looking for a score.'

'Maybe. But dealers don't usually strangle their clients.' The bruising was clearly visible on the girl's exposed throat.

'A rape gone wrong?' suggested Maura.

'Not unless he dressed her again.' He shook his head. 'I don't believe this was a random killing, and neither do you. We're a few hundred yards from the warehouse where Laura Novak was killed, not to mention the fact that it was Beverly Brown who reported the fire.'

'Could she have seen something else that night?' Maura mused. 'But if so, why didn't she report it?'

'Maybe she didn't realize what she'd seen. Maybe she was protecting someone.'

'Or maybe she was frightened,' Maura said slowly.

'With good reason.' He thought of the two little

girls, now motherless like Harriet Novak. Whoever this bastard was, he had to be stopped.

And what of Harriet? Gemma was right; time was running out. He tried to put aside the fear that Harriet was already dead, that they would find her body tossed away like a bit of rubbish, as Beverly Brown had been.

'If this was the same killer,' said Maura, 'why no attempt to hide the victim's identity this time? Or to hide the body? She wasn't even covered.'

Kincaid glanced round the barren waste. 'Lack of means? Lack of opportunity?' He grimaced as a gust of wind blew grit in his eyes and a fat raindrop splashed against his cheek. The rain had been teasing since mid-morning, advancing and retreating like a shy schoolgirl, but now the sky to the west looked thunderous. 'Let's get that tarpaulin up,' he called out to the uniformed officers. 'The Home Office pathologist won't be happy if her trace evidence gets washed away.'

When a car pulled through the cordon of patrol cars and Kate Ling got out, he found he wasn't surprised.

'Duncan,' she said as she reached them. 'If you really want to see me every few days, you could just buy me a drink.'

'Hullo, Kate. You remember Inspector Bell, from the other day?'

Already pulling on her gloves, Kate nodded at Maura. 'I hear you got an ID on the warehouse corpse.'

'News travels fast in exalted circles,' Kincaid told her. 'That's about all we've got so far, and now . . .' He gestured at the body before them. 'This young woman was a resident at the women's shelter opposite the warehouse.'

Kate squatted, graceful even in such an awkward position, and gently tilted the girl's head back with her gloved fingers. 'There are obvious signs of manual strangulation, as I'm sure you're aware.' She pulled back the eyelids, then stretched her hand across the throat, matching her own hand to the bruises. Her finger and thumb fell short on either side by half an inch. 'Not a particularly large hand, either, but he – or she – seems to have been strong enough to subdue her single-handedly.'

'Right-handed?'

'Looks that way.'

'Could she have been sedated?' asked Maura.

'Did she shoot up, you mean?' Kate pushed up the right sleeve of the girl's sweater, then repeated the process with the left. 'There are some tracks, but nothing that looks terribly recent. Unless she injected somewhere else.'

'Can you tell if she fought her attacker?'

The pathologist lifted the hands in turn, examining the fingertips.

Beverly's nails were bitten to the quick, and one cuticle bore a smear of dried blood. 'Hers?' Kincaid asked, bending down to look more closely.

'I think so, but . . .' Kate isolated the middle finger on the right hand. 'Even as short as her nails are, it looks as though she may have managed to scratch her attacker. I'd guess there are enough skin cells for analysis, but you know I can't tell you much more until I get her on the table. I can't even be absolutely certain that strangulation was the cause of death.'

He raised an eyebrow. 'Time of death? Come on, live dangerously, Doc.'

'You never give up, do you?' asked Kate, flashing him a grin. Then she turned back to the body, checking the exposed skin of the arms for lividity, testing the limbs and neck for rigor. 'I'll have to get a temp, but off the cuff I'd say at least twelve hours. But if you quote me, I'll deny it.' She stood up and reached for her instruments. 'Oh, and livor mortis seems to be very well defined. I don't think she was moved from this spot.'

'Well,' said Kincaid. 'At least this time we have an idea where to start.'

Gemma had driven Kit back to school, insisting that he finish his afternoon classes. He hadn't objected. He hadn't spoken at all during the drive from the court to Notting Hill, and his silence worried Gemma more than any angry tirade.

When she stopped the car, she said, 'It'll be all right, Kit. We'll work things out.'

He'd given her a look that told her he knew it was an empty promise, and when she tried to hug him, he pulled away. As she watched him walk through the school gates, she felt a rush of helplessness, followed by a fury that left her trembling.

Not trusting herself to talk to Kincaid over the

phone, Gemma had rung Doug Cullen for directions to the crime scene. She'd left her afternoon free as she hadn't known how long the court proceedings would take, and she decided that anything pending could wait a bit longer. She was going to Southwark.

Now she ducked under the tape strung round the edge of the rubble-strewn ground, then stood for a moment, picking out Kincaid's figure among the group huddled round a tarpaulin on the far side of the area. The sky had darkened with storm clouds and the photographer's flash briefly illuminated the faces of Kate Ling and Maura Bell.

Kincaid looked up then, and when he saw her, he came quickly to meet her.

His smile of greeting faded as he saw her face. 'Gemma. Is everything okay? How did it go?'

'It was a disaster. It was bloody well dreadful, if you want to know.' All her pent-up anger and worry spilled out in a flood of bitter words. 'It couldn't have been worse if we were axe murderers. Eugenia seemed plausible, while we looked like irresponsible parents – not that the judge could see that we had any qualifications to *be* Kit's parents. Without proof that you're Kit's natural father—'

'I'll talk to her. I can explain—'

'And the worst thing about it was that at least part of what she said was true. Ian *is* irresponsible. And we're *not* always there for Kit. You weren't there for him today.'

Kincaid looked devastated, and Gemma knew that if she'd meant to wound him, she'd succeeded.

'I know I let him down,' he said in appeal. 'I'll make it up to him somehow. Surely the judge will see reason.' He gestured towards the group gathered round the body. 'I couldn't leave today. I had no choice.'

'You did have a choice. You chose the job,' she spat back at him. But even as she said it, she saw the mortuary attendants lift Beverly Brown's small form into a body bag, and she wondered whether she would have done the same.

When Kincaid and Maura Bell rang the bell at the shelter, the door buzzed open immediately. The stairs seemed steeper than the last time he'd climbed them, the stairwell more dank and airless. His legs felt leaden and his shirt, still damp from the sudden soaking they'd received at the graveyard, clung to his skin as tenaciously as Gemma's words haunted his conscience. As he followed Maura upwards, he was grateful to her for pretending she hadn't witnessed their very public row.

They found Kath Warren waiting for them in the first-floor corridor, an anxious expression on her face.

'We've just now rung the police,' she said. 'I didn't expect to see you so soon.'

'Why? What's happened?' Kincaid asked as they followed her back into the office. Kath moved a stack of files from a chair so that they could sit, but neither accepted the offer.

Jason Nesbitt was on the phone, but he quickly

rang off and stood up to shake their hands. 'It's Mouse,' he said. 'Beverly Brown. She seems to have gone walkabout on us. The girls woke up this morning and came looking for their mummy, so she must have gone out some time in the night.'

'I thought you had a sign-out system?' Kincaid said with a quick glance at Maura. He wanted to hear what Kath and Jason had to say before he revealed anything.

Kath looked uncomfortable. 'We do, but Bev didn't sign out, and Shawna, the girl on the desk last night, didn't see her leave.' She sighed. 'Shawna's not always as dependable as she might be. We may have to get rid of the telly in the staffroom.'

'Why have you waited until now to report her missing? Weren't you worried about her?' Maura sounded more puzzled than accusing, and Kincaid thought it a giant leap in finesse.

'It's not the first time this has happened,' Kath said reluctantly. 'The last time she managed to sneak back in before she was missed, and we only learned what had happened when the children talked about waking up in the night and missing her. The residents aren't given the security code, you see – they have to be buzzed in – but sometimes they wait and come in with someone else. We thought she'd turn up this morning, trying to bluff her way out of it, but . . .' She looked at the clock.

'What happens if the residents go absent without leave like that?' Kincaid asked.

'We try to give the women every chance, if we can see they're making an effort, but Bev's pushed it too far this time. It sets a bad example for the others. I'm afraid she'll have to go.'

Kincaid caught Maura's quick glance, and this time he nodded.

'That's one decision you'll be spared,' Maura said, watching their faces intently. 'Beverly won't be coming back. She's dead. Her body was found near here a few hours ago.'

There was an instant's silence that seemed to stretch, vibrating like a high-tension wire. Kath stared at them, one hand pressed to her mouth. Jason sank to the edge of the desk, his eyes wide.

'You're sure?' whispered Kath. 'You're sure it's her?'

'There's no question,' Kincaid said. 'I'm sorry.'

'Oh, shit. The daft little cow.' Jason had tears in his eyes now. 'Look, it's all my fault.'

The others all stared at him in surprise.

'She's a repeater. Mouse.' When Kincaid and Maura looked at him blankly, Jason made an effort to explain. 'She can't stay away from her husband. He's not a bad bloke, really – has a steady job as an electrician. They only row when she goes back on the drugs, and then he tries to shake some sense into her. After that, she comes in here for a few weeks, then they make it up, and she goes back to him. Until the next time.'

Kath was shaking her head. 'But, Jason—'

'I suspected it. I suspected she was seeing him

again. But I didn't say anything because I didn't want to get her in trouble. And now . . . he must have . . .' His mouth twisted with distress.

'Jason.' Kath went to him, touched his arm. 'It's not your fault. You couldn't have prevented this.'

'We will be interviewing Beverly's husband,' Kincaid put in, 'but I think you might be jumping to conclusions a bit here.' He had their attention now, and there was something interesting in the tableau they presented, Kath's hand hovering protectively over Jason's shoulder. 'Earlier this morning we identified the body in the warehouse fire as Laura Novak. That makes two women with a connection to this shelter who have died in the last four days. That's too much of a coincidence for my taste.'

Kath gasped as if she'd taken a body blow. 'Oh my God. Laura. But Laura . . . Laura hardly knew Bev. Why would— Oh God,' she said again. 'I can't believe Laura's dead. I thought she must have gone away somewhere, with her little girl.'

Kincaid noticed that the offering of comfort was one-sided. Jason made no move towards Kath but sat absently loosening the collar of his designer shirt, his face blank with shock.

'We'll need to get Beverly's husband's name and address, as well as any other contact information,' Kincaid began, but Kath interrupted him.

'But then, if Laura's dead . . . Where's Harriet?'

'We don't know,' Kincaid answered, but he was suddenly distracted. The tab on one of the files Kath had transferred from the chair to the corner of the desk had caught his eye. It was an odd name. Where had he heard it before?

The skies opened up just as Gemma reached her car, dumping a brief deluge as if providing fitting punctuation to her conversation with Kincaid. She sat, thinking, while the rain pounded roof and windscreen.

She'd been unfair. She knew she'd been unfair; she knew that with this new death, and Harriet still missing, he needed all his focus on the case, but she hadn't been able to stop herself.

Bloody hell, she was useless. She'd failed the missing six-year-old. She'd failed Harriet Novak. She'd failed Kit today in the hearing. Had she even, a mean little voice whispered in her mind, failed her own unborn child? Everyone said nothing could have prevented her miscarriage, but deep in her heart she'd never quite believed it.

No! She pounded her palms on the steering wheel until they smarted. She'd been down that road before – she certainly wasn't going that way again. There was too much at stake.

Then she realized the rain was letting up, the shower moving away as quickly as it had come. A few straggling drops splattered against the windscreen as a watery sunlight emerged. When Gemma rolled down the car window, the air smelled so clean and full of promise that she felt ashamed of herself for even such a brief descent into self-pity. She'd always prided herself on her determination; it was time she demonstrated some evidence of it. She wasn't going to give up, not on Kit, not on Harriet, and it was Harriet who needed her help most urgently.

Frowning, she tried to recall everything that she had learned about Elaine Holland since her first phone call from Winnie. Then she put the car into gear and drove to Ufford Street.

To her astonishment, as she pulled up at the kerb in front of Franny's house, she saw Winnie wheeling Franny's chair down the ramp. They both waved to her as she got out of the car.

'What's happened?' she asked, hurrying to them. 'Is everything all right?'

'We decided it was high time Franny got out for a bit,' explained Winnie. 'We're going for a drink at the Hope and Anchor.'

'Will you join us?' Franny smiled, and Gemma realized she did look better. Her eyes were clear, and her face seemed less pinched, as if a constant pain had eased.

'Nothing would suit me better.' Realizing that she'd been dreading entering the close confines of the house, Gemma thought it no wonder Franny seemed relieved.

They walked companionably down the street, Winnie pushing Franny's chair, and when they reached the pub the staff made a great fuss over settling them at a table. It was a slow time of the afternoon and the place was empty except for a few solitary patrons with newspapers and a man tinkling idly, softly, at the keys of the upright piano. He segued from bits of Gershwin to Cole Porter to random snatches that Gemma didn't recognize, and the sound made her feel unaccountably sad.

When they'd got their drinks – Pimm's for Winnie and Franny, a lemonade for Gemma, who wanted to keep a clear head – she told them everything that had happened since she'd seen them the previous day.

'Franny, I don't want to distress you,' she went on, 'but I want to talk about Elaine. I've just realized how many different stories she told about her background, and I thought if we could put them all together, we might find something in common.'

'I don't mind, really.' Absently, Franny rotated her glass in the centre of the beer mat. She wore a pearl-buttoned cardigan fastened to the throat, and her cheeks looked faintly pink from the warmth or the excitement of the outing. 'I feel . . . I don't know. Once I knew she wasn't coming back . . . It's as if I was carrying a weight, but I never realized it until it was lifted.' Her face fell. 'But Elaine – wherever she is – I don't like to think of Elaine with a child.'

Nor did Gemma. 'Elaine told Tony Novak that she was married to a commercial traveller, and that she worked at an estate agent's here in the Borough.

'She told her co-workers at Guy's that she grew up in Gloucestershire and only came to London when her parents died, but the girl I spoke to swore that Elaine's accent was native to the Borough.'

'And she told me that her parents had migrated

from Canada,' said Franny, 'that her mother committed suicide when she was a child, and that she took care of her ill father until he died.'

Gemma realized suddenly that the music had stopped and the piano player was gone. She had never seen his face. For a moment she wondered if she had imagined him, as Elaine had imagined entire lives. Aloud, she mused, 'We know the first story was a complete fabrication. Could one of the others have been the truth?'

'What I wonder,' said Winnie slowly, 'is whether she told Tony Novak her parents were dead.'

'You think that's the common thread, her parents' deaths?'

'There's something else.' Winnie fingered the silver cross she wore beneath her collar. 'Franny, before Roberta left did Elaine ever stay when Roberta brought you Communion on Sundays? Because I remember that when I first came, I never saw her, but after a few weeks she began to hover in the doorway, and then after another week or two she would come into the room, a bit like a stray animal gaining confidence. I assumed it was the Church she disliked, but what if it was the priest? What if she was afraid of the priest?'

Gemma frowned. 'I'm not following you.'

'Maybe Elaine was afraid of Roberta.'

'Elaine was never at home when Roberta came during the week,' said Franny. 'And now I come to think of it, the few times Roberta dropped in unannounced at the weekend, Elaine went straight up to her room without meeting her. And then on Sundays, of course, she was always out of the house.'

'That settles it, then.' Winnie's pleasant face glowed with missionary zeal. 'We'll ring Roberta straight away.'

Chapter Eighteen

We never knows wot's hidden in each other's hearts;
and if we had glass winders there, we'd need keep the
shutters up, some on us, I do assure you!

Charles Dickens
Martin Chuzzlewit

She hadn't thought of what she would do with the
child. She hadn't thought past wanting to hurt *him*, to
punish him for discarding her without even a thought
of apology, as if she had never been more than a
convenience.

Nor had she meant to come back to this house ever
again. She'd locked it up after her mother's funeral,
set up an account out of her parents' estate to pay the
council tax so that there'd be no connection with the
new name she'd taken, and walked away. Why she
hadn't sold the place, she'd never quite been able to
fathom. When she tried to think about it, her mind
slithered sideways and the memories crowded, cla-
mouring, at the gates she'd refused to breach.

But then Tony had betrayed her; she had taken his
daughter – oh so easily – and there had been nowhere

else to go. And the house had settled back around her, the smells and sounds fastening into her flesh like little claws, making it more and more difficult to separate the past from the present.

The room drew her – but no, there was another child in the room now, a different little girl who had been bad. Or had she? The confusion made her feel ill. She hadn't slept, despite the pills she'd taken from Franny, nor had she eaten much. The bits of food she'd found in the pantry stuck in her throat, dry as the dust of the years gone by.

When she tried to close her eyes, she saw the stairwell spinning, the bottom rushing towards her like a vortex. What had she done? No, she hadn't meant the girl to fall, hadn't pushed her, no, not this time.

Or had she?

All she knew for certain was that she had to get out, out of this house, before it devoured her. But where could she go? Not back to Franny's, not back to her job at the hospital – all that was finished, a life that seemed as distant as another universe. But . . . she had created a new life before; she could do it again. A new name, a new place, a new story – any story but this.

But what of the child? She climbed the stairs and stood outside the door. There was no sound from within. What would she find if she looked inside?

She should open the door, she knew, but the fear swept through her, leaving her trembling and sick. What child would she let out, if she opened the door?

Would she ever be free of the little girl who had lived in that room?

At last she turned and retraced her way down the stairs, and as she went out of the house, she locked the door behind her.

Rose wiped her hands against the legs of her jeans for perhaps the hundredth time. Her fingertips had begun to crack from the hours of contact with the dry and dusty paper, her throat felt parched as sandpaper, and her back ached as if she'd been carrying hose all day.

'Want some coffee?' Bill Farrell asked as he set another stack of folders down beside her. The initial reserve she'd felt with him had evaporated over the long day, and by now she'd almost forgotten to think of him as a senior officer.

'No, thanks,' she said, looking at the cups littering the room. 'If I have any more I'll have to run laps round the room while I read these bloody things.' She stared in dismay at the number of boxes yet to examine and tried not to rub the dirt on her fingers into her eyes.

At least the photo brought by Superintendent Kincaid had allowed them to organize their search more efficiently. Farrell had begun by separating out only applicants who were male and Caucasian for Rose's perusal – with the help of the photo he was able to narrow his selection to those applicants whose photos bore at least some resemblance to the man caught by the security camera.

But in the end it was Rose, rummaging through a fresh box on her own while Farrell had gone for more coffee, who found the file.

'Shit,' she whispered, looking from the application photo to the print, then staring back at the file in stunned astonishment.

When Farrell came back into the room, she was standing, waving the folder at him. 'You're not going to believe this. His name is Jimmy Braidwood.'

'What?' Farrell set his coffee down among the files on the table, careless of the sloshing, and coming to stand beside her, looked at the file. 'You're not serious? As in James Braidwood?'

James Braidwood had been the celebrated super-intendent of the London Fire Engine Establishment, and he had been killed in the great Tooley Street fire of 1861, crushed under a falling wall. 'Yeah. Although it's just "Jimmy" on the application, not "James". No wonder this guy has such a thing about Victorian fires.'

'And you're sure it's him?'

She looked again at the photos, comparing them both with her memory of the man glimpsed so briefly at the scene of the fire, and a rush of nausea made her swallow hard. 'Yes. And look,' she added, flipping through the file. 'He passed both the written and physical exams. It says he was rejected on his psycho-logical assessment. There's a note attached by the interviewer.'

She read it aloud. '"*Mr Braidwood demonstrates a profound lack of the cooperative skills needed in today's firefighting environment. He also displays a marked bias*' *against females and persons of colour, and in my opinion suffers from delusions concerning an imagined connection with the legendary James Braidwood, and is a likely candidate for anti-social behaviour."'*

Farrell whistled. 'Good God. The bastard's a psychopath.'

Rose's queasiness gave way to an icy calm. 'We knew that,' she said with cold conviction, thinking of Bryan Simms's burned and broken body.

Bill Farrell took the file from her and flipped back to the opening page. 'At the time of application, he was employed by a private security firm—'

'The uniform.' Rose saw again the flash of dark blue sleeve.

'And it gives his home address as Blackfriars Road. If we're right, he's certainly set his fires close to home.'

'And he's escalating in leaps and bounds. What I don't understand is why he killed Laura Novak. Could she have somehow learned what he was doing?'

'There's no obvious connection between them.' Farrell looked again at the CCTV photo, his brow creased in concentration. 'From the video, it looks as if he happened to see the door that Chloe Yarwood had left open. But he works for a security firm, so he might have known, or guessed, that the premises across the street had a surveillance camera—'

'So he checks the side entrance, just in case, and finds it unlocked, too,' said Rose. 'What if . . . We know that Laura Novak had a connection with the women's shelter, which overlooks that door. Maybe she was at the shelter for some reason, saw Braidwood go in, and confronted him.'

'If she saw him, why didn't she just call the police?' argued Farrell. 'And that doesn't account for the conversation Chloe Yarwood overheard, unless Laura knew him. His uniform alone wouldn't have been enough to prompt her comment.' He shook his head. 'I don't think we can go any further without more evidence. We'll have to—'

'I think we're running out of time, sir.' Rose faced him, tense with the sense of foreboding that had plagued her since the first fire. 'He took a huge risk yesterday. I think he's been working up to something, something big, and now he's out of control.'

'What could . . .' Farrell stared at her, enlightenment and dismay dawning in his face. 'You think he means to recreate Tooley Street, where Braidwood died a hero. Not just with similar fires, but the real thing. Hay's Galleria?'

'What would be more fitting?' Hay's Wharf, known as 'the Larder of London' had, like Cotton's Wharf, been one of the great Victorian riverside warehouses. It lay between Tooley Street and the Thames, and had been beautifully restored as Hay's Galleria, a Bankside complex filled with restaurants, shops and craft stalls. A fire there would be disastrous, and if started in daylight, as the last fire had been, could cost many lives.

'Dear God. If you're right, we'll have to bring him in now, and hope we can find evidence. But we can't talk to him without the police.' Farrell pulled out his mobile phone. 'I'm calling Kincaid.'

Kincaid had accompanied Maura Bell back to Borough Station, leaving the uniformed officers to search Beverly Brown's meagre belongings and contact social services regarding care of the children. But while Bell and Cullen tried to find an address for one Gary Brown, husband of the late Beverly, thought by Kath Warren to live somewhere in Walworth, he stood at the window overlooking Borough High Street and thought.

He knew he'd come across the name on the shelter file somewhere else in the course of the case; it was simply a matter of dredging through all the accumulated information until he found the right bit.

When it came to him, he turned and said to Cullen, 'Hey, Doug. Gemma copied out a list of names you found at Laura Novak's. Did you keep the original?'

'Sorry, guv. I left it for forensics, in case it had prints. Was it important?'

'I don't know yet.' He remembered Gemma showing him the copy she'd made in her notebook. Would she have it with her now? He rang her to ask, but before she could reply Maura called out that she'd found an address for Gary Brown and that Brown had a previous conviction for assault. 'Gemma, hang on a second,' he said. Then, covering the mouthpiece, he called out, 'Somebody find me a pen and some paper.' When Cullen complied, he copied the list of names

Gemma read to him. One of the six, Clover Howes, was the name he'd seen on the file at the shelter.

Ringing off, he said to Cullen and Maura, 'I'm going back to the shelter. There's something we've missed here. I'd be willing to wager that these other women on the list were shelter clients, but what was Laura Novak's interest in them?'

'You think Kath Warren can tell us?' asked Cullen.

'It's worth a try. Maura, if you want to follow up on Brown—'

'I'll be damned if you send me haring after the husband if you've got a better lead.' She gave him a ferocious glare. 'That's bollocks. I'm going with you.'

'Right, then. Brown can wait. Doug?'

'Count me in.'

They found Kath Warren alone in the office, tidying up in preparation for the end of the day. Lines of exhaustion aged her usually pert face, and she looked up at them anxiously. 'If this is about the children,' she said, 'we're still waiting for social services. I'll stay until they come. We haven't been able to locate any other family to contact.'

'No, Kath, sit down a minute, please,' Kincaid said, motioning her back to her desk. 'We just have a few more questions we need to ask you.' She sat slowly, and Kincaid took the chair that had previously been occupied by the stack of files while Cullen and Maura stood unobtrusively at the back of the room.

He unfolded the list from his pocket and handed it to Kath. 'Are these women all clients of the shelter?'

'What . . .' Kath glanced at the sheet, and he

thought she paled beneath her make-up. 'Where did you get this?'

'From Laura Novak's desk. Why would Laura have made a list of these names?'

Kath looked dismayed. 'I'd no idea Laura knew. This wasn't something we were eager to advertise to the board of directors.'

'What did Laura know, Kath? What's special about these women?'

The paper trembled in Kath's hand. 'I told you the other day. Sometimes, when we place women in new situations, in spite of all our precautions, their abusers find them. These women – all of these women – were tracked down by their husbands or boyfriends. One of them, Clover Howes, is dead. Her husband assaulted her with a poker.'

'That's why you were moving her file,' Kincaid said slowly. 'Six women? In what time period, Kath?'

'A year.' She put the sheet of paper down on her desk and smoothed it flat. 'Six in the last year.'

'That's pushing the law of averages, I'd say. And you didn't tell your board about this?'

'We . . . we wanted to try to resolve it. We suspected that one of the regular clients, like Beverly, might have been selling information to the other women's partners. Or even one of our own staff. I told you we'd had suspicions about Shawna, who works nights. We know she's taken bribes from the residents to overlook minor infractions.'

'Like sneaking out at night?' Kincaid guessed.

'Or alcohol in the rooms, that sort of thing. But we had no proof of anything more.'

'Wait a minute.' The pieces had begun to fall into place all too clearly. Motive, means, opportunity – and the fact that when Kath Warren said *we* she wasn't using the royal first person. He stood and leaned over the desk. 'Kath, where's Jason?'

'Oh.' Kath looked round as if expecting Jason to pop up. 'He left early. A family emergency, a sick auntie in Kent. He had to drive down on Saturday as well.'

'Really? That's very interesting.'

'Why? What are you talking about?' Kath sounded baffled, but she'd shrunk back from him.

Kincaid thought of the subtle relationship cues he had seen between the two of them, and changed tack. 'Tell me what happened on Thursday night, Kath. What was Jason doing here?'

'He wasn't here,' she protested, more firmly than he'd expected.

'How can you be so sure?'

She looked at him, then at Cullen and Bell, who had moved up quietly to flank him on either side, and seemed to come to a decision. 'Because I was. And he never came.'

'Was he supposed to?' asked Maura, with surprising sympathy.

Kath swallowed and looked down at her hands, as if avoiding their eyes made her shame easier to bear. 'He was supposed to meet me here at half past ten. I'd told Shawna she could take a couple of hours off to see her boyfriend. But I waited and waited, and Jason never came. So if you're thinking he had something to do with Laura's death, you're wrong.'

Kincaid thought of Laura, making a list of women and checking off names as she discovered what had happened to them; of Laura, dropping Harriet at Mrs Bletchley's before ten o'clock, making up a story for Harriet and the child minder, because she meant to investigate something that was not appropriate to discuss with a child, and she didn't know how long it would take. She had meant to go home that night, after she'd had a look round the shelter office on her own – that's why she'd left the washing up in the kitchen sink – and she'd meant to go to work the next morning. But she never got to do either.

'Kath,' Kincaid said, 'what time did you actually get here on Thursday night?'

'A few minutes after half past ten. I got held up at home, with the kids.'

Had Jason come in early, quietly, seen Laura Novak digging through the files? Perhaps she'd been asking questions already that had made him suspect she knew something, so he moved back into the shadows, watching, and when she left, he had followed her. Or had he gone ahead and waited, knowing she would pass by him on her way home?

What had happened then? Had he ducked into the shelter of the warehouse door and, discovering it unlocked, pulled Laura in when she walked past? Or had he confronted her in the street? Perhaps as they began to argue he had pushed her against the door and it had swung open, and a terrible opportunity had presented itself.

You, of all people, when you knew what would happen, Laura had shouted in the darkness of the warehouse. Jason had known all too well what would happen to women trying to make new lives, if their abusers found them.

Kincaid thought of Jason's designer clothes, no doubt bought with money earned from others' misery, and he remembered the way Beverly Brown had flinched away from him when he passed. Kincaid had assumed it was fear of men, but perhaps it had been fear of one man in particular. Poor little Mouse, up that night with a fretfully ill child, what else had she seen from her window? And how had Jason lured her to a rendezvous in a deserted graveyard?

He thought of Jason's easy tears when they'd told him of Beverly's death, of his casting suspicion on Beverly's husband by his willing assumption of guilt, and fury coursed through him.

Jason had choked Beverly Brown, as he'd choked Laura before battering her, but in Laura's case he must have hoped he could prevent any connection being made between the shelter and the victim. Why he had set the fire after taking so much trouble to disguise Laura's identity, Kincaid still hadn't worked out, but he knew enough.

'We're going to need Jason's address, Kath; then we'll take you straight to the station so that you can make your statement. After all' – his smile held no humour – 'we wouldn't want you making any urgent phone calls.'

Gemma and Franny listened intently as Winnie spoke to Roberta from her mobile phone. Winnie had given a brief synopsis of what had happened and then had described Elaine. 'Yes,' she said now. 'Elaine Holland, that's right.'

Winnie's body slumped as she listened to the reply, her face growing glummer by the minute. 'Right, Roberta, thanks. Not to worry. I'll ring you la—' she'd begun when Gemma grabbed her arm.

'Winnie, wait. Tell her to hold on. Look, there's no point giving her Elaine's name. I doubt that's any more real than anything else she's said about herself. Does Roberta have a fax?'

'There's one in the vicarage office.'

'I've a copy of Elaine's photo. Tell Roberta to expect a fax. We can go to the police station.'

'No. I've a fax in the church office. We can send it from there,' offered Winnie, her eyes beginning to sparkle again. She passed this on to Roberta, adding that they would soon call her back.

As they walked from the pub back to the church, their progress slowed by Franny's chair, Gemma's impatience was tempered by dread. She feared they were wrong, and she feared that if they were right, they were too late.

When they reached the church office, Franny suddenly put her hands on the chair's wheels and brough it to a jerking halt. She twisted round so that she could look at Winnie.

'Winnie.' Her face had lost its animation, and she looked small and frightened. 'I'm not sure I want to know. Maybe it would be better if I could just go on thinking of her as she was. As Elaine.'

Winnie seemed to consider this. 'Do you think so?' she asked. 'I can take you home, if you want.' She held Franny's gaze, her face gentle with understanding, and after a moment Franny sighed.

'I can't, can I? I know too much to go back, and it was never real. None of it was real.' She wheeled the chair forward on her own, and Winnie and Gemma followed.

The tiny office was cramped with Franny's chair and warm from the heat that had built up during the afternoon. As Winnie fed the photo into the fax machine, Franny looked away until Gemma had tucked it back into her bag.

'There's a speaker phone,' said Winnie. 'Shall I . . .'

Gemma nodded. Winnie dialled, and after a moment Roberta's voice filled the room, rich and warm, with the huskiness of the chronic asthmatic.

'It's just coming through now, Winnie. Let me . . .' Roberta fell silent.

'Roberta,' said Winnie, 'are you still on the line?'

'Dear God,' whispered Roberta.

'What?'

'I'm sorry, love.' Her voice came through more strongly. 'It's just . . . I'd never have thought.'

'Do you know her?'

Gemma could hardly breathe.

'It's Elizabeth Castleman,' said Roberta. 'Her parents were parishioners of mine. They were elderly and had Elizabeth late, I suppose. They died, both of them, several years ago, after extended illnesses. Elizabeth looked after them.'

'Roberta, what is it?' prompted Winnie, hearing the hesitation in her friend's voice.

'They were churchgoing people. You know it's not our place to judge, Winnie, but their ideas were . . . harsh. And their house, it was a terrible place. Old, dirty and neglected. I paid pastoral visits the last year or two, and I always dreaded them. I remember Mrs Castleman telling me they cared nothing for material things, that it was the spirit that mattered, but there was no love in that house.'

'And Elizabeth?' Winnie asked quietly.

'She must have been past her mid-twenties and still caring for them. Like a moth trapped under a glass, I always thought her. Pale and futile. Then Mr Castleman died in his sleep, and a few weeks later Mrs Castleman fell down the stairs. It often happens that way with elderly couples, even those bound more by habit than fondness. But . . . I don't know. I don't feel comfortable speculating even now.'

Gemma leaned nearer the speaker. 'Roberta, this is Winnie's friend, Gemma. I know Winnie's explained that this is a police inquiry and a little girl's life may be at stake. Please tell us if there's anything you remember that might help.'

After a moment, Roberta's gusty sigh came over

the line. 'It's just that I'd visited the day before Mr Castleman died, and he seemed very strong. I know that doesn't mean anything, heart failure can happen at any time. But . . . I remember Elizabeth, standing in the corner, watching with such intensity as if she were waiting for him to die. Then Mrs Castleman, only a few weeks later, such a dreadful accident.'

Franny clasped a hand to her mouth, and Winnie sank onto the corner of her desk, her eyes wide with horror.

'You think she killed them,' said Gemma.

'I . . . I suspected it. But I told myself it was purely fancy in both cases. I wanted to be charitable. I let it go.'

'Roberta, what happened to the house?'

'I don't know. I never heard it had been sold. And Elizabeth just disappeared not long after her mother's funeral. I always assumed she'd moved away from the area, found somewhere free of old memories.'

'Where is it?'

'Why, it's just off Copperfield Street, near All Hallows Churchyard. Not far from you at all.'

Jason Nesbitt lived on a council estate near the junction of The Cut and Waterloo Road, not far from Ufford Street. The estate was early-sixties purpose-built, with all the concrete-block charm that implied. Some of the small balconies had been cleaned and decked out with late-season flowers; most held a jumble of rusting household items, the overflowing detritus of crowded

low-income living. All the walls were liberally decorated with graffiti.

They had dropped a shaken but still protesting
Kath Warren at the station to give her statement, and
Kincaid had called for uniformed back-up to meet
them at the council estate. If Kincaid was right and
Jason Nesbitt had killed at least two people, he wasn't
going to take his team in unprotected.

They found the flat at the back of the estate. The
paint on the door was bubbled and flaking, and half
the number hung askew. There was no bell.

'Definitely no urban regeneration going on here,'
muttered Cullen, a sure sign that he was nervous.

Kincaid pounded on the door. He'd expected reluctance or a refusal to answer at all. He'd sent one of
the uniformed officers round the back to cover the
balcony and windows, and fully intended to wait at
the front until they could get a warrant, if there was
no response to his knocking, but the door swung open
almost immediately.

Jason stared out at them, then gave a panicked
glance towards the rear of the flat. His hair stood on
end, his tie was loose, and the tail of his lilac shirt
hung half out of his trousers. 'Keep it down, will you?
Me mum's asleep in the back.' His carefully cultivated
accent seemed to have slipped, as well as his tie.
'Look, I've already told you everything I—'

'And you've been very helpful, so I'm sure you
won't mind if we come in and ask a few more questions,' Kincaid said.

'I've got to go. My auntie's not well . . .' The blood

ran from Jason's face as he glimpsed the two uniformed officers behind Cullen and Bell. 'What—'

'I don't think you lads need come in quite yet,'
Kincaid told the uniforms, then stepped neatly by
Jason. When Cullen and Bell followed, Jason retreated
to the centre of the room.

The place was a tip, and stank of alcohol, old
cigarettes and unwashed flesh. Not Jason, Kincaid
thought, as the young man had always appeared scru-
pulously clean at work. At the back of the room an
open suitcase lay on the floor, half filled, not with
clothes but with expensive electronics.

'Taking the telly too, are you, Jason?' Kincaid
asked conversationally.

Maura looked round the room appraisingly. 'I'm
surprised someone hasn't relieved you of this stuff, in
this neighbourhood. Or of your car.' They'd spotted
his latest-model Renault, reluctantly described by Kath
Warren, on the side street nearest the flat.

'Is this what you normally pack for a visit to
your sick auntie?' Kincaid poked about in the suitcase. 'Kent, I think Kath said? And you drove to Kent
on Saturday as well. You're a very conscientious
nephew.'

Jason swivelled another panicky glance at the
front door, then the rear of the flat. 'Look, tell me
what you want, then bugger off, okay? I've got to go.'

'Were you in such a hurry on Saturday too?' Kincaid asked mildly. 'Friday must have been hard for
you, waiting, with the police all over everything like
flies. Where did you keep Laura's clothes, in the boot

of your car? And yours, too – you must have got blood all over one of your expensive shirts. A shame, that.' Kincaid felt his phone vibrate, an unwelcome distraction. He ignored it and let the call go to voicemail.

'Is there really an aunt in Kent?' asked Maura, taking the ball. 'Or did you just drive out of London and dump the stuff? Only thing is, you'd be surprised what people manage to find and take to the police. Nosy buggers, humans.'

A sheen of sweat had appeared on Jason's brow, and his eyes rolled wildly. 'Don't know what you're talking about,' he said, but his voice cracked.

'And then there's the forensics,' Maura went on with a smile. 'In spite of all the shows on the telly, people still underestimate the forensics. You will have left traces in your car, Jason, and we will find them. A smudge of Laura's blood, a single hair. Oh, and we found a fingerprint in the blood on the bit of wood you used to bludgeon Laura – a good print, very clear.'

'And that's not to mention Beverly Brown,' Kincaid added. 'The pathologist found skin cells under her fingernails. That's the problem with choking people: they do tend to struggle a bit. Did she see you arguing with Laura that night, from her window?'

'I don't know what you're talking about,' Jason shouted at them, his voice rising into a sob.

'There's one thing I don't understand, though. Why did you start the fire in the warehouse when you'd already bashed Laura's face in?'

'I didn't start any fire,' said Jason, shaking his

head, spittle forming on his lips. 'You don't understand. You have to let me . . . I have to go . . .'

The smell of urine reached Kincaid's nose, and he looked away from the spreading stain on Jason's trousers, feeling sick. 'You don't seem to understand, Jason. I doubt you're going anywhere for a long time. We're processing a warrant for your arrest for the murders of Laura Novak and Beverly Brown. We may be able to charge you as an accessory in the death of Clover Howes as well.

'What did Laura find out, Jason? Did one of the women's husbands have an attack of conscience and talk to her? Or did she threaten to track them all down until one of them admitted the truth?'

Emotions flitted across Jason's mobile face – fear, caution, then venom won out. 'Laura was an interfering bitch who could never keep her nose out of things that didn't concern her,' Jason spat at them, his face contorting with hatred. 'She should have—'

'Jason!' The woman's voice came from behind Kincaid. 'Jason, I told you to keep yer bloody noise down, din't I?'

Kincaid turned and stared, appalled. Past middle age, blowsy, the woman had a rats' nest of peroxided hair and a mask of make-up that had slipped down her face as if she were melting. She was clad only in a stained wrap that revealed far too much of her sagging breasts, and she reeked of gin, but not even the weight and the paint could completely disguise the resemblance to her son.

'Jason, did you get me ciggies, like I asked yer?' She looked round at the detectives blearily. 'Who're these wankers? Get 'em out of me frigging sitting room before I knock yer silly.'

'Shut up, Mum.' Jason looked at the others, and his mouth twisted in a bitter smile. 'You self-righteous bastards,' he said, levelly now. He made a gesture encompassing the flat and his mother. 'You fucking, self-righteous bastards. Why don't you ask yourselves what you would do to get out of this?'

The window of the flat above the Indian takeaway was flung wide. A curtain at its edge moved lightly with the breeze, then hung still again. The sound of a radio could be heard, faintly, above the noise of the busy road.

Rose and Bill Farrell stood on the pavement, studying the place as unobtrusively as they could manage. They were both wearing civvies, and had left the FIT van in the next street. They didn't want to put the wind up Braidwood until they'd had a chance to talk to him.

'Someone's living there,' said Farrell. 'Let's have a word in the takeaway.' They went in, assaulted by the smell of hot oil and spices, and Rose felt herself salivate from hunger while her stomach cramped with anxiety over what they might discover. She let Farrell go up to the counter.

'We wondered if you knew the guy who lives upstairs?' Farrell asked the dark-skinned Indian behind the cash register. 'We were looking for a Jimmy Braidwood.'

'Don't know his name. Funny bloke. Never speaks. No hi, how are you, how's the weather – you know what I mean?'

'No chit chat,' offered Rose, smiling, and the man smiled back.

'I have to remember that. Chit-chat.' He looked at them more closely. 'You official or something? No badges, but you have that look.'

Farrell produced his identification. 'Fire investigator. Do us a favour, though, don't tell your neighbour we were asking about him before we've had a chance to talk to him.'

'The guy's done something wrong, I don't want to talk to him.' The man's teeth flashed white as he grinned. 'You take him away, maybe I get a pretty neighbour. But if you want to talk to him, you better talk soon.' He glanced at the clock on the shop wall. 'Guy usually leaves for work about now. Some security job.'

Farrell and Rose both thanked him, but the lingering smile he reserved for Rose.

'I should take you round with me more often,' Farrell teased as they stepped out onto the pavement again.

'Now what do we do?' asked Rose. They had left messages for Kincaid and for Jake Martinelli, explaining their situation, but neither had yet responded.

Farrell rubbed his beard. 'I say we go ahead. We're just going to have a friendly chat, see what he has to say for himself – assuming it is Jimmy Braidwood in this flat. I've told Kincaid and Martinelli to meet us here, and Martinelli to bring the dog just in case this guy's left any trace of accelerants about.'

'Won't we need a warrant?'

'Not if he lets us in, and for that we'll depend on your charm. Like I said, it's just a friendly visit.'

Rose couldn't quite see how you could accuse someone of arson in a friendly way, and as much as she liked Bill Farrell, she wished briefly for Kincaid's comforting presence.

There was no bell at the flat's street entrance, and the door opened easily. From the bottom of the stairs, they could see that the door at the top stood open, and as they began to climb Rose realized she no longer heard the radio.

Farrell stopped at the top landing and rapped on the door frame. 'Mr Braidwood?'

As Rose slipped up behind him, she saw a small room, drab and dingy, but neat as an army barracks. A man stood at an ironing board in trousers and cotton vest, carefully ironing a pale-blue uniform shirt. He was thin, thinner than she'd realized, but his bare arms were well muscled. His acne-pitted cheeks were hollow, and his eyes, when he glanced at Rose, seemed curiously flat and passed over her without a sign of recognition.

She shuddered and made an effort to keep her expression pleasantly neutral.

'What can I do for you?' said Braidwood. Turning off the iron, he put it on the end of the table, then slipped into his shirt, buttoning each button with careful deliberation. 'I'm afraid I don't have much to offer in the way of hospitality.'

He didn't invite them to sit but didn't seem to object when Farrell led the way further into the room. Rose could see now that the walls held a collection of framed Victorian prints, many from the *Illustrated London News*, showing Southwark warehouses and docks, and the horse-drawn engines of the original London Fire Establishment.

'We're from the fire brigade,' said Farrell. 'We'd like to ask you a few questions about the fire in Southwark Street last Thursday night.' When Braidwood merely looked at him, Farrell went on. 'A security camera recorded you looking in the open warehouse door a short time before the building burned.'

'I may have,' Braidwood answered slowly. 'But is that a crime, M . . . What did you say your name was? Farrell?'

'Most people would have reported an unsecured door,' countered Farrell, 'especially someone in your profession.'

'My profession?' Braidwood gazed at them and Rose couldn't tell if the flat eyes were interested or mocking. 'How is it that you know my name and my job from a CCTV film?'

'We know quite a bit more than that, Mr Braidwood,' said Rose. 'You see, I saw you at last night's fire, directing firefighters to save someone who didn't exist – deliberately putting firefighters at risk. It seemed to me that only a person with a grudge against the fire brigade would do such a thing, so we started looking through the files for applicants who had been fairly recently rejected. We found you, and your file photo matched the CCTV film as well as my description.

'We also found that you have an obsession with James Braidwood and with Victorian fires. You like to recreate them, and you are especially fascinated by Tooley Street, where James Braidwood died.'

Braidwood's eyes held open dislike now, and a spark of respect. 'That's very clever of you, but it doesn't prove anything about anything.'

'Oh, but we will,' said Farrell. 'Now that we know who you are and where you are, we'll be rechecking every bit of forensic evidence from those fires – not just the last two, but the half-dozen before that. And then we'll be checking your shifts and your move-ments against the times of the fires; we'll be checking into your background, and we'll be searching your premises for trace evidence connecting you to the fires. So, you see, we're all going to be very busy together for a good while.'

'Don't mock me,' snapped Braidwood, and for just an instant Rose glimpsed the blazing anger that hid behind the flat, expressionless eyes. 'You think you're so clever,' he went on. 'But you're not clever enough. I've always been one step ahead of you.

'Do you think I'll let you paw through my life, my things, as if I were some sort of exhibit?

'Yes, I started those fires – although Southwark

Street was an unexpected gift, divine intervention, I like to think.'

'And the woman who died in the fire?'

Braidwood shrugged. 'Not down to me. I didn't know she was there until they pulled her out the next day. But it was a nice touch, I thought. I would have tried it again.' He turned to Rose. 'Now, as to your firefighter, he really should have been more careful. The fire brigade is not what it used to be,' he added with a sigh.

Bill dug his fingers into Rose's shoulder, paralyzing her before she could react.

'I told them that,' Braidwood went on, 'but they wouldn't listen.'

Rose could feel the tension in Farrell's fingers. He said with great sincerity, 'I'm sure they'll listen now, Mr Braidwood.'

Braidwood showed his yellowed teeth, and the menace in the smile made Rose really afraid for the first time. 'Oh, I'm sure they will. The question is, will *you* live to tell them what fools they were?'

Reaching down behind his ironing board, he lifted a gallon can and in one fluid motion twisted off the top and sloshed the liquid all over himself. Then he swept his arm out in an arc, flinging the liquid towards them, and threw the can into the door. As the fumes hit Rose – it was acetone, dear God, acetone – she saw what Braidwood was lifting from the corner of the sofa where it had been concealed behind a cushion. It took her brain an instant to process such a familiar thing in an unexpected circumstance, then it all clicked and she shouted with terror. It was a road flare, and she saw his hand grip the cap to twist it.

'Rose, out!' Farrell was shouting in her ear. 'Out the window. Jump, Goddamn it! Jump!' He was pushing her and she was climbing, sliding, and then with a gasp dropping to the pavement, wrenching her ankle as she fell.

She was looking up at Bill, half out the window, hands grasping the sill, when there was a great *whomp* and a ball of flame blew out the window, and Bill was falling, crumpling to the ground. She hobbled to him, pushing bystanders out of the way, shouting, 'I'm a firefighter, let me through.' One of his legs was twisted at an odd angle, and the tops of his hands and his forehead were burned, but he was conscious and shouting, 'That crazy bastard!! He's going to burn down the whole damn road. Get the pumper! Make it pumps two—'

'I'm calling, Bill, I'm calling,' said Rose, who had managed to fumble her phone from her pocket and make her fingers push the right buttons. 'Just lie still, please; they're on their way, and there's an ambulance coming, too.'

'That crazy bastard,' he said again, but with less force, and she knew the shock and pain were setting in.

Looking up, Rose saw Kincaid and Martinelli running towards her, and then they were lifting her, hugging her, and shouting questions over each other.

But before she answered, Rose knelt and put her

arms around Martinelli's dog, burying her face in Scully's soft coat until she had choked back the sobs.

Then she looked up once more at the fire blazing above her and, just for an instant, she thought she saw Jimmy Braidwood, dancing in the window like a human torch.

Gemma slowed the car as she passed the small rectangle of All Hallows Churchyard. Some part of her mind noted the gate's graceful iron flowers, echoed by the stone arch beyond it, even as she searched for the street name Roberta had given them.

'Here,' said Winnie beside her, pointing, and Gemma made a sharp, screeching left turn.

Scanning the faded numbers, she quickly found the one she sought and stopped the car with an abrupt stamp on the brake. 'This is it. This must be it.'

She and Winnie slid out of the car and stood staring at the house before them in dismay. Its flat front was as inhospitable as a prison, its windows opaque with years of grime. To one side, a wall the height of the ground floor sported coils of spiked wire and a frosting of broken glass.

'It looks like no one's been here for years,' said Gemma. But as she looked more closely she saw that the doorstep was free of accumulated rubbish and that the windowpane nearest the door had a spot about the size of a fifty-pence piece rubbed clear of grime. 'No, I take that back,' she whispered. 'She has been here, and recently.'

'What should we—' began Winnie, but Gemma was already striding towards the door.

She pounded the tarnished knocker against the wood, calling out, 'Elaine Holland! Police! Open up!'

The house seemed to stare back at them in malevolent silence. Gemma tried the door, but the latch held fast. She pounded once more, then stepped back, her hand smarting from the effort. There was no sign of a watching eye at any of the windows.

'Can you get a warrant?' asked Winnie worriedly.

'Warrants take hours.' Gemma moved back several more paces until she stood in the street and could survey the entire house and its heavily fortified yard. 'And there's certainly no other way to get in.' The wall was impossible to scale, the windows small-paned, and she suspected that even if she could gain access to a latch, the windows wouldn't open. Still, it was worth a try, and if Elaine was inside it might get a reaction.

There was nothing in the street of suitable size and weight so she opened the boot of her car and pulled out a spanner. She cracked the pane above the centre sash smartly, then tapped the glass out. No one in the neighbouring houses stirred – the entire street seemed eerily abandoned.

Gemma could see the latch now. She reached in and clicked it open, then pushed upwards on the sash, straining until her arms ached. The window didn't budge. 'Okay, that's out. These windows haven't been opened for a very long time.'

'Then we'll have to wait,' Winnie said. 'Although I hate to think—'

'No. We're not going to wait.' Gemma rubbed her sweaty palms against the jacket of her best suit, flipped open her mobile phone, and pressed the speed dial for 999.

When Control answered, she gave her name, rank and location. 'There's smoke coming out of the house,' she said, 'and we think a child is trapped inside. I can't rouse the resident.' She suspected the panic in her voice sounded genuine enough.

Winnie gaped at her as she hung up, then looked frantically back at the house. 'But, Gemma, I don't—'

'When they get here, tell them you saw smoke coming from the back of the house, over the roof.' Gemma could already hear the two-tone of the siren and she sprinted to her car, moving it up well out of the way.

Rejoining Winnie, she said, 'I'll be in enough trouble without blocking access,' but she was grinning with the euphoric rush of having taken action.

The fire brigade pump ladder careered round the corner, siren sounding, and screeched to a stop. As the crew jumped out, Gemma showed the officer her badge and gave her explanation once more. One of the firefighters banged on the door and tried the latch, but the door didn't move.

'A fire? Are you sure?' asked the officer. He'd had time to examine the prospect himself and had seen no sign of smoke.

'Yes.' Gemma pointed over the roof. 'I definitely saw smoke coming from the back.'

'All right. On your head be it.' The officer studied

the map brought to him by his driver, then added, 'No way to get in from the back. Place is a regular fortress.' He gestured at his men. 'Okay, lads. Let's have some fun.'

One of the firefighters took an axe to the door, reducing the heavy barrier to kindling within a few minutes. The leading firefighters rushed in, Gemma and Winnie right on their heels. Ignoring the furious shouts of the officer, Gemma ran from room to room. There was no sign of Elaine or Harriet, or any evidence that the house had recently been occupied at all.

'Thought you said there was a fire,' said one of the firefighters, coming out of the kitchen. 'Have to admit the bloody old place is a fire trap, though.'

'Upstairs. It was upstairs, at the back. The smoke was curling over the top of the house.'

'Right, then.' He motioned to his partner. 'Let's have a look-see.' They climbed, Gemma trying to make herself invisible as she trod in their wake, with Winnie behind her.

The first-floor rooms were empty, and to Gemma the air seemed impregnated with age and illness, barely masked by the odour of dust. She felt an unwanted stab of pity for the child who had grown up in this place, but the pity only fuelled her rage towards the woman that little girl had become.

'She's gone,' murmured Winnie. 'Elaine's gone, isn't she?'

Gemma sensed she was right – there was no watchfulness here – and her heart gave a lurch of despair. Had she taken Harriet with her?

But another, narrower flight of stairs continued upwards. Following the firefighters, Gemma looked back only once, to give Winnie a reassuring glance, then had to drag her mind away from the vision of old Mrs Castleman tumbling down the dark chute.

When they reached the top landing they found only one door, locked. The leading firefighter pounded, then looked at Gemma and shrugged. She nodded. 'Step back then, ladies,' he said, and swung his axe.

The old locks were no match for the force of the blade. The door swung wide and the smell hit them like a blow, a sickening miasma of human waste, illness and fear. Peering past the bulk of the firefighters' shoulders, Gemma took in the chest with its ewer and basin, the bookcase, the bucket in the corner. She pushed forward, and the firefighter let her past.

Then she saw the bed, and the frightened, feverish eyes of the little girl who lay huddled beneath the tattered blanket.

'Jesus Christ,' said the firefighter, shaking his head, his weather-beaten face creased with horror. 'I'll swear to any amount of smoke you like.'

But all Gemma's focus was on the child, still alive, still aware. Safe. Moving to the bed, she dropped to her knees. 'It's all right, sweetheart. It's all right now,' she whispered, and then she lifted Harriet in her arms.

Chapter Nineteen

Grief never mended no broken bones, and as good
people's wery scarce, what I says is, make the most on
'em.

Charles Dickens
The Pickwick Papers

The weather had changed at last, bringing a light frost
in the night, followed by a bright, crisp day. As
Gemma drove through north-east London, she saw
that the city had suddenly taken on an autumn tint,
and above the faint flush of colour in the trees the sky
looked impossibly blue.

She followed the familiar road that led to Leyton,
where her parents had their bakery. But today her
destination was Abney Park Cemetery in nearby Stoke
Newington. She'd promised Kincaid she'd meet him at
Bryan Simms's funeral, but she'd been delayed at work
by a meeting with her guvnor. Knowing she'd missed
the church service, she'd headed directly to the cemetery instead.

Abney Park, like Kensal Green near Notting Hill,
was one of the great Victorian cemeteries, built when

420

churchyards could no longer hold the multitudes of dead. As she drove through the gates into the rambling grounds, she stopped and glanced at the map she'd downloaded from the Internet, comparing it with the directions to Bryan Simms's grave.

But as she scanned the page, James Braidwood's name jumped out at her. The great Victorian fireman was buried here, she saw, under a monument on the main drive. Putting the car into gear, she drove on, gazing at the marble tomb as she bumped past it.

What, she wondered, would happen to the remains of Jimmy Braidwood, who had had no family to claim him?

She soon saw that her map was superfluous, as parked cars filled the roads like arterial blood pumping out from a heart. She followed the main drive until she saw the crowds, then found a spot for her little Ford and walked back, leaving the road for a rough, grassy track. Her long russet coat provided welcome protection against the chill breeze.

As she crested a rise, she looked down upon a sea of mourners, almost all in navy-blue uniforms. The fire service had turned out to honour its own.

She stood at the back of the crowd for a few minutes, listening as an occasional snatch of the burial service drifted to her on the wind. Then she moved to one side and edged her way through the packed bodies until she could see the mourning party.

The pall-bearers, all firefighters, stood to one side, ramrod straight in their dress uniforms. On the other side of the grave were Bryan Simms's family, recognizable by their dark skins. Her throat tightened and she blinked until the feeling eased. The tears made her feel a hypocrite – she had never met the young man. And yet she knew that he had been brave, that he had been loved by friends and family, and that he had died needlessly. Surely that was reason enough to grieve for anyone.

A glimpse of the clergyman in his vestments made her think of Winnie, and of their conversation the previous day as they'd parted outside Guy's Hospital.

'Gemma, I wanted to tell you straight away,' Winnie had said. 'I'm going back to Glastonbury. It's sooner than expected, but Roberta's doctor says she's well enough to come back to London, especially with the cooler weather coming . . . and I think everything that's happened has made her feel her parish needs her.'

'But you've done so much—'

'No, no.' Winnie shook her head, cutting off Gemma's protest. 'I've done no more than Roberta would have done, had she been here.' She touched Gemma's arm gently. 'I'll miss you especially; we've become so close these last days. But I miss my parish, and I miss Jack. It's time for me to go home.' She smiled and hugged Gemma hard. 'We won't lose touch, though. We're family, after all.'

Gemma had returned the hug, then let Winnie go, but the sharp pinch of separation was still with her. It seemed to her that the past year had been made up of losses. First her baby. Then Hazel, gone so far away and now Winnie. Was that what you learned as you grew older, that life was made up of a series of losses?

And now Kit . . . She couldn't bear the thought of giving Kit up to his grandmother, and the disastrous court hearing on Monday had made the possibility seem very real.

It wasn't Kincaid's fault – she knew that. It was the bloody job, and she'd have been forced to do the same in his position. And yet . . . unreasonable as it was, she still felt he had let them down, and she knew he sensed her disappointment.

This added to the constraint that had begun to build between them over the question of trying for another baby. She knew the tiny crack could grow into a chasm if they weren't careful, but she somehow couldn't bring herself to bridge the gap. It wasn't that she didn't want to talk to him, but that she didn't understand her own hesitation well enough to explain it to anyone else.

The priest's voice rose, bringing her back to the scene before her, and he lifted his hand in final benediction. As the uniformed pall-bearers stepped forward to give their last salute, Gemma saw that one was female. This must be Rose Kearney, whom Gemma had not met, but she knew that Kincaid had been particularly drawn to her. Tall, fair and coltish, even with her blonde hair restrained in a knot something about the young woman struck a chord in Gemma's memory.

The mourners shifted and began to drift away.

Gemma caught sight of Kincaid at last, standing a few yards back from the pall-bearers. As she began to make her way down the slope, she saw Rose Kearney come up to him and, after a brief conversation, slip her arms around him. Kincaid returned the hug, a little awkwardly, then they stepped apart.

Another firefighter approached, the dark-haired fire investigator with the sniffer dog whom Gemma had seen briefly the day of the first fire. After a moment, he and Rose walked away side by side.

Kincaid turned and saw her. 'Gemma! I thought you hadn't made it.'

'That was Rose, wasn't it?' she said as she reached him.

'Oh.' He flushed as he realized she'd seen the embrace. 'That wasn't what—'

'No, no, I know that. It's just . . .' She studied him. 'You don't see it, do you?'

'See what?' He frowned, puzzled, and she thought of the strange ways that grief could disguise itself in the labyrinth of the human heart. Kit's mother had had that same fair grace, that same look of innocence burnished by intelligence.

'It's Vic,' she said, touching his cheek. 'She reminds you of Victoria.'

Kincaid left the cemetery with every intention of driving straight back to the Yard. Instead, he found himself winding west through the early-afternoon traffic and then on the M4, heading towards Reading.

He rang Cullen. 'Listen,' he said when Cullen picked up. 'I . . . I've got some personal business. Cover for me for a couple of hours, will you?'

Cullen hesitated, as if about to ask a question, then said, a touch too heartily, 'Right. Let me know when you're on your way in.'

It occurred to Kincaid to be thankful he'd signed out a motor pool Rover rather than driving the Midget to the funeral – his mother-in-law had always hated that car.

How could he not have seen that Rose reminded him of his ex-wife? It was more than a fleeting physical resemblance. He thought of Vic as she had been at twenty-two or twenty-three. She'd had that same air of quiet gravity, of taking life just a little too seriously.

The realization jabbed him like a pike, opening a wound he thought he'd plastered over, and then, to his astonishment, he'd found himself thinking of Eugenia.

What must it be like to lose a child, to have every reminder of that child bring fresh pain, and yet to know that the loss of that pain was a death in itself?

When he reached Reading, he exited the motorway and drove to the quiet suburb where Vic had spent her childhood, and where Bob and Eugenia Potts still lived. He pulled up in front of the house and stopped the car.

The brick semi-detached was one of identical dozens built in the sixties, when they had represented the ideal of middle-class afffluence. Now, they seemed merely dreary, and stultifyingly dull. The house hadn't changed, although the garden seemed more neglected than when he'd been there last. It was here Eugenia had brought Kit when his mother died; it was from here that Kit had run away.

Kincaid had always wondered how such an environment could have produced Vic – it had seemed as unlikely as a stone hatching a butterfly. And yet there must have been something in this household, in this family, that had nourished her uniqueness.

The net curtain at the front window twitched; identical curtains were probably twitching all along the street. It was his cue to charge the citadel or die trying. He brushed a bit of imaginary fluff from his lapel – his best dark suit, along with the sober Rover, might buy him a point or two – and got out of the car.

Bob Potts opened the door before Kincaid could ring. His father-in-law's hair had thinned to reveal a shiny pink scalp; his grey cardigan bagged at the elbows. He had become an old man. 'Duncan,' he said. 'You shouldn't have . . . This isn't a good—'

'Bob, please. Just give me a few minutes. Let me talk to you both.'

'You don't understand. I don't want her upset.' Bob Potts had spent forty years trying to prevent his wife from being upset, and the effort had sucked him dry. 'She—'

'Hear me out. What can it—'

'Let him in.' The voice came from the darkened room beyond the door.

As Bob stepped back, his shoulders drooping in

resignation, Kincaid followed. It took his eyes a moment to adjust to the dimness, then he made out his mother-in-law, seated in the worn armchair near the fire. One of the electric bars was lit, an unheard-of concession for a crisp and sunny afternoon, and the room was stuffily warm.

She, too, had aged visibly. He had not seen her since the spring, since the first letter had come from her solicitor, and his own solicitor had banned any direct contact between them. Her frame seemed to have shrunk, and the flesh sagged at her cheeks and jaws.

'Duncan. You had better sit down,' she said. Eugenia had never been one to forget the proprieties, even under duress. 'I'm surprised you could find the time to drive to Reading when you couldn't manage to appear at Christopher's hearing.'

Kincaid bit back a retort. He'd long ago learned the folly of trying to justify himself to Eugenia, especially where his job was concerned. 'I want to talk to you both about Kit. I want to see if we can reach an understanding, without lawyers, for his sake.'

'Why should we make any concession to you?' she asked, a gleam of malice in her eyes.

'This isn't a chess game,' he snapped, his anger flaring. 'This is a child we're talking about, and a child's life. We need to consider what's best for him.'

'And that has *nothing* to do with you. Christopher is our grandson, and only we have the right to make decisions concerning him.'

'Yes,' Kincaid said, as levelly as he could manage. 'He is your grandson. But he's my son, and I will not let you continue to make his life a misery.'

The spark of anger faded from Eugenia's eyes, and her face settled into a frozen mask. 'I will not discuss this with you. Now, get out of our house.'

'Why can't you face the truth? Is it because you still blame me for Vic's death?' He realized he was shouting and made an effort to lower his voice. 'Eugenia, please. Listen to me. I understand how you feel. I understand that every time you look at Kit you see Vic, and that it hurts you terribly, but that you can't bear the pain to stop because that's all you have left of her.

'But you have to let him go. Kit is not his mother, and he deserves to live his own life. You have to let him go . . . and you have to let her go. It's the only way you'll heal.'

She stared at him in silence, her eyes hollow, and for an instant he thought he'd reached her. Then she said, 'How dare you tell me what I feel? You always were an arrogant bastard. You know nothing, *nothing*, do you hear me?'

Bob cleared his throat, a nervous stutter of sound. 'You'd better go now, Duncan. You'd better do as she says.'

Kincaid stood. 'All right. But let me tell you this. I will do whatever it takes to keep my son with me – whatever it takes. And if you keep on with this, you will rue the consequences. Do you understand me?'

When neither of them replied, he turned away and

let himself out of the house. As he got into the car and pulled away from the kerb he realized his hands were shaking from the flood of fury and adrenalin.

He felt oddly and surprisingly liberated, as if he'd crossed some unexpected Rubicon. He had meant it. He would do whatever it took to keep Kit with him, even if it meant sacrificing his job, or his life as he knew it.

He would never know, now, if Tony Novak had been justified in taking his daughter, but he knew that, were he faced with giving Kit up to his grandparents, he would do the same.

It was evening by the time he reached Notting Hill again. Dusk was stealing round the brown house with the cherry-red door, and a welcoming light shone out from the windows.

The dogs barked as he came in, then leapt at his knees, tails wagging. He greeted them and went through to the kitchen. Gemma stood by the table, still in her work clothes, going through the post.

'Where are the boys?' he asked, kissing her cheek.

'Upstairs.' She looked up at him, frowning in concern. 'Where have you been? You didn't answer your phone, and Doug said you were out.'

'I went to see Bob and Eugenia. They're not going to budge, Gemma. They mean to take him away from us, and I won't let them do it. I don't care what it takes. If we have to go away somewhere, make a fresh start, would you—'

'You would do that for me?' It was Kit, standing in the kitchen doorway.

Kincaid turned and saw his son's face lit with surprise, and a wondrous dawning hope. 'Yes. You're my son, Kit. I won't let you go.'

'What . . .' Kit hesitated, then seemed to come to a decision. 'What if I had the test? Would that help?'

'It might. But I thought you didn't want—'

'And if it's not true, if I'm not really your son, will you still—'

'Kit, do you think I love Toby any less because we don't share genes?' He glanced at Gemma and saw that her eyes were bright with tears. 'What matters is that we're family. We stick together, okay?'

Kit took a breath and grinned. 'Right. Okay. Then I'll do it.'

They celebrated with the boys' favourite takeaway pizza and a riotous game of Scrabble in the sitting room, the boys' shouts punctuated by the dogs' barking. Kit radiated an infectious joy new to Kincaid, and he wondered if he was seeing his son for the first time as he'd been before grief entered his life.

Toby, charged up by an excitement he didn't understand, bounced round the room like a table-tennis ball, until Gemma laughingly shepherded him upstairs for his bath.

Later, when both boys were in bed and Gemma lay curled in Kincaid's arms, she said, 'Will the test be enough, do you think?'

'I hope so. We'll see.'

She turned a little, until he could just make out her profile in the dark. 'And did you mean what you said, about being willing to give up everything?'

Kincaid felt he'd stood at the edge of a chasm and found himself willing to leap. If he'd been given a reprieve by Kit's decision, at least he knew he possessed enough courage for the plunge. 'I think so, yeah.'

'Even the job?'

He traced a finger along her bare shoulder. 'I'd like to think I'm more than the job.'

'Oh, I think you're much more than that,' she said softly, and kissed him.

It was only much later, as he lay drowsily beside her, listening to her breathing steady into the slow rhythm of sleep, that the realization struck him. When he'd asked her if she would be willing to give up the life they'd built, for Kit's sake, she had not given him an answer.

Harriet had had to stay two days in hospital, for observation. Her arm had been set, and the doctors had said she needed fluids and rest. She didn't remember much of the first day, only her father, sitting beside her bed, gaunt and unshaven. He'd cried when he'd told her about her mum, gripping her good hand as if it might keep him from drowning, but Harriet couldn't find anything to say.

It seemed to her that she'd known, somehow, that

her mother was gone, when she'd cried for her as she lay on the bed in the dark house. Now she just felt numb, as if it had all happened to someone else, or to her a long time ago. Her mind wouldn't go any further than that; she couldn't visualize what her life was going to be like without her mother in it.

She slept again, and when she woke she had visitors. Her father spoke to them, then went out, leaving her alone with the newcomers. She recognized the policewoman with the pretty red hair who had found her, and the priest who'd been with her, with her kind face and funny collar.

With them was a small Asian woman in a wheelchair. When the others had greeted Harriet, the woman rolled her chair up to the bed and took Harriet's hand. Her thin face bore lines of pain, as if she'd been ill, but there was also something calm in it that Harriet found comforting.

'I'm so sorry about your mother, Harriet,' the woman said, her soft voice strained with the effort. 'And I'm so sorry about what happened to you.'

Harriet didn't understand who she was or why it should matter to her so much, but she nodded as if she did.

The woman looked relieved and smiled. She pulled something wrapped in tissue paper from her bag. 'This is for you – not for here, of course, because you can't light it – but for when you get home.'

Harriet couldn't manage the tissue paper with one hand, so the woman helped her pull it away, lifting out a candle in a square of pale green glass. It smelled sweet and made Harriet think of something nice, but she couldn't quite remember what it was. 'Thank you,' she said, and the woman seemed pleased.

'We'd better let you get some rest,' said the priest, and as they moved towards the door her father came back into the room.

'Have you . . . Is there any news of her?' he asked the policewoman in a low voice.

'No, nothing yet,' she answered.

'And . . .' Her father shifted uneasily and rubbed at his chin. 'Will I— Will there be . . . charges?'

'No,' the policewoman said again. 'No, I don't think so. You only took your daughter away from school, after all.'

When they'd gone Harriet thought about asking her dad what he'd meant, but instead she drifted off to sleep again.

She had one more visitor, on the second day. Her dad had gone down to the canteen for coffee when Mrs Bletchley sidled in the door, looking warily round the room. She wore what Harriet knew to be her best dress, and there was a smear of orange lipstick like a gash across her mouth.

She gave Harriet a brusque nod, then stood awkwardly at the foot of the bed. 'Just came to say sorry about your mum,' she blurted at last. 'A good woman, your mother. You shouldn't forget it. She remembered them as was less fortunate than her.' Mrs Bletchley nodded again, as if satisfied with her pronouncement, then frowned at Harriet. 'Don't suppose you'll be coming to stay, now.'

'No,' Harriet answered cautiously. 'I shouldn't think so.'

'Well. That's that, then.' Mrs Bletchley turned away but stopped at the door. 'You could maybe pop in sometimes, after school,' she said, not looking at Harriet, but there was an odd expression on her face.

Harriet struggled to cover her surprise. 'I . . . I suppose so,' she said. Mrs Bletchley made a funny sort of screwed-up face, then nodded once more as she went out, leaving Harriet to try to make sense of it all. When her dad came back, she didn't mention the odd visit. It seemed, somehow, to be something that should be kept between her and Mrs Bletchley . . . and her mum.

Her dad came to the hospital for her in his car on the evening of the second day, and she saw that the back was filled with all the bits and pieces from his flat. They drove to Park Street, and when he pulled up in front of the house Harriet saw Ms Karimgee still working at her desk next door. She lifted her hand in a wave, and Ms Karimgee waved back.

They went into the house in silence. Harriet walked from room to room, wondering what to do. None of the ordinary things seemed right. Where did she begin this new life, without her mother?

Hearing sounds from the kitchen, she went in and saw her father at the sink, doing the washing up. She stood, stricken with the realization that she'd never see her mum in that spot again, and the world felt as if it were caving in beneath her feet.

Her dad turned and saw her. He dropped the pan

and dishcloth and came to her, scooping her into his arms. Cradling her carefully so as not to jar her arm, he sat down in the kitchen chair and held her in his lap. Her head just fitted beneath his chin, and she could feel his heart beating in his chest.

'We'll be all right, won't we, Harriet?' he whispered, smoothing her hair. 'We'll take care of each other.'

'Yes,' she said. 'We will.'